The Further
Chronicles
of Conan

ROBERT JORDAN

The Further Chronicles of Conan

CONAN THE MAGNIFICENT
CONAN THE TRIUMPHANT
CONAN THE VICTORIOUS

TOR®
fantasy

A TOM DOHERTY ASSOCIATES BOOK
NEW YORK

THE FURTHER CHRONICLES OF CONAN

Copyright © 1999 by Conan Properties, Inc.

This is an omnibus edition consisting of the novels *Conan the Magnificent,* copyright © 1984 by Conan Properties, Inc., first Tor edition May 1984; *Conan the Triumphant,* copyright © 1983, 1984 by Conan Properties, Inc., first Tor edition October 1983; and *Conan the Victorious,* copyright © 1984 by Conan Properties, Inc., first Tor edition November 1984.

A Tor Book
Published by Tom Doherty Associates, LLC
175 Fifth Avenue
New York, NY 10010

www.tor.com

Tor® is a registered trademark of Tom Doherty Associates, LLC.

ISBN 0-765-30301-9 (PBK)
EAN 978-0765-30301-1 (PBK)

First Edition: October 1999
First Paperback Edition: September 2004

Printed in the United States of America

0 9 8 7 6 5 4 3 2 1

Contents

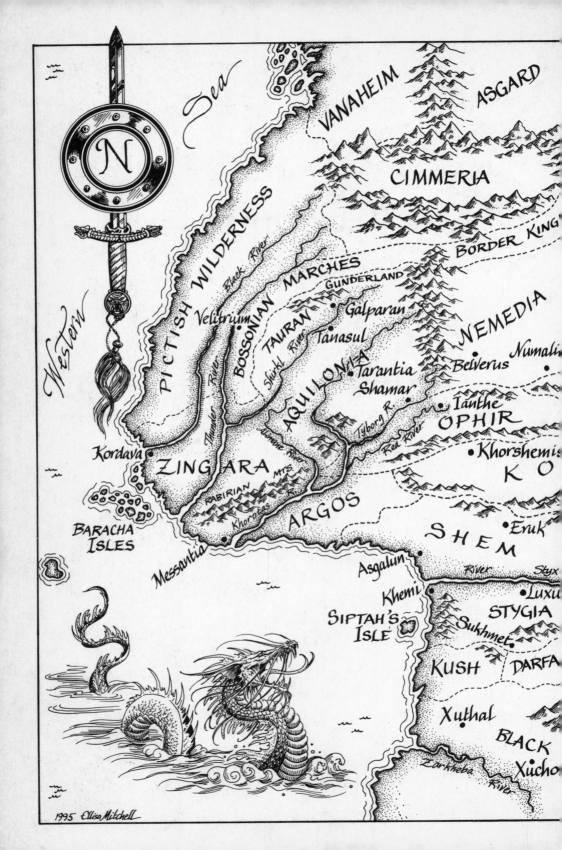

TUNDRAS
Haloga
HYPERBOREA
DESERTS
BRYTHUNIA
STEPPES
KEZANKIAN MTS.
HYRKANIA
CORINTHIA
ZAMORA
TURAN
Sultanapur
KARPASH MTS.
Shadizar
Arenjun
VILAYET SEA
KHITAI
Isle of Iron Statues
KHAURAN
Akit
Aghrapur
KHORAJA
DESERTS
Samara
IBARS MTS.
Shangara
Xapur
Zaporaska River
Zamboula
Khawarism
Kuthchernes
Pteion
Ilbars River
Kassali
KESHAN
PUNT
VENDHYA
KINGDOMS
ZEMBABWEI
IRANISTAN

Conan the Magnificent

Prologue

Icy air hung deathly still among the crags of the Kezankian mountains, deep in the heart of that arm of those mountains which stretched south and west along the border between Zamora and Brythunia. No bird sang, and the cloudless azure sky was empty, for even the ever-present vultures could find no current on which to soar.

In that eerie quiesence a thousand fierce, turbanned Kezankian hillmen crowded steep brown slopes that formed a natural amphitheater. They waited and merged with the silence of the mountains. No sheathed tulwar clattered against stone. No booted foot shifted with the impatience that was plain on lean, bearded faces. They hardly seemed to breathe. Black eyes stared down unblinkingly at a space two hundred paces across, floored with great granite blocks and encircled by a waist-high wall as wide as a man was tall. Granite columns, thick and crudely hewn, lined the top of the wall like teeth in a sun-dried skull. In the center of that circle three men, pale-skinned Brythunians, were bound to tall stakes of black iron, arms stretched above their heads, leather cords digging cruelly into their wrists. But they were not the object of the watcher's attention. That was on the tall, scarlet-robed man with a forked beard who stood atop a tunnel of massive stone blocks that pierced the low wall and led back into the mountain behind him.

Basrakan Imalla, dark face thin and stern beneath a turban of red, green and gold, threw back his head and cried, "All glory be to the true gods!"

A sigh of exaltation passed through the watchers, and their response rumbled against the mountainsides. "All glory be to the true gods!"

Had Basrakan's nature been different, he might have smiled in satisfaction. Hillmen did not gather in large numbers, for every clan warred against every other clan, and the tribes were riddled by blood feuds. But he had gathered these and more. Nearly ten times their number camped amid the jagged mountains around the amphitheater, and scores of others joined them every day. With the power the true gods had given him, with the sign of their favor they had granted him, he had done what no other could. And he would do more! The ancient gods of the Kezankians had chosen him out.

"Men of the cities," he made the word sound obscene, "worship false gods! They know nothing of the true gods, the spirits of earth, of air, of water. And of fire!"

A wordless roar broke from a thousand throats, approbation for Basrakan and hatred for the men of the cities melting together till even the men who shouted could not tell where one ended and the other began.

Basrakan's black eyes burned with fervor. Hundreds of Imallas wandered the mountains, carrying the word of the ancient gods from clan to clan, kept safe from feud and battle by the word they carried. But it had been given to him to bring about the old gods' triumph.

"The people of the cities are an iniquity in the sight of the true gods!" His voice rang like a deep bell, and he could feel his words resonate in the minds of his listeners. "Kings and lords who murder true believers in the names of the foul demons they call gods! Fat merchants who pile up more gold in their vaults than any clan of the mountains possesses! Princesses who flaunt their half-naked bodies and offer themselves to men like trulls! Trulls who drench themselves in perfumes and bedeck themselves in gold like princesses! Men with less pride than animals, begging in the streets! The filth of their lives stains the world, but we will wash it away in their blood!"

The scream that answered him, shaking the gray granite beneath his feet, barely touched his thoughts. Deep into the warren of caverns beneath this very mountain he had gone, through stygian passages lit only by the torch he carried, seeking to be closer to the spirits of the earth when he offered them prayers. There the true gods led him to the subterranean pool where eyeless, albescent fish swam around the clutch of huge eggs, as hard as the finest armor, left there countless centuries past.

For years he had feared the true gods would turn their faces from him for his study of the thaumaturgical arts, but only those studies had enabled him to transport the slick black spheres back to his hut. Without the knowledge from those studies he could never have succeeded in hatching one of the nine, could never have bound the creature that came from it to him, even as imperfectly as he had. If only he had the Eyes of Fire . . . no, *when* he had them all bonds, so tenuous now, would become as iron.

"We will kill the unbelievers and the defilers!" Basrakan intoned as the tumult faded. "We will tear down their cities and sow the ground whereon they stood with salt! Their women, who are vessels of lust, shall be scourged of their vileness! No trace of their blood shall remain! Not even a memory!" The hook-nosed Imalla threw his arms wide. "The sign of the true gods is with us!"

In a loud, clear voice he began to chant, each word echoing sharply from the mountains. The thousand watching warriors held their collective breath. He knew there were those listening who sought only gold looted from the cities rather than the purification of the world. Now they would learn to believe.

The last syllable of the incantation rang in the air like struck crystal. Basrakan ran his eyes over the Brythunian captives, survivors of a party of hunters who had entered the mountains from the west. One was no more than sixteen, his gray eyes twisted with fear, but the Imalla did not see the Brythunians as human. They were not of the tribes. They were outsiders. They were the sacrifice.

Basrakan felt the coming, a slow vibration of the stone beneath his feet, before he heard the rough scraping of claws longer than a man's hand.

"The sign of the true gods is with us!" he shouted again, and the creature's great head emerged from the tunnel.

A thousand throats answered the Imalla as the rest of the thick, tubular body came into view, more than fifteen paces in length and supported on four wide-set, massive legs. "The sign of the true gods is with us!" Awe and fear warred in that thunderous roar.

Blackened plates lined its short muzzle, overlapped by thick, irregular teeth designed for ripping flesh. The rest of that monstrous head and body were covered by scales of green and gold and scarlet, glittering in the pale sun, harder than the finest armor the hand of man could produce. On its back those scales had of late been displaced by two long, leathery boils. Drake, the ancient tomes called it, and if those volumes were correct about the hard, dull bulges, the sign of the true gods' favor would soon be complete.

The creature turned its head to stare with paralyzing intensity directly at Basrakan. The Imalla remained outwardly calm, but a core of ice formed in his stomach, and that coldness spread, freezing his breath and the words in his throat. That golden-eyed gaze always seemed to him filled with hatred. It could not be hatred of him, of course. He was blessed by the true gods. Yet the malevolence was there. Perhaps it was the contempt of a creature of the true gods for mere mortal men. In any case, the wards he had set between the crudely hewn granite columns would keep the drake within the circle, and the tunnel exited only there. Or did it? Though he had often descended into the caverns beneath the mountain—at least, in the days before he found the black drake eggs—he had not explored the tenth part of them. There could be a score of exits from that tangle of passages he had never found.

Those awesome eyes turned away, and Basrakan found himself drawing a deep breath. He was pleased to note there was no shudder in it. The favor of the old gods was truly with him.

With a speed that seemed too great for its bulk, the glittering creature moved to within ten paces of the bound men. Suddenly the great, scaled head went back, and from its gaping maw came a shrill ululation that froze men's marrow and turned their bones to water. Awed silence fell among the watchers, but one of the prisoners screamed, a high, thin sound with the reek of madness in it. The boy fought his cords silently; blood began to trickle down his arms.

The fiery-eyed Imalla brought his hands forward, palms up, as if offering the drake to the assemblage. "From the depths of the earth it comes!" he cried. "The spirits of earth are with us!"

Mouth still open, the drake's head lowered until those chill golden eyes regarded the captives. From those gaping jaws a gout of rubescent flame swept across the captives.

"Fire is its breath!" Basrakan shouted. "The spirits of fire are with us!"

Two of the prisoners were sagging torches, tunic and hair aflame. The youth, wracked with the pain of his burns, shrieked, "Mitra help me! Eldran, I—"

The iridescent creature took two quick paces forward, and a shorter burst of fire silenced the boy. Darting forward, the drake ripped a burning body in half. The crunching of bones sounded loudly, and gobbets of charred flesh dropped to the stone.

"The true gods are with us!" Basrakan declaimed. "On a day soon, the sign of the gods' favor will fly! The spirits of air are with us!" The old tomes had to be right, he thought. Those leathery bulges would burst, and wings would grow. They would! "On that day we will ride forth, invincible in the favor of the old gods, and purge the world with fire and steel! All praise be to the true gods!"

"*All praise be to the true gods!*" his followers answered.

"All glory to the true gods!"

"All glory to the true gods!"

"Death to the unbelievers!"

The roar was deafening. *"DEATH TO THE UNBELIEVERS!"*

The thousand would stay to watch the feeding, for they were chosen by lot from the ever-growing number encamped in the surrounding mountains, and many had never seen it before. Basrakan had more important matters to tend to. The drake would return to its caverns of its own accord when the bodies were consumed. The Imalla started up a path, well worn now in the brown stone by many journeys, that led from the amphitheater around the mountainside.

A man almost as tall as Basrakan and even leaner, his face burning with ascetic fanaticism above a plaited beard, met him and bowed deeply. "The blessings of the true gods be on you, Basrakan Imalla," the newcomer said. His turban of scarlet, green and gold marked him as Basrakan's acolyte, though his robe was of plain black. "The man Akkadan has come. I have had him taken to your dwelling."

No glimmer of Basrakan's excitement touched his stern face. The Eyes of Fire! He inclined his head slightly. "The blessings of the true gods be on you, Jbeil Imalla. I will see him now."

Jbeil bowed again; Basrakan went on, seemingly unhurried, but without even the inclination of his head this time.

The path led around the slope of the mountain to the village of stone houses, a score in number, that had grown up where once stood the hut in which Basrakan had lived. His followers had spoken of building a fortress for him, but he had no need of such. In time, though, he had allowed the construction of a dwelling for himself, of two stories and larger than all the rest of the village placed together. It was not a matter of pride, he often reminded himself, for he denied all pride save that of the old gods. The structure was for *their* glory.

Turbanned and bearded men in stained leather vests and voluminous trousers, the original color of which was a mystery lost in age and dirt, bowed as he passed, as did women covered from head to foot in black cloth, with only a slit for their eyes. He ignored them, as he did the two guards before his door, for he was openly hurrying now.

Within, another acolyte in multi-hued turban bent himself and gestured with a bony hand. "The blessings of the true gods be on you, Basrakan Imalla. The man Akkadan—"

"Yes, Ruhallah." Basrakan wasted not even moments on honorifics. "Leave me!" Without waiting to be obeyed, the tall Imalla swept through the door Ruhallah had indicated, into a room sparsely furnished with black-lacquered tables and stools. A hanging on one wall was a woven map of the nations from the Vilayet Sea west to Nemedia and Ophir.

Basrakan's face darkened at the sight of the man who waited there. Turban and forked beard proclaimed him hillman, but his fingers bore jeweled rings, his cloak was of purple silk and there was a plumpness about him that bespoke feasting and wine.

"You have spent too much time among the men of the cities, Akkadan," Basrakan said grimly. "No doubt you have partaken of their vices! Consorted with their women!"

The plump man's face paled beneath its swarthiness, and he quickly hid his beringed hands behind him as he bowed. "No, Basrakan Imalla, I have not. I swear!" His words tumbled over each other in his haste. Sweat gleamed on his forehead. "I am a true—"

"Enough!" Basrakan spat. "You had best have what I sent you for, Akkadan. I commanded you not to return without the information."

"I have it, Basrakan Imalla. I have found them. And I have made plans of the palace and maps—"

Basrakan's shout cut him short. "Truly I am favored above all other men by the true gods!"

Turning his back on Akkadan, he strode to the wall hanging, clenched fists raised in triumph toward the nations represented there. Soon the Eyes of Fire would be his, and the drake would be bound to him as if part of his flesh and will. And with the sign of the true gods' favor flying before his followers, no army of mortal men would long stand against them.

"All glory to the true gods," Basrakan whispered fiercely. "Death to all unbelievers!"

I

N ight caressed Shadizar, that city known as 'the Wicked,' and
veiled the happenings which justified that name a thousand
times over. The darkness that brought respite to other cities
drew out the worst in Shadizar of the Alabaster Towers, Shadizar of the
Golden Domes, city of venality and debauchery.

In a score of marble chambers silk-clad nobles coerced wives not
theirs to their beds, and many-chinned merchants licked fat lips over
the abductions of competitors' nubile daughters. Perfumed wives, fanned
by slaves wielding snowy ostrich plumes, plotted the cuckolding of hus-
bands, sometimes their own, while hot-eyed young women of wealth or
noble birth or both schemed at circumventing the guards placed on their
supposed chastity. Nine women and thirty-one men, one a beggar and
one a lord, died by murder. The gold of ten wealthy men was taken
from iron vaults by thieves, and fifty others increased their wealth at the
expense of the poor. In three brothels perversions never before contem-
plated by humankind were created. Doxies beyond numbering plied
their ancient trade from the shadows, and twisted, ragged beggars preyed
on the trulls' wine-soaked patrons. No man walked the streets unarmed,
but even in the best quarters of the city arms were often not enough to
save one's silver from cutpurses and footpads. Night in Shadizar was in
full cry.

Wisps of cloud, stirred by a warm breeze, dappled the moon sitting
high in the sky. Vagrant shadows fled over the rooftops, yet they were
enough for the massively muscled young man, swordbelt slung across
his broad chest so that the worn hilt of his broadsword projected above

his right shoulder, who raced with them from chimney to chimney. With a skill born in the savage wastes of his native Cimmerian mountains he blended with the drifting shades, and was invisible to the eyes of the city-born.

The roof the muscular youth traveled came to an end, and he peered down into the blackness hiding the paving stones of the street, four stories below. His eyes were frozen sapphires, and his face, a square-cut lion's mane of black held back from it by a leather cord, showed several ordinary lifetimes' experience despite its youth. He eyed the next building, an alabaster cube with a freize of scrollwork running all the way around it an arm's length below the roof. From deep in his throat came a soft growl. A good six paces wide, the street was, although it was the narrowest of the four that surrounded the nearly palatial structure. What he had not noticed when he chose this approach—eying the distances from the ground—was that the far roof was sloped. Steeply! Erlik take Baratses, he thought. And his gold!

This was no theft of his own choosing, but rather was at the behest of the merchant Baratses, a purveyor of spices from the most distant realms of the world. Ten pieces of gold the spice dealer had offered for the most prized possession of Samarides, a wealthy importer of gems: a goblet carved from a single huge emerald. Ten pieces of gold was the hundredth part of the goblet's worth, one tenth of what the fences in the Desert would pay, but a run of bad luck with the dice had put the Cimmerian in urgent need of coin. He had agreed to theft and price, and taken two gold pieces in advance, before he even knew what was to be stolen. Still, a bargain sworn to must be kept. At least, he thought grimly, there was no guard atop the other building, as there were on so many other merchants' roofs.

"Crom!" he muttered with a last look at Samarides' roof, and moved back from the edge, well back into the shadows among the chimneys. Breathing deeply to charge his lungs, he crouched. His eyes strained toward the distant rooftop. Suddenly, like a hunting leopard, he sprang forward; in two strides he was sprinting at full speed. His lead foot touched the edge of the roof, and he leaped, hurling himself into the air with arms outstretched, fingers curled to grab.

With a crash he landed at full length on the sloping roof. And immediately began to slide. Desperately he spread his arms and legs to slow himself; his eyes searched for a projection to grasp, for the smallest nub that might stop his fall. Inexorably he moved toward the drop to the pavement.

No wonder there was no watchman on the roof, he thought, furious at himself for not questioning that lack earlier. The rooftiles were glazed to a surface like oiled porcelain. In the space of a breath his feet were over the edge, then his legs. Abruptly his left hand slid into a gap where a tile was missing. Tiles shattered as his weight smashed his vainly gripping hand through them; fragments showered past him into the gloom beneath. Wood slapped his palm; convulsively he clutched. With a jerk that wrenched at the heavy muscles of his shoulder he was brought up short to swing over the shadowed four-story drop.

For the first time since his leap he made a sound, a long, slow exhalation between his teeth. "Ten gold pieces," he said in a flat voice, "are not enough."

Suddenly the wooden roof-frame he was grasping gave with a sharp snap, and he was falling again. Twisting as he dropped, he stretched, caught the finger-joint-wide ledge at the bottom of the frieze by his fingertips, and slammed flat against the alabaster wall.

"Not nearly enough," he panted when he had regained his breath. "I've half a mind to take the accursed thing to Zeno after this." But even as he said it he knew he would not go to the Nemedian fence. He had given his word.

At the moment, he realized, his problem lay not in how to dispose of the emerald goblet, but in how to leave his present position with a whole skin. The only openings piercing the alabaster wall at this height were ventilation holes the size of his fist, for the top floor and the attic were given over to storage and quarters for servants and slaves. Such needed no windows, to the mind of Samarides, and if they had them would only lean out and spoil the appearance of his fine house. No other ledges or friezes broke the smoothness of the walls, nor were there balconies overlooking the street. The roof he had first leaped from might as well have been in Sultanapur, the roof above as well have been beyond the clouds. That, the dangling youth reluctantly concluded, left only the windows of the third floor, their arched tops a good armspan lower than his feet.

It was not his way to dally when his course was decided. Slowly, hanging by his fingertips, he worked his way along the narrow ledge. The first two arched windows to pass beneath his feet glowed with light. He could not risk meeting people. The third, however, was dark.

Taking a deep breath, he let go his hold and dropped, his body brushing lightly against the wall. If he touched the wall too much, it would push him out and away to fall helplessly. As he felt his legs come in front of the window, he moved his feet inward, toward the window sill. Stone smashed against his soles, his palms slapped hard against the sides of the window, and he hung precariously, leaning outward. The thickness of the wall, the depth of the window, denied even a fingernail's hold. Only the outward pressure of his hands kept him from hurtling to the street.

Muscles knotted with the strain, he drew himself forward until he could step within Samarides' dwelling. As his foot touched the carpet-strewn floor, his hand went to the worn leather of his sword hilt. The room was dark, yet his night-accustomed eyes could make out the dim shapes of cushioned chairs. Tapestries, their colors reduced to shadings of gray, hung on the walls, and a dimly patterned carpet covered the marble floor. With a sigh he relaxed, a trifle, at least. This was no sleeping chamber, with someone to awaken and scream an alarm. It was about time something went right on this night of continuous near-disaster.

There were still problems, though. He was unsure whether the worst of these was how to get out of the dwelling—or how to get to his goal. Samarides' house was arranged around a central garden, where the gem merchant spent a great deal of his time among the fountains. The only door of the room in which he displayed his treasures opened onto the ground-floor colonnade around that garden.

It would have been easy to climb down from the roof to the garden, and Baratses had told him exactly the location of the door to the treasure room. Now he must make his way through the corridors, and risk coming on servants or guards.

Opening the door a crack, he peered into the hall, lit by gilded brass oil lamps hung on chains from bronze wall sconces. Tables inlaid with mother-of-pearl stood at intervals along walls mosaicked in intricate patterns with thousands of tiny, multihued tiles. No one trod the polished marble floor. Silently he slipped into the corridor.

For a heartbeat he stood, picturing the plan of the house in his mind. The treasure room was in *that* direction. Ears straining for the slightest hint of another's footstep, he hurried through the halls with a tread as light as a cat. Back stairs led downward, then others took him down again. Their location and the fact that their dark red tiles were dull and worn marked them as servant's stairs. Twice the scuff of sandals from a crossing corridor gave warning, and he pressed his back to a wall, barely breathing, while unseeing servants in pale blue tunics scurried by, too intent on their labors to so much as glance down the branching way.

Then he was into the central garden, the high, shadowed walls of the house making it a small canyon. Splash and burble echoed softly from half-a-score fountains, scattered among fig trees and flowering plants and alabaster statuary. The treasure room lay directly opposite him across the garden.

He took a step, and froze. A dim shape hurried toward him down one of the garden paths. Silently he moved further to the side, away from the light spilling from the doorway. The approaching figure slowed. Had he been seen, he wondered. Whoever was coming moved very slowly, now, seeming almost to creep, and made no sound at all. Abruptly the figure left the slated walk and moved toward him again. His jaw tightened; no other muscle of him moved, not so much as an eyelid blinking. Closer. Ten paces. Five. Two.

Suddenly the strangely still-dim figure froze, gasped. The big youth sprang. One hand cut off sound by covering the mouth that uttered it. His other arm pinned the figure's arms. Teeth dug into his calloused palm, and his captive flung about wildly, kicks thudding against his legs.

"Erlik take you!" he hissed. "You fight like a woman! Stop that, and I'll not hurt—"

It penetrated his mind that the body he held was rounded, if firm. He side-stepped to the edge of the light from the doorway, and found himself studying large, brown eyes that were suddenly frowning above his hand. It *was* a woman, and a pretty one, with satiny, olive skin and her hair braided tightly about her small head. The biting stopped, and he loosed his grip on her jaw. He opened his mouth to say he would not harm her if she gave no outcry, but she cut him off.

"I am a sorceress," she whispered hoarsely, "and I know you, Conan, far-traveler from Samaria, or Cymria, or some such place. You think you are a thief. Release me!"

The hairs on the back of his neck stirred. How could she know? He seemed to have a talent for running afoul of sorcerers, a talent he would just as soon lose. His grip was loosening when he became aware of the amused gleam in her big eyes, and the way her small, white teeth were biting a full lower lip. For the first time he took in her garb, snug, dull black from neck to toes. Even her feet were covered in ebon cloth, with the big toe separated like the thumb on a mitten.

Holding her out from him by her upper arms, he was unable to suppress a smile. Slender, she was, and short, but the close fit of her odd garments left no doubts as to her womanhood. She kicked at him, and he caught it on his thigh.

"Sorceress?" he growled softly. "Then why do I think you'll change your story should I take a switch to your rump?"

"Why do I think that at the first blow I'll howl loudly enough to bring half the city?" she whispered back. "But truly I don't wish to. My name is Lyana, and I've heard of you, Conan. I've seen you in the streets. And admired you. I just wanted to sound mysterious, so I could compete with your other women." She shifted in his grasp, and her round breasts, large on her diminutive slimness, seemed even more prominent. Her tongue wet her lips, and she smiled invitingly. "Could you please put me down? You're so strong, and you're hurting me."

He hesitated, then lowered her feet to the ground.

"What is this garb you wear, Lyana?"

"Forget that," she breathed, swaying closer. "Kiss me."

Despite himself his hands came up to clasp her face. Before his fingers touched her cheeks, she dropped to her knees and threw herself into a forward tumble past him. Stunned, he still managed to whirl after her. One tiny foot flashing from the middle of her roll caught him under the ribs, bringing a grunt, slowing him enough for her to come to her feet facing the wall . . . and she seemed to go up it like a spider.

With an oath Conan leaped forward. Something struck his arm, and he grabbed a soft, black-dye rope, hanging from above.

"Mitra blast me for a fool!" he grated. "A thief!"

Soft laughter floated down from close enough over his head to make him peer sharply upwards. "You are a fool." The girl's soft tones brimmed with mirth. "And I am indeed a thief, which you'll never be. Perhaps, with those shoulders, you could be a carter. Or a cart horse."

Snarling, Conan took hold of the rope to climb. A flicker caught the corner of his eye, and he felt more than heard something strike the ground by his foot. Instinctively, he jumped back, losing his grip on the rope. His grab to regain it brushed only the free end as it was drawn up.

"It would have struck you," the girl's low voice came again, "had I intended it so. Were I you, I'd leave here. Now. Fare you well, Conan."

"Lyana?" he whispered roughly. "Lyana?" Mocking silence answered him.

Muttering under his breath, he searched the ground around his feet, and tugged a flat, black throwing knife from the dirt. He tucked it behind his swordbelt, then stiffened as if stabbed.

The girl was a thief, and she had come from the direction of the treasure room. Cursing under his breath he ran, heedless of the rare shrubs and plants he passed.

An arched door led into the chamber where Samarides kept his most valuable possessions, and that door stood open. Conan paused a moment to study the heavy iron lock. That the girl had opened it he had no doubt, but if she had been within, then any traps must have been disabled, or else be easily avoided.

The Cimmerian hesitated a moment longer, then started across the chamber, floored in diamond-shaped tiles of alternating red and white. The emerald goblet, he had been told, stood at the far end of the room on a pedestal carved of serpentine. At his second step a diamond tile sank beneath his foot. Thinking of cross-bows mounted on the wall— he had encountered such before—he threw himself flat on the floor. And felt another tile sink beneath his hand. From the wall came a rattling clink and clatter he had been a thief long enough to recognize. The sinking tiles had each released a weight which was pulling a chain from a wheel. And that in turn would activate . . . what?

As he leaped to his feet a bell began to toll, then another. Cursing, he ran the length of the room. Twice more tiles sank beneath him, and by the time he reached the dull green mottled pedestal, four bells clanged the alarm. The pedestal was bare.

"Erlik take the wench!" he snarled.

Spinning, he dashed from the chamber. And ran head-on into two spear-carrying guards. As the three fell to the floor it flashed into Conan's head that it was just as well he had not dallied to choose something to make up for the loss of the goblet. His fist smashed into the face of one guard, nose and teeth cracking in a spray of red. The man jerked and sagged, unconscious. The other scrambled to his feet, spear ready to thrust. Had he delayed, Conan thought, they could likely have held him in the chamber long enough for others to arrive. His sword flickered from its sheath, caught the spear just behind the head, and the second guard found himself holding a long stick. With a shout the man threw the pole at Conan and fled.

Conan ran, too. In the opposite direction. At the first doorway of the house he ducked inside, bursting into the midst of servants nervously chattering about the still ringing bells. For an instant they stared at him, eyes going wider and wider, then he waved his sword in the air and roared at the top of his lungs. Shrieking men and women scattered like a covey of Kothian quail.

Confusion, the Cimmerian thought. If he spread enough confusion he might get out of there yet. Through the house he sped, and every servant he met was sent flying by fierce roars and waving blade, till cries of "Help!" and "Murder!" and even "Fire!" rang down every corridor. More than once the young Cimmerian had to duck down a side hall as guards clattered by, chasing after screams and yelling themselves, until he began to wonder how many men Samarides had. Cacophony run riot filled the house.

At last he reached the entry hall, surrounded on three sides by a balcony with balustrades of smoke-stone, beneath a vaulted ceiling worked in alabaster arabesques. Twin broad stairs of black marble curved down from that second-floor balcony to a floor mosaicked in a map of the world, as Zamorans knew it, with each country marked by representations of the gems imported from it.

All of this Conan ignored, his eyes locked on the tall, iron-studded doors leading to the street. A bar, heavy enough to need three men for the lifting, held them shut, and the bar was in turn fastened in place by iron chains and massive locks.

"Crom!" he growled. "Shut up like a fortress!"

Once, twice, thrice his broadsword clashed against a lock, with him wincing at the damage the blows were doing to his edge. The lock broke open, and he quickly pulled the chain through the iron loops holding it against the bar. As he turned to the next chain, a quarrel as thick as two of his fingers slammed into the bar where he had been standing. He changed his turn into a dive to the floor, eyes searching for the next shot.

Instantly he saw his lone opponent. Atop one flight of stairs stood a man of immense girth, whose skin yet hung in folds as if he had once been twice so big. Lank, thinning hair surrounded his puffy face, and he wore a shapeless sleeping garment of dark blue silk. Samarides. One of the gem merchant's feet was in the stirrup of a heavy crossbow, and he laboriously worked the handles of a windlass to crank back the bow-string, a rope of drool running from one corner of his narrow mouth.

Quickly judging how long it would be before Samarides could place another quarrel in the crossbow, Conan bounded to his feet. A single furious blow that struck sparks sent the second lock clattering to the floor. Sheathing his sword, the Cimmerian tugged the chain free and set his hands to the massive bar.

"Guards!" Samarides screamed. "To me! Guards!"

Muscles corded and knotted in calves and thighs, back, shoulders and arms, as Conan strained against the huge wooden bar. By the thickness of a fingernail it lifted. Sweat popped out on his forehead. The thickness of a finger. The width of a hand. And then the massive bar was clear of the support irons.

Three slow, staggering steps backwards Conan took, until he could turn and heave the bar aside. Mosaic tiles shattered as it landed with a crash that shook the floor.

"Guards!" Samarides shrieked, and pounding feet answered him.

Conan dashed to the thick, iron-studded doors and heaved one open to crash against a wall. As he darted through, another quarrel slashed past his head to gouge a furrow in the marble of Samarides' portico. Tumult rose behind him as guards rushed into the entry hall, shouting to Samarides for instructions, and Samarides screamed incoherently back at them. Conan did not look back. He ran. Mind filled with anger at a young woman thief with a too-witty tongue, he ran until the night of Shadizar swallowed him.

II

That quarter of Shadizar called the Desert was a warren of crooked steets reeking of offal and despair. The debaucheries that took place behind closed doors in the rest of the city were performed openly in the Desert, and made to pay a profit. Its denizens, more often in rags than not, lived as if death could come with the next breath, as it quite often did. Men and women were scavengers, predators or prey, and some who thought themselves in one class discovered, frequently too late, that they were in another.

The tavern of Abuletes was one of the Desert's best, as such was accounted there. Few footpads and fewer cutpurses were numbered among its patrons. Graverobbers were unwelcome, though more for the smells that hung about them than for how they earned their coin. For the rest, all who had the price of a drink were welcome.

When Conan slapped open the tavern door, the effluvia of the street fought momentarily with the smell of half-burned meat and sour wine in the big common room where two musicians playing zithers for a naked dancing girl competed unsuccessfully with the babble of the tavern's custom. A mustachioed Nemedian coiner at the bar fondled a giggling doxy in a tall, red-dyed wig and strips of green silk that did little to cover her generously rounded breasts and buttocks. A plump Ophirean procurer, jeweled rings glittering on his fingers, held court at a corner table; among those laughing at his jokes—so long as his gold held out, at least—were three kidnappers, swarthy, narrow-faced Iranistanis, hoping he would throw a little business their way. A pair of doxies, dark-eyed twins, hawked their wares among the tables, their girdles of coins clinking as their hips swayed in unison.

Before the Cimmerian had taken a full step, a voluptuous, olive-skinned woman threw her arms around his neck. Gilded brass breast-plates barely contained her heavy breasts, and a narrow girdle of gilded chain, set low on her well-rounded hips, supported a length of diaphanous blue silk, no more than a handspan in width, that hung to her braceleted ankles before and behind.

"Ah, Conan," she murmured thoatily, "what a pity you did not return earlier."

"Have some wine with me, Semiramis," he replied, eying her swelling chest, "and tell me why I should have come back sooner. Then we can go upstairs—" He cut off with a frown as she shook her head.

"I ply my trade this night, Cimmerian." At his frown, she sighed. "Even I must have a little silver to live."

"I have silver," he growled.

"And I cannot take coin from you. I will not."

He muttered an oath under his breath. "You always say that. Why not? I don't understand."

"Because you're not a woman." She laughed softly and traced a finger along his jaw. "A thing for which I am continually grateful."

Conan's face tightened. First Lyana had made a fool of him this night, and now Semiramis attempted the same. "Women never say their minds straight out. Very well. If you've no use for me tonight, then I'm done with you as well." He left her standing with her fists on her hips and her mouth twisted in exasperation.

At the bar he dug into his purse and tossed coppers onto the cracked wooden surface. As he had known it would, the sound of coins penetrated the wall of noise in the room and drew Abuletes, wiping his fat fingers on the filthy apron he wore over a faded yellow tunic. The tavernkeeper made the coins disappear with a deft motion.

"I want wine for that," Conan said. Abuletes nodded. "And some information."

" 'Tis enough for the wine," the tavernkeeper replied drily. He set a wooden tankard, from which rose the sour smell of cheap wine, before the big youth. "Information costs more."

Conan rubbed his thumb over a gouge in the edge of the bar, made by a sword stroke, drawing the fat man's piggish eyes to the mark. "There were six of them, as I recall," he said absently. "One with his knife pricking your ribs, and ready to probe your guts if you opened your mouth without his leave. What was it they intended? Taking you into the kitchen, wasn't it? Didn't one of them speak of putting your feet in the cookfire till you told where your gold is cached?"

"I have no gold," Abuletes muttered unconvincingly. He could spot a clipped coin at ten paces, and was reliably rumored to have the first copper he had ever stolen buried somewhere in the tavern.

"Of course not," Conan agreed smoothly. "Still, it was Hannuman's own luck for you I saw what was happening, when none else did. 'Twould have been . . . uncomfortable for you, with your feet in the coals and naught to tell them."

"Aye, you saw." The fat man's tone was as sour as his wine. "And laid about you with that accursed sword, splintering half my tables. Do you know what they cost to replace? The doxies were hysterical for all the blood you splattered around, and half my night's custom disappeared for fear you'd cut them down as well."

Conan laughed and drank deeply from the tankard, saying no more. Never a night passed without blood shed on the sawdust-strewn floor, and it was no rare sight to see a corpse being dragged out back for disposal in an alley.

Abuletes' face twisted, and his chin sank until his chins doubled in number. "This makes it clear between us. Right?"

The Cimmerian nodded, but cautioned, "If you tell me what I want to hear. I look for a woman." Abuletes snorted and gestured to the doxies scattered through the common room. Conan went on patiently. "She's a thief, about so tall," he marked with one big hand at the height of his chest, "and well rounded for her size. Tonight she wore black leggings and a short tunic, both as tight as her skin. And she carried this." He laid the thowing knife on the bar. "She calls herself Lyana."

Abuletes prodded the black blade with a grimy-knuckled finger. "I know of no woman thief, called Lyana or aught else. There was a man, though, who used knives like this. Jamal, he was named."

"A woman, Abuletes."

The fat tapster shrugged. "He had a daughter. What was her name? Let me see." He rubbed at a suety cheek. "Jamal was shortened a head by the City Guard, it must be ten years back. His brothers took the girl in. Gayan and Hafid. They were thieves, too. Haven't heard of them in years, though. Too old for the life now, I suppose. Age gets us all, in the end. Tamira. That was her name. Tamira."

The muscular youth stared expressionless at Abuletes until the fat tavernkeeper fell silent. "I ask about a girl called Lyana, and you spin me a tale of this Tamira. And her entire Mitra-accursed family. Would you care to tell me about her mother? Her grandfather? I've a mind to put your feet in the fire myself."

Abuletes eyed Conan warily. The man with the strange blue eyes was known in the Desert for his sudden temper, and for his unpredictability. The tavernkeeper spread his hands. "How hard is it to give a name not your own? And didn't I say? Jamal and his brothers wore the black garments you spoke of. Claimed it made them all but invisible in the dark. Had all sorts of tricks, they did. Ropes of raw silk dyed black, and I don't know what all. No, Tamira's your female thief, all right, whatever she calls herself now."

Black ropes, Conan thought, and suppressed a smile. Despite his youth he had had enough years as a thief to learn discretion. "Perhaps," was all he said.

"Perhaps," the tapster grumbled. "You mark me on it. She's the one. This makes us even, Cimmerian."

Conan finished his wine in three long gulps and set the empty tankard down with a click. "If she *is* the woman I seek. The question now is where to find her and make certain."

Abuletes threw up his pudgy hands. "Do you think I keep track of every woman in the Desert? I can't even keep track of the trulls in my own tavern!"

Conan turned his back on the tavernkeeper's grinding teeth. Tamira and Lyana, he was sure, were one and the same woman. Luck must be with him, for he had expected days of asking to find a trace of her. Denizens of the Desert left as few tracks as the animals of that district's namesake. Surely discovering so much so quickly was an omen. No doubt he would leave the tavern in the morning and find her walking past in the street. Then they would see who would make a fool of whom.

At that moment his eye fell on Semiramis, seated at a table with three Kothian smugglers. One, with his mustache curled like horns and big gilded hoops in his ears, kneaded her bare thigh as he spoke to her urgently. Nodding in sudden decision, Conan strode to the table where the four sat.

The Kothians looked up, and Semiramis frowned. "Conan," she began, reaching toward him cautioningly.

The big Cimmerian grasped her wrist, bent and, before anyone could move, hoisted her over his shoulder. Stools crashed over as the Kothians leaped to their feet, hands going to sword hilts.

"You northland oaf!" Semiramis howled, wriggling furiously. Her fist pounded futilely at his back. "Unhand me, you misbegotten spawn of a camel! Mitra blast your eyes, Conan!"

Her tirade went on, getting more inventive, and Conan paused to listen admiringly. The Kothians hesitated with swords half drawn, disconcerted at being ignored. After a moment Conan turned his attention to them, putting a pleasant smile on his face. That seemed to unsettle the three even more.

"My sister," he said mildly. "She and I must speak of family matters."

"Erlik flay your hide and stake your carcass in the sun!" the struggling woman yelled. "Derketo shrivel your stones!"

Calmly Conan met each man's gaze in turn, and each man shivered, for his smile did not extend to those glacial blue orbs. The Kothians measured the breadth of his shoulders, calculated how encumbered he would be by the woman, and tossed the dice in the privacy of their minds.

"I wouldn't interfere between brother and sister," the one with hoops in his ears muttered, his eyes sliding away. Suddenly all three were engrossed in setting their stools upright.

Semiramis' shouts redoubled in fury as Conan started for the rickety stairs that led to the second floor. He smacked a rounded buttock with his open palm. "Your sweet poetry leads me to believe you love me," he said, "but your dulcet tones would deafen an ox. Be quiet."

Her body quivered. It took him a moment to realize she was laughing. "Will you at least let me walk, you untutored beast?" she asked.

"No," he replied with a grin.

"Barbarian!" she murmured, and snuggled her cheek against his back.

Laughing, he took the stairs two at a time. Luck was indeed with him.

The Katara Bazaar was a kaleidoscope of colors and a cacophony of voices, a large, flagstone-paved square near the Desert where sleek lordlings, perfumed pomanders at their nostrils, rubbed shoulders with unwashed apprentices who apologized with mocking grins when they jostled the well-born. Silk-clad ladies, trailed by attentive slaves to carry their purchases, browsed unmindful of the ragged urchins scurrying about their feet. Some vendors displayed their goods on flimsy tables sheltered by faded lengths of cloth on poles. Others had no more than a blanket spread beneath the hot sun. Hawkers of plums and ribbons, oranges and pins, cried their wares shrilly as they strolled through the throng. Rainbow bolts of cloth, carved ivories from Vendhya, brass bowls from Shadizar's own metalworkers, lustrous pearls from the Western Sea and paste "gems" guaranteed to be genuine, all changed hands in the space of a heartbeat. Some were stolen, some smuggled. A rare few had even had the King's tax paid on them.

On the morning after his attempt at Samarides' goblet—the thought made him wince—Conan made his way around the perimeter of the bazaar, searching without seeming to among the beggars. Mendicants were not allowed within the confines of the great square, but they lined its edges, their thin, supplicating cries entreating passersby for a coin. There was a space between each ragged man and the next, and unlike beggars elsewhere in Shadizar these cooperated to the extent of maintaining that distance. Too many too close together would reduce each man's take.

Exchanging a copper with a fruitmonger for two oranges, the big

Cimmerian squatted near a beggar in filthy rags, a man with one leg twisted grotesquely at the knee. A grimy strip of cloth covered his eyes, and a wooden bowl with a single copper in the bottom sat on the flagstones before him.

"Pity the blind," the beggar whined loudly. "A coin for the blind, gentle people. Pity the blind."

Conan tossed one orange into the bowl and began stripping the peel from the other. "Ever think of going back to being a thief, Peor?" he said quietly.

The "blind" man turned his head sightly to make sure no one else was close by and said, "Never, Cimmerian." His cheerful voice was pitched to reach Conan's ear and no further. He made the orange disappear beneath his tunic of patches. "For later. No, I pay my tithe to the City Guard, and I sleep easy at night knowing my head will never go up on a pike over the West Gate. You should consider becoming a beggar. 'Tis a solid trade. Not like thieving. Mitra-accursed mountain slime!"

Conan paused with a segment of orange half-lifted to his mouth. "What?"

Barely moving his head, Peor motioned to a knot of six Kezankian hillmen, turbanned and bearded, their dark eyes wide with ill-concealed amazement at the city around them. They wandered through the bazaar in a daze, fingering goods but never buying. From the scowls that followed them, the peddlers were glad to see their backs, sale or no. "That's the third lot of those filthy jackals I've seen today, and a good two turns of the glass till the sun is high. They should be running for the rocks they crawled out from under, what with the news that's about this morning."

The beggar got little chance between sunrise and sunset to say anything beyond his pleading cry, and the occasional fawning thanks. It could not hurt to let him talk, Conan thought, and said, "What news?"

Peor snorted. "If it was about a new method of winning at dice, Cimmerian, you'd have known of it yesterday. Do you think of anything but women and gambling?"

"The news, Peor?"

"They say someone is uniting the Kezankian tribes. They say the hillmen are sharpening their tulwars. They say it could mean war. If 'tis so, the Desert will feel the first blow, as always."

Conan tossed the last of the orange aside and wiped his hands on his thighs. "The Kezankians are far distant, Peor." His grin revealed strong white teeth. "Or do you think the tribesmen will leave their mountains to sack the Desert? It is not the place I would chose, were I they, but you are older than I and no doubt know better."

"Laugh, Cimmerian," Peor said bitterly. "But when war is announced the mob will hunt for hillman throats to slit, and when they cannot find enough to sate their bloodlust, they'll turn their attentions to the Desert. And the army will be there—'to preserve order.' Which means to put to the sword any poor sod from the Desert who thinks of actually re- sisting the mob. It has happened before, and will again."

A shadow fell across them, cast by a woman whose soft robes of emerald silk clung to the curves of breasts and belly and thighs like a caress. A belt woven of golden cords was about her waist. Ropes of pearls encircled her wrists and neck, and two more, as large as a man's thumb- nail, were at her ears. Behind her a tall Shemite, the iron collar of a slave on his neck and a bored expression on his face, stood laden with packages from the Bazaar. She dropped a silver coin in Peor's bowl, but her sultry gaze was all for Conan.

The muscular youth enjoyed the looks women gave him, as a normal matter, but this one examined him as if he were a horse in the auction barns. And to make matters worse a scowl grew on the Shemite's face as though he recognized a rival. Conan's face grew hot with anger. He opened his mouth, but she spoke first.

"My husband would never approve the purchase," she smiled, and walked away with undulating hips. The Shemite hurried after her, cast- ing a self-satisfied glance over his shoulder at Conan as he went.

Peor's bony fingers fished the coin from the bowl. With a cackle that showed he had regained at least some of his humor, he tucked it into his pouch. "And she'd pay a hundred times so much for a single night with you, Cimmerian. Two hundred. A more pleasant way to earn your coin than scrambling over rooftops, eh?"

"Would you like that leg broken in truth?" Conan growled.

The beggar's cackles grew until they took him into a fit of coughing. When he could breathe normally again, he wiped the back of his hand across his thin-lipped mouth. "No doubt I would earn even more in my bowl. My knee hurts of a night for leaving it so all day, but that fall was the best thing that ever happened to me."

Conan shivered at the thought, but pressed on while the other held his good mood. "I did not come today just to give you an orange, Peor. I look for a woman called Lyana, or perhaps Tamira."

Peor nodded as the Cimmerian described the girl and gave a carefully edited account of their meeting, then said, "Tamira. I've heard that name, and seen the girl. She looks as you say."

"Where can I find her?" Conan asked eagerly, but the beggar shook his head.

"I said I've seen her, and more than once, but as to where she might be . . ." He shrugged.

Conan put a hand to the leather purse at his belt. "Peor, I could manage a pair of silver pieces for the man who tells me how to find her."

"I wish I knew," Peor said ruefully, then went on quickly. "But I'll pass the word among the Brotherhood of the Bowl. If a beggar sees her, you'll hear of it. After all, friendship counts for something, does it not?"

The Cimmerian cleared his throat to hide a grin. Friendship, indeed! The message would come to him through Peor, and the beggar who sent it would be lucky to get as much as one of the silver pieces. "That it does," he agreed.

"But, Conan? I don't hold with killing women. You don't intend to hurt her, do you?"

"Only her pride," Conan said, getting to his feet. With the beggars' eyes as his, he would have her before the day was out. "Only her pride."

Two days later Conan threaded his way through the thronging crowds with a sour expression on his face. Not only the beggars of Shadizar had become his eyes. More than one doxy had smiled at the ruggedly handsome young Cimmerian, shivered in her depths at the blue of his eyes, and promised to watch for the woman he sought, though never without a pout of sultry jealousy. The street urchins, unimpressed by broad shoulders or azure eyes, had been more difficult. Some men called them the Dust, those homeless, ragged children, countless in number and helpless before the winds of fate, but the streets of Shadizar were a hard school, and the urchins gave trust grudgingly and demanded a reward in silver. But from all those eyes he had learned only where Tamira had been, and never a word of where she was.

Conan's eyes searched among the passersby, seeking to pierce the veils of those women who wore them. At least, the veils of those who were slender and no taller than his chest. What he would do when he found her was not yet clear in his mind beyond the matter of seeking restitution for his youthful pride, but find her he would if he had to stare into the face of every woman in Shadizar.

So intent was he on his thoughts that the drum that cleared others from the street, even driving sedan chairs to the edge of the pavement, did not register on his mind until it suddenly came to him that he stood alone in the middle of the street. Turning to see where the steady thump came from, he found a procession bearing down on him.

At its head were two spearmen as tall as he, ebon-eyed men with capes of leopard skin, the clawed paws hanging across their broad, bare chests. Behind came the drummer, his instrument slung by his side to give free swing to the mallets with which he beat a cadence. A score of men in spiked helms and short, sleeveless mail followed the drummer. Half bore spears and half bows, with quivers on their backs, and all wore wide, white trousers and high, red boots.

Conan's eyes went no further down the cortege than the horsemen who came next, or rather the woman who led them, mounted on a prancing black gelding a hand taller than any her followers rode. Tall she was, and well rounded, a delight both callimastian and callipygean. Her garb of tight tunic and tighter breeches, both of tawny silk, with a scarlet cloak thrown well back across her horse's rump, did naught to hide her curves. Light brown hair, sun-streaked with gold, curled about her shoulders and surrounded a prideful face set with clear gray eyes.

She was a woman worth looking at, Conan thought. And besides, he knew of her, as did every thief in Shadizar. The Lady Jondra was known for many things, her arrogance, her hunting, her racing of horses, but among thieves she was known as the possessor of a necklace and tiara that had set more than one man's mouth watering. Each was set with a flawless ruby, larger than the last joint of a big man's thumb, surrounded by sapphires and black opals. In the Desert men taunted each other with the stealing of them, for of all those who had tried, the only one not taken by the spears of her guards had died with Jondra's own arrows in his eyes. It was said she had been more furious that the thief entered her chambers while she was bathing than at his bungled attempt at theft.

Conan prepared to step from the procession's path, when the spearmen, not five paces from him now, dropped their spears to the ready. They did not slow their pace, but came on as if the threat should send him scurrying for cover.

The big Cimmerian's face tightened. Did they think him a dog, then, to beat from their way? A young man's pride, dented as much as he could stand in recent days, hardened. He straightened, and his hand went to the worn, leather-wrapped hilt of his broadsword. Dead silence fell among the crowd lining the sides of the street.

The spearmen's eyes widened at the sight of the young giant standing his ground. The streets always cleared before their mistress, the drum usually sufficing, and never more than the gleam of a spearpoint in the sunlight required at most. It came to each in the same instant that this was no apprentice to be chivvied aside. As one man they stopped and dropped into a crouch with spears presented.

The drummer, marching obliviously, continued his pounding until he was between the two spearmen. There his mallets froze, one raised and one against the drumhead, and his eyes darted for a way out. The three men made a barricade across the street that perforce brought the rest of Lady Jondra's cortege to a halt, first the mailed hunters, then the horsemen, and so back down the line, till all stood stopped.

The ludicrousness of it struck Conan, and he felt mirth rising despite himself. How did he get himself into these predicaments, he wondered.

"You there!" a husky woman's voice called. "You, big fellow with the sword!" Conan looked up to find the Lady Jondra staring at him over the heads of her spearmen and archers. "If you can stop Zurat and Tamal in their tracks, perhaps you can face a lion as well. I always need men, and there are few who deserve the name in Shadizar. I will take you into my service." A tall, hawk-faced man riding next to her opened his mouth angrily, but she cut him off with a gesture. "What say you? You have the shoulders for a spearman."

The laughter broke through, and Conan let it roar, though he was careful not to take his eyes from the spearmen or his hand from his sword. Jondra's face slowly froze in amazement. "I am already in service," he managed, "to myself. But, my lady, I wish you good day and will no longer block your passage." He made a sweeping bow—not deep enough to lose sight of the spear points—and strode to the side of the street.

For an instant there was stunned silence, then the Lady Jondra was shouting. "Zurat! Tamal! March on! Junio! The beat!"

The spearmen straightened, and the drummer stiffly took up his cadence again. In moments the procession was moving. Jondra rode past stiffly, her eyes drifting to the big Cimmerian as if she did not realize what she did. The hawk-faced man rode beside her, arguing volubly, but she seemed not to hear.

A knot of barefooted street urchins, all color long faded from their tattered tunics, suddenly appeared near Conan. Their leader was a girl, though at an age when her scrawniness could pass for either sex. Half a head taller than her followers, she swaggered to the muscular youth's side and studied the array of hunters. The lion dogs passed, heavy, snarling brutes with spiked collars, pulling hard on the leashes held by their handlers.

"Dog like that could take your leg off," the girl said. "Big man, you get a spear in your belly, and who's going to pay us?"

"You get paid when you've found her, Laeta," Conan replied. The trophies of the hunt were borne by, skins of leopards and lions, great scimitar antelope horns, the skull of a huge wild ox with horns as thick and long as a man's arm, all held aloft for the view of the onlookers.

She cast a scornful glance at him. "Did I not say as much? We found the wench, and I want those two pieces of silver."

Conan grunted. "When I am sure it's her."

This was not the first report of Tamira he had had. One had been a woman more than twice his age, another a potter's apprentice with only one eye. The last of Jondra's procession passed, pack animals and high-wheeled ox-carts, and the throng that had stood aside flowed together behind like water behind a boat.

"Take me to her," Conan said.

Laeta grumbled, but trotted away down the street, her coterie of hard-eyed urchins surrounding her like a bodyguard. Under every ragged tunic, the Cimmerian knew, was a knife, or more than one. The children of the street preferred to run, but when cornered they were as dangerous as a pack of rats.

To Conan's surprise they moved no closer to the Desert, but rather farther away, into a district peopled by craftsmen. The din of brass-smiths' hammers beat at them, then the stench of the dyers' vats. Smoke from kiln fires rose on all sides. Finally the girl stopped and pointed to a stone building where a sign hanging from chains showed the image of a lion, half-heartedly daubed not too long past with fresh carmine.

"In there?" Conan asked suspiciously. Taverns attracted likes, and a thief would not likely be welcome amid potters and dyers.

"In there," Laeta agreed. She chewed her lip, then sighed. "We will wait out here, big man. For the silver."

Conan nodded impatiently and pushed open the tavern door.

Inside, the Red Lion was arranged differently from the usual tavern. At some time in the past a fire had gutted the building. The ground floor, which had collapsed into the cellar, had never been replaced. Instead, a balcony had been built running around the inside of the building at street level, and the common room was now in what had been the cellar. Even when the sun was high on the hottest day, the common room of the Red Lion remained cool.

From a place by the balcony rail just in front of the door, Conan ran his gaze over the interior of the tavern, searching for a slender female form. A few men stood on the balcony, some lounging against the railing with tankard in hand, most bargaining quietly with doxies for time in the rooms abovestairs. A steady stream of serving girls trotted up and down stairs at the rear of the common room with trays of food and drink, for the kitchen was still on the ground level. Tables scattered across the stone floor below held potters whose arms were flecked with dried clay and leather-aproned metal workers and apprentices with tunics stained by rainbow splashes.

The ever-present trulls, their wisps of silk covering no more here than they did in the Desert, strolled the floor, but as he had expected Conan could see no other women among the tables. Satisfied that Laeta was mistaken or lying, he started to turn for the door. From the corner of his eye he saw a burly potter, with a round-breasted doxy running her fingers through his hair, look away from her bounty to glance curiously at a spot below where the big Cimmerian stood. Another man, his leather apron lying across the table before him and a squealing jade on his knees, paused in his pawing of her to do the same. And yet another man.

Conan leaned to look over the railing, and there Tamira sat beneath him, demurely clothed in pale blue robes, face scrubbed to virginal freshness . . . and a wooden mug upended at her mouth. With a sigh she set the mug on the table upside-down, a signal to the serving girls that she wanted it refilled.

Smiling, Conan slipped the flat throwing knife from his belt. A flicker of his hand, and the black blade quivered in the upturned bottom of her mug. Tamira started, then was still except for the fingers of her left hand drumming on the tabletop. The Cimmerian's smile faded. With a muttered oath he stalked to the stairs and down.

When he reached the table the throwing knife had disappeared. He ignored the wide-eyed looks of men at nearby tables and sat across from her.

"You cost me eight pieces of gold," were his first words.

The corners of Tamira's mouth twitched upward. "So little? I received forty from the Lady Zayella."

Conan's hand gripped the edge of the table till the wood creaked in protest. Forty! "Zarath the Kothian would give a hundred," he muttered, then went on quickly before she could ask why he was then only to receive eight. "I want a word with you, wench."

"And I with you," she said. "I didn't come to a place like this, and let you find me, just to—"

"Let me find you!" he roared. A man at a nearby table hurriedly got up and moved away.

"Of course, I did." Her face and voice were calm, but her fingers began to tap on the table again. "How could I fail to know that every beggar in Shadizar, and a fair number of the trulls, were asking after my whereabouts?"

"Did you think I would forget you?" he asked sarcastically.

She went on as if he had not spoken. "Well, I will not have it. You'll get in my—my uncles' attention. They'll not take kindly to a stranger seeking after me. I led you here, well away from the Desert, in the hopes they'll not hear of our meeting. You'll find yourself with a blade in your throat, Cimmerian. And for some reason I don't quite understand, I would not like that."

Conan looked at her silently, until under his gaze her large, dark eyes began blinking nervously. Her finger-drumming quickened. "So you do know my country of birth."

"You fool, I am trying to save your life."

"Your uncles look after you?" he said abruptly. "Watch over you? Protect you?"

"You will find out how carefully if you do not leave me alone. And what's that smug grin for?"

"It's just that now I know I'll be your first man." His tone was complacent, but his every muscle tensed.

Tamira's mouth worked in silent incredulity, and scarlet suffused her cheeks. Suddenly a shriek burst from her lips, and the throwing knife was in her hand. Conan threw himself from his bench as her arm whipped forward. Beyond him an apprentice yelped and stared disbelieving at the tip of his nose, from which a steady drip of red fell to put new blotches on his dye-stained tunic.

Warily Conan got to his feet. Tamira shook her small fists at him in incoherent fury. At least, he thought, she did not have another of those knives. It would be out, otherwise. "But you must ask me," he said as if there had been no interruption. "That will make up for the eight gold pieces you stole from me, when you ask me."

"Erlik take you!" she gasped. "Mitra blast your soul! To think I worried . . . to think I . . . You're nothing but an oaf after all! I hope my uncles do catch you! I hope the City Guard puts your head on a pike! I hope—I hope—oh!" From head to toe she shook with rage.

"I eagerly await our first kiss," Conan said, and dodged her mug, aimed at his head.

Calmly turning his back on her wordless shouts, he strolled up the stairs and out of the tavern. As soon as the door closed behind him, his casual manner disappeared. Urgently he looked for Laeta, and smiled when she appeared with her palm out.

Before she could ask he tossed her two silver coins. "There's more," he said. "I want to know everywhere she goes, and everyone she sees. A silver piece every tenday for you, and the same for your followers." Baratses' gold was disappearing fast, he thought, but with luck it should last just long enough.

Laeta, with her mouth open to bargain, could only nod wordlessly.

Conan smiled in satisfaction. He had Tamira now. After his performance she thought he was a buffoon intent on seduction to salve his pride. He doubted if she even remembered her slip of the tongue. Almost she had said he would get in her way. She planned a theft, and wanted no encumbrance. But this time *he* would get there first, and *she* would find the empty pedestal.

IV

Much of the Zamoran nobility, the Lady Jondra thought as she strolled through her palace garden, deplored that the last of the Perashanids was a woman. Carefully drawing back the vermilion silk sleeve of her robe, she dabbled her fingers in the sparkling waters of a fountain rimmed with gray-veined marble. From the corner of her eye she watched the man who stood next to her. His handsome, dark-eyed face radiated self-assurance. A heavy gold chain, each link worked with the seal of his family, hung across the crisp pleats of his citrine tunic. Lord Amaranides did not deplore her femininity at all. It meant that all the wealth of the Perashanids went with her hand. If he could manage to secure that hand.

"Let us walk on, Ama," she said, and smiled at his attempt to hide a grimace for the pet name she had given him. He would think the smile was for him, she knew. It was not in him to imagine otherwise.

"The garden is lovely," he said. "But not so lovely as you."

Instead of taking his proffered arm she moved ahead down the slate-tiled walk, forcing him to hurry to catch up to her.

Eventually she would have to wed. The thought brought a sigh of regret, but duty would do what legions of suitors had been unable to. She could not allow the Perashanid line to end with her. Another sigh passed her full lips.

"Why so melancholy, my sweetling?" Amaranides murmured in her ear. "Let me but taste your honey kiss, and I will sweep your moodiness away."

Deftly she avoided his lips, but made no further discouraging move.

Unlike most nobly born Zamoran women, she allowed few men so much
as a kiss, and none more. But even if she could not bring herself to stop
her occasional tweaking of his well-stuffed pomposity, Amaranides must
not be put off entirely.

At least he was tall enough, she thought. She never allowed herself
to contemplate the reason why she was taller than most Zamoran men,
but she had long since decided that her husband must be taller than she.
Amaranides was a head taller, but his build was slender. With an idle
corner of her mind she sketched the man she wanted. Of noble lineage,
certainly. An excellent horseman, archer and hunter, of course. Physi-
cally? Taller than Amaranides by nearly a head. Much broader of shoulders, with a deep, powerful chest. Handsome, but more ruggedly so than
her companion. His eyes . . .

Abruptly she gasped as she recognized the man she had drawn in her
mind. She had dressed him as a Zamoran nobleman, but it was the sky-
eyed street-ruffian who had disrupted her return from the hunt. Her
face flooded with scarlet. Blue eyes! A barbarian! Like smoky gray fires
her own eyes blazed. That she could consider allowing such a one to
touch her, even without realizing it! Mitra! It was worse done without
realizing it!

". . . And on my last hunt," Amaranides was saying, "I killed a truly
magnificent leopard. Finer than any you've taken, I fancy. It will be a
pleasure for me to teach you the finer points of hunting, my little sweet-
meat. I . . ."

Jondra ground her teeth as he rattled blithely on. Still, he *was* a
hunter, not to mention nobly born. If he was a fool—and of that there
was little doubt in her mind—then he would be all the more easily
managed.

"I know why you've come, Ama," she said.

". . . Claws as big as . . ." The nobleman's voice trailed off, and he
blinked uncertainly. "You know?"

She could not keep impatience from her voice. "You want me for
your wife. Is that not it? Come." Briskly she set out through the garden
toward the fletcher's mound.

Amaranides hesitated, then ran after her. "You don't know how happy
you've made me, sweetling. Sweetling? Jondra? Where are you . . . ah!"

Jondra fended off the arms he tried to throw around her with a recurved bow she had taken from a gilded rack standing on a grassy sward.
Calmly she slipped a leather bracer onto her left arm for protection
from the bowstring. Another bow, a second bracer, and two quivers,

clustered fletchings rising above their black-lacquered sides, hung on the rack.

"You must . . . equal me," she said, gesturing toward a small round target of thickly woven straw hanging at the top of a wide wooden frame, which was three times the height of a man, a hundred paces distant. She had intended to say 'best,' but at the last could not bring herself to it. In truth, she did not believe *any* man could best her, either with a bow or on horseback. "I can marry no man who is not my equal as an archer."

Amaranides eyed the target, then took the second bow with a smug smile. "Why so high? No matter. I wager I'll beat you at it." He laughed then, a shocking bray at odds with his handsome features. "I've won many a purse with a bow, but you will be my finest prize."

Jondra's mouth tightened. Shaking back the hanging sleeves of her robes, she nocked an arrow and called, "Mineus!"

A balding man, in the short white tunic of a servant, came from the bushes near the frame and tugged at a rope attached near the target. Immediately the target, no bigger than a man's head, began to slide down a diagonal, and as it slid it swung from side to side on a long wooden arm. Clearly it would take a zig-zag path, at increasing speed, all the way to the ground.

Jondra did not raise her bow until the target had traversed half the first diagonal. Then, in one motion, she raised, drew and released. With a solid thwack her shaft struck, not slowing the target's descent. Before that arrow had gone home her second was loosed, and a third followed on its heels. As the straw target struck the ground, she lowered her bow with an arrow nocked but unreleased. It was her seventh. Six feathered shafts decorated the target. "The robes hamper me somewhat," she said ruefully. "With your tunic, you may well get more than my six. Let me clothe myself in hunting garb—are you ill, Ama?"

Amaranides' bow hung from a limp hand. He stared, pale of face, at the target. As he turned to her, high color replaced the pallor of his cheeks. His mouth twisted around his words. "I have heard that you delight in besting men, but I had not thought you would claim yourself ready to wed just to lure me to . . . this!" He spat the last word, hurling the bow at the riddled target. "What Brythunian witch-work did you use to magic your arrows?"

Her hands shook with rage as she raised her bow and drew the nocked arrow back to her cheek, but she forced them to be steady. "Remove yourself!" she said grimly.

Mouth falling open, the dark-faced nobleman stared at the arrow pointed at his face. Abruptly he spun about and ran, dodging from side to side, shoulders hunched, as if simultaneously attempting to avoid her arrow and steel himself against its strike.

She followed every skip and leap, keeping the arrow centered on him until he had disappeared among the shrubs. Then she released the breath in her tight lungs and the tension on her bowstring together. Thoughts she had disciplined from her mind came flooding back.

Lord Karentides, her father, had been a general of the Zamoran Army, as well as the last scion of an ancient house. Campaigning on the Brythunian border he chose a woman from among the prisoners, Camardica, tall and gray-eyed, who claimed to be a priestess. In the normal course of events there would have been nothing strange in this, for Zamoran soldiers often enjoyed themselves with captive Brythunian women, and the Brythunian slaves in Zamora were beyond counting. But Karentides married his captive. Married her and accepted the ostracism that became his.

Jondra remembered his body—his and . . . that woman's—lying in state after the fever that slew so many in the city, sparing neither noble nor beggar. She had been raised, educated, protected as what she was, heiress to vast wealth, to blood of ancient nobility. The marks were on her, though—the height and the accursed eyes of gray—and she had heard the whispers. Half-breed. Savage. Brythunian. She had heard them until her skill with a bow, her ready temper and her disregard of consequences silenced even whispers in her hearing. She was the Lady Jondra of the House Perashanid, daughter of General Lord Karentides last of a lineage to rival that of King Tiridates himself, and ware to anyone who mentioned aught else.

"He would not have hit it once, my lady," a quiet voice said at her elbow.

Jondra glanced at the balding servant, at the concern on his wrinkled face. "It is not your place to speak so, Mineus," she said, but there was no rebuke in her voice.

Mineus' expression folded into deference. "As you say, my lady. If my lady pleases, the girl sent by the Lady Roxana is here. I put her in the second waiting room, but I can send her away if that is still your wish."

"If I am not to wed," she said, replacing her bow carefully on the rack, "I shall have need of her after all."

The second waiting room was floored with a mosaic of arabesques in green and gold, in the middle of which stood a short, slender girl in a short tunic of dark blue, the color Lady Roxana put on her serving maids. Her dark hair was worked in a simple plait that fell to the small of her back. She kept her eyes on the tiles beneath her small feet as Jondra entered the room.

An ebony table inlaid with ivory held two wax tablets fastened face-to-face with silken cords. Jondra examined the seals on the cords carefully. Few outside the nobility or the merchant classes could write, but servants had been known to try altering their recommendations. There were no signs of tampering here. She cut the cords and read.

"Why do you wish to leave the Lady Roxana's service?" she asked abruptly. "Lyana? That's your name?"

"Yes, my lady," the girl answered without raising her head. "I want to become a lady's maid, my lady. I worked in the Lady Roxana's kitchens, but her handmaidens trained me. The Lady Roxana had no place for another handmaiden, but she said that you sought one."

Jondra frowned. Did the chit not even have enough spirit to meet her eyes? She abhorred a lack of spirit, whether in dogs or horses or servants. "I need a girl to tend my needs on the hunt. The last two found the rigors too great. Do you think your desire to be a lady's maid will survive heat and flies and sand?"

"Oh, yes, my lady."

Slowly Jondra walked around the girl studying her from every angle. She certainly *looked* sturdy enough to withstand a hunting camp. With fingertips she raised the girl's chin. "Lovely," she said, and thought she saw a spark in those large, dark eyes. Perhaps there was some spirit here after all. "I'll not have my hunts disrupted by spearmen panting after a pretty face, girl. See you cast no eyes at my hunters." Jondra smiled. There had definitely been a flash of anger that time.

"I am a maiden, my lady," the girl said with the faintest trace of tightness in her voice.

"Of course," Jondra said noncommittally. Few serving girls were, though all seemed to think the condition made them more acceptable to their mistresses. "I'm surprised the Lady Roxana allowed you to leave her, considering the praises she heaps on your head." She tapped the wax tablet with a fingernail. "In time I will discover if you deserve them. In any case, know that I will allow no hint of disobedience, lying, stealing or laziness. I do not beat my servants as often as some, but transgression in these areas will earn you stripes." She watched the sparks in the girl's eyes replaced with eagerness as the meaning of her words broke through.

"My lady, I swear that I will serve you as such a great lady deserves to be served."

Jondra nodded. "Mineus, show her to the servants' quarters. And summon Arvaneus."

"It shall be done, my lady."

She dismissed the matter from her mind then, the sounds of Mineus leading the girl from the room seeming to fade to insignificance. Replacing the tablets on the ebony table, she crossed the room to a tall, narrow cabinet of profusely carved rosewood. The doors opened to reveal shelves piled with scrolls of parchment, each bound with a ribbon. Hastily she pawed through the pale cylinders.

The incident with Amaranides had crystallized a decision. That the whispers about her parentage were still being bruited about was reason enough to end her consideration of marriage. Instead . . .

Amaranides had said she liked to best men. Could she help it that men, with their foolish pride, could not accept the fact that she was better than they, whether with bow or horse or on the hunt? Well, now she would best them properly. She would do what none of them had either the skill or the courage to do.

She untied the ribbon about a scroll and searched down the parchment until she found what she sought.

The beast, my lady, is said to be scaled like a serpent, but to move on legs. Winnowing out obvious exaggerations caused by fear, I can reliably report that it has slain and eaten both men and cattle. Its habitat, my lady, seems, however, to be the Kezankian Mountains near the border between Zamora and Brythunia. With the current unrest of the hill tribes, I cannot suggest . . .

The parchment crumpled in her hands. She would bring this strange beast's hide back as her trophy. Let one of Amaranides' ilk suggest he could do as much. Let him just dare.

Tamira scurried down palace corridors in Mineus' wake, barely hearing when the balding old man told her of her duties, or when he spoke to other servants. Until the very last moment she had not been certain her plan would work, even after so much planning and labor.

Forty gold pieces she had obtained from Zayella, and all had gone in preparation for this. Most went to Roxana's chamberlain, who provided the use of the Lady's private seal. There would be no checking though, to trip her up, for the Lady Roxana had departed the city a day past.

Tamira allowed herself a smile. In a day or two she would have Jondra's fabulous necklace and tiara.

"Give attention, girl," Mineus said impatiently. "You must know this to help prepare for the Lady Jondra's hunt."

Tamira blinked. "Hunt? But she just returned from a hunt."

"You saw me speak to Arvaneus, the chief huntsman. No doubt you will depart as soon as supplies are gathered."

Panic flashed through her. It had been none of her intention to actually go on one Jondra's forays. There was no point to her sweating in a tent while the jewels remained in Shadizar. Of course, they would be there when she returned. But so might the Lady Roxana. "I—I have to see . . . about my belongings," she stammered. "I left clothing at the Lady Roxana's palace. And my favorite pin. I must fetch—"

Mineus cut her short. "When you've had instructions as to your duties in preparing for the hunt. Not only must you see that my lady's clothing and jewels are packed, but you must see to her perfumes, the soaps and oils for her bathing, and—"

"She—my lady takes her jewels hunting?"

"Yes, girl. Now pay attention. My lady's rouges and powders—"

"You mean a few bracelets and brooches," Tamira insisted.

The old man rubbed his bald spot and sighed. "I mean nothing of the sort, girl. Of an evening my lady often adorns herself to dine in her finest. Now, since you seem distracted for some reason, I will see you through your tasks."

For the rest of the morning and into the afternoon Tamira was prodded and pushed from one labor to the next, always under Mineus' watchful eye. She folded Jondra's garments of silks and laces—three times she folded them before reaching Mineus' satisfaction—and packed them in wicker panniers. Rare perfumes from Vendhya and powders from far Khitai, rouges from Sultanapur, costly oils and unguents from the corners of the world, all she wrapped in soft cloths and packed, with the balding old man hovering close to remind her that every vial and jar must be handled as gently as a swaddling child. Then, staggering under the weighty panniers, she and another serving-woman carried them down to the stableyard, where the pack-animals would be loaded on the morrow.

On each trip through Jondra's chambers, the chests for transporting the noblewoman's jewelry, thick sided boxes of iron, made her mouth water. They sat so tantalizingly against a tapestry-hung wall. But they were empty iron now, for they would not be filled until the last instant. Still, the gems would be going with her. She could not help smiling.

Aching from the unaccustomed labor, Tamira found that Mineus had led her to a side door of the palace. "Fetch your belongings, girl," he said, "and return quickly. There will be more work."

Before she could speak she had been thrust outside, and the door closed in her face. For a long moment she stared wonderingly at the red-painted wood. She had forgotten her panic-induced invention of possessions. Her original plan called for remaining inside Jondra's palace until the necklace and tiara were in her hands. In that way Conan would never discover what she was up to. The huge barbarian seemed intent on . . .

It dawned on her that she *was* outside the palace, and she spun around to study the narrow street. A turbanned Kezankain hillman squatted disconsolately against a wall across the street, and a few ragged urchins played tag on the rough paving stones. She heaved a sigh of relief. There was neither a beggar nor a doxy in sight. Her uncles could provide a bundle to satisfy Mineus. Keeping a careful watch for Conan's many eyes, she hurried down the street.

Unseen by her, three of the urchins broke off their play and trailed after her.

The hillman watched her go with lustful eyes, then reluctantly returned to his surveillance of the palace.

V

At a corner table in Abuletes' common room, Conan glowered into a leathern jack half-filled with cheap Kothian wine. Semiramis, in a girdle of coins and two strips of thin scarlet silk, was seated in the lap of a Turanian coiner across the crowded room, but for once that was not the reason for the Cimmerian's dour face. What remained of Baratses' two gold pieces had been lessened at dice the previous night. With all of his mind on Tamira, he had given no thought to how to get more. And worst, he had had no word from Laeta. It was only a day since he had set the urchin to watch Tamira, but he was certain—as certain as if he had been told by the dark-eyed thief herself—that she moved already on the theft she planned. The theft he had vowed to beat her to. And he had no word!

Grimacing, he raised his wine and gulped the remainder of it down. When he lowered the jack a tall, bony man stood across the table from him. A fine black Khauranian cloak, edged with cloth of gold, was pulled tightly around him as if to hide his identity.

"What do you want, Baratses?" Conan grumbled. "I keep the two gold pieces for the attempt, and you should be thankful to have it made so cheaply."

"Do you have a room in this . . . establishment?" The spice merchant's black eyes darted about the raucous tavern as if he expected to be attacked at any moment. "I would talk with you in privacy."

Conan shook his head in disbelief. The fool had obviously dressed himself in what he considered plain fashion, but just as obviously he was no denizen of the Desert. His passage had certainly been noted, and footpads no doubt awaited nine deep in the street for his departure, but here, where he was safe from such, he feared robbery.

"Come," Conan said, and led the way up the rickety wooden stairs at the back of the common room.

His own room was a simple box of rough wooden planks, with a narrow window shuttered in a vain attempt to keep out the stench of the alley behind the tavern. A wide, low bed, a table with one short leg, and a lone stool were all the furnishings. The Cimmerian's few possessions—aside from the ancient broadsword he always wore—hung on pegs in one wall.

Baratses glanced around the room disdainfully, and Conan bristled. "I cannot afford a palace. Yet. Now, why are you here? Something more to be stolen? You'll give a fair price this time, or find someone else."

"You've not yet fulfilled your last commission, Cimmerian." Though the door was closed, the merchant kept his cloak clutched about him. "I have the rest of your gold here, but where is my goblet? I know Samarides no longer possesses it."

"Nor do I," Conan replied ruefully. "Another was there before me." He hesitated, but could not rid himself of the belief that the man deserved at least some information for his two gold pieces. "I have heard the Lady Zayella has the goblet now."

"So she offered you more than I," Baratses murmured. "I had heard you had some odd concept of honor, but I see I was wrong."

The Cimmerian's eyes grew icy. "Do not call me liar, merchant. Another took the goblet."

"The room is close," Baratses said. "I am hot." He twitched the cloak from his shoulders, swirling it before him.

Instinct flared a warning in Conan. As the cloak moved aside his big hand slapped down to grasp Baratses' wrist, stopping a black-bladed Karpashian dagger a handspan from his middle. "Fool!" he said.

Blood and teeth sprayed from the merchant's face beneath Conan's fist. The dagger dropped from nerveless fingers and struck the floor no more than an instant before Baratses himself.

The big Cimmerian frowned at the man lying unconscious before him. A sheath on Baratses' forearm had held the black blade. Conan bent to remove that, and tossed it and the dagger atop the cloak. "An attempt on my life," he muttered finally, "surely earns me the gold you brought."

Unfastening the merchant's purse from his belt, Conan emptied it onto his palm. There was no gold, only silver and copper. He counted it and grimaced. Three coppers more than a single gold piece. It seemed his death had been intended whether he had the goblet or not. Pouring the coins back into the purse, he added it to the dagger and sheath.

On the floor Baratses stirred and moaned.

Knotting his fist in the bony man's tunic, Conan lifted him erect and shook him till his eyes fluttered open. Baratses let out a gurgling groan as his tongue explored splintered teeth.

"I do not have the goblet," the Cimmerian said grimly. Easily he hoisted the merchant's feet clear of the floor. "I have never had the goblet." He took a step and smashed Baratses against the shutter, which burst open. The bloody-faced man dangled above the alley at arm's length from the window. "And if I ever see you again, I'll break the rest of your teeth." Conan opened his hand.

Baratses' wail cut off as he landed with a squelch in equal parts of mud, offal and the emptyings of chamber pots. A scrawny dog, disturbed at its rootings, began to bark at him furiously. Scrambling shakily to his feet, Baratses stared wildly about him, then broke into a slipping, sliding run. "Murder!" he screamed. "Murder!"

Conan sighed as he watched the merchant disappear down the alley. His cries would bring no aid in the Desert, but once he was beyond those cramped streets the City Guard would come quickly enough. And listen attentively to a respectable merchant's tale. Perhaps it would have been better had he slit the man's throat, yet murder had never been his way. He would have to leave the city for a time, until the furor died down. The fist that had broken Baratses' teeth pounded the window frame. And by the time he returned Tamira would have accomplished her theft. He might never even know what it was, much less in time to get there first.

Hastily he made his preparations. The contents of Baratses' purse were added to his own. The dagger in its sheath he fastened to his left forearm, then settled the black cloak about his broad shoulders. It fit a trifle snugly, but was ten times better than what he had.

He frowned at a lump over his chest, and felt inside the cloak. A small pouch of cloth was sewn there. From it he drew a small silver box, its lid set with blue gems. Inferior sapphires, his experienced eye told him. He flipped it open; his lip curled contemptuously at the sickly verduous powder within. Pollen from the green lotus of Vendhya. It seemed Baratses liked his dreams to come when he desired them. The small quantity in his hand would bring ten gold pieces. Upending the silver box, he tapped it against the heel of his hand to make sure all of the pollen fell to the floor. He did not deal in such things.

Quickly he ran an eye over the rest of his possessions. There was nothing there worth the bother of bundling. Near two years of thievery, and this was all he had to show for it. A fool like Baratses could throw away on stolen dreams as much as he could earn in a night of risking his life. Pushing open the door, he slapped the worn leather hilt of his broadsword with a mirthless laugh. "This is all I need anyway," he told himself.

At the bar Abuletes came slowly in response to the big Cimmerian's beckoning gesture. "I need a horse," Conan said when the fat innkeeper was finally before him. "A good horse. Not one ready for the boneyard."

Abuletes' black eyes, deepset in wells of suet, went from the cloak on Conan's shoulders to the stairs. "You need to leave Shadizar quickly, Cimmerian?"

"There's no body to be found," Conan reassured him. "Just a disagreement with a man who can get the ear of the City Guard."

"Too bad," Abuletes grunted. " 'Tis cheaper to dispose of a body than to purchase a horse. But I know a man—" Suddenly he glared past Conan's shoulder. "You! Out! I'll have none of you filthy little thieves in my place!"

Conan glanced over his shoulder. Laeta stood just inside the door, glaring fiercely back at the tavernkeeper. "She has come to see me," the Cimmerian said.

"She?" Abuletes said incredulously, but he was speaking to Conan's back.

"You have news of Tamira?" Conan asked when he reached the girl. It was like his luck of late, he thought, that the news would come when he could not use it.

Laeta nodded, but did not speak. Conan dug two silver pieces from his purse, but when she stretched out a hand for them he lifted them out of her reach and looked at her questioningly.

"All right, big man," she sighed. "But I had better get my coin. Yestermorn your wench went to the palace of the Lady Jondra."

"Jondra!" So she was after the necklace and tiara. And he had to leave the city. Grinding his teeth, he tossed the coins to Laeta. "Why didn't you tell me then?"

She tucked the silver under her torn tunic. "Because she left again. And," she added reluctantly, "we lost her trail in the Katara Bazaar. But this morning I set Urias to watch Jondra's palace, and he saw her again. This time she left dressed like a serving girl and riding a supply cart in Jondra's hunting party. The lot of them departed the city by the Lion Gate. A good six turns of the glass ago, it was. Urias took his time telling me, and I'm docking him his share of this silver for it."

Conan studied the girl, wondering if she had spun this tale. It seemed too fantastic. Unless . . . unless Tamira had discovered Jondra was taking the fabled necklace and tiara with her. But on a hunt? No matter. He had to leave Shadizar anyway. As well ride north and see for himself what Tamira was up to.

He started to turn away, then stopped, looking at Laeta's dirt-smudged face and big, wary eyes, truly seeing her for the first time. "Wait here," he told her. She eyed him quizzically, but stood there as he walked away.

He found Semiramis leaning against the wall at the back of the common room, one foot laid across her knee so she could rub it. Quickly he separated out half the coin in his purse and pressed it into her hand.

"Conan," she protested, "you know I'll not take money from—"

"It's for her," he said, jerking his head toward Laeta, who was watching him suspiciously. Semiramis arched a questioning eyebrow. "In another year she'll not be able to pass as a boy any longer," he explained. "Already she's putting dirt on her face to hide how pretty she is. I thought, maybe, that you . . ." He shrugged awkwardly, unsure of what he did mean.

Semiramis raised herself on tiptoes and brushed her lips against his cheek.

"That's no kiss," he laughed. "If you want to say goodbye—"

She laid her fingers against his lips. "You are a better man than you try to pretend, Cimmerian." With that she slipped by him.

Wondering if women were made by the same gods as men, he watched her approach Laeta. The two spoke quietly, looked at him, then moved toward an empty table together. As they sat, he suddenly recalled his own needs. He strode back to the bar and caught the tavernkeeper's arm as the fat man passed.

"About this horse, Abuletes . . ."

VI

Dark hung silently over Shadizar, at least in the quarter where lay the Perashanid palace. A hatchet-faced man in a filthy turban and stained leather jerkin, his beard divided into three braids, moved from the shadows, freezing when the barking of a dog rent the night. Then quiet came again.

"Farouz," the bearded man called softly. "Jhal. Tirjas."

The three men named appeared from the dark, each followed by half a score other turbanned Kezankian hillmen.

"The true gods guide our blades, Djinar," one man murmured as he passed hatchet-face.

Booted feet thudding on the paving stones, each small column hurried toward its appointed goal. Farouz would take his men over the garden's west wall, Jhal over the north. Tirjas was to watch the front of the palace and assure that no one left . . . alive.

"Come," Djinar commanded, and ten grim hillmen hurried after him to the east wall of the palace garden.

At the base of the wall two of his men bent to present cupped hands for his booted feet. Boosted thus, Djinar caught the top of the wall and scrambled over to drop inside. Moonlight put a silver glow on the trees and flowers of the garden. He wondered briefly at the labor involved. So much sweat, and for plants. Truly the men of the cities were mad.

Soft thuds announced the arrival of his companions. Swords were drawn with the susurration of steel on leather, and from one man came a fierce mutter. "Death to the unbelievers!"

Djinar hissed for silence, unwilling to speak lest his feelings at being

54

within a city became plain in his voice. So many people gathered in one place. So many buildings. So many walls, closing him in. He motioned the hillmen to follow.

Silently the stony-eyed column slipped through the garden. No doors barred their entrance to the palace. It was going well, Djinar thought. The others would be entering the palace at other places. No alarm had been given. The blessings of the old gods must be on them, as Basrakan Imalla had said.

Abruptly a man in the white tunic of a servant appeared before him, mouth opening to shout. Djinar's tulwar moved before he could think, the tip of the curved blade slicing open the other man's throat.

As the corpse twitched in a pool of crimson, spreading across the marble floor, Djinar found his nervousness gone. "Spread out," he commanded. "None must live to give an alarm. Go!"

Growling deep in their throats, his men scattered with ready blades. Djinar ran as well, seeking the chamber that had been described to him by a sweating Akkadan beneath the iron gaze of Basrakan Imalla. Three more servants, roused by pounding boots, fell beneath his bloody steel. All were unarmed, one was a woman, but all were unbelievers, and he gave them no chance to cry out.

Then he was at his goal, and it was as the plump man had said. Large square tiles of red, black and gold covered the floor in geometric patterns. The walls were red and black brick to the height of a man's waist. Furnishings he did not notice. That lamps were lit so that he could see them was all that was important.

Still gripping his sanguine sword, Djinar hurried to the nearest corner and pushed against a black brick four down from the top row and four out from the corner. He gave a satisfied grunt when it sank beneath his pressure. Quickly he moved to the other three corners in turn; three more black bricks sank into the wall.

A clatter of boots in the corridor brought him to his feet, tulwar raised. Farouz and other hillmen burst into the room.

"We must hurry," Farouz snarled. "A bald-headed old man broke Karim's skull with a vase and escaped into the garden. We'll never find him before he raises an alarm."

Djinar bit back an oath. Hurriedly he positioned four men on their knees, forming the corners of a square beside widely separated golden tiles. "Press all together," he ordered. "Together, mind you. Now!"

With sharp clicks the four tiles were depressed as one. A grinding noise rose from beneath their feet. Slowly, two thick sections of the floor swung up to reveal stairs leading down.

Djinar darted down those stairs, and found himself in a small chamber carved from the stone beneath the palace. Dim light filtered from above, revealing casket-laden shelves lining the walls. In haste he opened a casket, then another. Emeralds and sapphires on golden chains. Opals and pearls mounted in silver brooches. Carved ivories and amber. But not what he sought. Careless of the treasures he handled, the hillman spilled the contents of caskets on the floor. Gems and precious metals poured to the marble. His feet kicked wealth enough for a king, but he gave it not a second glance. With a curse he threw aside the last empty casket and ran back up the stairs.

More hillmen had come, crowding the room. Now some pushed past him to the chamber below. Squabbling, they stuffed their tunics with gems and gold.

"The Eyes of Fire are not here," Djinar announced. The men below, panting with greed, paid no mind, but those in the chamber with him grew long faces.

"Perhaps the woman took them with her," suggested a man with a scar where his left ear had been.

Farouz spat loudly. "It was you, Djinar, who said wait. The strumpet goes to hunt, you said. She will take her guards, and we shall have an easier time of it."

Djinar's thin lips curled back from his teeth. "And you, Farouz," he snarled. "Did you cry for us to press on? Did you spend no time in the places where women barter their flesh for coin?" He clamped his teeth on his rage. The feeling of walls trapping him returned. What was to be done? To return to Basrakan Imalla empty-handed after being commanded to bring the Eyes of Fire . . . He shuddered at the thought. If the Zamoran jade had the Eyes of Fire, then she must be found. "Does none of these vermin still live?"

Mutters of negation filled the room, but Farouz said, "Jhal keeps a wench alive till his pleasure is spent. Do you now abandon the Imalla's quest to join him?"

Djinar's dagger was suddenly in his hand. He tested the edge on a well-calloused thumb. "I go to ask questions," he said, and strode from the room.

Behind him the hubbub of argument over the looting rose higher.

VII

Conan let his reins fall on the neck of his horse, moving at a slow walk, and took a long pull on his water-skin. His expression did not change at the stale taste of the tepid fluid. He had drunk worse at times when the sun did not beat down so strongly from a cloudless sky as it did now, though it had risen not three handspans above the horizon. His cloak was rolled and bound behind his saddle pad, and a piece of his tunic was held on his head like a kaffiyeh by a leather cord. Rolling hills, with here and there an outcrop of rock or a huge, half-buried boulder, stretched as far as the eye could discern, with never a tree, nor any growth save sparse patches of rough grass.

Twice since leaving Shadizar he had crossed the tracks of very large bodies of men, and once he had seen Zamoran infantry in the distance, marching north. He kept himself from their sight. It did not seem likely that Baratses had influence enough to set the army on his trail, but a man in Conan's profession quickly learned to avoid chance encounters with large numbers of soldiers. Life was more peaceful, less complicated without soldiers. Of the Lady Jondra's hunting party he had seen no sign.

Plugging the spout of the skin, he slung it from his shoulder and returned to a study of the tracks he followed now. A single horse, lightly laden. Perhaps a woman rider.

He booted the roan into a trot, its quickest pace. He intended to have a word with Abuletes when he returned to Shadizar, a quiet converse about messages sent to horse traders. The tavernkeeper's friend had denied having another animal beside this gelding on its last legs, and bargained as if he knew the big youth had reason to leave Shadizar quickly. Conan dug in his heels again, but the animal would move no faster.

Snarls, growing louder as he rode, drifted to him over the next rise. Topping the swell of ground, he took in the scene below in one glance. Half a score of wolves quarreled over the carcass of a horse. Some eyed him warily without ceasing their feast. Twenty paces away the Lady Jondra crouched precariously atop a boulder, her bow clutched in one hand. Five more of the massive gray beasts waited below, their eyes intent on her.

Suddenly one of them took a quick step forward and leaped for the girl on the rock. Desperately she drew her feet up and swung the bow like a club. The wolf twisted in mid-air; powerful jaws closed on the bow, ripping it from her grasp. The force of it pulled her forward, slipping down the side of the boulder. She gave a half-scream, grabbed frantically at the stone, and hung there, closer now to the creatures below. She pulled her legs up, but the next leaper would reach them easily.

"Crom," Conan muttered. There was no time for planning, or even for conscious decisions. His heels thudded into the roan's ribs, goading it into a sliding charge down the hillside. "Crom!" he bellowed, and his broadsword whispered from its worn shagreen scabbard.

The wolfpack gained its feet as one, gray forms crouching to await him. Jondra stared at him in wild disbelief. The roan, eyes wide and whinnying in terror, suddenly broke into a gallop. Two of the wolves darted for the horse's head, and two more dashed in behind to snap at its hamstrings. A forehoof shattered a broad gray-furred head. Conan's blade whistled down to split the skull of a second wolf. The roan kicked back with both hind legs, splintering the ribs of a third, but the fourth sank gleaming fangs deep into one of those legs. Screaming, the horse stumbled and fell.

Conan stepped from his saddle pad as the animal went down, just in time to meet leaping gray death with a slashing blade. Half cut in two the great wolf dropped. Behind him Conan heard the roan scramble to its feet, whinnying frantically, and the solid thuds of hooves striking home. There was no opportunity to so much as glance at his mount, though, or even to look at Jondra, for the rest of the pack swarmed around him.

Desperately the big Cimmerian cut and hacked at deadly shapes that darted and slashed like gray demons. Blood splashed cinereous fur, and not all of it was theirs, for their teeth were like razors, and he could not keep them all from him. With cold certainty he knew he could not afford to go down, even for an instant. Let him once get off his feet, and he was meat for the eating. Somehow he managed to get the Karpashian dagger into his left hand, and laid about him with two blades. All thought left him save battle; he fought with as pure a fury as the wolves themselves, asking no quarter and giving none. To fight was all he knew. To fight, and let the losers go to the ravens.

As suddenly as the combat had begun it was ended. One instant steel battled slashing fangs, the next massive gray forms were loping away over the hills, one limping on three legs. Conan looked around him, half wondering that he still lived. Nine wolves lay as heaps of blood-soaked fur. The roan was down again, and this time it would not rise again. A gaping wound in its throat dripped blood into a dark pool that was already soaking into the rocky soil.

A scrabbling sound drew Conan's eyes. Jondra slid from the boulder and took her bow from the ground. Snug tunic and riding breeches of russet silk delineated every curve of her full-breasted form. Lips pursed, she examined the gouges in the bow's glued layers of bone and wood. Her hands shook.

"Why did you not put arrows into a few?" Conan demanded. "You might have saved yourself before I came."

"My quiver . . ." Her voice trailed off at the sight of her half-eaten horse, but she visibly steeled herself and went to the carcass. From under the bloody mass she tugged a quiver. A crack ran down one side of the black lacquerwork. Checking the arrows, she discarded three that were broken, then slung the quiver on her back. "I had no chance to reach this," she said, adjusting the cords that held the lacquered box on her back. "The first wolf hamstrung my gelding before I even saw it. It was Hannuman's own luck I made it to that rock."

"This is no country for a woman to ride alone," Conan grumbled as he retrieved the rolled cloak and wiped his bloody blade on his saddle pad. He knew he should take a different course with this woman. He had, after all, ridden halfway across Zamora for the express purpose of getting close enough to steal her gems. But there he stood with his horse dead, a dozen gashes that, if not serious still burned and bled, and no mind to walk easily with anyone.

"Guard your tongue!" Jondra snapped. "I've ridden—" Suddenly she seemed to see him fully for the first time. Taking a step back, she raised the bow before her as if it were a shield. "You!" Her voice was a breathless whisper. "What do you do here?"

"What I do is walk, since my horse is slain in the saving of your life.

For which, I mind me, I've heard no word of thanks, nor an offer to bind my wounds in your camp."

Mouth dropping open, Jondra stared at him, astonishment warring with anger on her face. Drawing a deep breath, she shook herself as if waking from a dream. "You saved my life . . ." she began, then trailed off. "I do not even know your name."

"I am called Conan. Conan of Cimmeria."

Jondra made a small bow, and her smile trembled only a little. "Conan of Cimmeria, I offer you my heartfelt thanks for my life. As well, I offer the use of my camp for as long as you choose to stay." She looked at the wolf carcasses and shuddered. "I have taken many trophies," she said unsteadily, "but I never thought to be one. The skins are yours, of course."

The Cimmerian shook his head, though it pained him to abandon useful pelts. And valuable ones, too, could they be gotten back to Shadizar. He hefted his waterskin, showing a long rent made by slashing jaws. A last few drops of water dripped to the ground.

"Without water, we can waste no time with skinning in this heat." He shaded his eyes with a broad palm and measured how far the sun had yet to rise to reach its zenith. "It will get hotter before it cools. How far is it to your camp?"

"On horses we could be there by the time the sun is high, or shortly after. On foot . . ." She shrugged, making her heavy breasts move under the tight silk of her tunic. "I walk little, and so am no judge."

Conan made an effort to keep his mind on the matter at hand. "Then we must start now. You will have to keep up, for if we stop in this heat we shall likely never move again. Now, which way?"

Jondra hesitated, clearly as unused to taking commands as to walking. Haughty gray eyes dueled with cool sapphire blue; it was gray that fell. Without another word, but with an irritated expression painted on her features, the tall noblewoman fitted a shaft to her bow and began walking, headed south of the rising sun.

Conan stared after her before following, and not for the pleasant rolling motion of her rump. The fool woman had not wanted him behind her. Did she fear he would take her by force? And why had she seemed shaken by fear when she recognized him? Slowly, however, his questions were submerged in the pleasure of watching her make her way over the rolling hills. The silk riding breeches fit her buttocks like skin, and the view as she toiled upslope ahead of him was enough to make any man forget himself.

The sun climbed on, a ball of luteous fire baking the air dry. Shimmers rose from the rocky ground, and boot soles burned as if they rested on coals. Every breath sucked moisture from the lungs, dried the throat. Across the sky marched the sun, to its zenith and beyond, roasting the flesh, baking the brain.

The sun, Conan realized as he labored uphill in Jondra's wake, had replaced the woman as the center of his thoughts. He tried to calculate the time he had left to find water, the time before the strength of his thews began to fail. The effort of wetting his cracking lips was wasted, for the dampness did not last beyond the doing. He saw no use in offering up prayers. Crom, the Lord of the Mound, the god of his harsh native land, listened to no prayers, accepted no votive offerings. Crom gave a man but two gifts, life and will, and never another. Will would carry him till dark, he decided. Then, having survived a day, he would set about surviving the night, and then the next day, and the next night.

Of the girl he was not so sure. Already she had begun to stagger, tripping over stones she would easily have stepped over when they left the horses. Abruptly a rock smaller than her fist turned under her boot, and she fell heavily. To hands and knees she rose, but no further. Her head hung weakly, and her sides heaved with the effort of drawing a decent breath from the bone-dry air.

Scrambling up beside her, Conan pulled her to her feet. She hung limply from his hands. "Is this the right direction, girl? Is it?"

"How—dare—you," she managed through cracked lips.

Fiercely he shook her; her head lolled on her neck. "The direction, girl! Tell me!"

Unsteadily she looked around them. "Yes," she said finally. "I—think."

With a sigh, Conan lifted her over his shoulder.

"Not—dignified," she panted. "Put—me—down."

"There's no one to see," he told her. And perhaps never would be, he told himself. A well-honed instinct for direction would keep him moving on the path Jondra had set as long as he was able to move; an instinct for survival and an indomitable will would keep him moving long after the limits of ordinary human endurance had been breeched. He would find her camp. If she actually followed the true path. If he had not waited too late to question her. If . . .

Putting his doubts and Jondra's weak struggles alike from his mind, Conan set out slightly to the south of the line the sun had followed in rising. Constantly his eyes searched for signs of water, but in vain. It was too much to hope for palm fronds waving above a spring. Now, however, he could not find even the plants that would show him where to dig for a seep hole. No trace of green met his eyes save the short, wiry grass that could grow where a lizard would die of thirst. The sun blazed its way westward.

Conan's gaze swept toward the horizon. No smoke marked a campsite, no track disturbed the stony flanks of the hills before him. A steady, ground-eating pace he kept, tirelessly at first, then, as shadows lengthened before him, with an iron determination that denied the possibility of surrender. With water the coming night would have been a haven. Without it, there would be no stopping, for if they stopped they might well never take another step.

Darkness swooped, with no twilight. The stretching shadows seemed to merge and permeate the air in moments. The searing heat dissipated quickly. Stars blinked into being, like flecks of crystal on black velvet, and with them came a chill that struck to the bone as fiercely as had the sun. Jondra stirred on his shoulder and murmured faintly. Conan could not make out what she said, nor waste the energy to wonder what it had been.

He began to stumble, and he knew it was not only the dark. His throat was as dry as the rocks that turned under his feet, and the cold gave little relief to the sun-cracked skin of his face. All he could see were the unwinking stars. Locking his eyes on the horizon, a thin line where sable merged into ebon, he trudged on. Abruptly he realized that three of those stars did seem to shimmer. And they lay below the horizon. Fires.

Forcing his feet to move faster, Conan half-ran toward the camp, for such it must be, whether Jondra's or another. Whoever's camp it was, they must go in, for they had to have water. With his free hand he loosened his sword in its scabbard. They needed water, and he meant to have it.

The "stars" clearly became fires built high, surrounded by two-wheeled carts and round tents, with picket lines of animals beyond. Conan stumbled into the firelight; men in short mail tunics and baggy white trousers leaped to their feet. Hands reached for spears and tulwars.

The Cimmerian let Jondra fall and put a hand to his sword hilt. "Water," he croaked. The one word was all he could manage.

"What have you done?" a tall hawk-faced man demanded. Conan worked for the moisture to ask what the man meant, but the other did not wait. "Kill him!" he snarled.

Conan's broadsword slid smoothly free, and it was not the only steel bared to gleam in the light of the fires. Some men raised their spears to throw.

"No!" The faint command came in a thirst-hoarsened voice. "No, I say!"

Conan risked a glance from the corner of his eye. One of the mail-shirted men held a water-skin solicitously to Jondra's lips, and her shoulders were supported by Tamira, in the short, white tunic of a servant.

Not lowering his sword—for few of the others had lowered theirs—Conan began to laugh, a dry, rasping sound of relief. It hurt his throat, but he did not care.

"But, my lady," the hawk-faced man protested. Conan remembered him, now, at Jondra's shoulder that day in Shadizar.

"Be silent, Arvaneus," Jondra barked. She took two more thirsty gulps from the waterskin, then pushed it aside and held out an imperious hand, demanding to be helped to her feet. The man with the waterskin hastened to comply. She stood unsteadily, but pushed him aside when he tried to support her. "This man saved me from wolves, Arvaneus, and carried me when I could not walk. While you huddled by the fires, he saved my life. Give him water. Tend his hurts, and see to his comfort."

Hesitantly, eying Conan's bare blade, the man with the waterskin handed it to the big Cimmerian.

Arvaneus spread his hands in supplication. "We searched, my lady. When you did not return, we searched until dark, then built the fires high that you might see them and be guided to the camp. At first light we would have—"

"At first light I would have been dead!" Jondra snapped. "I will retire to my tent now, Arvaneus, and give thanks to Mitra that my survival was not left to you. Attend me, Lyana." Her rigid-backed departure was spoiled slightly by a stumble, and she muttered a curse as she ducked into her scarlet-walled pavillion.

Conan cast an eye about the encampment—the tulwars and spears were no longer in evidence—and sheathed his own blade. As he was raising the waterskin, he met Arvaneus' gaze. The huntsman's black eyes were filled with a hatred rooted in his marrow. And he was not the only one staring at the Cimmerian. Tamira's glare was one of frustration.

"Lyana!" Jondra called from her tent. "Attend me, girl, or . . ." The threat was implicit in her tone.

For the barest moment Tamira hesitated, giving Conan a well-honed look, then she darted for the tent.

Arvaneus' face was still a mask of malignity, but Conan neither knew the reason nor cared. All that mattered was that he would now surely reach the necklace and tiara before the young woman thief. That and nothing more. With a rasping chuckle he tilted up the waterskin and drank deeply.

VIIII

The tall, gray-eyed young man kicked his horse into a trot as the lay of the country told him he neared his village. The last wisps of morning fog lingered among the towering forest oaks, as it often did in this part of Brythunia, not far from the Kezankian Mountains. Then the village itself came in view. A few low, thatch-roofed houses of stone, those of the village's wealthiest men, were dotted among the wattle structures that clustered around two dirt streets that lay at right angles to each other.

People crowded the street as he rode into the village. "Eldran!" they shouted, and dogs ran beside his horse, adding their barking to the uproar. "You have come! Boudanecea said you would!" The men were dressed as he, their tunics embroidered at the neck, with cross-gaitered fur leggings that rose to the knee. The women's dresses were longer versions of the tunics, but in a profusion of scarlets and yellows and blues where the men's were brown and gray, and embroidered at hem and at the ends of the sleeves as well.

"Of course I've come," he said as he dismounted. "Why should I not?" They gathered about him, each trying to get close. He noticed that every man wore a sword, though few did in the normal course of days, and many leaned on spears and carried their round shields of linden wood rimmed with iron. "What has happened here? What has the priestess to do with this?" A tumult answered him, voices tumbling over each other like brook water over stones.

". . . Burned the farmsteads . . ."

". . . Men dead, women dead, animals dead . . ."

". . . Some eaten . . ."

". . . Devil beast . . ."

". . . Went to hunt it . . ."

". . . Ellandune . . ."

". . . All dead save Godtan . . ."

"Hold!" Eldran cried. "I cannot hear you all. Who spoke of Ellandune? Is my brother well?"

Silence fell, save for the shuffling of feet. No one would meet his eyes. A murmur spread from the rear of the crowd, and they parted for the passage of a tall woman with a face serene and ageless. Her hair, the black streaked with gray, hung to her ankles and was bound loosely back with a white linen band. Her dress was of pristine linen as well, and the embroideries were of the leaves and berries of the mistletoe. A small golden sickle hung at her belt. She could walk anywhere in Brythunia and the poorest man in the land would not touch that sickle, nor the most violent raise a finger against her.

Eldran's clear gray eyes were troubled as they met hers of dark brown. "Will you tell me, Boundanecea? What has happened to Ellandune?"

"Come with me, Eldran." The priestess took his arm in a strong grasp. "Walk with me, and I will tell you what I can."

He let her lead him away, and none of the rest followed other than with sympathetic eyes that made fear rise in him. In silence they walked slowly down the dusty street. He kept a rein on his impatience, for he knew of old she would not be rushed.

Before the gray stone house where she lived, Boudanecea drew him to a halt. "Go in, Eldran. See Godtan. Speak with him. Then I will tell you."

Eldran hesitated, then pushed open the door of pale polished wood. A short, slight woman met him inside, dressed like Boudanecea, but with her dark, shiny hair braided in tight spirals about her head as a sign that she was still an acolyte.

"Godtan," was all he could say. What of Ellandune, he wanted to shout, but he had begun to fear the answer.

The acolyte silently drew aside a red woolen door-hanging and motioned him to enter the room. A stomach-wrenching melding of smells drifted out. Medicinal herbs and poultices. Burned meat. Rotting meat. He swallowed and ducked through. She let the hanging fall behind him.

It was a simple room, with a well-swept floor of smooth wooden planks and a single window, its curtains pulled back to admit light. A table with a glazed pottery basin and pitcher stood beside the bed on which lay the naked shape of a man. Or what had once been a man.

The right side of his face was burned away, a fringe of gray hair bordering what remained. From the shoulder to the knee his right side was a mass of charred flesh, crimson showing through cracks in the black. There were no fingers on the twisted stick that had once been his right arm. Eldran remembered that right arm well, for it had taught him the sword.

"Godtan." The name caught in his throat. "Godtan, it is I, Eldran."

The horribly burned man's remaining eye flickered weakly open, swiveled toward him. Eldran groaned at the madness in it.

"We followed," Godtan said, his voice a gurgling croak. "Into—the mountains. Kill it. We were—going to—. We didn't—know. The colors—of it. Beau—tiful. Beautiful—like death. Scales—turned—our arrows—like straws. Spears wouldn't—. Its breath—is fire!"

That mad eye bulged frantically, and Eldran said, "Rest, Godtan. Rest, and I'll—"

"No!" The word came from that twisted mouth with insistence. "No rest! We—fled it. Had to. Hillmen—found us. Took Aelric. Took—Ellandune. Thought—I was—dead. Fooled them." Godtan gave a rasping bark; Eldran realized with a shiver that it was meant to be laughter. "One—of us—had to—bring word—what happened. I—had to." His one eye swiveled to Eldran's face, and for a moment the madness was replaced by bewilderment and pain. "Forgive—me. I—did not—mean—to leave him. Forgive—Eldran."

"I forgive you," Eldran said softly. "And I thank you for returning with word of what happened. You are still the best man of us all."

A grateful smile curved the half of Godtan's mouth that was left, and his eye drifted shut as if the effort of keeping it open were too great.

Grinding his teeth, Eldran stalked from the building, slapping the door open so that it banged against the wallstones. His eyes were the gray of forged iron, hard and cold from the quenching, and when he confronted Boudanecea his fists were clenched till the nails dug into his palms in an effort to control his anger.

"Will you tell me now?" he grated.

"The beast of fire," she began, but he cut her off.

"A tale for children! Tell me what happened!"

She shook a fist under his nose, and her fury blazed back at him as strongly as his own. "How think you Godtan took his burns? Think, man! A tale for children, you call it. Ha! For all the breadth of your shoulders I've alway had trouble thinking of you as a man grown, for I helped your mother birth you, and wrapped your first swaddling cloths about you with these hands. Now you bring my doubts home again. I know you have the fierce heart of a man. Have you the brain as well?"

Despite his chill rage Eldran was taken aback. He had known Boudanecea since his childhood, and never had he seen her lose her temper. "But, Godtan . . . I thought . . . he's mad."

"Aye, he's mad, and as well he is. All the way from the Kezankians he came, like that, seeking to tell us the fate of his companions, seeking the help of his people. Seeking my help. But none of my spells or potions can help him. The greenrot had set in too deeply by the time I saw him. Only a necromancer could help him now." She touched the golden sickle at her belt to ward off the evil of the thought, and he made the sign of the sickle.

"So the . . . the devil beast came," Eldran said.

Her long hair swayed as she nodded. "While you were in the west. First one farmstead was burned, all of the building, and only gnawed fragments of people or cattle left. Men made up stories to settle their minds, of a fire that killed the family and the animals, of wolves getting at the remains when the fire burned down. But then a second farmstead was destroyed, and a third, and a fourth, and . . ." She took a long breath. "Twenty-three, in all, and all at night. Seven on the last night alone. After that the hotheads took matters into their own hands. Aelfric. Godtan. Your brother. A score of others. They talked like you when I spoke of the beast of fire after the first farmstead. A tale for children. Then they found spoor, tracks. But they still would not believe me when I said no weapon forged by the hands of ordinary men could harm the creature. They made their plans in secret, and sneaked from the village before dawn to avoid my eye."

"If no weapon forged by man . . ." Eldran's hands worked futilely. "Boudanecea, I will not let it rest. The hillmen must pay for my brother, and the beast must be slain. Wiccana aid me, it must! Not only for revenge, but to stop it coming again."

"Aye." The priestess breathed the word. "Wait here." In what would have been hurry for one without her stately dignity, she disappeared into her house. When she returned she was followed by a plump acolyte with merry brown eyes. The acolyte carried a flat, red-lacquered chest atop which were neatly folded white cloths and a pitcher of white-glazed pottery. "From this moment," Boudanecea told him, "you must do exactly as you are told, and no more. For your life, Eldran, and your sanity, heed. Now, come."

They formed a procession then, the priestess leading and the acolyte following behind Eldran. The women marched with a measured tread, and he found himself falling into it as if an invisible drum beat the steps.

The hair of the back of his neck stirred as he realized where they were taking him. The Sacred Grove of Wiccana, eldest of the sacred groves of Brythunia, where the boles of the youngest oaks were as thick and as tall as the largest elsewhere in the forest. Only the priestesses and acolytes went to the sacred groves now, though once, countless centuries in the past, men had made that journey. As sacrifices to the goddess. The thought did not comfort Eldran.

Limbs as thick as a man's body wove a canopy above their heads, and the decaying leaves of the past season rustled beneath their feet. Abruptly a clearing appeared before them, where a broad, low grassy mound lay bare to the sky. A rough slab of granite, as long and as wide as the height of a man, lay partially buried in the side of the mound before them.

"Attempt to move the stone," Boudanecea commanded.

Eldran stared at her. He was head and shoulders taller than most men of the village, well muscled and with broad shoulders, but he knew the weight was beyond him. Then, remembering her first instructions, he obeyed. Squatting beside the great stone, he tried to dig down with his hands to find the lower edge. The first handfuls moved easily, but abruptly the dirt took on the consistency of rock. It looked no different than before, yet his nails could not scratch it. Giving up on that, he threw his weight against the side of the slab, attempting to lever it over. Every sinew of him strained, and sweat ran in rivulets down his face and body, but the granite seemed a fixed part of the mound. It did not stir.

"Enough," Boudanecea said. "Come and kneel here." She indicated a spot before the slab.

The acolyte had laid open the top of the chest, revealing stoppered vials and bowls of a glaze that seemed the exact green of mistletoe. Boudanecea firmly turned Eldran's back to the plump woman and made him kneel. From the white pitcher she poured clear water over his hands, and wiped them with soft white cloths. Other cloths were dampened and used to wipe sweat from his face.

As she cleansed his face and hands the graying priestess spoke. "No man or woman can move that stone, nor enter that mound save with Wiccana's aid. *With* her aid . . ."

The acolyte appeared at her side, holding a small green bowl. With her golden sickle Boudanecea cut a lock of Eldran's hair. He shivered as she dropped it into the bowl. Taking each of his hands in turn, she pricked the balls of his thumbs with the point of the sickle and squeezed a few drops of his blood on top of the hair. The acolyte and bowl hurried from his view again.

Boudanecea's eyes held his. He could hear the plump woman clinking vials, murmuring incantations, but he could not look away from the priestess' face. Then the acolyte was back, and Boudanecea took from her the bowl and a long sprig of mistletoe, which she dipped into the bowl.

Head back, the priestess began to chant. The words she spoke were no words Eldran had ever heard before, but the power of them chilled him to the bone. The air about him became icy and still. A thrill of terror went through him as he held out his hands, palms up, without instruction. It was as if he suddenly had known that he must do it. Mistletoe slapped his hands, and terror was replaced by a feeling of wholeness and wellbeing greater than any he had ever known before. Boudanecea chanted on, her paean rising in tone. The dampened sprig of mistletoe struck one cheek, then the other. Abruptly his body seemed to have no weight; he felt as if he might drift on the lightest breeze.

Boudanecea's voice stilled. Eldran wavered, then staggered to his feet. The peculiar sense of lightness remained with him.

"Go to the stone." Boudanecea's voice hung like chimes in the crystallized air. "Move the stone aside."

Silently Eldran moved to the slab. It had not changed that he could see, and rather than feeling stronger, he seemed to have no strength at all. Still the compulsion of her words was on him. Bending beside the stone, he fitted his hands to it, heaved . . . and his mouth fell open as the stone rose like a feather, pivoted on its further edge, and fell soundlessly. He stared at the stone, at his hands, at the sloping passage revealed in the side of the mound, at Boudanecea.

"Go down," she told him. Tension froze her face, and insistence made her words ring more loudly. "Go down, and bring back what you find."

Taking a deep breath, Eldran stumbled down the slanting, dirt-floored passage. No dust rose beneath his feet. Broad, long slabs of stone had been carefully laid for walls and roof to the passage, their crude work showing their age. Quickly the passage widened into a round chamber, some ten paces across, walled and roofed in the same gray stone as the way down. There were no lamps, but a soft light permeated the room. Nor were there the cobwebs and dust he had expected. A smell of freshly grown green things hung in the air, a smell of spring.

There could be no doubt as to what he was to bring up, for the chamber was bare save for a simple pedestal of pale stone, atop which rested a sword of ancient design. Its broad blade gleamed brightly, as if it had just come, newly made and freshly oiled, from the smith's hand. The bronze hilt was wrapped with leather that could have have been tanned that season. Its quillons ended in claws that seemed designed to hold something, but they were empty now.

A sense of urgency came on him as he stared at the sword. Seizing it, he half-ran back to the sunlight above.

As he took his first step onto the ground of the clearing he heaved a sigh of relief. And suddenly he felt as he had before coming there. All the strange sensations were gone. Almost against his will he looked over his shoulder. The great stone rested where it had originally lain, with no sign that it had ever been disturbed. Even the place where he had dug beside it was no longer there.

A shudder ran down his bones. Only the weight of the sword in his hand—an ordinary seeming, if ancient, blade—remained to convince him something had actually happened. He clung hard to sanity, and did not wonder about what that something had been.

"Flame Slayer," Boudanecea said softly. Her hand stretched toward the sword, but did not touch it. "Symbol of our people, sword of our people's heroes. It was forged by great wizards nearly three thousand years ago, as a weapon against the beasts of fire, for the evil of Acheron had launched a plague of them, creations of their vile sorceries, upon the world. Once those claws held two great rubies, the Eyes of Fire, and the sword could control the beasts as well as slay them. For it *can* slay the beast."

"Why didn't you tell me of it?" Eldran demanded. "Why did you bring me here unknowing, like a sheep to. . . ." His voice trailed off, for he did not like the thoughts that image brought back.

"It is part of the *geas* laid on the sword," the priestess replied, "and on we who keep it. Without the aid of a priestess, no one can reach the sword. But no priestess may speak of the sword to any who does not hold it. Great care must be taken in choosing to bring a man to the blade, for as well as its uses against the beasts of fire it can be a locus of great power to one who knows the ways of such things."

He hefted the sword curiously. "Power? Of what kind?"

"Do you seek power, Eldran?" she asked gravely. "Or do you seek to slay the beast?"

"The beast," he growled, and she nodded approval.

"Good. I chose you when first I knew what the beast was. You are acknowledged the finest man in Brythunia with sword or horse or bow. It is said that you move through the forest, and the trees are unaware of your passage, that you can track the wind itself. Such a man will be needed to hunt down the beast of fire. And this you must remember. Do not allow the sword to leave your possession, even while you sleep, or you will never regain its hilt. Instead the sword will, Wiccana alone knows how, return to its place beneath the stone. Many times it has been lost, but always, when it is needed and the stone is lifted aside, the sword is there. That will not help you should you lose it, though, for the sword may be given to any man but once in his life."

"I will not lose it," Eldran said grimly. "It will do its work, and I will return it here myself. But now I must take it from here." He began to move toward the trees, out of the sacred grove; his first nervousness was returning, as if this was not a place for men to remain long. "There is no time to waste, so I must choose the rest of my party quickly."

"Rest?" Boudanecea exclaimed, halting him at the edge of the trees. "I intended you to go alone, one swift hunter to slay the—"

"No. There must be blood price for Aelric and Ellandune, and for any others who fell to the hillmen. You know it must be so."

"I know," she sighed. "Your mother was like my own sister. I had hoped to hold her grandson one day, hoped for it many a day before this. Now I fear I never shall."

"I will come back," he said, and laughed suddenly, shocking himself. "You will get to see me wed yet, Boudanecea."

She raised the mistletoe in benediction, and he bowed his head to accept it. But even as he did he was listing in his mind the men he would take into the mountains with him.

IX

E asing himself in his high-pommeled Zamoran saddle, Conan studied the country toward which the hunting party traveled. The flat, rolling hills through which they rode had changed little in the three days since his rescue of Jondra, except that the short grass was more abundant here and a brown tangle of thornbushes occasionally covered a stony slope. Ahead, though, the hills rose quickly higher, piling up on one another till they melded into the jagged, towering peaks of the Kezankians.

These were an arm of that range that stretched south and west along the border between Zamora and Brythunia. Conan knew of no game in them that would attract a hunter like Jondra save for the great spiral-horned sheep that lived amid the sheer cliffs in the heart of the range. In the heart of the mountain tribes, as well. He could not believe she meant to venture there.

The hunting party was a vile-tempered snake twisting its way among the low hills, avoiding the crests. Spearmen muttered oaths as their sandaled feet slipped on stony slopes, exchanging insults with mounted archers. Pack animals brayed and muleteers cursed. Ox drivers shouted and cracked their long whips as the oxen strained to pull the high-wheeled supply carts. The string of spare horses, raising an even taller plume of dust than all the rest of the party, was the only part of the column not adding to the tumult. Jondra rode before it all with Arvaneus and half a score other mounted hunters, oblivious of the noise behind them. It was no way to enter the country of the hill tribes. Conan was only thankful the dogs had been left behind in Shadizar.

Tamira, perched precariously atop lashed bundles of tenting on a lurching cart, waved to him, and Conan moved his horse up beside the cart. "You surprise me," he said. "You have avoided me these three days past."

"The Lady Jondra finds many labors for me," she replied. Eying the carter, walking beside his oxen, she edged more to the rear of the high-wheeled vehicle. "Why did you follow me?" she whispered fiercely.

Conan smiled lazily. "Followed you? Perhaps I seek the country air. Invigorating rides are good for the lungs, I'm told."

"Invigorating—" She spluttered indignantly. "Tell me the truth, Cimmerian! If you think to cut me out—"

"Already I have told you my plans for you," he broke in.

"You . . . you are serious?" she said, a rising note of incredulity in her voice. As if fearing he might seize her on the instant, she wiggled to the far side of the cart and peered at him over the top of the rolled tenting. "The Lady Jondra requires that her handmaidens be chaste, Cimmerian. You may think that saving her life will gain you license, but she is a noble, and will forget her gratitude in a moment if you transgress her rules."

"Then I will have to be careful, won't I?" Conan said, letting his horse fall behind. She peered after him anxiously as the cart trundled on. Conan wore a satisfied smile.

He was sure she did not believe that he had no interest in Jondra's jewels—she was no fool, or she could not have thieved as long as she had in Shadizar—but she would at least think his mind was divided between the gems and her. Most women, he had found, would believe that a man lusted after them on the slightest provocation. And if Tamira believed that, she would be nervously looking over her shoulder when she should be getting her hands on the gems.

A blackened hillside caught the big Cimmerian's eye, off from the line of march, and he turned his horse aside from curiosity. Nothing was left of the thornbushes that had once covered the slope save charred stumps and ashes. It did not have the look of lightning strike, he thought, for the bolt would have struck the hilltop, not its side.

Abruptly his mount stopped, nostrils flaring, and gave a low, fearful whicker. Conan tried to urge the animal closer, but it refused, even taking a step back. He frowned, unable to see anything ominous. What would frighten a horse he had been told was trained for the hunting of lions?

Dismounting, he dropped his reins, then watched to be sure the animal would stand. Its flanks shivered, but training held it. Satisfied, Conan approached the burn. And loosened his sword, just in case.

At first his booted feet stirred only ashes over blackened soil and rock. Then his toe struck something different. He picked up a broken wild ox horn with a fragment of skull attached. The horn was charred, as were the shreds of flesh adhering to the bone, but the piece of skull itself was not. Slowly he searched through the entire burn. There were no other bones to be found, not even such cracked bits as hyenas would leave after scavenging a lion's kill. He extended his search to the area around the char.

With a clatter of hooves Arvaneus galloped up, working his reins to make his horse dance as he stared down at Conan. "If you fall behind, barbar," the hawk-faced man said contemptuously, "you may not be so lucky as to find others to take you in."

Conan's hands tightened on the horn. The gems, he reminded himself firmly. "I found this in the ashes, and—"

"An old ox horn," the huntsman snorted, "and a lightning strike. No doubt it signifies some portent to one such as you, but we have no time for wasting."

Taking a deep breath, Conan went on. "There are tracks—"

"I have trackers, barbar. I have no need of you. Better you do fall behind. Leave us, barbar, while you can." Wheeling his mount in a spray of rocks and dirt, Arvaneus galloped after the fast-disappearing column.

There was a sharp crack, and Conan discovered that the ox horn had broken in his grip. "Zandru's Nine Hells!" he muttered.

Tossing the shattered remnants of horn aside, he knelt to examine the track he had found. It was only part of an animal's print, for the stony soil did not take tracks well. At least, he thought it was an animal's print. Two toes ending in long claws, and scuffings that might have indicated the rest of the foot. He laid a forefinger beside one of the claw marks. The claw had been easily twice as large as his finger.

He had never heard of a beast that made tracks as large as these. At least, he thought, Jondra did not hunt this. Nor did he think he would warn her of it. What he knew of her suggested she would leap at the chance to hunt an unknown creature, especially if it was dangerous. Still, he would keep his own eyes open. Swinging into the saddle, he galloped after the hunting party.

Sooner than Conan expected, he caught up with them. The column was halted. Men held the horses' heads to keep them silent, and the carters held the oxen's nose-rings so they would not low. Tamira paused in beating dust from her short white tunic to grimace at Conan as he walked his horse past the cart of tenting. From somewhere ahead came a faint, steady pounding of drums.

At the front of the line Jondra and a handful of her hunters lay on their bellies near the crest of a hill. Leaving his horse at the foot of the slope, Conan made his way up to them, dropping flat before his head overtopped the hill. The drumbeat was louder here.

"Go, barbar," Arvaneus snarled. "You are not needed here."

"Be silent, Arvaneus," Jondra said softly, but there was iron in her tone.

Conan ignored them both. A third of a league distant another column marched, this one following a knife-edge line, caring not whether it topped hills or no. A column of the Zamoran Army. Ten score horsemen in spiked helms rode in four files behind a leopard-head standard. Behind came twenty drummers, mallets rising and falling in unison, and behind them . . . The Cimmerian made a rough estimate of the numbers of sloped spears, rank on rank on rank. Five thousand Zamoran infantry made a drum of the ground with their measured tread.

Conan turned his head to gaze at Jondra. Color came into her cheeks beneath his eyes. "Why do you avoid the army?" he asked.

"We will camp," Jondra said. "Find a site, Arvaneus." She began moving backwards down the slope, and the huntsman slithered after her.

Conan watched them go with a frown, then turned back to peer after the soldiers until they had marched out of sight beyond the hills to the north.

The camp was set up when Conan finally left the hill, conical tents dotting a broad, flat space between two hills. Jondra's large tent of bright scarlet stood in the center of the area. The oxen had been hobbled, and the horses tied along a picket line beyond the carts. No fires were lit, he noted, and the cooks were handing out dried meat and fruit.

"You, barbar," Arvaneus said around a strip of jerky. "I see you waited until the work was done before coming in."

"Why does Jondra avoid the army?" Conan demanded.

The hawk-faced man spit out a wad of half-chewed meat. "The *Lady* Jondra," he snapped. "Show a proper respect toward her, barbar, or I'll . . ." His hand clutched the hilt of his tulwar.

A slow smile appeared on Conan's face, a smile that did not extend to suddenly steely eyes. There were dead men who could have told Arvaneus about that smile. "What, huntsman? Try what is in your mind, if you think you are man enough." In an instant the black-eyed man's curved blade was bare, and, though Conan's hand had not been near his sword hilt, his broadsword was out in the same breath.

Arvaneus blinked, taken aback at the big Cimmerian's quickness. "Do you know who I am, barbar?" There was a shakiness to his voice, and his face tightened at it. "Huntsman, you call me, but I am the son of Lord Andanezeus, and if she who bore me had not been a concubine I would be a lord of Zamora. Noble blood flows in my veins, barbar, blood fit for the Lady Jondra herself, while yours is—"

"Arvaneus!" Jondra's voice cracked like a whip over the camp. Pale faced, the noblewoman came to within a pace of the two men. Her close-fitting leather jerkin was laced tightly up the front, and red leather boots rose to her knees. Arvaneus watched her with a tortured expression on his face. Her troubled gray eyes touched Conan's face, then jerked away. "You overstep yourself, Arvaneus," she said unsteadily. "Put up your sword." Her eyes flickered to Conan. "Both of you."

Arvaneus' face was a mosaic of emotion, rage and shame, desire and frustration. With a wordless shout he slammed his blade back into its scabbard as if into the tall Cimmerian's ribs.

Conan waited until the other's sword was covered before sheathing his own, then said grimly, "I still want to know why you hide from your own army."

Jondra looked at him, hesitating, but Arvaneus spoke up quickly, urgently. "My lady, this man should not be among us. He is no hunter, no archer or spearman. He does not serve you as . . . as I do."

With a deep chuckle, Conan shook his black-maned head. "It is true I am my own man, but I am as good a hunter as you, Zamoran. And as for the spear, will you match me at it? For coin?" He knew he must best the man at something, or else contend with him as long as he remained with the hunters. And he carefully had not mentioned the bow, of which he knew little beyond the holding of it.

"Done!" the huntsman cried. "Done! Bring the butts! Quickly! I will show this barbarian oaf the way of the spear!"

Jondra opened her mouth as if to speak, then closed it again as the camp erupted in a bustle of men, some scurrying to clear a space for the throwing, others rushing to the carts to wrestle with a heavy practice butt. The thick bundle woven of straw was a weighty burden to carry on a hunting expedition, but it did not break arrows or spear points, as did casting and shooting at trees or at targets on a hillside.

A shaven-headed man with a long nose leaped on an upturned keg. "I'll cover all wagers! I give one to twenty on Arvaneus, twenty to one on the barbarian. Don't crowd." A few men wandered over to him, but most seemed to take the outcome as foregone.

Conan noticed Tamira among those about the keg. When she left she strolled by him. "Throw your best," she said, "and I'll win a silver piece. . . ." She waited until his chest began to expand with pride, then finished with a laugh, ". . . Since I wagered on the other."

"It will be a pleasure to help you lose your coppers," he told her dryly.

"Stop flirting, Lyana," Jondra called sharply. "There's work for you to be doing."

Tamira made a face the tall woman could not see, bringing a smile to Conan's face despite himself, then scurried away.

"Will you throw, barbar?" Arvaneus asked tauntingly. The tall huntsman held a spear in his hand and was stripped to the waist, revealing hard ropes of muscle. "Or would you rather stay with the serving girl?"

"The girl is certainly more pleasing to look on than your face," Conan replied.

Arvaneus' face darkened at the ripple of laughter that greeted the Cimmerian's words. With the blade of his spear the Zamoran scratched a line on the ground. "No part of your foot may pass this line, or you lose no matter how well you throw. Though I doubt I must worry about that."

Doffing his tunic, Conan took a spear handed to him by another of the hunters and moved to the line. He eyed the butt, thirty paces away. "It does not look a great distance."

"But see the target, barbar." The swarthy huntsman smiled, pointing. A lanky spearman was just finishing attaching a circle of black cloth, no bigger than a man's palm, to the straw.

Conan made his eyes go wide. "Aaah," he breathed, and the hawk-faced man's smile deepened.

"To be fair," Arvaneus announced loudly, "I will give you odds. One hundred to one." A murmur rose among the watchers, and all in the camp were there. "You did mention coin, barbar. Unless you wish to acknowledge me the better man now."

"They seem fair odds," Conan said, "considering the reputation you have with yourself." The murmur of astonishment at the odds offered became a roar of laughter. He considered the weight of his purse. "I have five silver pieces at those odds." The laughter cut off in stunned silence. Few there thought the hawk-faced man might lose, but the sheer magnitude of his unlikely loss astounded them.

Arvaneus seemed unmoved. "Done," was all he said. He moved back from the line, took two quick steps forward, and hurled. His spear streaked to the center of the black cloth, pinning it more firmly to the butt. Half a score of the hunters raised a cheer, and some began trying to collect their bets now. "Done," he said again, and laughed mockingly.

Conan hefted his spear as he stood at the line. The haft was as thick as his two thumbs, tipped with an iron blade as long as his forearm. Suddenly he leaned back, then whipped forward, arm and body moving as one. With a thud that shoved the butt back his spear buried its head not a finger's width from the other already there. "Mayhap if it were further back," he mused. Arvaneus ground his teeth.

There was silence in the camp till the man on the keg broke it. "Even odds! I'll give even odds on Arvaneus or—what's his name? Conan?— or on Conan! Even odds!"

"Shut your teeth, Telades!" Arvaneus shouted, but men crowded around the shaven-headed man. Angrily the huntsman gestured toward the butt. "Back! Move it back!" Two men rushed out to drag it a further ten paces, then returned quickly with the spears.

Glaring at Conan, Arvaneus took his place back from the line again, ran forward and threw. Again his spear struck through the cloth. Conan stepped back a single pace, and again his throw was one single continuous motion. His spear brushed against Arvaneus's, striking through the black cloth even more closely than the first time. Scattered shouts of delighted surprise rose among the hunters. The Cimmerian was surprised to see a smile on Jondra's face, and even more surprised to see another on Tamira's.

Arvaneus's face writhed with fury. "Further!" he shouted when the spears were returned once more. "Further! Still further!"

An expectant hush settled as the butt was pulled to sixty paces distant. It was a fair throw for the mark, Conan conceded to himself. Perhaps more than a fair throw.

Muttering under his breath, the huntsman set himself, then launched his spear with a grunt. It smacked home solidly in the butt.

"A miss!" Telades called. "It touched the cloth, but a miss! One to five on Conan!"

Arm cocked, Conan hurtled toward the line. For the third time his shaft streaked a dark line to the cloth. A tumultuous cry went up, and men pounded their spears on the ground in approbation.

Telades leaped from his keg and capered laughing through the crowd to clasp Conan's hand. "You've cost me coin this day, northerner, but 'twas worth every copper to see it done."

Eyes bulging in his head, Arvaneus gave a strangled cry. "No!" Suddenly he was running toward the butt, pushing men from his path. He began wrestling the heavy mass of straw further away. "Hit this, barbar dog!" he shouted, fighting his weighty burden still. "Erlik take you and your accursed cheating tricks! Hit this!"

"Why, 'tis a hundred paces," Telades exclaimed, shaking his head. "No man could—" He cut off with a gasp as Conan took a spear from the hand of a nearby hunter. Like antelope scattering before a lion, men ran to get from between the Cimmerian and the distant target.

Arvaneus voice drifted back to them, filled with hysterical laughter. "Hit this, barbar! Try!"

Weighing the spear in his hand, Conan suddenly moved. Powerful legs drove him forward, his arm went back, and the spear arched high into the air. The hawk-faced huntsman stared open-mouthed at the spear arcing toward him, then screamed and hurled himself aside. Dust lifted from the butt as the spear slashed into the straw beside the two already there.

Telades ran forward, peering in disbelief, then whirled to throw his arms high. "By all the gods, he hit cloth! You who call yourselves spearmen, acknowledge your master! At a hundred paces he hit the cloth!"

A throng of hunters crowded around Conan, shouting their approval of his feat, striving to clasp his hand.

Abruptly the shouts faded as Jondra strode up. The hunters parted before her, waiting expectantly for what she would say. For a moment, though, she stood, strangely diffident, before speaking.

"You asked me a question, Cimmerian," she said at last, looking over his shoulder rather than at him. "I do not give reasons for what I do, but you *did* save my life, and your cast was magnificent, so I will tell you alone. But in private. Come." Back rigid and looking neither to left nor right, she turned and walked to her scarlet tent.

Conan followed more slowly. When he ducked through the tent flap, the well-curved noblewoman stood with her back to the entrance, toying with the laces of her leather jerkin. Fine Iranistani carpets, dotted with silken pillows, made a floor, and golden lamps stood on low, brass tables.

"Why, then?" he said.

She started, but did not turn around. "If the army is out in such force," she said distractedly, "they must expect trouble of some sort. They would surely try to turn back a hunting party, and I do not want the trouble of convincing some general that I will not be ordered about by the army."

"And you keep this secret?" Conan said, frowning. "Do you think your hunters have not reasoned some of this out themselves?"

"Is Lyana as you said?" she asked. "Pleasing to look on? More pleasing than I?"

"She is lovely." Conan smiled at the stiffening of her back, and added judiciously, "But not so lovely as you." He was young, but he knew enough of women to take care in speaking of one woman's beauty to another.

"I will pay Arvaneus's wager," Jondra said abruptly. "He does not have five hundred pieces of silver."

The tall Cimmerian blinked, taken aback by her sudden shift. "I will not take it from you. The wager was with him."

Her head bowed, and she muttered, seemingly unaware that she spoke aloud. "Why is he always the same in my mind? Why must he be a barbarian?" Suddenly she turned, and Conan gasped. She had worked the laces from her jerkin, and the supple leather gaped open to bare heavy, round breasts and erect, pink nipples. "Did you think I brought you to my tent merely to answer your questions?" she cried. "I've allowed no man to touch me, but you will not even stretch out a hand. Will you make me be as shameless as—"

The young noblewoman's words cut off as Conan pulled her to him. His big hands slid beneath her jerkin, fingers spreading on the smooth skin of her back, to press her full breasts against him. "I stretch out both hands," he said, working the leather from her shoulders to fall to the carpets.

Clutching at him, she laid her head against his broad chest. "My hunters will know . . . they will guess what I . . . what you . . ." She shivered and held to him harder.

Gently he tipped her head back and peered into her eyes, as gray as the clouds of a mountain morning. "If you fear what they think," he said, "then why?"

The tip of her small pink tongue wet her lips. "I could never have made that spear cast," she murmured, and pulled him down to the silken cushions.

X

Conan tossed aside the fur coverlet and got to his feet with an appreciative look at Jondra's nude form. She sighed in her sleep, and threw her arms over her head, tightening the domes of her breasts in such a way as to make him consider not dressing after all. Chuckling, he reached for his tunic instead. The locked iron chests containing her gems got not a wit of his attention.

Three days since the spear casting, he reflected, and for all her fears of what her hunters might think, it would take a man both blind and deaf to be still unaware of what occurred between Jondra and him. She had not let him leave her tent that first night, not even to eat, and the past two had been the same. Each morning, seemingly oblivious of the hunters' smiles and Arvaneus's glares, she insisted that Conan "guide" her while she hunted, a hunt that lasted only until she found a spot well away from the line of march where there was shade and a level surface large enough for two. The chaste, noble Lady Jondra had found that she liked lying with a man, and she was making up for lost opportunities.

Not that her absorbtion in the flesh was total. That first day she had been unsatisfied on their return with how far the column had traveled. Up and down the line she galloped, scoring men with her tongue till they were as shaken as if she had used her quirt. Arvaneus she took aside, and what she said to him no one heard, but when he galloped back his lips were a tight, pale line, and his black eyes smouldered. There had not been another day when the progress of the column failed to satisfy her.

Settling his black Khauranian cloak around his shoulders, Conan stepped out into the cool morning. He was pleased to see that the cook-fires had at last been made with dried ox dung, as he had suggested. No smoke rose to draw eyes to them, and that was more important than ever, now. A day to the north of where they camped, at most two days amid the now steep-sloped hills, lay the towering ranges of the Kezankian, dark and jagged against the horizon.

The camp itself squatted atop a hill amidst trees twisted and stunted by arid, rocky soil. Every man wore his mail shirt and spiked helm at all times, now, and none went so far as the privy trenches without spear or bow.

A sweating Tamira, dodging from fire to fire under the watchful eye of the fat cook, gave Conan a grimace as she twisted a meat-laden spit half a turn. Arvaneus, sitting cross-legged near the fires, sullenly buried his face in a mug of wine when he saw the Cimmerian.

Conan ignored them both. His ears strained for the sound he thought he had heard. There. He grabbed Tamira's arm. "Go wake J . . . your mistress," he told her. Hands on hips, Tamira stared at him wryly. "Go," he growled. "There are horsemen coming from the south." A look of startlement passed over her face, then she darted for the big scarlet tent.

"What offal do you spout now?" Arvaneus demanded. "I see nothing."

Telades came running across the camp to the hawk-faced man's side. "Mardak claims he hears horses to the south, Arvaneus."

With an oath the huntsman tossed his mug to the ground and scrambled to his feet. A worried frown creased his face. "Hillmen?" he asked Telades, and the shaven-headed man shrugged.

"Not likely from the south," Conan said. "Still, it couldn't hurt to let the rest of the camp know. Quietly."

"When I need your advice," Arvaneus snarled, but he did not finish it. Instead he turned to Telades. "Go among the men. Tell them to be ready." His face twitched, and he added a muttered, "Quietly."

Unasked, the Cimmerian added his efforts to those of Telades, moving from man to man, murmuring a word of warning. Mardak, a grizzled, squint-eyed man with long, thin mustaches also was passing the word. The hunters took it calmly. Here and there a man fingered the hilt of his tulwar or pulled a lacquered quiver of arrows closer, but all went on with what they were doing, though with eyes continually flickering to the south.

By the time Conan returned to the center of the camp, ten horsemen had topped the crest of the next hill and were walking their horses toward the camp.

Arvaneus grunted. "We could slay all of them before they knew we were here. What are they, anyway? Not hillmen."

"Brythunians," Telades replied. "Is there really cause to kill them, Arvaneus?"

"Barbarian scum," the hawk-faced hunter sneered. "They don't even see us."

"They see us," Conan said, "or they'd never have crossed that crest. And what makes you think we see all of them?"

The two Zamorans exchanged surprised looks, but Conan concentrated on the oncoming men. All wore fur leggings and fur-edged capes, with broadswords at their waists and round shields hung behind their saddles. Nine of them carried spears. One, who led them, carried a long, recurved bow.

The Brythunian horsemen picked their way up the hill and drew rein short of the camp. The man with the bow raised it above his head. "I am called Eldran," he said. "Are we welcome here?"

A sour look on his face, Arvaneus stood silent.

Conan raised his right hand above his head. "I am called Conan," he said. "I welcome you, so long as you mean harm to none here. Dismount and share our fires."

Eldran climbed from his horse with a smile. He was almost as tall as Conan, though not so heavily muscled. "We cannot remain long. We seek information, then we must move on."

"I seek information as well," Jondra said as she strode between the men. Her hair, light brown sun-streaked with blonde, was tousled, and her tight riding breeches and tunic of emerald silk had an air of having been hastily donned. "Tell me. . . ." Her words died as her eyes met those of Eldran, as gray as her own. Her head was tilted back to look up at him, and her mouth remained open. Finally she said unsteadily, "From . . . from what country are you?"

"They're Brythunians," Arvaneus spoke up. "Savages."

"Be silent!" Jondra's enraged scream caught the men by surprise. Conan and Eldran stared at her wonderingly. Arvaneus's face paled. "I did not speak to you," she went on in a voice that shook. "You will be silent till spoken to! Do you understand me, huntsman?" Not waiting for his answer, she turned back to Eldran. The color in her cheeks was high, her voice thin but cool. "You are hunters, then? It is doubly dangerous for you to hunt here. The Zamoran army is in the field, and there are always the hillmen."

"The Zamoran army does not seem to find us," the Brythunian answered. His still-mounted men laughed. "As for the hillmen . . ." There was an easiness to his voice, but grim light flashed in his eyes. "I have given my name, woman, but have not heard yours."

She drew herself up to her greatest height, still no taller than his shoulder. "It is the Lady Jondra of the House Perashanid of Shadizar, to whom you speak, Brythunian."

"An honorable lineage, Zamoran."

His tone was neutral, but Jondra flinched as if he had sneered. Strangely, it seemed to steady her in some fashion. Her voice firmed. "If you are a hunter, perhaps you have seen the beast I hunt, or its sign. I am told its body is that of a huge serpent, covered with scales in many colors. Its track—"

"The beast of fire," one of the mounted Brythunians murmured, and others made a curving sign in the air before them as if it were a charm.

Eldran's face was tight. "We seek the beast as well, Jondra. Our people know it of old. Perhaps we can join forces."

"I need no more hunters," Jondra said quickly.

"The creature is more difficult to slay than you can imagine," the tall Brythunian said urgently. His hand gripped tightly at the hilt of his sword, a weapon of ancient pattern with quillons ending in claws like an eagle's. "It's breath is fire. Without us you can but die in the seeking of it."

"So say you," she said mockingly, "with your children's tales. I say I will slay the beast, and without your aid. I also say that I had better not find you attempting to poach my kill. This trophy is mine, Brythunian. Do you understand me?"

"Your eyes are like the mists of dawn," he said, smiling.

Jondra quivered. "If I see you again, I'll put arrows in both of *your* eyes. I'll—"

Suddenly she grabbed a bow from one of her archers. Brythunian spears were lowered, and their horses pranced nervously. Hunters reached for their tulwars. In one smooth motion Jondra drew and released, into the air. Far above the camp a raven gave a shrill cry and began to flutter erratically, dropping toward a far hill.

"See that," Jondra exclaimed, "and fear my shafts."

Before the words were out of her mouth the distant raven jerked downward, turning over as it plummeted to reveal a second arrow transfixing its feathered corpse.

"You are a fine shot," Eldran said as he lowered his bow. Smoothly he swung into his saddle. "I would stay to shoot with you, but I have hunting to do." Without a backward glance he wheeled his horse and rode down the hill, his men following as if unaware that their backs were bare to the camp's archers.

That thought occurred quickly to Arvaneus. "Archers," he began, when Jondra whirled on him, glaring. She said no word, nor needed to. The huntsman backed away from her, eyes down, muttering, "Your forgiveness, my lady."

Next she turned her attentions to Conan. "You," she breathed. "He spoke to me like that, and you did nothing. Nothing!"

The big Cimmerian eyed her impassively. "Perhaps he is right. I found signs of a beast that may kill with fire. And if he is right about that, perhaps he is right about the difficulty of killing it. Perhaps you should return to Shadizar."

"Perhaps, perhaps, perhaps!" She spat each word. "Why was I not told of these signs? Arvaneus, what do you know of this?"

The huntsman darted a malice-filled gaze at Conan. "A fire begun by lightning," he said sullenly, "and a few old bones. This one is frightened by his own shadow. Or by the shadow of the mountains."

"That is not true, is it?" Jondra's eyes were doubtful on Conan's face. "You do not make invention for fear of dying at the hillmen's hands, do you?"

"I do not fear death," Conan said flatly. "The dark will come when it comes. But none save a fool seeks it out needlessly."

The noblewoman tossed her head haughtily. "So," she said, and again, "So." Without another look at Conan, she stalked away, calling loudly, "Lyana! Prepare my morning bath, girl!"

Arvaneus grinned at Conan malevolently, but the Cimmerian youth did not see him. Matters had become complex far beyond his simple plans on leaving Shadizar, Conan thought. What was he to do now? There was one way he knew to concentrate his mind for the solution of a problem. Producing a small whetstone from his pouch, he drew his sword and settled cross-legged to touch up the edge on the ancient blade and think.

Basrakan Imalla glared at the raven lying dead on his chamber floor and tugged at the forks of his beard in frustration. The watch-ravens were not easily come by. Nestlings must be secured, and only one pair in twenty survived the incantations that linked them so that one of the two saw and experienced what the other did. Time to secure the birds, time to work the spells. He had no time for replacing the accursed bird. Likely the other had fallen to a hawk. And he had so few of them.

With a grunt he kicked the dead bird, smashing it into the bare stone wall. "Filthy creature," he snarled.

Tugging his crimson robes straight, he turned to the six tall perches that stood in the center of the floor. On five of the perches ravens sat, tilting their heads to watch him with eyes like shiny black beads. Their wings, clipped so they could not fly, drooped listlessly. There were few furnishings in the room other than those perches. A table inlaid with mother-of-pearl bore a brass lamp and a scattering of implements for the dark arts. A shelf along one wall held the volumes of necromantic lore that he had gathered in a lifetime. No one entered that room, or the others reserved to his great work, save him, and none save his acolytes knew what occurred there.

Lighting a splinter of wood at the lamp, Basrakan began to trace an intricate figure in the air before the first bird. The tiny eyes followed the flame, which was mirrored in their black surfaces. As he traced, Basrakan chanted words from a tome copied on vellum made of human skin rather than sheepskin, words that floated in the air till the walls seemed to shimmer. With each word the tracing grew more solid, till an unholy symbol in fire hung between himself and the raven.

The raven's beak opened with painful slowness, and creaking words, barely recognizable, emerged. "Hills. Sky. Trees. Clouds. Many many clouds."

The sorcerer clapped his hands; the fiery image vanished, and the words ceased to come. It was often thus with the creatures. By the spells that held them they would speak of men before all else, but if there were no men they would mutter about whatever they happened to see, go on forever if he did not silence them.

The same ritual before the next bird gained him the same reply, with only the terrain changed, as did the next and the next. By the time he reached the last raven he was hurrying. An important matter awaited his attention in the next room, and he was certain by now what the creature would report. Chanting, he traced the symbol in fire, preparing even as it came into being to clap his hands.

"Soldiers," the raven croaked. "Many many. Many many."

Barakan's breath caught in his throat. Never more than now had he regretted the inability of the ravens to transmit numbers. "Where?" he demanded.

"South. South of mountains."

Thoughtfully the stern-faced Imalla stroked his beard. If they came from the south, they must be Zamorans. But how to deal with them? The bird that had actually seen the soldiers could be made to return and guide his warriors back to them. The men would see it as a further sign of the favor of the old gods, for birds were creatures of the spirits of the air. And it would the first victory, the first of many against the unbelievers.

"Return!" Basrakan commanded.

"Return," the raven croaked agreement, and he broke the link.

How many soldiers, he wondered as he strode from the chamber, and how many warriors of the true gods to send against them?

As he passed through the next chamber, he paused to ponder the girl who cowered against a wall paneled in polished oak, as rare and costly in these mountains as pearls. Her dark eyes streamed tears, and her full mouth quivered uncontrollably. Her skin was smooth and supple, and his view of it was not hampered by garments.

Basrakan grimaced in disgust and wiped his hands on the front of his scarlet robes. Only eighteen, and already she was a vessel of lust, attempting to ensnare the minds of men. As did all women. None were truly pure. None were worthy of the ancient gods.

Shaking himself from his dark reverie, the holy man hurried on. He had no fear for the girl's wandering. The *geas* he had put on her would not allow her to leave that chamber until he gave her permission, until he found her worthy.

In the corridor he found Jbeil Imalla just entering his abode. The lean man bowed, his black robes rustling stiffly. "The blessings of the true gods be on you, Basrakan Imalla. I come with ill tidings."

"Ill tidings?" Basrakan said, ignoring the greeting. "Speak, man!"

"Many warriors have joined our number, but most of them have never seen the sign of the true gods' favor." Jbeil's dark eyes burned with the fervor of the true believer above his plaited beard, and his mouth twisted with contempt for those less full of faith than himself. "Many are the voices crying out to witness a sacrifice. Even some who have seen now whisper that the creature sent by the ancient gods has abandoned us, since it has not been seen in so many days. A few, among the newcomers, say that there *is* no sign, that it is all a lie. These last speak now in private places, among themselves, but they will not forever, and I fear the hearts of the doubters may be easily swayed."

Basrakan's teeth ground in frustration. He had had the same fears of abandonment himself, and scourged himself at night, alone, for his lack of belief. He had tried to summon the beast of fire, tried and failed. But it was still there, he told himself. Still beneath the mountain, waiting to come forth once more. Waiting for—his breath caught in his throat—a sign of their faith.

"How many warriors are gathered?" he demanded.

"More than forty thousand, Imalla, and more come every day. It is a great strain to feed so many, though they are, of course, the faithful."

Basrakan pulled himself to his full height. Renewed belief shone on his dark narrow face. "Let the warriors know that their lack of faith is not secret." He intoned the words, letting them flow from him, convinced they were inspired by the true gods. "Let them know that an act of faith is demanded of them if they would have the sight they crave. A bird will come, a raven, a sign from the spirits of the air. Half of those gathered are to follow it, and it will guide them to unbelievers, soldiers of Zamora. These they must slay, letting none escape. Not one. If this is done as it is commanded, the sight of the true gods' favor will be granted to them."

"A bird," Jbeil breathed. "A sign from the spirits of the air. Truly are the ancient gods mighty, and truly is Basraken Imalla mighty in their sight."

Basrakan waved away the compliment with a negligent hand. "I am but a man," he said. "Now, go! See that it is done as I have commanded."

The black-robed man bowed himself from the sorcerer's presence, and Basrakan began to rub at his temples as soon as he was gone. So many pressures on him. They made his head hurt. But there was the girl. Showing her the evil within her, saving her from it, would ease the pain. He would chastise the lust from her. His face shining with the ascetic look of one who suffered for his duty, Basrakan retraced his steps.

XI

Djinar lay on his belly in the night and studied the hunter's camp, lying still and quiet on the next hill. His dark robes blended with the shadows of his own stony hilltop. Only smouldering beds of ashes remained of the cook fires, leaving the camp in darkness, its tents and carts but dim mounds, save for the soft glow of lamps within a large tent of scarlet. The moon rode high over the jagged peaks to the north, but dense dark clouds let its pale light through only an occasional brief rent. A perfect night for attack. He tugged at the triple braids of his beard. Perhaps the ancient gods *were* with them.

It had certainly seemed so during the days when the trail of the hunting party led north like an arrow aimed at the encampment of Basraken Imalla. Could it be that the Eyes of Fire were drawn in some fashion to the Imalla, that the true gods stirred themselves among men, even through the Zamoran slut? A chill like the trickle of an icy mountain stream ran down Djinar's spine, and the hairs on the back of his neck rose. It seemed to him that the ancient gods walked the earth within sight of his eyes. Rocks grated behind him; Djinar gasped, and almost fouled himself.

Farouz dropped down beside him on the stony ground.

"Sentries?" Djinar asked finally. He was pleased at the steadiness of his voice.

The other man snorted in contempt. "Ten of them, but all more asleep than awake. They will die easily."

"So many? The soldiers set guards in such numbers, but not hunters."

"I tell you, Djinar, they all but snore. Their eyes are closed."

"A score of eyes," Djinar sighed. "All it takes is one pair to be alert. If the camp is awakened, and we must ride uphill at them . . ."

"Bah! We should have attacked when first we found them, while they were yet on the march. Or do you still fear the Brythunian dogs? They are gone long since."

Djinar did not answer. Only because Sharmal had gone off alone to answer a call of nature had the Brythunians been seen, ghosting along the trail of the hunters from Shadizar. There was no great love lost between Brythunian and Zamoran, it was true, but either would turn aside from slaying the other to wet his blade with the blood of a hillman. Farouz would have placed them between their two enemies—at least two score of the Brythunians; half again so many Zamorans—without a thought save how many he could kill.

"If your . . . caution brings us to failure," Farouz muttered, "do not think to shield yourself from Basrakan Imalla's wrath by casting blame on others. The truth will be known."

Farouz, Djinar decided, would not survive to return to the Imalla's encampment of the faithful. The old gods themselves would see the justice of it.

Again boots scrabbled on the rocks behind him, but this time Djinar merely looked over his shoulder. Sharmal, a slender young man with his wispy beard worked into many thin braids, squatted near the two men. "The Brythunian unbelievers ride yet to the east," the young man said.

"They did not stop at dark?" Djinar demanded, frowning. He did not like behavior out of the ordinary, and men did not travel by night without pressing reason, not in sight of the Kezankians.

"When I turned back at sundown," Sharmal answered, "they still rode east. I . . . I did not wish to miss the fighting."

"If there is to be any," Farouz sneered.

Djinar's teeth ground loudly. "Mount your horses," he commanded. "Surround the camp and advance slowly. Strike no blow until I call, unless the alarm be given. Well, Farouz? You speak eager words. Can your arm match them?"

With a snarl Farouz leaped to his feet and dashed down the hill to where their shaggy, mountain-bred horses waited.

Djinar followed with a grim smile and climbed into the high-pommeled saddle. Carefully he walked his mount around the side of the hill, toward the camp atop the next stony rise. The rattle of unshod hooves on rock did not disturb him, not now. He guided his horse upslope. To the core of him he was convinced the Zamorans would not rouse. The ancient gods were with him. He and the others were one with the dark. He could make out a sentry, leaning on his spear, unseeing, unaware of one more shadow that drifted closer. Djinar loosed his tulwar from its scabbard. The true gods might walk the camp before him, but there was another presence as well. Death. He could smell it. Death for many men. Death for Farouz.

Smiling, Djinar dug in his heels; his mount sprang forward. The sentry had time to widen his eyes in shock; then the curved blade with the strength of Djinar's arm and the weight of the charging horse behind it took the man's head from his shoulders. Djinar's cry rent the darkness. "By the will of the true gods, slay them! No quarter!" Screaming hillmen slashed out of the night with thirsty steel.

Conan's eyes slitted open, where he lay wrapped in his cloak and the night beneath the sky. After her behavior he had chosen not to go to Jondra's tent, despite the lamps that remained invitingly lit even now. It had not been thoughts of the silken body that had wakened him, though, but a sound out of place. He could hear the breathing of the sentry nearest him, a breathing too deeply regular for a man alert. The fools would not hear his advice, he thought. They listened, but would not hear. There were other things they did not hear, as well. The sentry's half-snore was overlaid by another sound; stones slid and clicked on the hillside. On *all* sides of the hill.

"Crom!" he muttered. In a continuous motion he threw aside his black cloak, rose to his feet and drew steel. His mouth opened to shout the alarm, and in that instant there was need no longer.

On the heels of the hollow 'thunk' of a blade striking flesh came, "By the will of the true gods, slay them! No quarter!"

Chaos clawed its way out of the dark, hillmen appearing on every side screaming for the blood of unbelievers, hunters scrambling from their tents crying prayers to their gods for another dawn.

The big Cimmerian ran toward the sentry he had listened to. Shocked to wakefulness the hunter tried to lower his long-pointed spear, but a slashing stroke across the face from a tulwar spun him shrieking to the ground.

"Crom!" Conan roared.

The hillman jerked at his reins, spun his shaggy mount above the downed sentry toward the huge man who loomed out of the night. "The true gods will it!" he yelled. Waving his bloody blade above his turban, he booted his shaggy mount into a charge.

For the space of a heartbeat Conan halted, planted his feet as if preparing to take the charge. Suddenly he sprang forward, ducking under the whistling crescent of steel, his own blade lancing into the hillman's middle. The shock of the blow rocked the Cimmerian to his heels as the hillman seemed to leap backwards over his horse's rump to crash to earth.

Placing his foot on the chest of the corpse, Conan pulled his sword free. Warned by a primitive sense, by a pricking between his shoulderblades, he whirled to find another mounted foe, and a tulwar streaking for his head. But his steel was rising as he turned, its razor edge slicing through the descending wrist. Tulwar and hand flew, and the keening hillman galloped into the night with the fountaining stump of his wrist held high, as if he could thus keep the blood from pouring out of him.

Already two high-wheeled carts were towering bonfires, and flames swiftly ate five of the round tents. Over all hung the din of battle, the clang of steel on steel, the screams of the wounded, the moans of the dying. Another cart burst afire. The burnings cast back the night from struggling pairs of men who danced with sanguine blades among the bodies that littered the hilltop. Of those who lay still, more wore the mail shirts and spiked helms of Zamorans than wore turbans.

All this Conan took in in an instant, but one sight among all the others drew his eyes. Jondra, drawn from her sleeping furs and naked save for a quiver slung over her shoulder, stood before her crimson walled tent, nocking arrows and firing as calmly as if she shot her bow at straw targets. And where her shafts went hillmen died.

Another had become aware of her, the Cimmerian saw. A hillman at the far end of the camp suddenly gave an ululating cry and kicked his mount into a gallop for the bare-skinned archer.

"Jondra!" Conan shouted, but even as he did he knew she could not hear above the tumult. Nor would all his speed take him to her side in time.

Tossing his sword to his left hand, he flung himself in two bounds back to the sentry who lay with his face a ruined mask staring at the sable sky. Ruthlessly he put a foot on the man's outstretched arm, ripped free the heavy hunting spear from the death-grip that held it. With desperate quickness he straightened, turned and threw, freezing as the spear left his hand. No will or thought was left for motion, for all rode with that thick shaft. The hillman's mount was but two strides from Jondra, his blade heartbeats from her back, but still she neither heard nor turned. And the hillman convulsed as a forearm-long blade transfixed his chest. His horse galloped on, and he slowly toppled backwards, falling like a sack before the woman he meant to slay. Jondra started as the body hit the ground almost at her feet, but for a moment continued to fumble at her empty quiver in search of another arrow. Abruptly she tossed aside her bow and snatched the tulwar from the dead man's hand.

Conan found he could breathe again. He took a step toward her . . . and something sliced a line of fire across his back. The big youth threw himself into a forward roll and came to his feet searching for his attacker. There were men behind him, both hillmen and hunters, but all save Arvaneus and Telades were killing or being killed, and even as he looked they engaged turbanned foes. He had no time to seek out particular enemies, Conan thought. There were enough for all. The dark blood-rage rose in him, cold enough to burn.

When he turned back Jondra was gone, but thoughts of her were buried deep now in the battle-black of his mind. Some men are said to be born for battle; Conan had been born on the field of battle. The scent drawn in with his first breath had been the coppery smell of fresh-spilled blood. The first sound to greet his ears had been the clash of steel. The first sight his eye beheld had been ravens circling in the sky, waiting till living men departed and they ruled what remained.

With the battle fury that had been his birthright he strode through the flames and screams of the encampment, and death rode on his steel. He sought the turbanned men, the bearded men, and those he found went before Erlik's Black Throne with eyes of azure fire their last memory of the world of men. His ancient broadsword flashed banefully in the light of burning tents, flashed till its encrimsoned length could flash no more, but seemed rather to eat light as it ate life. Men faced him, men fell before him, and at last men fled him.

The time came when he stood alone, and no turbans could his questing eye find but those on dead men. There were standing men, he realized as the haze of battle-rage thinned and cleared his eyes, Zamoran hunters gathered in a loose circle about him, staring in wonder tinged with fear. He turned to face each man in turn, and each fell back a step at his gaze. Even Arvaneus could not hold his ground, though his face flushed with anger when he realized what he had done.

"The hillmen?" Conan demanded hoarsely. He stripped the rough woolen cloak from a hillman's corpse and wiped his blade clean.

"Gone," Telades said in a high voice. He paused to clear his throat. "Some few fled, I think, but most . . ." His gesture took in the entire hilltop, strewn with bodies and burned-out tents, illumined by flaming carts. "It was your work that saved us, Cimmerian."

"Hannuman's Stones!" Arvaneus roared. "Are you all women? It was your own arms saved you, swords in your own hands! If the barbar slew one or two, it was his skin he sought to save."

"Do not speak the fool," Telades retorted. "You of all men should not speak against him. Conan fought like a demon while the rest of us struggled to realize that we were awake, that it was not a nightmare we faced." A murmur of agreement came from the circle of men.

Face twisted darkly, Arvaneus opened his mouth, but Conan cut him off. "If some of them escaped, they may return with others. We should be gone from this place, and quickly."

"There stands your hero," Arvaneus sneered. "Ready to run. Few hillman bands are larger than the number which attacked us, and most of them now wait for the worms. Who else will come against us? I, for one, think we slew all of the mountain dogs."

"Some did flee," Telades protested, but Arvaneus spoke on over him.

"I saw none escaping. If I had, they wouldn't have lived to escape. If we run like rabbits, then like rabbits we run from shadows."

"Your insults begin to disturb me, huntsman," Conan said, hefting his sword. "In the past I have forborne killing you for one reason or another. Now, it is time for you to still your tongue, or I will still it for you."

Arvaneus stared stiffly back at him, his tulwar twitching in his hand, but he did not speak. The other hunters moved back to give room.

Into the silence Jondra stepped, a robe of brocaded sky-blue silk covering her to the ankles and held tightly at her neck with both hands. She studied the two men confronting each other before speaking. "Conan, why do you think the hillmen will return?"

She was attempting to ignore the tension, the Cimmerian knew, and so disarm it, but he thought the answer to her question was more important than killing Arvaneus. "It is true that bands of hillmen are usually small, but in Shadizar it is said the Kezankian tribes are gathering. The soldiers we saw marching north bear this out, for it is also said the army is being sent to deal with them. To go risks nothing; to stay risks that the few who fled may bring back a thousand more."

"A thousand!" the hawk-faced man snorted. "My lady, it is well known how the hill tribes war constantly with one another. A thousand hillmen in one place would kill each other in the space of a day. And if, by some miracle, so many were gathered together, their attention would surely be on the soldiers. In any case, I cannot believe in this bizarre rumor of a gathering of the tribes. It goes against all that I know of the hillmen." Jondra nodded thoughtfully, then asked, "And our injured? How many are they, and how badly hurt?"

"Many nicks and cuts, my lady," Arvaneus told her, "but only fourteen hurt badly enough to be accounted as wounded, and but two of those seriously." He hesitated. "Eleven are dead, my lady."

"Eleven," she sighed, and her eyes closed.

" 'Twould have been more, my lady, save for Conan," Telades said, and Arvaneus rounded on him.

"Cease your chatter of the barbar, man!"

"Enough!" Jondra barked. Her voice stilled the hunters on the instant. "I will reach a decision on what is to be done tomorrow. For now the wounded must be tended, and the fires put out. Arvaneus, you will see to it." She paused to take a deep breath, looking at no one. "Conan, come to my tent. Please?" The last word was forced, and as she said it she turned away quickly, her robe flaring to give a glimpse of bare thighs, and hurried from the circle of men.

Conan's visits to Jondra's tent and sleeping furs had been an open secret, but an unacknowledged one. Studiously the men all avoided looking at Conan, or at each other, for that matter. Arvaneus seemed stunned. Tamira alone met his eyes, and she glared daggers.

With a shake of his head for the vagaries of women, the big Cimmerian sheathed his sword and followed Jondra.

She was waiting for him in her scarlet tent. As he ducked through the tent-flap, she slipped the silk robe from her shoulders, and he found his arms full of sleek bare skin. Full breasts bored into his ribs as she clutched at him, burying her head against his broad chest.

"I . . . I should not have spoken as I did earlier," she murmured. "I do not doubt what you saw, and I do not want you to stay away from my bed."

"It is well you believe me," he said, smoothing her hair, "for I saw as I said. But now is no time to speak of that." She sighed and snuggled closer, if that was possible. "It is time to speak of turning back. Your hunters have taken grievous hurt from the hillmen, and you are yet a day from the mountains. Do you enter the mountains with carts and oxen, you'll not escape further attention from the tribes. Your men will be slain, and you will find yourself the slave of an unwashed tribesman whose wives will beat you constantly for your beauty. At least, they will until the harsh life and the labor leaches your youth as it does theirs."

Word by word she had stiffened in his arms. Now she pushed herself from him, staring up at him incredulously. "It has been long years," she said in breathless fury, "since I apologized to any man, and never have I b . . . asked one to my bed before you. Whatever I expected for doing so, it was not to be lectured."

"It must be spoken of." He found it hard to ignore the heavy, round breasts that confronted him, the tiny waist that flared into generous hips and long legs, but he forced himself to speak as if she were draped in layers of thick wool. "The hillmen are roused. Ants might escape their notice, but not men. And should you find this beast you hunt, remember that it is a hunter as well, and one that kills with fire. How many men will you see roasted alive to put a trophy on your wall?"

"A folk tale," she scoffed. "If hillmen cannot frighten me off, do you think I will run before a myth?"

"Eldran," he began with a patience he no longer felt, but her screach cut him off.

"No! I will not hear of that . . . that Brythunian!" Panting, she struggled to gain control of herself. At last she drew herself up imperiously. "I did not summon you here for argument. You will come to my bed and speak only of what we do, or you will leave me."

Conan's anger coiled to within a hair's breadth of erupting, but he managed to keep his reply to a mocking, "As my lady wishes." And he turned his back on her nudity.

Her furious cries followed him into the fading night, echoing across the camp. "Conan! Come back here, Mitra blast you! You cannot leave me like this! I command you to return, Erlik curse you forever!"

No man looked up from his labor, but it was clear from the intensity with which they minded their work that none was deaf. Those prodding burning bundles from the carts with spears abruptly redoubled their efforts to save what had not already caught fire. The newly set sentries suddenly peered at the failing shadows as if each hid a hillman.

Tamira was passing among the wounded, lying in a row on blankets in the middle of the camp, holding a waterskin to each man's mouth. She looked up with a bright smile as he passed. "So you'll sleep alone again tonight, Cimmerian," she said sweetly. "A pity." Conan did not look at her, but a scowl darkened his face.

One of the carts had been abandoned to burn, and flaming bundles lay scattered about the others. The fat cook capered among the men, waving a pewter tray over his head and complaining loudly at their use of his implements for shoveling dirt onto the fires. Conan took the tray from the rotund man's hands and bent beside Telades to dig at the rocky soil.

The shaven-headed hunter eyed him sideways for a time, then said carefully, "There are few men would walk out on her without reason."

Instead of answering the unasked question, Conan snarled, "I've half a mind to tie her to her horse so you can lead her back to Shadizar."

"You've half a mind if you think that you could," Telades said, throwing a potful of dirt and small stones on a fiery bale, "or that we would. The Lady Jondra decides where to go, and we follow."

"Into the Kezankians?" Conan said incredulously. "With the tribes stirring? The army didn't come north for the weather."

"I've served the House Perashanid," the other man said slowly, "since I was a boy, and my father before me, and his before him. The Lady Jondra *is* the house, now, for she is the last. I cannot desert her. But you could, I suppose. In fact, perhaps you should."

"And why would I do that?" Conan asked drily.

Telades answered as though the question had been serious. "Not all spears are thrown by the enemies you expect, northlander. If you do stay, watch your back."

Conan paused in the act of stooping for more dirt. So the spear that grazed his back had not been cast by a hillman's hand. Arvaneus, no doubt. Or perhaps some other, long in the Perashanid's service, who did not like the last daughter of the house bedding a landless warrior. That was all he needed. An enemy behind him—at least one—and the hillmen surrounding. Tomorrow, he decided, he would make one last try at convincing Jondra to turn back. And Tamira, as well. There were gems aplenty in Shadizar for her to steal. And if they would not, he would leave them and go back alone. Furiously he scooped dirt onto the tray and hurled it at the flames. He would! Erlik take him if he did not.

In the gray dawn Djinar stared at the pitiful following that remained to him. Five men with shocked eyes and no horses.

"It was the giant," Sharmal muttered. His turban was gone, and his face was streaked with dirt, and dried blood from a scalp wound. His eye focused on something none of the rest could see. "The giant slew who he would. None could face him." No one tried to quiet him, for the mad were touched by the old gods, and under their protection.

"Does any man think we can yet take the Eyes of Fire from the Zamoran woman?" Djinar asked tiredly. Blank stares answered him.

"He cut off Farouz's hand," Sharmal said. "The blood spurted from Farouz's arm as he rode into the night to die."

Djinar ignored the youth. "And does any man doubt the price we will pay for failing Basrakan Imalla's command?" Again the four who retained their senses kept silent, but again the answer was in their dark eyes, colored now by a tinge of horror.

Sharmal began to weep. "The giant was a spirit of the earth. We have displeased the true gods, and they sent him to punish us."

"It is decided, then." Djinar shook his head. He would leave much behind, including his favorite saddle and two young wives, but such could be more easily replaced than blood from a man's veins. "In the south the tribes have not yet heeded Basrakan's call. They care only for raiding the caravans to Sultanapur and Aghrapur. We will go there. Better the risk no one will take us in than the certainty of Basrakan's anger."

He did not see Sharmal move, but suddenly the young man's fist thudded against his chest. He looked down, perplexed that his breath seemed short. The blow had not been that hard. Then he saw the hilt of a dagger in the fist. When he raised his eyes again, the other four were gone, unwilling to meddle in the affairs of a madman.

"You have been attained, Djinar," Sharmal said in a tone suitable for instructing a child. "Better this than that you should flee the will of the true gods. Surely you see that. We must return to Basrakan Imalla, who is a holy man, and tell him of the giant."

He had been right, Djinar thought. Death had been in that camp. He could smell it still. He opened his mouth to laugh, and blood poured out.

XII

Amid the lengthening shadows of mid-afternoon, some sem-
blance of normality had returned to the hunter's camp. The
fires were out, and those carts that could not be salvaged had
been pushed to the bottom of the hill, along with supplies too badly
burned for use. Most of the wounded were on their feet, if not ready
for another battle, and the rest soon would be. The dead—including
now the two most seriously wounded—had been buried in a row on the
hillside, with cairns of stones laid atop their graves to keep the wolves
from them. Zamoran dead, at least, had been treated so. Vultures and
ravens squawked and contended beyond the next hill, where the corpses
of hillmen had been dragged.

Sentries were set now not only about the hilltop camp itself, but on
the hills surrounding. Those distant watchers, mounted so they could
bring an alarm in time to be useful, had been Conan's idea. When he
put the notion forward Jondra ignored it, and Arvaneus scorned it, but
the sentries were placed, if without acknowledgement to the Cimmerian.

It was not for pique, however, that Conan stalked through the camp
with a face like a thunderhead. He cared nothing who got credit for the
sentries, so long as they were placed. But all day Jondra had avoided
him. She had hurried about checking the wounded, checking the meals
the cook prepared, meddling in a score of tasks she would normally have
dismissed once she ordered them done. All in the camp save Conan she
had kept at the run. And every particle of it, he knew, was to keep from
talk with him.

Tamira trotted by in her short white tunic, intently balancing a flagon of wine and a goblet on a tray, and Conan caught her arm. "I can't stop now," she said distractedly. "She wants this right away, and the way she's been today I have no wish to be slow." Suddenly the slender thief chuckled. "Perhaps it would have been better for us all if you *hadn't* slept alone last night."

"Never mind that," Conan growled. "It's time for leaving, Tamira. Tomorrow will see us in the mountains."

"Is that what you said to Jondra to anger her so?" Her face tightened. "Did you ask her to go back with you, too?"

"Fool girl, will you listen? A hunting trophy is no reason to risk death at the hands of hillmen, nor are those gems."

"What of Jondra?" she said suspiciously. "She won't turn back."

"If I can't talk her into it, I will go without her. Will you come?"

Tamira bit her full under-lip and studied his face from beneath her lashes. Finally, she nodded. "I will. It must be in the night, though, while she sleeps. She'll not let me leave her service, if she knows of it. What would she do without a handmaiden to shout at? But what of your own interest in the rubies, Cimmerian?"

"I no longer have any interest," he replied.

"No longer have," Tamira began, then broke off with a disbelieving shake of her head. "Oh, you must think I am a fine fool to believe that, Cimmerian. Or else you're one. Mitra, but I do keep forgetting that men will act like men."

"And what does that mean?" Conan demanded.

"That she's had you to her bed, and now you will not steal from her. And you call yourself a thief!"

"My reasons are no concerns of yours," he told her with more patience than he felt. "No more than the rubies should be. You leave with me tonight, remember?"

"I remember," she said slowly. As her large brown eyes looked up at him, he thought for a moment that she wanted to say something more.

"Lyana!" Jondra's voice cracked in the air like a whip. "Where is my wine?"

"Where is my wine?" Tamira muttered mockingly, but she broke into a run, dodging around Telades, who labored under one end of a weighty brass-bound chest.

"Mayhap you shouldn't have angered her, Cimmerian," the shaven-headed hunter panted. "Mayhap you could apologize." The man at the other end of the chest nodded weary agreement.

"Crom!" Conan growled. "Is everyone in the camp worrying about whether I . . ." His words trailed off as one of the sentries galloped his horse up the hill. Unknowingly, easing his broadsword in its scabbard, he strode to where the man was dismounting before Jondra. The hunters left off their tasks to gather around.

"Soldiers, my lady," the sentry said, breathing heavily. "Cavalry. Two, perhaps three hundred of them, coming hard."

Jondra pounded a fist on a rounded thigh. Her salmon silk tunic and riding breeches were dusty and sweat-stained from her day's labors. "Erlik take all soldiers," she said tightly, then took a deep breath that made her heavy breasts stir beneath the taut silk of her tunic. "Very well. If they come, I'll receive their commander. Arvaneus! See that any man who's bandaged is out of sight. If the soldiers arrive before I return, be courteous, but tell them nothing. Nothing, understand me! Lyana! Attend me, girl!" Before she finished speaking she was pushing through the assembled hunters, not waiting for them to move from her path.

The hawk-faced huntsman began shouting commands, and hunters and carters scattered in all directions, hastening to prepare the camp for visitors. Moving the wounded inside tents was the least of it, for most of them could walk without assistance, but Jondra's industriousness had left bales and bundles, piles of cooking gear and stacks of spears scattered among the remaining tents till the camp seemed struck by a whirlwind.

Ignoring the bustle behind him, Conan settled into a flat-footed crouch at the edge of the camp, his eyes intent on the direction from which the sentry had come. More than once his hand strayed unconsciously to the worn hilt of his ancient broadsword. He did not doubt that the sentry had seen Zamoran soldiers and not hillmen, but he had as little regard for one as for the other. Relations between the army and a thief were seldom easy.

A ringing clatter of shod hooves on loose stone heralded the soldiers' approach well before the mounted column came into sight. In ranks of four, with wellaligned lance-points glittering in the afternoon sun, they wended their way along the small valleys between the hills. A banner led them, such as Zamoran generals were wont to have, of green silk fringed with gold, its surface embroidered in ornate gold script recounting victories. Conan snorted contemptuously at the sight of the honor standard. At that distance he could not read the script, but he could count the number of battles listed. Considering the number of true battles fought by Zamoran arms in the twenty years past, that banner gave honor to many a border skirmish and brawl with brigands.

At the foot of the hill the column drew up, two files wheeling to face the camp, the other two turning their mounts the other way. The standard bearer and the general, marked by the plume of scarlet horsehair on his golden helmet and the gilding of his mail, picked their way up the hill through the few stunted trees and scattered clumps of waist-high scrub.

At Arvaneus' impatient signal two of the hunters ran forward, one to hold the general's bridle, the other his stirrup, as he dismounted. He was a tall man of darkly handsome face, his upper lip adorned by thin mustaches. His arrogant eye ran over the camp, pausing at Conan for a raised brow of surprise and a sniff of dismissal before going on. The Cimmerian wondered idly if the man had ever actually had to use the jewel-hilted sword at his side.

"Well," the general said suddenly, "where is your mistress?"

Arvaneus darted forward, his face set for effusive apologies, but Jondra's voice brought him to a skidding halt. "Here I am, Zathanides. And what does Zamora's most illustrious general do so far from the palaces of Shadizar?"

She came before the general with a feline stride, and her garb brought gasps even from her hunters. Shimmering scarlet silk, belted with thickly woven gold and pearls, moulded every curve of breasts and belly and thighs, rounded and firm enough to make a eunuch's mouth water.

It was not the raiment that drew Conan's attention, however. On her head rested a diadem of sapphires and black opals, with one great ruby larger than the last joint of a big man's thumb lying above her brows. Between her generous breasts nestled that ruby's twin, depending from a necklace likewise encrusted with brilliant azure sapphires and opals of deepest ebon. The Cimmerian's gaze sought out Tamira. The young woman thief was demurely presenting to Zathanides a tray bearing a golden goblet and a crystal flagon of wine, with damp, folded cloths beside. She seemed unaware of the gems she had meant to steal.

"You are as lovely as ever, Jondra," the general said as he wiped his hands and tossed the cloths back onto the tray. "But that loveliness might have ended gracing some hillman's hut if I hadn't found this fellow Eldran."

Jondra stiffened visibly. "Eldran?"

"Yes. A Brythunian. Hunter, he said." He took the goblet Tamira filled for him, gracing her with a momentary smile that touched only his lips. "I wouldn't have believed his tale of a Zamoran noblewoman in this Mitra-forsaken place if it had not been for his description. A woman as tall as most men, ravingly beautiful of face and figure, a fair shot with a bow. And your gray eyes, of course. I knew then it could be none but you." He tilted back his head to drink.

"He dared describe me so? A fair shot?" She hissed the words, but it had been "ravingly beautiful" that made her face color, and the mention of her eyes that had clenched her fists. "I hope you have this Eldran well chained. And his followers. I . . . I have reason to believe they are brigands."

Conan grinned openly. She was not a woman to take kindly to being bested.

"I fear not," Zathanides said, tossing the empty goblet back to Tamira. "He seemed what he called himself, and he was alone, so I sent him on his way. In any case, you should be thankful to him for saving your life, Jondra. The hillmen are giving trouble, and this is no place for one of your little jaunts. I'll send a few men with you to see that you get back to Shadizar safely."

"I am no child to be commanded," Jondra said hotly.

The general's heavy-lidded eyes caressed her form, and his reply came slowly. "You are certainly no child, Jondra. No, indeed. But go you must."

Jondra's eyes flickered to Conan. Abruptly her posture softened, and her voice became languorous. "No, I am not a child, Zathanides. Perhaps we can discuss my future plans. In the privacy of my tent?"

Startlement passed over Zathanides' face to be replaced by pleasure. "Certainly," he said with an unctuous smile. "Let us . . . discuss your future."

Arvaneus' swarthy face was a blend of despair and rage as he watched the pair disappear into the scarlet tent. Conan merely scooped up a handful of rocks and began tossing them down the hill one by one. Telades squatted next to him.

"More trouble, Cimmerian," the shaven-headed man said, "and I begin to wonder if you are worth it."

"What have I to do with anything?" Conan asked coldly.

"She does this because of you, you fool northlander."

"She makes her choice." He would not admit even to himself that this flirting with Zathanides sat ill with him. "She's not the first woman to choose a man for wealth and titles."

"But she is no ordinary woman. I have served her since she was a child, and I tell you that you were the first man to come to her bed."

"I know," Conan said through gritted teeth. He was unused to women casting him aside; he liked neither the fact of it nor the discussing of it.

A woman's scream came from the tent, and the Cimmerian threw another stone. The tightness of his jaw eased, and a slight smile touched his lips. Arvaneus took a single step toward the scarlet pavilion, then

froze in indecision. From where she knelt by the tent flap, Tamira cast
an agonized glance at Conan. All the rest of the camp seemed stunned
to immobility. Another shriek rent the air.

Telades leaped to his feet, but Conan caught the hunter's arm. "I
will see if she requires aid," he said calmly, tossing aside his handful of
stones. Despite his tone the Cimmerian's first steps were quick, and by
the time he reached the tent he was running.

As he ducked through the tent-flap, the story was plain. Jondra struggled among the cushions, her scarlet robe rucked up above her rounded
hips, long legs kicking in the air, while Zathanides lay half atop her
fumbling with his breeches and raining kisses on her face. Her small
fists pounded futilely at his back and sides.

With a snarl Conan grasped the man by the neck of his gilded mail
shirt and the seat of his breeches, lifting him straight into the air. Zathanides gave a shout, then began cursing and struggling, clawing at his
sword, but the huge Cimmerian easily carried him to the entrance and
threw him from the tent to land like a sack.

Conan took a bare instant to assure himself that Jondra was unharmed. Her jewelry was discarded on the cushions, and her robe was torn
to expose one smooth shoulder, but she seemed more angry than hurt
as she scrambled to her feet, pushing her silk down over her sleek nudity.
Then he followed Zathanides outside. The general had risen to one
knee, his mouth twisted with rage, and his sword came out as Conan
appeared. The Cimmerian's foot lashed out. The jeweled sword went
flying; Zathanides yelped and clutched his wrist. The shout of outraged
pain faded as Conan's blade point touched the general's throat.

"Stop!" Jondra cried. "Conan, put up your sword!"

Conan lowered his steel slowly, though he did not sheath it. It had
been she who was assaulted, and by his thinking Zathanides' life was
hers to dispose of as she saw fit, or even to spare. But he would not
disarm himself until the man was dead or gone.

"I'll have your head, barbarian," Zathanides snarled as he got painfully to his feet. "You'll discover the penalty for attacking a Lord of
Zamora."

"Then you will discover the penalty for . . . for manhandling a Lady
of Zamora," Jondra said coldly. "Tread warily, Zathanides, for your
head and Conan's will share the same fate, and the choice is yours."

Zathanides' dark eyes bulged, and spittle dripped from the corner of
his mouth. "Make what charges you will, you half-breed Brythunian
trull. Do you think there is anyone in Zamora who has not heard the
stories of you? That you bed a man before you take him in service as a

hunter? Who will believe that one such as I would touch such a slut, such a piece of—"

He cut off and took a step back as Conan's sword lifted again, but Jondra grabbed the Cimmerian's massive arm, though both her hands could not come near encircling it. "Hold, Conan," she said unsteadily. "Make your choice, Zathanides."

The dark-faced general scrubbed at the spittle on his chin with the back of his hand, then nodded jerkily. " 'Tis you who has made a choice, Jondra. Keep your savage lover. Enter the mountains if you will, and find a hillman." Stamping to where his jewel-hilted blade lay, he snatched it from the ground and slammed it home in the sheath at his side. "For all I care, you can go straight to Zandru's Ninth Hell!"

Satisfaction glimmered beneath Conan's anger as he watched the general's stiff-backed march to his horse. Zathanides might wish to abandon Jondra to her fate, but too many of his own soldiers knew that he had found her. The attempted rape might well be covered up—especially if other nobles felt about Jondra as the general did—but failing in his attempt to turn a woman back from the mountains would place his manhood in an unfavorable light indeed. At least, that was the way the Cimmerian believed a man of Zathanides' ilk would look at the matter. Conan felt he could safely wager that the next day would see the appearance of a force under orders to escort the hunting party to Shadizar, without regard for what Jondra had to say.

As Zathanides and his standard bearer galloped down the hill, Arvaneus approached the crimson-walled tent, his manner at once arrogant and hesitant. "My lady," he said hoarsely, "if you command it, I will take men and see that Lord Zathanides does not survive the night."

"If I command it," Jondra replied in an icy tone, "you will sneak in the night and murder Zathanides. Conan did not await my command. He faced Zathanides openly, without fear of consequences."

"My lady, I . . . I would die for you. I live only for you."

Jondra turned her back on the impassioned huntsman. Her eyes fastened on Conan's broad chest as if afraid to meet his gaze. "You begin to make a habit of saving me," she said softly. "I see no reason for us to continue to sleep apart." Arvaneus's teeth ground audibly.

Conan said nothing. If his thoughts concerning Zathanides were correct, then he should be gone from the camp before the night ended, for the general's instructions would certainly include the death of one large northlander. Too, there was his plan of departing with Tamira. Leaving from Jondra's bed would necessitate explanations he did not want to make.

The tall noblewoman drew a shuddering breath. "I am no tavern wench to be toyed with. I will have an answer now."

"I did not leave your bed for wanting to," he said carefully, and cursed his lack of diplomatic skill when her chin went up and her eyes flared. "Let us not argue," he added quickly. "It will be days before the wounded have their strength back. They should be days of rest and enjoyment." Days spent in her return to Shadizar, he thought, but his satisfaction vanished at her scornful laugh.

"Can you be so foolish? Zathanides will brood on his manhood and the pride he lost here, then convince himself that he can escape any charges I might bring. Tomorrow will see more soldiers, Conan, no doubt with orders to take me back in chains if I'll go no other way. But they will need to seek me in the mountains." Abruptly her face stilled, and her voice hardened. "You are *not* so foolish as that. You know as well as I the soldiers will return. You would have waited and seen me carried back to Shadizar like a bundle. Well, go, if you fear the mountains. Go! I care not!" As abruptly as she had turned her back on Arvaneus, she turned to face the huntsman again. "I intend to press on at first light," she told the hawk-faced man, "and to move quickly. All baggage must be discarded except what can be carried on pack animals. The wounded and all men who cannot be mounted will turn back with the ox-carts. Perhaps their trail will confuse Zathanides for a time. . . ."

As her list of instructions went on, Arvaneus shot a look over her shoulder at Conan, smug satisfaction mingled with a promise of violence. There would be more trouble from that quarter. Or rather, the Cimmerian reminded himself, there would be if he continued with the hunters, which he had no intention of doing. And since such was his plan, it was time for him to be making preparations for his leave-taking.

Slowly Conan moved away from the noblewoman's flow of commands. With studied casualness he drifted beyond the cookfires. The fat cook, frowning over a delicate dish for Jondra's table, never looked up as the Cimmerian rooted among the supplies. When Conan walked on, he carried two fat leather pouches of dried meat in the crook of his arm. Taking one quick look to make certain he was unobserved, he cached the meat beneath a thornbush on the edge of the encampment. Soon he had added four waterbags, and blankets of blue-striped wool. He was inured to sleeping with naught but his cloak for protection from the cold, or even without it, but he could not think a city woman like Tamira was so hardy.

The horses had to wait until the point of leaving—they certainly could not be saddled now without drawing unwanted attention—but he walked to the picket line anyway. It was easier to choose out a good mount when there was light to see. The big black he had been riding would do for him; Tamira needed a horse with good endurance as well, though. He had intended to move down the line of animals without stopping, so as to give no hint of his interest, but as he came to a long-legged bay mare—just the sort he would choose for Tamira—his feet halted of their own accord. On the ground at the mare's head rested a high-pommeled saddle, a bulging waterbag, and a tightly tied leather sack.

"In the night, Tamira?" he said softly. "Or while I sit waiting for darkness to come?" The picture of the rubies lying on the cushions of Jondra's tent was suddenly bright in his mind.

With a calm he did not feel, Conan strode through the camp, his eyes seeking Tamira. Once more the encampment was an anthill, hunters scurrying at Jondra's commands. For an instant the noblewoman paused, gazing at Conan as if she wished to speak, but when he did not slow she turned angrily back to supervising the preparations for the next morning. Nowhere did Conan see Tamira. But that, he thought grimly, might mean he was not too late.

Conan knew how he would have entered the scarlet tent, had he chosen to steal the rubies with the camp aroused. A glance told him no one was watching, and he quickly slipped behind Jondra's pavilion. Down the back of the tent a long slit had been made. Parting it a fingerwidth, he peered in. Tamira knelt within, rooting among the cushions. With a muffled laugh she drew out the sparkling length of the necklace. The tiara was gripped in her other hand.

Soundlessly Conan slipped through the slit. The first announcement of his presence Tamira received was his hand closing over her mouth. His free arm encircled her, pinning her arms and lifting her before she had time to do more than gasp into his palm. She had dropped the gems, he saw, but that was the end of his moment of peace. Tamira exploded into a wriggling, kicking, biting bundle. And footsteps were approaching the front of the tent.

With a muttered oath the Cimmerian ducked back through the slit with his struggling burden. Behind the tent was no place to stop, however, not if someone was going to enter the tent, not with Tamira as likely as not to scream that *he* had been thieving. Cursing under his breath, he scrambled down the stony slope until he found a clump of scrub brush that hid them from the camp. There he tried to set her down, but she kicked him fiercely on the ankle, rocks slid beneath his foot, and he found himself on the ground with Tamira beneath him, her eyes starting from her head from the force of the fall.

"You great oaf!" she wheezed after a moment. "Do you try to break my ribs?"

"I did not kick myself," he growled. "I thought we agreed to leave in the night. What were you doing in Jondra's tent?"

"Nothing was said about the rubies," she retorted. "I haven't changed my plans for them, even if you have. Perhaps," she finished angrily, "you find what Jondra gives you more valuable than rubies, but as I am not a man I have a different view of the matter."

"Leave Jondra out of this," he snapped. "And do not try to change the subject. You have a horse waiting this very instant."

Tamira shifted uneasily beneath him, and her eyes slid away from his. "I wanted to be ready," she muttered. "For the night."

"Do you think I'm a fool," he said, "that I take you for a fool? The saddle cannot escape discovery till nightfall. But if someone planned to steal the rubies and leave the camp within the turn of a glass . . . You could not have been planning such a thing, could you?"

"They would not have held you to blame." Her tone was sullenly excusatory. "Jondra would not blame you if she found you with the rubies in your pouch. And if she did, it would be less than you deserve."

"Jondra," he breathed. "Always Jondra. What is it to you whose bed I share? You and I are not lovers."

Tamira's large brown eyes grew even wider. Scarlet suffused her cheeks, and her mouth worked for a long moment before sound finally came out. "We most certainly are not!" she gasped. "How dare you suggest such a thing? Let me up! Get off me, you great ox! Let me up, I say!" Her small fists punctuated her words, pounding at his shoulders, but suddenly her fingers had tangled in his hair, and she was pressing her lips to his.

Conan blinked once in surprise, then returned her kiss with as much fervor as she was putting into it. "Don't think this will convince me to stay," he said when they broke apart for air. "I'm not such a fool."

"If you stop," she moaned, "then you *are* a fool."

With one last silent reminder that he would *not* be a fool, Conan gave up talk and thought alike for pleasures at once simpler and more complex.

he was not a fool, Conan told himself once more as he guided his horse along a trail halfway up a nameless peak on the fringe of the Kezankians. If he kept saying it, he thought he might convince himself in time. Before and behind him stretched the hunting party, all mounted and many leading pack animals, wending their way deeper into the hillman domains. The sun stood barely above the horizon. They had left the camp in the hills before the first glimmer of dawn. The ox-carts with the wounded would be on their way back to Shadizar.

Lost in his own thoughts, Conan was surprised to find that Jondra had reined aside to await him. He had not spoken to her since she turned her back on him, but he noted that at least she was smiling now.

She drew her horse in beside his. The trail was wide enough for the animals to walk abreast. "The day is fine, is it not?" she said brightly.

Conan merely looked at her.

"I hoped you would come to me in the night. No, I promised myself I would not say that." Shyly she peered at him through lowered lashes. "I knew you could not leave me. That is . . . I thought . . . you *did* stay because of me, did you not?"

"I did," he said glumly, but she appeared not to notice his tone.

"I knew it," she said, her smile even more radiant than before. "Tonight we will put the past behind us once and for all." With that she galloped up the line of mounted men to resume her place at their head.

Conan growled deep in his throat.

"What did she want?" Tamira demanded, guiding her mount up beside his. It was the same bay mare she had chosen out for her flight. She glared jealously after the noblewoman.

"Nothing of consequence," Conan replied.

The young woman thief grunted contemptuously.

" 'Tis likely she thinks you are still here because of the over-generous charms she displays so freely. But you came because of me. Didn't you?"

"I came for you," Conan told her. "But unless you want to see how strongly Jondra wields a switch, you had best not let her see us talking too often."

"Let her but try."

"Then you intend to explain to her that you are not Lyana the hand-maiden, but Tamira the thief?"

"If she faced me in a fair fight," the slender woman began with a toss of her head, then broke off in a laugh. "But it is not talk I want from you. She can have that. Till tonight, Conan."

The big Cimmerian sighed heavily as she let her horse fall behind his. It was no easy task he had ahead of him, and all because he could not allow a woman who had shared his bed—much less two of them—to enter the Kezankians while he rode back to Shadizar. He supposed those men who called themselves civilized and him barbarian could have man-aged it easily. It was beyond him, though, and his pride was enough to make him believe he could bring both safely out of the mountains. Of course, he knew, soon or late each woman would find out about the other. At that point, he was sure, he would rather face all the hillmen of the Kezankians than those two females.

The thought of hillmen brought him back to his surroundings. If he did not keep watch, they might not even make it fully into the moun-tains, much less out. His eyes scanned the steep brown mountain slopes around him, dotted with tress bizarrely sculpted by wind and harsh clime. He searched the jagged peaks ahead. No signs of life did he discern, but the breeze brought a sound to him, faint yet disturbing. It came from behind.

He reined his horse around to look back, and felt the hair stir on the back of his neck. Far below and far distant among the foothills a battle raged. He could make out little save dust rising as smoke from the hills and the small forms of men swarming like ants, yet for an instant he saw what he could swear was a Zamoran honor standard atop a hill. Then it was ridden down, and the men who rode over it wore turbans. Most of the other shapes he could make out were turbanned as well.

"What is the matter?" Jondra shouted, galloping down the trail. She had to force her way through a knot of hunters gathered behind Conan. "Why are you halted?"

" 'Tis a battle, my lady," Telades said, shading his eyes with one hand to peer down at the hills. "I cannot say who fights."

"Hillmen," Conan said. "From the look of it hillmen are killing some part of the Zamoran army."

"Nonsense!" Arvaneus snapped. "The army would sweep any hillman rabble aside. Besides, the tribes never gather in such numbers, and . . . and . . ." The force of his words weakened as he spoke, and he finished lamely with, "It is impossible to make out details at this distance. That could be anyone fighting. Perhaps it is not a battle at all."

"Perhaps it is a folk dance," Conan said dryly.

Jondra touched his arm. "Is there aught we can do to aid them?"

"Not even if we had wings," the big Cimmerian replied.

Relief was writ plain on the faces of the hunters at his reply, but it was relief tinged with fear. It was all very well to talk of entering the Kezankians and risking the wrath of the hill tribes. To actually see that wrath, even at a distance, was something else, and most especially when it seemed to be dealt out by more hillmen than a man might expect to see in a lifetime of roaming the mountains.

Jondra looked from face to face, then put on a smile. "If so many hillmen are down there, then we shall have the mountains to ourselves." Her words had little effect on the hunters' expressions. A raven appeared, flying around the side of the mountain. "There," Jondra said, drawing her bow from its lacquered case behind her saddle. "Should there be a hillman or two left in the mountains, we'll deal with them as easily as this." Her bowstring slapped against her forearm leather; the raven's wings folded, and the bird dropped like a stone. Conan thought he heard her mutter something about "Brythunian" as she recased her bow. "Now let us ride," she commanded, and galloped back up the trail.

Slowly the column of hunters formed again behind the noblewoman. As Tamira passed Conan, she gave him an anxious, wide-eyed look. Perhaps he *was* a fool, he thought, but he could be no other than what he was. With a reassuring smile for the young woman thief, he joined the file of horsemen picking its way up the mountain.

Eldran ran a judicious eye over the two score men following him through a field of boulders deeper into the mountains, and said, "We stop for a rest."

"About time," said a round-cheeked man with gray streaking the long hair that was held back from his face by a leather cord. "We've ridden since before first light, and I'm not so young as I once was."

"If you tell me about your old bones one more time, Haral," Eldran laughed, and the others joined in, though their laughter was strained. Haral's age and plumpness were belied by the scars on his face, and the wolf whose fur trimmed his cloak had been slain with his bare hands. "A short stop only," Eldran went on. "These mountains feel ill, and I would be done with what we came for and out of them quickly."

That cooled their mirth, as he had intended it should. The laugh had been good for easing the disquiet, and perhaps more than disquiet, that had fallen over them all since they entered the mountains, but they must be ever mindful of what they were about and where they were if they were to leave with their lives.

As the others sat or lay or even walked a bit to stretch their legs, Eldran reclined with his reins wrapped loosely about one hand. He had had his own difficulties in keeping his mind cleanly on his purpose in the Kezankians. Even through the unease that hung about him like a miasma, a tall Zamoran beauty with arrogance enough for a score of kings had a way of intruding on his thoughts when he was not careful. But was she truly Zamoran, he wondered. Her manner, acting as if she ruled whatever ground she stood on, said yes. But those eyes. Like the mists of morning clinging to the oaks of the forest. No Zamoran ever had such eyes, as gray as his own.

Angrily he reminded himself of his purpose, to avenge his brother and those who went with him into the Kezankians, never to return. And to avenge as well those who had died attempting to defend their farmholds against the beast of fire. To make certain that more deaths did not come from the beast. If he and every man with him died, it would be small price for success. They had all agreed to that before ever they left Brythunia.

A raven circled high above him. Like the bird he and Jondra had shot, he thought. Angrily he leaped to his feet. Could nothing put the woman from his mind? Well, he would not be reminded of her longer by that accursed bird. He pulled his bow from its wolf-hide case behind his saddle.

"Eldran!" From a space clear of boulders higher on the mountain, a bony man with a pointed nose waved to him frantically. "Come quickly, Eldran!"

"What is it, Fyrdan?" Eldran called back, but he was scrambling up the slope as he spoke. Fyrdan was not one to become excited over nothing. Others of the band followed.

"There," the bony man said, flinging out an arm to point as Eldran joined him.

Eldran cupped his hands beside his eyes to improve his seeing, but there was little to make out save boiling dust and the tiny figures of struggling men on the hills far below. "Hillmen," he said finally.

"And Zamorans," Fyrdan added. "I saw the banner their general carried go down."

Slowly Eldran's hands dropped to his sides. "Forgive me, Jondra," he said softly.

"Perhaps the soldiers had not fetched her yet," Haral said. "Perhaps these are the other soldiers we saw."

Eldran shook his head. "The others were further west. And I watched their camp until their general left to find her."

"A Zamoran wench," Fyrdan said scornfully. "There are plenty of good Brythunian women eager for a tumble with . . ." His words trailed off under Eldran's glare.

"We will speak no more of the woman," the gray-eyed man said. "We will talk of other things, things that must be said. We have tracked the beast here to its home ground, and its spoor is on the mountains themselves. The very rocks are baneful, and the air reeks of maleficence. Let no man say he has not felt it as I have."

"Next you will be claiming second sight," Haral grumbled, then added with a chuckle, "Unless you've changed greatly since last we swam together, you cannot qualify to become a priestess." No one echoed his jollity; grave eyes watched Eldran, who went on in grim tones.

"I have no need of second sight to scent death. Who follows me from here must resign himself that his bones will go unanointed. I will not think ill of any man who turns back, but let him do it now."

"Do you turn back?" Haral asked gently. Eldran shook his head. "Then," the plump man said, "I will not either. I am old enough to choose the place of my dying, an it comes to that."

"My brother rode with yours, Eldran," Fyrdan said. "My blood burns as hot for vengeance as yours." One by one the others made it known that they, too, would go on, and Eldran nodded.

"Very well," he said simply. "What will come, will come. Let us ride."

The raven was gone, he saw as he made his way back down to the trail. Birds of ill omen, they were, yet he could not find gladness in him for its absence. It had reminded him of Jondra, and whether she lived or no he could not think he would ever see her again. But then, he thought bleakly, there would be ravens beyond counting deeper in the Kezankians, and bones aplenty for them to pick.

XIV

Basrakan Imalla stalked the floor of his oaken-paneled chamber with head bowed as if his multi-hued turban were too heavy. His blood-red robes swirled with the agitation of his pacing. So many worries weighing on his shoulders, he thought. The path of holiness was not an easy one. There was the matter of another dead raven in the next chamber. Men, it had said before dying. But how many, and where? And to have two of the birds slain in only a few days. Did someone know of the ravens' function? Someone inimical to him? Another had reported men as well. Not soldiers; the birds could distinguish them. But the inability to count meant there could be ten or a hundred. It might even be the same party seen by the dead raven. He would have to increase his patrols and find these interlopers, however many groups of them there were.

At least the bird that accompanied the men he had sent against the soldiers had reported victory. No, not merely victory. Annihilation. But even with that came burdens. The warriors he had sent forth camped now, so said the raven. Squabbling among themselves over the looting of the dead, no doubt. But they would return. They had to. He had given them a victory, a sign from the old gods.

Unbidden the true source of his worries rushed back to mock him, though he tried as he had so often in days past to force it from him. A sign from the old gods. The sign of the ancient gods' favor. Seven times, now, he had tried to summon the drake, each attempt carefully hidden from the eyes even of his own acolytes, and seven times he had failed. Unrest grew in the camps for the lack of the showing. And those he had sent after the Eyes of Fire had not returned. Could the old gods have withdrawn their grace from him?

Wrapping his arms around him, he rocked back and forth on his heels. "Am I worthy, O gods of my forefathers?" he moaned. "Am I truly worthy?"

"Our question exactly, Imalla," a voice growled.

Basrakan spun, and blinked to find three hillmen confronting him. He struggled to recover his equilibrium. As he drew himself up, two of the bearded men shrank back. "You dare disturb me?" he rasped. "How did you pass my guards?"

The man who had stood his ground, his mustaches curled like the horns of a bull, spoke. "Even among your guards there are doubts, Imalla."

"You are called Walid," Basrakan said, and a flicker of fear appeared in the other's black eyes.

There were no sorceries involved, though. This Walid had been reported to him as one of the troublemakers, the questioners. It had taken him a moment to remember the man's description. He had not thought the troublemaking had gone so far as this, however. But he had prepared for every eventuality.

With false calmness he tucked his hands into the long sleeves of his crimson robe. "What doubts do *you* have, Walid?"

The man's thick mustache twitched at the repetition of his name, and he half turned his head as if looking for support from his companions. They remained well behind him, meeting neither his eyes nor Basrakan's. Walid drew a deep breath. "We came here, many of us, because we heard the old gods favored you. Those who came before us speak of a fabulous beast, a sign of that favor, but I have seen no such creature. What I *have* seen is thousands of hillmen sent to battle Zamoran soldiers, who have ever before slaughtered us when we fought them in numbers. And I have seen none of those warriors return."

"That is all?" Basrakan asked.

His suddenly mild tone seemed to startle Walid. "Is it not enough?" the mustached man demanded.

"More than enough," Basrakan replied. Within his sleeves his hands clasped small pouches he had prepared only a day past, when the unrest among the gathered tribes first truly began to worry him. Now he praised his foresight. "Much more than enough, Walid."

Basrakan's hands came out of his sleeves, and in a continuous motion he scattered the powder from one pouch across Walid. As the powder struck, the Imalla's right hand made arcane gestures, and he chanted in a tongue dead a thousand years.

Walid stared down at his chest in horror for a moment as the chilling incantation went on, then, with a shout of rage and fear, he grabbed for his tulwar. Even as his hand touched the hilt, though, fire spurted from his every pore. Flame surrounded him as clothes and hair turned to ash. His roar of anger became a shrill shriek of agony, then the hiss of boiling grease. A plume of oily black smoke rose from the collapsing sack that had been a man.

The other two men had stood, eyes bulging with terror, but now one burst for the door, and the other fell to his knees crying, "Forgiveness, Imalla! Forgiveness!"

In two quick strides Basrakan was on them, throwing the powder over the fleeing man and the kneeling one alike. His long-fingered hands gestured, and the chant rose once more. The running man made it to the door before fire engulfed him. The other fell on his face, wriggling toward Basrakan, then he, too, was a living pyre. Their screams lasted only moments, blending into a shrill whistle as flame consumed their bones.

At last even the black smoke guttered out. Only small heaps of dark, oily ash were left on the floor, and sooty smudges on the ceiling. The fierce-eyed Imalla viewed the residues of his accusers with satisfaction, but it faded quickly to grim anger. These men would have brothers, cousins, and nephews, scores of male relatives who, while they might fear to confront Basrakan openly, would most certainly now be a source of further dissention. Some might even go beyond words. The tribesmen lived and died by the blood feud, and nothing could turn them from it save death.

"So be it," he pronounced intently.

Dark face as cold and calm as if he had a lifetime for the task, Basrakan gathered a sampling from each pile of ash, scraping them into folded scraps of parchment with a bone knife four times blessed in rites before the ancient gods of the Kezankians. Ash from each dead man went into a thick-walled mortar of plain, unworked gold. The sorcerer's movements quickened as he added further ingredients, for speed now was essential. Powdered virgin's eye and ground firefly. Salamanders' hearts and the dried blood of infants. Potions and powders, the ingredients of which he dared not even think of. With the thigh bone of a woman strangled by her own daughter he ground the mixture, twelve times widdershins, intoning the hidden names of the ancient gods, names that chilled the marrow and made vapors of frost hang in the air. Twelve times the other way. Then it was done, this first step, leaving the golden vessel filled almost to the brim with black powder that seemed to swirl like smoke in its depths.

Gingerly, for the blending was deadly to the touch now, Basrakan carried the mortar to a cleared space on the pale stone floor. There, dipping a brush tipped with virgins' eyelashes into the moist mixture, he carefully scribed a precise pattern on the smooth stone. It was a cross, its arms of equal length exactly aligned to north and south, east and west. Tipping each arm was a circle, within which he drew the four idiograms of the ancient gods, the secret signs of earth, air, water, and fire. Next a triangle, its apex at the meeting of the arms of the cross, enclosed the symbol for the spirits of fire, and that same character was placed on each point of the triangle.

Basrakan paused, staring at what he had wrought, and his breath came fast. He would not admit to fear despite a tightening in his bowels, but this was more dangerous than anything he had yet attempted. An error in any phase, one completed or one to come, and the rite would rebound on him. Yet he knew there was no turning back.

Deftly he tipped the last of the powder into a silver censer on the end of a silver chain. Ordinary flint and steel provided the spark and set it smouldering. Aligning his feet carefully on the broad base of the triangle, he swung the censer in an intricate pattern. Wisps of smoke wafted upward from the silver ball, and Basrakan's incantation rose with the odoriferous vapors. With each swing of the censer one crystalline word rang in the air, words that even the fiery-eyed Imalla could not hear, for they were not meant for human ears, and the human mind could not comprehend them.

Around him the very air seemed to glisten darkly. Smoke from the censer thickened and fell to the stone floor, aligning itself unnaturally with the pattern drawn there. Basrakan's chant came faster, and more loudly. The words pealed hollowly, like funereal tolling from the depths of a cavern. Within the ropes of smoke now covering the configuration came a glow, ever fiercer and hotter, till it seemed as if all the fires of the earth's bowels were bound in those roiling thongs of black. Sweat rolled down Basrakan's thin cheeks from the heat. The glow became blinding, and his words rose higher and higher, the walls shivering under their impact.

Suddenly Basrakan ceased his cry. Silence came, and in that instant, glow and smoke and drawn pattern all vanished. Even the smoke from the censer failed.

Done, Basrakan thought. Weariness filled him. Even his bones felt weak. But what had had to be done, had been done.

A tremor shook him as his eye fell on the remains of his accusers. On each pile of ash, from which all that could be burned had been burned, danced pale flames. Even as he watched they licked into extinction. He drew a deep breath. This was no cause for fear, but rather for exaltation.

Jbeil burst into the chamber, panting, with one hand pressed hard to his side. "The bless . . . the bless . . . the blessings . . ."

"An Imalla must be dignified," Basrakan snapped. Returning confidence, returning faith, washed away the dregs of his fear. "An Imalla does not run."

"But the camps, Imalla," Jbeil managed past gulps of air. "Fire. Men are burning. Burning, Imalla! Warriors, old men, boys. Even babes unweaned, Imalla! They simply burst into flame, and not water or dirt can extinguish them. Hundreds upon hundreds of them!"

"Not so many, I think," Basrakan replied coolly. "A hundred, perhaps, or even two, but not so many as you say."

"But, Imalla, there is panic."

"I will speak to the people, Jbeil, and calm them. Those who died were of tainted blood. Did the means of their dying tell you nothing?"

"The fire, Imalla?" Jbeil said uncertainly. "They offended the spirits of fire?"

Basrakan smiled as if at a pupil who had learned his lesson well. "More than offended, Jbeil. Much more. And all males of their blood shared their atonement." A thought struck him, a memory of words that seemed to have been spoken days in the past. "My guards, Jbeil. Did you see them as you came in?"

"Yes, Imalla. As I came to you. The two who were at your door accompanied Ruhallah Imalla on some errand." His eyes took on a sly cast. "They ran, Imalla. Ruhallah knows little of dignity. Only the urgency of my message brought me to such haste."

"Ruhallah had his own urgency," Basrakan said so softly he might have been speaking to himself. He fixed the other man with an eye like a dagger. "Ruhallah is to blame for the fiery deaths this day. He and those false guards who flee with him. Ruhallah led those men of the blood that perished this day into false beliefs and tainted ways." It could be so, he thought. It must be so. Assuredly, it *was* so. "Ruhallah and the guards who flee with him must be brought back to face payment for what they have done." Few things amused Basrakan, but the next thought to visit him brought a smile to his thin lips. "They are to be given to the women of the men who died by fire this day. Let those who lost kith and kin exact their vengeance."

"As you command, Imalla, so will it be." Jbeil froze in a half-bow, and his eyes went wide. "Aaiee! Imalla, it had been driven from my mind by the burnings and . . ." Basrakan glared at him, and he swallowed and went on. "Sharmal has returned, Imalla. One of those you sent after the Eyes of Fire, Imalla," he added when the tall holy man raised a questioning eyebrow.

"They have returned?" Basrakan said, excitement rising in his voice. "The Eyes of Fire are mine! All praise to the old gods!" Abruptly he was coldly calm, only an intensity of tone remaining of the emotion that had filled his speech. "Bring the gems to me. Immediately, fool! Nothing should have kept you from that. Nothing! And bring the men, as well. They will not find their rewards small."

"Imalla," Jbeil said hesitantly, "Sharmal is alone, and empty handed. He babbles that the rest are dead, and other things, as well. But there is little of sense in any of it. He . . . he is mad, Imalla."

Basrakan ground his teeth, and tugged at his forked beard as if he wanted to pull it out by the roots. "Empty handed," he breathed at last, hoarse and icy. He could not be cheated of his desires now. He *would* not be. "What occurred, Jbeil? Where are the Eyes of Fire? I will know these things. Put this Sharmal to the question. Strip him of his skin. Sear him to the bone. I will have answers!"

"But, Imalla," Jbeil whispered, "the man is mad. The protection of the old gods is on him."

"Do as I command!" Basrakan roared, and his acolyte flinched.

"As . . . as you command, Imalla, so will it be." Jbeil bowed deeply, and moved backwards toward the door.

So much had happened, Basrakan thought, in such a short time. There was something he was forgetting. Something . . . "Jbeil!" The other man jerked to a halt. "There are strangers in the mountains, Jbeil. They are to be found, and any survivors brought to me for offering to the true gods. Let it be done!" He gestured, and Jbeil nearly ran from the room.

XV

W e will make camp now." Jondra announced while the sun still rose. Arvaneus' voice rose, echoing her command, and obediently her hunters dismounted and began seeing to the pack animals and their own mounts.

Conan caught her eye questioningly, and she favored him with a smile. "When hunting a rare animal," she said, "care must be taken not to bypass its feeding grounds. We will spend days in each camp, searching."

"Let us hope this animal is not also searching," Conan replied. The noblewoman frowned, but before she could speak Arvaneus came to stand at her stirrup.

"Do you wish the trackers out now, my lady?" he asked.

Jondra nodded, and a shiver of excitement produced effects to draw male eyes. "It would be wonderful to get a shot at my quarry on the first day. Yes, Arvaneus. Put out your best trackers."

She looked expectantly at Conan, but he pretended not to notice. His tracking skill was the equal of any of the hunters', but he had no interest in finding the creature Jondra sought. He wanted only to see the two women returned to the safety of Shadizar, and he could offer them no protection if he was out tracking.

Jondra's face fell when Conan did not speak, but the dark-eyed huntsman smiled maliciously. "It takes a great special skill to be a tracker," he said to no one in particular. "My lady." He made an elegant bow to Jondra, then backed away, calling as he straightened. "Trackers out! Telades! Zurat! Abu!" His list ran on, and soon he and nine others were trotting out of the camp in ten different directions. They went afoot, for the slight spoor that a tracker must read as a scribe read words on parchment could be missed entirely from the back of a horse.

With the trackers gone, the beauteous noblewoman began ordering the placement of the camp, and Conan found a place to settle with a honing stone, a bit of rag and a vial of olive oil. A sword must be tended to, especially if it would soon find use, and Conan was sure his blade would not be idle long. The mountains seemed to overhang them with a sense of foreboding, and something permeated the very stones that made him uneasy. The honing stone slid along his blade with quiet sussuration. Morning grew into afternoon.

The camp, Conan decided after a time, was placed as well as it could be under the circumstances. The stunted trees that were scattered so sparsely through the Kezankians were in this spot gathered into what might pass for a grove, though an exceedingly thin one. At least they added some modicum to the hiding of the camp.

Jondra's scarlet tent, which she had never considered leaving behind, stood between two massive granite boulders and was screened from behind by the brown rock of a sheer cliff. No other tents had been brought—for which small favor the Cimmerian was grateful—and the hunters' blankets were scattered in twos and threes in a score of well-hidden depressions. The horses were picketed in a long, narrow hollow that could be missed even by a man looking for it. To one unfamiliar with the land the encampment would be all but invisible. The trouble, he thought sourly, was that the hillmen were more than familiar with their mountains. There would be trouble.

As though his thought of trouble had been a signal, a sound sliced through the cool mountain air, and Conan's hand stopped in the act of oiling his sword blade. Through the jagged peaks echoed a shrill, ululating cry, piercing to the bone and the heart. He had never heard the like of that sound, not from the throat of any man or any creature.

The big Cimmerian was not alone in being disturbed by the hunting call—for such he was sure it was. Hunters sat up in their blankets, exchanging worried glances. Some rose to walk a few paces, eyes searching the steep, encircling slopes. Jondra came to the flap of her tent, head tilted questioningly, listening. She wore leather now, jerkin and breeches, as always fitting her curves like a second skin, but plain brown, suitable for the hunt. When the sound was not repeated she retreated inside once more.

"What in Mitra's thrice-blessed name was that?" Tamira said, dropping into a crouch near Conan. She adjusted her short white robe to provide a modicum of decency, and wrapped slim arms about her knees. "Can it be the creature Jondra hunts?"

"I would not be surprised if it was," Conan said. He returned to the oiling of his blade. "Little good those rubies will do you if you end in the belly of that beast."

"You try to talk me into fleeing," she retorted, "leaving you with a clear path to the gems."

"I have told you," he began, but she cut him off.

"A clear path to Jondra's sleeping furs, then."

Conan sighed and slid his broadsword into his sheath. "You were in my arms this night past, and she not for two days. And I said that I came into these thrice-accursed mountains for you. Do you now call me liar?"

Her eyes slid away from his, to the rugged spires of granite surrounding them. "Do you think the trackers will find it? This beast, I mean? Perhaps, if they do not, we will leave these mountains. I would as well steal the rubies while returning to Shadizar."

"I would as soon they found naught but sore feet," Conan said. He remembered the half-charred fragment of skull and horn. "This beast will not be so easy to slay as Jondra believes, I fear. And you will not steal the rubies."

"So you *do* mean to take them yourself."

"I do not."

"Then you intend to save them for your paramour. For Jondra."

"Hannuman's Stones, woman! Will you give over?"

Tamira eyed him sharply. "I do not know whether I want you to be lying or not."

"What do you mean by that?" he asked in puzzlement.

"I intend to steal the rubies, you understand, no matter what you say or do." Her voice tightened. "But if you did not come for the rubies, then you came for me. Or for Jondra. I am uncertain whether I wouldn't rather have the sure knowledge that all you wanted was the gems."

Conan leaned back against the boulder behind him and laughed until he wheezed. "So you don't believe me?" he asked finally.

"I've known enough men to doubt anything any of you says."

"You have?" he exclaimed in feigned surprise. "I would have sworn I was the very first man you'd known."

Color flooded her cheeks, and she leaped to her feet. "Just you wait until—"

Whatever her threat was to be, Conan did not hear its finish, for Telades hurried into the camp, half out of breath and using his spear as a walking staff. Men hastened to surround him, and the Cimmerian was first among them.

A hail of words came from the hunters.

"Did you find tracks?"

"We heard a great cry."

"What did you see?"

"It must have been the thing we hunt."

"Did you see the beast?"

Telades tugged off his spiked helm and shook his shaved head. "I heard the cry, but I saw neither animal nor tracks."

"Give your report to me," Jondra snapped. The hunters parted to let her through. Her eagerness was betrayed by the bow in her hand. "Or am I to wait until you've told everyone else?"

"No, my lady," Telades replied abashedly. "I ask forgiveness. What I saw was the army, my lady. Soldiers."

Again a torrent of questions broke over the man.

"Are you sure?"

"From the lot we saw fighting?"

"How could they get into the mountains ahead of us?"

Jondra's cool gray eyes swept across the assembled hunters, and the torrent died as though she had cracked a whip.

"Where are those soldiers, Telades?" Conan asked. Jondra looked at him sharply, but closed her mouth and said nothing.

"Not two leagues to the north and east of us," Telades replied. "Their general is Lord Tenerses. I got close enough to see him, though they did not see me."

"Tenerses," Conan mused. "I have heard of him."

"They say he hunts glory," the shaven-headed hunter said, "but it seems he thinks well enough to know when danger is about. His camp is so well hidden, in a canyon with but one entrance, that I found it only by merest chance. And I could not see how many men he has with him."

"Not one fewer than Zathanides," Conan said, "if what I have heard of him is true. He is a man with a sense of his own importance, this Tenerses."

Jondra broke in in flat tones. "If you two are quite finished discussing the army, I would like to hear the results I sent this man for in the first place. Did you find tracks, Telades, or did you not?"

"Uh, no, my lady. No tracks."

"There are still nine others," the noblewoman said half to herself. "As for these soldiers," she went on in a more normal tone, "they have naught to do with us, and we naught to do with them. I see no reason why they should be a subject of further discussion, nor why they should even become aware of our existence. Am I understood?"

Her gaze was commanding as it met each man's eyes in turn, and each man mumbled assent and grew intent in his study of the ground beneath his feet, until she came to Conan. Eyes of chilling azure looked back at her in unblinking calmness, and it was smoky gray orbs that dropped to break the mesmerizing contact.

When she looked at him again, it was through long eyelashes. "I must talk with you, Conan," she murmured. "In my tent. I . . . would have your advice on the hunt."

Over Jondra's shoulder Conan saw Tamira watching him intently, hands on hips. "Perhaps later," he said. When the noblewoman blinked and stared, he added quickly, "The mountains are dangerous. We cannot spare even one watcher." Before she could say more—and he could see from the sparks in her eyes that she intended to say *much* more—he retreated across the camp to his place by the boulder.

As he settled once more with his back to the stone, he noticed that both women were looking at him. And both were glaring. The old saying was certainly proving true, he thought. He who has two women oft finds himself in possession of none. And not one thing could he think to do about it. With a sigh he set back to tending his steel. Some men claimed their blades had the personalities of women, but he had never known a sword to suffer jealousy.

The other trackers began returning at decreasing intervals. Jondra allowed these no time to become involved in extraneous—to her—matters with the other hunters. She met each man as he entered the camp, and her sharp gaze kept the rest back until she finished her questioning and gave the tracker leave to go.

One by one the trackers returned, and one by one they reported . . . nothing of interest to Jondra. One, who had searched near Telades, had found the cheek-piece of a soldier's helmet. Another had seen a great mountain ram with curling horns as long as a man's arm. Jondra angrily turned her back on him before he finished telling of it. Several saw hillmen, and in numbers enough to make a prudent man wary, but none had found the spoor of the beast, or anything that might remotely be taken as a sign of its presence or passage. The gray-eyed noblewoman heard each man out, and strode away from each impatiently tapping her bow against her thigh.

The last to return was Arvaneus, trotting into the camp to lean on his spear with an arrogant smile.

"Well?" Jondra demanded as she stalked up to him. "I suppose you have seen nothing either?"

The hawkfaced huntsman seemed taken aback at her tone, but he recovered quickly and swept a bow before her. "My lady, what you seek, I give to you." He shot a challenging look at Conan as he straightened. "I, Arvaneus, son of Lord Andanezeus, give it to you."

"You have found it?" Excitement brightened her face. "Where, Arvaneus?"

"A bare league to the east, my lady. I found the marks of great claws as long as a man's hand, and followed them for some distance. The tracks were made this day, and there cannot be another creature in these mountains to leave such spoor as human eyes have never before seen."

The entire camp stared in amazement as Jondra leaped spinning into the air, then danced three steps of a jig. "It must be. It must. I will give you gold to make you wealthy for this, Arvaneus. Find this beast for me, and I will give you an estate."

"I want no gold." Arvaneus said huskily, his black eyes suddenly hot. "Nor estates."

Jondra froze, staring at him, then turned unsteadily away. "Prepare horses," she commanded. "I would see these tracks."

The huntsman looked worriedly at the sky. The sun, giving little warmth in these mountains, lay halfway to the western horizon from its zenith. "It is late to begin a hunt. In the morning, at first light—"

"Do you question my commands?" she snapped. "I am no fool to start a hunt for a dangerous beast with night approaching, but I will see those tracks. Now! Twenty men. The rest will remain in camp and prepare for the hunt tomorrow."

"As you command, my lady," Arvaneus muttered. He glared malevolently at Conan as Jondra turned to the big Cimmerian and spoke in a soft voice.

"Will you ride with me, Conan? I . . . I would feel much safer." The awkwardness of her words and the coloring of her cheeks gave her the lie. With obvious difficulty, she added, "Please?"

Wordlessly Conan rose and walked to the picket line. Arvaneus barked orders, and others joined the Cimmerian. As Conan was fastening his saddle girth, he became aware of Tamira, making a great show of idly petting the nose of a roan next to his tall black.

"Will you ride with me, Conan?" she mimicked softly. "I will feel so much safer." She twisted up her face as if to spit.

Conan let out a long breath. "I'd not like to see either of you dead, or a hillman's slave. You will be safer here than will she out there, so I go with her."

He stepped up into the high-pommeled Zamoran saddle. Tamira trotted alongside as he rode from the hollow where the horses were picketed. "You will be out there," she told him, "and so will she. You could return to find me gone, Conan. And the rubies. What is to keep me here?"

"Why, you'll be waiting for me," he laughed, booting his mount to a trot. A hurled rock bounced off his shoulder, but he did not look back.

XVI

The party of Zamoran hunters made their way in single file along the gullies and clefts that lined the mountains like wrinkles of ancient age on the face of the earth. Arvaneus led, since he knew the way, and Jondra rode close behind him. Conan, in turn, kept close to the tall noblewoman. There would be little time to spare when protection was needed. The mountains seemed to press in on them malignly, even when their way opened enough for a score of men or more to ride abreast.

The big Cimmerian's eyes searched the jagged crags and steep slopes around them constantly, and with instincts long buried in civilized men he probed for his enemies. No sign of hillmen did he see, no hint of them came to his senses, but menace still oozed from the stones. Outwardly he seemed at ease, but he was dry tinder waiting for a spark.

Abruptly Arvaneus drew rein where the walls of rock were steep and close. "There, my lady," the huntsman said, pointing to the ground. "Here is the first track I found."

Jondra scrambled from her saddle to kneel by a small patch of clay. The deep marks of two massive claws and part of a third were impressed there. "It is larger than I thought," she murmured, running two slender fingers into one impression.

"We have seen the tracks," Conan said. The oppressive air seemed thicker to him. "Let us return to the camp."

Arvaneus' lip curled in a sneer. "Are you afraid, barbar? My lady, there are more tracks further on. Some are complete."

"I must see that," Jondra exclaimed. Swinging into her saddle she galloped ahead, and Arvaneus spurred after her.

Conan exchanged a look with Telades—by the shaven-headed hunter's sour face he liked this as little as the Cimmerian—then they and the rest of the column of horsemen followed.

As it had often before, the narrow passage opened out. This time it led into a small canyon, perhaps a hundred paces wide, with five narrow draws cutting its steep brown walls. Conan eyed those openings suspiciously. Any enemy hidden in those would be on them before they had time to react. The hillmen's favorite tactic was the ambush.

On the floor of the canyon the spoor of the beast was plentiful. Tracks leading both in and out showed that the beast had explored the narrow cuts. Unease permeated the column; hunters shifted their spears nervously, or reached back to touch the cased bows behind their saddles, and horses danced and shied. Jondra uncased her bow as she dismounted at the track Arvaneus pointed out, and nocked an arrow before kneeling to examine it. The hawk-faced huntsman frowned at the ground around him, attempting with only partial success to control his mount's quick sidesteps.

Conan found himself wondering about that frown. Arvaneus had seen this canyon and the tracks that filled it only a short time before. What was there for him to frown about? The big Cimmerian's breath caught in his throat. Unless there were *more* tracks than he had seen before. If that was true they must leave immediately.

Conan opened his mouth, and a shrill ululation split the air, chilling the blood, making the horses buck and scream. Jondra's mount tore the reins from her hands and bolted, nostrils flaring and eyes rolling wildly, leaving the noblewoman standing like a statue of ice. With difficulty the Cimmerian pulled his big black around. "Crom," he breathed into the din filling the stone walls.

Into the canyon came a monstrous creature, huge, on massive legs. Multi-hued scales glittered in the sinking sun, broken only by dark, leathery-appearing bulges on its back. Adamantine claws gouged the stone beneath them. The broad head was thrown back, the widespread maw revealing jagged teeth like splinters of stone, and that piercing cry struck men to their souls.

The hunters were men who had faced death many times, and if it had never before confronted them in such form, still death was no stranger to them. As that malevolent howl ended they forced themselves into movement, fighting horses half-mad with terror to spread and surround the gargantuan form. The man nearest the beast leveled his spear like a lance and charged. With a clang as of steel against stone the spear struck, and the rider was shivered from his saddle. The great head lowered, and flame roared from that gaping mouth. Man and horse shrieked as one, a shrillness that never seemed to end, as they were roasted alive.

A gasp rose from the other hunters, but they were already launching their attack, men charging in from from either flank. Even had they wished to turn aside, the beast gave them no chance. More swiftly than any leopard it moved, claws sweeping bloody rags that had once been men to the ground, jaws crushing men and horses alike. Spears splintered like straws against the iridescent scales, and the cries of the dying drowned out all save thought, and fear became the only thought in the hunter's minds.

Through that howling maelstrom of certain death Conan galloped, swinging low out of his saddle to snatch an unbroken spear from the bloody ground. Those great golden eyes, he thought. The eyes had to be vulnerable, or the long, dark protuberances on its back. He forced his mount to turn—it struggled to run on, away from the horror—and the sight that met his eyes sent a quiver through him as not even the beast's hunting cry had.

Jondra stood not ten paces from the creature's head. Even as he saw her, an arrow left her bow. Squarely on one malevolent golden eye the shaft struck. And ricocheted away. The beast lunged, claws streaking toward her. Frantically she leaped back, but the tip of one claw snagged in the laces of her red leather jerkin, and she was jerked into the air to dangle before the creature's eyes. Ignoring the carnage around it, the shouting, screaming men, the beast seemed to study her.

A thrill of horror coursed through Conan. There was a light of intelligence in those auric globes. But if the brain behind them could reason, it was a form of reasoning too inhuman for the mind of man to know it. It did not see the beautiful woman as other than prey. The spike-toothed mouth opened, and Jondra was drawn closer.

Conan's spear came up. "Crom!" he bellowed, and his heels thudded his fear-ridden mount into a charge. His spearpoint held steady on one leathery bulge. He clamped his knees tightly on the animal against the shock he had seen throw others to the ground, but even so the force of the blow rocked through him, staggering his horse to its knees.

With sinuous grace and blinding speed the glittering beast twisted, smashing Conan with the leg from which Jondra dangled. Breath rushed from the big Cimmerian as he was lifted and hurled through the air. Stony ground rushed up to slam what little air remained from his chest. Desperately he fought to breathe, forced numbed muscles to move, rolled to hands and knees, staggered to his feet. Jondra lay on her back near him, writhing, bare breasts heaving as she struggled for air.

The beast turned its attention to the Cimmerian, Jondra's jerkin still tangled in its claws. What remained of his horse lay quivering beneath the creature; gobbets of flesh fell from its fanged jaws.

In what he knew was a futile gesture Conan drew his ancient broadsword. Steel made no mark on those infrangible scales. He could not move quickly enough to escape the creature's attack unburdened, much less carrying Jondra, and he could not leave her behind. Yet he would not die without fighting.

"Ho, Conan!" Swaying in his saddle, Telades rode toward the beast from behind. The mail over his chest was rent, and blood drenched him, but he gripped his spear firmly. "Get her away, northlander!" Pounding his boots into his horse's flanks, he forced it forward.

Iridescent scales flashed as the creature spun.

"No!" Conan shouted.

Flame engulfed the shaven-headed hunter, and the beast leaped to tear at smouldering flesh.

The Cimmerian would not waste Telades' sacrifice. Sheathing his blade, he scooped Jondra from the ground and darted into a narrow cleft, pursued by the sounds of crunching bone.

As the terrible grinding faded behind him, Jondra stirred in his arms. "I did not mean for them to die," she whispered. Her eyes were horror-laden pools.

"You wanted to hunt the beast," he said, not slowing his steady stride. Under other circumstances he would have searched for survivors. Now he thought only of getting Jondra far from that charnel scene, back to the relative safety of the camp.

Jondra pressed herself more firmly against his broad chest as if sheltering from storm winds in the safety of a huge boulder. "Telades gave his life for me," she murmured, shivering. "Truly, I did not wish it to be. Oh, Conan, what can I do?"

Conan stopped dead, and she huddled in his arms as though hiding from his icy blue gaze. "Leave these mountains," he said harshly. "Go back to Shadizar. Forget this beast, and always remember the men who died for your foolishness and pride."

Anger and arrogance flared across her face. Her fist rose, then abruptly fell limp. Tears leaked down her cheeks. "I will," she wept. "Before all the gods, I swear it."

"It will not repay Telades' sacrifice," he said, "but it will at least mean that you value what he did."

Gently she touched Conan's cheek. "Never have I wanted a man to guide me, but you almost make me . . ." Small white teeth bit her full underlip, and she dropped her eyes. "Will you come back to Shadizar with me?" she said softly, shifting in his grasp again so that her full, round breasts were exposed to his gaze.

"Perhaps," he replied gruffly, and began walking once more, with his full concentration on the twists of the cleft and the stony ground beneath his feet. Only a fool would refuse a woman like the one he held. And only a fool would disregard the advice he had given. But Telades had become a friend, and the man had died for him as well as for her.

A part of the Cimmerian's code demanded that Telades' death, offered in place of his own, should be repaid, just as another part of that code demanded that he see Jondra and Tamira to safety. At the moment the second seemed much more easily accomplished than the first! How, he thought, could he slay a beast that steel could not harm? If he took no notice of the charms Jondra displayed in his arms, it was no wonder.

XVII

T amira was the first person Conan saw when he strode into the
camp with his arms full of half-naked noblewoman and the sun
a bloody ball balanced on jagged peaks. The slender young
thief regarded him with fists on hips and a jaundiced eye for the way
Jondra clung to him. Then Jondra looked around dazedly, revealing her
tear-stained face. Tamira's jaw dropped, and she dashed into the red-
walled tent to return with a cloak.

As Conan stood Jondra upright, the smaller woman enfolded her in
soft blue wool. When he released his hold on her, the noblewoman sank
to her knees. Tamira knelt beside her, drawing Jondra's head to her
shoulder and glaring up at the big Cimmerian.

"What happened?" she demanded hotly.

"We found the beast she hunts. Hunted. Have any of the others
returned?"

Dark eyes widening with sudden fear, Tamira shook her head.
"None. They . . . they could not all be dead?"

"Of course not," Conan said. He would be very surprised ever to see
another of them alive, but there was no point in terrifying the wench
more than she already was. Better to find work to occupy her mind.
"See to her," he told Tamira. "She never stopped crying for a hundred
paces together all the way back here."

"And no wonder," Tamira replied hotly, "with no better care than
you've taken of her." She bundled the unresisting noblewoman off to
her tent, leaving Conan standing open-mouthed.

He would never understand women, he decided. Never. Then he

became aware of the remaining hunters gathered around him, looking at him worriedly. Looking to him for commands, he realized with some surprise. Firmly he put all thoughts of women from his mind.

"At dawn," he told them, "we leave for Shadizar. But first we must survive until then. No man sleeps tonight, unless he wants to risk waking with his throat cut. And no fires. Break open the supply packs."

With as much haste as Conan could manage, the hunters prepared themselves. All of the arrows were shared out, three quivers per man, and each man had an extra spear, as well as a waterbag and a pouch of dried meat. A coward or two might flee, with the means at hand, but he would not condemn the others to death if flight was required.

An assault from hillmen might come at any time, from any quarter save the cliff that backed Jondra's tent. Even if the first thrust were beaten off, they could not afford to be there when daylight came, pinned like bugs beneath a butcher bird's claws. They would attempt to retreat after an attack, or during, if it could not be driven back. And if they were on the point of being overwhelmed, every man would have to see to his own survival as best he could.

Worst of all would be an attack by the beast. As he moved through the darkening twilight from man to man, Conan left each with same final words. "Do not try to fight the beast. If it comes, run, and hope your gods feel kindly toward you."

Not far from Jondra's tent Conan settled into a flat-footed squat. Did the worst come, the others had only themselves to think of. He would need to be close to the women if he was to get them away.

A crunch of stone underfoot announced Tamira's approach, and he shifted his pair of spears to make a space for her.

"She's asleep," the slender woman sighed as she dropped to the ground beside him. "She wore herself out with tears. And who's to question it, after what she saw?"

"It happened by her command," Conan said quietly, "and for her pride. That Brythunian told her of the beast, and I told her what I had discovered of it."

"You are a hard man, Cimmerian. As hard as these mountains."

"I am a man," he told her simply.

For a time Tamira was silent. Finally she said, "Jondra says you are returning to Shadizar with her."

Conan gave a sour grunt. "It seems she talked a lot for a woman on the point of exhaustion."

"She plans to have apartments constructed for you in her palace."

"Ridiculous."

"She intends to dress you all in silk, with wristlets and armbands of gold to show off your muscles."

"What?" He thought he heard a giggle beside him in the deepening dark, and glared at her. "Enjoy your jokes, girl," he growled. "I, myself, do not find them funny."

"You were *her* first man, too, Conan. You cannot know what that means to a woman, but I do. She cares for you. Or perhaps it is for the image of you that she cares. She asked me if there were other men like you. She even compared you with Eldran, that Brythunian. She pretended not to remember his name, but she did."

Something in her voice struck him. "Mitra blind me if you don't pity her." His tone was incredulous.

"She knows less of men than I," the slender thief replied defensively. "It is a hard thing to be a woman in a world with men."

"It would be harder in a world without them," he said drily, and she fisted him in the ribs.

"I don't find *your* jokes," she began, but his hand closed over her mouth.

Intently he listened for the sound he was sure he had heard before. There. The scrape of a hoof—an *unshod* hoof—on stone.

"Go to the tent," he whispered, giving her a push in the right direction. "Rouse her, and be ready to flee. Hurry!"

At that instant a cry broke the night. "By the will of the true gods!" And hordes of hillmen swarmed through the camp on shaggy mountain horses, curved tulwar blades gleaming in the pale moonlight as they rose and fell.

Conan hefted a spear and threw at the nearest target. A turbanned rider, transfixed, screamed and toppled from his galloping horse. Another hillman, calling loudly on his gods, closed with raised steel. There was no chance for the Cimmerian to throw his second spear. He dropped flat and swung it like a club at the legs of the charging animal. With a sharp crack the haft of the spear struck; horse and rider somersaulted. Before the hillman could rise, Conan put a forearm's length of spear through his chest.

All about the Cimmerian steel clanged against steel. Men shouted battle cries, shouted death rattles. In that deadly, bloody tempest an ingrained barbarian sense gave Conan warning. Pulling the spear free, he whirled in time to block a slashing tulwar. Deftly he rotated his spear point against the curved blade, thrust over it into his bearded attacker's throat. Dying, the hillman clutched the weapon that killed him with both hands. His horse ran out from under him, and as he fell he wrenched the spear from Conan's grip.

"Conan!" Tamira's shriek cut through the din to the Cimmerian's ears. "Conan!"

Desperately the Cimmerian's eyes sought for the slender woman . . . and found her, lifted to a hillman's saddle by a fist in her hair. Grinning broadly through his beard, the tribesman tauntingly lowered his blade toward her throat. With one hand she frantically attempted to fend off the razor edge, while the other clutched at his robes.

Conan's broadsword came into his hand. Two bounds took him to Tamira's side; the hillman's head went back, and his mouth fell open as the Cimmerian's steel slid smoothly between his ribs. Lifeless fingers loosened in Tamira's hair, and Conan caught her as she fell. Trembling arms snaked round his neck; she sobbed limply against his chest.

With a corpse on its back the horse galloped on, and in the space of a breath Conan had taken in the situation in the camp. The fight went badly. Had gone badly, for there was little of it left. Few of the turban-ned warriors remained in the camp, and they were occupied with mu-tilating the dead. Murderous cries from the dark told of hillmen spreading in pursuit of hunters. Jondra's tent was in flames.

A chill went through the big Cimmerian. As he watched, the last of the tent collapsed, sending a shower of sparks into the night. If Jondra was in that, there was no hope for her. He hoped that she had gotten out, but he could not help her now. He had a woman to care for, and no time to spare for another.

Bending to catch Tamira behind the knees, he heaved her onto his shoulder like a sack. A half-formed protest came through her weeping, but the flow of tears did not slow. None of the tribesmen slashing at corpses noticed the muscular youth or his well-curved burden as he faded into the night.

Like a spirit Conan moved from shadow to shadow. Darkness alone, however, was no shield, he knew. From the clouded velvet sky a nacreous moon shed little light, but enough to make movement plain to a dis-cerning eye, and Tamira's short, white robe made matters no better. The night-clad rocks were filled with the clatter of galloping hooves on stone, the shouts of hunting hillmen. They hunted, and, given time, they would find.

The Cimmerian kept moving, always away from the noise of the hill-men, and his eyes searched for a hiding place. A line of deeper blackness within the dark caught his gaze. He made his way to it and found a horizontal fracture in the face of a cliff. It was wide enough to hold Tamira, deep enough for her to remain hidden from all but someone sticking an arm into it.

Lowering the girl from his shoulder, he thrust her into the crack. "Stay quiet," he told her in low tones, "and do not move. I'll be back as quickly as I can. Listen to me, woman!"

"He . . . he was going to kill me," she sobbed. "He was l-laughing." She clutched at him, but he gently removed her hands from his shoulders.

" 'Tis over, now. You are safe, Tamira."

"Don't leave me."

"I must find Jondra. Remain here till I return, and I will get the three of us out of these mountains." He had thought his voice full of confidence—certainly more confidence than he felt, at the moment—but she drew back from him into the crack in the cliff.

"Go then," she said sullenly. He could not see her, but her tears seemed to dry up suddenly. "Well? Go, if you want to."

He hesitated, but Jondra was still to be found, and whether alive or dead he did not know. Tamira would be safe here until he could return. "I will come back quickly," he said, and slipped away into the night.

Tamira peered from the crevice, but though her night vision was like that of a cat, she could see nothing. Conan had disappeared. She settled back sulkily.

She had nearly been killed, had been taunted with her own death, and he went after *her* when it should have been clear even to a blind man that she needed the comfort of his arms. But then, were not all men blind? It was not fair that he could affect her so much, while he cared so little. Once she had been able to think calmly and logically about any man. Once—it seemed a hundred years ago—before she allowed the young Cimmerian giant to . . . Even alone in the dark she blushed at the thought.

She would not think of him any more, she decided. Drawing herself to the front of the crack, she tried once more to pierce the darkness. It was futile, like attempting to peer through a raven's wing. A chill wind whined through the mountains, and she pulled her knees up, huddling, painfully aware of how little warmth was to be had from her short tunic.

Where *had* he gone? To look for Jondra, he claimed, but how did he intend to find her in the night? Was the noblewoman even alive? The tent had been aflame, Tamira remembered. Nothing could have survived in that. Except . . . the iron chests containing Jondra's jewels.

Tamira's eyes gleamed with delight, and she bit her lip to suppress a giggle. "Let him search for Jondra," she whispered. "He'll return to find me gone. Gone from the mountains, and the rubies with me."

With the suppleness of a cat she rolled from the crevice, came to her feet in the night. The cold breeze ruffled her white tunic about her thighs. For an instant she considered the problem of that garment's paleness.

"Well, I cannot go naked," she said finally, then clamped her teeth shut. She could not afford to make a sound, now.

Silently she glided into the dark, moving with all the stealthy skill she possessed. No matter what was said in Shadizar, in the taverns of the Desert, concerning Conan, she *was* the best thief in the city.

A sound halted her, a grating as of boots on rock, and she wished she had her daggers. Whoever it was, she thought contemptuously, he was clumsy. Noiselessly she moved away from he-who-stepped-on-rocks . . . and was buried beneath a rush of smelly robes and unwashed flesh.

She kicked at the cursing men who swarmed over her, struck at them until her wrists were caught in a grip like a vise. Hands fumbled at her body. She saw a bearded face, merciless and hard, and a curved dagger raised high. A scream choked in her throat. So many men to kill one woman. It was unfair, she thought dully. Her tunic was grasped at the neck and ripped open to the waist.

"See!" a voice said hoarsely. "It is as I said. A woman, and young."

The hard face did not change. "A lowland woman! A vessel of lust and corruption!"

"Even so," a third man said, "remember the Imalla's commands. And remember Walid's fate before you think to disobey." The hard-faced man blinked at that, and frowned.

"Take me to the Imalla," Tamira gasped. She knew that Imallas were holy men among the hill tribes. Surely a holy man would protect her.

The hard face split in an evil grin. "Let it be as the wench wishes. Mayhap she will come to regret not choosing my blade." And he began to laugh.

XVIII

In the canescent pre-dawn light Conan flattened himself on a narrow granite ledge as a file of hillmen rode by on a narrow path below, between steep walls. Their numbers had thinned as the night waned, but there were still too many of the bearded men to suit him. As the last of the horsemen disappeared up the twisting track, the big Cimmerian scrambled from fingerhold to fingerhold, down from the ledge, and set off at a trot in the opposite direction, toward the campsite that had become a bloody shambles so short a time before, toward Tamira's hiding place.

Two hundred paces down the trail he passed the remains of one of the Zamoran hunters. He could not tell which. The headless body, covered with blackened blood and bright green flies, lay with limbs twisted at unnatural angles. Conan gave the corpse not a glance as he went by. He had found too many others during the night, some worse than this, and at each one he had only been grateful it was not Jondra. Now worry for Tamira filled his mind. He was sure she was safe—even in daylight that crack would not be easily noticed—but she had been alone for the entire night, a night filled with hillmen and the memories of murder.

Along the slope of a mountain he trotted, eyes ever watchful. Dropping to his belly, he crawled to the top of a rough stone outcropping. Below him lay the camp, blackened ground and ash where Jondra's tent had stood against the cliff. Half a score bodies, many in more than one piece, were scattered among the stunted trees—Zamoran bodies only, for the hillmen had carried their own dead away. There was no sound but the somber droning of flies.

Conan took a deep breath and went over the ridgetop, half sliding down the other side on loose rocks and shale. The dead he let lie, for he had no time to waste on burials or funeral rites. Instead he concentrated on what might be of use to the living. A spear, whole and overlooked by the hillmen. A waterbag unslashed and bulging damply. A pouch of dried meat.

The tribesmen had been thorough in their looting, however, and there was little to find. Broken spearpoints, the cook's pots, even the rope used for picketing horses had been taken, and the ashes of Jondra's tent had been sifted for anything not consumed by the flames. He did find his black Khauranian cloak, tucked where he had left it beneath the edge of a boulder. He added it to the pitiful pile.

"So you are a thief, a looter!"

At the hoarse words Conan grabbed up the spear and whirled. Arvaneus shuffled toward him, black eyes glittering, knuckles white on his spear haft. The huntsman's head was bare; dust covered him, and his baggy white breeches were torn.

"It is good to see another of Jondra's party alive," Conan said. "All thought you were slain by the beast."

The huntsman's eyes slid off to the side, skipped from body to body. "The beast," he whispered. "Mortal men could not face it. Any fool could see that. That cry . . ." He shivered. "They should have fled," he went on plaintively. "That was the only thing to do. To try to fight it, to stay even a moment . . ." His gaze fell on the pile Conan had made, and he tilted his head to look sidelong at the big Cimmerian. "So you are a thief, stealing from the Lady Jondra."

Hair stirred on the back of Conan's neck. Madness was not something he had encountered frequently, especially in one he had known when sane. "These supplies may save Jondra's life," he said, "when I find her. She is lost, Arvaneus. I must find her quickly if she is to get out of these mountains alive."

"So pretty," Arvaneus said softly, "with her long legs, and those round breasts meant to pillow a man's head. So pretty, my Lady Jondra."

"I am going now," Conan said, stretching out one hand to pick up his cloak. He was careful not to take his eyes from Arvaneus, for the other man still gripped his spear as if ready to use it.

"I watched her," the swarthy huntsman went on. The mad light in his eyes deepened. "Watched her run from the camp. Watched her hide from the hillmen. She did not see me. No. But I will go to her, and she will be grateful. She will know me for the man I am, not just as her chief huntsman."

Conan froze when he realized what Arvaneus was saying. The Cimmerian let out a long breath, and chose his words carefully. "Let us go to Jondra together. We can take her back to Shadizar, Arvaneus. She will be very grateful to you."

"You lie!" The huntsman's face twisted as if he was on the point of tears; his hands flexed on his spear haft. "You want her for yourself! You are not good enough to lick her sandals!"

"Arvaneus, I—"

Conan cut his words short as the huntsman thrust at him. Whipping his cloak up, the Cimmerian entangled the other man's spear point, but Arvaneus ripped his weapon free, and Conan was forced to leap back as gleaming steel lanced toward him once more. Warily, the two men circled, weapons at the ready.

"Arvaneus," Conan said, "there is no need for this." He did not want to kill the man. He needed to know where Jondra was.

"There is need for you to die," the hawkfaced man panted. Their spearpoints clattered as he felt for weakness and Conan deflected his probes.

"We have enemies enough around us," Conan told him. "We should not do their killing for them."

"Die!" Arvaneus screamed, rushing forward, spear outthrust. Conan parried the thrust, but the huntsman did not draw back. He came on, straight onto the Cimmerian's spearpoint. Arvaneus' weapon dropped to the ground, but he took yet another step forward, clawed hands reached for Conan, impaling himself further. Surprise flooded his face; jerkily he looked down at the thick wooden shaft standing out from his chest.

The big Cimmerian caught Arvaneus as he collapsed, eased him to the stony ground. "Where is she?" Conan demanded. "Erlik blast you, where is Jondra?"

Laughter wracked the huntsman. "Die, barbar," he rasped. "Die." Blood welled up in his mouth, and he sagged, eyes glazing.

With a muttered curse Conan got to his feet. At least she was alive, he thought. If it was not all a fantasy constructed by a man mind. Gathering up his supplies, he set out for Tamira's hiding place.

From the shaded shelter of huge stone slabs, split from the cliff behind her by an earthquake centuries gone, Jondra stared longingly at the tiny pool of water far below and licked her lips. Had she known it was there while dark still covered the Kezankians, she would not have thought twice before assuaging her thirst. But now . . . She peered to the east, to a sun still half-hidden by the jagged peaks. It was full enough light to expose her clearly to the eyes of any watchers.

And expose, the voluptuous noblewoman thought wryly, was exactly the right word. Save for the dust of flight on her legs, she was quite naked.

"Not the proper dress for a noble Zamoran woman while hunting," she whispered to herself. But then, Zamoran nobles were seldom roused from their slumber by murderous hillmen or tents burning around them. Nor did they take part in the hunt as the prey.

She turned once more to study the pool, and licked lips that were dry again in moments. To reach it she would have to traverse a steep, rocky slope with not so much as a blade of grass for cover. At the bottom of the slope was a drop; she could not be sure how far from this angle, but it did not look enough to cause difficulty. The pool itself beckoned her enticingly. A patch of water she could doubtless wade in three strides without sinking to her knees, with three stunted trees on its edge, and at that moment it seemed more inviting than her palace gardens.

"I will not remain here until my tongue swells," she announced to the air. As if the sound of her own voice had spurred her to action, she crawled from the shelter of the stone slabs and started down the slope.

At first she moved carefully, picking her way over the loose stone. With every step, however, she became more aware of her nudity, of the way her breasts swayed with every movement, of how her skin flashed palely in the sunlight. First night and then the stone slabs had provided some illusion of being less naked. She had often lain naked in her garden, luxuriating in the warmth of the sun, but here sunlight stripped the illusion as bare as she. Here she could not know who watched her. Reason told her if there was a watcher, she had greater problems than nudity, but reason prevailed nothing against her feelings. Curling one arm over her breasts helped little, and she found herself crouching more and more, hurrying faster, taking less care of where she put her feet.

Abruptly the stones beneath her turned, and she was on her back, sliding amid a cloud of dust. Desperately she clawed for a hold, but each stone she grasped merely set others sliding. Just as she was ready to moan that matters could not get worse, she found herself falling. Only for long enough to be aware of the fall did she drop, then a jolt pulled her up short. The slide of rocks and dirt she had begun did not cease, however. A torrent of rubble showered down on her. Covering her face with her arms, spitting to clear dust from her mouth, she reflected that she would be a mass of bruises from shoulders to ankles after this day.

The rain of dirt and stones slowed and halted, and Jondra examined her position with a sinking feeling. The first shock was that she hung upside down, against the face of the drop she had been sure would present no difficulty. A twisted tree stump no thicker than her wrist held her ankle firmly in the V it formed with the face of the drop. Beneath her a pile of rubble from her fall reached just high enough for her to touch the stones with her fingertips.

Deliberately she closed her eyes and took three deep breaths to calm herself. There had to be a way out. She always found a way to get what she wanted, and she did *not* want to die hanging like a side of mutton. She would, she decided, just have to get hold of the stump and lift her ankle free.

At her first attempt to bend double a jolt of pain shot from her ankle, and she fell back gasping. The ankle was not broken, she decided. She would not accept that it was. Steeling herself against the pain, she tried again. Her fingers brushed the stump. Once more, she thought.

A rustle drew her eyes toward the pool, and terror chilled her blood. A bearded hillman stood there in filthy yellow tunic and stained, baggy trousers. He licked his lips slowly, and his staring black eyes burned with lust. He started toward her, already loosening his garments. Suddenly there was a noise like a sharp slap, and the hillman stopped, sank to his knees. Jondra blinked, then saw the arrow standing out from his neck.

Frantically she searched for the shaft's source. A movement on a mountain caught her eye, a moment's view of something that could have been a bow. Three hundred paces, the archer in her measured calmly, while the rest of her nearly wept for relief. Whichever of her hunters it was, she thought, she would gift him with as much gold as he could carry.

But she was not about to let anyone, least of all a man in her service, find her in such a helpless position. Redoubling her efforts, she split several splinters of wood from the stump and chipped her fingernails, but got no closer to freeing herself.

Suddenly she gasped in renewed horror at the sight of the man who appeared walking slowly toward her. This was no hillman, this tall form with fur leggings and clean-shaven face and gray eyes. She knew that face and the name that went with it, though she would have given much to deny it. Eldran. Vainly she tried to protect her modesty with her hands.

"You!" she spat. "Go away, and leave me alone!"

He continued his slow advance toward her, one hand resting lightly on the hilt of his broadsword, his fur-lined cloak slung back from his shoulders. No bow or quiver was in evidence. His eyes were fixed on her, and his face was grim.

"Stop staring at me!" Jondra demanded. "Go away, I tell you. I neither need nor want your help."

She flinched as three hillmen burst silently from the rocks behind the Brythunian, rushing at him with raised tulwars. Her mouth opened to scream . . . and Eldran whirled, the broadsword with its clawed quillons seeming to flow into his hand. In movements almost too fast for her to follow the four danced of death. Blood wetted steel. A bearded head rolled in the dust. And then all three hillmen were down, and Eldran was calmly wiping his blade on the cloak of one.

Sheathing the steel, he stepped closer to her. "Perhaps you do not want my help," he said quietly, "but you do need it."

Jondra realized her mouth was still open and snapped it shut. Then she decided silence would not do, but before she could speak the big Brythunian had stepped onto the pile of rubble, taken hold of her calves and lifted her clear of the stump that had held her. One arm went behind her knees, and she was swung up into his arms. He cradled her there as easily as did Conan, she thought. He was as tall as the Cimmerian, too, though not so broad across the shoulders. For the first time since the attack she felt safe. Color abruptly flooded her face as the nature of her thoughts became clear to her.

"Put me down," she told him. "I said, put me down!"

Silent, he carried her to the pool and lowered her gently by its edge. "You are down," he said. She winced as he felt her ankle. "A bad bruise, but it should heal in a few days."

There was dried blood on his forehead, she saw. "How came you by that? Have you met other hillmen?"

"I must get my bow," he said curtly, and stalked away.

As well if he did not return, she thought angrily, but the thought brought a twinge of anxiety. Suppose he did *not* return. Suppose he decided to abandon her, naked and alone in this wilderness. When he reappeared she gave a small sigh of relief, and then was angry with herself for that.

He set his bow and a hide quiver of arrows down, then turned to her with a bleak face. "We met other hillmen, yes. Two score men followed me into these accursed mountains, and I failed to keep them safe until we accomplished our purpose. Hillmen, hundreds of them, found our camp. I do not know if any of my companions still live." He sighed heavily. "I surmise the same fate befell you. I wish I could promise to see you to safety, but there is a task I have yet to accomplish, and it must take precedence even over you. I will do what I can for you, though. I must regret that I cannot take days to sit here and just look at you."

It came to her that he *was* looking at her, looking as if he intended to commit what he saw to memory. It also came to her that she was naked. Quickly she scrambled to her knees, crouching with her arms over her breasts. "A civilized man would turn his back," she snapped.

"Then the men you call civilized do not appreciate beauty in a woman."

"Give me your cloak," she commanded. "I am no tavern wench to be stared at. Give it to me, I say!"

Eldran shook his head. "Alone in the heart of the Kezankians, naked as a slave girl on the auction block, and still you demand and give orders. Take garments from the hillmen, if you wish, but do so quickly, for we must leave this place. There are others of their sort about. If you do not wish me to watch, I will not." Taking up his bow again, he nocked an arrow, and his eyes scanned the mountain slopes. "Hurry, girl."

Face flushed with anger and some other emotion she did not quite understand, Jondra refused even to look at the corpses. "Their garments are filthy and bloodstained," she said, biting off each word. "You must provide me decent garb. Such as your cloak!"

"Wiccana has cursed me," the Brythunian said as if she had not spoken, "that she made your eyes touch my soul. There are many women in my native land, but I must come to here, and see you. I look into your eyes, and I feel your eyes touch me, and there are no other women. It is you I want to bear my children. A petulant, pampered woman whose very blood is arrogance. Why should I so want a woman such as you? Yet my heart soars at the sight of you."

Jondra's mouth worked in soundless fury. Petulant! Bear his children! And he went on, saying unbearable things, things she did not want to hear. Her hand found a fist-sized rock by the water, and, with no more thought than white-hot rage, she hurled it. She gave a shocked gasp when Eldran crumpled bonelessly. A thin line of blood trickled down his temple.

"Eldran?" she whispered.

Frantically she crawled to his unmoving form, held a hand before his mouth. He still breathed. Relief filled her, stronger than she would have believed possible. She hesitated over touching the bloody gash where the stone had struck, then instead gently smoothed back his curling brown hair.

Suddenly her hand jerked back as if burned. What was she doing? She had to be gone before he regained consciousness. At best he would start his ranting again, about her bearing his children and the like. At worst . . . She remembered the ease with which he had carried her—and firmly pushed away the memory of feeling protected while he did so. He was strong. Strong enough to force his will with her. She must go quickly.

The first of her needs was water, and she dropped down beside the pool to drink until she felt she would burst at one more swallow. The cool water invigorated her. Limping, she walked back to Eldran. He must be the source of what she needed. Truly she could not bring herself to touch the hillmen's garments, but things of his were another matter.

His bow she snatched up with an excited murmur, and raised it to test the pull. In astonishment she stared from the bow to the man on the ground. She had never met the man who could pull a stronger bow than she, but this bow she could not draw a handspan. Reluctantly she laid it on the ground beside him.

The sword she did not touch, for she had no skill with the weapon. Instead she slipped the tall Brythunian's dagger from his belt. Once she made slits in his fur-lined cape for her head and arms, it made a passable tunic, when belted with one of the rawhide thongs that had tied his fur leggings. The leggings themselves she cut to wrap around her feet, then tied with pieces of the other thong.

And then she was ready to go. For long moments she knelt by Eldran's side, hesitating. Some men never awoke from head injuries. What if he needed care?

"Jondra?" he murmured. Though his eyes remained closed, his hands reached out as if searching for her. She started back from it as from a snake. He must care for himself, she decided.

At the start she kept her pace slow, for the mountainous terrain was rough at best. Her ankle would give no trouble if she did not overtax it, she thought. But after a time her thoughts drifted to Eldran, too. He had been near to waking when she left. He would be dazed, at first, but not too dazed to know she was gone, nor to remember what she had done. He was a hunter. Her hunters could track. There was no reason to suppose the Brythunian could not. And Eldran had two good legs on which to walk.

Almost without realizing it she began to press for speed. The ache in her ankle grew, but she ignored it. Eldran would be following her. She had to keep ahead of him. Her breath came, in gulps. Her mouth was dry as if she had never drunk, and her throat as well. She was a hunter, too, she told herself. She knew how to watch for prey; she could also watch for a pursuer. Constantly she studied her backtrail, till she spent nearly as much time looking over her shoulder as looking ahead.

Rounding a thick, stone spire, she had taken three staggering, limping strides before she saw the half-score hillmen, sitting their horses and staring at her in amazement.

"A gift from the old gods!" one of them shouted, and booted his horse forward.

Jondra was too tired to struggle as he tangled a hand in her hair and pulled her belly-down across his mount before his saddle pad. Weeping in exhausted despair, she sagged unresisting as the hillman flipped up the tail of Eldran's cloak and fondled her bare buttocks.

"He will save me," she sobbed softly into the shaggy fur beneath her face. "He will save me." And a part of her mind wondered why the countenance she conjured was that of the Brythunian.

XIX

Conan's teeth ground as he stared into the crevice where he had hidden Tamira. Staring, he knew, would do no good. She was not likely to appear from the mere force of his looking.

Forgetting the crack in the stone, he examined the ground and frowned. There was little that was enlightening. The ground was too stony to take footprints, but he had learned to track in the mountains of Cimmeria, and the ground in one set of mountains was not too unlike that in another. Here a rock was scraped. There another had its dark bottom turned up to the light. The story he found was perplexing. Tamira had left. That, and nothing more. He could find no sign that hillmen or anyone else had come to take her. She had simply gone. Nor had she waited long after his own departure to do so, for he could see remnants of the night's dew on some of the overturned stones.

"Fool wench," he growled. "Now I have two of you to find." And when he found the thief, he vowed, he would wear out a switch.

Carrying his spear at the trail, Conan set out at a lope, easily following the scattered sign. As he did he felt like cursing. It was clear where she had headed. The camp. The rubies. Perhaps she finally had them, for he remembered the iron chests had not been in the ashes of Jondra's tent.

Suddenly he stopped, frowning at the rocky ground. There had been a struggle here, among several people. He picked up a torn scrap of white cloth. It was a piece of a servant's tunic, like the one Tamira had been wearing. He crumpled it in his fist.

"Fool wench," he said again, but softly.

Warily, now, he went on, eyes searching as much for hillmen as for signs of passage. After a time he became aware that he was following three tracks. Two were of men on horseback, one the set he followed, one much fresher. Newest of all were the tracks of several men afoot. Hillmen did not travel far without their shaggy horses, and there were not enough of them to be soldiers. He could think of no other group at large in the mountains, for if any of the Zamoran hunters remained alive they were certainly seeking the lowlands as fast as they could.

Suspicions roused, he looked even more carefully for likely ambush sites. The Kezankians had a wealth of such places, which did not make his task easier. Sharp bends around precipitous slopes and narrow passages between sheer walls were common. Yet it was a small valley bordered by gentle slopes that first halted him.

From the end of a deep ravine that opened into the valley, he studied it. Motionless, he stood close against the rock wall. It was motion which drew the eye more than anything else. Stunted trees dotted the slopes, but in numbers too small to provide cover. From the valley floor to the peaks there were few boulders or depressions to hide attackers, and those lay half-way to the summit on both sides. Hillmen liked to be close for their ambushes, to allow their prey little time to react. Everything his eyes could see told him the valley was safe, but instinct prickled in the back of his skull. Instinct, which had saved him more than once, won out.

Swiftly he retreated down the ravine. At a place where the wall had collapsed in a fan of rock, nearly blocking the way, he climbed up and out. Patient as a hunting cat he moved from boulder to boulder, twisted tree to twisted tree, following every fold and dip in the land.

Finally he found himself on the slope above the valley. Below him, crouched behind a jagged boulder with bow in hand, was a man. Conan grunted softly in surprise. Though he lacked fur leggings, the embroidered tunic marked the ambusher as a Brythunian. In fact, Conan knew him for the leader of those who had come to Jondra's camp in the hills. Frowning, he eased silently down the incline. Just above the watcher he stopped, settled his cloak about his shoulders and sat with his spear leaning against his shoulder.

"Whom do you wait for, Eldran of Brythunia?" he asked conversationally.

The Brythunian did not start. Instead he looked calmly over shoulder. "You, Conan of Cimmeria," he said. "Though I will admit I did not know it was you who followed us."

"Not you," Conan said. "Hillmen. And you can tell the rest of your men to come out. Unless you think they really have need to watch my back."

Grinning, Eldran sat up. "So we both know what we are about." He waved his arm, and one by one seven men in fur-leggings and embroidered tunics appeared on the slope, trotting to join them. "Do you, too, seek to rescue Jondra, then, Cimmerian?"

Conan drew a long breath. "So she is in the hands of the hillmen. Yes, I seek her, though it was another woman, also a captive, I first set out to find. But you speak as if you also wish to rescue Jondra. This puzzles me, considering the warmth of your last meeting with her."

"We have met since, she and I," Eldran said ruefully, "and there was even less warmth on her part. Some time after, I found where she had fallen captive to hillmen." He fingered his rough gray woolen cloak, dirty and torn; it was a hillman's cloak, Conan saw, stained and dirty. "There are matters I must discuss sharply with that woman."

One of the other Brythunians, a bony man with a pointed nose, spat. "I still say forget the woman. We came to slay the beast of fire, and we must do it if we all die. We have no time for foreign women."

Eldran did not reply, though his face tightened. Another of them murmured, "Peace, Frydan," and the bony man subsided, albeit with an ill grace.

"So you hunt the beast as Jondra did," Conan said. "She learned better after twenty of her hunters died, torn apart or burned alive. Only she, myself and one other survived that enounter, and we barely. I would see the thing dead, too, Brythunian, but there are easier ways to kill yourself."

"The Zamoran wench finds the beast," Frydan muttered disgustedly, "while we find only tracks. Mayhap we do need her."

Again Eldran ignored him. "Jondra hunted for a trophy," he said. "We hunt to avenge dead kin, and to prevent more deaths. Your steel could not prevail against the beast of fire, Conan, nor any mortal-wrought metal. But this," he laid a hand on the hilt of his broadsword, "was forged by mages for that very purpose."

The big Cimmerian eyed the weapon with sudden interest. Objects of sorcery were not beyond his experience. Betimes he could feel the aura of their power in his hands. If this weapon was indeed as Eldran said, then his debt to Telades could yet be repaid. "I would heft the weapon that could slay that creature," he said, but the gray-eyed Brythunian shook his head.

"Once it leaves my possession, Cimmerian, it will journey, Wiccana alone knows how, back to the place where it was given me, and I shall never regain it in this life. Such is the way of its ensorcelment."

"I understand," Conan said. Perhaps it was as the Brythunian said, and perhaps not, but did Eldran fall, he vowed, he would see that wherever the blade journeyed, it came first to his hand. One way or another, if he lived, the debt to Telades would be paid. "But before the beast, the women. Agreed?"

"Agreed," Eldran replied. "As our trails have converged, perhaps we will find both women together. Haral continued after the hillmen who have Jondra, and he will mark the way so we may follow quickly."

Conan got to his feet. "Then let us tarry no longer if we would save them before they are harmed." Yet as they filed down the slope his heart was grim. Women captives did not receive kind treatment from hillmen. Let them only have courage, he thought. Let them only survive till he could find them.

For the twentieth time Tamira examined her bonds, and for the twentieth time knew the futility of such study. Leather cuffs about her wrists and ankles were attached to stout chains fastened in the ceiling and floor of the windowless, stone-walled chamber, holding her rigidly spread-eagled in mid-air. The slender thief's sweat-slick nudity glistened in the light from bronze lamps. The air was chill; the sweat came from fear, fear more of something half-sensed in the room than of her captivity.

Jondra hung suspended as she was, facing her, and Tamira exchanged glances with the noblewoman. The taller woman's body also gleamed, every curve of breast and hip and thigh highlighted. Tamira hoped she also shared the other woman's calmness of face, though it was slightly spoiled by Jondra's constant wetting of her lips.

"I am the Lady Jondra of the House Perashanid of Zamora," Jondra said, her voice quaking. "A generous ransom will be paid for my safe return, and that of my serving woman. But we must be clothed and well-treated. Did you hear me? I will give our weight in gold!"

The crimson-robed man who labored at their feet, drawing a strange pattern on the floor with powders poured from small clay bowls, did not glance up. He gave no sign at all that he had heard, as he had given no sign since they were brought to him. He murmured constantly as he drew, words that Tamira could barely hear, and could not understand at all.

Tamira tried not to listen, but the steady drone bored into her ears.

She clenched her teeth to keep them from chattering. Basrakan Imalla, the men who had thrown her at his feet had called him. She would have wept for her belief that a holy man would protect her, but she feared that if she began she might never stop.

"I am the Lady Jondra of the House. . . ." Jondra licked her lips nervously. Her head tossed as she attempted to jerk at her bonds; a quiver ran down the length of her, but no more. "I will give you twice our weight in gold." Her voice was fringed with panic, and the tone of panic grew with every word. "Three times! Four! Any amount you wish! Anything! But whatever you intend, do not do it! Do not! Oh, Mitra protect me, do not!"

The beautiful noble sobbed and struggled wildly, and her fear sparked Tamira's own to flame. The thief knew now what she sensed in the chamber, what she had not allowed herself to even think of. Sorcery. The very walls reeked of sorcery. And something else, now that she let herself feel it. A malevolent hatred of women. Sobs wracked her, and tears streamed from beneath eyelids squeezed shut as if she could hide behind them.

"You are vessels of iniquity!" The harsh voice cut through Tamira's weeping. Unwillingly she looked. Basrakan stood stroking his forked beard, and his black eyes glittered despite at them. "All women of the cities are unclean vessels of lust. The old gods themselves will prove it on your bodies. Then I will chastise you of your vileness, that you may go to the ancient gods of these mountains in purity."

Shuddering, Tamira tore her eyes from him, and found herself looking down at the design he had drawn, an elongated diamond with concave sides. A short, black candle on one of the points flickered beneath her, another beneath Jondra. The configuration of lines within the diamond pulled at her gaze, drew it hypnotically. Her thoughts fragmented, became a maze, and unrecognizable images came into her mind, images that brought terror. Shrieking in the depths of her mind she tried to flee, to find a refuge, but all was chaos and horror.

Suddenly the maze itself shattered. Gasping, she found that she could look away from the diamond. The stern-faced Imalla had seated himself cross-legged at one end of the unholy pattern. He struck a small gong of burnished brass that stood by his side, and she realized it had been that sound which had released her from the maze. Again the gong sounded, and he began a new chant. Once more the gong chimed. And again. Again.

She told herself that she would not listen, but her bones seemed to vibrate with his words, with the reverberations of the brass. The air within the chamber grew chill; it thickened and stirred. Its caress on her body was palpable, like the feathery stroking of soft hands that touched her everywhere at once. And the heat, rising.

In disbelief she stared down at the candle beneath her. The flame stood firm, untroubled by the breezes she felt stirring, yet it could not possibly be the source of the waves of heat that seemed to rise from it. But the heat came, from somewhere, licking through her limbs, making her belly roll and heave, changing. She tried to shake her head, tried to deny the desire that curled and coiled within her. Dimly she heard a groan of negation from Jondra. Vaguely she saw the noblewoman, head thrown back, hips jerking uncontrollably, and she knew that she writhed as well.

Her lips parted; a moan was wrenched from her. "Conan!" With the tattered shreds of reason left to her, she recognized an answering cry from Jondra. "Eldran!" It would not stop. Her blood boiled.

With a crash the doors of the chamber flew open. Tamira gasped as if plunged into icy water; all sensation of desire fled from her in an instant. Weeping replaced it, tears for the uncleanness that seemed to cover her.

Basrakan leaped to his feet. "Do you desire death, Jbeil?" he snarled. "Do you desire to join Sharmal?"

The gaunt man in the door bowed deeply. "Forgiveness, Basrakan Imalla," he said hastily, "but it is the Eyes of the Fire."

Basrakan pulled him erect by fistfuls of black robe. "Speak, fool! What of the Eyes?"

"Sharmal claims that a woman brings the Eyes into the mountains. And he describes her." Jbeil flung a hand, pointing to Jondra.

Through her tears Tamira met the noblewoman's eyes, and got a confused stare and a shake of the head in return.

Basrakan's blood-red robes swirled as he spun. Tamira would have flinched from his gaze if she could. Before it had been malign. Now she could read in them skin being flayed, flesh stripped from bone. Her skin. Her flesh.

"Two camps of outsiders were destroyed this night past." The Imalla's voice was quiet, like the first brush of a knife against a throat. "This woman came from one of them, Jbeil. Find every scrap that was taken from that camp. Find the Eyes of Fire. Find them, Jbeil."

Jbeil ran from the chamber as if his own throat had felt that blade's caress.

Basrakan's eyes, like ebon stones, were locked on Jondra, but Tamira could not break her own gaze from them. As she stared helplessly, she found herself praying to every god she knew that whatever Basrakan sought was brought to him. Quickly.

XX

From the scant shelter of a sparse clump of twisted trees above the hillman village, Conan frowned at a two-story stone structure in its center. Armed men swarmed in hundreds about the score of crude stone huts, but it was the slate-roofed building that held his eyes. Around him lay the Brythunians, and they, too, watched.

"I have never heard of a dwelling like that among hillmen," Eldran said quietly. "For the Kezankians, it is a palace."

"I have never heard of so many hillmen in one place," Frydan said nervously. His eyes were not on the village, but on the surrounding mountains. Half a score camps were visible from where they lay, one close enough for the breeze to bring the sour smell of cooking and the shouts of men searching through the low tents. They had seen more clusters of the low, earth-colored tents in reaching their present vantage. "How many are there, Haral?"

"A score of thousands, perhaps." The plump Brythunian's voice was a study in casualness. "Perhaps more. Enough to go around, in any case." Frydan stared at him, then closed his eyes wearily.

Through a gap between mountains Conan caught sight of crude stone columns. "What is that?" he asked, pointing.

Haral shook his head. "I have done little looking about, Cimmerian. I saw the woman, Jondra, taken into that building below, and since I have watched and waited for Eldran."

"Rescuing her will not be easy," Conan sighed. "Are you sure you did not see another woman captive?" Once more Haral shook his head, and the Cimmerian resumed his study of what lay below.

155

"It would take an army to go down there," Frydan protested. "Eldran, we did not come to die attempting to rescue a Zamoran wench. We seek the beast of fire, or do you forget? Let us be about it." Some of the other Brythunians murmured agreement.

"I will have her out of there," Eldran replied quietly, "or die in the trying."

An awkward silence hung over them for a moment, then Haral abruptly said, "There is an army in these mountains."

Frydan's mouth twisted sarcastically. "The Zamorans? I am sure they would come to help us if we only asked."

"Perhaps they would," Conan said with a smile, "if they were asked properly." The others looked at him doubtfully, obviously wondering if he made a joke, so he went on. "Their general is one Tenerses, I understand, a lover of glory and easy victories. He has been sent into the mountains to put down a gathering of the hill tribes. Well, here it is."

Even Haral was skeptical. "Unless this Tenerses is a fool, Cimmerian, he'll not attack here. Why, he'd be outnumbered four to one at the very least."

"That is true," Conan agreed. "But if he thought there were but a thousand or so hillmen, and they on the point of leaving before he could gain his victory . . ." He grinned at the others, and slowly, as the idea caught hold, they grinned back. All save Fyrdan.

"The tribesmen would all rush to meet his attack," Eldran said, "giving us as good as a clear path to Jondra's prison. Perhaps your woman—Tamira?—is there as well. Both sets of tracks came to this village."

Conan's smile faded. He had stopped counting hillman camps when he reached twenty, but Tamira could be in any one of ten thousand dingy tents. He could do nothing save rescue Jondra and hope to find the slender thief after. It was a faint hope at the moment, but he had no more. "Who will go to lure Tenerses?" he said grimly.

"Fyrdan has a silver tongue," Eldran said, "when he wishes to use it so."

"We should be about our charge. It is what we came for," the bony man said stiffly.

Eldran put a hand on his shoulder. "I cannot leave this woman," he said quietly.

Frydan lay still for a moment, then sighed and sat up. "If I can steal one of the sheep these hill scum call a horse, I will reach the Zamorans in half a turn of the glass. A moment to snare this general with my tale and get his block-footed soldiers marching." He squinted at the sun, approaching its zenith. "The earliest I could get them here is mid-afternoon, Eldran. With luck."

"Wiccana will give you her luck, and guide your words," Eldran said.

Conan turned from the leavetaking among the Brythunians to resume his study of the stone building. "I will get you out," he vowed under his breath. "Both of you."

Pain had long since come and gone in Tamira's shoulders, wracked by her suspension. Even the numbness that replaced pain had faded into the background, leaving only fear. She did not have to look at Jondra to know the noblewoman's eyes were directed, as were hers, at Basrakan, the man who held their fate on the tip of his tongue. She could as soon have grown wings as taken her eyes from his dark presence.

The Imalla sat, now, on a low stool. Idly he stroked his forked beard and watched the two bound women with eyes as black as bottomless pits. For the first turn of the glass he had stalked the room, muttering dire threats and imprecations at those who moved slowly to obey him, to obey the will of the true gods, muttering about the Eyes of Fire. Twice so long he had sat quietly, and Tamira wished he would pace again, rant, anything but look at her. His eyes no longer glittered; they seemed devoid of life or even the barest shreds of humanity. In their depths she read tortures that did not even have names. That which called itself Tamira cowered in the furthest recesses of her mind in a vain attempt to escape that diabolic ebon gaze, but she could not look away.

At the doors came a scratching. It was like the slash of a knife in the dead silence. Tamira shuddered; Jondra whimpered and began to sob softly.

Basrakan's scarlet robes rippled as he rose fluidly. His voice was filled with preternatural calmness. "Bring the Eyes to me."

One door opened a crack, and Jbeil entered diffidently. "I have not your knowledge, Basrakan Imalla," the gaunt man said as if he dared not breathe, "but these fit the description my poor ears heard." The gems he extended in his hands gleamed in the lamp light.

Tamira's eyes widened. The black-robed man held Jondra's necklace and tiara.

Basrakan put out a hand; the jewelry was laid in his palm. From beneath his blood-red robes he produced a dagger. Almost delicately he picked at the settings around the two great rubies. Gold, sapphires and black opals he threw aside like trash. Slowly his hands rose before his face, each cupping one sanguine gem.

"They are mine at last," he said as if to himself.

"All power is mine." His head swiveled—no other muscle moved—to regard the two naked women suspended in chains. "Before this sun sets the doubters will have their proof. Confine these women, Jbeil. This day they will be given to the old gods."

Tamira shivered, and for an instant she teetered on the brink of unconsciousness. Given to the old gods. Sacrificed—it could mean no other. She wanted to cry out, to plead, but her tongue clove to the roof of her mouth. Wildly she stared at the swarthy, turbanned men who appeared to take her from her bonds. Her limbs would not work; she could not stand unaided. As she was carried from the room, her eyes sought desperately for Basrakan, the man who had the power of life and death here, the man who could, who must change his edict. The stern-faced Imalla stood before a table on which rested the rubies, his long fingers busy among vials and flasks.

The door closed, shutting off Tamira's view, and a wordless wail of despair rose in her throat. She tried to find moisture in her mouth so that she might beg the cold-eyed men who bore her unheeding of her nudity. To them she might as well not be a woman. Sacrificial meat, she shrieked in her mind.

Inexorably, she was carried on, down winding stone steps into musty corridors. A thick iron-bound door opened, and she was thrown to land heavily on hard-packed earth. With a hollow boom the door slammed.

Escape, she thought. She was a thief, a skilled thief, used to getting into places designed to keep her out. Surely she could get out of one meant to keep her in. Awkwardly, for the stiffness of her arms and legs, she pushed up to her knees and surveyed her prison. The dirt floor, rough stone walls, the obdurate door. There was nothing else. Dim light filtered down from two narrow slits near the ceiling, twice the height of a tall man above her head. Her momentary burst of hope faded away.

A whimper reminded her that she was not alone. Jondra lay huddled on the dirt, her head in her arms. "He will never find me," the noble-woman wept bitterly.

"He will find us," Tamira said stoutly, "and save us." To her shock she realized that, though all her other hopes were gone, one still remained. She had never asked favor or aid from any man, but she knew with unshakeable certainty that Conan would find her. She clung to an image of him breaking down the heavy, iron-bound door and bearing her away, clutched at it the way a drowning man would clutch a raft.

Jondra did not stop her slow, inconsolable sobbing. "He does not know where I am. I hit him with a rock, and . . . I do not want to die."

Tamira crawled to the taller woman and shook her by a shoulder. "If you give up, then you are dead already. Do you think I did not know terror to my soul in that chamber above?" She made a disgusted sound deep in her throat. "I've seen virgin girls on the slave block with more courage than you. All of that vaunted pride was camouflage for a sniveling worm ready to crawl on her belly."

Jondra glared up at her with some spark of her old spirit, but there was still a plaintive note in her voice. "I do not want to die."

"Nor do I," Tamira replied, and abruptly the two women were clinging to each other, trembling with their fear yet drawing strength each from the other. "You must say it," Tamira whispered fiercely. "Say it, and believe it. *He will save us.*"

"He will save us," Jondra said hoarsely.

"He will save us."

"He will save us."

Basrakan intoned the last word, and his eyes opened wide with awe at the rush of strength through his veins. He felt as if a single bound would take him the length of the room. He drew a deep breath and thought he could detect each separate odor in the room, sharp and distinct. So this was what it was to be bonded with the drake.

On the table the glow faded from the rubies, from the lines of power drawn there in virgins' blood and powdered bone and substances too dreadful for mortal men to speak their names. But the glow that permeated Basrakan's very marrow did not fade. Triumph painted his face.

"We are one," he announced to the chamber, to the dangling chains where the women had hung. "Our fates are one. It *will* obey my summons now."

Tamira started as the door opened, crashing back against the stone wall. She felt Jondra tense as Basrakan appeared in the opening.

"It is time," the Imalla said.

"He will save us," Tamira whispered, and Jondra echoed, "He will save us."

"They are stirring," Eldran said.

Conan nodded, but did not take his eyes from the two-story stone structure below. From all the camps hillmen were moving, thick lines of them filing toward the stone columns that peeked through the gap between mountains. In the village five score turbanned men stood before the stone building. A red robed man with a forked beard and multi-hued turban stepped out, and a muffled roar rose from the waiting hill-men, the words of it lost with the distance.

The Cimmerian stiffened as Jondra appeared, naked, arms bound behind her, a guard to either side with drawn tulwar. And behind her came Tamira, tied and bare as well.

"They are together," Eldran said excitedly. "And unharmed, so far as I can see. Alive, at least, praise Wiccana."

"So far," Conan said.

The skin between the Cimmerian's shoulderblades prickled. There was much about the scene below that did not please him, much beside the way the women were being treated. Where were they being taken, and why? Why?

The hundred hillmen formed a rough, hollow circle about the red-robed man and the two women. The procession joined the streams flowing toward the distant columns.

"This feels ill," Conan said. Unconsciously he eased his ancient broadsword in its worn shagreen sheath. "I do not think we can wait longer."

"Just a little longer," Haral pleaded. "Fyrdan will bring the soldiers soon. He will not fail."

"Not soon enough, it seems," Conan said. He got to his feet and dusted his hands together. "I think I will take a stroll among the hill-men."

With a grin, Eldran straightened. "I feel the need of stretching my legs as well, Cimmerian."

"You young fools!" Haral spluttered. "You'll get your heads split. You'll . . . you'll . . ." With a growl he stood up beside them. "We'll need turbans, if we're to pass for hillmen long enough to keep our heads." The others were on their feet now, too.

"There is a camp just down the mountain," Conan said, "and none in it save women and children, that I can see."

"Then let us be about our walk," Eldran said.

"These old bones aren't up to this any more," Haral complained.

The small file of men started down the mountain.

". . . For the time of our glory has come," Basrakan cried to the throngs of turbanned men jammed shoulder to shoulder on the mountainsides about the amphitheater. Their answering roar washed over him. "The time of the old gods' triumph is upon us!" he called. "The sign of the true gods is with us!"

He spread his arms, and the flow of power through his bones made him think he might fly. Loudly he began to chant, the words echoing from the slopes. Never had so many seen the rite, he thought as the invocation rang out. After this day there would be no doubters.

His dark eyes flickered to the two naked women dangling from their wrists against the iron posts in the center of the circle of crude stone pillars. It was fitting, he thought, that those who brought him the Eyes of Fire should be the sacrifice now, when the new power that was in him was made manifest to his people. They struggled in the bonds, and one of them cried a name, but he did not hear. The glory of the old gods filled him.

The last syllable hung in the air, and vibration in the stone beneath his feet told Basrakan of the coming. He drew breath to announce the arrival of the sign of the true gods' favor.

From the masses on the slopes shouts and cries drifted, becoming louder. Basrakan's face became like granite. He would have those who dared disturb this moment flayed alive over a slow fire. He would . . . There were men within the circle! Abruptly the words penetrated his mind.

"Soldiers!" was the cry. "We are attacked!"

Walking hunched to disguise his height, with his cloak drawn tightly around him, Conan pushed through the pack of hillmen quickly, giving no man more than an instant to see his face. Grumbles and curses followed him. A roughly wound turban topped his black mane, and his face was smeared with soot and grease from a cooking pot, but he was grateful that men saw what they thought they should see, no matter what their eyes told them. The wide circle of crude stone columns was only a few paces away. Conan kept his head down, but his eyes were locked on the two women. A few moments more, he thought.

A murmur ran through the crowd, growing louder. Far down the mountain someone shouted, and other voices took up the cry. It had been more than the big Cimmerian expected to go undetected so long. Best to move before the alarm became general. Grasping his sword hilt firmly, Conan tore off the turban and leaped for the circle of columns.

As he passed between two of the roughly hewn pillars he realized what words were being shouted. "Soldiers! We are attacked! Soldiers!"

Over and over from a thousand throats. Fyrdan, he thought, laughing. They might live through this yet.

Then he was running across the uneven granite blocks, blade bared. The red-robed man, forked beard shaking with fury, shouted at him from atop a tunnel built of stone that seemed to reach back into the mountain, but Conan did not hear. Straight to the blackened iron posts he ran. Tears sprang into Tamira's eyes when she saw him.

"I knew you would come," she laughed and cried at the same time. "I knew you would come."

Swiftly Conan sawed apart the leather cords on her wrists. As she dropped, he caught her with an arm around her slim waist, and she tried to twine her arms about his neck.

"Not now, woman," he growled. In a trice he had her slender nudity bundled in his cloak. From the corner of his eye he saw that Eldran had treated Jondra the same. "Now to get out," he said.

Haral and the other Brythunians were within the columned circle, all facing outwards with swords in hand. From outside, bearded faces stared at them, some with disbelief, some with anger. And some, Conan saw in amazement, some with fear. Tulwar hilts were fingered, but none moved to cross the low granite wall atop which the columns stood.

From afar came the sounds of Zamoran drums beating furiously. The clash of steel drifted faintly in the air, and the shouts of fighting men.

"Mayhap we can just stay here till the soldiers come," Haral said unsteadily.

A ripple ran through the hillmen pressed against the circle's perimeter.

"Stay back!" the red-robed man cried. "The unbelievers will be dealt with by—".

Screaming at the top of their lungs, a score of turbanned warriors leaped into the circle with steel flashing against the Brythunians. By ones and twos, others joined them. Conan wished he knew what held the rest back, but there was suddenly no time for thought.

The Cimmerian blocked a tulwar slash aimed at his head, booted another attacker full in the belly. The second man fell beneath the feet of a third. The Cimmerian's steel pivoted around his first opponent's curved blade to drive through a leather-vested chest. He wanted to spare a glance for Tamira, but more hillmen were pressing on him. A mighty swing of his ancient broadsword sent a turbanned head rolling on the granite blocks, then continued on to rip out a bearded throat in a spray of blood.

Battle rage rose in him, the fiery blood that drowned reason. Hillmen rushed against him, and fell before a whirlwind of murderous steel. His eyes burned like azure flames, and all who looked into them knew they saw their own death. In some small corner of his mind sanity remained, enough to see Eldran, facing three hillmen and pushed almost to the low stone wall, fighting with broadsword in one hand and tulwar in the other. Haral and another Brythunian stood back to back, and a barricade of corpses slowed others who tried to reach them.

Abruptly the hillman who faced Conan backed away, dark eyes going wide with horror as he stared past the Cimmerian's shoulder. The tribesmen outside the circle were silent, pressing back from the stone columns. Conan risked a backward glance, and clamped his teeth on an oath.

Slowly the iridescent form of the beast of fire moved from the stone tunnel, its great golden eyes coldly surveying the arena filled with men who slowed and ceased their struggles as they became aware of it. One of the leathery bulges on its back had split; the edge of what appeared to be a wing, like that of a great bat, protruded. And almost beneath its feet crouched Tamira and Jondra.

"Behold!" the red-robed mage cried, flinging wide his arms. "The sign of the true gods is with us!"

For an instant there was silence save for the dimly heard sounds of distant battle. Then Eldran shouted. "Cimmerian!" The Brythunian's arm drew back; the ancient broadsword with its strange, clawed quillons arced spinning through the air.

Conan shifted his own sword to his left hand, and his right went up to catch the hilt of the thrown blade.

As if his movement, or perhaps the sword, had drawn its eyes, the brightly scaled beast stepped toward the Cimmerian. Memory of their last encounter was strong in Conan, and as the spike-toothed maw opened he threw himself into a rolling tumble. Flame roared. The hillman he had faced screamed as beard, hair and filthy robes blazed.

Conan knew well the quickness of the beast. He came to his feet only to dive in a different direction, one that took him closer. Fire scorched the stone where he had stood. The glittering creature moved with the speed of a leopard, Conan like a hunting lion. With a mutter of hope that Eldran spoke truly about the weapon, the big Cimmerian struck. A shock, as of sparks traveling along his bones, went through him. And the blade sliced through one golden eye, opening a gaping wound down the side of the huge scaled head, a wound that dripped black ichor.

Atop the stone tunnel the red-robed man screamed shrilly and threw his hands to his face. The beast reared back its head and echoed the scream, the two sounds merging, ringing through the mountains.

Conan felt his marrow freezing as the cry lanced into him, turning his muscles to water. Anger flared in him. He would not wait so to die. Fury lent him strength. "Crom!" he roared. Rushing forward, he plunged the ensorceled weapon into the creature's chest.

With a jerk, the beast's movement tore the hilt from his hand. Onto its hind legs it rose, towering above them all. If its cry had been one of pain before, now it was a shriek of agony, a scream that made the very stones of the mountains shiver.

The red-robed man was down on his knees, one hand to his face, the other clutching his chest. His black eyes on the scaled form were pools of horror. "No!" he howled. "No!"

Slowly the monstrous shape toppled. The stones of the tunnel cracked at its fall. A damp, leathery wing emerged from the broken bulge on its back, quivered once and was still. From beneath the beast extended a corner of scarlet robe, rivulets of crimson blood and black ichor falling from it.

From the hillmen on the slopes a keening went up, an eery wail of despair. Suddenly the thousands of them broke into fear-ridden flight. Even now they tried to avoid the circle of columns, but their numbers were too great, their panic too strong. Those close to the low stone wall were forced over it, screaming denial, by the press of human flesh. The circle became a maelstrom, hundreds trampling each other in their eagerness to flee.

Like a rock Conan breasted the flood, his eyes searching desperately for Tamira and Jondra. The men streaming around him had no thought left but escape, no desire but to claw through the pack, grinding underfoot anyone who slowed them. No man raised a hand against the Cimmerian except to try to pull him from their path. None touched a weapon, or even seemed to see him with their terrified eyes. They would not stop to harm the women deliberately, but if either woman went down beneath those trampling feet . . .

Eldran's height made him stand out as he waded through the shorter hillmen with Jondra in his arms. The Brythunian scrambled over the low stone wall and disappeared in the wash of dirty turbans.

Then Conan caught sight of the gold-edged black cloak, well beyond the circle, being borne around the mountain by the tide of flight. "Fool woman," he growled.

The clash of steel was closer, driving fear deeper into the hearts of men still trying to flee. There was no room to draw or swing a sword, but here and there daggers were out now, and hillman spilled hillman's blood to carve a way through to safety. With hammering fists and sword-hilt, Conan hewed his own path through the mob, ruthless in his need to reach Tamira. Screaming men went down before his blows, and those who fell beneath the feet of that frenzied horde did not rise again.

The hillman village came into sight. Around the two-story stone building swarmed a hell of panting, desperate men dragging screaming black-swathed women with squalling babes in their arms and children clutching their long skirts. Here knots of men could break off from the seething mass to seek their camps. Others paused in flight to grab what they could from the stone huts. Bright steel flashed and reddened, and possessions changed hands thrice in the space of a breath.

Conan's sword and the breadth of his shoulders kept a space clear about him, but he barely even saw the men who slunk away from him like curs. He could no longer find Tamira among the now spreading streams of hillmen.

Abruptly the slender woman thief dashed from the stone structure that towered over the others in the village. She gasped and snugged the gold-edged black cloak tightly about her as Conan grabbed her arm.

"What in Mitra's name are you doing?" the Cimmerian demanded fiercely.

"My clothes," she began, and shrieked when he raised his sword.

Deftly Conan brought his blade over her head to run through a black-robed man who ran from the building with a dagger in his hand and murder in his eye. The hillman's multi-hued turban rolled from his head as he fell.

"I was just," Tamira began again, holding the cloak even more tightly, but she cut off with a squeal as Conan swung her over his shoulder.

"Fool, fool woman," he muttered, and with a wary eye for other hillmen with more than flight on their minds, he headed for the mountain heights.

Behind him, clangor rose as the Zamoran army topped the rise overlooking the village.

Epilogue

Leaning back against a boulder, Conan allowed himself a real smile for the first time in days. They were at the edge of the mountains, and in their journey they had seen no hillman who was not fleeing. Certainly there had been none interested in attacking outsiders.

". . . And when Tenerses realized how many hillmen he faced," Fyrdan was saying, "he began shouting for me and his torturer all in one breath."

"There was little fun where we were, either," Haral told him. "These old bones cannot take this adventuring any more."

Jondra and Tamira, still swathed in their borrowed cloaks, huddled close to a small fire with their heads together. They showed more interest in their own talk than that of the men.

"It was hard enough with the Zamorans," the bony man laughed. "I thought I would have my hide stripped off on the instant. Then that . . . that sound came." He shivered and pulled his cloak closer about him. "It turned men's bowels to water. The hillmen stood for only a moment after that, then broke."

"That was Conan," Eldran said from where he examined the two shaggy horses they had found wandering, saddled but riderless, in the mountains. There had been others that they could not catch. "He slew the beast of fire, and it . . . screamed."

"And the Zamoran gained his victory," Haral said, "and his glory. It will be years before the hill tribes so much as think of uniting again. He

166

will be acclaimed a hero in Shadizar, while the Cimmerian gets nothing."

"Let Tenerses have his glory," Conan said. "We have our lives, and the beast is dead. What more can we ask?"

Eldran turned suddenly from the horses. "One more thing," he said sharply. "A matter of debt. Jondra!"

Jondra stiffened and looked over her shoulder at the tall Brythunian. Tamira rose swiftly, carefully holding the black cloak closed, and moved to Conan's side.

"I know of no debt I owe you." The gray-eyed noblewoman's voice was tight. "But I would speak with you about garments. How long am I to be forced to wear no more than this cloak? Surely you can find me *something* more."

"Garments are a part of your debt," Eldran told her. He ticked off items on his fingers. "One cloak lined with badger fur. One pair of wolf fur leggings. And a good Nemedian dagger. I will not speak of a crack on the head. Since I see no chance of having them returned, I will have payment."

Jondra sniffed. "I will have their weight in gold sent to you from Shadizar."

"Shadizar?" Eldran laughed. "I am a Brythunian. What do I care of gold in Shadizar?" Abruptly he leaped, bearing the tall noblewoman to the ground. From his belt he produced long leather thongs like those used to tie leggings. "If you cannot pay me," he said into her disbelieving face, "then I will have you in payment."

Conan rose to his feet, one hand going to his sword hilt, but Tamira laid both of her small hands atop his. "Do nothing," she said softly.

The big Cimmerian frowned down at her. "Do you hate her so?"

Tamira shook her head, smiling. "You would have to be a woman to understand. Her choice is to return to being a wealthy outcast, scorned for her blood, or to be the captive of a man who loves her. And whom she loves, though she cannot bring herself to admit it. It is a choice any woman could make in an instant."

Conan admitted to himself that Jondra did not seem to be struggling as hard as she might, though she almost made up for it with her tirade. "You Brythunian oaf! Erlik blast your soul! Unhand me! I'll have your head for this! Derketo shrivel your manhood! I will see you flayed alive! Ouch! My ransom will be more wealth than you've ever seen if I am unharmed, Mitra curse you!"

Eldran straightened from her with a grin. She was a neat bundle in the cloak, now, snugly tied from shoulders to ankles with the leather thongs. "I would not take all the wealth of Zamora for you," he said. "Besides, a slave in Brythunia can have no interest in gold in Shadizar." He turned his back on her indignant gasp. "You understand, Cimmerian?"

Conan exchanged a glance with Tamira; she nodded. "I have had it explained to me," he answered. "But now it is time to take my leave."

"Wiccana watch over you, Cimmerian," Eldran said. Frydan and Haral echoed the farewell.

Conan swung into the saddle of one of the two horses. "Tamira?" he said, reaching down both hands. As he lifted her up behind him, her cloak became disarrayed, exposing soft curves and satin skin, and she had to press herself to his back to preserve her modesty.

"Be more careful," she complained.

The big Cimmerian only smiled, and spoke to the others. "Fare you well, and take a pull at the hellhorn for me if you get there before me."

As their shaggy mount carried them away from the small camp, Tamira said, "Truly you do not have to worry for her, Conan. I'll wager by the end of the year she has not only managed to make him free her, but that they are wed as well."

Conan only grunted, and watched for the first appearance of the lowlands through the gap ahead.

"It is a pity we must go back to Shadizar empty handed, is it not?"

Still Conan did not reply.

"No doubt some hillman has the rubies, now," Tamira sighed heavily. "You must understand, I do not hold it against you. I would like to see you once we return to Shadizar. Perhaps we could meet at the Red Lion."

"Perhaps we could." Delving into the pouch at his belt Conan drew out the two great rubies from Jondra's regalia. They seemed to glow with a crimson light on his calloused palm. "Perhaps I might spend some of what I receive for these on you." Tamira gasped; he felt her rumaging within the cloak, and smiled. "Did you think I would not know of the pouch sewn inside my own cloak?" he asked. "I may not have been raised as a thief, but I have some skill with my fingers."

A small fist pounded at his shoulder. "You said you would not steal from her," the slender thief yelped.

"And so I did not," he answered smoothly. "I stole them from you."

"But you would not steal from her because you slept with her, and you . . . I . . . we . . ."

"But did *you* not say that should not trouble a thief?" he chuckled.

"Do not go to sleep," Tamira said direly. "Do not even close your eyes. Do you hear me, Cimmerian? You had better heed my words. Do you think I'll allow . . ."

Conan tucked the rubies back into his pouch, then thoughtfully moved the pouch around on his belt where it would be harder for her to reach. He might not receive the triumphal parade that Tenerses would get, but his would not be a bad return to Shadizar. Laughing, he booted his horse into a gallop.

Conan
the
Triumphant

Prologue

The great granite mound called Tor Al'Kiir crouched like a malevolent toad in the night, wearing a crown of toppled walls and ruined columns, memories of failed attempts by a score of Ophirean dynasties to build there. Men had long since forgotten the origin of the mountain's name, but they knew it for a place of ill luck and evil, and laughed at the former kings who had not had their sense. Yet their laughter was tinged with unease for there was that about the mountain that made it a place to avoid even in thought.

The roiling black clouds of the storm that lashed Ianthe, that sprawling golden-domed and alabaster-spired city to the south, seemed to center about the mountain, but no muffled murmur of the thunder that rattled roof-tiles in the capital, no flash of light from lightnings streaking the dark like dragons' tongues, penetrated to the depths of Tor Al'Kiir's heart.

The Lady Synelle knew of the storm, though she could not hear it. It was proper for the night. Let the heavens split, she thought, and mountains be torn asunder in honor of *his* return to the world of men.

Her tall form was barely covered by a black silk tabard, tightly belted with golden links, that left the outer curves of breasts and hips bare. None of those who knew her as a princess of Ophir would have recognized her now, dark eyes glittering, beautiful face seemingly carved from marble, spun-platinum hair twisted about her head in severe coils and bearing a coronet of golden chain. There were four horns on the brow of that coronet, symbol that she was High Priestess of the god she had chosen to serve. But the bracelets of plain black iron that encircled her wrists were a symbol as well, and one she hated, for the god Al'Kiir accepted only those into his service who admitted themselves to be his slaves. Ebon silk that hung to her ankles, the hem weighted by golden beads, stirred against her long, slender legs as, barefoot, she led a strange procession deeper into the mountain through rough hewn passages, lit by dark iron cressets suggesting the form of a horrible, four-horned head.

A score of black-mailed warriors were strange enough, their faces covered by slitted helmets bearing four horns, two outthrust to the sides and two curling down before the helmet, making them seem more demons than men. The quillons of their broadswords were formed of four horns as well, and each wore on his chest, picked out in scarlet, the outline of the monstrous horned head only hinted by the fiery iron baskets suspended by chains from the roof of the tunnel.

Stranger still was the woman they escorted, clothed in Ophirean bridal dress, diaphanous layers of pale cerulean silk made opaque by their number, caught at the waist with a cord of gold. Her long hair, black as a raven's wing, curling about her shoulders, was filled with the tiny white blossoms of the tarla, symbol of purity, and her feet were bare as a sign of humility. She stumbled, and rough hands grasped her arms to hold her erect.

"Synelle!" the black-haired woman called woozily. A hint of her natural haughtiness came through her drug-induced haze. "Where are we, Synelle? How did I come here?"

The cortege moved on. Synelle gave no outward sign that she had heard. Inwardly her only reaction was relief that the drug was wearing off. It had been necessary in order to remove the woman from her palace in Ianthe, and it had made her easier to prepare and bring this far, but her mind must be clear for the ceremony ahead.

Power, Synelle thought. A woman could have no real power in Ophir, yet power was what she craved. Power was what she would have. Men thought that she was content to order the estates she had inherited, that she would eventually marry and give stewardship of those lands— ownership in all but name—to her husband. In their fools' blindness they did not stop to think that royal blood coursed in her veins. Did ancient laws not forbid a woman taking the crown, she would stand next in succession to the childless King now on the throne in Ianthe. Valdric sat his throne, consumed with chivying his retinue of sorcerers and physicians to find a cure for the wasting sickness that killed him by inches, too busy to name an heir or to see that, for this failure to do so, the noble lords of Ophir struggled and fought to gain the seat his death would vacate.

A dark, contented smile touched Synelle's full red lips. Let those proud men strut in their armor and tear at one another like starving wolfhounds in a pit. They would wake from their dreams of glory to find that the Countess of Asmark had become Queen Synelle of Ophir, and she would teach them to heel like whipped curs.

Abruptly the passage widened into a great, domed cavern, the very memory of which had passed from the minds of men. Burning tapers on unadorned walls hacked from the living stone lit the smooth stone floor, which bore only two tall, slender wooden posts topped with the omnipresent four-horned head. Ornament had been far from the minds of those who had burrowed into a nameless mountain in a now forgotten age.

They had meant it as prison for the adamantine figure, colored like old blood, that stood dominating the grotto, as it would have dominated the greatest place ever conceived. A statue it seemed, yet was not.

The massive body was as that of a man, though half again as tall as any human male, save for the six claw-tipped fingers on each broad hand. In its malevolent, horned head were three lidless eyes, smouldering blackly with a glow that ate light, and its mouth was a broad, lipless gash filled with rows of needle-sharp teeth. The figure's thick arms were encircled by bracers and armlets bearing its own horned likeness. About its waist was a wide belt and loinguard of intricately worked gold, a coiled black whip glistening metallically on one side, a monstrous dagger with horned quillons depending on the other.

Synelle felt the breath catch in her throat as it had the first time she had seen her god, as it did each time she saw him. "Prepare the bride of Al'Kiir," she commanded.

A choking scream broke from the bridal-clothed woman's throat as she was hurried forward by the guards who held her. Quickly, with cords that dug cruelly into her soft flesh, they bound her between the twin posts on widely straddled knees, arms stretched above her head. Her blue eyes bulged, unable to tear themselves away from the great form that overtowered her; her mouth hung silently open as she knelt, as if terror had driven even the thought of screaming from her.

Synelle spoke. "Taramenon."

The bound woman started at the name. "Him, also?" she cried. "What is happening, Synelle? Tell me! Please!" Synelle gave no answer.

One of the armored men came forward at the summons, carrying a small, brass-bound chest, and knelt stiffly before the woman who was at once a princess of Ophir and a priestess of dark Al'Kiir.

Muttering incantations of protection, Synelle opened the chest and drew out her implements and potions, one by one.

As a child had Synelle first heard of Al'Kiir, a god forgotten by all but a handful, from an old nurse-maid who had been dismissed when it was learned what sort of evil tales she told. Little had the crone told her before she went, but even then the child had been enraptured by the power said to be given to the priestesses of Al'Kiir, to those women who would pledge their bodies and their souls to the god of lust and pain and death, who would perform the heinous rites he demanded. Even then power had been her dream.

Synelle turned from the chest with a small, crystal-stoppered vial, and approached the bound woman. Deftly she withdrew the clear stopper and, with its damp end, traced the sign of the horns on the other woman's forehead.

"Something to help you attain the proper mood for a bride, Telima." Her voice was soft and mocking.

"I don't understand, Synelle," Telima said. A breathy quality had come into her voice; she tossed her head with a gasp, and her hair was a midnight cloud about her face. "What is happening?" she whimpered.

Synelle returned the vial to its resting place in the chest. Using powdered blood and bone, she traced the sign of the horns once more, this time in broad strokes on the floor, with the woman at the posts at the horns' meeting. A jade flask contained virgin's blood; with a brush of virgin's hair she anointed Al'Kiir's broad mouth and mighty thighs. Now there was naught left save to begin.

Yet Synelle hesitated. This part of the rite she hated, as she hated the iron bracelets. There were none to witness save her guards, who would die for her, and Telima, who would soon, in one way or another, be of no import to this world, but she herself would know. Still it must be done. It must.

Reluctantly she knelt facing the great figure, paused to take a deep breath, then fell on her face, arms outspread.

"O, mighty Al'Kiir," she intoned, "lord of blood and death, thy slave abases herself before thee. Her body is thine. Her soul is thine. Accept her submission and use her as thou wilt."

Trembling, her hands moved forward to grasp the massive ankles; slowly she pulled herself across the floor until she could kiss each clawed foot.

"O, mighty Al'Kiir," she breathed, "lord of pain and lust, thy slave brings thee a bride in offering. Her body is thine. Her soul is thine. Accept her submission and use her as thou wilt."

In ages past, before the first hut was built on the site of Acheron, now eons gone in dust, Al'Kiir had been worshipped in the land that would become Ophir. The proudest and most beautiful of women the god demanded as offerings, and they were brought to him in steady streams. Rites were performed that stained the souls of those who performed them and haunted the minds of those who witnessed them.

At last a band of mages vowed to free the world of the monstrous god, and had the blessings of Mitra and Azura and gods long forgotten placed on their foreheads. Alone of that company had the sorcerer Avanrakash survived, yet with a staff of power had he sealed Al'Kiir away from the world of men. That which stood in the cavern beneath Tor Al'Kiir was no statue of the god, but his very body, entombed for long ages.

Two of the guards had removed their helmets and produced flutes. High, haunting music filled the cavern. Two more stationed themselves behind the woman kneeling between the posts. The rest unfastened their scabbarded broadswords from their belts and began to pound the stone floor in rhythm to the flutes.

With boneless sinuosity Synelle rose and began to dance, her feet striking the floor in time with the pounding of the scabbards. In a precise pattern she moved, cat-like, each step coming in an ancient order, and as she danced she chanted in a tongue lost to time. She spun, and weighted black silk stood straight out from her body, baring her from waist to ankles. Sensuously she dipped and swayed from the looming shape of the god to the kneeling woman.

Sweat beaded Telima's countenance, and her eyes were glazed. She seemed to have lost awareness of her surroundings and she writhed uncontrollably in her bonds. Lust bloomed on her face, and horror at the realization of it.

Like pale birds Synelle's hands fluttered to Telima, brushed damp dark hair from her face, trailed across her shoulders, ripped away one single layer of her bridal garb.

Telima screamed as the men behind her struck with broad leather straps, again and again, criss-crossing from shoulders to buttocks, yet her jerking motions came as much from the potion as from the lashing. Pain had been added to lust, as required by the god.

Still Synelle danced and chanted. Another layer of diaphanous silk was torn from Telima, and as her shrieks mounted the chant wove into them, so that the cries of pain became part of the incantation.

The figure of Al'Kiir began to vibrate.

Where neither time, nor place, nor space existed, there was a stirring, a half awakening from long slumber. Tendrils of pleasurable feeling caressed, feeble threads of worship that called. But to where? Once appetites had been fed to satiation. Women had been offered in multitudes. Their essences had been kept alive for countless centuries, kept clothed in flesh forever young to be toys for the boundless lusts of a god. Memories, half dreams, flickered. In the midst of eternal nothingness was suddenly a vast floor. A thousand women born ten thousand years before danced nude. But they were merely shells, without interest. Even a god could not keep frail human essence alive forever. Petulance, and dancers and floor alike were gone. From whence did these feelings come, so frequently of late after seemingly endless ages of absence, bringing with them irritating remembrance of what was lost? There was no direction. A shield was formed and blessed peace descended. Slumber returned.

Synelle slumped to the stone floor, panting from her exertions. There was no sound in the cavern except for the sobs of the midnight-haired beauty kneeling in welted nudity.

Painfully the priestess struggled to her feet. Failure again. So many failures. She staggered as she made her way to the chest, but her hand was steady as she removed a dagger that was a normal sized version of the blade at the god's belt.

"The bowl, Taramenon," Synelle said. The rite had failed, yet it must continue to its conclusion.

Telima moaned as Synelle tangled a hand in her black hair and drew her head back. "Please," the kneeling woman wept.

Her sobs were cut off by the blade slashing across her throat. The armored man who had borne the chest thrust a bronze bowl forward to catch the sanguinary flow.

Synelle watched with disinterest as final terror blazed in Telima's eyes and faded to the glaze of death. The priestess's thoughts were on the future. Another failure, as there had been so many in the past, but she would continue if a thousand women must die in that chamber. She would bring Al'Kiir back to the world of men. Without another glance at the dead woman, she turned to the completion of the ceremony.

I

The long pack train approaching the high crenellated granite walls of Ianthe did not appear to be moving through a country officially at peace. Twoscore horsemen in spiked helms, dust turning their dark blue wool cloaks gray, rode in columns to either side of the long line of sumpter mules. Their eyes constantly searched even here in the very shadow of the capital. Half carried their short horse-bows at the ready. Sweaty-palmed muledrivers hurried their animals along, panting with eagerness to be done now that their goal was in sight.

Only the leader of the guards, his shoulders broad almost to the point of busting his metal jazeraint hauberk, seemed unconcerned. His icy blue eyes showed no hint of the worry that made the others' eyes dart, yet he was as aware of his surroundings as they. Perhaps more so. Three times since leaving the gem and gold mines on the Nemedian border, the train had been attacked. Twice his barbarian senses had detected the ambush before it had time to develop, the third time his fiercely wielded broadsword smashed the attack even as it began. In the rugged mountains of his native Cimmeria, men who fell easily into ambush did not long survive. He had known battle there, and had a place at the warriors' fires, at an age when most boys were still learning at their father's knees.

Before the northeast gate of Ianthe, the Gate of Gold, the train halted. "Open the gates!" the leader shouted. Drawing off his helm, he revealed a square-cut black mane and a face that showed more experience than his youth would warrant. "Do we look like bandits? Mitra rot you, open the gates!"

A head in a steel casque, a broken-nosed face with a short beard, appeared atop the wall. "Is that you, Conan?" He turned aside to call down, "Swing back the gate!"

Slowly the right side of the iron-bound gate creaked inward. Conan galloped through, pulling his big Aquilonian black from the road just inside to let the rest of the train pass. A dozen mail-clad soldiers threw their shoulders behind the gate as soon as the last pack-laden mule ran by. The huge wooden slab closed with a hollow boom, and a great bar, thicker than a man's body, crashed down to fasten it.

The soldier who had called down from the wall appeared with his casque beneath his arm. "I should have recognized those accursed eastern helmets, Cimmerian," he laughed. "Your Free-Company makes a name for itself."

"Why are the gates shut, Junius?" Conan demanded. "'Tis at least three hours till dark."

"Orders, Cimmerian. With the gates closed, perhaps we can keep the troubles out of the city." Junius looked around, then dropped his voice. "It would be better if Valdric died quickly. Then Count Tiberio could put an end to all this fighting."

"I thought General Iskandrian was keeping the army clear," Conan replied coolly. "Or have you just chosen your own side?"

The broken-nosed soldier drew back, licking his thin lips nervously. "Just talking," he muttered. Abruptly he straightened, and his voice took on a blustering tone. "You had better move on, Cimmerian. There's no loitering about the gates allowed now. Especially by mercenary companies." He fumbled his casque back onto his head as if to give himself more authority, or perhaps simply more protection from the Cimmerian's piercing gaze.

With a disgusted grunt Conan touched boot to his stallion's ribs and galloped after his company. Thus far Iskandrian—the White Eagle of Ophir, he was called; some said he was the greatest general of the age— had managed to keep Ophir from open civil war by holding the army loyal to Valdric, though the King seemed not to know it, or even to know that his country was on the verge of destruction. But if the old general's grip on the army was falling . . .

Conan scowled and pressed on. The twisted maze of maneuverings for the throne was not to his liking, yet he was forced to keep an understanding of it for his own safety, and that of his company.

To the casual observer, the streets of Ianthe would have showed no sign that nobles' private armies were fighting an undeclared and unacknowledged war in the countryside. Scurrying crowds filled narrow side streets and broad thoroughfares alike, merchants in their voluminous robes and peddlers in rags, silk-clad ladies shopping with retinues of basket-carrying servants in tow, strutting lordlings in satins and brocades with scented pomanders held to their nostrils against the smell of the sewers, leather-aproned apprentices tarrying on their errands to bandy words with young girls hawking baskets of oranges and pomegranates, pears and plums. Ragged beggars, flies buzzing about blinded eyes or crudely bandaged stumps, squatted on every corner—more since the troubles had driven so many from their villages and farms. Doxies strutted in gilded bangles and sheer silks or less, often taking a stance before columned palaces or even on the broad marble steps of temples.

Yet there was that about the throng that belied the normalcy of the scene. A flush of cheek where there should have been only calm. A quickness of breath where there was no haste. A darting of eye where there was no visible reason for suspicion. The knowledge of what occurred beyond the walls lay heavily on Ianthe even as the city denied its happening, and the fear that it might move within the walls was in every heart.

When Conan caught up to the pack train, it was slowly wending its way through the crowds. He reined in beside his lieutenant, a grizzled Nemedian who had had the choice of deserting from the City Guard of Belverus or of being executed for performing his duty too well, to the fatal detriment of a lord of that city.

"Keep a close watch, Machaon," the Cimmerian said. "Even here we might be mobbed if this crowd knew what we carried."

Machaon spat. The nasal of his helm failed to hide the livid scar that cut across his broad nose. A blue tattoo of a six-pointed Kothian star adorned his left cheek. "I'd give a silver myself to know how Baron Timeon comes to be taking this delivery. I never knew our fat patron had any connections with the mines."

"He doesn't. A little of the gold and perhaps a few gems will stay with Timeon; the rest goes elsewhere."

The dark-eyed veteran gave him a questioning look, but Conan said no more. It had taken him no little effort to discover that Timeon was but a tool of Count Antimides. But Antimides was supposedly one of the few lords of Ophir *not* maneuvering to ascend the throne at the death of the King. As such he should have no need of secret supporters, and that meant he played a deeper game than any knew. Too, Antimides also had no connection with the mines, and thus as little right to packsaddles loaded with gold bars and chests of emeralds and rubies. A second reason for a wise man to keep his tongue behind his teeth till he knew more of the way things were, yet it rankled the pride of the young Cimmerian.

Fortune as much as anything else had given him his Free-Company in Nemedia, but in a year of campaigning since crossing the border into Ophir they had built a reputation. The horse archers of Conan the Cimmerian were known for their fierceness and the skill of him who led them, respected even by those who had cause to hate them. Long and hard had been Conan's climb from a boyhood as a thief to become a captain of mercenaries at an age when most men might only dream of such a thing. It had been, he thought, a climb to freedom, for never had he liked obeying another's commands; yet here he played the game of a man he had never even met, and it set most ill with him. Most ill, indeed.

As they came in sight of Timeon's palace, a pretentiously ornamented and columned square of white marble with broad stairs, crowded between a temple of Mitra and a potter's works, Conan suddenly slid from his saddle and tossed his reins and helmet to a surprised Machaon.

"Once this is all safely in the cellars," he told his lieutenant, "let those who rode with us have until dawn tomorrow for carousing. They've earned it."

"The baron may take it badly, Conan, you leaving before the gold is safely under lock and key."

Conan shook his head. "And I see him now, I may say things best left unsaid."

"He'll likely be so occupied with his latest leman that he'll not have time for two words with you."

One of the company close behind them laughed, a startling sound to come from his sephulcral face. He looked like a man ravaged nearly to death by disease. "Timeon goes through almost as many women as you, Machaon," he said. "But then, he has wealth to attract them. I still don't see how you do it."

"If you spent less time gaming, Narus," Machaon replied, "and more hunting, perhaps you'd know my secrets. Or mayhap it's because I don't have your spindly shanks."

A dozen of the company roared with laughter. Narus' successes with women came with those who wanted to fatten him up and nurse him back to health; there seemed to be a surprising number of them.

"Machaon has enough women for five men," laughed Taurianus, a lanky, dark-haired Ophirean, "Narus dices enough for ten, and Conan does enough of both for twenty." He was one of those who had joined the company since its arrival in Ophir. But nine of the original score remained. Death had done for some of the rest; others had simply tired of a steady diet of blood and danger.

Conan waited for the laughter to subside. "If Timeon's got a new mistress, and it's about time for him to if he's running true to form, he'll not notice if I'm there or no. Take them on in, Machaon." Without waiting for a reply the Cimmerian plunged into the crowd.

Other than staying away from Timeon until he was in better temper, Conan was unsure of what he sought. A woman, perhaps. Eight days the journey to the mines and back had taken, without so much as a crone to gaze on. Women were forbidden at the mines; men condemned to a life digging rock were difficult enough to control without the sight of soft flesh to incite them, and after a year or two in the pits the flesh would not have to be that soft.

A woman, then, but there was no urgency. For a time he would simply wander and drink in the bustle of the city, so different even with its taint from the open terror that permeated the countryside.

Ophir was an ancient kingdom; it had coexisted with the mage-ridden empire of Acheron, gone to dust these three millenia and more, and had been one of the few lands to resist conquest by that dark empire's hordes. Ianthe, its capital, might have been neatly planned and divided into districts at some time in its long history, but over the centuries the great city of spired towers and golden-domed palaces had grown and shifted, winding streets pushing through haphazardly, buildings going up wherever there was space. Marble temples, fronted by countless rows of fluted columns and silent save for the chants of priests and worshippers, sat between brick-walled brothels and smoking foundries filled with the clanging of hammers, mansions and alabaster between rough taverns and silversmiths' shops. There was a system of sewers, though more often than not the refuse thrown there simply lay, adding to the effluvia that filled the streets. And stench there was, for some were too lazy even to dispose of their offal in the sewers, emptying chamber pots and kitchen scraps into the nearest alley. But for all its smells and cramped streets, for all its fears, the city was alive.

A trull wearing a single strip of silk threaded through her belt of coins smiled invitingly at the big youth, running her hands through her dark curls to lift well-rounded breasts, wetting her lips for the breadth of his shoulders. Conan answered her inviting smile with one that sent a visible shiver through her. Marking her as likely for later, though, he moved on, the doxy's regretful gaze following him. He tossed a coin to a fruit-girl and took a handful of plums, munching as he went, tossing the seeds into a sewer drain when he saw one.

In the shop of a swordsmith he examined keen blades with an expert eye, though he had never found steel to match that of his own ancient broadsword, ever present at his side in its worn shagreen scabbard. But the thought of a woman rose up in him, the memory of the whore's thighs. Perhaps there was some small urgency to finding a woman after all.

From a silversmith he purchased a gilded brass necklace set with amber. It would go well on the neck of that curly-head wench, or if not her, about the neck of another. Jewelry, flowers and perfume, he had learned, went further with any woman, be she the most common jade of the streets or a daughter of the noblest house, than a sack of gold, though the trull would want her coins as well, of course. The perfume he obtained from a one-eyed peddler with a tray hung on a strap about his scrawny neck, a vial of something that smelled of roses. Now he was ready.

He cast about for a place to throw the last of his plum pits, and his eye fell on a barrel before the shop of a brass smith, filled with scraps of brass and bronze obviously ready for melting down. Lying atop the metallic debris was a bronze figure as long as his forearm and green with the verdigris of age. The head of it was a four-horned monstrosity, broad and flat, with three eyes above a broad, fang-filled gash of a mouth.

Chuckling, Conan straightened the statuette in the barrel. Ugly it was, without doubt. It was also naked and grotesquely male. A perfect gift for Machaon.

"The noble sir is a connoisseur, I see. That is one of my best pieces."

Conan eyed the smiling, dumpy little man who had appeared in the doorway of the shop, with his plump hands folded over a yellow tunic where it was strained by his belly. "One of your best pieces, is it?" Amusement was plain in the Cimmerian's voice. "On the scrap heap?"

"A mistake on the part of my apprentice, noble sir. A worthless lad." The dumpy fellow's voice dripped regretful anger at the worthlessness of his apprentice. "I'll leather him well for it. A mere two gold pieces, and it is—"

Conan cut him off with a raised hand. "Any more lies, and I may not buy it at all. If you know something of it, then speak."

"I tell you, noble sir, it is easily worth—" Conan turned away, and the shopkeeper yelped. "Wait! Please! I will speak only the truth, as Mitra hears my words!"

Conan stopped and looked back, feigning doubt. This fellow, he thought, would not last a day among the peddlers of Turan.

There was sweat on the shopkeeper's face, though the day was cool. "Please, noble sir. Come into my shop, and we will talk. Please."

Still pretending reluctance, Conan allowed himself to be ushered inside, plucking the figure from the barrel as he passed. Within, the narrow shop was crowded with tables displaying examples of the smith's work. Shelves on the walls held bowls, vases, ewers and goblets in a welter of shapes and sizes. The big Cimmerian set the statuette on a table that creaked under its weight.

"Now," he said, "name me a price. And I'll hear no more mention of gold for something you were going to melt."

Avarice struggled on the smith's plump face with fear of losing a purchaser. "Ten silvers," he said finally, screwing his face into a parody of his former welcoming expression.

Deliberately Conan removed a single silver coin from his pouch and set it on the table. Crossing his massive arms across his chest, he waited.

The plump man's mouth worked, and his head moved in small jerks of negation, but at last he sighed and nodded. "'Tis yours," he muttered bitterly. "For one silver. It's as much as it is worth to melt down, and without the labor. But the thing is ill luck. A peasant fleeing the troubles brought it to me. Dug it up on his scrap of land. Ancient bronzes always sell well, but none would have this. Ill favored, they called it. And naught but bad luck since it's been in my shop. One of my daughters is with child, but unmarried; the other has taken up with a panderer who sells her not three doors from here. My wife left me for a carter. A common carter, mind you. I tell you, that thing is . . ." His words wound down as he realized he might be talking himself out of a sale. Hurriedly he snatched the silver and made it disappear under his tunic. "Yours for a silver, noble sir, and a bargain greater than you can imagine."

"If you say so," Conan said drily. "But get me something to carry it through the streets in." He eyed the figure and chuckled despite himself, imagining the look on Machaon's face when he presented it to him. "The most hardened trull in the city would blush to look on it."

As the smith scurried into the back of his shop, two heavy-set men in the castoff finery of nobles swaggered in. One, in a soiled red brocade tunic, had had his ears and nose slit, the penalties for first and second offences of theft. For the next he would go to the mines. The other, bald and with a straggly black beard, wore a frayed wool cloak that had once been worked with embroidery of silver or gold, long since picked out. Their eyes went immediately to the bronze figure on the table. Conan kept his gaze on them; their swords, at least, looked well tended, and the hilts showed the wear of much use.

"Can I help you?" the shopkeeper asked, reappearing with a coarsely woven sack in his hand. There was no 'noble sir' for this sort.

"That," slit-ear said gruffly, pointing to the statuette. "A gold piece for it."

The smith coughed and spluttered, glaring reproachfully at Conan.

"It's mine," the Cimmerian said calmly, "and I've no mind to sell."

"Two gold pieces," slit-ear said. Conan shook his head.

"Five," the bald man offered.

Slit-ear rounded on his companion. "Give away your profit, an you will, but not mine! I'll make this ox an offer," he snarled and spun, his sword whispering from its sheath.

Conan made no move toward his own blade. Grasping the bronze figure by its feet, he swung it sideways. The splintering of bone blended with slit-ear's scream as his shoulder was crushed.

The bald man had his sword out now, but Conan merely stepped aside from his lunge and brought the weighty statuette down like a mace, splattering blood and brains. The dead man's momentum carried him on into the tables, overturning those he did not smash, sending brass vases and bowls clattering across the floor. Conan whirled back to find the first man thrusting with a dagger held left-handed. The blade skittered off his hauberk, and the two men crashed together. For the space of a breath they were chest to chest, Conan staring into desperate black eyes. This time he disdained to use a weapon. His huge fist traveled more than half the length of his forearm, and slitear staggered back, his face a bloody mask, to pull shelves down atop him as he crumpled to the floor. Conan did not know if he was alive or dead, nor did he care.

The smith stood in the middle of the floor, hopping from one foot to the other. "My shop!" he wailed. "My shop is wrecked! You steal for a silver what they would have given five gold pieces for, then you destroy my place of business!"

"They have purses," Conan growled. "Take the cost of your repairs from—" He broke off with a curse as the scent of roses wafted to his nose. Delving into his pouch, he came out with a fragment of vial. Perfume was soaking into his hauberk. And his cloak. "Erlik take the pair of them," he muttered. He hefted the bronze figure that he still held in one hand. "What about this thing is worth five gold pieces? Or worth dying for?" The shopkeeper, gingerly feeling for the ruffians' purses, did not answer.

Cursing under his breath Conan wiped the blood from the figure and thrust it into the sack the smith had let drop.

With a shout of delight the smith held up a handful of silver, then drew back as if he feared Conan might take it. He started, then stared at the two men littering his floor as if realizing where they were for the first time. "But what will I do with them?" he cried.

"Apprentice them," Conan told him, "I'll wager they won't put anything valuable in the scrap barrel."

Leaving the dumpy man kneeling on the floor with his mouth hanging open, Conan stalked into the street. It was time and more to find himself a woman.

In his haste he did not notice the heavily veiled woman whose green eyes widened in surprise at his appearance. She watched him blend into the crowd then, gathering her cloak about her, followed slowly.

II

The *Bull and Bear* was almost empty when Conan entered, and the half-dread silence suited his mood well. The curly-haired trull had been leaving with a customer when he got back to her corner, and he had not seen another to compare with her between there and this tavern.

An odor of stale wine and sweat hung in the air of the common room; it was not a tavern for gentlefolk. Half a dozen men, carters and apprentices in rough woolen tunics, sat singly at the tables scattered about the stone floor, each engrossed in his own drinking. A single doxy stood with her back to a corner, not plying her trade but seeming rather to ignore the men in the room. Auburn hair fell in soft waves to her shoulders. Wrapped in layers of green silk, she was more modestly covered than most noble ladies of Ophir, and she wore none of the gaudy ornaments such women usually adorned themselves with, but the elaborate kohl of her eyelids named her professional, as did her presence in that place. Still, there was a youthful freshness to her face that gave him cause to think she had not long been at it.

Conan was so intent on the girl that he failed at first to see the graying man, the full beard of a scholar spreading over his chest, who muttered to himself over a battered pewter pitcher at a table to one side of the door. When he did, he sighed, wondering if the wench would be worth putting up with the old man.

At that moment the bearded man caught sight of Conan, and a drunken, snaggle-toothed grin split his wizened face. His tunic was patched in a rainbow of colors, and stained with wine and food.

"Conan," he cried, gesturing so hard for the big youth to come closer that he nearly fell from his stool. "Come. Sit. Drink."

"You look to have had enough, Boros," Conan said drily, "and I'll buy you no more."

"No need to buy," Boros laughed. He fumbled for the pitcher. "No need. See? Water. But with just a little . . ." His voice trailed off into mumbles, while his free hand made passes above the pitcher.

"Crom!" Conan shouted, leaping back from the table. Some in the room looked up, but seeing neither blood nor chance for advantage all went back to their drinking. "Not again while you're drunk, you old fool!" the Cimmerian continued hastily. "Narus still isn't rid of those warts you gave him trying to cure his boil."

Boros cackled and thrust the pitcher toward him. "Taste. 'S wine. Naught to fear here."

Cautiously Conan took the proffered pitcher and sniffed at the mouth of it. His nose wrinkled, and he handed the vessel back. "You drink first, since it's your making."

"Fearful, are you?" Boros laughed. "And big as you are. Had I your muscles . . ." He buried his nose in the pitcher, threw back his head, and almost in the same motion hurled the vessel from him, gagging, spluttering and spitting. "Mitra's mercies," he gasped shakily, scrubbing the back of a bony hand across his mouth. "Never tasted anything like that in my life. Must have put a gill or more down my gullet. What in Azura's name is it?"

Conan suppressed a grin. "Milk. Sour milk, by the smell."

Boros shuddered and retched, but nothing came up. "You switched the pitcher," he said when he could speak. "Your hands are swift, but not so swift as my eye. You owe me wine, Cimmerian."

Conan dropped onto a stool across the table from Boros, setting the sack containing the bronze on the floor at his side. He had little liking for wizards, but properly speaking Boros was not such a one. The old man had been an apprentice in the black arts, but a liking for drink that became an all-consuming passion had led him to the gutter rather than down crooked paths of dark knowledge. When sober he was of some use in curing minor ills, or providing a love philtre; drunk, he was sometimes a danger even to himself. He was a good drinking companion, though, so long as he was kept from magic.

"Here!" the tavernkeeper bellowed, wiping his hands on a filthy once-white apron as he hurried toward them. With his spindly limbs and pot belly, he looked like a fat spider. "What's all this mess on the floor? I'll have you know this tavern is respectable, and—"

"Wine," Conan cut him off, tossing coppers to clatter on the floor at his feet. "And have a wench bring it." He gestured to the strangely aloof doxy. "That one in the corner will do."

"She don't work for me," the tavernkeeper grunted, bending to collect the pitcher and the coins. Then he got down on hands and knees to fetch one copper from under the table and grinned at it in satisfaction. "But you'll have a girl, never fear."

He disappeared into the rear of the building, and in short moments a plump girl scurried out, one strip of blue silk barely containing her bouncing breasts and another fastened about her hips, to set a pitcher of wine and a pair of dented tankards before the two men. Wriggling, she moved closer to Conan, a seductive light in her dark eyes. He was barely aware of her; his eyes had gone back to the auburn-haired jade.

"Fool!" the serving wench snapped. "As well take a block of ice in your arms as that one." And with a roll of her lips she flounced away.

Conan stared after her in amazement. "What is Zandru's Nine Hells got into her?" he growled.

"Who understands women?" Boros muttered absently. Hastily he filled a tankard and gulped half of it. "Besides," he went on in bleary tones once he had taken a deep breath, "now Tiberio's dead, we'll have too much else to be worrying about . . ." The rest of his words were drowned in another mouthful of wine.

"Tiberio dead?" Conan said incredulously. "I spoke of him not too hours gone and heard no mention of this. Black Erlik's Throne, stop drinking and talk. What of Tiberio?"

Boros set his tankard down with obvious reluctance. "The word is just now spreading. Last night it was. Slit his wrists in his bath. Or so they say."

Conan grunted. "Who will believe that, and him with the best blood claim to succeed Valdric?"

"Folk believe what they want to believe, Cimmerian. Or what they're afraid not to believe."

It had had to come, Conan thought. There had been kidnappings in plenty, wives, sons, daughters. Sometimes demands were made, that an alliance be broken or a secret betrayed; sometimes there was only silence, and fear to paralyze a noble in his castle. Now began the assassinations. He was glad that a third of his Free-Company was always on guard at Timeon's palace. Losing a patron in that fashion would be ill for a company's reputation.

" 'Tis all of a piece," Boros went on unsteadily. "Someone attempts to resurrect Al'Kiir. I've seen lights atop that accursed mountain, heard whispers of black knowledge sought. And this time there'll be no Avan-rakash to seal him up again. We need Moranthes the Great reborn. It would take him to bring order now."

"What are you chattering at? No matter. Who's next in line after Tiberio? Valentius, isn't it?"

"Valentius," Boris chuckled derisively. "He'll never be allowed to take the throne. He's too young."

"He's a man grown," Canon said angrily. He knew little of Valentius and cared less, but the count was a full six years older than he.

Boros smiled. "There's a difference between you two, Cimmerian. You've put two hard lifetimes' experience into your years. Valentius has led a courtier's life, all perfumes and courtesies and soft words."

"You're rambling," Conan barked. How had the other man read his thoughts? A fast rise had not lessened his touchiness about his compar-ative youth, nor his anger at those who thought him too young for the position he held. But he had better to do with his time than sit with a drunken failed mage. There was that auburn-haired wench, for instance. "The rest of the wine is yours," he said. Snatching up the sack with the bronze in it, he stalked away from the table, leaving Boros chortling into his wine.

The girl had not moved from the corner or changed her stance in all the time Conan had been watching her. Her heart-shaped face did not change expression as he approached, but her downcast eyes, blue as a northland sky at dawn, widened like those of a frightened deer, and she quivered as if prepared for flight.

"Share some wine with me," Conan said, motioning to a table nearby.

The girl stared at him directly, her big eyes going even wider, if such were possible, and shook her head.

He blinked in surprise. That innocent face might belie it, but if she wanted directness . . . "If you don't want wine, how does two silvers take you?"

The girl's mouth dropped open. "I don't . . . that is, I . . . I mean . . ." Even stammering, her voice was a soprano like silver bells.

"Three silvers, then. A fourth if you prove worth it." She still stared. Why was he wasting time with her, he wondered, when there were other wenches about? She reminded him of Karela, that was it. This girl's hair was not so red, nor her cheekbones so high, but she recalled to him the woman bandit who had shared his bed—and managed to disrupt his life—every time their paths had crossed. Karela was a woman fit for any man, fit for a King. But what use raking up old memories? "Girl," he said gruffly, "if you don't want my silver, say so, and I'll take my custom elsewhere."

"Stay," she gasped. It was an obvious effort for her to get the word out.

"Innkeeper," Conan bellowed, "a room!" The wench's face went scarlet beneath the rouge on her cheeks.

The spidery tapster appeared on the instant, a long hand extended for coin. "Four coppers," he growled, and waited until Conan had dropped them into his palm before adding, "Top of the stairs, to the right."

Conan caught the furiously blushing girl by the arm and drew her up the creaking wooden stairs after him.

The room was what he had expected, a small box with dust on the floor and cobwebs in the corners. A sagging bed with a husk-filled mattress and none-too-clean blankets, a three-legged stool, and a rickety table were all the furnishings. But then, what he was there for went as well in a barn as in a palace, and often better.

Dropping the sack on the floor with a thump, he kicked the door shut and put his hands on the girl's shoulders. As he drew her to him he peeled her silken robes from her shoulders to her waist. Her breasts were full, but upstanding, and pink-nippled. She yelped once before his mouth descended on hers, then went stiff in his arms. He could as well have been kissing a statue.

He drew back, but held her still in the circle of his arms. "What sort of doxy are you?" he demanded. "A man would think you'd never kissed a man before."

"I haven't," she snapped, then began to stammer. "That is, I have. I've kissed many men. More than you can count. I am very . . . experienced." She bared her teeth in what Conan suspected was meant to be an inviting smile; it was more a fearful rictus.

He snorted derisively and pushed her out to arms' length. Her hands twitched toward her disarrayed garments, then were still. Heavy breathing made her breasts rise and fall in interesting fashion, and her face slowly colored again. "You don't talk like a farm wench," he said finally. "What are you? Some merchant's runaway daughter without sense enough to go home?"

Her face became a frozen mask of arrogant pride. "You, barbarian, will have the honor of taking a noblewoman of Ophir to . . . to your bed." Even the stumble did not crack her haughty demeanor.

Taken together with her manner of dress—or undress, rather—it was too much for the Cimmerian. He threw back his head and bellowed his laughter at the fly-specked ceiling.

"You laugh at me?" she gasped. "You dare?"

"Cover yourself," he snapped back at her, his mirth fading. Anger sprouted from stifled desires; she was a tasty bit, and he had been looking forward to the enjoyment of her. But a virgin girl running away from a noble father was the last thing he needed, or wanted any part of. Nor could he walk away from her if she needed help, either. That thought came reluctantly. Softhearted, he grumbled to himself. That was his trouble. To the girl he growled, "Do it, before I take my belt to your backside."

For a moment she glared at him, sky-blue eyes warring with icy sapphire. Ice won, and she hastily fumbled her green robes back into place, muttering under her breath.

"Your name," he demanded. "And no lies, or I'll pack you to the Marline Cloisters myself. Besides the hungry and the sick, they take in wayward girls and unruly children, and you look to be both."

"You have no right. I've changed my mind. I do not want your silver." She gestured imperiously. "Stand away from that door."

Conan gazed back at her calmly, not moving. "You are but a few words away from a stern-faced woman with a switch to teach you manners and proper behavior. Your name?"

Her eyes darted angrily to the door. "I am the Lady Julia," she said stiffly. "I will not shame my house by naming it in this place, not if you torture me with red-hot irons. Not if you use pincers, and the knout, and . . . and . . ."

"Why are you here, Julia, masquerading as a trull, instead of doing needlework at your mother's knee?"

"What right have you to demand . . . ? Erlik take you! My mother is long dead, and my father these three months. His estates were pledged for loans and were seized in payment. I had no relations to take me in, nor friends who had use for a girl with no more than the clothes on her back. And you will call me Lady Julia. I am still a noble-woman of Ophir."

"You're a silly wench," he retorted. "And why this? Why not become a serving girl? Or a beggar, even?"

Julia sniffed haughtily. "I would not sink so low. My blood—"

"So you become a trull?" He noted she had the grace to blush. But then, she did that often.

"I thought," she began hesitantly, then stopped. When she resumed her voice had dropped to a murmur. "It seemed not so different from my father's lemans, and they appeared to be ladies." Her eyes searched his face, and she went on urgently. "But I've done nothing. I am still . . . I mean . . . Oh, why am I telling any of this to you?"

Conan leaned against the door, the crudely cut boards creaking at his weight. If he were a civilized man, he would abandon her to the path she was following. He would have his will of her and leave her weeping with her coins—or cheat her of them, for that was the civilized way. Anything else would be more bother than she was worth. The gods alone knew what faction she might be attached to by blood, for all they had not helped her so far, or what faction he might offend by aiding her.

His mouth twisted in a grimace, and Julia flinched, thinking it was for her. He was thinking too much of factions of late, spending too much time delving the labyrinthine twists of Ophirean politics. This he would leave to the gods. And the wench.

"I am called Conan," he said abruptly "and I captain a Free-Company. We have our own cook, for our patron's kitchens prepare fussed-over viands not fit for a man's stomach. This cook, Fabio, needs a girl to fetch and serve. The work is yours, an you want it."

"A pot girl!" she exclaimed. "Me!"

"Be silent, wench!" he roared, and she rocked back on her heels. He waited to be certain she would obey, then nodded in satisfaction when she settled with her hands clasped at her throat. And her mouth shut. "Do you decide it is not too far beneath you, present yourself at Baron Timeon's palace before sunfall. If not, then know well what your future will be."

She let out one startled squeak as he took the step necessary to crush her to his chest. He tangled his free hand in her long hair, and his mouth took its pleasure with hers. For a time her bare feet drummed against his shins, then slowly her kicking stopped. When he let her heels thud to the floor once more, she stood trembling and silent, tremulous azure eyes locked on his face.

"And I was gentle compared to some," he said. Scooping up the sack containing the bronze, he left her standing there.

oros was gone from the common room when Conan returned below, for which the Cimmerian was just as glad.

The spidery innkeeper rushed forward, though, rubbing his hands avariciously. "Not long with the girl, noble sir. I could have told you she'd not please. My Selina, now . . ."

Conan snarled, and the fellow retreated hastily. Crom! What a day, he thought. Go out searching for a wench and end up trying to rescue a fool girl from her own folly. He had thought he had out-grown such idiocy long ago.

Outside the street was narrow and crooked, little more than an alley dotted with muddy potholes where the cracked paving stones had been pried up and carried away, yet even here were there beggars. Conan tossed a fistful of coppers into the nearest out-thrust bowl and hurried on before the score of others could flock about him. A stench of rotted turnip and offal hung in the air, held by stone buildings that seemed to lean out over the way.

He had not gone far when it dawned on him that the mendicants, rather than chasing after him crying for more, had disappeared. Such men had the instincts of feral animals. His hand went to his sword even as three men stepped into the cramped confines of the street before him. The leader had a rag tied over where his right eye had been. The other two wore beards, one no more than a straggly collection of hairs. All three had swords in hand. A foot grated on paving stone behind the Cimmerian.

He did not wait for them to take another step. Hurling the bag containing the bronze at the one-eyed man, he drew his ancient broadsword and dropped to a crouch in one continuous motion. A blade whistled over his head as he pivoted, then his own steel was biting deep into the side of the man behind. Blood spurting, the man screamed, and his legs buckled.

Conan threw himself into a dive past the collapsing man, tucking his shoulder under, and rolled to his feet with his sword at the ready just in time to spit one-eye as he rushed forward with blade upraised. For an instant Conan stared into a lone brown eye filling with despair and filming with death, then one of the others was crowding close, attempting to catch the big Cimmerian while his sword was hung up in the body. Conan snatched the poignard from one-eye's belt and slammed it into his other attacker's throat. The man staggered back with a gurgling shriek, blood pumping through the fingers clutching his neck to soak his filthy beard in crimson.

All had occurred so quickly that the man impaled on Conan's blade was just now beginning to fall. The Cimmerian jerked his blade free as one-eye dropped. The first attacker gave a last quiver and lay still in a widening sanguinary pool.

The man with the straggly beard had not even had time to join the fight. Now he stood with sword half-raised, dark eyes rolling from one corpse to another and thin nose twitching. He looked like a rat that had just discovered it was fighting a lion. "Not worth it," he muttered. "No matter the gold, it's not worth dying." Warily he edged backwards until he came abreast of a crossing alley; with a last frightened glance he darted into it. In moments even the pounding of his feet had faded.

Conan made no effort to follow. He had no interest in footpads, of which the city had an overabundance. These had made their try and paid the price. He bent to wipe his sword, and froze as a thought came to him. The last man had mentioned gold. Only nobles carried gold on their persons, and he was far from looking that sort. Gold might be paid for a killing, though the life of a mercenary, even a captain, was not usually considered worth more than silver. Few indeed were the deaths that would bring gold. Except . . . assassination. With a shout that rang from the stone walls Conan snatched up the sack-wrapped statuette and was running in the same motion, encarmined blade still gripped in his fist. With him out of the way it might be easier to get through his company to Timeon. And that sort of killing had already begun. His massive legs pumped harder, and he burst out of the alley onto a main street.

A flower-girl, screeching at the giant apparition wielding bloody steel, leaped out of his way; a fruit peddler failed to move fast enough and caromed off Conan's chest, oranges exploding from his basket in all directions. The peddler's imprecations, half for the huge Cimmerian and half for the apprentices scurrying to steal his scattered fruit, followed Conan down the crowded street, but he did not slow his headlong charge. Bearers, scrambling to move from his path, overturned their sedan chairs, spilling cursing nobles into the street. Merchants in voluminous robes and serving girls shopping for their masters' kitchens scattered screaming and shouting before him.

Then Timeon's palace was in sight. As Conan pounded up the broad alabaster stairs, the two guards he had set on the columned portico rushed forward, arrows nocked, eyes searching the street for what pursued him.

"The door!" he roared at them. "Erlik blast your hides! Open the door!"

Hurriedly they leaped to swing open one of the massive bronze doors, worked with Timeon's family crest, and Conan rushed through without slowing.

He was met in the broad entry hall by Machaon and half a score of the company, their boots clattering on polished marble tiles. Varying degrees of undress and more than one mug clutched in a fist showed they had been rousted from their rest by his shouts, but all had weapons in hand.

"What happens?" Machaon demanded. "We heard your shouts, and—"

Conan cut him off. "Where is Timeon? Have you seen him since arriving?"

"He's upstairs with his new leman," Machaon replied. "What—"

Spinning, Conan raced up the nearest stairs, a curving sweep of alabaster that stood without visible support. Pausing only an instant Machaon and the others followed at a dead run. At the door to Timeon's bedchamber, tall and carved with improbable beasts, Conan did not pause. He slammed open the door with a shoulder and rushed in.

Baron Timeon leaped from his tall-posted bed with a startled cry, his round belly bouncing, and snatched up a long robe of red brocade. On the bed a slender, naked girl clutched the coverlet to her small yet shapely breasts. Ducking her head, she peered shyly at Conan through a veil of long, silky black hair that hung to her waist.

"What is the meaning of this?" Timeon demanded, furiously belting the robe about his girth. After the current fashion of the nobility, he wore a small, triangular beard on the point of his chin. On his moon face, with his found, protuberant eyes, it made him look like a fat goat. An angry goat, now. "I demand an answer immediately! Bursting into my chambers with sword drawn." He peered suddenly at the blade in Conan's hand. "Blood!" he gasped, staggering. He flung his arms around one of the thick intricately carved posts of his bed as if to hold himself erect, or perhaps to hide himself behind. "Are we attacked? You must hold them off till I escape. That is, I'll ride for aid. Hold them, and there'll be gold for all of you."

"There's no attack, Lord Timeon," Conan said hastily "At least, not here. But I was attacked in the city."

Timeon glanced at the girl. He seemed to realize he had been far from heroic before her. Straightening abruptly, he tugged at his robe as if adjusting it, smoothed his thinning hair. "Your squabbles with the refuse of Ianthe have no interest for me. And my pretty Tivia is too delicate a blossom to be frightened with your tales of alley brawls, and your gory blade. Leave, and I will try to forget your ill manners."

"Lord Timeon," Conan said with forced patience, "does someone mean you harm, well might they try to put me out of the way first. Count Tiberio is dead this last night at an assassin's hand. I will put guards at your door and in the garden beneath your windows."

The plump noble's water blue eyes darted to the girl again. "You will do no such thing. Tiberio took his own life, so I heard. And as for assassins—" he strode to the table where his sword lay, slung the scabbard into a corner and struck a pose with the weapon in hand—"should any manage to get past your vigilance, I will deal with them myself. Now leave me. I have . . ." he leered at the slender girl who still attempted unsuccessfully to cover herself, "matters to attend to."

Reluctantly Conan bowed himself from the room. The instant the door was shut behind him, he growled, "That tainted sack of suet. An old woman with a switch could beat him through every corridor of this palace."

"What are we to do?" Machaon asked. "If he refuses guards . . ."

"We guard him anyway," Conan snorted. "He can take all the chances he wants to with us to protect him, and he will so long as there's a woman to impress, but we cannot afford to let him die. Put two men in the garden, where he can't see them from his windows. And one at either end of this hall, around the corners where they can hide if Timeon comes out, but where they can keep an eye on his door."

"I'll see to it." The scarred warrior paused. "What's that you're carrying?"

Conan realized he still had the bronze, wrapped in its sack, beneath his arm. He had forgotten it in the mad rush to get to Timeon. Now he wondered. If the men who had attacked him had not been trying to open a way to the baron—and it now seemed they had not—perhaps they had been after the statuette. After all, two others had been willing to kill, and die, for it. And they had thought it worth gold. It seemed best to find out the why of it before giving Machaon a gift that might bring men seeking his life.

"Just a thing I bought in the city," he said. "Post those guards immediately. I don't want to take chances, in case I was right the first time."

"First time?" Machaon echoed, but Conan was already striding away.

The room Conan had been given was spacious, but what Timeon thought suitable for a mercenary captain. The tapestries on the walls were of the second quality only, the lamps were polished pewter and brass rather than silver or gold, and the floor was plain red tiles. Two arched windows looked out on the garden, four floors below, but there was no balcony. Still, the mattress on the big bed was goose down, and the tables and chairs, if plain varnished wood, were sturdy enough for him to be comfortable with, unlike the frail, gilded pieces in the rooms for noble guests.

He tossed the rough sacking aside and set the bronze on a table. A malevolent piece, it seemed almost alive. Alive and ready to rend and tear. The man who had made it was a master. And steeped in abomination, Conan was sure, for otherwise he could not have infused so much evil into his creation.

Drawing his dagger, he tapped the hilt against the figure. It was not hollow; there could be no gems hidden within. Nor did it have the feel or heft of bronze layered over gold, though who would have gone to *that* much trouble, or why, he could not imagine.

A knock came at the door while he was still frowning at the horned shape, attempting to divine its secret. He hesitated, then covered it with the sack before going to the door. It was Narus.

"There's a wench asking for you," the hollow-cheeked man said. "Dressed like a doxy, but her face scrubbed like a temple virgin, and pretty enough to be either. Says her name is Julia."

"I know her," Conan said, smiling.

Narus' mournful expression did not change, but then it seldom did. "A gold to a silver there's trouble in this one, Cimmerian. Came to the front and demanded entrance, as arrogant as a princess of the realm. When I sent her around back, she tried to tell me her lineage. Claims she's noble born. The times are ill for dallying with such."

"Take her to Fabio," Conan laughed. "She's his new pot girl. Tell him to put her peeling turnips for the stew."

"A pleasure," Narus said, with a brief flicker of a smile, "after the way her tongue scourged me."

At least one thing had gone well with the day, Conan thought as he turned from the door. Then his eye fell on the sacking covered bronze on the table, and his moment of jollity faded. But there were other matters yet to be plumbed, and the feeling at the back of his neck told him there would be deadly danger in doing so.

IV

The sly-faced man who called himself Galbro wandered nervously around the dusty room where he had been told to wait. Two great stuffed eagles on perches were the only decoration, the amber beads that had replaced their eyes seeming to glare more fiercely than ever any living eagle's eyes had. The lone furnishings was the long table supporting the leather bag in which he had brought what he had to sell. He did not like these meetings; despite all the silver and gold they put in his purse, he did not like the woman who gave him the coin. Her name was unknown to him, and he did not want to know it, nor anything else about her. Knowledge of her would be dangerous.

Yet he knew it was not the woman alone who made him pace this time. That man. A northlander, Urian said he was. From whencever he came, he had slain five of Galbro's best and walked away without so much as a scratch. That had never happened before, or at least not since he came to Ophir. It was an ill omen. For the first time in long years he wished that he was back in Zingara, back in the thieves' warren of alleys that ran along the docks of Kordava. And that was foolish, for if he was not shortened a head by the guard, his throat would be slit by the denizens of those same alleys before he saw a single nightfall. There were penalties attached to playing both sides in a game, especially when both sides discovered that you cheated.

A light footstep brough him alert. *She* stepped into the room, and a shiver passed through him. No part of her but her eyes, dark and devoid of softness, was visible. A silver cloak that brushed the floor was gathered close about her. A dark, opaque veil covered the lower half of her face, and her hair was hidden by a white silk head-cloth, held by a ruby pin, the stone as large as the last joint of his thumb.

The ruby invoked no shreds of greed within him. Nothing about her brought any feeling to him except fear. He hated that, fearing a woman, but at least her coin was plentiful. His taste for that was all the greed he dared allow himself with her.

With a start he realized she was waiting for him to speak. Wetting his lips—why did they dry so in her presence?—he opened his bag, spread his offerings on the table. "As you can see, my lady, I have much this time. Very valuable."

One pale, slender hand extended from the cloak to finger what he had brought, object by object. The brass plaque, worked with the head of the demon that so fascinated her, was thrust contemptuously aside. He schooled his face not to wince. Leandros had labored hard on that, but of late she accepted few of the Corinthian's forgeries. Three fragments of manuscript, tattered and torn, she studied carefully, then lay to one side. Her fingers paused over a clay head, so worn with age he had not been certain it was meant to be the creature she wanted. She put it with the parchments.

"Two gold pieces," she said quietly when she was done. "One for the head, one for the codexes. They but duplicate what I already have."

A gold for the head was good—he had hoped for no more than coppers at best—but he had expected two for each of the manuscripts. "But, my lady," he whined, "I can but bring you what I find. I cannot read such script, or know if you already possess it. You know not what difficulties I face, what expenses, in your service. Five of my men slain. Coin to be paid for thefts. Men to be—"

"Five men dead?" Her voice was a whipcrack across his back, though she had not raised it.

He squirmed beneath her gaze; sweat rolled down his face. This cold woman had little tolerance for failure, he knew, and less for men who drew attention to themselves, as by leaving corpses strewn in the streets. He had Baraca as example for that. The Kothian had been found hanging by his feet with his skin neatly removed, yet still alive. For a few agonized hours of screaming.

"What have you been into, Galbro," she continued, her low words stabbing like daggers, "to lose five men?"

"Naught, my lady. A private matter. I should not have mentioned it, my lady. Forgive me, please."

"Fool! Your lies are transparent. Know that the god I serve, and whom you serve through me, gives me the power of pain." She spoke words that his brain did not want to comprehend; her hand traced a figure in the air between them.

Blinding light flashed behind his eyes, and agony filled him, every muscle in his body writhing and knotting. Helpless, he fell, quivering in every limb, bending into a backbreaking arch till only his head and drumming heels touched the floor. He tried to shriek, but shrieks could not pass the frozen cords of his throat, nor even breath. Blackness veiled his eyes, and he found a core within him that cried out for death, for anything to escape the all-consuming pain.

Abruptly the torment melted away, and he collapsed in a sobbing heap.

"Not even death can save you," she whispered, "for death is one of the realms of my master. Behold!" Again she spoke words that seared his mind.

He peered up at her pleadingly, tried to beg, but the words stuck in his throat. The eagles moved. He knew they were dead; he had touched them. But they moved, wings unfolding. One uttered a piercing scream. The other swooped from its perch to the table, great talons gripping the wood as it tilted its head to regard him as it might a rabbit. Tears rolled uncontrollably down his thin cheeks.

"They would tear you to pieces at my command," the veiled woman told him. "Now speak. Tell me all."

Galbro began to babble. Words spilled from his mouth like water from a fountain. The bronze figure, described in minute detail. How he learned of it, and the attempts to secure it. Yet even in his terror he held back the true description of the giant northlander. Some tiny portion of him wanted to be part of killing this man who had endangered him; a larger part wanted whatever the veiled woman might pay for the piece. Did she know how to obtain it without him she might decide his usefulness was at an end. He knew she had others like him who served her, and Baraca reminded him of the deadliness of her wrath. When his torrent of speech ended, he lay waiting in dread.

"I dislike those who keep things from me," she said at last, and he shivered at the thought of her dislike. "Secure this bronze, Galbro. Obey me implicitly, and I will forgive your lies. Fail . . ."

She did not have to voice the threat. His whirling mind provided a score of them, each worse than the last. "I will obey, my lady," he sobbed, scrubbing his face in the dust of the floor. "I will obey. I will obey."

Not until her footsteps had faded from the room could he bring himself to stop the litany. Raising his head he stared wildly about the room, filled with joyous relief that he was alone and still alive. The eagles caught his eye, and he moaned. They were still again, but one leaned forward with wings half raised as if ready to swoop at him from its perch. The other still clung to the table, head swiveled to pierce him with its amber gaze.

He wanted to flee, yet he knew with a sinking feeling that he could not run far enough or fast enough to escape her. That accursed northlander was responsible for this. If not for him everything could have gone on as before. Rage built in him, comforting rage that overlaid his terror. He would make the northlander pay for everything that had happened to him. That big man would pay.

Synelle waited until she was in her palanquin—unadorned for anonymity—with the pale gray curtains safely drawn before lowering her veil. The bearers carried her from the courtyard of the small house where she had met Galbro without a word needed from her. Tongueless, so they could not speak of where they had borne her, they knew the need to serve her perfectly as well as did the sly-faced thief.

It was well she always went to these meetings prepared. A cloth on which Galbro had wiped his sweat, obtained by another of her minions, a few feathers plucked from the eagles, these had given her the means to quell the thief. She could rest at her ease knowing the man's soul was seared with the need for absolute obedience. And yet for once the gentle swaying of the platform did not lull her as she lolled on silken cushions.

Something about the sly little man's description of the bronze produced an irriating tickle in the back of her mind. She had encountered many representations of Al'Kiir's head, many medalions and amulets embossed with his head or the symbol of the horns, but never before a complete figure. It sounded so detailed, perhaps an exact duplicate of the actual body of the god. Her face went blank with astonishment. In one of the manuscript fragments she had gathered there was . . . something. She was sure of it.

She parted the forward curtains a slit. "Faster!" she commanded. "Erlik blast your souls, faster!"

The bearers increased their pace to a run, forcing their way through the crowds, careless of the curses that followed them. Synelle would do more than curse if they failed to obey. Within, she pounded a small fist against her thigh in frustration at the time it took to cross the city.

As soon as the palanquin entered the courtyard of her mansion, before the bearers could lower it to the slate tiles, Synelle leaped out. Even in her haste hate flickered through her at the sight of the house. As large as any palace in the city, it still was not a palace. The white stuccoed walls and red-tiled roof were suitable for the dwelling of a merchant. Or a woman. By ancient law no woman, not even a princess, could maintain a palace within the walls of Ianthe. But she would change that. By the gods, if what she thought were true she would change it within the month. Why wait for Valdric to die? Not even the army could stand against her. Iskandrian, the White Eagle of Ophir, would kneel at her feet along with the great lords of Ophir.

Dropping her cloak for a serving maid to tend to, she raised her robes to her hips and ran, heedless of servants who stared at bare, flashing limbs. To the top floor of the mansion she ran, to a windowless room where only one other but herself was allowed, and that one with her mind ensorceled to forget what lay within, to die did anyone attempt to force the awful knowledge from her.

Golden sconces on the walls held pale, perfumed candles, yet all their light could not thrust back an air of darkness, the feel of a shrine to evil. Shrine it was, in a way, though there was no idol, no place for votive offerings. Three long tables, polished till they gleamed, were all the furnishings the room contained. On one were flasks of liquids that bubbled in their sealed containers or glowed with eery lights, vials of powders noxious and obscene, the tools of her painfully learned craft. The second was covered with amulets and talismans; some held awesome powers she could detect but not yet wield. Al'Kiir would give them to her.

It was to the third table she hurried, for there were the fragments of scroll, the tattered pages of parchment and vellum that she had slowly and carefully gathered over the years. There was the dark knowledge of sorceries the world had attempted to forget, sorceries that would give her power. Hastily she pawed through them, for once careless of flakes that dropped from ancient pages. She found what she sought, and easily read in a language dead a thousand years. She was perhaps the last person in the world capable of reading that extinct tongue, for the scholar who had taught her she had had strangled with his own beard, his wife and children smothered in their beds to be doubly sure. Death guarded secrets far better than gold.

An eager gleam lit her dark eyes, and she read again the passage she had found.

Lo, call to the great god, entreating him, and set before the image, the
succedaneum, the bridge between worlds, as a beacon to glorify the way
of the god to thee.

She had thought this spoke of the priestess as bridge and beacon,
placing herself before the image of Al'Kiir, but that which lay beneath
the mountain was not an image. It was material body of the god. It must
be the image that was to be placed before the priestess during the rites.
The image. The bronze figure. It had to be. A thrill of triumph coursed
through her as she swept from the room.

In the corridor a serving girl busily lighting silver lamps hung from
the walls awkwardly made obeisance clutching her coal-pot and tongs.

Synelle had not realized how close the fall of darkness came. Twilight
was almost on the city; precious time wasted away as she stood there.
"Find Lord Taramenon," she commanded, "and bid him come to my
dressing chamber immediately. Run, girl!" The serving girl ran, for the
Lady Synelle's displeasures brought punishments best not thought of.

There was no need to ask if the handsome young lord was in her
mansion. Taramenon wished to be king, a foolish desire for one with
neither the proper blood lines nor money, and one he believed he had
hidden from her. It was true he was the finest sword in Ophir—she had
made a point of binding the best bladesmen of the land to her service—
but that counted little in the quest for a throne. He followed Synelle in
her own seeking because he believed in his arrogance that she would
find it impossible to rule without a husband by her side, because he
thought in his pride that he would be that husband. Thus he would gain
his crown. She had done nothing to dissuade him from the belief. Not
yet.

Four tirewomen, lithe matched blondes in robes that seemed to be
but vapors of silk, paused only to bend knee before hurrying forward,
moving as gracefully as dancers, as Synelle entered her dressing chamber. Her agents had gone to great efforts to find the four, sisters of
noble Corinthian blood with but a year separating each from the next;
Synelle herself had seen to the breaking and training of them. They
followed her submissively and silently as she strolled about the room,
removing her garments without once impeding her progress in any way.
In nakedness more resplendent than any satins or silks, long-limbed,
full-breasted and sleek, Synelle allowed them to minister to her. One
held an ivory-framed mirror while another used delicate fur brushes to
freshen the kohl on Synelle's eyelids and the rouge on her lips. The

others wiped her softly with cool, damp clothes, and annointed her with rare perfume of Vendhya, priced at one gold coin the drop.

The heavy tread of a man's boots sounded in the antechamber, and the tirewomen scurried to fetch a lounging robe of scarlet velvet. Synelle refused to hold out her arms for them to slip it on until the steps were at the very door.

Taramenon gasped at the tantalizing flash of silken curves, quickly sheathed, that greeted his entrance. He was tall, broad of shoulders and deep of chest, with an aquiline nose and deep brown eyes that had melted the hearts of many women. Synelle was glad that he did not follow the fashion in beards, being rather clean shaven. She was also pleased to note the quickening of his breath as he gazed at her.

"Leave me," she commanded, belting tight the red satin sash of her robe. The girls filed obediently from the room.

"Synelle," Taramenon said thickly as soon as they were gone, and stepped forward as if to take her in his arms.

She stopped him with an upraised hand. There was no time for such frivolity, no matter how amusing it might usually be to make him writhe with a desire she had no intention of slaking. Her studies told her there were powers to be gained from allowing a man to take her, and dedicating that taking to Al'Kiir, but she knew Taramenon's plans for her. And she had seen too many proud, independent women give themselves to a man only to discover they had given pride and independence as well. Not for her listening breathlessly for a lover's footstep, smiling at his laughter, weeping at his frowns, running to tend to his wants like the meanest slave. She would not risk such an outcome. She would never give herself to any man.

"Send your two best swordsmen after yourself to find and follow Galbro," she said, "without allowing him to become aware of it. He seeks a bronze, an image of Al'Kiir the length of a big man's forearm, but it is too important to trust to him. When he has located it for them, they are to secure it and bring it to me at once. Do you understand, Taramenon? Are you listening?"

"I listen," he said hoarsely, a touch of anger in his voice. "When you summoned me to your dressing chamber, at this hour, I thought something other than an accursed figure was on your mind."

A seductive smile caressed her full lips, and she moved closer to him, until her breasts were pressed against him. "There will be time for that when the throne is secure," she said softly. Her slender fingers brushed his mouth. "All the time in the world." His arms began to come up around her, but she stepped smoothly out of his embrace. "First the throne, Taramenon, and this bronze you call accursed is vital to attaining that. Send the men tonight. Now."

She watched a multitude of emotions cross his face, and wondered yet again at how transparent were the minds of men. No doubt he thought his features unreadable, yet she knew he was adding this incident to a host of others, cataloguing the ways he would make her pay for them once she was his.

"It will be done, Synelle," he growled at last.

When he was gone her smile turned to one of ambition triumphant. Power would be hers. The smile became full-throated laughter. It would be hers, and hers alone.

V

The night streets of Ianthe were dark and empty, yet near the palace of Baron Timeon a shadow moved. A cloaked and hooded figure pressed itself to the thickly-ornamented marble walls, and cool green eyes, slightly tilted above high cheekbones, surveyed the guards marching their rounds among the thick, fluted columns of alabaster. All very well, those guards, but would he who lay sleeping within remember his own thief's tricks?

The cloak was discarded, revealing a woman in tight-fitting tunic and snug breeches of buttery leather, with soft red boots on her feet. Moonlight shimmered on titian hair tied back from her face with a cord. Quickly she undid her sword belt and refastened it with her Turanian scimitar hanging down her back, then checked the leather sack hanging at her side. Strong, slender fingers tested the niveous marble carvings of the wall, and then she was climbing like a monkey.

Below the edge of the flat roof she paused. Boots grated on slate tiles. He remembered. Yet for all the reputation this Free-Company was building in the country, they were yet soldiers. Those on the roof walked regular paths, as sentries in a camp. The measured tread came closer, closer. And then it was receding.

As agile as a panther, she was onto the roof, running on silent feet, losing herself in the shadows of two score chimneys. At the drop of the central garden around which the entire palace was arranged, she fell to her belly and peered down. There were the windows of his sleeping chamber. They were dark. So he did sleep. She would have expected him to be carousing with yet another in a long line of all too willing

wenches. It was one of the things she remembered most about him, his
eye for women and theirs for him.

Knowledge had been easily come by. Not even bribes had been necessary. All that had been required was for her to pretend to be a serving
woman—though that had been no small a task in itself, given her lush
beauty; serving maids with curves like hers soon found themselves pro-
moted to the master's bed—and chat to the women of Baron Timeon's
palace in the markets. They had been eager to tell about the great house
in which they served, about their fat master and his constantly changing
parade of women, about the hard-eyed warriors who had hired themselves to him. Especially about the warriors they had been willing to
talk, giggling and teasing each other about returning from the stable
with hay covering the back of a robe and stolen moments in secluded
corners of the garden.

She would have wagered there were guards in that garden as well as
on the roof, but those did not worry her. From the leather sack she
produced a rope woven of black-dyed silk, to the end of which was
fastened a padded grapnel. The metal prongs hooked on the scrollwork
along the roof-edge; the rope fell invisibly into the darkness below. It
was just long enough to reach the window she sought.

A short climb downward, and she was inside the room. It was as black
as Zandru's Seventh Hell. A dagger found its way into her hand . . . and
she stopped dead. What if there were some error in her information?
She did not want to kill the wrong man. She had to be sure.

Mentally cursing her own foolishness, she felt in the darkness for a
table, for a lamp . . . and yes, a coal-box and tongs. She puffed softly on
the coal till it glowed, held it to the wick. Light bloomed, and she gasped
at the apparition on the table beside the brass lamp. Horned malevolence
glared at her. It was but a bronze figure, yet she sensed evil in the thing,
and primeval instinct deep within her told her that evil was directed at
women. Could the man she sought have changed so much as to keep
such monstrosity in his chamber? The man she sought!

Heart pounding, she spun, dagger raised. He still slept, a young giant
sprawled in his slumber. Conan of Cimmeria. Soft-footed she crept
closer to his bed, her eyes drinking him in, the planes of his face, the
breadth of his shoulders, the massive arms that had . . .

Stop, she commanded herself. How many wrongs had this man com-
mitted against her? She had lived on the plains of Zamora and Turan
with the freedom of the hawk till Conan had come, and brought with
him the destruction of her band of brigands. For his stupid male honor
and the matter of a silly oath she had made him swear in a moment of

anger, he had allowed her to be sold into slavery, into a zenana in Sultanapur. Every time the switch had kissed her buttocks, every time she had been forced to dance naked for the pleasure of the fat merchant who had been her master and his friends, all these could be laid at Conan's feet.

When at last she had escaped and fled to Nemedia, become the queen of the smugglers of that country, he had appeared again. And before he was done she must needs pack her hard-acquired wealth on sumpter animals and flee again.

She had escaped him, then, but she could not escape his memory, the memory of his building fires in her, fires that she came to crave like the smoker of the yellow lotus craved his pipe. That memory had hounded her, driven her into riotous living and excesses that shocked even the jaded court of Aquilonia. Only when all her gold was gone had she known freedom again. Once more she had taken up the life she loved, living by her wits and her sword. She had sought a new country, Ophir, and raised a new band of rogues.

How many months gone had the first rumors come to her of a huge northerner whose Free-Company was a terror to all who opposed him? How long had she tried to convince herself that it was not the same man who always brought ruin to her? Once more she found herself within the same borders as he, but this time she would not flee. She would be free of him at last. With a sob she raised the dagger high and brought it down.

A strange sound penetrated Conan's dreams—a woman's sob, he thought drowsily—and brought him awake. He had just time to see a shape beside his bed, see the descending dagger, and then he was rolling aside.

The dagger slashed into the mattress where his chest had been, and the force of the missed stab brought his attacker down on top of him. Instantly he seized the shape—the back of his brain noted a curious softness—and hurled it across the room. In the same motion he leaped from the bed, seized the worn leather-wrapped hilt of his broadsword and slung the scabbard aside. It was then that he saw his assailant clearly for the first time.

"Karela!" he exclaimed.

The auburn-haired beauty rising warily from the floor near the wall snarled at him. "Yes, Derketo blast your eyes! And would she had made you sleep just one moment more."

His gaze went to the dagger thrust into his mattress, and his eyebrows raised. But all he said was, "I thought you went to Aquilonia to live the life of a lady."

"I am no lady," she breathed. "I am a woman! And woman enough to put an end to you once and for all!" Her hand went to her shoulder, and suddenly she was rushing at him, brandishing three feet of curved razor-sharp steel.

Anger blazed in Conan's icy blue eyes, and he swung his sword to meet hers with a crash. Shock appeared on Karela's face, her mouth dropping open with incredulity as her blade was nearly wrenched from her grasp. She took a step back, and from that moment was ever defending from his flashing edge. He did not force her back, but every pace backwards she took, he followed. And she could not but move backwards, away from the force of those blows, panting, desperate to attack yet with no slightest opportunity. If he made certain that his sword struck only hers, he also made certain that every blow had his full strength behind it, rocking her to her heels. The cool smile on his face, calm even as he battled her, struck to her heart. It mocked her, wounding more deeply than ever steel could.

"Derketo take you, you over-muscled barbar," she rasped.

With a sharp ring her scimitar was hurled from her. For a breath she froze, then dove for the fallen blade.

Conan tossed his broadsword aside and seized the back of her tunic as she leaped. Fabric already strained by more than generous callimastian curves split down the front; her momentum carried her partly out of her tunic, stripping her half-way to the waist. In an instant Conan had twisted his fistful of cloth, trapping her arms at her sides. He found he had caught a spitting, kicking wildcat. But, he noted, a wildcat who still had the finest, roundest set of breasts he had seen in many a day.

"Coward!" she shouted. "Spawn of a diseased goat! Fight me blade to blade, and I'll spit you like the capon you are!"

Easily he pulled her over to the bed, seated himself, and jerked her across his knees. Easily he controlled her frenzied thrashings.

"Oh, no!" she gasped. "Not that! Cimmerian, I'll cut your heart out! I'll slice your manhood for—"

Her diatribe was cut off with a howl as his big hand landed forcefully on her taut-breeched buttocks.

A fist thumped against the heavy wooden door, and Machaon's voice sounded from the corridor. "What's happening in there, Conan? Are you all right?"

"All is well," Conan replied. "I'm tending to an unruly wench."

That provoked furious struggles from Karela, futile against his iron grasp. "Release me, Cimmerian," she growled, "or I'll see you hanging by your heels over a slow fire. Unhand me, Derketo shrivel your manhood!"

Conan answered her with a smack that brought another howled curse. "You tried to kill me, wench," he said slowly, punctuating each word with his calloused palm. "You've been untrustworthy from the first day I laid eyes on you. In Shadizar you'd have let me be slain without a word of warning." Karela's shrieked imprecation became incoherent; she kicked frantically at the air, but he did not pause. "In the Kezankian Mountains you betrayed me to a sorcerer. I saved your life there, but in Nemedia you bribed my jailors with gold to torture me. Why? Why a knife for my heart while I lay sleeping? Have I ever harmed you? Is your soul filled with treachery, woman?"

A half-formed plea among her cries penetrated his rage, killing his anger and staying his hand. Karela pleading? Whatever she had done or tried to do, that was not right. As he could not kill her, neither could he bring himself to break her pride completely. He pushed her off his lap to fall with a thump to her knees.

Her tear-streaked face twisted with sobs, Karela's slender hands stole back gingerly to her buttocks. Then, as if suddenly remembering Conan's presence, she tore them away again; moist green eyes glared daggers at him. "May Derketo blast your eyes, Cimmerian," she said jerkily, "and Erlik take your soul for a plaything. No man has ever treated me as you do and lived."

"And no one," he said quietly, "man or woman, has ever dealt with me as treacherously as you have without incurring my enmity. And yet I cannot find it in me to hate you. But this! Murder was never your way, Karela. Was it for gold? You've always loved gold above all else."

"It was for me!" she spat at him, pounding a small fist on her thigh. Her eyes squeezed shut, and her voice dropped to a whisper. "Your presence turns my muscles to wine. Your eyes on me sap my will. How can I not want you dead?"

Conan shook his head in wonderment. Never had he pretended to understand women, least of all this fierce female falcon. Once more he was convinced that whatever gods had created men had not been the gods who created women.

As she knelt there in disarray, naked to the waist, Conan felt other stirrings than amazement. She was a woman of marvelous curves to brighten the eye, a wonderful blend of softness and firmness to delight the touch. Always she had been able to rouse his desire, though she often attempted to use that to bend him to her will. Abruptly he decided that learning why and how she had come to Ophir could wait. Gently he drew her between his knees.

Her clear green eyes, still tremulous, fluttered open. "What are you doing?" she demanded unsteadily.

He lifted the tattered tunic from her and threw it aside.

Small white teeth bit into her full underlip, and she shook her head. "No," she said breathlessly. "I will not. No. Please."

Easily he lifted her to the bed, disposed of her soft boots, peeled the tight breeches from her long legs.

"I hate you, Conan." But there was a curious note of pleading in her voice for such a statement. "I came to kill you. Do you not realize that?"

He plucked her dagger from his mattress and held it in two fingers before her gaze. "Take it, if you truly wish me dead."

For the space of three breaths his eyes held hers. Convulsively she turned her face aside. Conan smiled and, casually tossing the dagger to the floor, set about producing cries from her that had naught to do with pain.

VI

Sunlight steaming through the windows woke Conan. He opened his eyes and found himself staring at Karela's dagger, once more driven to the hilt into his mattress. The blade held a fragment of parchment. Karela was gone.

"Blast the woman," he muttered, ripping the parchment free. It was covered with a bold, sprawling hand.

Another debt added to those you already owe me. The next time you will die, Cimmerian. I will not run from another country because of you. By the Teats of Derketo I swear, I will not.

Frowning, he crumpled the parchment in his fist. It was like the woman, leaving before he woke, with threats but without answers to any of his questions. He had thought she was done with threats altogether; she had enjoyed the night as well as he, of that she had left no doubt.

Hurriedly he dressed and headed into the bowels of the palace. He was still settling his swordbelt about his waist when he entered the long room where his company took their meals, near the kitchen Timeon had given over to them. The simple hearty provender Fabio prepared offended his own cooks, so the lord said. Some score and a half of the mercenary warriors, unarmored but weapons as always belted on, were scattered among crude trestle-tables that had been rooted out of storage in the stables. Machaon and Narus sat by themselves, their attention to the leather jacks of ale in their fists and the wooden bowls of stew before them not so great that they did not note his entrance.

"Ho, Cimmerian," Machaon called out loudly. "How was that, ah, unruly wench last night?" A sprinkling of rough laughter made it clear he had shared his story with the rest.

Could not the accursed fool keep his tongue behind his teeth, Conan thought. Aloud he said, "Double the guards on the roof, Machaon. And see they keep eyes and ears open. A parade of temple virgins would be undetected up there as it is."

Narus laughed dolefully into his ale as Conan straddled a bench across from them. "The wench was *too* unruly, was she? 'Tis the way of all women, to be least accomodating when you want them most."

"Do you have to beat all of them?" Taurianus called, a jealous edge to his bantering tone. "I thought her shrieks would bring the roof down."

"Food!" Conan bellowed. "Must I die of hunger?"

"There's a morsel in that kitchen," Machaon chuckled, "I could consume whole." He nudged Narus as Julia hurried from the kitchen, balancing with some difficulty a bowl of stew, a loaf of bread and a mug of ale.

She was much changed from the last time Conan had seen her. Her long auburn hair was tied with a green ribbon, and pulled back from a face bare of rouge or kohl but streaked with sweat from the heat of the kitchen fires. Her long robe of soft white wool, soot smudged and damp with soapy water, was meant to be modest, he assumed, but it clung to her curves in a way that drew the eye of every man in the room.

"You must speak to that man," she said as she set Conan's meal before him. He stared at her questioningly, and she flung out an arm dramatically toward the kitchen. "That man. Fabio. He threatened me . . . with a switch. Tell him who I am."

Conan scooped up a horn spoon full of stew. In one form or another it served the men of the company for both meals of the day, morning and night. "You work in the kitchens," he said. "That is Fabio's domain. Did a queen somehow come to scrub his pots he'd switch her an she did it badly. You'd best learn to do as he tells you."

Julia sputtered in indignation, the more so when Machaon laughed.

"You've too many airs, wench," the grizzled veteran chortled. "Besides, you're well padded for it." And he applied a full-fingered pinch to punctuate his claim.

Squealing, the auburn-haired girl leaped. To seize Conan's bowl and upend it over Machaon's head. Narus convulsed with laughter so hard that he began coughing.

"Fool girl," Conan growled. "I was eating that. Fetch me another, and quick about it."

"Fetch your own," she snapped back. "Or starve, if you wish to eat with the likes of him." Spinning on her heel, she stalked into the kitchen, her back rigid.

A stunned Machaon sat raking thick gobbets of stew from his face with his fingers. "I've a mind to take a switch to that conceited jade myself," he muttered.

"Go easy with her," Conan said. "She'll learn in time, whether she will or no. She is used to a gentler way of life than that which faces her now."

"I'd like to gentle her," Machaon replied. "But I'll keep my hands from her as she's yours, Cimmerian."

Conan shook his head. "She's not mine. Nor yours either, till she says she is. There are bawds aplenty in the town, is that your need."

The two men stared at him perplexedly, but they nodded, and he was satisfied. They might think he was in truth laying claim to the girl— though doubtless wondering why he wished to make a secret of it—but they would not demand more of her than she was willing to give. And they would speak it among the company, giving her protection with the others as well. He was not sure why he did not, save for Karela. It was difficult for him to think too much of other women when that fiery wench was about.

In any case, she was likely to give him ten times the trouble Julia did, and without trying half so hard. Karela was a woman who kept her word. If he did not find a way to stop her she would put steel between his ribs yet. Worse, she had a mind for vengeance like a Stygian. It would be like her to destroy the Free-Company, if she could, before killing him.

"Have either of you heard rumors of a woman bandit?" he asked in a carefully casual tone.

"I'll have to bathe to get clean of this," Machaon growled, picking a lump of meat from his hair. He popped it into his mouth. "I've heard no such tales. Women are meant for other things than brigands."

"Nor I," Narus said. "Women are not suited to the violent trades. Except perhaps that red-haired jade we encountered in Nemedia. She claimed to be a bandit, though I'd never heard of her. The buxom trull was offended I did not know her fame. Remember?"

"She's no trull," Conan said, "and she'll carve your liver does she hear you name her so." Immediately the words were gone he wished he had held his tongue.

"She's here!" Machaon exclaimed. "What was her name?"

"Karela," Narus said. "A temper like a thornbush, that one has."

Machaon laughed suddenly. "She was the wench last night." He shrugged at Conan's glare. "Well, there's no woman in the palace who'd need her bottom warmed to crawl into your blankets. It must have been her. I'd not bed her without my sword and armor, and mayhap a man to watch my back."

"It was her," the Cimmerian said, and added grudgingly, "She tried to put a dagger in me."

"That sounds like the woman I remember," Narus chortled. "From the yells, I'd say you taught her better manners."

"Twould be sport," Machaon crowed, "to stuff her and our Julia into a sack together."

Tears ran down Narus' face from his laughter. "I would pay coin to see that fight."

"Erlik take the pair of you," Conan snarled. "There's more danger in that woman than sport. She thinks she has a grievance against me, and she will cause trouble for the company if she can."

"What can a woman do?" Narus said. "Nothing."

"I would not like to wager my life on that," Conan told him. "Not when the woman is Karela. I want you to ask questions in the taverns and the brothels. 'Tis possible she's changed her name, but she cannot change the way she looks. A red-haired woman bandit with a body like one of Derketo's handmaidens will be known to someone. Tell the others to keep their eyes open as well."

"Why can you not manage her grievance as you did last night?" Machaon asked. "A smack on the bottom and to bed. Oh, very well—" he raised his hands in surrender as Conan opened his mouth for more angry words—"I will ask questions in the brothels. At least it gives me an excuse to spend more time at the House of the Doves."

"Forget not the House of the Honeyed Virgins," Narus added.

Conan scowled wordlessly. The fools did not know Karela as he did. He hoped for the sake of the company that they had time to learn before it was too late. Abruptly he became aware of the horn spoon of stew he still held, and put it in his mouth. "Fabio's cooking horse again," he said when he'd swallowed.

Narus froze with his own spoon half lifted. "Horse?" he gasped. Machaon stared at his bowl as if he expected it to leap from the table at him.

"Horse," Conan said, tossing his spoon to the rough planks. Narus gagged. Not until he was out of the room did the Cimmerian permit a smile to grow on his face. The meat tasted like beef to him, but those two deserved the worrying they were going to do over what Fabio was feeding them.

"Conan!" Julia ran out of the door he had just exited, bouncing off his chest as he turned. Her hands clutched her robe at the waist, twisting nervously. "Conan, you didn't . . . that is, last night . . . I mean . . ." She stopped and took a deep breath. "Conan, you must speak to Fabio. He struck me. Look." Half-turning she lifted her robe to expose the alabastrine rounds of her buttocks.

Conan was barely able to make out a pink stripe across the undercurve. He raised his gaze to her face. Her eyes were closed; the tip of her tongue continually wetted her full lips.

"I'll speak to him," he said gravely. Her eyes shot open, and a smile blossomed on her face. "I'll tell him he must strike harder than that to make any impression on a stubborn pot-girl."

"Conan!" she wailed. Hastily she covered herself, smoothing the pale wool over her hips. Her eyes became as hard as sapphires. "You had a woman in your . . . your chamber last night. I . . . I was passing in the corridor, and I heard."

He smiled, and watched a blush spread over her cheeks. So she had had her ear pressed to his door, had she? "And what concern is that of yours?" he asked. "You are here to scrub pots and stir the stew, to fetch and carry for Fabio. Not to be wandering parts of the palace where you have no business."

"But you kissed me," she protested. "And the way you kissed me! You cannot make me feel like that, then calmly walk away. I'm a woman, curse you! I'm eighteen! I will not be dismissed like a plaything."

For the second time in the space of hours, he mused, a woman was protesting her womanhood to him. But what a contrast between them. Karela was bold and defiant even as she melted with passion; Julia frightened despite her bluff front. Karela knew well the ways of men and women; Julia was ravaged by a kiss. Karela knew who she was and what she wanted; Julia . . .

"Do you want to come to my bed?" he said softly, taking her chin in his hand and tilting her face up. Scarlet suffused her face and neck, but she did not try to wrench free. "Say yes, and I'll carry you there this moment."

"The others," she whispered. "They'll know."

"Forget them. 'Tis you must chose."

"I cannot, Conan." She sobbed when he released her, and leaned toward him as if seeking his touch. "I want to say yes, but I fear to. Can you not just . . . take me? Men do such things, I know. Why must you put this burden I do not want on me?"

Barely four years seperated them, yet at that moment he felt it could as well be four hundred. "Because you are not a slave, Julia. You say you are a woman, but when you are truly a woman you will be able to say yes or no, and know it is what you mean to say. But till then . . . well, I take only women to my bed, not frightened girls."

"Erlik curse you," she said bitterly. Instantly she was contrite, one hand raised to touch his cheek. "No, I didn't mean that. You confuse me so. When you kissed me you made me want to be a woman. Kiss me again, and make me remember. Kiss me, and give me the courage I need."

Conan reached for her, and at that instant a bellow of pain and rage echoed down the halls. He spun, grabbing instead for the leather-wrapped hilt of his sword. The cry came again, from above he was certain.

"Timeon," he muttered. His blade came into his hand, and he was running, shouting as he ran. "Rouse yourselves, you poxed rouges! 'Tis the baron screaming like a woman in birth! To arms, curse you!"

Servants and slaves ran hysterically, shrieking and waving their arms at his shouts. Men of the company knocked them aside without compunction as they poured out of the corners where they had been taking their ease. Helmets were tugged on and swords waved as a growing knot of warriors followed the big Cimmerian up marble stairs.

In the corridor outside Timeon's chamber the two guards Conan had caused to be set there stood staring dumbfounded at the ornately carved door. Conan slammed into that door at a dead run, smashing it open.

Timeon lay in the middle of a multi-hued Iranistani carpet, his body wracked by convulsions, heels drumming, plump hands clawing at his throat. His head was thrown back, and every time he managed to fight a breath he loosed it again in a scream. Tivia, his leman, stood with her back to a wall, clutching a cloak about her tightly, her eyes, large and dark, fixed on the helplessly jerking man in an expression of horror. An overturned goblet lay near Timeon, and a puddle of wine soaking into the rug.

"Zandru's Hells!" Conan growled. His eye lit on Machaon, forcing his way through the men crowding the hall. "A physician, Machaon. Quickly! Timeon's poisoned!"

"Boros is in the kitchens," the tattoed man called back. Conan hesitated, and the other saw it. "Curse it, Cimmerian, it'll take half the day to get another."

Timeon's struggles were growing weaker; his screams had become moans of agony. Conan nodded. "Fetch him, then."

Machaon disappeared, and Conan turned back to the man on the floor. How had the fool gotten himself poisoned? The answer might mean life or death to him and the rest of the company. And he had to have the answer before the matter was turned over to the King's torturers. Valdric might ignore the great part of what was happening in his country, but he would not ignore the murder of a noble in the very shadow of his throne.

"Narus!" Conan shouted. The hollow-faced man stuck his head into the room. "Secure the palace. No one leaves, nor any message, till I say. Hurry, man!"

As Narus left Machaon hurried Boros into the room. The former mage's apprentice looked sober at least, Conan was glad to see.

"He's poisoned," the Cimmerian said.

Boros looked at him as he might at a child. "I can see that."

Fumbling in his pouch the gray-bearded man knelt beside Timeon. Quickly he produced a smooth white stone the size of a man's fist and a small knife. With difficulty he straightened one of the baron's arms, pushed up the sleeve of his robe, and made a deep cut. As blood welled up he pressed the white stone to the cut. When he took his hands away the stone remained, tendrils of black appearing in it.

"Bezoar-stone," Boros announced to the room. "Sovereign for poison. A physician's tool, strictly speaking, but I find it useful. Yes."

He tugged at his full beard and bent to study the stone. It was full black, now, and as they watched it became blacker, as a burned cinder, as a raven's wing, and blacker still. Suddenly the stone shattered. In the same moment a last breath rattled in Timeon's throat, and the fat baron was still.

"He's dead," Conan breathed. "I thought you said that accursed stone was sovereign for poison!"

"Look at it!" Boros wailed. "My stone is ruined. 'Twould take poison enough to kill ten men to do that. I could not have saved him with a sack full of bezoar-stones."

"It is murder, then," Narus breathed. A murmur of disquiet rippled through the men in the corridor.

Conan's hand tightened on his sword. Most of the three-score who followed him now he had recruited in Ophir, a polyglot crew from half a dozen lands, and their allegiance to him was not as strong as that of the original few. They had faced battle with him often—such was the way of the life they led, and accepted by them—but unless he found the

murderer quickly fear of being put to the question would do what no
enemy had ever been able to. Send them scattering to the four winds.

"Do you want me to find who put the poison in the wine?" Boros
asked.

For a moment Conan could only gape. "You can do that?" he demanded finally. "Erlik blast you, are you sober enough? An you make
some drunkard's mistake, I'll shave your corpse."

"I'm as sober as a priest of Mitra," Boros replied. "More so than
most. You, girl. The wine came from that?" He pointed to a crystal
flagon, half-filled with ruby wine, on a table near the bed. Tivia's mouth
opened, but no words came out. Boros shook his head. "No matter. I
see no other, so the wine must have come from there." Climbing to his
feet with a grunt, he delved into his pouch once more.

"Is he truly sober?" Conan said quietly to Machaon.

The grizzled man tugged nervously at the three thin gold rings dangling from the lobe of his right ear. "I think so. Fabio likes his company,
but doesn't let him drink. Usually."

The Cimmerian sighed. Avoiding the hot irons meant trusting a man
who might give them all leprosy by mistake.

With a stick of charcoal Boros scribed figures on the tabletop around
the flagon of wine. Slowly he began to chant, so softly that the words
were inaudible to the others in the room. With his left hand he sprinkled
powder from a twist of parchment over the flagon; his right traced ob-
scure patterns in the air. A red glow grew in the crystal container.

"There," Boros said, dropping his hands. "A simple thing, really."
He stared at the flagon and frowned. "Cimmerian, the poisoner is close
by. The glow tells."

"Crom," Conan muttered. The men who had been in the doorway
crowded back into the hall.

"The closer the wine is the one who poisoned it," Boros said, "the
more strongly it will glow."

"Get on with it," Conan commanded.

Picking up the flask, Boros moved closer to Machaon. The glow remained unchanged. As he moved past the door, briefly thrusting the
flask toward the men outside, it dimmed. Abruptly the bearded man
pressed the wine-filled vessel against Narus' chest. The hollow-cheeked
man started back; the glow did not brighten.

"A pity," Boros murmured. "You look the part. And that leaves
only . . ."

All eyes in the room went to Tivia, still standing with her back
pressed against the wall. Under their gaze she started, then shook her

head vigorously, but still said nothing. Boros padded toward her, holding the flagon of glowing wine before him. With each step the light from the wine became brighter until, as he stopped not a pace from the girl, the crystal he held seemed to contain red fire.

She avoided looking at the luminous vessel. "No," she cried. "Tis a trick of some sort. He who placed the poison in the wine put a spell on it."

"Sorcerer as well as poisoner?" Boros asked mildly.

With an oath Conan strode across the room. "The truth, girl! Who paid you?" She shook her head in denial. "I've no stomach for torturing woman," he continued, "but mayhap Boros has some spell to force the truth from you."

"Well, let me see," the old man mused. "Why, yes, I believe I have just the thing. Aging. The longer you take to tell the truth, the older you'll become. But it works rapidly, child. I should speak quickly, were I you, or you may well leave this room a toothless crone. Pity."

Tivia's eyes swiveled desperately from the grim-faced Cimmerian to the kindly-appearing man, calmly stroking his beard, who had voiced the awful threat. "I do not know his name," she said, sagging against the wall. "He wore a mask. I was given fifty pieces of gold and the powder, with fifty more to come when Timeon was dead. I can tell you no more." Sobbing, she slid to the floor. "Whatever you do to me, I can tell you no more."

"What do we do with her now?" Machaon asked. "Give her over to the judges?"

"They'll have her beheaded for slaying a noble," Narus said. "A shame, that. She's too pretty to die like that, and it should hardly count a crime to kill a fool like Timeon."

"Giving her to the judges won't help us," Conan said. He wished he could carry on this conversation with Machaon and Narus in privacy, but the door was open and most of the company had jammed themselves into the corridor. Shut them out now and there might not be a dozen left when the door was opened again. He took a deep breath and went on. "We've lost our patron to an assassin. Ordinarily that would be the death knell for a Free-Company." Uneasy mutters rose in the hall, and he lifted his voice to a roar. "Ordinarily, I said. But Timeon was a supporter of Count Antimides to succeed Valdric. Perhaps we can take service with Antimides, if I deliver the murderer to his hands." At least it was a chance, he thought. Antimides might well find them employment simply to keep secret his own ambitions.

"Antimides?" Machaon said doubtfully. "Cimmerian, 'tis said he's one of the few nobles who does *not* seek the throne at Valdric's death." There were murmured agreements from the hall.

"Timeon spoke too freely in his cups," Conan said. "Of how Antimides was so clever he had fooled everyone. Of how he himself would be one of the most powerful lords of Ophir once Antimides took the throne."

"Well enough," Machaon said, "but will Antimides take us in service? If he pretends to be aloof from the struggle to succeed Valdric, how will he have need for a Free-Company?"

"He'll take us," Conan said with more confidence than he felt. "Or find us service. I'll take oath on it." Besides, he thought, it was the only course they had open.

"That aging spell," Narus said suddenly. "It seems a strange sort of spell, even for folk as strange as sorcerers are reputed to be. Why would you learn a thing like that?"

"Cheese," Boros replied with a chuckle. "I had a taste for well-aged cheese when I was young, and I created the spell for that. My master flogged me for wasting time. In truth, I doubt it would work on a human."

"You tricked me," Tivia gasped. "Whoreson dog!" she shrieked, launching herself at the bearded man with fingernails clawed. Conan caught her by the arms, but she still struggled to get to the old man, who stared at her in amazement. "I'll pluck your eyes, you old fraud! You dung beetle's offspring! I'll take your manhood off in slices! Your mother was a drunken trull, and your father a poxed goat!"

"Get me a cord to tie her wrists," Conan said, then added, "And a gag." Her tirade was becoming obscene to the point where Machaon was listening with interest. The Cimmerian glared at Narus, who looked abashed as he hurried to fetch what Conan required. It was all he needed, to have to carry a shrieking girl through the streets. Narus returned with strips of cloth, and, muttering to himself, Conan bound his writhing prisoner.

VII

Conan drew few stares as he made his way through Ianthe, even with a wiggling, cloak-wrapped woman over his massive shoulder. Or because of the woman. In the streets of the capital, eaten by fear and riddled with suspicion, no one wanted to interfere in something that might even possibly involve them in the troubles beyond the walls of the city. They could see a kidnapping take place or murder done and walk by looking the other way. Who the young giant might be, or why he carried a woman like a sack of grain, no one wanted to know. It could be dangerous to know. It could be dangerous even to appear curious. Therefore none looked too closely at the big Cimmerian of his burden.

He had already been to Antimides' palace. With more than a little difficulty—for the well-fed chamberlain, as proud in his manner as any noble of the land, had seen no reason to give any information whatsoever to a stranger, and a barbarian at that—he learned that the count was a guest of the King. King Valdric liked Antimides' conversation, claiming it was better tonic than any of his physicians or sorcerers could compound. Lord Antimides would be remaining at the royal palace for several days. It was remarkable how free the chamberlain had become with his tongue once a big hand had lifted him until his velvet shoes dangled clear of the floor.

The royal palace of Ophir was a fortress rather than the marble and alabaster edifices erected in the city by nobles. It was not by chance that the King dwelt behind massive granite walls while his lords spent their days in the capital in manors more suited to pleasure than defense. More than once the throne of Ophir had only been held secure by a King taking refuge behind those walls, betimes even refuge from his own nobles. They, having no strong points within Ianthe, had always been forced to abandon the city to the King. And as control of Ianthe was the key to keeping the crown, it was said that whoever held the royal palace held Ophir.

The guards at the towering barbican gate before the royal palace stirred themselves at Conan's approach. A paunch-bellied sergeant, the small triangular beard that was in favor among the nobles waggling on his chins, stepped forward and raised a hand for the Cimmerian to halt.

"What's this, then? Do you mercenaries now think to give us your left-over women?" He chuckled over his shoulder to the pikemen behind him, enjoying his own wit. "Off with you. The royal palace is no place for your drunken carousing. And if you must bind your women, keep them from sight of the army or we will be forced to take cognizance of it."

"She's a gift for Count Antimides," Conan replied, and managed a conspiratorial wink. "A tasty pastry from my patron. Perhaps he wishes to curry favor with a great lord." Tivia redoubled her squirming; unintelligible noises came from behind the twist of rag gagging her.

"She seems not to like the idea," the sergeant chortled.

Conan grinned back at him. "I wager Lord Antimides will know what to do with her, whether she likes it or not."

"That he will. Wait you here." Belly shaking with mirth, the soldier disappeared through the gate. In a few moments he was back with a slender man, his black hair streaked with gray, in a tabard of gold and green, Antimides' colors.

The slender man turned a supercilious gaze on the big Cimmerian. "I am Ludovic," he said sharply, "Count Antimides' steward. You've come to see the count? Who are you?" He appeared to ignore Conan's burden.

"I am Conan of Cimmeria, Captain of the Free-Company in service to Baron Timeon."

Ludovic stroked his beard thoughtfully with a single finger, his eyes traveling to the wriggling girl over Conan's shoulder, then nodded. "Follow me," he commanded. "Perhaps the count will grant you a brief time."

Conan's mouth tightened. All this obsequiousness and play-acting was enough to turn his stomach. But he followed the slender man under the portcullis and into the royal palace.

If a fortress from the outside, the seat of the Kings of Ophir was still a palace within. Gleaming white marble walls, floors covered with a profusion of many-hued mosaicks, fluted alabaster columns. Golden lamps depending on silver chains from high vaulted ceilings, painted with scenes from Ophir's glorious history. Gardens, surrounded by shaded colonnades and filled with rare blossoms from the far corners of the world. Courtyards, tiled with greenstone, where ladies of the court in diaphanous gowns that concealed little of their curves dabbled pale fingers in the babbling waters of ornate fountains.

Their passage left a wake of giggles and murmurs, and stares at the towering Cimmerian and the burden across his broad shoulder. No fear was there here in noticing the unusual, and commenting on it. High-born, hot-eyed women speculated loudly on the pleasures to be found in being carried so—without the cords, of course.

The slender man scowled and increased his pace, muttering under his breath. Conan followed and wished the steward would go faster still.

Finally Ludovic stopped before a wide door carved with the ancient arms of Ophir. "Wait," he said. "I will see if the count will give you audience."

Conan opened his mouth, but before he could speak, the slender man disappeared through the door, carefully closing it behind him. Audience, he thought disgustedly. Antimides already acted as if he wore the crown.

The door swung open, and Ludovic beckoned him. "Hurry, man. Count Antimides can spare you but a few moments."

Muttering to himself Conan bore his burden within. Immediately he saw the room, his eyebrows lifted in surprise. Perhaps to the casual observer the room would not seem odd, but to one who knew Antimides' ambitions it was clearly a small throne room. An arras depicting a famous battle scene, Moranthes the Great defeating the last army of Acheron in the passes of the Karpash Mountains, hung across one wall. On a dais before the great tapestry was a massive chair with a high back, its dark wood carved with a profusion of leopards and eagles, the ancient symbols of Ophirean Kings.

If the chair seemed not grand enough by itself for a throne, the man seated there made it so. Deep-seated, piercing black eyes flanked a strong, prominent nose. His mouth was hard above a firm chin with its precisely trimmed fashionable beard. Long fingers bearing swordsman's callouses played with a ruby chain hanging across the chest of a robe of cloth-of-gold, slashed to show emerald silk beneath.

"My lord count," Ludovic said, bowing to the man on the dais, "this is the man calling himself Conan of Cimmeria."

" 'Tis my name," Conan said. He lowered Tivia to the thick-carpeted floor, layered in costly multi-colored rugs from Vendhya and Iranistan. She crouched there silently, fright seeming at last to have stilled her rage.

"Count Antimides," Ludovic pronounced grandly, "wishes to know why you have come to him."

"The girl is Tivia," Conan replied, "late mistress of Baron Timeon. Until she did poison him this morn."

Antimides raised a finger, and Ludovic spoke again. "But why have you brought her to him? She should be given to the King's justices."

Conan wondered why the count did not speak for himself. But the ways of nobles were as strange as those of sorcerers. And there were more troublesome matters to concern him. Time for his gamble had come. "As Baron Timeon supported Count Antimides in his quest to succeed Valdric, it seemed proper to bring her before the count. My Free-Company is now without a patron. Perhaps the count can find—"

"My quest!" Antimides burst out, his face choleric with rage. "How dare you accuse me of . . ." He broke off, grinding his teeth. Ludovic stared at him in obvious surprise. Tivia, her mouth working futilely at her gag, seemed transfixed by his gaze. "You, jade," he breathed. "So you poisoned your master, and were caught at it by this barbar mercenary. Pray that justice is mercifully swift for you. Take her away, Ludovic."

Desperately and futilely Tivia attempted to force words past the cloth gagging her. She flung herself against her bonds as the steward seized her, but the slender man bore her behind the arras with little effort. A door opened and closed behind the hanging, and her cries were cut off.

The Cimmerian reminded himself that Tivia was a self-confessed murderer, and for gold. Still, it pained him to have a hand in a woman's death. In his belief women were not meant to die violently; such was for men. He forced himself to stop thinking of her, and put his attention on the hawk-eyed man on the dais. "Count Antimides, there is still the matter of my Free-Company. Our reputation is well known, and—"

"Your reputation!" Antimides snarled. "Your patron assassinated, and you speak of your reputation. Worse, you come to me with vile accusations. I should have your tongue torn out!"

"Pray, Antimides, what accusations are these to put you in such a rage?"

Both men started at the questions; so intent had they been on each other that neither had noticed the entrance of another. Now that Conan saw her, though, he drank her in appreciatively. Long of leg and full of breast, an exotic beauty blending the extraordinary combination of hair like fine, spun silver and large, dark eyes that spoke of deep wells of untapped passion, she moved with sinuous grace, her shimmering scarlet robe, barely opaque and slit up one thigh to a rounded hip, clinging to the curves of breast and thigh.

"Why do you come here, Synelle?" Antimides demanded. "I will not be bothered by your sharp tongue today."

"I have not seen this chamber since you came to the royal palace, Antimides," she said with a dangerous smile. "Seeing it, a suspicious mind might think you sought the crown after all, no matter your public pronouncements of disdain for those who strive beyond the city walls." Antimides' face darkened, and his knuckles grew white on the arms of the chair; Synelle's smile deepened. "But as to why I came. It is said in the palace that a giant northlander came to you bearing a woman wrapped like a package from a fish-monger. Surely I could not miss seeing that? But where is this gift? She is a gift, is she not?"

"This does not concern you, Synelle," Antimides grated. "Go back to your woman's concerns. Have you not needlework waiting?"

Synelle merely arched her eyebrows and moved closer to Conan. "And this is the barbarian? He is certainly as large as was reported. I have a liking for big men." Shivering ostentatiously, she fingered the small, overlapping steel plates on his hauberk. "Are you a mercenary, my handsome northlander?"

He smiled down at her, preening under her sultry look despite himself. "I am captain of a Free-Company, my lady. My name is Conan."

"Conan." Her lips caressed the name. "And why do you come to Antimides, Conan?"

"Enough, Synelle," Antimides barked. "That lies between me and this barbar." He had shot a hard look at the big Cimmerian, a warning to silence.

Conan bristled, and glared back. "I came seeking employment for my company, my lady, but the count has nothing for us." Did the fool think he had no sense? Speaking of Timeon, and the baron's connection to Antimides, would gain him naught and perhaps cost much.

"Nothing?" Pity dripped from Synelle's voice. "But why do you not enter my service?" She raised her eyes boldly to his, and he thought he read a promise in them. "Would you not like to . . . serve me?"

Antimides snorted derisively. "You outdo yourself, Synelle. Are you not satisfied with Taramenon? Do you need an entire company of rogues to satisfy you? Or do you think to contend for the throne your-self?" He roared with laughter at his own wit, but jealous anger colored his glare at Conan.

Synelle's face hardened, and Conan thought she bit back words. At last she spoke in icy tones. "My house is as ancient as yours, Antimides. And did the succession depend on blood alone, I would stand first after Valdric." She drew a deep, shuddering breath, and her smile returned. "I *will* take your company in service, Conan. At twice the gold Antimides would give."

"Done," Conan said. It was not the sort of service he had sought, but the men of his company would at least be pleased with the gold.

The stern-faced count seemed bewildered over what had happened. "Can you be serious, Synelle?" he asked incredulously. "What use have you for such men? You throw your gold away like a foolish girl, on a whim."

"Are not my holdings subject to bandit attacks as others are, now that the army keeps to the cities? Besides," she added with a smouldering look at the Cimmerian, "I like his shoulders." Her voice hardened. "Or do you try to deny me even the right to take men-at-arms in service?"

"Women who need men-at-arms," Antimides replied hotly, "should make alliance with a man who can provide them."

"Why, so I have," she said, her mercurial mood becoming all gaiety. "Come with me, Conan. We have done here."

Conan followed as she moved from the chamber, leaving a fuming Antimides on his wooden throne.

In the corridor she turned suddenly, her mouth open to speak. Conan, caught by surprise, almost walked into her. For a moment she stood, words forgotten and dark eyes wide, staring up at him. "Never have I seen such a man," she whispered then, as if to herself. "Could you be the one to . . ." Her words trailed off, but she still stood gazing at him as if in a trance.

A woman-wise smile appeared on Conan's face. He had not been sure if her flirting in the other room had been for his benefit or Antimides, but of this he had no doubt. Lifting her into his arms, he kissed her. She returned his kiss with fiery lips, cupping his face with both hands, straining her body to him.

Abruptly she pulled back, horror filling her eyes; her hand cracked against his face. "Loose me!" she cried. "You forget yourself!"

Confused, he set her feet back on the floor. She took two quick steps back from him, one trembling hand to her lips.

"Your pardon, my lady," he said slowly. Did the woman play a game with him?

"I will not have it," she breathed unsteadily. "I will not." Slowly her composure returned, and when she went on her voice was as cold as it had ever been for Antimides. "I will forget what just happened, and I advise you to do the same. I have a house on the Street of Crowns where you may quarter your company. There are stables behind for your horses. Ask for it, and you will be directed. Go there, and await my instructions. And forget, barbarian, as you value your life."

Did women ever know their own minds, Conan wondered as he watched her stiff back recede down the corridor. How then did they expect men to know them? His consternation could not last long, however. Once more he had managed to save his company. For a time, at least, and that was all a man could ask. All that was left was to convince them there was no disgrace in taking service with a woman. Thinking on that he set about finding his way out of the palace.

VIIII

The massive walls and great outer towers of the royal palace had stood for centuries unchanged, but the interior had altered with every dynasty till it was a warren of corridors and gardens. Soon Conan felt he had visited all of them without making his way to the barbican gate.

Servants rushing through the halls on their duties would not even pause at question from the young barbarian in well-used armor. They were nearly as arrogant as the nobles who lounged in the fountained courts, and inquiries made to richly-clad folk got him little from the haughty men except gibes that brought him close to drawing his sword a time or two. The sleek, languorous women gave inviting smiles and even offers as open as those of any trull on the streets. Such might have appealed had he not been in haste to return to the Free-Company, but even they had only amusement for his ignorance of the palace, tinkling laughter and directions that, followed, sent him in circles.

Conan stepped into yet another courtyard, and found he was staring at King Valdric himself, trailing his retinue as he crossed the greenstone tiles. The King looked worse than Narus, the young Cimmerian thought. Valdric's gold-embroidered state robes hung loosely on a shrunken body that had once weighed half again as much as it did now, and he used the tall, gem-encrusted scepter of Ophir as a walking staff. His golden crown, thickly set with emeralds and rubies from the mines on the Nemedian border, sat low on his brow; and his eyes, sunken deep in a hollow-cheeked face, held a feverish light.

The retinue consisted mainly of men with the full beards of scholars, leavened with a sprinkling of nobles in colorful silks and soldiers of rank in gilded armor, crested helms beneath their arms. The bearded men held forth continuously, competing loudly for Valdric's ear as the procession made its slow way across the courtyard.

"The stars will be favorable this night for an invocation to Mitra," one cried.

"You must be bled, your majesty," another shouted. "I have a new shipment of leeches from the marshes of Argos."

"This new spell will surely cast the last of the demons from you," a third contributed.

" 'Tis time for your cupping, my King."

"This potion . . ."

"The balance of fluxes and humors . . ."

Conan made an awkward bow, though none of them seemed to notice him. Kings, he knew, were particular about such things.

When he straightened, King and retinue had gone; but one, a white-haired soldier, had stayed behind and was looking at him. Conan knew him immediately, though he had never met the man. Iskandrian, the White Eagle of Ophir, the general who kept the army aloof from the struggle to succeed Valdric. Despite his age and white hairs, the general's leathery face was as hard as the walls of the palace, his bushy-browed gray eyes clear and sharp. The calloused hand that rested on his sword hilt was strong and steady.

"You're the one who brought the girl to Antimides," the white-haired general said abruptly. "What is your name?"

"Conan of Cimmeria."

"Mercenary," Iskandrian said drily. His attitude toward mercenaries was well known. To his mind no foreign warrior should tread the soil of Ophir, not even if he *was* in service to an Ophirean. "I've heard of you. That fat fool Timeon's man, are you not?"

"I am no one's man but my own," Conan said hotly. "My company did follow Baron Timeon, but we have lately taken the Lady Synelle's colors." At least, they would once he drummed the fact into their heads.

Iskandrian whistled between his teeth. "Then, mercenary, you have gotten yourself a problem along with your lady patron. You've a set of shoulders like an ox, and I suppose women account you handsome. 'Twill light a fire in Taramenon's head to have a man like you near Synelle."

"Taramenon?" Conan remembered Antimides mentioning that name as well. The count had implied this Taramenon had some interest in Synelle, or she in him.

"He is the finest swordsman in Ophir," Iskandrian said. "Best sharpen your blade and pray to your gods for luck."

"A man makes his own luck," Conan said, "and my sword is always sharp."

"A good belief for a mercenary," Iskandrian laughed. "Or a soldier." A frown quickly replaced his mirth. "Why are you in this part of the palace, barbarian? You are far from the path from Antimides' chambers to the gate."

Conan hesitated, then shrugged ruefully. "I am lost," he admitted, and the general laughed again.

"That does not sound like what I've heard of you. But I'll get you a guide." With a wave of his hand he summoned a servant, who bowed low before Iskandrian and ignored Conan. "Take this man to the barbican gate," the general commanded.

"My thanks," the Cimmerian told him. "Yours are the first words I have heard in some time that were neither mocking nor lies."

Iskandrian eyed him sharply. "Make no mistake, Conan of Cimmeria. You have a reputation for daring and tactical sense, and were you Ophirean, I'd make you one of my officers. But you are a mercenary, and an outlander. Do I have my way, the day will come when you'll leave Ophir with all the haste you can muster or have your ashes scattered here." With that he stalked away.

By the time Conan got back to Timeon's palace, he was uncertain if he had ever had so many opposed to him before. Iskandrian seemed to like him personally, and would see him dead given the chance. Antimides hated him to the bone, and without doubt would like to put him on his funeral fires whether he went to them alive or dead. Synelle he was unsure of; what she said she wanted and what her body said she wanted were opposites, and a man could be shaved at the shoulders for involving himself with such a one as that. Karela claimed that she desired him dead, for all she had not taken the opportunity granted her, and she had a knack of making her desires come true that would make a statue sweat in the circumstances. Then there was the thrice-accursed horned figure. *Had* the second group of attackers been after it, as those first two had been? If they were, he could wager good coin on future attempts, though he still had no clue as to why.

Of course, he could rid himself of the threat of attack by ridding himself of the bronze, but that smacked too much of fright to suit him. Let him but discover why it was worth killing and dying for, and he would willingly shed himself of it, but it was not his way to run from trouble. The Cimmerian almost laughed when he realized that the murder of Timeon was the only trouble to come his way of late that had been resolved.

The guards on the white-columned portico looked at him expectantly, and he put on a smile for their benefit. "All is well," he told them. "We have a patron, and gold to tempt the wenches."

He left them slapping each other's back in relieved laughter, but once he was inside his own smile disappeared. Did they know half of what faced them, they would likely throw down their bows on the spot and desert.

"Machaon!" he called, the name echoing in the high-ceilinged entry hall.

Narus, on the balcony above, shouted down. "He's in the garden. How went matters with Antimides?"

"Assemble the men here," Conan told him, hurrying on.

The tattooed veteran was in the garden as Narus had said, on a bench with a girl, his arms wrapped around her and hers around him. Trust Machaon, the Cimmerian thought with a chuckle, even when waiting to see if they must flee the country. It was about time he found something for merriment in the day.

"Leave her be," he said jovially. "There'll be time for wenches lat—" He broke off as the girl leaped to her feet. It was Julia, cheeks scarlet and breasts heaving.

Clutching her skirts with both hands she looked helplessly at him, turned suddenly tear-filled eyes on Machaon, then ran wailing past the Cimmerian into the palace.

Machaon flung up his hands as Conan rounded on him angrily. "Hear me out before you speak, Cimmerian. She came about me, teasing, and taunted me about kissing her. And she did not try to run when I did it, either."

Conan scowled. He had saved her from a life as a trull, given her honest employment, for this? "She's no camp-follower, Machaon. If you want her, then court her. Don't grab her like a doxy in a tavern."

"Mitra's mercies, man! Court her? You speak as if she were your sister. Zandru's Hells, I've never taken a woman against her will in my life."

The young Cimmerian opened his mouth for an angry retort, and found that none came. If Julia wanted to be a woman fully-fledged, who was he to say her nay? And Machaon was certainly experienced enough to make her enjoy her learning.

"I'm trying to protect someone who apparently doesn't want it any more, Machaon," he said slowly. His reason for seeking out the grizzled man returned to him. "Events have turned as I said they would. We have our patron." Machaon barked a laugh and shook a fist over his head in triumph. "Narus is bringing some of the men to the entry hall. You fetch the rest, and I'll tell the company."

The wide, tapestry-hung hall filled rapidly, threescore men—less the guards posted, for there was no reason to be foolish—crowding it from wall to wall. All looking expectantly to him, Conan thought as he watched them from a perch on the curving marble stair. Boros was among them, he saw, but after the gray-bearded man had ferreted out Tivia for him, he was willing to let him remain. So long as he remained sober and stayed away from magic, at least.

"The company has a new patron," he announced, and the hall exploded in cheers. He waited for the tumult to subside, then added, "Our payment is twice what we were getting." After all, he thought while they renewed their shouts of glee, Synelle had offered to double Antimides' best offer; why would she not do the same for Timeon's? "Listen to me," he called to them. "Quiet, and listen to me. We'll be quartering in a house on the Street of Crowns. We leave here within the hour."

"But whom do we serve?" Taurianus shouted. Others took up the cry.

Conan drew a deep breath. "The Lady Synelle." Flat silence greeted his words.

At last Taurianus muttered disgustedly, "You'd have us serve a woman?"

"Aye, a woman," the Cimmerian answered. "Will her gold buy less when you clink it on the table in a tavern? And how many of you have worried as to how we'd fare if, when someone does succeed Valdric, it turned out we followed the wrong side? We'll be out of that. A woman cannot succeed to the throne. There'll be naught to do but guard her holdings from bandits and spend her gold."

"Twice as much gold?" Taurianus said.

"Twice as much." He had them, now. He could see it in their faces. "Get your belongings together quickly. And no looting! Timeon has heirs somewhere. I want none of you rogues hauled before the justices for theft."

Laughing again, the company began to disperse, and Conan dropped to a seat on the stair. At times it seemed as much of a battle to hold the company together as to fight any of the foes they had been called on to face.

"You handled that as well as any king," Boros said, creakily climbing the stairs.

"Of kings I know little," Conan told him. "All I know are steel and battle."

The gray-bearded man chuckled drily. "How do you think kings get to be kings, my young friend?"

"I neither know nor care," the Cimmerian replied. "All I want is to keep my company together. That and no more."

Sweat glistened on the body of the naked woman stretched taut on the rack, reflecting the flames of charcoal-filled iron cressets of the damp-streaked stone walls of the royal palace dungeon. Nearby, the handles of irons thrust from a brazier of glowing coals, ready in case they were called for. From the way she babbled her tale, punctuating it periodically with screams as the shaven-headed torturer encouraged her with a scourge, they would not be needed.

She had taken money to poison Timeon, but she did not know the man who paid her. He was masked. She became frightened when the first dose of poison showed no effect on the baron, and had placed all she had been given in his wine at once. Before all the gods, she did not know who had paid her.

Antimides listened quietly as the torturer did his work. It amazed him how the struggle for even a chance at life could continue when the person involved had to know there was no hope of it. Time and again, with men and women alike, had he seen it. As soon as he had spoken and seen the expression on Tivia's face, he was aware that she recognized his voice, that she knew him for the man behind the black silk mask. Yet even with the rack and the whip she denied, praying that he would spare her if he thought his secret was safe.

It was odd, too, how dangers suddenly multiplied just when he was in sight of his goal. Had the girl administered the poison in daily doses as directed the finest physician would have said Timeon died of natural causes, and he would have been free of a fool who drank too much and talked too freely when drunk. Then there was the barbarian with the outlandish name, bringing her to him, drawing attention to him when he least wanted it. No doubt that could be laid to Timeon's tongue. But what were the chances the man would fail to tell Synelle what he knew or suspected?

He, Antimides, had been the first to learn of Valdric's illness, the first to prepare to take the throne at his death, and all, he was certain, without being suspected by anyone. While the others fought in the countryside, he remained in Ianthe. When Valdric finally died, they who thought to take the throne, those few who managed to survive his assassins, would find that he held the royal palace. And he who held the royal palace held the throne of Ophir. Now all of his careful plans were endangered, his secrecy threatened.

Something would have to be done about Synelle. He had always had plans for that sharp-tongued jade. Prating about her bloodlines. Of what use were bloodlines in a wench, except with regard to the children she could produce? He had planned to take great pleasure in breaking her to heel, and in using those bloodlines she boasted of to make heirs with an even stronger claim to the throne than himself. But now she had to be done away with, and quickly. And the barbarian as well.

He perked an ear toward Tivia. She was repeating herself. "Enough, Raga," he said, and the shaven-headed man desisted. Antimides pressed a gold coin into the fellow's thick-thingered hand. Raga was bought long since, but it never hurt to ensure loyalties. "She's yours," Antimides told the man. Raga beamed a gap-toothed smile. "When you are done, dispose of her in the usual fashion."

As the count let himself out of the dungeon Tivia's shrieks were rising afresh. Lost in his planning for Synelle and the barbarian, Antimides did not hear.

IX

The house on the Street of Crowns was a large square, two stories high, around a dusty central court, with the bottom floor of the two sides being given over to stables. A wooden-roofed balcony, reached by stairs weakened from long neglect, ran around the courtyard on the second level. Dirty red roof tiles gleamed dully in the late afternoon sun; flaking plaster on the stone walls combined with shadows to give the structure a leprous appearance. An arched gate, its hinges squealing with rust, led from the street to the courtyard, where a dusty fountain was filled with withered brown leaves.

"Complete with rats and fleas, no doubt," Narus said dolefully as he dismounted.

Taurianus sat his horse and glared about him. "For this we left a palace?" A flurry of doves burst from an upper window. "See! We're expected to sleep in a roost!"

"You've all grown too used to the soft life in a palace," Conan growled before the mutters could spread. "Stop complaining like a herd of old women, and remember the times you've slept in the mud."

" 'Twas better than this, that mud," Taurianus muttered, but he climbed down from his saddle.

Grumbling men began carrying blanket rolls and bundles of personal belongings in search of places to settle themselves. Others led their horses into the stables; curses quickly floated out as to the number of rats and cobwebs. Rotund Fabio hurried in search of the kitchens, trailed by a half-running Julia, her arms full of soot-blackened pots and bundles of herbs, strings of garlic and peppers dangling from her shoulders.

Boros stood at the gate staring about him in amazement, though he certainly slept in little better as a matter of course. Synelle, Conan thought, had much to learn about what was properly provided a Free-Company.

They had attracted entirely too much attention for Conan's taste during their search for the house. Three-score armored men on horseback, laden with sacks and cloak-wrapped bundles till they looked like a procession of country peddlers, could not help but draw eyes even in a city that assiduously attempted to avoid seeing anything that might be dangerous. The Cimmerian would just as soon they could all have become invisible till the matter of Timeon's death was forgotten. And he was none too eager to look into any of those bundles, many of which clinked and seemed heavier than they had a right to be. For all his injunction against looting he was sure they were filled with silver goblets and trinkets of gold. More of those following him than not, the Ophireans most certainly, were light-fingered at the best of times.

Giving his horse over to one of the men, the big Cimmerian went in search of a room for himself, his blanket roll over one shoulder and the sack containing the bronze under his arm. Save for weapons and armor, horse and change of clothes, they were all the possessions he had.

Soon he found a large, corner room on the second floor, with four windows to give it light. A wad of straw in one corner showed that a rat had been nesting there. Two benches and a table stood in the middle of the floor, covered with heavy dust. A bed, sagging but certainly large enough even for his height, was jammed against a wall. The mattress crackled with the sound of dried husks when he poked it, and he sighed, remembering the goose-down mattress in Timeon's palace. Think of the mud, he reminded himself sternly.

Machaon's voice drifted up from the courtyard. "Conan, where are you? There's news!"

Tossing his burdens on the bed, Conan hurried out onto the balcony. "What word? Has Synelle summoned us?"

"Not yet, Cimmerian. The assassins were busy last night. Valentius fled his palace after three of his own guards turned their blades on him. 'Tis said others of his men cut them down, but the lordling now seems affrightened of his own shadow. He has taken refuge with Count Antimides."

Conan's eyebrows went up. Antimides. The young fool had unknowingly put himself in the hands of one of his rivals. Another lord removed from the race, this one by his own hand, in a manner of speaking. Who stood next in the blood-right after Valentius? But what occurred among the contending factions, he thought, no longer concerned him or his company.

"We're done with that, Machaon," he laughed. "Let them all kill each other."

The grizzled veteran joined his laughter. "An that happens, mayhap we can make you King. I will settle for count, myself."

Conan opened his mouth to reply, and suddenly realized a sound that should not be there had been impinging on his brain. Creaking boards from the room he had just left. No rat made boards creak. His blade whispered from its sheath, and he dove through the door, followed by Machaon's surprised shout.

Four startled men in cast-off finery, one just climbing in the window, stared in shock at the appearance of the young giant. Their surprise lasted but an instant; as he took his first full step into the room, swords appeared in their fists and they rushed to attack.

Conan beat aside the thrust of the first to reach him, and in the same movement planted a foot in the middle of his opponent's dirty gray silk tunic. Breath left the man in an explosive gasp, and he fell in a heap at the feet of a thick-mustached man behind him. The mustached man stumbled, and the tip of Conan's blade slashed his throat in a fountain of blood. As the dying man fell atop the first attacker, a man with a jagged scar down his left cheek leaped over him, sword hacking wildly. Conan dropped to a crouch—whistling steel ruffled the hair atop his head—and his own blade sliced across scar-face's stomach. With a shriek the man dropped in a heap, both hands clutching at thick ropes of entrails spilling from his body. A sword thrust from the floor slid under the metal scales of Conan's hauberk, slicing his side, but the Cimmerian's return blow struck through gray-tunic's skull at the eyes.

"Erlik curse you!" the last man screamed. Sly-faced and bony, he had been the last into the room, and had not joined in the wild melee. "Eight of my men you've slain! Erlik curse all your seed!" Shrieking, he dashed at Conan with frenzied slashes.

The Cimmerian wanted to take this man alive, in condition to answer questions, but the furious attack was too dangerous to withstand for long. A half-mad light of fear and rage gleamed in the man's sweaty face, and he screamed with every blow he made. Three times their blades crossed, then blood was spurting from the stump of sly-face's neck as his head rolled on the floor.

With a clatter of boots mercenaries crowded into the room, led by

Machaon, all with swords in hand. "Mitra, Cimmerian," the tattooed man said, scanning the scene of carnage. "Couldn't you have saved just one for us?"

"I didn't think of it," Conan replied drily.

Julia forced her way through the men. When she saw the bodies her hands went to her face, and she screamed. Then her eyes lit on Conan, and her composure returned as quickly as it had gone. "You're wounded!" she said. "Sit on the bed, and I will tend it."

For the first time Conan became aware of a razor's edge of fire along his ribs, and the blood wetting the side of his hauberk. " 'Tis but a scratch," he told her. "Get these out of here," he added to Machaon, gesturing to the corpses.

Machaon told off men to cart the dead away.

Julia, however, was not finished. "Scratch or not," she said firmly, "if it is not tended you may grow ill. Fetch me hot water and clean clothes," she flung over her shoulder, as she attempted to press Conan toward the bed. "Clean, mind you!" To everyone's surprise two of the mercenaries rushed off at her command.

Amused, Conan let her have her way. Muttering to herself she fussed over getting his metal-scaled leather tunic off. Gently she palped the flesh about the long, shallow gash, a thoughtful frown on her face. She seemed unconcerned about his blood on her fingers.

"It seems you are ahead once more," Machaon said ruefully, before leaving them alone.

"What did he mean by that?" she asked absently. "Don't talk. Let the wound lie still. There are no ribs broken, and I will not have to sew it, but after it is bandaged you must take care not to exert yourself. Perhaps if you lie—" She broke off with a gasp. "Mitra protect us, what is that evil thing?"

Conan followed her suddenly frightened gaze to the bronze figure, lying on the bed and now out of the sack. "Just something I bought as a gift for Machaon," he said, picking it up. She backed away from him. "What ails you, girl? The thing is but dead metal."

"She is right to be affrighted," Boros said from the door. His eyes were fixed on the bronze as on a living demon. "It is evil beyond knowing. I can feel the waves of it from here."

"And I," Julia said shakily. "It means me harm. I can feel it."

Boros nodded sagely. "Aye, a woman would be sensitive to such. The rites of Al'Kiir were heinous. Scores of men fighting to the death while the priestesses chanted, with the heart of the survivor to be ripped from his living body. Rites of torture, with the victim kept alive and screaming on the altar for days. But the most evil of all, and the most powerful, was the giving of women as sacrifices. Or as worse than sacrifices."

"What could be worse than being sacrificed?" Julia asked faintly.

"Being given to the living god whose image that is," Boros answered, "to be his plaything for all eternity. Such may well have been the fate of the women given to Al'Kiir."

Julia swayed, and Conan snapped, "Enough, old man! You frighten her. I remember now that you mentioned this Al'Kiir once before, when you were drunk. Are you drunk now? Have you dredged all this from wine fumes in your head?"

"I am deathly sober," the gray-bearded man replied, "and I wish I were pickled in wine like a corpse. For that is not only an image of Al'Kiir, Cimmerian. It is a necessary, a vital part of the worship of that horrible god. I thought all such had been destroyed centuries ago. Someone attempts to bring Al'Kiir again to this world, and did they have that unholy image they might well succeed. I, for one, would not care to be alive if they do."

Conan stared at the bronze gripped in his big hand. Two men had died attempting to take it from him in the shop. Three more perished in the second attack, and that that had been for the same thing he no longer doubted. Before he himself died, sly-face had accused Conan of slaying about eight of his men. The numbers were right. Those who wanted to bring back this god knew the Cimmerian had the image they needed. In a way he was relieved. He had had stray thoughts that some of these attacks, including the one just done, were Karela's work.

The men fetching the hot water and bandages entered the room; Conan thrust the image under his blanket roll and signed the others to silence until they were gone.

When the three were alone again, Julia spoke. "I'll tend your wound, but not if you again remove that evil thing from its hiding. Even there I can sense it."

"I'll leave it where it is," the young Cimmerian said, and she knelt beside him and busied herself with bathing and bandaging his wound. "Go on with your telling, Boros," he continued. "How is it this god cannot find his own way to the world of men? That seems like no god to fear greatly, for all his horns."

"You make jokes," Boros grumbled, "but there is no humor in this. To tell you of Al'Kiir I must speak of the distant past. You know that Ophir is the most ancient of all the kingdoms now existing in the world, yet few men know aught of its misty beginnings. I know a little. Before even Ophir was, this land was the center of the worship of Al'Kiir. The strongest and handsomest of men and the proudest and most beautiful of women were brought from afar for the rites of which I have spoken. But, as you might imagine, there were those who opposed the worship of Al'Kiir, and foremost of these were the men who called themselves the Circle of the Right-Hand Path."

"Can you not be shorter about it?" Conan said. "There's no need to dress the tale like a story-teller in the marketplace."

Boros snorted. "Do you wish brevity, or the facts? Listen. The Circle of the Right-Hand Path was led by a man named Avanrakash, perhaps the most powerful practitioner of white magic who has ever lived."

"I did not know there was such a thing as white magic," Conan said. "Never have I seen a sorcerer who did not reek of blackness and evil as a dunghill reeks of filth."

This time the old man ignored him. "These men made contact with the very gods, 'tis said, and concluded a pact. No god would stand against Al'Kiir openly, for they feared that in a war between gods all that is might be destroyed, even themselves. Some—Set, supposedly, was one—declared themselves apart from what was to happen. Others, though, granted those of the Right-Hand Path an increase in powers, enough so that they in concert could match a single god. You can understand that they would not give so much to a single man, for that would make him a demigod at the least, nor enough to all of them that they could not be vanquished easily by as few as two of the gods in concert."

Despite himself Conan found himself listening intently. Julia, her mouth hanging open in wonderment, held the ties of the Cimmerian's bandages forgotten as she followed Boros' words.

"In the battle that followed, the face of the land itself was changed, mountains raised, rivers altered in their courses, ancient seas made desert. All of those who marched against Al'Kiir, saving only Avanrakash, perished, and he was wounded to the death. Yet in his dying he managed with a staff of power to sever Al'Kiir from the body the god wore in the world of men, to seal the god from that world.

"Then came rebellion among the people against the temples of Al'Kiir, and the first King of Ophir was crowned. Whole cities were razed so that not even their memory remains. All that kept so much as the name of Al'Kiir in the minds of men was destroyed.

"The earthly body of the god? Men tried to destroy that as well, but the hottest fires made no mark, and the finest swords shattered against it. Finally it was entombed beneath a mountain, and the entrances sealed up, so that with time men should forget its very existence.

"They both succeeded and failed, they who would have destroyed the god's name and memory, for the name Tor Al'Kiir was given to the mountain, but for centuries gone only a scattered few have known the source of that name, though all men know it for a place of ill luck, a place to be avoided.

"I believed I was the last to have the knowledge I possess, that it would go to my funeral fires with me. But I have seen lights in the night atop Tor Al'Kiir. I have heard whispers of knowledge sought. Someone attempts to bring Al'Kiir back to this world again. I was sure they would find only failure, for the lack of that image or its like, but do they get their hands on it, blood and lust and slavery will be the portion of all men."

Conan let out a long breath when the old man at last fell silent. "The answer is simple. I'll take the accursed thing to the nearest metalworker's shop and have it melted down."

"No!" Boros cried. A violent shudder wracked him, and he combed his long beard with his fingers in agitation. "Without the proper spells that would loose such power as would burn this city from the face of the earth, and perhaps half the country as well. Before you ask, I do not know the necessary spells, and those who do would be more likely to attempt use of the image than its destruction."

"That staff," Julia said suddenly. "The one Avanrakash used. Could it destroy the image?"

"A very perceptive question, child," the old man murmured. "The answer is, I do not know. It might very well have that power, though."

"Much good that does," Conan muttered. "The staff is no doubt rotted to dust long ago."

Boros shook his head. "Not at all. 'Tis a staff of power, after all, that Staff of Avanrakash. Those men of ancient times revered its power, and made it the scepter of Ophir, which it still is, though covered in gold and gems. It is said 'twas the presence of that scepter, carried as a standard before the armies of Ophir, that allowed Moranthes the Great to win his victories against Acheron. If you could acquire the scepter, Conan . . ."

"I will not," Conan said flatly, "attempt to steal King Valdric's scepter on the off chance that it might have some power. Zandru's Nine Hells, the man uses the thing as a walking staff! It's with him constantly."

"You must understand, Cimmerian," Boros began, but Conan cut him off.

"No! I will put the thrice-accursed beneath the floor boards yonder until I can find a place to bury it where it will never be found. Crack not your teeth concerning any of this until I can do so, Boros. And stay away from the wine till then as well."

Boros put on a cloak of injured dignity. "I have been keeping this particular secret for nearly fifty years, Cimmerian. You've no need to instruct me."

Conan grunted, and let Julia lift his arm to finish her bandaging. It was yet another rotten turnip to add to the stew before him. How to destroy a thing that could not be destroyed, or as well as could not, given the lack of trustworthy sorcerer, and such were as rare as virgin whores. Still, he was worried more about Karela than any of the rest. What, he wondered, was that flame-haired wench plotting?

X

Karela reined in her bay mare at the edge of the tall trees, thick with the shadows of the setting sun, and studied the small peak-roofed hut in the forest clearing. A single horse was tethered outside, a tall black warmount colorfully caprisoned for a noble, though its scarlet and black bardings bore the sign of no house. A lone man was supposed to meet her there, but she would wait to make sure.

The snap of a fallen twig announced the arrival of a man in coarse woolen tunic and breeches of nondescript brown that blended well with the shadows. The sound was deliberate, she knew, that she, being warned, would not strike with the Turanian scimitar she wore on her belt at his sudden appearance; Agorio could move in the woods as silently as the fall of a feather, did he choose. Both the man's ears had been cropped for theft, and his narrow face bore a scar that pulled his right eye into a permanent expression of surprise. "He came alone, my lady, as you instructed," he said.

Karela nodded. They were not so good as her hounds of the Zamoran plains, the men who followed her now. Most had been poachers, and petty thieves if the opportunity presented itself, when she found them, and they had little liking for the discipline she forced on them, but given time, she would make them as good and as feared as any band of brigands that ever rode.

She rode slowly into the clearing, sitting her saddle as proudly as any queen. She disdained to show more caution than she had already. As she dismounted she drew her curved sword, and pushed open the crude plank door of the hut with the blade.

Within was a single room with the rough furnishings to be expected in such a place, dimly lit by a fire on the hearth. Dust covered everything, and old, dried cobwebs hung from the bare, shadowed rafters. A man with a plain scarlet surcoat over his armor stood in the center of the dirt floor, his thumbs hooked casually in the wide, low-slung belt that supported his scabbarded longsword. He was almost as tall as Conan, she noted, with shoulders nearly as broad. A handsome man, with an eye for women from the smile that came to his lips when she entered.

She kicked the door shut with her heel and waited for him to speak. She did not sheath her blade.

"You are not what I expected, girl," he said finally. His dark eyes caressed the curves beneath her snug-fitting jerkin and breeches. "You are quite beautiful."

"And you've made your first mistake." There was danger in her voice, though the man did not seem to realize it. "No man calls me girl. I'll have the answers to some questions before we go further. Your message came to me through ways I thought known only to a trusted few. How did you come to know of them? Who are you, and why would you send me fifty golds, not knowing if I'd come or not?" For that was the amount that had accompanied the message.

"Yet you did come," he said, radiating cool confidence. From beneath his surcoat he produced two bulging leather purses and tossed them to the table. They clinked as they landed. "And here are a hundred more pieces of gold, if you will undertake a commission for me, with as many to follow at its completion."

Her tone hardened. "My questions."

"Regrettably I cannot answer," he said smoothly. "You need have no fear of being seized, my inquisitive beauty. I came alone, as I said I would. There are no men in the trees about us."

"Except my own," she said, and was pleased to see surprise flicker across his face.

He recovered his aplomb quickly. "But that is to be expected. When I heard of a bandit band led by a . . . a woman, I knew they must be very good indeed to long survive. You see, you're becoming famous. Put up your blade. Eastern, is it not? Are you from the east, my pretty brigand? You have not the coloring of the eastern beauties I have known, though you are as lovely as all of them together."

His smile deepened, a smile she was sure sent he expected to send tingles through every woman favored with it. And likely had his expectations met, she admitted. She also knew that only her danger at his manner—girl, indeed! My pretty brigand. Ha!—armored her against it. She held hard to that anger, prodded at it. She did, however, sheathe her sword.

"I'll not tell you my history," she growled, "when I get not even your name in return. At least you can tell me what I am to do for these two hundred gold pieces."

His smoldering-eyed study of her did not end, but at least it abated. "Baron Inaros is withdrawing from his keep to his palace in Ianthe. He is not involved in the current struggles. Rather, he is afraid of them. 'Tis the reason for his move, seeking the safety of the capital. His guards will be few in number, not enough to trouble a bold band of brigands. For the two hundred you will bring me his library, which he brings with him in two carts. And of course you may keep anything else you take from his party."

"A library!" Karela burst out. "Why would you pay two hundred pieces of gold, two hundred and fifty, in truth, for a collection of dusty scrolls?"

"Let us simply say I am a collector of rarities, and that there are works in Inaros' possession I am willing to pay that price for."

Karela almost laughed. This man as a collector of rare parchments was one thing she would not believe. But there was no profit in calling him liar. "Very well," she said, "but I will have two hundred gold pieces upon delivery of these, ah, rarities." It was her turn to smile. "Are you willing to pay *that* price?"

He nodded slowly, once more eyeing her up and down. "I could almost consider it cheap, though you'd best not try to press me too far, or I may take my commission to another who, if not so pretty, is also not so greedy. Now let us seal the bargain."

"What," she began, but before she could finish he took a quick step and seized her. Roughly he crushed her against him; she could not free an arm enough to draw her sword.

"I have a special way of sealing pacts with women," he chuckled. "Struggle if you wish, but you will enjoy it before 'tis done." Suddenly he froze at the sharp prick of her dagger point against his neck.

"I should slit your throat," she hissed, "like the pig you are. Back away from me. Slowly."

Obediently he stepped backwards, his face a frozen mask of rage. As soon as he was clear of her dagger stroke, his hand went to his sword.

She flipped the dagger, catching it by the point.

"Will you wager your life that I cannot put this in your eye?" His hand fell back to his side.

Desperately Karela fought her own desire to kill him. He deserved it clearly, to her thinking, but how could she keep it secret that she had slain a man come to hire her? Such things never remained buried long. All who heard the tale would think she had done it for the coins on the table, and there would be no more offers of gold.

"You codless spawn of a diseased camel!" she spat in frustration. "But recently I saw a figure that reminds me of you. An ugly thing to curdle any woman's blood, as you are. All horns and fangs, with twice as much manhood as any man, and like to think with that manhood, as you do, were it alive. If you have any manhood."

He had gone very still as she spoke, anger draining from his face, and there was barely contained excitement in his voice as he spoke. "This figure? How many horns did it have? How many eyes? Was it shaped otherwise like a man?"

Karela stared at him in amazement. Was this some attempt to draw her off guard, it was most surely a strange one. "What interest can you have in it?"

"More than you can possibly know. Speak, woman!"

"It was like a man," she said slowly, "except that it had too many fingers and toes, and claws on all of them. There were four horns, and three eyes. And a reek of evil as strong as yours."

His smile returned, but not for her this time. To her surprise it was a smile of triumph. "Forget Inaros," he said. "Bring me that figure, and I will give you *five* hundred pieces of gold."

"Think you I'd still take your gold," she said incredulously, "after this?"

"I think you'd take five hundred pieces of it if it came from Erlik himself. Think, woman. Five hundred!"

Karela hesitated. It was a tempting amount. And to think she could earn it at the Cimmerian's expense made it more so. But to deal with this one. "Done," she was surprised to hear herself say. "How shall we meet again, when I have the thing?"

He tugged off his brilliant red surcoat, revealing gilded armor beneath. "Have a man wearing this over his tunic stand before the main gate of the royal palace when the sun is at its zenith, and on that day at dusk I will come to this hut with the gold."

"Done," Karela said again. "I will leave you, now, and I advise you to wait the time it takes to count one thousand—an you can count— before following, else you will discover whether that pretty armor will avail you against crossbow bolts." With that she backed from the hut, and scrambled into her saddle.

As she rode into the forest she found that she almost felt like singing. Five hundred pieces of gold and another stroke against the Cimmerian, if a small one. But there would be greater, the first already under way. This time it would be Conan who was forced to flee, not her. He would flee, or he would die.

Synelle paced the floor of her sleeping chamber like a caged panther, hating her agitation yet unable to quell it. Silver lamps lit the room against the night at the windows, lending a sheen to the gossamer hangings about her bed. Her pale hair hung damp with sweat, though the night was cool. Normally she guarded her exotic beauty jealously, never allowing a curl to be out of place or the slightest smudging of rouge even when she was alone, but now turmoil filled her to the exclusion of all else.

For the hundreth time she stopped before a mirror and examined her full, sensuous lips. They looked no different than they always had, but they felt swollen. With a snarl of rage she resumed her pacing, her long robe of canescent silk clinging to every curve of her body. She was aware of every particle of the sleek gray material sliding on the smoothness of her skin.

Ever since that . . . that barbarian had kissed her she had been like this. She could not stop thinking about him. Tall, with shoulders like a bull and eyes like a winter lake. A crude, unmannered lout. Wild and untamed, like a lion, with arms that could crush a woman in his embrace. She felt like bubbling honey inside. She could not sleep; already this night she had tossed for hours in torment, filled to the brim with feelings she had never before experienced.

Why had she even taken the Free-Company in service? Only to spite Antimides, as had always given her pleasure in the past. There was no reason to keep it, except that Antimides would certainly think he had won in some fashion if she dismissed them. And there was the barbarian.

Desperately she tried to force her mind away from Conan. "I will not give myself to him!" she cried. "Not to any man! Never!"

There were other things to think about. There had to be. The women. Yes. Of the bronze image of Al'Kiir, she was certain now. The men Taramenon had sent after Galbro would bring it to her. But she needed a woman for the rite, and not any woman would do. This woman must be beautiful above all others about her, proud to the point of fierceness. Proud women there were, but plain or old or disqualified on a score of other points. Beautiful women abounded, and some had pride, but where was the fierceness? Without exception they would tremble at a man's anger, give way to his will eventually, for all they might resist a time.

Why did they have to be so? Yet she could understand a little now. What woman could resist a man like the barbarian. Him again! She pounded a small fist on her sleek thigh in frustration. Why did he continually invade her thoughts?

Suddenly her face firmed with determination. She strode to a marble-topped table against the tapestried wall, touched her fingers to a twist of parchment there. Within were three long, black, silky hairs, left on her robe when the barbarian . . . Her hand trembled. She could not think of that now; her mind must be clear. It must be.

Why did it have to be him? Why not Taramenon? Because he had never affected her as Conan did? Because she had toyed with him so long that only the pleasure of toying remained?

"It will be Conan," she whispered. "But it will be as I wish." Her hand closed on the parchment, and she swept from the room.

Slaves, scrubbing floors in the hours when their mistress was not usually about, scrambled from her path, pressing their faces to the marble tiles in obeisance. She took no more notice of them than she did of the furnishings.

Straight to her secret chamber she went, closing the door behind her and hurriedly lighting lamps. Triumph sped her movements, the certainty of triumph soon to be realized.

At the table covered with beakers and flasks she carefully separated one hair from the packet. One would be enough, and that would leave two in case further magicks must be worked on the huge barbarian.

On a smooth silver plate she painted the sign of the horns, the sign of Al'Kiir, in virgin's blood, using a brush made from the hair of an unborn child and handled with a bone from its mother's finger. Next two candles were affixed to the plate one on either side, and lit. Black, they were, made from the rendered tallow of murdered men, stolen from their graves in blessed ground.

Haste was of the essence, now, but care, too, lest disaster come in place of what she sought. Gripping her tongue between her teeth, she painted the final symbols about the edge of the plate. Desire. Lust. Need. Wanting. Passion. Longing.

Quickly she threw aside the brush, raised her hands above her head, then lowered them before her, palms up, in a gesture of pleading. In the arcane tongue she had learned so painfully, Synelle chanted, soft spoken words that rebounded from the pale walls like shouts, invoking powers linked to Al'Kiir yet not of him, powers of this world, not of the void where he was imprisoned. In the beginning she had attempted to use those powers to make contact with Al'Kiir. The result had been a fire that gutted a tower of her castle, lying halfway to the Aquilonian border, a burning with flames that no water could extinguish, flames that died only when there was not even a cinder left to burn. For long after that she had feared to try again, not least for the stares directed at her and the whispers of sorcery at the castle of Asmark. To cover herself she had brought charges of witchcraft against a woman of the castle, a crone of a scullery maid who looked the part of a witch, and had her burned at the stake. Synelle had learned care from that early mistake.

Slowly the candles guttered out in pools of their own black tallow, and Synelle lowered her hands, breathing easily for the first time in hours. The painted symbols on the plate, the hair, all were ash. A cruel smile touched her lips. No more was there need to fear her desires. The barbarian was hers, now, to do with as she would. Hers.

XI

Conan's skin crawled as he walked across the dusty courtyard of the house where his company was quartered. The hairs on his body seemed to move by themselves. Bright sunlight streamed from the golden globe climbing into the mourning sky; chill air seemed to surround him. It had been so ever since he woke, this strangeness, and he had no understanding of why.

Fear the big Cimmerian dismissed as a cause. He knew his fears well, and had them well in hand. No fear could ever affect him so, who had, in his fear years, faced all manner of things that quelled the hearts of other men. As for the image, and even Al'Kiir, he had confronted demons and sorcerers before, as well as every sort of monster from huge flesh-eating worms to giant spiders dripping corrosive poison from manibles that could pierce the finest armor to a dragon of adamantine scales and fiery breath. Each he had conquered, and if he was wary of such, he did not fear them.

"Cimmerian," Narus called, "come get yourself a cloak."

"Later," Conan shouted back to the hollow-faced, who was rooting with others of the company in the great pile of bales and bundles that had been delivered by carts that morning.

Synelle had finally seen to the needs of the Free-Company she had taken in service. Bundles of long woolen cloaks of scarlet, the color of her house, had been tumbled into the courtyard, along with masses of fresh bedding and good wool blankets. There had been knee-high Aquilonian boots of good black leather, small mirrors of polished metal from Zingara, keen-bladed Corinthian razors, and a score of other things, from a dozen countries, that a soldier might need. Including a sack of gold coin for their first pay. The mercenaries had turned the morning into a holiday with it all. Fabio had kept Julia running all morning, staggering under sacks of turnips and peas, struggling with quarters of beef and whole lamb carcasses, rolling casks of wine and ale to the kitchens.

Fabio found Conan by the dry fountain. The fat, round cook was mopping his face with a rag. "Conan, that lazy wench you saddled me with has run off and hidden somewhere. And look, she hasn't swept a quarter of the courtyard yet. Claims she's a lady. Erlik take her if she is! She has a mouth like a fishwife. Flung a broom at my head in my own kitchen, and swore at me as vilely as I've ever heard from any man in the company."

Conan shook his head irritably. He was in no mood to listen to the man's complaints, not when he felt as if ants were skittering over his body. "If you want the courtyard swept," he snapped, "see to it yourself."

Fabio stared after him, open-mouthed, as he stalked away.

Conan scrubbed is fingers through his hair. What was the matter with him? *Could* that accursed bronze, the evil of it that Julia claimed to sense, have affected him from beneath the floor while he slept?

"Cimmerian," Boros said, popping out of the house, "I've been seeking you everywhere."

"Why?" Conan growled, then attempted to get a hold of himself. "What do you want?" he asked in a slightly more reasonable tone.

"Why, that image, of course." The old man looked around, then lowered his voice. "Have you given any thought to destroying it? The more I think on it, the more it seems the Staff of Avanrakash is the only answer."

"I am not stealing the Erlik-accursed scepter," Conan grated. When he saw Machaon approaching, the Cimmerian felt ready to burst.

The grizzled mercenary eyed the bigger man's grim face quizzically, but said only, "We're being watched. This house, that is."

Conan gripped his swordbelt tightly with both hands. This was business of the company, perhaps important business, and he had worked too long and too hard for that to allow even his own temper to damage it.

"Karela's men?" he asked in what was almost his normal voice. It took a great effort to maintain it.

"Not unless she's begun taking fopling youths into her band," Machaon replied. "There are two of them, garbed and jeweled for a lady's garden, with pomanders stuck to their nostrils, wandering up and down the street outside. They show an especial interest in this house."

Young nobles, Conan thought. They could be Antimides' men, if the count was concerned as to how much Conan was talking of what he knew. Or they could be seeking the image, though nobles hardly meshed with the sort who had tried for it thus far. They might even be this Taramenon, Synelle's jealous suitor, and a friend, come to see for themselves what manner of man the silvery-haired beauty had taken in service. Too many possibilities to reason out, certainly not in his present state of mind.

"If we seize them when next they pass," he began, and the two listening to him recoiled.

"You must be mad," Boros gasped. " 'Tis the image, Cimmerian. It affects you ill. It must be destroyed quickly."

"I know not what this old magpie is chattering about," Machaon said, "but seizing nobles . . . in broad daylight from a street in the middle of Ianthe . . . Cimmerian, it would take more luck than ten Brythunian sages to get out of the city with our heads still on our shoulders."

Conan squeezed his eyes shut. His brain whirled and spun, skittering through fogs that veiled reason. This was deadly dangerous; he *must* be able to think clearly, or he could lead them all to disaster.

"My Lord Conan?" a diffident voice said.

Conan opened his eyes to find a barefoot man in the short white tunic of a slave, edged in scarlet, had joined them. "I'm no lord," he said gruffly.

"Yes, my lor . . . uh, noble sir. I am bid tell you the Lady Synelle wishes your presence at her house immediately."

Images of the sleek, full-breasted noblewoman flickered into Conan's mind, clearing aside all else. His unease was washed away by a warm flow of desire. Sternly he reminded himself that she no doubt wanted to consult with him about the company's duties, but the reminder could as well have been whispered into a great storm of the Vilayet Sea. When first he kissed her, she had responded. Whatever her words said, her body had told the truth of her feelings. It *must* have.

"Lead on," Conan commanded, then strode through the gate and into the street without waiting. The slave had to scurry after him.

Conan gave little heed to the man half-running beside him to keep up as he moved swiftly through throng-filled streets. With every stride his visions of Synelle grew stronger, more compelling, and his breath came faster. Each line of her became clear in his mind, the swell of round breasts above a tiny waist his big hands could almost span, the curve of sleek thighs and sensuously swaying hips. She filled his mind, clouded his eyes so that he saw none of the teeming crowds nor remembered anything of his journey.

Once within Synelle's great house the man in the short tunic rushed ahead to guide Conan up stairs and through corridors, but the Cimmerian was certain he could have found the way by himself. His palms sweated for the smooth satin of her skin.

The slave bowed him into Synelle's private chamber. The pale-skinned beauty stood with one small hand at her alabaster throat, dark eyes seeming to fill a face surrounded by silken waves of spun-platinum hair. Diaphanous silk covered her ivory lushness, but concealed nothing.

"Leave us, Scipio," she said unsteadily.

Conan was unaware of the slave leaving, closing the door behind him. His breath was thick in his throat; his nails dug into calloused palms. Never had he taken a woman who did not want him, yet he knew he was at the brink. One gesture from her, one word that he might take as invitation; it would be enough. Battle raged within the giant Cimmerian, ravening lust warring with his will. And for the first time in his life he felt his will begin to bend.

"I called you here, barbarian," she began, then swallowed and began again. "I summoned you to me. . . ."

Her words faded away as he covered the floor between them. His hands took her shoulders gently; how great the struggle not to rip that transparently mocking garment from her. As he gazed down at her up-turned face, he read fear there, and longing. Her melting eyes were bottomless pools into which he could fall forever; his were azure flames.

"Do not fear me," he said hoarsely. "I will never harm you."

She pressed her cheek to his chest, crushing her full breasts against him. Unseen by him a small smile curved her lips, softening, though not supplanting, the fear in her eyes. "You are mine," she whispered.

"When first I kissed you," Conan panted, "you wanted me. As I want you. I knew I had not imagined it."

"Come," she said, taking his hand as she backed from him. "My bed lies beyond that archway. I will have wine brought, and fruits packed in snow from the mountains."

"No," he growled. "I can wait no longer." His hand closed on sheer silk; the robe shredded from her ripe nakedness. Careless of her protests of servants who might enter, he pulled her to the floor. Soon she protested no more.

XII

T he sun was rising toward its height once more as Conan left
Synelle's house, and he wondered wearily at the passing of
unnoticed hours. But she had so occupied him with herself that
there had been no room for time. Had she not been gone from her bed
at his waking, he might not be leaving yet. For all of a day and a night
together, and little sleeping in it, a knot of desire still burned in his
belly, flaring whenever he thought of her. Only the need to see to his
Free-Company, and her absence, had stirred him to dress and go.

Bemused he strode through the crowded streets as if they were empty
of all but him, seeing only the woman who still held his mind in thrall
with her body. Merchants in voluminous hooded robes and tarts in little
save gilded bangles scurried from his way lest they be trampled; satin-
clad nobles and long-bearded scholars abandoned dignity to leap aside
when they incredulously saw he would not alter his path. He heard the
curses that followed him, but the stream of abuse from scores of throats
did not register. It was so much meaningless babble that had naught to
do with him.

Suddenly a man who had not stepped aside bounced off Conan's
chest, and the Cimmerian found himself staring into an indignant face
as the memory of Synelle's silken thighs dimmed, but did not fade. The
man was young, no older than he himself, but his tunic of blue brocade
slashed with yellow, the golden chain across his chest, his small, fashionable beard, the pomander clutched in his hand, all named him nobly
born.

"You there, thief," the youthful lord sneered. "I have you now."

"Get out of my way, fool," Conan growled. "I've no time or desire to play lordlings' games." The man wore a sword strapped around his waist, the Cimmerian noted, unusual with the garb he wore.

Conan tried to step around the brocaded youth, but another young noble, with thin mustachios in addition to his beard, stepped in front of him with a swagger. Jeweled rings bedecked all his fingers, and he, too, wore a sword. "This outlander," he said loudly, "has robbed my friend."

Conan wondered for whose benefit he was speaking so; no one in the teeming street paid the three any mind. In fact, a large space had opened about them as passersby studiously avoided their vicinity. Whatever sport these two sought, he wanted none of it. He wished only to see that all was well with his company and return as quickly as possible to Synelle. Synelle of the alabaster skin as soft as satin.

"Leave be," he said, doubling a massive fist, "or I'll set your ears to ringing. I've stolen nothing."

"He attacks," the mustachioed lordling cried, and his sword swept from its sheath as his fellow flung his rose-scented pomander at Conan's face.

Even with his brain fogged by a woman's memory the big Cimmerian had survived far too many battles to be taken so easily by surprise. The blade that was meant to take his head from his shoulders passed through empty air as he leaped aside. Anger washed his mind clean of all but battle rage. The sport these fops sought was his death, a killing for which, with the times as they were and the fact that he was an outlander, they would not be brought to book. But they had chosen no easy meat. Even as Conan's own steel was coming into his fist, he booted the first young noble who had accosted him squarely in the crotch; the youth shrieked like a girl and crumpled, clutching himself.

Whirling, Conan beat aside the thrust the mustachioed lordling had meant for his back. "Crom!" he bellowed. "Crom and steel!" And he waded ferociously into the combat, his sword a flashing engine of destruction.

Step by step his opponent was forced back, splashes of blood appearing on his tunic as his desperate defenses failed to turn aside the Cimmerian's blade quickly enough. Disbelief grew on his face, as if he could not understand that he faced a man better with the sword than he. Recklessly he attempted to go over to attack. Only once more did Conan's steel strike, but this time it split the lordling's skull to his black mustachios.

As the body fell the grate of the boot on pavement gave Conan warning, and he turned to block the first noble's slash. Chest to straining chest they stood, blades locked.

"I am better than ever Demetrios was," his youthful attacker sneered. "In this hour you will meet your gods, barbar."

With a heave of his mighty shoulders Conan sent the other staggering back. "Run to your mother's breast, youngling," he told him, "and live to do your boasting to women. If you know their use."

With a cry of fury the man rushed at Conan, a blur of steel before him. Eight times their blades met, striking sparks with the force of the blows, filling the street with a ringing as of a blacksmith's hammer and anvil. Then the Cimmerian's broadsword was slicing through ribs and flesh to the heart beneath.

Once more, for a moment, Conan stared into those dark eyes. "You were better," he said, "but not by enough."

The young lord opened his mouth, but blood spilled out instead of words, and death dulled his eyes.

Hastily Conan freed his blade and cleaned it on the tunic of blue brocade. The space about them still was clear, and as if an invisible wall separated him and the two dead from those hurrying by, no one so much as glanced toward them. Given the mood of the city, it was more likely than not that no one of them would admit to what he had seen, short of being put to the question by the King's torturers, but there was no point in standing there until a score of Iskandrian's warriors appeared. Sheathing his sword, Conan melded into the crowd. Within a few paces they had closed around him, cloaking him in their number.

No more did thoughts of Synelle clog his mind. With the death of the second of his attackers he had remembered Machaon telling him of two young nobles watching the house where the Free-Company was quartered. That two different lordlings should attack him on the very next day was beyond his belief. The one had called loudly that Conan had robbed the other, as if inviting witnesses. Hardly the act of one intending murder, but perhaps slaying him had been but part of their plan.

Had they succeeded, who in Ianthe would have taken the part of a dead barbarian over that of two from noble houses? The people rushing by had done their best to ignore what happened, but if collared by a noble and pressed, which of them would not remember that Conan had been accused of theft and had then attacked the two, proving his guilt? With a King's Justice and a column of Ophirean infantry, Demetrios and his friend could have descended on the Free-Company, demanded the object they claimed had been stolen—and which they could no doubt describe as well as Conan—and have the house torn apart to find it. The bronze would have been in the hands of those who sought to use it. Boros might try to speak of evil gods and rites beneath Tor Al'Kiir, or Julia, but no ear would pay heed to the pratings of a drunken former apprentice mage, nor the babblings of a pot-girl.

Conan quickened his pace, brimming with an urgent need to assure himself that the image still lay beneath the floorboards of his sleeping chamber. He had become convinced of one thing. He would not have another night of rest in Ophir until that malevolent figure was beyond the reach of men.

The black candles guttered out, and Synelle lowered her hands with a satisfied sigh. The spell binding the barbarian had been altered. He was still held, but with more subtle desires than before.

With a weary groan she sagged to a low stool, wincing with the movement, and brushed spun silver hair back from her face. She pulled her cloak—that unadorned covering of scarlet wool had been all she had taken time to snatch in her flight, and it *had* been flight—about her nakedness. Her breasts were swollen and tender, her thighs and bottom bruised by Conan's fierce desires.

"How could I have known what would be unleashed in him?" she whispered. "Who could have thought a man could be so . . ." She shivered uncontrollably.

In the barbarian's arms she had felt gripped by a force of nature as irresistible as an avalanche. Fires he had built in her, feeding them till they raged out of control. And when the leaping flames had consumed all before them, when he had quenched and slaked what he had aroused, he stoked still new fires. She had tried to bring that endless cycle to a halt, more than once she had tried—memories flooded her, memories of incoherent cries when words could not be formed and reason clung by the slenderest of threads to but a single corner of her passion-drugged mind—but her sorcery had not only wakened lust in him, it had magnified that lust, made it insatiable, overwhelming. His powerful hands had handled her like a doll. His hands, so strong, so knowing and sure of her.

"No," she muttered angrily.

She would not think of his hands. That way led to weakness. She would remember instead the humiliation of crawling weakly from her own bed when the barbarian fell at last to slumber, slinking like a thief for fear of waking him, of waking the desire that would bloom in him when his eyes touched her. On the floor of her secret chamber she had slept, curled on the hard marble with only the cloak for covering and lacking even the mat the meanest of her slaves would have, too exhausted to think or dream. Remember that, she told herself, and not the pleasures that sent tendrils of heat through her belly even in remembrance.

A ragged cry broke from her throat, and she staggered to her feet to pace the room. Her eye fell on the silver plate, black tallow hardening at its edges, the ash of blood and hair lying on its surface. The spell *was* altered. Not again would she have to face a night where she was a mote caught in the stormwind of the giant barbarian's desires. Her breathing slowed, grew more normal. He was still hers, he would still bring her to rapture, but his lusts would be more controllable. Controllable by her, that is.

"Why did I fear it so long?" she laughed softly. Taken altogether, this thing of men was quite wonderful. "They must simply be controlled, and then their vaunted strength and power can avail them nothing."

That was the lesson women had not learned, that she had only just come to. If women would not be controlled by men, then they must rather control men. She had always coveted power. How strange and beautiful that power should be the key to safety in this as well!

A knock at the door shattered her musings. Who would dare disturb her there? The rapping came again, more insistent this time. Gathering her cloak across her breasts with one hand, she flung open the door, tongue ready to flay whoever had violated her sanctorum.

A surprised, "You!" slipped out instead.

"Yes, me," Taramenon said. His face was tight with barely controlled anger. "I came to speak to you last night, but you were . . . occupied."

Laying a hand gently on his chest, she pushed him back—how easily he moved, even in his rage—and closed the door firmly behind her. No man, not even he, would ever enter that chamber.

"It is well you are here," she said as if he had had no accusation in his words. "There are matters of which we must speak. A woman must be found—"

"You were with him," the tall nobleman grated. "You gave that barbarian swine what was promised to me."

Synelle drew herself to her full height, and flung cold fury at him like a dagger. "Whatever I gave was *mine* to give. Whatever I did was *mine* to do, and none with right to gainsay me."

"I will slay him," Taramenon moaned in anguish, "like a dog in the dirt."

"You will slay whom I tell you to slay, when I tell you to slay them." Synelle softened her voice; shock had driven anger from Tara- menon's face. There was still uses for the man, and she had long since learned means of controlling him that had naught to do with sorcery. "The barber will be useful for a time. Later you may kill him if you wish."

The last had been a sudden thought. Conan was a wonderful lover, but why limit herself to one? Men did not limit themselves to one woman. Yet the young giant would always hold a place in her affections for the vistas of pleasure he opened to her; when she was Queen of Ophir she would have a magnificent tomb erected for him.

"I found the brigand you wanted," Taramenon muttered sullenly. "A woman."

Synelle's eyebrows arched. "A *woman* bandit? A hardened trull, no doubt, with greasy hair and gimlet eye."

"She is," he replied, "the most beautiful woman I have ever seen."

Synelle flinched, and her jaw tightened. Why had the fool forced his presence on her before her tire-maids could see to her toilet? "So long as she brings me the scrolls from Inaros' library, I care not what she looks like." He chuckled, and she stared at him. Suddenly he was more relaxed, as if he thought he was in command. "If you think to make sport of me," she began dangerously.

"I did not send her after Inaros' scrolls," Taramenon said.

Words froze in her throat. When she found speech again she hissed at him. "And pray tell me why not?"

"Because I sent her after the image of Al'Kiir that you speak. She knows where it is. She described it to me. It will be I who provide you with what you so desperately need. Did you think you could hide your impatience, your eagerness beyond that you've ever shown for all the parchments and artifacts you have gathered placed together? I bring it to you, Synelle, not that barbar animal, and I expect at least the reward that he got."

Her pale, dark-eyed beauty became icy still. She let her cloak gap open to the floor; Taramenon gasped, and sweat beaded his forehead. "You will come to my bed," she began softly, but abruptly her words became lashes of a whip tipped with steel, "when I summon you there. You will come, yes, perhaps sooner than you dream, certainly sooner than you deserve, but at *my* command." Slowly and calmly she covered herself once more. "Now when will the image be delivered to your hand?"

"The signal that she has it," he mumbled sulkily, "will be a man in my red surcoat standing before the main gate of the royal palace at noon. That night at dusk I will meet her at a hut in the forest."

Synelle nodded thoughtfully. "You say this woman is beautiful? A beautiful woman who does what men do, who leads men rather than belonging to them. She must have great pride. I shall be at that meeting with you, Taramenon." From the corner of her eye she saw a slave creeping down the corridor toward them, and rounded on him, furious at the interruption. "Yes?" she snapped.

Falling to his knees, the man pressed his face to the marble tiles. "A message, my gracious lady, from the noble Aelfric." Without lifting his head he held up a folded parchment.

Synelle frowned and snatched the message. Aelfric was Seneschal of Asmark, her ancestral castle, a man who served her well, but who liked as well the fact that she seldom visited or troubled him. It was not his way to invite her attention. Hastily she broke the lump of wax sealed with Aelfric's ring.

To My Most Gracious Lady Synelle,

With pain I send these tidings. In the day past have vile brigands most cowardly struck at my Lady's manor-farms, burning fields, touching barns, driving oxen and cattle into the forests. Even as your humble servant writes these dire words, the night sky glows red with newfires. I beseech my Lady to send aid, else there will be no crops left, and starvation will be the lot of her people.

I remain obediently,
your faithful servitor,
Aelfric

Angrily she crumpled the letter in her fist. Bandits attacking *her* holdings? When she held the throne she would see every brigand in the country impaled on the walls of Ianthe. For now Aelfric would have to fend for himself.

But wait, she thought. With the power of Al'Kiir she could seize the throne, overawe both lords and peasants, yet would it not be even better had she some incident to point to that showed she was more than other women? Did she take Conan's warriors into the countryside and quell these bandits herself. . . .

She prodded the slave with her foot. "I am leaving for the country. Tell the others to prepare. Go."

"Yes, my lady," the slave said, backing away on his knees. "At once, my lady." Rising, he bowed deeply and darted down the hall.

"And you, Taramenon," she went on. "Set a man to watch for this woman's signal and bring me word, then ride you for Castle Asmark. Await me there, and this night your waiting will be ended." She almost laughed at the lascivious anticipation that painted his visage. "Go," she said, in the same tone she had used with the slave, and Taramenon ran as quickly as the other had.

It was all a matter of maintaining proper control she told herself. Then she went in search of writing materials, to send a summons to the barbarian.

XIII

Conan straightened from checking his saddle girth and glared about him at the assemblage pausing for yet another rest at Synelle's command. Three and twenty high-wheeled carts, each drawn by two span of yoked oxen, were piled high with what the Countess of Asmark considered necessary for removing to her castle in the country, rolled feather mattresses and colorful embroidered silk cushions casks of the rarest wines from Aquilonia and Corinthia and even Khauran, packages of delicate viands that might not be readily available away from the capital, chests upon chests of satins and velvets and laces.

Synelle herself traveled in a gilded litter, borne by eight muscular slaves and curtained with fine silken net to admit the breeze yet keep the sun from her alabastrine skin. Her four blonde tire-women crouched in the shade of a cart, fanning themselves against the midday heat. Their lithe sleekness drew many eyes among the thirty mercenaries surrounding the carts, but the women were attuned only to listening for the next command from the litter. Nearly three score other servants and slaves hunkered out of the sun or tended to errands, drivers for the oxen, maids, seamstresses, even two cooks who were at that moment arguing vociferously over the proper method of preparing hummingbirds' tongues.

"Watch the trees, Erlik take you!" Conan shouted. Abashedly the mercenaries tore their eyes from the blondes to scan the forest that ran along two sides of the broad, grassy meadow where they had halted.

The Cimmerian had opposed halting; he had opposed each stop they had made thus far. Slowed by the oxcarts, they would not arrive at Synelle's castle until the following afternoon did they make the best speed the lumbering animals were capable of. Even one night in the forests with this strange cortege was more than he might wish for, much less risking a second such camp. A pavillion would have to be erected for Synelle to sleep in, another in which she would bathe, and yet a third for her tire-women's mats. There would be a fire to warm Synelle, fires for the cooks, fires to keep the maids from becoming affrighted of the night, and all no doubt large enough to announce their presence and location to anyone with eyes.

Machaon led his horse over to Conan. "I've word of Karela, Cimmerian," he said. "I crossed paths last night at the *Blue Bull* with a weedy scoundrel, a panderer who lost his women, and thus his income, to another, and whose tongue was free after his third pitcher of ale. I meant to speak of it earlier, but what with our patron's summons arriving hard on your heels this morn I forgot."

"What did you hear?" Conan asked eagerly.

"She uses her own name again, for one thing. She has not been long in Ophir, but already some twenty rogues follow her, and she is making reputation enough that Iskandrian has put twenty pieces of gold on her head."

"Such a small price must anger her," Conan laughed. "I fear not it will remain so low for long. But what of getting a message to her, or finding her? What did he say of that?"

"After a time the fellow seemed to realize he was babbling, and shut his teeth." At the Cimmerian's look of disappointment Machaon smiled. "But he let fall enough for me to question others. North of Ianthe, an hour's ride on a good horse, part of an ancient keep still stands, over-grown by the Sarelian Forest. There Karela camps her band on most nights. I am sure of it."

Conan grinned broadly. "I'll make her admit she has no grievance against me if I have to paddle her rump until she does."

"A treatment I could recommend for others," the tattooed man said with a significant look at the litter.

Conan followed his look and sighed. "We have been halted long enough," was all he said.

As the young Cimmerian walked toward the net-curtained palanquin he tried to make some slight sense of these last two days, not for the first time that morning. The previous day and night seemed like a dream, but a fever-born dream of madness, with lust burning all else from his mind. Had what he remembered—Synelle's sweat-slicked thighs and wanton moans flashed in his mind—actually happened? It all seemed distant and dim.

When he answered her summons this morn, he had felt no such all-consuming desire. He wanted her, wanted her more than he had ever wanted any woman, more than he had wanted all the many women of his life together, but there had been a sense of restraint within him, strictures unnatural to his nature holding him in check. He did not lose control of himself with women—were his memories of the day before true?—but neither did he face them feeling bound with stout ropes.

And he had deferred to her! When, as haughty and regal as any queen, she commanded him as to how to order his men on the march, his urge had been to snort and tell her brusquely that such matters were his province. Instead he had found himself almost pleading with her, painfully convincing her that she should leave the command of his company to him. He had met kings and potentates and not acted so. How did this woman affect him in this manner? This time, he vowed, it would be different.

He stopped before Synelle's curtained litter and bowed. "If it pleases my lady, we should be moving on." Inwardly he snarled at himself. He was no man to break vows, and this had gone as swiftly as if it had never been made. What was the matter with him? Yet he could change nothing. "It is dangerous, my lady, to stay still so long with bandits and worse about."

A delicate hand parted the mesh curtain, and Synelle looked out at him calmly, a small smile curling her full lips. Her traveling garb of cool linen clung to her, revealing the curves and shadows of her. Conan's mouth went dry, and his palms dampened, at the sight.

"It would not be so dangerous," she said, "had you obeyed me and brought your entire company."

Conan gritted his teeth. Half of him wanted to tell this fool woman that she should leave the trade of arms to those who knew it; the other half wanted to stammer an apology. "We must be moving, my lady," he said finally. It had been an effort to say only that, and he feared he did not want to know what else he might have said.

"Very well. You may see to it," she said, letting the curtain fall.

Conan bowed again before turning away.

His stomach roiled as he strode back to his horse. Perhaps he *was* going mad. "To horse!" he roared, swinging into his saddle. "Mount and prepare to move! Oxdrivers to your animals!" Chattering men and giggling women darted along the row of carts. "Keep those maids off the carts!" he shouted. "We need what speed we can manage, and no extra weight for the animals! Move you!"

Harness creaked as massive beasts took up the strain; mercenaries scrambled to their mounts in a rattle of armor.

Conan raised his arm to signal the advance, and at that instant a mass of horsemen in chain-mail charged from the trees. Shrieks rose from terrified women, and the oxen, sensing the humans' fear, bellowed mournfully. This was what the Cimmerian had feared since leaving Ianthe, but for that reason he was ready for it.

"Bows!" he commanded, and short, curved horse-bows came into thirty hands beside his own.

Those powerful bows, unknown in the west except for Conan's Free-Company, could not be drawn as ordinary bows were. Nocking an arrow with a three-fingered grip on the bowstring, the huge Cimmerian placed those fingers against his cheek and thrust the bow out from him.

There were close to a hundred of them, he estimated as he drew, wearing the sign of no house and carrying no banners or pennons, yet armored too well for bandits. He loosed, and thirty more shafts flew after his. They were still too distant to pick individual targets, but the mass of them made target enough. Saddles emptied, but the onrushing men-at-arms, their wordless battle cries rising, came on. By the time Conan let his third arrow fly—the feathered shaft lanced through the eye-slit of the foremost horseman's white-plumed helmet; the man threw his hands to his face and rolled backwards over the rump of his still racing horse—the enemy had closed too much for bows to be of further use.

"Out swords!" he called, thrusting his bow back into its lacquered wooden scabbard behind his saddle. As he drew sword and thrust his left arm through the leather straps of his round shield with its spiked boss, he realized his helm still hung from his pommel. Battle rage was on him; let them see who killed them, he thought. "Crom!" he shouted. "Crom and steel!"

At the pressure of his knees, the big Aquilonian black burst forward into a gallop. Conan caught sight of Synelle, standing by her litter with her mouth open in a scream he could not hear for the blood pounding in his ears, then his mount was smashing into another horse, riding the lighter animal down, trampling its armored rider beneath steel-shod hooves.

The huge Cimmerian caught a blade on his shield, and his answering stroke severed the arm wielding it at the shoulder. Immediately he reversed to a backslash that cut deep into the neck of another foe.

Dimly he was aware of others of his men about him in the frenzied melee, but such were of necessity a series of individual combats; only when the vagaries of battle drew two comrades together did men of one side or the other stand together against their enemy.

A chain-mailed man rode close with broad-sword raised high to chop, and Conan drove the spike on his shield into the man's chest, ripping him from the saddle with one jerk of a massive arm. War-trained, his big black lashed out with flashing fore-hooves at foemen's horses as he hacked deeper into the press with his murderous steel.

From beyond the swirling frenzy of slashing, shouting, dying men came a cry. "Conan! For the Cimmerian!"

About time, a cool corner of Conan's brain thought, and Narus, with twenty more mercenaries following, charged into the rear of the enemy. There was no time for more thought, for he was trading furious sword-strokes with a man whose chain-mail was splashed with blood not his own. He saw one of his men go down, head half-severed. The killer came galloping past, waving his gory blade and screaming a warcry. Conan kicked a foot free of its stirrup and booted the shouting man from his horse. The Cimmerian's blade freed itself from his opponent's and thrust under the other's chin, shattering the steel links of his mail coif and bringing a scarlet gout from his ruined throat. The man Conan had kicked from his saddle scrambled to his feet as his fellow fell, but the young giant's broadsword struck once, battering down his upraised steel, twice, and his headless corpse dropped across his comrade's body.

"Crom and steel!"

"Conan! Conan!"

"For the Cimmerian!"

It was too much for the mailed attackers, embattled before and behind, a huge northland beserker in their midst and no knowing in the fog of battle how many it was they faced. First a single man fled the combat, then another. Panic rippled through them, and cohesion was gone. By twos and threes they fought to get away. As they scattered some of the mercenaries set out in pursuit, echoing the halloing cry of hunters riding down deer.

"Back, you fools!" Conan bellowed. "Back, Black Erlik rot you!"

Reluctantly the mercenaries gave over the chase, and in moments the last of the mailed men still able to flee had melted into the forest. The men of the company who had pursued trotted back, waving gory swords and rasing shouts of victory.

"A most excellent plan, Cimmerian," Narus laughed as he galloped up, "having us trail behind as a surprise for unwelcome guests." His jazeraint hauberk was splattered with blood, no drop of which was his. The gaunt-faced man, disease-riddled though he appeared, was equal to Machaon with a blade, and none but Conan was their master. "Ten to one in gold they never knew how many hit them."

"A difficult wager to settle," Conan said, but half his mind on the other. "Machaon," he called, "what's the butcher's price?"

"I'm taking a count, Cimmerian." Quickly the tattooed veteran finished and rode to join them. "Two dead," he retorted, "and a dozen who'll need the carts to get back to Ianthe."

Conan nodded grimly. Well over a score of the enemy lay on the hoof-churned ground, meadow grass and soil now seeming plowed, and only a few moved weakly. As many more were scattered back to the trees, sprouting feathered shafts. In the grim world of the mercenary it was little better than an even trade, for enemies were always there and easily found, but new companions were hard to come by.

"See if one of them lives enough to answer questions," the Cimmerian commanded. "I would know who sent them against us, and why."

Hurriedly Machaon and Narus dismounted. Moving among the bodies, stopping occasionally to heave one over, they returned supporting between them a bloodstreaked man with a wicked gash down the side of his face and neck.

"Mercy," he gasped faintly. "I cry mercy."

"Then name he who sent you," Conan demanded. "Were you to kill us all, or one in particular?"

The Cimmerian had no intention of slaying a wounded and helpless man, but the prisoner clearly feared the worst. Almost eagerly he said, "Count Antimides. He bid us slay you and seize the Lady Synelle. Her we were to bring to him naked and in chains."

"Antimides!" Synelle hissed. The men shifted uneasily to see her picking her way across the bloody ground; such sights as lay about them, men hacked and torn by the savagery of battle, were not for women's eyes. Synelle did not seem to notice. "He dares so much against me?" she continued. "I will have his eyes and his manhood! I will—"

"My lady," Conan said, "those who attacked us may rejoin and seek you again." And he also, he added to himself, though that did not concern him as much as the other. "You must return to Ianthe, and quickly. You must ride one of the horses."

"Back to the city?" Synelle nodded vigorously. "Yes. And when I get there Antimides will learn the price of an attack on my person!" Her eyes were bright with eagerness for that teaching.

Conan began seeing to preparations, ordering men who hurried to obey. The warriors, at least, knew their vulnerability should the enemy return, perhaps with reinforcements. "Machaon, tell off ten men to ride with the carts. Unload everything except the Lady Synelle's jewelry and clothes to lighten the oxen's loads. Leave the litter here, so they can see she's no longer with the carts. Crom, of course we bring in our dead! Spread the wounded among the carts so they're not crowded, and have the maids tend them. Yes, their wounded as well."

"No!" Synelle snapped. "Leave Antimides' men! Fetch me naked and chained, will they? Let them die!"

Conan's hands tightened on his reins until his knuckles were white. His temples throbbed like drums. "Load their wounded, too," he said, and drew a shuddering breath. Almost he had not been able to get the words out.

Synelle looked at him strangely. "A strong will," she said musingly. "And yet there could be pleasure in—" Abruptly she stopped, as if she thought she had said too much, but the Cimmerian could understand nothing of it.

"My lady," he said, "you must ride astride. We have no side-saddle."

She held out a hand to him. "Your dagger, barbarian."

When she took it from him it felt as though sparks jumped from her hand to his. Deftly she slit the front of her robe. Narus led forward a horse, and she mounted with flashing limbs, exposed to the tops of her pale thighs, nor did she do anything to cover them once in the saddle. Conan could feel her eyes on him as solidly as a touch, but of which sort he could not tell. He tore his gaze from her long legs, and heard a laugh softly, the sound burning in his brain.

"We ride!" he commanded hoarsely, and galloped toward Ianthe, the rest streaming behind.

XIV

Karela kept the hood of her dark blue woolen cloak pulled well forward; there were those about her in the crowd-filled streets of Ianthe who would put aside their habit of ignoring what occurred around them for a chance at Iskandrian's reward.

She snorted at the thought. Twenty pieces of gold! A thousand times so much had been placed on her head by the Kings of Zamora and Turan. The merchants of those countries had offered more, and would have considered it cheap to rid their caravans of her depredations at the price. High Councils had had debated methods of dealing with her, armies had pursued her, and no man took passage from one city to another without offering prayers that she would spare his purse, all with equal futility. Now, she found herself reduced to an amount of coin that spoke of petty irritation. The humiliation of it was so great that barely could she keep her mind on her purpose for entering the city.

The house where Conan's company of rogues was gathered lay just ahead. That morning she had watched him ride out with half his company. A short time later another large contingent of his men had departed by another gate and trailed after the first. Wily Cimmerian! She had long since gotten over the foolishness of failing to respect his abilities. He would be taken in no ordinary trap. But then she was no ordinary woman.

Unbidden, her thoughts went back to that woman of the nobility he had been escorting. Did she know him, he had already visited the wench's bed. He had always had an eye for willing wenches, and few were those who were not willing did he once smile at them. The red-haired woman wished she could get her hands on this Synelle. Lady, indeed. She would not soil her hands with the like of those who called themselves ladies. Karela would show her what a real woman looked like, then send her back to Conan as a present, stuffed naked into a sack. When someone had offered her gold to burn the jade's farms, she had not stopped to ask why or query who the man with the deep-set, commanding eyes was behind his mask of black silk. It had been a chance to strike at Conan, and his precious Synelle, and she leaped at it. She would prick him and prick him until he was forced to flee, and if he would not . . .

Angrily she pulled her mind back to the matter at hand. She no longer cared what women he took, she told herself. Such interest in the man had brought her naught but grief. With the men he had taken to protect his new trull, he could not have left many behind. She looked through the arched gateway as she passed. Yes. There were only a handful to be seen, playing at dice against the side of the fountain in the courtyard. He who had made the cast cursed, and the others laughed as they scooped up his losings.

Karela raised a hand to her face as if brushing away a fly, and two men pushing a handcart toward her, its flat bed piled high with wooden boxes held in place by ropes, suddenly turned it into the alley beside the house. Karela followed them. The men glanced at her questioningly; she nodded, and they turned to watch the street.

One, a dark-faced Zamoran with drooping mustaches, whom she had taken on out of memory of better days, said softly, "No one looks."

In the space of two breaths Karela scrambled up the carefully arranged boxes and into a window on the second floor. It was Conan's room. Her sources of information had discovered that for her easily enough.

Her lip curled contemptuously as she looked around the bare chamber. So this was what he had come to since forsaking a palace in Nemedia. She had never heard the straight of his departing that land when he had been offered honors and wealth by the King, but it brought a measure of continuing satisfaction that he had not profited from the adventures which ended in her flight. It did her good to think of him brought low. Yet the blankets were folded neatly on the bed. There were no cobwebs on the ceiling, no dust in the corners, and the floor had been freshly swept. A woman, she thought, and not likely it was his fine Synelle. The Cimmerian gathered a zenana about him like an easterner.

Sternly she reminded herself of her lack of interest in Conan's women. She had come for that obscene bronze figure, and nothing more. But where to begin searching? There did not look to be many places for hiding. Beneath the bed, perhaps.

Before she could take a step, the door opened and a girl wearing plain white robes walked in. There was something oddly familiar about her face and hair, though Karela could swear she had never seen the girl before.

"Keep your silence, wench," Karela commanded. "Close the door and answer my questions quickly, and you'll come to no harm."

"Wench!" the girl said, her eyes flashing indignantly. "What are you doing here . . . wench? I think I'll let you see if you like Fabio's switch. Then you can answer questions for me."

"I told you," Karela began, but the girl was already turning back to the door. With a curse the woman bandit jumped across the room and grappled with her, managing to kick the door shut as she did.

She expected the girl to surrender, or try to scream for help at most, but with a sqawl of rage the other woman buried her hands in Karela's red hair. The two women fell to the floor in a kicking, nail-clawing heap.

Derketo, Karela thought, she did not want to kill the jade, but she had defended herself too long with a sword to remember well this woman-fighting. She almost screamed as the other sank teeth into her shoulder; handfuls of her hair were at the point of being ripped from her head. Desperately she slammed a knee into the girl's belly. Breath left the other woman in a gasp, and Karela wriggled forward to kneel on her arms. Her dagger slipped into her hand, and she held it before the girl's face.

"Now be silent, Derketo take you!" she panted. The girl glared up at her defiantly, but held her tongue.

Abruptly Karela realized what was familiar about the girl. The eyes were different, but the color of her hair, the shape of her face. Conan had found himself an imitation of herself. She could not think whether to laugh, or cry, or slit the wench's throat. Or wait for the Cimmerian and slit his. No interest, she told herself again. No interest at all.

"What is your name?" she grated. That would never do. She made an effort to sound more friendly, if that was possible while brandishing a dagger in the wench's face. "What's your name, girl? I like to know who I'm talking to."

The woman beneath her hesitated, then said, "Julia. And that is all you will get from me."

Karela dressed her face with a smile. "Julia, Conan has a bronze figure that I must have, a filthy thing with horns. An you've seen it, you'll not have forgotten. No woman could. Tell me where it is, and I'll leave you unharmed when I go."

"I'll tell you nothing!" Julia spat. But her eyes had flickered to a corner of the room.

There was nothing there at all that Karela could see. Still. . . . "Very well, Julia, I must search without your help then. But I'll have to bind you. Now hear my warning well. Do you try to fight or flee, either one, this," she gestured with her blade, "will find a home in your heart. Do you understand?"

Julia's face was still filled with fury, but she nodded, albeit with obvious reluctance.

Carefully Karela cut away Julia's robe. The girl flinched, but otherwise did not change her hate-filled expression. As Karela was slicing strips from the robe with her dagger she could not help noticing her naked prisoner's body. The Cimmerian always had had a liking for full-breasted women, she thought sourly. But hers were better. That was, if she had still been interested in him in that way, which she was not.

"Roll over," she commanded, nudging Julia with her foot. When the girl obeyed, Karela swiftly tied her hands and feet. The wench groaned through clenched teeth as she pulled the bindings together in the small of the naked woman's back, but the threat of the dagger was enough to keep the protest muted. Not comfortable, Karela thought savagely, but then the girl had not truly answered her question. A wadding of cloth fastened with another strip of cloth did her a gag, but before Karela left she lifted Julia's face by a handful of hair. "Conan likes round bottoms," she said with a biting smile. "You have a bottom like a boy."

Julia jerked wildly at her bonds and made angry sounds behind her gag, but Karela was already studying the corner the girl's eyes had indicated. There *was* nothing there. Neither crack in the plaster nor new work gave sign that anything had been hidden behind the wall, and no opening in the fly-specked ceiling . . . A board sagged beneath her foot, and she smiled.

Swiftly she knelt and levered up the floorboard with her dagger. The malevolent bronze lay beneath, nestled in decades of dirt and rat droppings. Fitting, she thought. She reached for the horned figure, but her fingers stopped, quivering, a handsbreadth away. She could not bring herself to touch it. The evil she had felt before still radiated from it, twisting her stomach. Contact with it would surely have her wretching. Hastily she fetched a blanket from the bed, folded it around the bronze, and gathered it up like a sack, holding the weighty burden well away from her. Even so she could sense the abomination of the thing, but so long as she did not have to look at it she could stand carrying it.

At the window she paused. "Thank Conan for me," she told the struggling girl. "Tell him I thank him for five hundred pieces of gold."

With that she dropped through the window and scampered down the boxes. In the alley she hid the blanket-wrapped figure inside a box on the cart. And the relief it was to get rid of it, she thought, even after so brief a contact.

"We'll meet in one turn of the glass," she told the mustached Zamoran, "at the Carellan Stables."

As she slipped back into the crowded street, the hood of her cloak once more shielding her face, she glanced regretfully at the sun. Too late today to post a man before the royal palace. On the morrow, though, the signal would be sent, and by nightfall she would have her five hundred pieces of gold. She wished fervently that she could see the Cimmerian's face when he learned how much he had lost.

XV

Silvery hair and slit robe alike flowing behind her, Synelle raced through the wide corridors of her great house, heedless of the horrified cries of servants and slaves at her dusty dishevelment, unhearing of their pleas after her welfare and concern for her precipitate return. Conan had left ten of his archers, now standing watch at the entrances, to protect her, then rode off before she could stop him. To deal with Count Antimides, one of those left behind had told her. But she would not wait for him to deal with the Mitra-accursed wretch. Antimides had struck at her—at her!—and his destruction, utter and complete, was her right and hers alone. The means of it must be exquisite, so that when the truth of it could at last be proclaimed to the world the expunging of that excrescence would be told and retold for centuries. His desire for the crown and and chains he had meant to emprison her in, that was it.

From a wall she snatched a mirror of silvered glass. With that under her arm, she swept into her secret chamber. From amidst the scintillant flasks and seething beakers of vile substances she took a vial of Antimides' blood. He had been a useful, if unknowing, tool until now, adding to the confusion and weakening those she would eventually have to cow, but always had she been aware that he might become dangerous to her. That blood had been obtained from an ensorceled serving girl, one who often shared Antimides' bed and passed on to Synelle, for the bewitchment that held her, all she learned of the great lord's plans, and kept against just such a day as this. Necromantic spells that could hold a corpse incorruptible for a thousand years kept it liquid.

With great care she sketched the crown of Ophir on the mirror in the count's blood. Below that she drew a sanguine chain.

"See yourself with the crown you seek upon your head, Antimides," she whispered. "But only for a time. A brief, painful time." Laughing cruelly, she bent back to her dark work.

"We attract attention," Machaon announced to no one in particular.

The file of nineteen armored horsemen in spiked helms with round shields slung on the arms, led by Conan, made its way slowly through the streets of Ianthe, and the crowds who parted before them did indeed stare. Deadly intensity hung about them like a cloud, stunning even those who would have looked away, numbing their reticence to see.

"There will be trouble for this," Narus said dolefully. He rode next in line behind Machaon. "Even can we slay Antimides—and the gods alone know how many guards he has—Iskandrian will not look the other way for our killing of a noble within the very walls of the capital. We shall have to flee Ophir, if we can."

"And if we do not slay him," Conan said grimly, "then still we must flee. Or would you ever be sitting with your back to a wall for protection, ever looking across your shoulder for his next attack?"

And more attacks there would be, the Cimmerian was sure. Whatever Antimides' reason for wanting to seize Synelle, he could only be seeking Conan's death to still his tongue. The attacks would continue until Conan was dead, or Antimides was.

"I didn't say we should not kill him," Narus sighed. "I simply said we must flee afterwards."

"If we must flee in any case," Taurianus demanded, "why should we then take this risk? Let the lord live, and let us be gone from Ianthe with all our blood in us." The lanky man looked more glum even than Narus, and the dark hair that straggled from under his helm was damp with anxious sweat.

"You'll never make a captain, Ophirean," the gaunt-faced mercenary replied. "A Free-Company lives by its name, and dies by it, as well. Can we be attacked with impunity, then the company is as dead as if we have all had our weazands slit, and we are no better than vagabonds and beggars."

Taurianus muttered under his breath, but spoke no more complaints aloud.

"There is Antimides' palace," Machaon said abuptly. He frowned

suspiciously at the sprawling, golden-domed edifice of marble and alabaster. "I see no guards. I do not like this, Cimmerian."

Antimides' palace was second in size within Ianthe only to the royal
palace itself, a massive structure of columns and terraces and spired towers, with broad, deep steps leading up from the street. There were no
guards in sight on those steps, and one of the great bronze doors stood
ajar.

A trap perhaps, Conan thought. Had Antimides learned of his failure
already? Was he inside with his guards gathered close about him for
protection? Such would be a foolish move, sure to have been protested
by any competent captain. Yet a lord with Antimides' arrogance might
well have bludgeoned his guard commander into complacent compliance
long since.

He turned in his saddle, studying the men behind. The seven besides
Machaon and Narus who had crossed the border from Nemedia with
him were there. They had followed him far, and loyally.

Long and hard had he labored to build this company, and to keep it,
yet fairness made him say, "What numbers we face inside I do not know.
Does any man wish to leave, now is the time."

"Speak not foolishness," Machaon said. Taurianus opened his mouth,
then closed it again without speaking.

Conan nodded. "Four men to hold the horses," he ordered as he
dismounted.

With steady, purposeful tread they climbed the white marble steps,
drawing swords as they did. Conan stepped through the open door, its
broad bronze face scribed hugely with the arms of Antimides' house,
and found himself in a long, dome-ceilinged hall, with grand, alabaster
stairs sweeping up to a columned balcony that encircled the hall.

A buxom serving girl in plain green robes that left her pretty legs
bare to the tops of her thighs dashed out of a door to one side of the
hall, a large, weighty bag over her shoulders. A scream bubbled out of
her when she saw the armed and armored men invading the palace.
Dropping the bag, she sped wailing back the way she had come.

Narus thoughtfully eyed the array of golden goblets and silver plate
that had spilled out of the bag. "A guess as to what happens here?"

"Antimides fleeing our righteous wrath?" Machaon hazarded hope-
fully.

"We cannot afford let him escape us," Conan said. He did not believe
the count would flee, but there was strangeness here that worried him.
"Spread out. Find him."

They scattered in all directions, but warily, swords at the ready. Too many battles had they faced, too many traps had been sprung around them, for complacency. The continued survival of a mercenary lay in his readiness to give battle on an instant. Any instant.

A lord's chambers would be above, the Cimmerian thought. He took the curving stairs upward.

Room by room he searched, finding no one, living or dead. Everywhere there were signs of hasty flight, and of a desire to carry away everything of value. Marks where tapestries had been pulled from the walls and carpets taken up. Tables overturned, whatever they had borne gone. Golden lamps wrenched halfway from brackets that had resisted being pried from the walls. Oddly, every mirror he saw was starred with long cracks.

Then he pushed open a door with his sword, and looked into a room that seemed untouched. Furniture stood upright, golden bowls and silver vases in place, and tapestries depicting heroic scenes of Ophir's past hung from the walls. The one mirror in the room was cracked, however, as the others were. An intricately carved chair was set before it, the high back to the door, but the voluminous, gold-embroidered green silk sleeve of a man's robe hung over one gilded wooden arm.

With the strides of a great hunting cat the giant Cimmerian crossed the room, presented his sword to the throat of the man seated there. "Now, Antimides—" Conan's words died abruptly, and the hairs on the back of his neck stirred.

Count Antimides sat with eyes bulging from an empurpled face and blackened tongue protruding between teeth clenched and bared in a rictus of agony. The links of a golden chain were buried in the swollen flesh of his neck, and his own hands clutched the ends of that chain, seeming even in the iron grip of death to strain at drawing it tighter.

"Crom!" Conan muttered. He would not believe that fear of his vengeance had been enough to make Antimides sit before a mirror and watch as he strangled himself. The Cimmerian had met sorcery often enough before to know the smell of it.

"Conan! Where are you?"

"In here!" he replied to the shout from the hall.

Machaon and Narus entered with a slender, frightened youth in filthy rags that had been fine satin robes not long past. His wrists bore the bloody marks of manacles; the palor of his skin and the thinness of his face spoke of long days in darkness and missed meals.

"Look what we found chained below," the tattooed man said.

Not so much of a youth, Conan saw at second glance; there was that in the man's manner—a petulant thrust of a too-full lower lip; a sulkiness of eye and stance—that gave an air of boyishness.

"Well, who is he?" the Cimmerian asked. "You speak as if I should know him."

The youthful appearing man lifted his chin with almost feminine hauteur. "I am Valentius," he said in a high voice that strained for steadiness, "count now, but King to be. I give you my thanks for this rescue." His dark eyes flickered uncertainly to Narus and Machaon. "If rescue it indeed is."

Narus shrugged. "We told him why we are here," he said to Conan, "but he does not believe. Or not fully."

"There are two guards below with their gullets slit," Machaon said, "but we've seen no one living. There is madness in this place, Cimmerian. Has Antimides truly fled?"

For an answer Conan jerked his head toward the high-backed chair. The other three hesitated, then moved quickly to look.

Shockingly, Valentius giggled. "However did you make him do this? No matter. 'Tis fitting for his betrayal of my trust." His fine-featured face darkened quickly. "I came to him for aid and shelter, and he laughed at me. At me! Then he clapped me in irons and left me to rot and fight rats for my daily bowl of swill. So pious, he was. So unctuous. He would not have my blood on his hands, he said, and laughed. He would leave that to the rats."

"I've seen death on many fields, Conan," Machaon said, "but this is an ugly way to slay a man, for all he deserved killing." His knuckles were white on his sword hilt as he gazed on the corpse. Narus formed his fingers into a sign to ward off evil.

"I did not kill him," Conan told them. "Look at his hands on the chain. Antimides slew himself."

Valentius laughed again, shrilly. "However 'twas done, it was done well." Moods shifting like quicksilver, his face screwed up viciously, and he spat in the corpse's bloated face. "I but regret I could not see the doing."

Conan exchanged glances with his two friends. This was the man with the best blood claim to succeed Valdric on the throne of Ophir. The young Cimmerian shook his head in disgust. The urge to be rid of the youth quickly was strong, but did he simply leave him the fool would have his throat cut in short order. Perhaps that would be the better for Ophir, but such was not his decision to make.

To Valentius he said, "We will take you to the royal palace. Valdric will give you protection."

The slender young man stared at him, wild-eyed and trembling. "No! No, you cannot! Valdric will kill me. I am next in line for the throne. He will kill me!"

"You speak foolishness," Conan growled. "Valdric has no care for aught but saving his own life. 'Tis likely in a day he'll not even remember you are in the palace."

"You do not understand," Valentius whined, wringing his hands. "Valdric will look at me, knowing that he is dying, knowing that I will be King after. He will think of the long years I have before me, and he will hate me. He will have me slain!" He looked desperately from one face to the next, and finished with a sullenly muttered, " 'Tis what I would do, and so will he."

Machaon spat on the costly Turanian carpet. "What of blood kin?" he asked gruffly "What of friends, or allies?"

The cringing man shook his head. "How can I know who among them to trust? My own guards turned on me, men who have served my house faithfully for years." Suddenly his voice quickened, and his dark eyes took on a sly light. "You protect me! When I am King, I will give you wealth, titles. You shall have Antimides' palace, and be count in his stead. You and your men shall be the King's personal bodyguard. Riches beyond imagining I shall grant you, and power. Choose a woman, noble or common, and she will be yours. Two, do you wish them, or three! Name the honor you desire! Give it name, and I shall grant it!"

Conan grimaced. It was true that there could be no better service for a Free-Company than what Valentius offered, but he would sooner serve a viper. "What of Iskandrian?" he said. "The general takes no part in these struggles, follows no faction."

Valentius nodded reluctantly. "If you will not serve me," he said sulkily.

"Then let us leave this place," Conan said, "and quickly. It would be ill to be found standing over Antimides' corpse." As the others hurried from the room, though, he paused for one last look at the dead man. Whatever sorcery Antimides had enmeshed himself in, the Cimmerian was glad it did not touch him. With a shiver he followed the others.

XVI

Dusk was falling as Conan returned to the house where his company was quartered, and the gray thickening of the air, the coming blackness, fitted his mood well. Iskandrian had taken Valentius under his protection at the army's barracks readily enough, but the old general had listened to their story with a suspicious eye on the Cimmerian. Only for Valentius' agreement that Antimides appeared to have strangled himself had the mercenaries left those long, stone buildings unchained, and the petulant glare the young lord gave Conan as he said the words was as clear as a statement that he would have spoken differently could he but be sure he would not himself be implicated.

And then there had been Synelle. Conan had found her in a strange mixture of fury and satisfaction. She already knew of Antimides' death, though he was not aware the word had spread so quickly; that accounted for her contentment. But she had upbraided him savagely for riding away without her permission, and for taking the time to bring Valentius to Iskandrian's care.

The last seemed to infuriate her more than the first. He was in her service, not that of the fopling Valentius, and he would do well to remember it. To his own amazement he had listened meekly, and worst of all had had to fight with himself to stop from begging her forgiveness. He had never begged anything from man or woman, god or demon, and it made his stomach turn to think how close he had come.

He slammed open the door of his room, and stopped dead. In the dimness Julia, naked and bound hand and foot, frowned up at him with her mouth working frantically at a gag.

"Machaon!" he shouted. "Narus!" Hastily he untied her gag. Her bonds had been tightly tied, and she had pulled them tighter with her struggles. He had to wield his dagger carefully to cut only the strips of cloth and not her flesh. "Who did this?" he demanded as he labored to free her.

With a groan she expelled a damp wad of cloth from her mouth, and worked her jaw before speaking. "Do not let him see me like this," she pleaded. "Hurry! Hurry!"

Machaon, Narus and Boros tumbled through the door, all shouting questions at once, and Julia screamed. As Conan severed the last binding, she jerked free of him and scrambled to the bed, snatching a blanket to cover herself.

"Go away, Machaon!" she cried, cowering back. Rubiate color suffused her cheeks. "I will not have you see me so. Go away!"

" 'Tis gone," Boros said drunkenly, pointing to the corner where Conan had hidden the bronze figure.

For the first time the Cimmerian realized the board was lifted aside, and the space beneath it empty. A chill as of death oozed through him. It seemed meet that this day should end so, with disaster peering at him like the vacant eye-sockets of a skull.

"Mayhap," Boros muttered, "do we ride hard, we can be across the border before it's used. I've always wished to see Vendhya, or perhaps Khitai. Does anyone know a land more distant?"

"Be quiet, you old fool," Conan growled. "Julia, who took the bronze? Crom, woman, stop worrying about that accursed blanket and answer me!"

Not ceasing her efforts to make the blanket cover all of her bountiful curves, and less precariously, Julia glared at him and sniffed. " 'Twas a trull in men's breeches and wearing a sword." She glanced at Machaon out of the corner of her eye. "She said I have a boy's bottom. My bottom is as round as hers, only not so big."

Conan ground his teeth. "Her eyes," he asked impatiently. "They were green? Her hair red? Did she say anything else?"

"Karela?" Machaon said. "I thought she meant to kill you, not steal from you. But why is Boros so affrighted by this thing she took? You've not got us meddling with sorcerers again, Cimmerian?"

"You know her," Julia said accusingly. "I thought so from what she said about my . . ." She cleared her throat and began again. "All I remember of what she said is that she swore by Derketo and thanked you for five hundred pieces of gold. Have you truly given her so much? I remember my father's lemans, and I'd not think this Karela was worth a silver."

Conan pounded a huge fist on his thigh. "I must find her, Machaon, without delay. She has stolen a bronze figure that came to me by happenstance, a thing of evil power that will wreak destruction undreamed of, does she sell it to those I fear she will. Give me precise directions to find that ruined keep."

Julia moaned. "That is what she meant about gold? She takes the hellish thing to those Boros spoke of? Mitra protect us all, and the land!"

"I understand not a word of all this," Machaon said, "but one thing I do know. An you enter the Sarelain Forest in the night, you'll break your neck. That tangle is bad enough to travel in daylight. 'Twould take a man born there to find his way in the dark."

"I can find her," Boros said, swaying, "so long as she has the bronze. Its evil is in truth a beacon." He pushed his sleeves up bony arms. "A simple matter of—"

"An you attempt magic in your condition," Conan cut him off, "I'll put your head on a spike over the River Gate with my own hands." The gray-bearded man looked hurt, but subsided, muttering under his breath. Conan turned to Machaon. "There is no time to waste. Daylight may be too late."

Machaon nodded reluctantly, but Narus said, "Then take a score of us with you. Her band—"

"—would hear so many coming and melt away," the Cimmerian finished for him. "I go alone. Machaon?"

Slowly the tattooed veteran spoke.

Machaon was right, Conan thought as an unseen branch whipped across his face for what seemed the hundredth time. A man could easily break his neck in that blackness. He forced his horse on through the heavy thicket of vines and undergrowth, hoping he moved in the right direction. As a boy he had learned to guide himself by the stars, but the sky was seldom visible, for the forest was ancient, filled with huge oaks whose thick interwoven branches formed a canopy with few openings above his head.

"You've come far enough," a voice called from the dark, "unless you want a quarrel in your ribs!"

Conan put a hand to his sword.

"None of that!" another man said, then chuckled. "Me and Tenio grew up in this forest, big man, poaching the King's deer by night. He sees better than I do, and you might as well be standing under a full moon for all of me."

"I seek Karela," Conan began, but got no further.

"Enough talk," the first voice said. "Take him!"

Suddenly rough hands were pulling the big Cimmerian from his horse, into the midst of a knot of men. He could not even see well enough to count how many, but he seized an arm and broke it, producing a scream. There was no room to draw his sword, nor light to see where to strike; he snatched his dagger instead and laid about him, bringing yells and curses when he slashed flesh. In the end their numbers were too great, and he was pressed to the dirt by the weight of them, his wrists bound behind him and a cord tied between his ankles for a hobble.

"Anybody hurt bad?" panted the man who had chuckled earlier.

"My arm," someone moaned, and another voice said, "Bugger your arm! He near as cut my ear off!"

Cursing the dark—not all had cat's eyes—they pulled Conan to his feet and pulled him through the trees, dragging him, when the hobble caught roots and tripped him, until he managed to get his feet under him again.

Abruptly a blanket was pulled aside before him, and he was thrust into a stone-walled room lit by rush torches in rusted iron sconces on the walls. A huge hearth with a roaring fire of logs as big as a man's leg, a great iron pot suspended on pivoting arm above it, filled one wall. Blankets at the windows—narrow arrow-slits, in fact—kept the light from spilling into the surrounding forest. A dozen men, as motley a collection of ruffians as Conan had ever seen, sprawled on benches at crude trestle tables, swilling wine from rough clay mugs and wolfing down stew from wooden bowls.

Karela got to her feet as Conan's captors crowded in after him, complaining loudly about their wounds and bruises. Her dark leather jerkin, worn over tight breeches of pale gray silk tucked into red boots, was laced snugly, yet gaped enough at the top to reveal the creamy upper slopes of her full, heavy breasts. A belt worn low on her well-rounded hips supported her scimitar.

"So," she said, "you're more fool than I thought you, Cimmerian. You'll force me to kill you yet."

"The bronze, Karela," he said urgently. "You must not sell it. They're trying—"

"Silence him!" she snapped.

"—to raise Al'Kiir," he managed to get out, then a club smashed against the back of his head, and darkness claimed him.

XVIII

The fool, Karela thought as she stared at Conan's huge prostrate form. Was his masculine arrogance so great that he could believe all he must needs do to retrieve the figure was ride up and take it? She knew him for a priceful man, and knew as well that the pride was justified. By himself, with naught but his broadsword, he was more than a match for . . .

Abruptly she cursed to herself. The Cimmerian was no longer the same man who had emprisoned a part of her and carried it away with him. She had been thinking of him as he was when she first knew him, a thief and a loner with naught but his wits and the strength of his sword arm. Now he commanded men, and men who, she reluctantly admitted, were a more dangerous pack than the hounds she led.

"Was he alone?" she demanded. "An you've led his Free-Company here, I'll have your hides for boots!"

"Didn't see nobody else," Tenio muttered. "That means there weren't nobody else." A small, ferrety man with a narrow face and sharp nose, he spat a tooth into his palm and glared at it. "I say kill him." Some of those nursing broken ribs and knife gashes growled assent.

Marusas, her Zamoran, produced a dagger in his long, calloused fingers. "Let us wake him, instead. He looks strong. He would scream a long time before he died."

Instantly all of the men were shouting, arguing for one course or the other.

"Kill him now! He's too dangerous!"

"He's just a man. Flay him, and he'll scream like any other."

"You didn't fight him out there! You don't know!"

"He cut me to the bone with ten of us on him, and broke Agorio's arm!"

"Silence, you dogs !" Karela roared, and the bickering ceased as they turned to stare at her. "I say who dies, and I say he doesn't. Not yet, at least! Do any of you mangy curs care to dispute me? To your kennels!"

She put a hand to her scimitar hilt, and a dangerous light glowed in her green eyes. One by one they dropped their eyes from hers, muttered, and shuffled back to their drinking or to tend their wounds. Jamaran, a huge, shaven-headed Kushite with shoulders broader than Conan's and the thick fingers of a wrestler, was the last to remain glowering at her, his dark face twisted with anger. A split of his cheek showed where Conan's fist had landed in the struggle.

"Well, Jamaran?" she said. She knew he wanted to replace her, and take her to his bed as well, though he did not know she was aware of his desires. He had thoughts about the proper place for women; sooner or later she would have to show him the error of his ways or slay him. "Are you ready to dispute my rule?"

Surprise glimmered on his face, and was quickly supplanted by a sneering smile. "Not yet," he growled. "I will tell you when, my red-haired pretty." His black eyes ran over her body like a caress, then with incredible lightness on his feet for a man of his size he stalked to the nearest table and snatched up a mug, tossing back his head to drink deeply.

Karela quivered in shocked outrage as she glared at his broad back. Never before had he been so open. She would have to kill him, she thought, after this. But it could not be done now. The temper of her band was too delicately balanced. As much as she hated admitting it, a wrong move now could wreck all she had labored for. With a snarl she released her sword.

It was not like the days in Zamora, she thought grimly. Then none of her band dared to challenge her word, or to think of her as a woman. It was all Conan's fault. He had changed her in some way she did not understand, some way she did not want to be changed. He had woven a thread of weakness into her fabric, and other men could sense it.

As if her thoughts of him had been a call the Cimmerian groaned and stirred.

"Gag him," she ordered. "Move, Derketo curse you! I'll not be bothered by his babblings!"

Conan shook himself as Tenio and Jamaran knelt beside him. "Karela," he said desperately, "listen to me. These men are dangerous. They mean to bring an evil—"

Tenio tried to shove a rag into his mouth, and screamed as the Cimmerian sank teeth into his hand. Jamaran smashed a fist into Conan's jaw; the ferret-faced man jerked his hand free, sprinkling drops of blood as he shook it. Before Conan could speak again Jamaran had thrust the wadding home and bound it. As he got to his feet the shaven-headed man kicked Conan in the ribs and pulled back his booted foot for another. Tenio drew his dagger with his undamaged hand, a murderous gleam in his eyes.

"Stop that," Karela commanded. "Did you hear me? Leave him!"

Slowly, reluctantly, the two drew away from the Cimmerian.

She could feel those sapphire eyes on her. He shook his head furiously, fighting the gag, making angry noises behind it. Shivering, she turned her back to stare into the fire.

Karela knew she could not afford to let herself listen to the young giant. He had always been able to talk her into anything. Did he put his hands on her, her will melted. This time, she told herself, this time it would be different.

The night went slowly for her, and she was aware that it was because of Conan's eyes on her back. The rest of the bandits took themselves off to sleep, most simply pulling blankets about them on the stone floor, but sleep would not come near Karela. Like a leopard in a cage she paced, and the goad that made her pace was an unblinking icy blue gaze. She would have had him blindfolded, except that she would not admit even to herself that simply his eyes on her could affect her so greatly.

Finally the titian-haired beauty settled before the great hearth and studied the leaping flames as if they were the most important thing in the world. Yet even then she could not escape the Cimmerian, imagining him writhing in the fire, imagining him suffering all the tortures of the damned, all the tortures he so richly deserved. She could not understand why that seemed to make her feel even worse, or why from time to time she had to surreptitiously wipe tears from her cheeks.

At first light she sent Tenio riding for Ianthe with the scarlet surcoat. The rest of the day she spent in ignoring Conan. Food and drink she denied him.

"Let him eat and drink when I have gone," she commanded.

The men scattered about the room, most devoting their energies to dice or cards, gave her muttered assent and strange looks. She did not care. Not for the briefest moment would she allow the Cimmerian to be ungagged in her presence. Not until she had the five hundred pieces of gold in her hands to taunt him with. Not until she managed to settle herself, and that seemed strangely difficult to do.

Then the sun was making its downward journey. Time for Karela to leave for the hut. The bronze she had left, still wrapped in the blanket from Conan's bed, outside beneath a tree. There was no one about to steal it, and she would not have it under the same roof with her could she avoid it.

As she was tying the blanket-swathed bundle behind her saddle—and muttering to herself for the sickness it made her feel in the pit of her stomach—Jamaran came out of the lone tower that remained of the ancient keep.

"That thing is valuable," he said challengingly. "Five hundred gold pieces, you say."

Karela did not answer him. This morning was no better time to kill him than last night had been.

"I should go with you," the huge man went on when she remained silent. "To make certain you return safely with the gold. This noble you go to may prove treacherous. Or perhaps something else might delay you, a woman alone with so much gold."

Karela's face tightened. Did the fool think she planned to run off with the coin? Or did he think to take the gold and her both? "No!" she snapped as she swung into the saddle. "You are needed here to help guard the prisoner."

"There are a score to watch him. So much gold—"

"Fool!" She made the word a sneering whiplash. "You must learn to think if you would lead men. That one inside, bound as he is, is more dangerous than any man you've ever seen. I but hope there are enough of you to keep him till I return."

Before Jamaran could speak the furious words she could read plainly on his face, Karela put spurs to her fleet eastern bay, and darted down a narrow path that was little more than a deer track. Many such crossed and criss-crossed in the thick forest, and she was soon gone beyond following.

In truth, she did not think all of her followers were necessary to keep Conan imprisoned. What she had told the big Kushite was true. The Cimmerian giant was dangerous enough to make even her wary, and she prided herself on walking carefully about no man. She had seen him struggle when defeat was inevitable, slay when his own death was certain, win when only doom lay ahead. Bound hand and foot, however, and guarded by twenty men, she did not doubt Conan would be waiting as she had left him when she returned.

Nor did she think Jamaran could take the gold—or what else he wanted from her—without her steel drinking his life in the attempt. But her pride would not allow the nameless noble to see the open disrespect the shaven-headed man now showed her. Besides, this noble would certainly have other commissions—he had already offered one, though changing it to acquiring the bronze—but he would not likely offer them if he thought she could not keep discipline in her own band.

When Karela reached the clearing where the rude hut stood, the sun was a bloody ball half-obscured by the treetops, and long shadows stretched toward the east. The scarlet-and-black caprisoned warhorse stood alone as before. Slowly she made a circuit of the clearing, within the shaded shelter of the trees. It was a desultory search, she was well aware, but she was also aware of the bronze tied behind her. More than once had she found herself riding forward on her saddle to avoid the brush against her buttocks of the rough wool that contained it. She knew a desperate urgency to be rid of the figure.

With a snorted laugh for her own sensitivity, Karela galloped into the clearing and dismounted. She carried the blanket gripped like a sack, and kicked open the rough door of planks. "Well, Lord Nameless, do you have my . . ." Her words trailed away in surprise.

The tall nobleman stood as he had at the first meeting, but this time he was not alone. A woman with a scarlet cloak pulled around her, the hood pulled well forward, stood beside him, cool dark eyes studying Karela over a veil of opaque silk.

Karela stared back boldly, tossing the blanket to the dirt floor at their feet. "Here is your accursed image. Now where is my gold?"

The veiled woman knelt, hastily pulling aside the folds of coarse wool. A reverent sigh came from her as the horned figure was revealed. With delicate hands she lifted it to the crude table. Karela wondered how she could bear to touch it.

"It is Al'Kiir," the veiled woman breathed. "It is what I sought, Taramenon."

Karela blinked. *Lord Taramenon?* If half what she had heard of his swordplay were true, he would be no easy opponent. She let her hand drift to the hilt of her scimitar. "There are five hundred pieces of gold to be handed over before it is yours."

The other woman's eyes swiveled to her.

"Is she what you seek also?" Taramenon asked.

The veiled woman nodded thoughtfully. "She seems so. How are you called, wench?"

"I am Karela, wench!" the red-haired bandit snapped, emphasizing the last word. "Now let me tell your fates, if you have not brought the coin agreed on. You, my fine lordling, I will sell into Koth, where your pretty face may please a mistress." Taramenon's face darkened, but the veiled woman laughed. Karela turned her attention to her. "And you I will sell into Argos, where you may dance naked in a tavern in Messantia, and please the patrons one by one for the price of a mug of ale."

"I am a princess of Ophir," the veiled woman said coldly, "who can have you impaled on the walls of the royal palace. Do you dare speak so to one before whom you should tremble?"

Karela sneered. "I not only dare speak so, by Derketo's Teats, if my gold is not forthcoming I'll strip you on the spot to see if an Argossean tavern will have you. Most Ophirean noblewomen are bony wenches who could not please a man did they try with all their might." Steel whispered across leather as her blade left its scabbard. "I'll have my gold now!"

"She will indeed do," the scarlet-cloaked woman said. "Take her."

Karela spun toward Taramenon, had an instant to see him watching with a bemused smile on his face, making no move toward her or his sword, then two men in the leather armor of light cavalry dropped from the dark rafters atop her. In a struggling heap she was borne to the packed-earth floor.

"Derketo blast you!" she howled, writhing futilely in their grip. "I'll spit you like capons! Codless jackals!"

Taramenon plucked her sword from her hand and tossed it into a corner. "You'll not be needing that any longer, girl."

Despite her frenzied striving, the cavalrymen dragged Karela to her feet. Fool! she berated herself. Taken like a virgin in a kidnapper's nets! Why had she not wondered why there was no horse for the woman?

"I suppose it's too much to hope for that she's a maiden," the woman said.

Taramenon laughed. "Much too much, I should say."

"Treacherous trull!" Karela snarled. "Catamite fopling! I'll peel your hides in strips! Release me, or my men will stake you out for the vultures! Are you fool enough to think I came alone?"

"Perhaps you did not," Taramenon said calmly, "thought I saw no one the last time you claimed to have men about this hut. In any case, my shout will bring fifty men-at-arms. Shall we see what your miserable brigands can do against them?"

"Enough, Taramenon," the veiled woman said. "Do not bandy words with the baggage. There was talk of stripping." She eyed Karela's tight breeches and snug-laced leather jerkin, and a note of malicious amusement entered her voice. "I would see that she is not . . . too bony for my purpose."

Taramenon laughed, and the three men set to with a will. Karela fought furiously, and when they were done there was blood on her nails and teeth, but she stood naked, heavy round breasts heaving with her effort. Lecherous male eyes probed her beauty, slid along the curves of lush thighs and narrow waist. Dark feminine eyes regarded her more coldly, and with a touch of jealousy lighting them. Pridefully the green-eyed woman stood as erect as the twisting of her arms behind her back would allow. She would not cringe like a shrinking girl on her wedding night for these of any others.

The tall nobleman touched his cheek, now decorated by four parallel sanquinary streaks, and examined the blood on his fingertips. Suddenly his hand flashed out; the force of his slap was such that Karela and the two men holding her all staggered.

"Do not damage her!" the veiled woman said sharply. "Your beauty is not ruined, Taramenon. Now bind her for transport."

"A taste of the strap will do her no damage, Synelle," the darkly handsome lord growled, "and I would teach her her proper place."

The name so shocked Karela that she missed the veiled woman's retort. Conan's patroness! Could the woman have learned of her own connection with the Cimmerian and be thinking to dispose of a rival? Well, she had the Cimmerian to bargain for her release, and if Derketo favored her she would have this treacherous noblewoman to hang by her heels beside him.

Karela opened her mouth to make her offer—Conan's freedom in return for her own—and a wadded rag pushed the words back into her throat. Like a starving panther she stuggled, but three men were too much for her. With ease that seemed to mock her they corded her into a neat package, wrists strapped to ankles, knees beneath her chin, thin straps laced around and around her, digging deep into her flesh. When one of the cavalrymen produced a large leather sack the memory of her plans for Synelle, including her method of returning her to Conan, flooded her face with scarlet.

"At least she can still blush," Synelle laughed as Karela was stuffed into the sack. "From her language, I thought she was lost to all decency. Carry her to the horses. We must hurry. Events procede more quickly than I would like, and we must meet them."

"I must return to the palace to pay my respects," Taramenon said. "I will join you as quickly as I can."

"Do so quickly," Synelle said smoothly, "or I may put Conan in your place."

As Karela's dark prison was heaved swaying into the air, she felt tears running down her cheeks. Derketo curse the Cimmerian! Once again he had brought her humilation. She hoped Jamaran would slit his throat. Slowly.

XVIII

Conan lay on the dirt-strewn stone floor as he had for a day and a night now, bound and biding his time with the patience of a jungle predator, all of his mind and energies given over to waiting and watching. Karela's injunction to give him food and water had been ignored, and he was dimly aware of hunger and thirst, but they affected him little. He had gone longer without either, and he knew he would have both once the men who guarded him were dealt with. Soon or late a mistake would be made, and he would take advantage. Soon or late, it would come.

Brass lamps had been lit against the deepening night, but with Karela gone no one had rehung blankets to cover the tall, narrow arrow slits. Rough clay jars of wine had been passed more freely with the red-haired woman's departure, and the four brigands who had not already staggered to one of the upper rooms of the tower for drunken sleep were engrossed in drinking more and gaming with dice. The fire on the long hearth burned low; the last of the thick logs that had been stacked against the wall had long since gone into the flames, and no more had been brought from outside. None of them had thought to tend the iron kettle suspended over the flames, and the smell of burning stew blended with the unwashed stench of bandits.

Abruptly Tenio hurled dice and leather dice-cup aside. "She should have returned by now," he muttered. "What keeps her?"

"Perhaps she keeps herself," Jamaran growled. His black eyes went to Conan, and he bared large, yellow teeth in a snarl. "Leaving us with this one she seems so affrighted of."

Marusas paused in the act of scooping up the dice. "You think she has run away with the gold? It sounds a tidy sum, but her share of our raids has been as much in the last month alone."

"Erlik take you, play!" snapped a man with a slitted leather patch tied over where his nose had been cut off. His pale eyes had a permanent look of suspicious anger, as if he knew and hated what men thought when they saw his disfigurement. "I'm twenty silvers down with coin on the table. Play, curse you!" The three ignored him.

Jamaran slammed a fist the size of a small ham on the table top. "And that's another thing. Why should a woman receive ten times the share that the rest of us do? Let her try our work alone and see what sport the men she tries to rob will have with her. Without us, she'd be no more than a cut-purse, bargaining when she was caught to escape having her cheek branded for a grant of the favors she is so stingy with now."

"Without her," Tenio rebutted, "what are we? How much did we get on our own? Now you moan about only fifty golds in a month, but you didn't never get ten before her."

"She's a woman!" the huge Kushite said. "A woman's place is in a man's bed, or cooking for him, not giving orders."

Marusas laughed and tugged at his drooping black mustaches. "I would like riding her myself. Much fun in breaking that one to bridle, eh?"

"'Tis more than the pair of you could do together," Tenio sneered. "I don't like taking orders from a woman no better than you, but she puts gold in my purse, more than I've seen before. And I know I'd have to keep her tied hand and foot or risk waking with my own dagger in my throat. Or worse."

"No cods at all on you," Jamaran snorted. He nudged the Zamoran with a huge elbow. "I always knew there was more woman than man in him. Likely spends all his hours in Ianthe at the House of the Yearling Lambs." The two of them roared with laughter, and patch-nose joined in as if despite himself.

All the blood left Tenio's face, and his narrow-bladed dagger flickered into his hand. "I don't take that from nobody," he snarled.

"From me you take what I give," Jamaran said, all mirth gone from his voice, "or I'll use that blade of yours to make *sure* you've no cods."

"Curse the lot of you for chattering old women!" patch-nose shouted. "Am I suddenly not good enough to dice with?"

Conan made a sound behind his gag; had his throat not been parched it would have been a chuckle. A while longer and they would kill each other, leaving him only his bonds to worry about.

Flinging his mug across the room in a spray of wine, Jamaran heaved himself from his bench and strode on legs as big around as a normal man's waist to stand over the Cimmerian. Conan's icy azure gaze calmly met the dark glower directed at him.

"Big man," Jamaran said contemptuously, and his foot thudding into Conan's ribs lifted the Cimmerian from the stone floor. "You seem not so big to me." Again his foot drove Conan back. "Why does Karela want you kept safe? Is she afraid of you? Or maybe she loves you, huh? Perhaps I'll let you watch while I enjoy her, if she comes back." Each sentence he punctuated with a massive booted foot, until Conan lay struggling for breath on the very edge of the hearth. The Cimmerian glared at Jamaran as the shaven-headed man squatted beside him, doubling a heavy fist. "Ten men have I beaten to their death with this. You will be number eleven. I do not think Karela will return—she's been gone too long already—but I'll wait a bit longer. I want her to see it. Watching a man killed that way does something to a woman." Laughing, the huge Kushite straightened. With a last kick he turned back to the table. "Where's my mug?" he roared. "I want wine!"

Cursing behind his gag Conan jerked himself out of the coals he had landed in, but his mind was not on his burns. So intent had he been on awaiting his chance for escape that their talk of Karela's lateness had barely impinged on his thoughts. He knew her well enough to be sure she had not fled with the gold. Boros' words came back to him. The most beautiful and proudest women of the land were sacrificed to Al'Kiir. Few were the women more beautiful than Karela, and to her pride he could well attest. The fool wench had not only taken those who wanted to raise the god the means to do so, she had delivered herself as a sacrifice. He was sure of it. Now he must rescue her from her own folly. But how? How even to free himself?

He shifted to ease his weight on a burn on his arm, and suddenly his lips curled in a smile around his gag. Careless of searing flame he thrust his bound wrists into the fire. Gritting his teeth on his gag against fiery agony, he strained mighty arms against the ropes, massive muscles knotting and writhing. Sweat beaded his face.

The reek of burning hemp came to him; he wondered how the others could fail to be aware of it, but none of the four so much as looked in his direction. They were immersed in their mugs of wine, and patchnose kept up his arguing for a chance to win back his loses. Abruptly, the ropes parted, and Conan pulled his half-cooked wrists from the flames, careful to keep them yet behind his back. His gaze sought his ancient broad-sword, leaning against the wall behind the drinking men.

There would be no chance to grasp it before he came to grips with the men between him and his steel.

With a crash patch-nose kicked over his bench. Conan froze. Snarling the man snatched up his mug and began to stalk back and forth across the room, muttering angrily about men who won and then would not gamble, and shooting dark glances at the other three, still intent on their drink. His eyes did not stray to the Cimmerian, lying rigid on the hearth-stone.

Slowly, so as to draw no attention, Conan slid his booted feet back until he could feel the heat of flames licking about them. To the smell of burning rope was added that of scorching leather, but the latter was no more noticed than the first. Then those cords were burned through as well. There was no time to waste on the gag. Rolling to his feet the big Cimmerian snatched a long, black fire-iron from the hearth.

Patch-nose was the first to see Conan free of his bonds, but the man had only time to goggle before wine sprayed out of his mouth and his skull was crushed by the fire-iron. Shouting, the others scrambled to their feet. Tenio produced his dagger, but Conan drove the fire-iron point-first through the ferret-faced man's chest and caught the blade as it dropped from the transfixed man's nerveless fingers. Marusas' sword leaped into his hand, then the Zamoran was staggering back, trying to scream around the dagger that had blossomed in fountains of scarlet in his throat.

Roaring, Jamaran leaped to grapple with the Cimmerian, throwing bearlike arms about his waist, heaving him into the air. Conan felt the man's huge fists locked in the small of his back, felt his spine begin to creak. Conan smashed his linked hands down on the nape of the huge man's bull neck, once, twice, thrice, to no effect. Jamaran's grip tightened inexorably. In moments, the Cimmerian knew, his back would snap. Desperately he slammed his palms against the other's ears.

With a scream Jamaran let him drop. Even as his heels hit the stone floor, Conan's bladed hand struck the huge Kushite's throat. Jamaran gagged, yet lashed out with a massive fist in the same instant. Conan blocked the blow, winding his arm around the shaven-headed man's to pull him close. With hammer-like blows the Cimmerian pounded the big man's body, feeling ribs splinter beneath his fist.

In the night a trumpet sounded the Ophirean army call for the attack. "Company one, ready torches!" a voice called. "Company two, attack! Take no prisoners!" Feet pounded on the floors above; frantic yells rose.

In his desperate struggle Conan had no time to worry about the new danger. Jamaran smashed his head against the Cimmerian's; Conan staggered, clinging to consciousness. The huge Kushite tried to enfold Conan once more in his crushing embrace, but Conan rammed a knee into his crotch, lifting the man to his toes with bulging eyes. Like thunderbolts the heels of Conan's hands struck Jamaran's chin. The shaven head went back with a loud crack as the Kushite's neck broke, and he fell in a boneless heap.

Conan ripped the gag from his mouth and threw it atop the body of the man who had threatened to beat him to death. A torch was thrust through one of the arrow slits, then another. Putting a hand on the table top Conan vaulted across it to grab his sword hilt, baring the blade by slinging the worn shagreen scabbard away. When soldiers spoke of taking no prisoners they generally slew whatever moved, without questioning whether it was enemy or captive. Conan did not mean to die easily.

A man darted in at the door, sword ready; Conan swung his steel . . . and stopped a hands-breadth away from splitting Machaon's skull. Narus rushed in behind the grizzled veteran, and two more of the company.

"You!" Conan exclaimed. "You are the Ophirean army?"

Narus shrugged and held up a battered brass trumpet. "An odd talent of mine, but useful from time to time." He looked around at the bodies on the stone floor. "Once more you leave nothing for the rest of us."

"There are more above," Conan said, but Narus shook his head.

"They lept from breaks in the walls, thinking we were who we claimed, and fled into the night."

"We've still bloody work to do," Conan told him. "Karela has been taken prisoner, and I mean to rescue her." Atop Tor Al'Kiir, he thought. Boros said he had seen lights there, and he had no other clue. "We must move quickly, if you will come with me."

"Mitra, Conan," Machaon growled, "will you let me say a word? There's no time for wenches, not even her. We came after you because Zandru's Hells have come to sup in Ophir."

"Al'Kiir." Conan's heart sank. "They've raised the god already."

"I know naught of gods," Machaon muttered, "but Valdric lies dead of the sickness that consumed him, and Iskandrian has seized the royal palace."

Conan started in surprise. "Iskandrian!"

"The old general has declared for Valentius," Narus explained. "And that young coxcomb has taken the name Maranthes II, as if a name could make him a great king. I hear he didn't wait for funeral rites or even a priest, but took the crown from Valdric's corpse before it was cold and put it on his own head."

"Will you stop your nattering, Narus!" Machaon barked. "Most of the nobles think as you did, Cimmerian. They gather their forces, but Iskandrian moves to put them down before they can. He marched with most of the Ianthe garrison an hour after he put Valentius on the throne. If that isn't enough, Taurianus is talking loudly that the company should join the nobles. He's telling everyone if Iskandrian wins it means the end of Free-Companies in Ophir." His tattooed face grew grim. "I'll tell you, Conan, he's right on that. Iskandrian will give short shrift to mercenaries."

"We'll worry about Iskandrian later," Conan said. "Karela comes first, and matters even more important than her. How many of the company did you bring, Machaon?"

"Seven, including Narus and myself, all of whom crossed the Nemedian border with us. Two I left to guard Julia. The mood of the others is bad, Cimmerian. You must return now if you mean to hold them together. Karela can take care of herself for a time if any woman can."

"We found your black picketed with this lot's mounts," Narus added.

"Crom!" Conan muttered. The numbers were not enough if they faced what he feared atop Tor Al'Kiir. "We ride for Ianthe, to gather the company and ride out again. No, not to join the nobles. To Tor Al'Kiir. There'll be time for questions later. To horse, Erlik blast your hides. To horse, and pray to whatever gods you can think of that we are in time."

XIX

I ron-shod hooves struck sparks from paving stones as Conan galloped through the dark and empty streets of Ianthe, seven men trailing behind with their cloaks standing out in the wind of their charge. Atop the malevolent granite hump of Tor Al'Kiir torches flickered, distant points of light in the moonless sky mocking his efforts at haste. He cursed to himself, regretting even the time it had taken to bribe the gate-watch for entry.

He wanted to shout at the sleepers who felt a momentary safety behind their walls of brick and stone. Mourning cloths draped from shuttered windows and shrouded public fountains; sprigs of sa'karian, black and white berries intermixed as symbol of death and rebirth, adorned every door. The capital of Ophir mourned its dead King in fear and uncertainty, yet none in that city knew that what they felt was as a flickering lamp flame to the storm-lashed fire-death of a great forest beside the terror that awaited their wakening.

As he galloped through the archway of the house where his company was quartered, Conan bellowed. "To me! Out with you, and to horse! Move, damn you to Zandru's Hells!" Stillness lay heavily on the blackened building; his words echoed hollowly from the courtyard walls as the others clattered in behind him. "Taurianus!" he called. "Boros!"

A door open with the protest of rusty hinges, showing a tiny light, and four figures moved into the court. Slowly the shadowy shapes resolved into Boros, Julia, and two of his company holding shielded lanterns. The armored men were the two remaining besides those behind him who had come with him from Nemedia.

"Where are the others?" Conan demanded.

"Gone," Boros answered hollowly. "Taurianus—Erlik roast his soul for eternity—convinced most of them you were dead, since you didn't return. Half followed him to join the nobles against Iskandrian. The rest?" His thin shoulders shrugged. "Faded away to hide as best they can. Without you, fear corroded their hearts."

Conan fought the urge to rain curses upon Taurianus' head. There was no time; the torches still burned atop the mountain. What must be done, must be done with the men he had. But he would lead no man blind to face sorcerers, and perhaps a god.

"Boros," he said grimly, "tell of Al'Kiir. But briefly, old man. The time of his coming is near, perhaps before first light, if we do not stop it."

Boros gasped and, tugging at his beard, spoke in a quavering voice, filled with all his years, of days before even ancient Ophir existed and the rites of Al'Kiir, of the Circle of the Right-Hand Path and the imprisonment of the demonic god, of those who would bring the abominable worship again into the world and the god whose horror they celebrated. When he was done there was silence, broken only by the call of an owl. Each man's breath was audible, and they all spoke of fear.

"If we go to Iskandrian with this tale," Conan said finally, "he will think it a ruse of the nobles and slay us, or emprison us for madmen until it is too late. But every word is as true and as dire as a spear thrust to the heart. Boros has told you what comes, what fate may lie in store for your sister, or wife or daughter, because she is comely and spirited. I ride to Tor Al'Kiir to stop it. Who rides with me?"

For a long moment only silence answered him, then Julia stepped forward, her chin held high. "If there is no courage among these who call themselves men, at least I will go with you."

"You will go to your sleeping mat," Machaon growled, "or I'll bind you in such a package as Karela made of you, to keep you safe against my return." The girl moved hurriedly behind Boros, eyeing the grizzled mercenary warily as if unsure how much of his threat he meant. Machaon nodded with satisfaction, then turned in his saddle to Conan. "I've seen more of wizards following you, Cimmerian, than one man has a right to expect in a lifetime. But I cannot see that once more will make any difference."

"An owl calling on a moonless night means death," Narus said glumly, "but I've never seen a god. I, too, ride with you, Cimmerian."

One by one, then, the other seven mercenaries pledged to follow also, voices cold with humiliation at being surpassed in courage by a girl, with anger and determination to protect some particular woman from the bloody rites. And still with fear. Yet they would come.

Conan eyed their scant number in the pale light of the lanterns and sighed. "We will be enough," he said, as much to convince himself as anything else, "because we must. We must. Claran, Memtes, get your horses." The two men named set their lanterns on the ground and ran for the stables. "We ride as soon as they return," he went on. "We must needs scale the mountain afoot, for our horses cannot climb those slopes, but—"

"Wait, Conan," Boros broke in. "Make haste slowly, or you but hasten to your death. You must acquire the Staff of Avanrakash."

"There is no time, old man," Conan said grimly. He twisted impatiently in his saddle to peer through the night toward the deeper blackness of Tor Al'Kiir. The torch lights still were there, beckoning him, taunting him to his core. What befell Karela while he sat his horse like a statue?

"Do you go forth to confront a lion," the bearded man chided, "would you then say there was no time to fetch spear or bow? That you must face it with bare hands? You go to face Al'Kiir. Think your courage and steel will avail you against a god? As well slit your own throat right here."

Conan's massive hands tightened on the reins in frustration until his knuckles cracked. He did not fear death, though he sought it no more than any other man, but his death would be of no use if Karela were still sacrificed, if Al'Kiir was freed again. Decision came swiftly, spurred by necessity. He tossed his reins to Machaon and dismounted.

"Take my horse with you to the mountain," he commanded as he tugged his hauberk off over his head. Such work as he had now to do was not best done in armor. He dropped to the gound to pull off his boots. "I will meet you at the crossroads at the foot of the mountain."

"Do you know where this staff the old man speaks of is to be found?" Machaon asked.

"In the throne room," Boros said. "By ancient law, at the death of a King the scepter and crown must be left on the throne for nine days and nine nights. Valentius has usurped custom by donning the crown so quickly, but he will not dare flout it altogether."

"The royal palace!" Machaon exclaimed. "Cimmerian, you are mad to think you can enter there. Come! We will do the best we can with honest steel."

"I was a thief once," Conan replied. "'Twill not be the first palace I've entered by ways other than the door." Stripped now to his breechcloth, he slung his swordbelt across his massive chest so that his sword hung down his back, dagger and pouch beneath his left arm. Claran and Memtes trotted their horses from the stable, hooves ringing on the thick slates of the court. "I will be at the crossroads, with the staff," the Cimmerian said, "without fail. Be you there also."

With ground-eating pantherish strides, Conan loped into the night. Behind him Machaon and the others clattered out of the courtyard and turned their mounts in the other direction, toward the North Gate, but he was already one with the darkness, a deadly ghost racing through unlit streets that were empty of other human forms. Every door was barred, every window shuttered, as the inhabitants of the city cowered in fear of what might come; only occasional scavenging dogs, gaunt-ribbed and half-wild, prowled the moonless streets, and they shied away from the huge shape that shared the way with them. Beneath his leathery-soled feet the paving stones felt like the rocks of his native Cimmeria, and the feel gave wings to his stride as when he raced up mountains as a boy. His great lungs pumped with the effort of his running, for this time he raced not for the pride of winning, but for Karela, and for every woman who would lose life or more if he failed.

Again an owl cried, and Conan's mind went to Narus' words. Perhaps the cry did mean death, his or someone else's. Crom, the fierce god of the harsh and icy land where he was born, gave a man life and will, but the grim Lord of the Mound never promised that life would be long, nor that will would always prevail. A man could but fight, and keep fighting so long as breath or life remained.

The Cimmerian did not slow until the massive walls of the royal palace loomed before him, crenelations and towertops only shadows against the ebon sky. The thick, iron-sheathed gates were closed and barred, the portcullis down, but he spared not a glance in that direction. Such was not his means of entry this night.

His fingers felt across the surface of the wall, featureless in the blackness. Long centuries past had the great wall been built, of stones each weighing more than twenty times as much as a big man. Only the largest trebuchet could hurl boulders weighty enough to trouble its solidity, but Conan did not mean to batter a way through. Those years had leeched at the mortar between the great stones, leaving gaps that made an easy path for one mountain-born.

With agile sureness Conan climbed, fingers and toes searching out the grooves where wind and rain and time had worn away the mortar, mighty muscles straining to pull him up where there was but room for

fingernails to grip. Below was only the long, bone-shattering drop to
pavement now swathed in the night, yet he did not slow in his swift
ascent of that sheer wall. Time pressed on him too greatly to allow room
for caution.

At the top of the wall he paused between two tall merlons topped
with stone leopards, ears straining for the scuff of boots on the rampart,
the creak of leather and armor. A combat there with guards would surely
doom his quest before it had truly begun. There was no sound. Conan
drew himself through the crennel. No guards were atop the wall. The
palace was silent as a tomb. It seemed Iskandrian had left only men for
the gates; the White Eagle would strike hard, as was his wont.

From the rampart a curving ramp led down toward the outer bailey.
There, however, he would surely be seen, no matter how few guards
had been left behind or how many servants hid in fear that too-ardent
service to him who now wore the crown might be punished if he lost
it. Rooftops must be his path. The nearest, a wing of the palace, lay but
an easy jump from the ramp for a vigorous man. Easy if the approaching
run could be made on level ground rather than down a steep ramp, and
if a three-story drop to the granite paving of the bailey were ignored.

Conan measured distances and angles, then took a deep breath and
sprinted down the ramp. At the sixth great stride he flung himself across
the chasm. Fingertips caught at the edge of the roof. One tile broke
free, spiraling into the dark to shatter on the stones below; for an instant
the Cimmerian hung by one hand. Slowly he hauled himself up, swung
to hook a leg over the edge. The tile he held to shifted under his hand.
Then he was flat on the roof, carefully setting aside the loose tile and
quieting his breath as he waited to see if the noise of the first tile's fall
drew attention. Still nothing stirred.

Like a jungle beast Conan was up and running, feet sure on the slanting tiles, climbing granite gargoyles to a higher level, leaping from a
balcony tiled in black and white marble to clutch at a high peaked gable,
edging with chest pressed flat against smooth granite along a ledge wide
enough only for the balls of his feet, then climbing again, past mullioned
windows and trefoils, until at last he scrambled through a narrow ventilation arch and looked down from great height on the vast throne room
of the royal palace.

Great golden lamps hung on thick chains of the same metal from the
vaulted ceiling, their bright flames lighting well the floor far below, a
floor mosaicked in huge representations of the leopards and eagles that
were the royal symbols of Ophir. In the middle of that floor was a black-

shrouded bier on which Valdric's body lay in state, clothed in ornate robes of gold embroidered purple set with pearls. No living man was there to keep vigil over the dead King.

Conan's eyes sought the throne. Like unto the great chair in which Antimides had sat it was, covered in leopards and eagles, but larger still and of solid gold. The beasts' eyes were rubies, and claws and talons clutched emeralds as large as the joint of a man's thumb. Of the crown there was no sign. Ancient law or no, the Cimmerian thought, Valentius had not found it in himself to part with the royal diadem for even nine days once he had gained it. Yet what he sought was there. Across the arms of the throne lay the scepter of Ophir, its golden length glittering with an encrustation of all manner of gems.

Carefully Conan let himself down inside the throne room, using the scrolls and arabesques carved in the marble walls to climb down until he reached their end, some twenty feet above the floor. Here great tapestries hung. He ripped loose a corner of one—a scene of a crowned King hunting deer from horseback—and let himself drop, swinging on it as at the end of a rope. His feet brushed the floor, and he released the tapestry to run to the throne.

Almost hesitantly he hefted the long scepter. So much had he risked on the word of a drunk, and so much depended on it. Hastily he produced his dagger and began prying away soft gold and sparkling jewels, letting them fall to the purple velvet cushion of the throne. At the sight of wood beneath he grunted in satisfaction, but continued until he had stripped away all the outer sheath. He was left with a plain wooden staff as long as his outstretched arms and as thick as his two thumbs together.

Yet could it be in truth the Staff of Avanrakash, he wondered. He felt no magical qualities in it, and it showed no signs of its supposed great age. In fact, had it been a walking staff he would have thought it cut no more than a few days previous.

"But it *was* within the scepter," he breathed, "and it is all I have." For luck he scooped a handful of gems from the cushion, not bothering to see what they were, and stuffed them into his pouch.

"A common thief," Taramenon said from the door to the throne room. "Will not Synelle be surprised when she returns to find your head on a spike atop the River Gate?"

Conan reached over his shoulder; his sword slid easily into his grasp. The staff clutched in his left hand, he strode toward the tall noble. He had no words to say, no time for words. Even so in a corner of his mind lust flared at the mention of the woman's name. Synelle. He could he have gone so long without thinking of her? How could he have gone so long without touching her? The frozen rage of battles forced the thoughts down, smothered them.

Taramenon threw aside his fur-trimmed scarlet cape and drew his own blade. "I but stepped in here a moment to spit in Valdric's face. To offer obeisance to a corpse that was half-rotted before even it died turned my stomach. Finding you is a pleasant surprise I did not expect." Abruptly rage contorted his face into an ugly mask. "I will tell her of your death when I see her this night. Your filthy hands will never touch her again, you barbarian swine!" Snarling he rushed forward, swinging his blade in a mighty chop at Conan's head.

The Cimmerian's broadsword met Taramenon's with a tremendous clash. The Ophirean's eyes widened at the force of the blow but on the instant he struck again. Again Conan's blade met his in a shower of sparks. Taramenon fought with all the deadly finesse of one who was the finest swordsman in Ophir, his longsword as agile and swift and deadly as a Kothian viper; Conan fought with the cold ferocity of a northland beserker, his steel the lightning of the Cimmerian crags. Conan had no time to waste in defense—he must conquer, and quickly, or the noise of the fight would draw others, and he might well be over-whelmed by sheer numbers—but his constant attack left no room to Taramenon for aught *but* defense.

Sweat rolled down the face of the finest blade in Ophir as he found himself forced back, ever back, by an implacable demon with a face of stone and icy blue eyes, eyes in which depths he could read his own death. Panic clouded Taramenon's face, and for the first time in his life he knew fear. "Guards!" he screamed. "A thief! Guards!"

In that brief instant of divided attention Conan's blade engaged that of the tall Ophirean, brought it down, around, thrust under it. Chain mail links snapped, razor steel sliced through muscle and bone, and the Cimmerian's sword hilt slammed against Taramenon's chest.

Conan stared into dark incredulous eyes. "Synelle is mine," he grated. "Mine!"

Blood bubbled from Taramenon's mouth, and he fell. Conan stared at the body in wonder before remembering to pull his sword free. Why had he said such a thing? Synelle was of no import in this. Karela was important, Al'Kiir and the staff and getting to the crossroads quickly. Yet images suppressed by events rose unbidden, sleek thighs and satin skin and swelling breasts and . . . Shaking his head woozily he half-staggered to Taramenon's discarded cape to clean his bloody blade and cut strips to bind the staff across his back. Was he going mad, he wondered. Visions of Synelle kept crowding his brain, as if time spent not thinking of her had to be made up. Desperately he forced them back. The crossroads, he thought. The crossroads, and no time.

Running to the half-torn-down tapestry, he began to climb. Synelle. The crossroads, and no time.

XX

Karela grunted as the sack in which she was carried was upended,
dumping her, still bound and naked, onto cold stone. After the
darkness light blinded her, filling her eyes with tears. The tears
infuriated her; she would not have those who had taken her prisoner
think they had reduced her to crying. Blinking, she was at last able to
make out the roughly cut stone walls of what seemed to be a small cave,
lit by rush torches in black iron sconces.

She was not alone, she realized. Synelle was there, and four other
women, alabastrine-skinned blondes who seemed to wear variations of
one face. The noblewoman was not dressed as when last Karela had seen
her. Now she wore bracelets of black iron chain on each wrist, and two
narrow strips of ebon silk, before and behind, leaving the outer curves
of hips and breasts bare, were all her garb save for a belt of golden links.
Karela stared when she saw the buckle. It was the head of the malevolent
bronze she had sold—tried to sell, she thought ruefully—but rendered
in gold. A chaplet of gold chain encircled Synelle's silvery tresses, se-
verely braided into a coronet, and on that golden band, too, were the
four horns of that demonic figure.

The other women were dressed as was Synelle, but the narrow belts
cinching their waists were of black iron, and dark metal enclosed their
ankles and necks as well. Their hair, neatly coiled about their heads,
bore no headdress. With bowed heads their humbly alert eyes watched
the exotically beautiful noblewoman.

Karela swallowed hard, and was reminded again how dry was her
throat. Had she the use of her mouth she would tell this Synelle she

could have Conan. It would be a lie—she would not be driven from her business with the Cimmerian by this pale-haired trull who called herself a lady—but lying seemed much the better part of valor at the moment.

Synelle nodded, and the four women in iron belts produced leather straps. Karela jerked futilely at her bonds despite herself. If only she had a dagger, or but a single hand free, or even her tongue to shout her defiance at them.

"Listen to me, wench," Synelle said. "These women will prepare you. If you fight, they will beat you, but in any event they will carry out my orders. I would have you as little marked as possible, so if you will submit, nod your head."

Karela tried to shout through her gag. Submit! Did this fool woman think she was some milksop maiden to be frightened by threats? Her green eyes hurled all her silent fury at Synelle.

Abruptly Synelle moved, placing a foot on Karela's knees, bound beneath her chin, to roll her onto her back and hold her there. "A taste, then. Cut well in."

The other women darted forward, their leather straps slicing beneath Karela's corded heels, raining blows on her helpless buttocks, drawn taut by her tying.

Her green eyes bulged in her head, and she had an instant to be grateful for the gag that held back her cries, then her head was nodding frantically. Derketo! There was no use in being beaten while lying trussed like a pig for market.

Synelle motioned the women back. "I was sure you would be reasonable."

Karela tried to meet the dark eyes staring down at her, then closed her own in humiliation. It was clear from the look on Synelle's face that she had never doubted that the red-haired woman could be brought to heel. Let them free her, Karela prayed, and she would show them the worth of pledge wrung from whips. She would . . .

Suddenly the cords binding her were severed. Karela caught a flash of a dagger. She moved to grab it . . . and sprawled in boneless agony on the stone floor, muscles stiff from long confinement barely able to do more than twitch. Slowly, painfully, she brought a hand up to drag the gag from her mouth. She wanted to weep. The dagger was gone from sight, and she had neither seen who had held it nor where it was hidden.

Even as she dropped the wadded cloth two of the women pulled her to her feet. She gasped with the pain; had they not supported her she could not have stood. One of the others began drawing an ivory comb through her tangled locks, while the last wiped her sweat away with soft, damp clothes.

Karela worked her mouth for the moisture to speak. "I'll not sell you to a tavern," she managed. "I'll tear your heart out with my bare hands."

"Good," Synelle said. "I feared your spirit might have been broken. Often the journey here, bound, is enough for that. It is well that it was not in your case."

Karela sneered. "You want the pleasure of breaking me yourself, then? You will not have it, because you cannot do it. And if you want Conan back—"

"Conan!" the noblewoman cut her off, dark eyes widening in surprise. "How do you come to know of the barbarian?"

"We were once," Karela began, then spluttered to a halt. She was tired, and spoke of things of which she had no wish to speak. "No matter how I know of him. If you want him, you'll cease your threats and bargain."

Synelle trilled with laughter. "So you think I merely attempt to dispose of a rival. I should be furious that such as you could think of yourself as my rival, but I find it merely amusing. I expect he is a man who has known many women in his time, and if you are one of that number I see he has little discrimination in his choosing. That is at an end, now." She held out a slender palm. "I hold the barbarian there, wench. He will crawl to me on his belly when I call him, dance like a bear for a tin whistle at my command. And you think to be my rival?" She threw back her head and laughed even harder.

"No woman could treat Conan so," Karela snapped. "I know, for I have tried, and by Derketo, I am ten times the woman you are."

"You are suitable for the rites," the silver-haired woman said coolly, "but I am High Priestess of Al'Kiir. Yet were I not, you would still not be woman enough to serve as my bowermaid. My tirewomen were nobly born in Corinthia, and she who draws my bath and rubs me with oils was a princess in far Vendhya, yet to obey my slightest wish is now the whole of their lives. What can a jade of a bandit be beside such as they, who are but my slaves?"

Karela opened her mouth for another retort, and gasped when a black-armored man in a horned helmet appeared in the entrance to the cavern. For an instant she had thought it was the creature the bronze represented. Foolishness, she berated herself. Such a creature could not exist.

"Has Taramenon come yet?" Synelle demanded of the man.

"No, my lady. Nor any message of him."

"He will suffer for this," Synelle said heatedly. "He defies me, and I will see him suffer for it!" Drawing a deep breath, she smoothed the already taut black silk over her rounded breasts. "We will proceed without him. When he comes, he is to be seized and bound. There are rites other than the gift of women."

"Taramenon, my lady?" the man said in shocked tones.

"You heard my command!" Synelle made a brusque gesture, and the armored figure bowed himself from her presence.

Karela had been listening intently, hoping for some fragment of information that might help her escape, but now she became aware of how the four women were dressing her, the tiny white tarla blossoms woven into her hair, the diaphanous layers of blue silk meant to be removed one by one for the titillation of a groom.

"What travesty is there?" she growled. "You *do* think me a rival, but if you mean to rid yourself of me in this way, you are mad! I'll marry no man! Do you hear me, you pasty-faced trull?"

A cruel smile curled Synelle's lips, and the look on her face sent a chill through Karela's blood. "You will marry no *man*," the haughty noble-woman said softly. "Tonight you will wed a god, and I will become ruler of Ophir."

The tall white marker at the crossroads, a square marble pillar inscribed with the distances to the borders of Nemedia and Aquilonia, loomed out of the night ahead of Conan. No sound broke the silence save his labored breath and the steady slap of his running feet on the paving stones. Beyond the marker reared the dark mass of Tor Al'Kiir, a huge granite outcropping dominating the flat country about it.

The big Cimmerian crouched beside the marble plinth, eyes straining at the blackness. There was so sign of his men. Softly he imitated the cry of a Nemedian nighthawk.

The muted jingle of tight-strapped harness announced the sudden appearance of Machaon and the rest, leading their horses. Memtes, bringing up the rear, gripped the reins of Conan's big Aquilonian black as well as those of his own mount. Bows and quivers were slung on their backs.

"I thought it best to keep from sight," the tattooed veteran told Conan quietly. "As we arrived, two score men-at-arms passed, chasing another band as large, and twice parties of light cavalry have gone by at the gallop. Scouts, the last, no doubt."

"Unless I miss my guess," Narus added in a low voice that would not travel far, "Iskandrian seeks action this night, and the nobles seek to avoid him until their strength is gathered. Never did I think that when the final battle for Ophir occurred, I would be scaling a mountain."

"Go to Taurianus, then," Conan growled, "if you seek glory!" Irritably he shook his black-maned head. Such edginess was not his usual manner, but his thoughts scarcely seemed his own. With a desperation foreign to him he fought to cling to his purpose of mind, struggled against images of Synelle and lust that threatened to overwhelm him.

"Is that the famous staff?" Machaon asked. "It has no look of magic to me."

"It is," the Cimmerian replied, "and it has." He hoped he did not lie. Unfastening the strips of cloth that held the length of wood, he clutched it in one hand and drew his sword with the other. "This is the last chance to change your minds. Let any man unsure of what he does step aside." The soft and deadly susuration of steel sliding from scabbards was his answer. Conan nodded grimly. "Then hide the horses in yon copse of trees and follow me."

"Your armor," Machaon said. " 'Tis on your saddle."

"There is no time," Conan said, and without waiting for the others he started up the stony slope.

Crom was not a god men prayed to; he gave nothing beyond his first gift. But now Conan offered a prayer to any god that would listen. If he died for it, let him be in time.

A silent file of purposeful men fell in behind him in his climb, on their way to beard a god in his den.

The lash struck across her shoulders again, and Karela gritted her teeth against the howl she wanted to let pass. Bound between posts topped with the obscene head of Al'Kiir, she knelt, all but the last layer of thin blue silk torn away from her sweat-slick body. It was not the pain from the incessant bite of leather that made her want to cry out, or not alone; she would have died before giving her tormentors the satisfaction of acknowledging that. But the burning stripes that made scarlet lattices on her body were as pin-pricks beside the flaming desire the ointment with which Synelle had anointed her brought unbidden. Uncontrollably Karela writhed, and wept for the humiliation of it.

The silvery-haired noble-woman danced before her, spinning and dipping, chanting words that defied hearing in rhythm to haunting flutes and the pounding of scabbarded swords on the stone floor of the vaulting cavern. Between Synelle and Karela stood the bronze she had stolen from Conan, but its evil was overpowered by the waves of horror that radiated from the huge sanguinary image that dominated the chamber. Three ebon eyes that seemed to drink in light held her own. She tried to tear her eyes from that hellborn gaze, she prayed for the strength to pull away, but like a bird hypnotized by a serpent she had no will left.

The lashes struck, again and again. Her hands quivered in her bonds with the effort of not shrieking, for that demonic scarlet figure had begun to vibrate, giving off a hum that blended with the flutes and wrenched at the core of her that made her a woman. Conan, she cried silently, where are you?

Stirring where neither time nor space existed, where endless nihility was all. Awakening, almost full, as pleasure overwhelming lanced through the impenetrable shield. Irritation, vaster than the minds of all men together could encompass, flared. Would these torments never cease, these returnings of ancient memories near gone and better forgotten? Would not.... Full awareness for the first time in eons, awareness cold enough to freeze suns and stay worlds in their motion. There was direction. A single pristine strand of crystalline desire and pain stretching into the infinite. Slowly, with a wariness born of long centuries of disappointment, from the midst of nothingness the gleaming thread of worship was followed.

Conan peered around the edge of a huge, moss-covered block of marble which had once been intended for construction. Crickets chirped in the dark, and a nightbird gave a haunting cry. All else was still.

Roofless walls of niveous stone and truncated alabaster columns, never completed and now wreathed by thick vines, covered the leveled top of the mountain. Among the columns were more than a score of men in black armor and horned helms, the torches a third of them carried casting flickering shadows over the weather-beaten ruins. He wanted to sigh with relief at the symbol picked out in scarlet on their chests. It was clearly the head of the image Karela had stolen, the head of Al'Kiir. Not until that moment had he allowed himself to fear he might be coming to the wrong place.

The black-armored man had to be guarding an entrance to chambers below, Conan thought, where the horrible rite was to take place. Boros had said the tomb lay buried in the heart of the mountain. At least, they were supposed to be standing guard. The sinister reputation of Tor Al'Kiir made it unlikely anyone would come there, most especially in the night, and that made them careless. Some leaned against pale fluted marble. Others sat and talked among themselves. No eye was directed outward to watch for intruders.

Conan signaled with his hands; long practiced, the nine men behind him slid soundlessly away. The Cimmerian counted silently, knowing how long it would take each man to reach his place.

"Now!" he shouted, and burst from concealment to hurl himself at the guards. As he had known it would, his shout and the appearance of a lone man charging froze them for an instant, long enough for nine bowstrings to twang, for nine feathered shafts to drink life.

The guards of Al'Kiir had been chosen for their skill, though, and even as their comrades were falling the survivors darted for cover behind the columns. But then Conan was among them. Thrusting the staff like a lance he took a man under the chin; throat cartiledge snapped loudly, and blood spilled from a mouth that could no longer scream.

"For Conan!" he heard behind him. "Conan!"

A blade thrust at him, and his ancient steel severed the arm that held it. He ducked beneath a decapitating cut and, wielding his broadsword like an axe, chopped through his attacker's mid-section almost to the spine. Kicking the body away, he straightened to find no black-armored man standing. His mercenaries stood among the bodies, gripping bloody swords and warily watching for more of the enemy.

"Are they all dead?" Conan demanded.

Machaon shook his head. "Two managed to run down there." He pointed to a dark opening where steps had led down into the mountain.

"Crom!" the Cimmerian muttered. With quick strides he moved to the opening and started down. Wordlessly the others followed.

Sweat trickling down her sleek form, Synelle moved in the ancient forms and patterns, her body swaying and bending in an exaltation of lust and pain. Time-forgotten words spilled from her mouth, echoed against the walls, supplicating and glorifying her dire god. The monstrous horned malevolence before which she danced pulsated like the string of a harp. The drone that came from it now drowned out the flutes and the pounding scabbards and even the slap of leather on flesh, yet seemed to merge with and amplify her voice.

A part of her mind noted that the auburn-haired woman, naked now to the lash, sagged in her bonds, but struggled still against surrender. Not once had a cry passed her lips. That was well, Synelle thought, not pausing an instant in either movements or incantation. She was certain that the success she seemed to be having was as much due to the stubborn pride of this Karela as to the bronze image. Much better than any of the haughty noblewomen, who in the end always wept and begged and offered their bodies to the men whipping them in exchange for even a moment's surcease.

One of her guards, his chain-mail rent and bloodied, burst into the chamber. "We are attacked, my lady!" he gasped. "Hundreds of them! They cry, for Conan!"

Synelle faltered, then desperately continued with dance and invocation. To stop now would mean disaster, doom better undreamed of. Yet her mind spun. Conan? It was impossible. But then it was impossible that any should dare brave the night slopes of Tor Al'Kiir. Then who . . .

Thoughts and words and movement died as one. All sound stopped as the great horned head turned toward her and three lidless eyes, black as death, regarded her like dark flames of unholy life.

Men in black chain-mail, their horned helmets making them seem more demons than men in the dim light of fires burned low in iron cressets, appeared as if from the walls to defend the rough-cut stone passage. Demons they might appear, yet they died like men. Into the midst of them Conan waded, his ancient broadsword tirelessly rising and falling in furious butchery, till its length was stained crimson and blood fell from it as if the steel itself had wounds. A charnel house he made, and those who dared confront him died. Many could not face that gory blade nor the deathly cold eyes of he who wielded it, and darted past the one man to face instead the nine behind.

The Cimmerian spared no thought for those who refused him combat. What they guarded and what he sought lay ahead, and he did not cease his slaying until he had hacked his way into a huge cavern. The blood chilled in his veins at what he saw.

Twenty more of the black-armored men stood there, but they were as frozen as he, and seemed as insignificant as ants beside what else the chamber contained. Karela, her lush nakedness welted, hanging by her wrists from two wooden pillars. Synelle, oddly garbed in black silk that clung damply to her, a horned chaplet on her brow. And beyond her a shape out of madmen's nightmares, its skin the color of dead men's blood. Al'Kiir awakened threw back his head, and from a broad fanged gash of a mouth came laughter to curdle the heart of heroes.

Even as the evil god's laughter stunned Conan's mind, Synelle's presence filled it. The staff fell from his fingers, and he took a step toward her.

The dark-eyed noblewoman pointed a slender finger at the young giant. As if commanding more wine she said, "Kill him."

The strange lethargy that had affected him of late when he was about her slowed Conan's hand, but his sword took the head of the first man to turn toward him before that man had his blade half-drawn. Nobles could prate while they lounged at their ease of chivalry in battle, though they rarely practiced it; a son of the bleak northland knew only how to fight to win.

The others came at him then, but he retreated to the entrance, wide enough for only three at a time to get near. With a frenzy-approaching madness he fought, and his steel did murderous work among them. Synelle filled his brain. He would get to Synelle if he must wade to his waist in blood.

A scream drew his eye beyond the men struggling to slay him. Al'Kiir had seized Synelle in a clawed hand that almost encircled her narrow waist, lifting her before that triad of ebon eyes for inspection.

Conan redoubled his efforts, and the fury of his attack, seeming reckless of death, forced the mail-clad men to fall back before him.

"Not me!" Synelle screamed, her face contorted in terror. "I am thy faithful slave, o mighty Al'Kiir! Thy priestess! She is the one brought for thy delight!"

Al'Kiir turned his horned head to Karela, and his lipless mouth curled in a fanged smile. He took a step toward her, reaching out.

"No!" Conan roared, desperation clawing at him. "Not Karela!" His foot struck something that rolled with the sound of wood on stone. The Staff of Avanrakash.

Ignoring the men who still faced him, Conan seized the staff from the floor and hurled it like a javelin. Straight to the chest of the monstrous figure the plain wooden staff flew, struck, and pierced. Al'Kiir's free hand tugged at the length of wood, but it could as well have been anchored with barbs. Black ichor poured out around it, and the horned god shrieked, a piercing cry that went on without end, shattering thought and turning muscles to water.

Steel clattered to the stone floor as blackmailed men dropped their swords and fled, pushing past Conan as if he held no weapon at all. And he, in turn, paid them no heed, for the scream that would not stop allowed room for awareness of nothing else.

Around the staff drops of ichor hardened like beads of obsidian, and the hardening widened, spreading steadily through the malevolent shape.

Synelle plucked frantically at the claw-tipped fingers that held her; her long legs kicked wildly. "Release me," she pleaded. "Release thy faithful priestess, o mighty Al'Kiir." Now she struggled with fingers of stone. Slowly, as if it moved with difficulty, the horned head turned to look at her. "Release me!" she screamed. "Release me! No! Mitra, save me!" Her kicking slowed, then her legs were frozen, her cries stilled. Her pale skin gleamed like polished marble in the light from the torches. There was silence.

Flight. Flight from pain great enough to slay a thousand worlds. Flight back to the hated prison of nothingness. Yet something had been brought along. It was clothed in the flesh it had once worn, and a beautiful, naked woman, dark of eye and silvery of hair, floated in the void, mouth working with screams that were not worth hearing. Evil joy, black as the depths of the pit. Long centuries of delight would come from this one before the pitiful spark that was human essence faded and was gone. But the pain did not end. It grew instead. The crystalline thread that linked this place of nonexistence with that other world was still intact, unseverable. Yet it must be ended, least endless eons of agony follow. It must be ended.

Conan shook his head as if waking from a fever dream, and ran to Karela. Quickly he severed her bonds, caught her as she would have fallen.

The beautiful red-haired bandit turned her sweat-streaked face up to him. "I knew you would come," she whispered hoarsely. "I prayed for you to rescue me, and I hate you for it."

The Cimmerian could not help smiling. Whatever had happened to her, Karela was unchanged. Sheathing his sword, he picked her up in his arms. Sighing weakly, she put her arms around his neck and pressed her face to his chest. He thought he felt the wetness of tears.

His gaze went to the stone shape pierced by the wooden staff, the sanguinary horned monstrosity clutching the alabaster figure of a struggling woman, her face frozen in horror for eternity. All the raging feelings and confusions that had filled him were gone as if they had never been. Bewitched, he thought angrily. Synelle had ensorceled him. He hoped that wherever she was she had time for regret.

Machaon and Narus ran into the chamber, bloody swords in hand,

and skidded to a halt, staring in awe. "I'll not ask what happened here," the gaunt-faced man said, "for I misdoubt I'd believe it."

"They flee from us, Cimmerian," Machaon said. "Ten of them together, and they ran down a side passage at the sight of us. Whatever you did took all the heart right out of them."

"The others?" Conan asked, and the tattooed mercenary shook his head grimly.

"Dead. But they collected their ferryman's fees and more."

Suddenly Narus pointed at the huge stone figure. "It's—it's—" He stammered, unable to get any more words out.

Conan spun. The petrified body of the god was quivering. A hum came from it, a hum that quickly rose in pitch until it pierced the ears like driven nails.

"Run!" the Cimmerian shouted, but could not hear his own words through the burning pain that clawed at his skull.

The other two men needed no urging, though. The three of them sped through the rough-hewn stone passages, Conan keeping up easily despite carrying Karela. In their headlong flight they leaped over the bodies of the dead, but saw no one living. And the mind-killing vibration followed them up sloping tunnels, level after level, up the stone steps to the ruins.

As the Cimmerian dashed out among the overgrown columns, the skull-piercing sound ceased. Birds and crickets had fled; the loudest noise to be heard was their own blood thrumming in their ears. Before a breath could be drawn in the silence, the mountain shook. Half-built columns toppled and mossy walls collapsed, blocks of marble large enough to crush a man splashing dirt like water, but the sound of their fall was swallowed by the rumbling that rose from the granite bowels of Tor Al'Kiir.

Dodging through clouds of dust and flying chips of shattered rock, Conan hurtled down the slope, Karela's naked form clutched to his chest. The side of a mountain in the night was no place to be during an earthquake, but neither was the midst of crumbling marble walls. He had a feeling the only safe place to be in *this* earthquake was as far from Tor Al'Kiir as it was possible to run. And run he did, over ground that danced like the deck of a ship in a storm, fighting to keep his balance for rocks bouncing beneath his feet and stones flying through the air like hail. He no longer knew if Machaon and Narus ran with him, nor could he spare a thought for them. They were men, and must take their risks. Conan had to get Karela to safety, for some primal instinct warned him that worse was to come.

With a sound like the splitting of the earth, the peak of Tor Al'Kiir erupted in fire, mountaintop and alabaster columns and marble walls alike flung high into a sky now lit by a fiery glow. The blast threw Conan into the air; he twisted so that his own huge frame took the bone-jarring impact of landing. It was no longer possible to gain his feet. He put his body over that of Karela, sheltering her from the stones that filled the air. As he did one image remained burned into his brain, a single flame towering a thousand paces from the destroyed top of Tor Al'Kiir, a single flame that took the form of the Staff of Avanrakash.

Epilogue

In the paleness before full dawn Conan peered toward Ianthe, towers thrusting into the early morning mist, glazed red roof tiles beginning to gleam with the light of a sun not yet risen. An army approached the city, men-at-arms with gaily colored pennons streaming, long columns of infantry with shields slung on their backs, tall plumes of dust rising beneath thousands of pacing hooves and tramping feet. A victorious army, he thought. But whose?

Avoiding looking at the steaming, cratered top of Tor Al'Kiir, he picked his way through the huge, misshapen boulders that now littered the mountain slope. A quarter of its height had the great granite mound lost in the night, and what lay at its new peak the Cimmerian neither knew nor wanted to know.

Narus voice came to him, tinged with a bitter note. "Women should not be allowed to gamble. Almost I think you changed dice on me. At least let my buy back—"

"No," Karela cut him off as Conan rejoined his three companions. She wore Narus' breeches, tight across the curves of her hips and voluminous in the legs, with his scarlet cloak wrapped about her shoulders and his sword across her knees. The inner slopes of her full breasts showed at the gap in the cloak. "I have more need of something to wear than of gold. And I did not switch the dice. You were too busy filling your filthy eyes and leering at the sight of me uncovered to pay mind of what you were doing."

Machaon laughed, and the gaunt man grunted, attempting to pull his hauberk down far enough to cover his bony knees.

"We must be moving," Conan announced. "There has been a battle, it seems, and whoever won there will be mercenaries without patrons or leaders, men to reform the company. Crom, there may be enough for you each to have your own Free-Company."

Machaon, sitting with his back against one of the building stones that had once stood atop the mountain, shook his head. "I have been longer in this trade, Cimmerian, than you have lived, and this night past has at last given me my full. I own some land in Koth. I shall put up my sword, and become a farmer."

"You?" Conan said incredulously. "A month of grubbing in the dirt, and you'll tear apart the nearest village with your bare hands, just for the need of a fight."

" 'Tis not quite as you imagine," the grizzled veteran chuckled. "There are ten men working the land now. I will be a man of substance, as such as counted among farmers. I shall fetch Julia from the city, and marry her if she will have me. A farmer needs a wife to give him strong sons."

Conan frowned at Narus. "And do you, too, intend to become a farmer?"

"I've no love of dirt," the hollow-faced man replied, snatching the dice from Karela, who had been examining them idly, "but . . . Conan, wizards I did not mind so much, and those men who looked like a snake had been at their mothers were no worse than a horde of blood-drunk Picts, but this god you found us has had my heart in my mouth more than I can remember since the Battle of Black River, when I was a fresh youth without need of shaving. For a time I seek a quiet city, with buxom wenches to bounce on a bed and," he rattled the dice in cupped hands, rolled them on the ground, "young lads with more coin than sense."

"They had best be very young," Karela laughed. "Do you intend to gain any of their coin. Eh, Cimmerian?" Narus glared at her and grumbled under his breath.

As Conan opened his mouth, a flash of white caught his eye, cloth fluttering in the breeze down slope. "Crom!" he muttered. It was Boros and Julia. "I'll wring his scrawny neck for bringing her here," he growled. The others scrambled to their feet to follow him down the mountainside.

When Conan reached the girl and the old man, he saw they were not alone. Julia knelt beside Taurianus, tearing strips from her white robes to try to staunch the blood oozing from a dozen rents in the Ophirean's hauberk. The man's hair was matted with dirt and blood, and a bubble of scarlet appeared at his lips with each labored breath.

Boros flung up his hands as soon as he saw Conan. "Do not blame me. I tried to stop her, but I have not your strength. I thought it best to come along and protect her as best I could. She said she was worried about Machaon."

"About all of them," Julia said, her face reddening. "Conan, we found him lying here. Can you not help him?"

The Cimmerian needed no close examination of Taurianus' wounds to see the man would not survive them. The ground about him was already blackened with his blood. "So the nobles lost," he said quietly. A mercenary fighting on the victorious side would not have crawled away to die.

The Ophirean's eyes fluttered open. "We caught the Eagle," he rasped, and continued with frequent pauses to struggle for breath. "We left our camp—with fires lit—and Iskandrian—fell on it—in the night. Then we took him—in the rear. We would have—destroyed him—but a giant flame—cleft the sky—and the white-haired devil—shouted the gods—were with them. Some cried—it was the Staff—of Avanrakash. Panic seized us—by the throat. We fled—and his warriors cut us down. Enjoy your time—Cimmerian. Iskandrian—is impaling—every mercenary—he catches." Suddenly he lurched up onto one elbow and stretched out a clawed hand toward Conan. "I am a better man—than you!" Blood welled in his mouth, and he fell back. Once he jerked, then was still, dull eyes staring at the sky.

"A giant flame," Narus said softly. "You are a man of destiny, Cimmerian. You make kings even you do not mean to."

Conan shrugged off the words irritably. He cared not who wore the crown of Ophir, except insofar as it affected his prospects. With Iskandrian at Valentius' side—perhaps, he thought, it was time to start thinking of the fopling as Moranthes II—there would be no chance to gather more men, and possibly no men left alive to gather. " 'Twill be Argos for me," he said.

"You!" Machaon snapped abruptly, and Julia jumped. "Did I not tell you to remain in Ianthe? Must I fetch a switch for you here and now? The life of a poor farmer's wife is hard, and she must learn to obey. Would you have our only pig die because you did not feed it when I told you?"

"You have no right to threaten me," the auburn-haired girl burst out. "You cannot . . ." Her words trailed off, and she sat back on her heels. "Wife? Did you say wife?" Taking a deep breath, she said earnestly, "Machaon, I will care for your pig as if it were my beloved sister."

"There's no need to go so far as that," Machaon laughed. His face sobered as he turned to Conan. "A long road we've traveled together, Cimmerian, but it has come to its ending. And as I've no desire to let Iskandrian rummage in my guts with a stake, I'll take my leave now. I wish to be far from Ianthe before this day is done."

"And I," Narus added. " 'Tis Tarantia for me, for they do say the nobles of Aquilonia are free with their coin and love to gamble."

"Fare you well," Conan told them. "And take a pull at the hellhorn for me, if you get there before me."

Julia ran to clasp Machaon's arm, and, with Narus, they started down the mountain.

"After that fool wench's display," Karela muttered, "I need a drink, or I'll be sick to my stomach."

Conan eyed her thoughtfully. "Events hie me to Argos, for 'tis said Free-Companies are being hired there. Come with me, Karela. Together, in a year, we'll rule the country."

The red-haired beauty stared at him, stricken. "Do you not understand why I cannot, Cimmerian? By the Teats of Derketo, man, you wake in me longings to be like that simpering wench, Julia! You make me embrace weakness, make me want to let you protect me. Think you I'm a woman to fold your blankets and cook your meals?"

"I've never asked such of you," he protested, but she ignored him.

"One day I would find myself walking a pace behind you, silent lest I should miss your words, and I'd plant a dagger in your back for it. Then I would likely weep myself to madness for the doing of what you brought on yourself. I will not have it, Conan. I will not!"

A sense of loss filled him, but pride would not allow it to touch his face. "At least you have gained one thing. This time I flee, and you remain in Ophir."

"No, Conan. The vermin that formed my band are not worth the effort of gathering them again. I go to the east." Her head came up, and her eyes glowed like emeralds. "The plains of Zamora shall know the Red Hawk again."

He fumbled in his pouch and drew out half the gems he had taken from the scepter of Ophir. "Here," he said gruffly. Karela did not move. "Can you not take a parting gift from a friend?" Hesitantly a slender hand came to his; he let the gems pour into it.

"You are a better man that you know, Cimmerian," she whispered, "and I am a fool." Her lips brushed his, and she was gone, running with the cloak a scarlet banner behind her.

Conan watched until she passed out of sight below.

"Even the gods cannot understand the brain of a woman," Boros crackled. "Men, on the other hand, rarely think with their brains at all."

Conan glared at the bearded man. He had forgotten Boros was still there. "Now you can return to the taverns and your drinking," he said sourly.

"Not in Ophir," Boros said. He tugged at his beard and glanced nervously toward the ruined mountaintop. "A god cannot be killed as if it were an ordinary demon. Al'Kiir still lives—somewhere. Suppose his body is buried yet up there? Suppose another of those images exists? I will not be in this country if someone else attempts to raise him. Argos, I think. The sea air will be good for my lungs, and I can take ship for distant lands if I hear evil word from Ophir."

"Not in my company," Conan growled. "I travel alone."

"I can work magicks to make the journey easier," Boros protested, but the Cimmerian was already making his way down the mountain. Chattering continuously the gray-bearded man scrambled after Conan, who refused to respond to his importunings.

Once more he was on his own, Conan thought, with only his sword and his wits, but he had been so often before. There were the gems in his pouch, of course. They would fetch something. And Argos lay ahead, Argos and thoughts he had never entertained before. If chance could bring a fool like Valentius to a throne, why could he not find a path? Why indeed? Smiling, he quickened his pace.

Conan
the
Victorious

Prologue

The Vendhyan night was preternaturally still, the air weighty and oppressive. No slightest breeze stirred, leaving the capital city of Ayodhya to swelter. The moon hung heavily in the sky like a monstrous yellow pustule, and most of the few who ventured out to see it shuddered and wished for even a single cloud to hide its sickly malevolence. There were whispers in the city that such a night, such a moon, were omens of plague, or of war, but certainly of death.

The man who called himself Naipal gave no heed to the whispers. Watching from the highest balcony of a vast palace of alabaster spires and golden domes, his by royal gift, he knew the moon was no omen of any sort. It was the stars that gave the night its promise, the passing of configurations that had blocked his way for months. He laid long, supple fingers on the long, narrow golden coffer held beneath his arm. Tonight, he thought, there would be one moment of transcendent danger, a moment when all his plans could crumble to dust. Yet there was no gain without risk, and the greater the gain, the greater the danger.

Naipal was not his true name, for in a land noted for its intrigues, those who followed his path were secretive beyond the ordinary. He was tall for a Vendhyan, and they were accounted a tall people among the nations of the East. That height gave him a presence that he deliberately diminished by wearing robes of somber hue, such as the dark gray he now wore, rather than the rainbow silks and satins affected by men of fashion. Also the shade of charcoal was his modestly small turban, with neither gem nor plume to set it off. His face was darkly handsome, seeming calm beyond the ability of any disaster to shatter, with heavy-lidded black eyes that spoke of wisdom to men and of passion to women.

Seldom did he allow himself to be seen, however, for in mystery there was power, though many knew that one called Naipal was court wizard to King Bhandarkar of Vendhya. This Naipal, it was said in Ayodhya, was a wise man, not only for his good and faithful service to the King since the strange disappearance of the former court wizard, but also for his modest lack of ambition. In a place where every man and woman brimmed with ambition and plotting, the lack was considered praise-worthy, if peculiar. But then, his sort did peculiar things. It was known, for instance, that he gave great sums to the poor, to the children of the streets. This was a source of some amusement to the nobles of the court, for they thought he did it to assume a guise of kindness. In truth he had thought long before giving the first coin. He had come from those streets and remembered well wretched nights crouched in an alley, too hungry to sleep. The truth would have showed a weakness; therefore he fostered the cynical rumors of his motives, for he allowed himself no weakness.

With a last look at the sky, Naipal left the balcony, firmly clutching the narrow coffer. Golden lamps, cunningly wrought in the shapes of birds and flowers, lit the high-ceilinged corridors of his palace. Exquisite porcelains and fragile crystal vases stood on tables of polished ebony and carven ivory. The carpets layered thickly beneath his feet in a welter of color were beyond price, and any one of the delicately-woven tapestries on the alabaster walls could have been exchanged for the daughter of a king. In public, Naipal made every effort to efface himself; in private, he reveled in all the pleasures of the senses. This night, however, after waiting so long, his eye did not touch any of the ornaments of his palace nor did he call for wine, nor musicians, nor women.

Down he went, into the depths of his palace and beyond, to chambers with walls that glowed with a faint pearlescence as though glazed by the hand of a master, chambers hewn from the bowels of the earth by his powers. Few of his servants were allowed to enter those deep-buried rooms and passages, and those few could not speak of what they did or saw for the simple lack of a tongue. The world at large did not know of those chambers, for those servants who did not descend into them, and so were allowed to keep their tongues, fearfully and wisely averted their eyes and would not so much as whisper of them on their sleeping pallets.

A downward-sloping corridor opened into a great square chamber, thirty paces on a side, with softly-gleaming canescent walls that were all of one piece, without join. Above, a pointed dome rose twenty times the height of a tall man. Centered beneath that dome was an arcane pattern in silver, buried in the near translucence of the floor and encompassing the greater part of the room. That silver graving gave off its own unholy radiance of frosty paleness. At nine precisely chosen spots on the perimeter of that figure were tripods of delicately worked gold, no higher than Naipal's knee and placed so that each leg seemed to continue a portion of the pattern. The air seemed sharp with dire forces, and the memories of foulness done.

Incongruously, the sixth part of the length of one wall was taken by a large grille of iron bars, with a locked door, also of iron, set in it. Near the strange latticework a table of polished rosewood held the implements and ingredients he would need this night, all arranged on black velvet as a gem merchant might display his wares. A large flat box of ornately carved ivory stood atop faceted crystal legs at one end of the velvet. The place of honor on that table, though, was held by a small, finely crafted ebony chest.

Setting the golden coffer beside a silken cushion before which stood another golden tripod, Naipal went to the table. His hand stretched toward the small black chest, but on sudden impulse he raised the ivory lid instead. Carefully he brushed aside layers of blue silk, as soft as the finest down, revealing a silvered mirror, its polished surface showing no image at all, not even a reflection of the chamber.

The mage nodded. He had expected no different, but knew he must not allow his certainties to stop him from proper precautions. This mirror was not so very unlike a scrying glass, but instead of being used to communicate or spy, it had very special properties. That silver surface would show no images save those that threatened his designs.

Once, soon after he became wizard in the court of King Bhandarkar, Mount Yimsha, abode of the dreaded Black Seers, had appeared in the mirror. It had been only curiosity at his ascension, he knew. They saw no threat in him, more fools they. In a day the image was gone, and never since had anything been reflected there. Not so much as a flicker. Such was the efficacy of his planning.

With a feeling of satisfaction, Naipal covered the mirror once more and opened the ebony chest. Within was that which made his satisfaction grow. In carven hollows in the sable wood lay ten stones, smooth ovals of so inky a hue that the ebony seemed less black beside them. Nine were the size of the last joint of a man's thumb, the last twice so large. These were the *khorassani*. For centuries men had died seeking them in vain, until their very existence became first part of legends, then the stuff of stories for children. Ten years it had taken Naipal to acquire them, a search filled with adventures and trials to make it fit for epics had it been known.

Reverently he placed the nine smaller *khorassani*, one atop each of the golden tripods that bordered the arcane figure within the floor. The tenth, the largest, he set on the tripod before the cushion. All was in readiness.

Naipal settled cross-legged onto the cushion and began to speak the words of power, commanding forces unseen. *"E'las eloyhim! Maraath savinday! Khora mar! Khora mar!"*

Again the words repeated, again and again unending, and the stone before him began to glow as though with fires imprisoned in its core. No illumination did it give, yet it seemed to burn with all light. Abruptly, with a hiss as of white-hot metal thrust into water, narrow streaks of fire leaped from the glowing stone, one to each of the nine *khorassani* surrounding the silver pattern. As suddenly as they were born, the blazing bars died, yet now all ten stones blazed with the same fury. Once more the slashing hiss sounded, and the encircling stones were linked by burning lines, while from each tripod another bar of terrible incandescence stretched both upward and downward. Within the confines of that fiery cage neither floor nor dome could any longer be seen, but only darkness stretching to infinity.

Naipal fell silent, studying his handiwork, then shouted, "Masrok, I summon you!"

A rushing came, as though all the winds of the world poured through vast caverns.

A thunderclap smote the chamber, and within the flamebarred cage there floated a huge eight-armed shape, twice as tall as any man and more, with skin like polished obsidian. Its only garb was a silver necklace from which depended three human skulls, and its body was smooth and sexless. Two of its hands held silver swords that shone with an unearthly light. Two more held spears with human skulls hanging below the points for decoration, and another grasped a needle-pointed dagger. Each weapon shared the glaucous, other-worldly glow. Large leathery ears twitched on the hairless head, and sharply slanted ruby eyes swiveled to Naipal.

Carefully the creature stretched to touch one silvery spear to the fiery bounds. A million hornets buzzed in rage, and lightnings flashed along the candent boundary, ceasing only when the spear point was withdrawn.

"Why do you still seek escape, Masrok?" Naipal demanded. "You cannot break our bargain so easily. Only lifeless matter can cross through that boundary from the outside, and nothing, not even you, can pass it from the inside. As you well know."

"If you make foolish errors, O man, there is no need for bargains." The booming words were pronounced stiffly around teeth that seemed designed for rending flesh, but a touch of arrogance came through. "Still, I will keep our pact."

"Most assuredly you will, and should from gratitude if for no other reason. Did I not free you from a prison that had held you for centuries?"

"Freedom, O man? I leave that prison only when summoned to this place by you, and here I am constrained to remain until commanded by you to return once more to that same prison. For this and promises, I aid you? I sent the demons to bear away your former master so that you could rise to what you consider power as the court wizard. I shield the eyes of the Black Seers of Yimsha while you attempt that which would draw their wrath upon your head. I do these things at your command, O man, and you dare speak to me of freedom?"

"Continue to obey me," Naipal said coldly, "and you will have your freedom entire. Refuse . . ." He flung open the golden coffer. From it he snatched a silvery dagger like the one the demon carried, even to the glow, and thrust it toward the demon. "When we made our pact, I demanded a token of you, and you gave me this with warnings as to the danger of its merest touch to human flesh. Did you think with a demon-weapon in my grasp I would not seek the secret of its powers? You hold human knowledge in contempt, Masrok, though it was mortal men who chained you in your adamantine prison. And in the knowledge of mere humans, in the ancient writings of human wizards, I found mention of weapons borne by demons, weapons of glowing silver, weapons that cannot miss what they strike at and slay whatever they strike. Even demons, Masrok. Even you!"

"Strike at me then," the demon snarled. "I marched to war beside gods, and against gods, when the highest achievement of man was to turn over a rock to eat the grubs beneath. Strike!"

Smiling thinly, Naipal returned the dagger to the coffer. "You are of no use to me dead, Masrok. I simply want you aware that there is worse I can do to you than leave you in your prison. Even for a demon, imprisonment is to be preferred to death."

The demon's rubescent eyes fixed malevolently on the mage. "What do you wish of me this time, O man? There are limits to what I can do unless you remove the constraints on my journeying."

"There is no need for that." Naipal drew a deep breath; the moment of danger was at hand. "You were imprisoned to guard the tomb of King Orissa beneath the lost city of Maharashtra."

"You have asked before, O man, and I will not tell you the location of tomb or city. I will not betray that if I am bound for all of time."

"I know well the limits of your aid to me. Listen to my command. You will return to that tomb, Masrok, and bring to me one of the warriors buried with King Orissa. Bring me one man of the army that formed his bodyguard in death."

For a moment Naipal thought the demon would accept the command without demur, but abruptly Masrok screamed, and as it screamed, it spun. Faster and faster it whirled until it was an ebon blur streaked with silver. No part of that blur touched the boundaries of its cage, but the hornets screamed and lightnings slashed walls of fiery lace. The chamber vibrated with the penetrating shriek and a blue-white glare filled the air.

Calm did not desert Naipal's face, yet sweat beaded his brow. He knew well the forces contained in that barrier and the power necessary to make it cry out and flare as it did. It was almost to the point of shattering; almost to the point of unleashing Masrok. Through the thousand deaths he would die when that happened, the greatest pain would be the failure of all his grand designs.

As abruptly as the tempest had begun, it ended. Masrok stood as truly carved from obsidian, crimson eyes glaring at the wizard. "You ask betrayal!"

"A small betrayal," Naipal said blandly, though it took all his reserves to manage it. "Not the location of the tomb. Merely a single warrior out of thousands."

"To escape two millennia of bondage is one thing, to betray what I was set to guard is another!"

"I offer freedom, Masrok."

"Freedom," was all the demon said.

Naipal nodded. "Freedom, after two thousand years."

"Two thousand years, O man? The span of a human life is but a moment's dreaming to me. What are years to one such as I?"

"Two thousand years," the mage repeated. For a long moment there was silence.

"Three others guard as I do," Masrok said slowly. "My other selves, all of us created from the same swirl of chaos in the very instant time itself was born. Three to my one. It will take time, O man."

By the barest margin was Naipal able to mask his exhaltation. "Do it as quickly as possible. And remember that when your service to me is done, you will have your freedom. I await your sign that the task is done. Now go, Masrok! I command it!"

Once more thunder smote the chamber, and the fiery cage stood empty.

With an unsteady hand, Naipal wiped the sweat from his brow, then hastily scrubbed it on his dark robes as though denying its existence. It was done. Another thread had been placed in a tapestry of great complexity. There were a thousand such threads, many being placed by men—and women—who had no idea of what they truly did or why, but when the pattern had finally been woven . . . A small smile touched his face. When it was woven, the world would bow to Vendhya, and Vendhya, unknowing, would bow to Naipal.

I

From a distance the city seemed jeweled, ivory and gold beside a sea of sapphire, justifying the name of Golden Queen of the Vilayet Sea. A closer view showed why others gave Sultanapur's byname as "the Gilded Bitch of the Vilayet."

The broad mole-protected harbor was crowded with the ships that gave Sultanapur cause to call itself Queen to Aghrapur's King, but for every roundship filled to the gunwales with silks from Khitai, for every galley that carried the scent of cinnamon and cloves from Vendhya, another vessel, out of Khoraf or Khawarism, reeked of stale sweat and despair, the odiferous brand of the slaver.

Gold-leafed domes proliferated on palaces of pale marble, it was true, and alabaster spires stretched toward the azure sky, but the streets were cramped and crooked in the best of quarters, for Sultanapur had grown haphazardly over centuries beyond counting. Half a score of times in those numberless years had the city died, its gilded palaces and temples to now-nameless gods gone to ruin. At each death, however, new palaces and new temples to new gods had grown like mushrooms on the rubble of the old, and like mushrooms, they crowded together where they would, leaving only rambling ways between for streets.

The city was dusty in a land that might know rain once in a year, and it, too, had as distinct a smell as the harbor. Without rain to wash the streets, the stenches of years hung in the hot air, a blend of spices and sweat, perfume and offal, a thousand aromas melded together till the parts could no longer be told one from the other. The whole was an ever-present miasma, as much a part of the city as any building.

Baths proliferated in Sultanapur: ornate marble structures with mosaicked pools, served by nubile wenches in naught but their sleek skins; wooden tubs behind taverns, where a serving girl might scrub a back for the price of a drink. It was the constant heat, however, and not the smell that made them a tradition. The wrinkled nose and the perfumed pomander were signs of the newcomer to Sultanapur, for those who dwelt there for any time no longer noticed the smell.

Newcomers there always were, for the Gilded Bitch of the Vilayet drew certain sorts of men from all corners of the known world. In a cool, fig-tree-shaded court or a shadowy tavern, an ebon-faced merchant from Punt might discuss with an almond-eyed Khitan the disposition of wines from Zingara, or a pale-cheeked Corinthian might speak with a turbaned Vendhyan of the ivory routes to Iranistan. The streets were a polyglot kaleidoscope of multi-hued grab in a hundred cuts from a score of lands, and the languages and accents to be heard among the babble of the marketplaces were too numerous for counting. In some instances the goods were honestly purchased. In others the purchase had been from the pirates who plagued the sea lanes, or coin had been passed to raiders of caravans or to smugglers on a dark coast. However obtained, on no more than half of what passed through Sultanapur was the King's custom paid. Sultanapur was a queen that took pride in her infidelity to her king.

For all that he was head and shoulders taller than most of those he passed, the muscular young man drew no special notice for his size as he made his way through streets filled with high-wheeled, ox-drawn wains squeaking on ungreased axles toward the docks. His tunic of white linen was tight across the breadth of his shoulders, and a broadsword swung at his side in a worn leather scabbard, but neither sword nor breadth of shoulders was enough to pick him out in Sultanapur. Big men, men who carried swords, were always sure of hire in a city where there was never a lack of goods or lives to guard.

Beneath a thick mane of black hair, held back from his face by a leather cord, were eyes as blue as the Vilayet and as hard as agates. Those eyes did cause stares from the few who noticed them. Some made a sign to ward off the evil eye as he passed, but those who did so did it surreptitiously. It was all very well to avoid the curse of those strange eyes, but to anger their possessor was another matter entirely when the leather wrappings of his sword-hilt were worn smooth with use and his bearing and face showed him little loath to add to that wear.

Aware of those who stared and made the sign of the horns, the youth ignored them. Two months in Sultanapur had made him used to such.

Sometimes he wondered how those men would take it if they found themselves in his native mountains of Cimmeria, where eyes of any shade but blue or gray were as rare as his own were in this southern land of Turan. As often since coming to this place where the blue Vilayet mocked with its wetness the dry air, he thought longingly of the windswept, snowy crags of his homeland. Longingly, but briefly. Before coming to Turan he had been a thief, but he found that the gold that came from thievery had a way of trickling through his fingers as fast as he got it. He meant to return to Cimmeria—someday—but with gold enough to scatter like drops of water. And in Sultanapur he had found an old friend and a new trade.

At a stone-walled tavern with a crescent moon roughly daubed in yellow on its front, the Cimmerian went in, cutting off much of the noise of the street as he pulled the heavy door shut behind him. The Golden Crescent was cool inside, for its thick walls kept out the heat of the sun as well as the clatter. Tables were scattered across the stone floor so that talk at one could not easily be heard at another, and the interior was lighted poorly apurpose, for here whom a man talked to or what he said was considered no one's business but his own. The patrons were mainly Turanians, though they seemed a mixed lot. Their garments ranged from threadbare once-white cotton to costly velvets and silks in gaudy shades of scarlet and yellow. Not even the most ragged of them lacked coin, though, as evidenced by the number of doxies seated on men's knees or displaying their wares among the tables in narrow strips of brightly colored silk.

Some of the men nodded to the Cimmerian, or spoke. He knew them by name—Junio and Valash and Emilius—for they followed the same trade as he, but he did no more than acknowledge their greeting for he had no interest in them this day. He peered into the dimness, searching for one woman in particular. He saw her at the same moment she saw him.

"Conan!" she squealed, and he found his arms full of satiny olive flesh. A length of red silk two fingers in width encircled her rounded breasts, and another twice as wide was tucked through a narrow girdle of gilded brass set low on sweetly curving hips. Black hair cascaded down her back to all but bare buttocks, and her eyes shone darkly. "I hoped you would come to see me. I have missed you sorely."

"Missed me?" he laughed. "It has been but four days, Tasha. But to mend your loneliness . . ." He freed a hand to delve into the leather purse at his belt and held up a blue topaz on a fine golden chain. For the next few minutes he was busy being kissed, fastening the chain about her neck, then being kissed again. And being kissed by Tasha, he thought, was more definite than a night in some women's arms.

Lifting the clear azure stone from its nest between her breasts, she admired it again, then gazed up at him through long lashes. "You must have had good luck with your fishing," she smiled.

Conan grinned. "We fishermen must work very hard for our coin, casting nets out, hauling them in. Luckily, the price of fish is very high right now." To gales of laughter from men close enough to hear, he led Tasha to an empty table.

All of the men who frequented the Golden Crescent called themselves fishermen, and it was even possible that some few actually were, upon occasion. For the vast majority, however, their "catches" were landed at night on deserted stretches of the coast where none of King Yildiz's excisemen were about to see whether it was fish or bales of silk and casks of wine that were offloaded. It was said that if all of the so-called fishermen in Sultanapur actually brought fish to market, the city would be buried to the tops of the tallest tower, and the Vilayet would be stripped of its finny denizens.

At a table near the back of the room, Conan dropped to a bench and pulled Tasha on to his lap. A sloe-eyed serving girl appeared at his elbow, wearing little more than the doxies, though in cotton rather than silk. She was as available as the other women, for those who could not or would not pay the trulls' prices, and the smile she beamed at the broad-shouldered Cimmerian said she would take Tasha's place in an instant.

"Wine," he said and watched the rhythmic sway of her almost-covered hips as she left.

"You did come to see me, did you not?" Tasha asked acidly. "Or is that why you did not come yesterday? You said you would return yesterday. Were you off comforting some thick-ankled serving wench?"

"I did not think her ankles were thick," Conan said blandly. His hand barely caught Tasha's wrist before her slap reached his face. She squirmed on his lap as though to rise, and he tightened his arm around her waist. "Who is sitting on my knee?" he asked. "That should tell you whom I want."

"Perhaps," she pouted, but at least she had stopped trying to get up.

He released her arm carefully. He had been made aware of her temper early on. She was quite capable of trying to rake his eyes out with her nails. But the passion that went into her rages she put into other things as well, and so he continued to seek her out.

The serving girl returned with a clay pitcher of wine and two battered

metal cups, taking away the coins he gave her. This time Tasha watched
her depart, with a glare that boded ill. It had been Conan's experience
that women, whatever they said, preferred men who were not easily
bullied, but now he thought a little oiling of the waters might be in
order.

"Now look you," he said. "We did not return to Sultanapur until
this very morning, for the wind turned against us. From the boat to here
I took only a few hours to find that bauble for you. If need be, I will
fetch Hordo to vouch for it."

"He would lie for you." She took the cup he filled for her, but instead
of drinking she bit her lower lip, then said, "He came looking for you.
Hordo, I mean. I forgot, before. He wants to see you right away. Something about a load of 'fish.' "

Conan hid a smile. It was a transparent attempt to make him leave
on a fool's errand. On leaving their vessel, the one-eyed smuggler had
spoken of his intentions to seek out a certain merchant's wife whose
husband was in Akif. The Cimmerian saw no reason to share that knowledge, however.

"Hordo can wait."

"But—"

"You, Tasha, I prize above any silk or gems. I will stay here. With
you."

She gave him a sidelong glance with bright eyes. "You hold me so
dear?" Lithely she snuggled closer to him and bent to murmur into his
ear between teasing nips with small white teeth. "I like your present
very much, Conan."

The sounds of the street intruded momentarily, indicating the entrance of another patron. With a gasp, Tasha crouched as though trying
to use him as a shield. Even for the Golden Crescent, he realized suddenly, it had become too quiet. The constant low murmur of conversation was gone. The Cimmerian looked at the door. In the dimness he
could barely make out the shape of a man, tall for a Turanian. One
thing was plain, however, even in the shadows by the door. The man
wore the tall pointed helmet of the City Guard.

The intruder walked slowly into the silent tavern, head swiveling as
if searching for someone, the fingers of one hand tapping on the hilt of
the curved sword at his hip. None of the men at the scattered tables
met his eyes, but he did not appear interested in any of them. He was
an officer, Conan could now see, a narrow-faced man, tall for a Turanian, with a thin mustache and a small beard waxed to a point.

The officer's fingers stopped tapping as his gaze lit on Conan's table, then began again as he drew closer. "Ah, Tasha," he said smoothly, "did you forget I said I would come to you today?"

Tasha kept her eyes down and answered in a near whisper, "Forgive me, Captain Murad. You see that I have a patron. I cannot . . . I . . . please."

"Find another woman," Conan growled.

The captain's face froze, but he did not take his eyes from Tasha. "I did not speak to you . . . fisherman. Tasha, I do not want to hurt you again, but you must learn to obey."

Conan sneered. "Only a fool needs fear in his dealings with women. If you prefer cringing curs, find yourself a dog to beat."

The guardsman's face paled beneath its swarthiness. Abruptly he seized Tasha's arm, jerking her from the Cimmerian's lap. "Leave my sight, scum, before I—"

The threat cut off as Conan leaped to his feet with a snarl. The narrow-faced man's eyes widened in surprise, as though he had expected the girl to be given up without a fight, and his hand darted for his sword hilt, but Conan moved faster. Not toward his own blade, however. Killing guardsmen was considered bad business for smugglers unless it was absolutely necessary, and in truth usually even then. Soldiers who palmed a coin and looked the other way could become tigers in defense of the King's laws when one of their own was slain. The Cimmerian's fist smashed into the other's chin before a fingerwidth of steel was bared. The officer seemed to attempt a tumbler's back flip and fell against a table, toppling it as he dropped to the floor. His helmet spun across the floor, but the Turanian lay where he had fallen like a sack of rags.

The tavernkeeper, a plump Kothian with small gold rings in the lobe of each ear, bent to peer at the officer. He scrubbed his fat hands nervously on his wine-stained apron as he straightened. "You've ruined my custom for a tenday, northlander. *If* I'm lucky. Mitra, man! You've killed the perfumed buffoon! His neck's snapped."

Before anyone else could speak or move the door to the street slammed open, and two more guardsmen strode through. They marched into the common room sneering as though it were a barracks square filled with peasant conscripts. The unnatural stillness of the tavern was disturbed by tiny shiftings and rustlings as men marked escape routes.

Conan quietly cursed under his breath. He was all but standing over the accursed fool's body. To move would only draw attention more quickly than it would come already. As for running, he had no intention of dying with a sword in his back. With a small gesture he motioned Tasha from him. He found the alacrity with which she obeyed a trifle disappointing.

"We seek Captain Murad," one of the guardsmen shouted into the silence. An oft-broken nose gave him a brawler's face. The other tugged at a straggly mustache and stared superciliously about the room. The Kothian tried to scuttle into the deeper shadows, but the broken-nosed soldier froze him with a glare. "You, innkeeper! This smuggling scum you serve seem to have no tongues. Where is Captain Murad? I know he came in here."

The Kothian's mouth worked soundlessly, and he scrubbed his hands all the harder in his apron.

"Find your tongue, fool, before I slit it! If the captain's with a wench, still he must hear the word I bring without delay. Speak, or I'll have your hide for boots!"

Abruptly the straggly-mustached soldier caught the speaker's tunic sleeve. "It's Murad, Tavik!" he exclaimed, pointing.

From the still form of the officer the guards' eyes rose inexorably to Conan, their faces hard. The Cimmerian waited calmly, seemingly unaffected by their stares. What would happen, would happen.

"Your work, big man?" Tavik asked coldly. "Striking an officer of the City Guard will cost you the bastinado. Abdul, see to waking the captain."

They had rested too long under the protection of their position with regard to the smugglers, the big youth thought. Tavik drew his curved sword, but held it casually, lowered by his side, as though he did not believe anyone there would actually make him use it. The other did not even reach for his weapon.

Abdul squatted beside Captain Murad's body, grasped the officer's arms, and stiffened. "He's dead," he breathed, then shouted it. "He's dead, Tavik!"

Conan kicked the bench he had been sitting on at Abdul, who was attempting to leap to his feet and unsheathe his sword at the same time. As the scraggly-mustached man danced awkwardly to avoid falling over the impediment, the Cimmerian's own blade was bared. At his companion's cry, Tavik had raised his blade high to slash, which might have been all very well had his opponent been unarmed. Now he paid for his error as Conan's steel sliced across his exposed belly. With a shrill scream, Tavik dropped his sword, fingers clutching in a vain attempt to keep in the thick ropes of his intestines as he followed the weapon to the stone floor.

Conan leaped back as he recovered from the killing stroke, his broadsword arcking down barely in time to block Abdul's thrust at his side. The force of the blow knocked the guardsman's tulwar wide, and doomed desperation filled his dark eyes in the moment before the Cimmerian's blade pierced his throat to stand out a handspan from the back of his neck. As Conan jerked his sword free from the collapsing corpse, Tavik gave one last kick and died.

Grimly the Cimmerian wiped his sword on Abdul's tunic and sheathed it. The common room, he realized, now held but half those it had at the beginning of his fight, and more were disappearing every moment through the doors that led to alleys beside and behind the building. No man or wench in the tavern but would want to be able to deny being in the Golden Crescent on the day three of the City Guard died there.

The Kothian tavernkeeper cracked the door to the street enough to peer out, then closed it with a groan. "Guardsmen," he muttered. "Half a score of them. And they look impatient. They'll be in here in a trice to see what's keeping those two. How am I to explain this happening in my tavern? What am I to tell them?" His hand snatched the gold coin Conan tossed him, and he was not too despondent to bite it before making it disappear beneath his apron.

"Tell them, Banaric," Conan said, "of the slavers from Khoraf who killed the captain in a quarrel, and then the guardsmen. A dozen slavers. Too many for you to interfere."

Banaric nodded reluctantly. "They might believe it. Maybe."

They were the last two in the tavern, Conan saw. Even Tasha had gone. And without a word, he thought sourly. In a matter of moments the entire day had gone rotten. At least he would not have to worry about being hounded by the City Guard. Or he would not if the Kothian told the story he had been paid to tell.

"Remember, Banaric," he said. "A dozen Khorafi slavers." He waited for the innkeeper's nod, then slipped out the back.

II

Conan hurried away from the Golden Crescent by the network of alleys, barely as wide as his shoulders and stinking of urine and offal, that crisscrossed the area of the tavern. His plans had been for a day in Tasha's arms, but that had certainly gone aglimmering. He slipped in the slime underfoot, barely caught himself, and cursed. Even if he managed to find the jade again, he was not sure he wanted to spend time with a woman who would take his gift and then run away—without so much as a kiss—just because of a little trouble. There were other women, and other uses for his time. Even after buying the topaz for her and tossing a gold piece to Banaric, Conan's purse was far from empty. The "fish" unloaded the night before on a secluded beach had been Khitan silks and the famed Basralla laces from Vendhya, and the prices paid for them were generous. He would spend a little coin on himself.

Deep into the heart of the sprawling city he went, far from the harbor district, yet all parts of Sultanapur had their share of bustling commerce. There were no ox-drawn carts here, but still the narrow streets were filled with humanity, for coppersmith's shop and bawdy house might lie cheek by jowl with rich merchant's dwelling, and tavern and potter's shop with temple. Buyers, sellers and worshipers were all jumbled in the throng.

Sleek ladies in veils of lace, trailed by servants to carry their purchases, jostled with apprentices bearing rolled rugs or stacked bolts of cloth on their shoulders. Filthy urchins with greedy fingers stalked the purses of fat men with velvet tunics and even greedier eyes. In a small square a juggler kept six lighted brands in the air at the same time while shouting curses at trulls in girdles of coin and little else who solicited those who paused to watch.

At every street crossing, fruit peddlers sold pomegranates, oranges and figs, some from trays held before them by a strap about the neck, some from wicker panniers on donkeys. From time to time the donkeys added their braying to the general tumult. Geese and chickens in reed cages honked and cackled, pigs tethered by a leg grunted disconsolately. Hawkers cried a hundred varied wares, and merchants bargained at the top of their lungs, shouting that such a price would ruin them, then going lower still.

A copper bought a large handful of figs that Conan ate as he strolled and looked, and occasionally made a purchase. From a swordsmith, working his forge beneath a striped awning with the ring of hammer on white-hot metal, the Cimmerian purchased a straight-bladed dagger and sheath that he tucked through his sword-belt in the small of his back. Finely carved amber beads went into his pouch with the thought that they would grace the neck of some other wench than Tasha. Unless, of course, she apologized prettily for running away as she had.

A narrow, shadowed shop, presided over by a skinny man with an unctuous manner and oily countenance, yielded a white hooded cloak of the thinnest wool, not for the cold that never came in Sultanapur, but to keep off the sun. He had looked for such a cloak for some time, but most men in Sultanapur wore turbans, and few cloaks with hoods were sold, not to mention cloaks large enough to fit across his shoulders.

A ragged man passed Conan, bearing on his back a large clay jar wrapped in damp cloths. The handle of a ladle protruded from the mouth of the jar, and brass cups clinked against each other as they dangled on chains along the jar's sides. The sight of him awoke in Conan the thirst that came from eating so many sweetly ripe figs, for the ragged man was a water seller. In a city so hot and so dry as Sultanapur, water had a price as surely as did wine.

Conan motioned the man aside and squatted against a wall while the water seller set down his jar. The chains reached far enough for a Turanian to stand and drink, but Conan must needs either squat or stoop. A copper passed into the water seller's bony hand, and Conan took his cup of water.

Not so cool by far as a mountain stream in Cimmeria, he thought, freshened by the runoff of the spring thaws. But such thoughts were worse than useless, serving only to make the heat seem to suck moisture from a man even faster. He drew up the hood of his new cloak to give himself a little shade. As he drank, fragments of talk drifted to him through the cacophony of the street. Tasha occupied his mind, and but fragments of fragments registered on his ear.

". . . Forty coppers the cask is outrageous . . ."

". . . At least ten dead, they say, and one a general . . ."

". . . A prince, I heard . . ."

". . . If my husband finds out, Mahmoud . . ."

". . . A Vendhyan plot . . ."

". . . While the *wazam* of Vendhya is in Aghrapur talking peace . . ."

". . . So I seduced his daughter to even the bargain . . ."

". . . The assassin was a northland giant . . ."

Conan froze with the brass cup at his lips. Slowly he raised his eyes to the water seller's face. The man, staring idly at the wall against which the Cimmerian crouched, seemed merely to await the return of his cup, but sweat beaded his dark forehead where there had been none before, and his feet shuffled as though he would be away quickly.

"What did you hear, water seller?"

The ragged man jumped, rocking his jar. He had to catch it to keep it from toppling. "Master? I . . . I hear nothing." A nervous laugh punctuated his words. "There are always rumors, master. Always rumors, but I listen only to the babblings of my own head."

Conan slid a silver piece into the man's calloused palm. "What did you hear just now?" He asked in a milder tone. "About a northlander."

"Master, I sell water. Nothing else." Conan merely continued looking at him, but the man blinked and swallowed as though at a snarl. "Master, they say . . . they say there are soldiers dead, City Guardsmen, and perhaps a general or a prince. They say Vendhyans hired it done, and that one of the slayers . . ."

"Yes?"

The water seller swallowed again. "Master, they say one of the slayers was a . . . a giant. A . . . a northlander."

Conan nodded. The tale obviously had its roots in the occurrence at the Golden Crescent. And if so much were common knowledge, in however distorted a fashion, how much else was known also? His name perhaps? He did not worry about the how of the story spreading. Smugglers did not usually turn against their own, but perhaps one in the tavern that morning had been caught and put to the question by the guardsmen who had been in the street. Mayhap Banaric had not felt a gold piece enough for a lie in the face of the guardsmen's certain anger at what they found. At the moment he had quite enough worry in how to avoid capture in a city where he stood out like a camel in a zenanna.

His eyes searched the street, and a possibility came to him. At least there were no guardsmen. Yet.

He emptied the cup with a gulp, but held it a moment longer. "It is a good thing to sell, water," he said. "Water and nothing else. Men who sell water and nothing else never have to look over their shoulders for fear of who might be there."

"I understand, master," the water seller gasped. "I sell water and nothing else. Nothing else, master."

Conan nodded and released the cup. The water seller heaved his jar onto his back so quickly that water slopped over the sides, and hurried into the streaming crowd. Before he was out of sight, Conan had already dismissed the ragged fellow from his mind. There would be a reward, likely as distorted as the numbers of guardsmen slain, and the water seller would sooner or later try for part of it, but with luck, he would remain silent for perhaps as much as an hour. In truth, the Cimmerian would settle for a tenth of that.

Drawing the hood of his cloak farther forward, Conan strode hurriedly down the street, searching for a vendor of a particular sort. A sort of vendor who did not seem to be present, he thought angrily. There were sellers of brass bowls and wicker baskets, of tunics and sandals and gilded jewelry, but not of what he sought. But he had seen apprentices carrying . . . There it was. A rug merchant's stall, filled with carpets in all sizes and colors, stacked, rolled and hanging on the walls.

As Conan entered, the plump merchant hurried forward, hands rubbing in anticipation and a professional smile on his face. "Welcome, master. Welcome. Here you may see the finest carpets in all of Sultanapur. Nay, in all of Turan. Carpets to grace the palace of King Yildiz himself, may Mitra bless him thrice daily. Carpets from Iranistan, from—"

"That one," Conan cut him off, pointing to a rug that lay near the front of the stall in a roll thicker than a man's head. He was careful to keep his face down. The sight of blue eyes would bring more than a sign for warding off the evil eye now.

"Indeed, master, you are truly a connoisseur. Without even the bother of unrolling it, you chose the finest carpet in my shop. For the trifle of one gold piece—"

This time the rug merchant's jaw dropped, for Conan immediately thrust a gold piece into the man's hands. It left him with little in his purse, but he had no time for bargaining, however odd that might strike the merchant.

The plump man's mouth worked as he attempted to regain his equilibrium. "Uh, yes, master. Of course. I will fetch apprentices to bear your purchase. Two should be enough. They are strong lads."

"No need," Conan told him. Sword and swordbelt were hastily stored just inside the folds of the rug. "I will carry it myself."

"But it is too heavy for one. . . ."

The merchant faded into astounded silence as Conan easily hoisted the rolled carpet to his left shoulder, then casually shifted it to a more comfortable position. The thick tube on his shoulder would give him an excuse to walk with back bent and head down, and thus seem not quite so tall. So long as he kept the hood of his cloak well forward, he might be able to pass as just one more of the scores of men bearing carpets through the streets for weavers or rug sellers.

He noticed the open-mouthed merchant staring at him. "A wager," Conan explained, and as he could not think of the possible terms of such a bet, he hurried from the shop. As he left, he could feel the man's popping eyes on his back.

Once out in the narrow street there was a temptation to walk as swiftly as he could, but he forced himself to move slowly. Few laborers or apprentices in Sultanapur moved more quickly than a slow stroll unless under the eyes of their master. Conan gritted his teeth and matched his pace to that of the real laborers he saw. Even so, he impatiently used the rug to fend his way through the streams of people. Most moved from his path with no more than a muttered curse. A growl from beneath his hood answered the few who shouted their curses and shook a fist or caught at his sleeve. Having gotten a closer look at him, each of the latter decided they were needed urgently elsewhere. Surreptitious glances under the edge of his hood told Conan he was almost halfway to the harbor.

A change in the noise of the street slowly came to the Cimmerian's awareness. Leg-tied pigs and tethered sheep still grunted and bleated unabated, and the cackling from high-stacked wicker cages filled with chickens continued unaltered. But a woman bargaining loudly for a shawl of Vendhyan lace paused, then turned her back to the throng and continued more quietly. A peddler of pins and ribbons faltered in his cry and drew back to the mouth of an alley before giving voice again. Others started or stuttered in their tradings, or cast nervous eyes about.

It was not he who excited them. Of that Conan was sure. There was something behind him, but he could not turn to look. He strained his ears to penetrate the wall of the farmyard babble and market chatter. Yes. Among the many feet that walked that street were some number that moved to a silent cadence. Marching feet. Soldiers' feet. The Cimmerian moved his right hand to the rolled carpet as though to balance it. The hand rested not a fingerwidth from the hilt of his sword, hidden in those folds.

"I tell you, Gamel," came a harsh voice at Conan's rear, "this big oaf is naught but a laborer. A weaver's man. Let us not waste our time with him."

A second speaker answered in tones smoother and touched with mockery. "And I say he is big enough, if he stood straight. This could well be the giant barbar the Venehyans hired. Will you forget the reward, Alsan? Can you forget a thousand gold pieces?"

"Gamel, I still say—"

"You there! Big fellow! Stand and turn!"

Conan stopped in his tracks. A thousand gold pieces, he thought. Surely Captain Murad could not be worth so much. But these men said he fit the description of the one for whom that amount would be paid, and he could not imagine that it could be someone else. Matters were occurring in Sultanapur of which he had no knowledge, but it seemed they concerned him all the same.

Slowly the Cimmerian turned, keeping the thick roll between the guardsmen and his face, making no effort this time to hurry people from the path of the swinging rug. The soldiers had continued to approach, apparently satisfied that he obeyed. By the time he was sideways to them, they had reached him.

A hand grabbed his arm. "All right, you," the harsh voice said. "Let's see your face."

Conan let the hand pull him around a handspan farther. Then, jerking his scabbarded broadsword from the rug, he dropped the heavy roll against the man who tugged. He was only vaguely aware of the thin-mustached guardsman falling with a scream and the snap of a broken leg. His eyes were all for the twenty more filling the narrow street behind the first.

For the merest instant all were frozen; Conan was the first to move. His hand swept out to topple wicker cages of wildly squawking chickens into the soldiers' midst. Chickens exploded from burst cages. Peddlers and shoppers, shrieking as mindlessly as the birds, fled in all directions, some even trying to trample a way through the soldiers, who in turn attempted to club people from their way. The pigs' grunts had become desperate squeals and sheep leaped and jerked at their bonds.

Conan jerked his blade free of its sheath as a guardsman burst out of the confusion and hurdled the downed man as he drew his tulwar. Side-stepping, the Cimmerian struck. The Turanian gagged loudly as he doubled over the steel that bit deep into his middle. Before the man could fall, Conan had freed his blade to slash at the cords binding the nearest sheep. Fleeing the flashing blade, the wooly animals darted toward the jumble of soldiers shouting for the way to be cleared and shoppers screaming for mercy, the whole spiced with scores of fluttering, squawking chickens. Two more soldiers struggled clear of the pack only to fall over the sheep. Conan waited no longer. He ran, pulling over more cages of chickens behind him as he did.

At the first corner he turned right, at the next, left. Startled eyes, already turned in the direction of the tumult, followed his flight. He had gained only moments, he knew. Most of those who saw him would deny everything when asked by the City Guard, for such was the way of life in Sultanapur, but some would talk. Enough to make a trail for the soldiers to follow. Ahead of him an ox-drawn, two-wheeled cart, piled high with lashed bales to a height greater than a man, passed his line of sight on a crossing street. Another high-wheeled cart followed behind, the ox-driver walking beside his animal with a goad, then another.

Abruptly Conan stopped before the stall of a potter. Before the potter's goggling eyes, he calmly reached up and wiped the blood from his sword on the man's yellow awning. Hurriedly resheathing his blade, Conan fastened the belt around his waist as he ran on. At the next crossing street he looked back. The potter, staring after him and pointing, stopped his shouting when he saw Conan's gaze on him. This man would certainly talk, even before the guardsmen asked. It was a risk he took, the Cimmerian knew, but if it failed, he would be no worse off than before. But it would work, he told himself. He had the same feeling that he had when the dice were going to fall his way.

Sure that the potter marked his direction, Conan turned in the direction from which the carts had come. As he started down the street, he let out a breath he had not been aware of holding. The feeling of certainty was assuredly working better than it usually did with dice. Still another ox-cart rumbled down the narrow street toward him.

Moving back against a wall to let the cart pass, he stepped around it to the far side as soon as it was by. When his legs were in line with the tall wheels, he slowed his pace to the trudge of the ox. The potter would tell the guardsmen of the direction he had gone, while he went off the opposite way. It was but another moment gained, but enough moments such as these could add up to a man's life.

As soon as the cart had crossed the street where the potter stood, Conan hurried on ahead. He had to get to the harbor and the jumble of docks, warehouses, and taverns, where he could find safety among the smugglers. And he had to find out why there was a reward of a thousand pieces of gold being offered for him. The first was the most urgent, yet it would not be so easy as simply walking there. He was far from inconspicuous, and the white cloak would soon be added to the description of the man for whom the reward was offered. Without the hood, though, his blue eyes would leave a trail easily followed by guardsmen seeking a big northlander. The question, then, was how to exchange the cloak for one of another color, but also with a hood, while not letting his eyes be seen.

He watched for a cloak he might buy or steal, but saw few with hoods and none large enough to avoid looking ludicrous on his broad shoulders. There was no point in drawing eyes by looking the clown when the purpose was to avoid them. As quickly as he could without gaining attention for his speed, pausing at every street crossing to look for guardsmen, he moved toward the harbor. Or tried to. Three times he was forced to turn aside by the sight of City Guardsmen, and once he barely had time to duck into a shop selling cheap gilded jewelry before half a score of guardsmen strode by. He was going north, he realized, parallel to the harbor district, and certainly not toward it.

Guardsmen's spears above the heads of the crowd before him turned him down a side street packed with humanity. Away from the harbor, he thought with a curse as he pushed through the crowd, then cursed again when shouts for the way to be cleared indicated the soldiers had entered the same street. They gave no sign that they had seen him, but that could not last for long, not with him standing a head taller than the next tallest man on the street. He lengthened his stride, then almost immediately slowed again. A score of spear points, glittering in the sunlight, approached from ahead.

This time he did not waste breath on curses. An alley, smelling strongly of offal and chamber pots, offered the only escape. As he ducked into it, he realized that he had been there before, in company with Hordo during his first days with the one-eyed man's band of smugglers. Stairs of crumbling brown brick, narrow yet, even so, all but filling the width of the alley, led to the floor above a fruit vendor's stall. Conan took them two at a time. A stooped man in robes of brown camel's hair jumped as the Cimmerian pushed open the rough wooden door without knocking.

The small room was sparsely furnished, with a cot against one wall and an upright chest with many small drawers against another. A table that leaned on a badly mended leg sat in the middle of the bare wooden floor, a single stool beside it. A few garments hung on pegs in the walls. All seemed old and weathered, and the stooped man was a match for his possessions. Sparse white hair and olive skin blotched with age and wrinkled like often-folded parchment made the fellow seem able to claim a century. His hands were like knobby claws as they clutched a packet of oilskin, and his dark eyes, hooded and glaring, were the only part of him that showed any spark of vitality.

"My apologies," Conan said quickly. He wracked his brain for the old man's name. "I did not mean to enter so abruptly, Ghurran." That was it. "I fish with Hordo."

Ghurran grunted and bent to peer fussily at the packets and twists of parchment atop the rickety table. "Hordo, eh? His joints aching again? He should find another trade. The sea does not suit his bones. Or perhaps you come for yourself? A love philtre, perhaps?"

"No." Half of Conan's mind was on listening for the soldiers below. Not until they were gone could he risk putting his nose outside. "What I truly need," he muttered, "is a way to become invisible until I reach the harbor."

The old man remained bent over the table, but his head swiveled toward the big youth. "I compound herbs, and occasionally read the stars," he said dryly. "You want a wizard. Why not try the love philtre? Guaranteed to put a woman helpless in your arms for the night. Of course, perhaps a handsome young man like you does not need such."

Conan shook his head distractedly. The parties of guardsmen had met at the mouth of the alley. A thin murmuring floated to him, but he could not make out any words. They seemed in no hurry to move on. All of this trouble, and he did not even know why. A Vendhyan plot, those he had overheard had said. "May their sisters sell for a small price," he muttered in Vendhyan.

"Katar!" Ghurran grunted. The old man lowered himself jerkily to his knees and fumbled under the table for a dropped packet. "My old fingers do not hold as once they did. What was that language you spoke?"

"Vendhyan," Conan replied without taking his mind from the soldiers. "I learned a little of the tongue, since we buy so much fish from Vendhyans." Most of the smugglers could speak three or four languages after a fashion, and his quick ear had already picked up considerable Vendhyan as well as smatterings of several others. "What do you know of Vendhya?" he went on.

"Vendhya? How should I know of Vendhya. Ask me of herbs. I know something of herbs."

"It is said that you will pay for herbs and seeds from far lands, and that you ask many questions of these lands when you buy. Surely you have purchased some herbs from Vendhya."

"All plants have uses, but the men who bring them to me rarely know those uses. I must try to draw the information from them, asking all they know of the country from which the herbs or seeds came in order to sift out a few grains that are useful to me." The old man got to his feet and paused for breath, dusting his bony hands on his robes. "I have bought some trifles from Vendhya, and I am told it is a land full of intrigue, a dangerous land for the unwary, for those who too easily believe the promises of a man or the flattery of a woman. Why do you wish to know of Vendhya?"

"It is said in the streets that a prince has been slain, or perhaps a general, and that Vendhyans hired the killing done."

"I see. I have not been out the entire day." Ghurran chewed at a gnarled knuckle. "Such a thing is unlikely at this time, for it is said that *wazam* of Vendhya, the chief advisor to King Bhandarkar, visits Aghrapur to conclude a treaty, and many nobles of the royal court at Ayodhya visit as well. Yet remember the intrigues. Who can say? You still have not told me why you are so interested in this."

Conan hesitated. The old man provided poultices and infusions for half the smugglers in Sultanapur. That so many continued to trust him was in his favor. "The rumor is that the assassin was a northlander, and the City Guard seems to think I am the man."

The parchment-skinned man tucked his hands into the sleeves of his robe and peered at Conan with his head tilted. "Are you? Did you take Vendhyan gold?"

"I did not," Conan replied. "Nor did I kill a prince, or a general." Assuredly no man he had faced that day had been either.

"Very well," Ghurran said. His lips tightened reluctantly. Then he sighed and took a dusty dark-blue cloak from the wall. "Here. This will make you somewhat less conspicuous than the one you wear now."

Surprised, Conan nonetheless quickly exchanged his white cloak for the other. Despite the dust and folds of hanging, perhaps for years, the dark-blue wool was finely woven and showed little wear. It was tight across the Cimmerian's shoulders, yet had obviously been made for a man bigger than Ghurran.

"Age shrinks all men," the stooped herbalist said as though he had read Conan's mind.

Conan nodded. "I thank you, and I will remember this." The sound of the soldiers had faded away while he was talking. He cracked the door and peered out. The narrow street was jammed with people, but none were guardsmen. "Fare you well, Ghurran. And again, my thanks."

Without waiting for the other man to speak again, Conan slipped out, descended the stairs and melded into the crowd. The harbor district, he thought. Once he reached that, there would be time to consider other matters.

The patrols of guardsmen were a nuisance to the young Turanian who made his way out of the harbor district and into an area that seemed favored, as nearly as he could tell, solely by beggars, bawds and cutpurses. He avoided the soldiers deftly, and none of the area's denizens favored him with a second glance.

A Corinthian mother had given him features that were neither Corinthian nor Turanian, but rather simply dark-eyed and not quite handsome. Clean-shaven at the moment, he could pass as a native of any one of a half a score of countries and had done so more than once. He was above medium height, with a rawboned lanky build that often fooled men into underestimating his strength, several times to the saving of his life. His garb was motley, a patched Corinthian doublet that had once been red, baggy Zamoran breeches of pale cotton, well-worn boots from Iranistan.

Only the tulwar at his side and his turban, none too clean and none too neatly wrapped, were Turanian, he thought sourly. Four years gone from his own country and before he was back a tenday, he found himself skulking about the dusty streets of Sultanapur trying to avoid the City Guard. Not for the first time since leaving home at nineteen, he regretted his decision not to follow in his father's footsteps as a spice merchant. As always, though, the regret lasted only until he could remind himself of how boring a spice merchant's life was, but of late that reminding took longer than it once had.

Turning into an alley, he paused to see if anyone took notice. A single footsore trull began to flash a smile at him, then valued his garb in her mind and trudged on. The rest of the throng streamed by without an eye turning his way. He backed down the stench-filled alley, keeping a watch on the street, until he felt a rough wooden door under his fingers. Satisfied that he was still unobserved, he ducked through the doorway into darkness.

Instantly a knife at his throat stopped him in his tracks, but all he did was say quietly, "I am Jelal. I come from the West." Anything else, he knew, and the knife wielder would have used his blade, not to mention the two other men he was sure were in the pitch-black room.

Flint struck steel, light flared, and a lamp that smoked and reeked of rancid oil was held to his face. Two, he saw, beside the one who still held a razor edge to his throat, and even the man with the lamp, a thick half-moon scar curling around his right eye, clutched a bared dagger.

The scar-faced man stepped aside and jerked his head toward a door leading deeper into the building. "Go on," he said. Only then was the knife lowered from Jelal's throat.

Jelal did not say anything. This was not the first such meeting for him, nor even the twentieth. He went on through the second door.

The windowless room he entered was what was to be expected in this quarter of the city, rough walls of clay brick, a dirt floor, a crude table tilted on a cracked leg. What was not to be expected were the beeswax candles giving light, the white linen cloth spread on the table top, or the crystal flagon of wine sitting on the cloth beside two cups of hammered gold. Nor was the man seated behind the table one to be expected in such a place. A plain dark cloak, nondescript yet of quality too fine for that region of Sultanapur, covered much of his garb. His narrow thin-nosed face, with mustaches and small beard neatly waxed to points, seemed more suited to a palace than a district of beggars. He spoke as soon as Jelal entered.

"It is well you come today, Jelal. Each time I must come out into the city increases the risk I will be seen and identified. You have made contact?" He waved a soft-skinned hand with a heavy gold seal-ring on the forefinger toward the crystal flagon. "Have some wine for the heat."

"I have made contact," Jelal replied carefully, "but—"

"Good, my boy. I knew that you would, even in so short a time. Four years in Corinthia and Koth and Khauran, posing as every sort of merchant and peddler, legal and otherwise, and never once caught or even suspected. You are perhaps the best man I have ever had. But I fear your task in Sultanapur has changed."

Jelal drew himself up. "My lord, I request to be reposted to the Ibari Scouts."

Lord Khalid, the man who ordered and controlled all the spies of King Yildiz of Turan, stared in amazement. "Mitra strike me, why?"

"My lord, you say I was never once suspected in four years, and it is true. But it is true because I not only acted the part, I *was* a merchant, or a peddler as the instant demanded, spending most of my days buying and selling, talking of markets and prices. My lord, I became a soldier in part to avoid becoming a merchant like my father. I was a good soldier, and I ask to serve Turan and the King where I can serve them best, as a soldier once more in the Ibari Mountains."

The spy master drummed his fingers on the table. "My boy, you were chosen for the very reasons you cite. Your service was all in the southern mountains, so no western foreigner is likely to ever have seen you as a soldier. Your boyhood training to be a merchant not only prepared you to play that part to perfection, but also, because of a merchant's need to winnow fact from rumor to find the proper market and price, it made sure that you could do the same with other kinds of rumors and give reports of great value. As you have. You serve Turan best where you are."

"But, my lord—"

"Enough, Jelal. There is no time. What do you know of events in Sultanapur this day?"

Jelal sighed. "There are many rumors," he began slowly, "reporting everything but an invasion. Piecing together the most likely, I should say that Prince Tureg Amal was killed this morning. Beyond that I should say the strongest rumor is that a northlander was involved. As it was not what I came to Sultanapur for, I put no more than half my mind to it, I fear."

"Half your mind, and you get one of two right." The older man nodded approvingly. "You are indeed the best of my men. I do not know where the rumor of a northlander was born. Perhaps someone saw such a man in the street."

"But the guardsmen, my lord. They seek—"

"Yes, yes. The rumors have spread even to them, and I've done nothing to change that state of affairs for the moment. Let the true culprits think they have escaped notice. It is not the first time soldiers have been sent chasing shadows, nor will it be the last. And a few innocent foreigners—if any of them can truly be called innocent—a few such put to the question, or even killed, is a small price to pay if it helps us take the true villains unaware. Believe me when I say the throne of Turan could be at stake."

Jelal managed a nod. He was aware from experience just how coldly practical this soft-appearing man could be, even if the stakes were considerably less than the Turanian throne. "And the prince, my lord? You said I was half right."

"Tureg Amal," Kalid sighed, "drunkard, wastrel, lecher, and High Admiral of Turan, died this morning of a poisoned needle thrust into his neck. Not by a northern giant, as the rumors say, but by a woman. A Vendhyan assassin, according to reports."

"An assassin?" Jelal said. "My lord, the prince's ways with women are well know. Could he not perhaps simply have driven some wench to murder?"

The spy master shook his head. "As much as I should prefer it so, no. The servants at Tureg Amal's palace have been questioned thoroughly. A Vendhyan woman was delivered to the palace this morning, supposedly a gift from a merchant of that country seeking added protection for his cargoes on the Vilayet. Within the hour the prince was dead, the keeper of his zenanna drugged, and the woman had disappeared unseen from a heavily guarded palace."

"It certainly sounds the work of an assassin," Jelal agreed, "but—"

"There could be worse," the older man cut him off. "The commander of the prince's bodyguard, one Captain Murad, was also slain this morning, along with two of his men, apparently in a tavern brawl. I do not like such coincidences. Perhaps it was unrelated, and perhaps they were silenced after effecting the woman's escape. And if men of the High Admiral's bodyguard took gold to aid in his death . . . well, that scandal could do more harm than the old fool's murder."

"Be that as it may, my lord, the other does not make sense. I understand that the *wazam* of Vendhya is in Aghrapur to negotiate a treaty with King Yildiz. Surely the King of Vendhya would not countenance an assassination while his chief counselor was in our capital, in our very hands. And if he did, why the High Admiral? The King's death would create turmoil, while the prince's creates only anger toward Vendhya."

"The King's death by a Vendhyan assassin would also create war with Vendhya," Khalid said dryly, "while Tureg Amal's . . ." He shrugged. "I do not know the why of it, my boy, but Vendhyans suck intrigue with their mothers' milk and do nothing without a purpose, usually nefarious. As for the *wazam*, Karim Singh sailed from Aghrapur yesterday. And the treaty? I was suspicious of it before, now I am doubly so. Less than five years ago they nearly went to war with us over their claims to Secunderam. Now, without a protest, the *wazam* puts his seal on a treaty that does not so much as mention that city. And one that favors Turan on several other points, as well. I had thought they sought to lull us while they prepared some stroke. Now I no longer know what to think." He began to roll the tip of his beard between his thumb and forefinger, the greatest outward sign of inner turmoil that he ever showed.

Reluctantly Jelal felt the puzzle catching at him, as it so often had before. The desire to return to soldiering was still there but pushed to the back of his mind. For the moment. "What can I do, my lord?" he asked at last. "The Vendhyan assassin is surely no longer in the city."

"That is true," the spy master replied, and his voice hardened as he spoke. "But I want answers. I need them. The King depends on me for them. What is Vendhya up to? Are we to expect a war? Captain Murad's death may lead to some answers. Use the contacts you have made with the lawless underside of Sultanapur. Find a trail to the answers I need and follow it all the way to Vendhya if you must. But bring me the answers."

"I will, my lord," Jelal promised. But to himself he promised that this was the last time. Whether he was returned to the Ibari Scouts or not, after this one last puzzle, he would be a spy no more.

IV

Despite the cloak Ghurran had given him, Conan kept close to the sides of the narrow, bustling streets, on the edges of the continuous flow of people. It was true that the dark-blue cloak would not bring a moment's glance from a guardsman looking for one of white linen, and the hood did hide his face and damning blue eyes, but the sheer size of him was difficult to miss. Few men in Sultanapur came close to his height or breadth of shoulder, and certainly none of them was among the crowds thronging the streets he traveled this day. The big Cimmerian stood out like a Remaira stallion among mules.

Five times after leaving the herbalist Conan was forced to turn aside for patrols of guardsmen, their precisely slanted spears glinting in the bright sun as though to give warning of their coming, but luck seemed at last to be with him. His progress toward the harbor was constant, if zig-zag. High-wheeled ox-carts began once more to be almost as numerous as people. The long stone shapes of warehouses rose about him, and the tall white towers of the city granaries. Men with the calloused hands and sweat-stained tunics of dockers and roustabouts outnumbered all but those with the rolling walk and forked queues of seafarers. Half the women were trulls in narrow girdles of jingling coin and thin silk or less, while most of the rest cast a sharp eye for a purse to cut or a bolt of silk or lace that could be snatched from a cart. Here, too, were people who knew him.

"An hour's pleasure, big man?" cooed a buxom doxy with hennaed hair piled high on her head and gilded brass hoops in her ears. She moved closer and pressed nearly bare breasts against his arm, dropping her voice for his ear alone. "You fool, the City Guard has already taken up three dockers just for being tall. And they are questioning outlanders, so you're doubly at risk. Now, put your arm around me, and we will go to my room. I can hide you till it all quiets. And I'll charge you but—oh, Mitra, I'll not charge you at all."

Conan grinned despite himself. "A generous offer, Zara. But I must find Hordo."

"I've not seen him, Conan. And you cannot risk looking. Come with me."

"Another time," he said, and she squealed as he pinched a plump buttock.

In short order a sailor in a tar-smeared tunic and a bearded warehouseman had repeated Zara's warning. A slender wench with a virgin's face and innocent eyes—and a cutpurse's curved blade with which she constantly toyed—echoed both warning and offer. None knew where Hordo was to be found, however. Conan almost accepted the slender woman's offer. The glass had been turned, he knew, and the sands were running out on him. Did he not find Hordo quickly, he must go to ground.

A short, wiry man, bent under the weight of a canvas sack on his shoulder, suddenly caught the Cimmerian's eye. Conan snagged the man's bony arm with one hand and hauled him out of the stream of people.

"What are you doing?" the Cimmerian's captive whispered between teeth clenched in a wooden smile. His sunken eyes darted frantically above a pointed nose, giving him the image of a mouse searching for a hole. "Mitra, Cimmerian! I stole this not twenty paces from here, and they'll see it's gone in another moment. Let me go!"

"I am looking for Hordo, Tarek," Conan said softy.

"Hordo? He's at Kafar's warehouse, I think." Tarek stumbled a step as Conan released him, then rotated his shoulder in a broad gesture. "You should not grab a man so, Cimmerian. It could be dangerous. And don't you know the City Guard—"

"—is seeking a big outlander," Conan finished for him. "I known."

A shout rose from the direction Tarek had come, and the little man darted away like the rodent he resembled. Conan went the other way, soon passing by a stall where a salt peddler in voluminous robes seemed to dance with his helpers, they jumping about to dodge while he tugged at his beard and kicked at them and shouted that the gods were unmerciful to send the same man blind apprentices and thieves as well. While the salt vendor leaped and screamed, two girls of no more than sixteen years hefted one of his canvas sacks between them and disappeared, unseen by him, into the throng.

Twice more the Cimmerian was forced to turn aside for a patrol of the City Guard, but Kafar's warehouse was not far, and he reached it quickly. It was not one of the long stone structures owned by merchants, but rather a nondescript building of two stories, daubed in flaking white clay, that might once have held a tavern or a chandler's shop. In truth it was a warehouse of sorts. A smugglers' warehouse. Gold in the proper palms kept the guardsmen away, for the time at least. When the bribes failed, though, because higher authority decided an example must be made, or more likely because someone decided the reward for confiscated contraband outweighed the bribes, the smugglers of Sultanapur would not be slowed for an instant. Scores of such warehouses could be found near the harbor, and when Kafar's was no more, two others would spring up in its place.

The splintery wooden door from the street let into a windowless room dimly lit by rush torches in crude iron sconces. Two of the torches had guttered out, but no one seemed to notice. A small knot of men, dressed in mismatched garb from a dozen countries, squatted in a semicircle, casting dice against a wall. Others sat on casks at a table of boards laid on sawhorses, engrossed in whispered talk over clay mugs of wine. A Kothian in a red-striped tunic sat off by himself on a three-legged stool near a door at the back of the room, idly flipping a dagger to stick up in the rough-hewn planks of the floor. The air in the room was hot and close, not only because of the torches, but because few of the half-score men there ever made acquaintance with water and most thought soap a fine gift for a woman, if nicely perfumed, but not a thing to be used.

Only the Kothian looked up at Conan's entrance. "Do you not know—" he began.

"I know, Kafar," Conan said curtly. "Is Hordo here?"

The Kothian jerked his head at the door behind him and returned to flipping his dagger. "The cellar," he said as the blade quivered in the floor once more.

It was the custom in such places to store the goods of each smuggler in a separate room, for no man among them trusted those not of his band to the point of letting him know what kind of "fish" he carried or to where. Closed doors, iron-bound and held shut with massive iron locks, lined the corridor in the rear of the building. At the end of the corridor, beside a wide door leading to the alley behind the warehouse, were stone stairs leading down.

As the Cimmerian started down the stairs, Hordo opened the door at the bottom. "Where in Zandru's Nine Hells have you been?" the one-eyed smuggler roared. "And what in Mitra's name have you been doing?" He was nearly as big as Conan, though his muscles were over-laid with fat and the years had weathered his face. Large gold hoops hung from his ears and a jagged scar ran from under his eye-patch of rough leather down into the thick black thatch of his beard, pulling the left side of his mouth into a permanent sneer. "I leave word with Tasha and the next thing I hear . . . Well, get on down here before the Guard seizes you right in front of me. If that fool wench failed to tell you I needed you, I'll have her hide."

Conan winced ruefully. So Tasha had been speaking the truth. If he had not thought she was lying from jealousy, he would have left the Golden Crescent before the captain arrived, and the City Guard would not be seeking his head. Well, it was far from the first time he had gotten into trouble from misreading a woman. And in any case, a man who used pain to frighten a woman to his bed deserved killing.

"It was not her fault, Hordo," he said, pushing past the bearded man into the cellar. "I had a trifle of trouble with—" He cut off at the sight of a stranger in the room, a tall, skinny man in a turban who stood beside a score of small wooden chests, like the tin-lined chests in which tea was shipped, stacked on the dirt floor against a dusty stone wall. Here, too, light came from rush torches. "Who is he?" the Cimmerian demanded.

"He's called Hasan," the one-eyed man replied impatiently. "A new 'fisherman.' Now! Is there any truth to these rumors, Cimmerian? I do not care if you've killed Tureg Amal; that old fool is no loss to the world. But if you have, you must get out of Sultanapur, perhaps out of Turan, and quickly. Even if you killed no one, you had best remain out of sight until they catch who did."

"The High Admiral?" Conan exclaimed. "I heard it was a general, though now that I think of it, someone did say a prince. Hordo, why would I kill the High Admiral of Turan?"

The lanky man spoke up suddenly. "The rumors say it was hired done. For enough gold I suppose a man might kill anyone."

Conan's face became stony. "You seem to be calling me liar," he said in a deadly quiet tone.

"Easy, Cimmerian," Hordo said, and added to the other man, "Are you trying to get yourself killed, Hasan? Offer this man coin for a killing, and 'twill be luck if you escape with no more than broken bones. And if he says he killed no one, then he killed no one."

"I did not say that exactly," Conan said uncomfortably. "There was a Guard captain, and two or three guardsmen." He glared at the turbaned man who had made a sound in his throat. "You have a comment about *that* as well?"

"You two fighting cocks settle your ruffs," Hordo snapped. "We have a load of 'fish' to carry. The man who wants it shipped will be here any instant, and I'll have no bloodshed, or snarling either, in front of him. He'll seek elsewhere if he thinks we will slay each other before delivering his chests." His bearded head swung like that of a bear. "I need my whole crew if we are to get the accursed things to the mouth of the Zaporoska in the time specified, and the only two who have heeded my call squabble like dockers with their heads full of wine."

"You told me we'd not sail again for three or four days," Conan said, walking over to examine the chests. Hasan moved warily out of his way, but it was the finely crafted boxes that interested him. "The crew are scattered among the taverns and bordellos," he went on, "hip deep in women, and with wine fumes where their wits were four hours gone. I could enjoy a quick journey out of Sultanapur now, but if we find all twenty by nightfall, I'll become an Erlikite."

"We must sail by dark," Hordo said. "The gold is more for being faster than agreed, but less for being slower." The scar-faced smuggler moved Hasan farther away from them with a look, then stepped closer to the Cimmerian and dropped his voice. "I do not doubt your word, Conan, but *is* it you the guardsmen seek? For this captain, perhaps?"

Conan shrugged, but did not stop his study of the chests. "I do not know," he replied for Hordo's ears alone. "The rumors say nothing of Murad, and my name is not mentioned." The largest dimension of the chests was the length of a man's forearm. Their sides were smooth and plain, and the flat, close-fitting lid of each was held by eight leaden seals impressed with the image of a bird he had never seen before. "The tongues of the street speak of Tureg Amal. Still, somewhere words have been spoken concerning what occurred at the Golden Crescent, or there would be no big northlander in the tale." He hefted one of the boxes, trying its weight. To his surprise, it was light enough to have been packed with feathers. "Men from the northern lands are not so common as visitors in Sultanapur for that."

"Aye," the one-eyed man agreed sagely. "And it is said that when two rumors meet, they exchange words. Also that a rumor changes on each journey from mouth to ear."

"Do you begin to quote aphorisms in your old age, Hordo?" Conan chuckled. "I know not the how or why of what has happened, but I do know that trouble sits on my shoulder until it is all made clear."

"I am not too old to try breaking your head," Hordo growled. "And when was the day trouble did not sit on your shoulder, Cimmerian?"

Conan ignored the question; he had long since decided a man could not live a free life and avoid trouble at the same time. "What is in these chests?" he asked.

"Spices," came an answer from the doorway.

The Cimmerian's hand went to his sword-hilt. The new-comer wore a dark gray cloak with a voluminous hood. As soon as he had closed the cellar door behind him, he threw back the hood to reveal a narrow, swarthy face topped by a turban twice as big around as was the fashion in Turan, fronted by heron feathers held by a pin of opal and silver. Rings covered his fingers with sapphires and amethysts.

"A Vendhyan!" Hasan burst out.

Hordo motioned him to silence. "I was afraid you were not coming Patil."

"Not coming?" The Vendhyan's tone was puzzled, but then he smiled thinly. "Ah, you feared that I was involved with the events spoken of in the streets. No, I assure you I had nothing to do with the very unfortunate demise of the High Admiral. Such affairs are not for me. I am but a humble merchant who must avoid paying the custom both of your King Yildiz and of my King Bhandarkar if I am to make my poor profit."

"Of course, Patil," Hordo said. "And you have come to the proper men to see that Yildiz's excisemen take not a single coin of yours. The rest of my crew is even now preparing our boat for a swift passage. Conan, go see that all is in readiness." He half-turned his back to the Vendhyan and made small frantic gestures that only Conan and Hasan could see. "We must be ready to sail quickly."

Conan knew very well what the gestures meant. He was to go upstairs and intercept any of Hordo's crew who came staggering in with their brains half-pickled in wine. Five or six sots stumbling in and making it clear to this Patil that they were part of the crew would do little to convince him they could make good on Hordo's promise of sailing quickly. But Conan did not stir. Instead he hefted the chest again.

"Spices?" he said. "Saffron, pepper, and all the other spices I could name come across the Vilayet from the east. What spice crosses from the west?"

"Rare condiments from islands of the Western Sea," Patil replied smoothly. "They are considered great delicacies in my country."

Conan nodded. "Of course. Yet despite that, I've heard nothing of such being smuggled. Have you, Hordo?"

The bearded man shook his head doubtfully; worry that Conan was putting the arrangement in jeopardy creased his face. Patil's face did not change, but he wet his lips with the tip of his tongue. Conan let the box fall, and the Vendhyan winced as it thudded on the packed earth.

"Open it," Conan said. "I would see what we carry across the Vila-yet."

Patil let out a squawk of protest directed at Hordo. "This is not a part of our agreement. Kafar told me that you were the most trustworthy of the smugglers, otherwise I would have gone elsewhere. I offer much gold for you to deliver my chests and myself to the mouth of the Za-poroska River, not for you to ask questions and make demands."

"He does offer a great deal of gold, Conan," Hordo said slowly.

"Enough to carry kanda leaf?" the Cimmerian asked. "Or red lotus? You have seen the wretches who would choose their pipes over wine, or a woman, or even over food. How much gold to carry that?"

Breathing heavily, Hordo scratched at his beard and grimaced. "Oh, all right. Open the chests, Patil. I care not what they contain so long as it is not kanda leaf or red lotus."

"I cannot!" the Vendhyan cried. Sweat made his dark face shine. "My master would be furious. I demand that—"

"Your master?" Hasan cut him off. "What kind of merchant has a master, Vendhyan? Or are you something else?"

Conan's voice hardened. "Open the chests."

Patil's eyes shifted in a hunted way. Suddenly he spun toward the door. Conan lunged to catch a handful of the Vendhyan's flaring cloak, and the swarthy man whirled back, his fist swinging at the Cimmerian's face. A tiny flicker of light warned Conan, and he leaped back from the blow. The leaf-shaped blade that projected from between Patil's fingers sliced lightly across Conan's cheek just below the eye. Conan's foot came down on the dropped chest, which turned and sent him sprawling on his back on the dirt floor.

The instant he was free of Conan's grasp, Patil darted to the door, flung it open and dashed through. Straight into three men who seemed each to be supporting the others as they walked, or rather staggered. All four went down in a thrashing, cursing heap.

Scrambling to his feet, Conan hauled the struggling men out of the tangle, heaving each aside as soon as he saw that it was one of Hordo's crew. The last was Patil, and the Vendhyan lay without moving. His large turban was knocked askew, and it came off completely as the Cimmerian rolled him onto his back. It was as Conan had feared. Patil's dark eyes stared at him emptily, twisted with pain, and the Vendhyan's teeth were bared in a frozen rictus. The would-be killer's fist was jammed against the center of his chest. Conan had no doubt the push-dagger's blade had been just long enough to reach the heart.

He brushed a hand across his cheek. The fingertips came away red, but the cut was little more than a scratch. It was luck, he thought, that the fellow had not simply stabbed at him. He might never have been aware of the small dagger until it found his own heart.

"Not the outcome you expected, is it?" he told the corpse. "But I would rather have you alive to talk."

Hordo pushed past him to grab the Vendhyan's robes. "Let us get this out of sight of anyone who wanders by the stairs, Cimmerian. No need to flaunt matters, especially as I'd not like anyone to think we killed this fool for his goods. Things like that can ruin a man's trade."

Together they dragged the body into the cellar and shut the iron-strapped door. The three smugglers who had inadvertently stopped the Vendhyan's escape lay sprawled against a wall, and two of them stared blearily at the corpse when it was dropped at their feet.

" 'S drunker 'n us," muttered an Iranistani wearing a stained and filthy headcloth.

" 'S not drunk," replied the man next to him, a Nemedian who might have been handsome had his nose not been slit for theft at some time in the past. " 'S dead."

The third man emitted a snore like a ripping sail.

"All three of you shut your teeth," Hordo growled.

Conan touched his cheek again. The blood was already congealing. He was more interested in the chest he had dropped, though. He set it upright on the floor and knelt to study the lead seals. The bird impressed in the gray metal was no more familiar now than before. Vendhyan, perhaps, though seemingly the chests went in the wrong direction for that. The seals could be simply a means of keeping the chests tightly closed or a way to tell if they had been opened. He had also seen such used as triggers to launch venom-tipped needles or poisonous vapors at those who pried where they were not wanted. Such were not usually found on smuggled goods, but then again, these were apparently no ordinary "fish."

"I'll take the chance," he muttered. His heart pounded as he pushed the point of his new dagger under one seal.

"Wait, you fool," Hordo began, but with a twist of his wrist, Conan sliced through the soft lead. "Some day your luck will be used up," the one-eyed man breathed.

Without replying, the Cimmerian quickly broke the other seals. The dagger served to lever up the tight-fitting lid. Both stared in disbelief at the contents of the chest. To the brim it was filled with small, dried leaves.

"Spices?" Hasan said doubtfully.

Conan cautiously stirred the leaves with his dagger, then scooped up a handful. They cracked brittlely in his grasp and gave off no aroma. "A man does not try to kill to hide spices," Conan said. "We'll see what is in the other chests."

He half-rose from his knees, swayed and sank back down. The heavy thumping in his chest continued unabated. He touched the cut on his face once more; it felt as though a piece of leather lay between fingers and cheek. "That blade." His tongue felt thick around the words. "There was something on it."

The blood drained from Hordo's face. "Poison," he breathed. "Fight it, Cimmerian. You must fight it! If you let your eyes close, you'll never open them again!"

Conan tried again to rise, to go over to the other chests, and again he almost fell. Hordo caught him, easing him to a sitting position against the wall.

"The chests," Conan said. "If I'm dying, I want to know why."

"Mitra curse the chests!" Hordo snapped. "And you're not dying! Not if we can get Ghurran here."

"I will go for him," Hasan said, then subsided under Hordo's glare.

"And how will you do that, who's never seen the man before? Prytanis!" Hordo stalked across the cellar, and with a hand the size of a small ham hauled the Nemedian to his feet by a fistful of tunic. His other hand slapped the slit-nosed fellow's face back and forth. "Grab your wits, Prytanis! Can you hear me? Listen, Erlik take you, or I'll break your skull!"

"I am listening," the Nemedian groaned. "By all the gods, do not hit my head so. It is breaking already."

"Then listen well if you do not want it shattered," Hordo growled, but he stopped his slapping. "Get you to Ghurran and fetch him here. Tell him it is poison and tell him there's a hundred gold pieces for him if he gets here in time. Do you understand that, you sotted spawn of a camel?"

"I understand," the Nemedian said unsteadily and staggered toward the door under the impetus of Hordo's shove.

"Then run, curse you! If you fail in this, I'll slit your belly and hang you with your own guts! Where do you think you're going?" the one-eyed man added as Hasan made to follow Prytanis from the cellar.

"With him," Hasan replied. "He's so drunk he will not remember what he's about beyond the first pitcher of wine he sees without some-one to keep him to the task."

"He will remember," Hordo rumbled, "because he knows I will do as I said. To the word. If you want to do something, put a cloak over Patil so we do not have to look at him."

"You do not have a hundred pieces of gold, Hordo," Conan said.

"Then you can pay it," the smuggler replied. "And if you die on me, I will sell your corpse for it."

Conan laughed, but the laughter quickly trailed off in coughing, for he had no breath to spare. He felt as weak as a child. Even if the others got him to his feet, he knew it would be all he could do to stand. The fear and despair in his friend's voice did not touch him, however. There was an answer he must have, and it lay there in the chests stacked against the wall. Or at least some clue to the answer must. The question was simple, yet finding the answer would keep him alive a while longer, for he would not allow himself to die without it.

He would not die without knowing why.

V

One by one, five more of Hordo's crew staggered into Kafar's cellar, most as drunk as the first three. Decidedly sickly looks came over their faces as they heard what had happened. It was not the death of the Vendhyan, nor even his attempt on Conan, but rather the means of that attempt. They were used to an honest blade and could even understand the knife in the back, but poison was something a man could not defend against. Cups that changed color when poisoned wine was poured into them were in the realm of wizards, and of princes who could afford to pay wizards.

Their green faces did not bother Conan, but the funereal glances they cast at him did. "I am not dead yet," he muttered. The words came pantingly now.

"Where in Zandru's Nine Hells is Ghurran?" Hordo growled.

As though to punctuate his words, the iron-strapped door banged open, and Prytanis led Ghurran into the cellar by a firm grip on a bony arm. The slit-nosed Nemedian appeared to have sobered to a degree, whether from his exercise in fetching Ghurran or from Hordo's threats.

A leather strap crossed the stooped herbalist's heaving chest, supporting a small wooden case at his side. Freeing his arm with a jerk, he scowled about the room, at the swaying drankards and the still-snoring Iranistani and the cloak-shrouded mound that was the Vendhyan. "For this I was dragged through the streets like a goat going to market?" he grated breathlessly. "To treat men fool enough to drink tainted wine?"

"Tainted wine on a blade," Conan managed. He leaned forward and his head spun. "Once already today you helped me. Can you do it again, Ghurran?"

The old man brushed past Hordo and knelt to peer into the Cimmerian's eyes. "There may be time," he murmured, then in a firmer voice said, "You have the poisoned blade? Let me see it."

It was Hasan who lifted the cloak enough to tug the push-dagger from the corpse's chest. He wiped the leaf-shaped blade on the cloak before handing it to Ghurran.

The herbalist turned the small weapon over in scrawny fingers. A smooth ivory knob formed the hilt, carved to fit the palm while the blade projected between the fingers. "An assassin's weapon in Vendhya," he said. "Or so I have heard such described."

Conan kept his eyes on the old man's parchment-skinned face. "Well?" was all he said.

Instead of answering, Ghurran held the blade to his nostrils and sniffed lightly. Frowning, he wet a long-nailed finger at his mouth and touched it to the blade. With even greater caution than he had shown before, he brought the finger to his lips. Quickly he spat, scrubbing the finger on his robes.

"Do something!" Hordo demanded.

"Poisons are something I seldom deal with," Ghurran said calmly. He opened the wooden box hanging at his side and began to take out small parchment packets and stone vials. "But perhaps I can do something." A bronze mortar and pestle, no larger than a man's hand, came from the box. "Get me a goblet of wine, and quickly."

Hordo motioned to Prytanis, who hurried out. The herbalist set to work, dropping dried leaves and bits of powder into the mortar, grinding them together with the pestle. Prytanis returned with a rough clay goblet filled to the top with cheap wine. Ghurran took it and poured in the mixture from the mortar, stirring it vigorously with his finger.

"Here," the old man said, holding the wine to Conan's mouth. "Drink."

Conan looked at the offering. A few pieces of leaf floated on the wine's surface along with the sprinkling of varicolored powders. "This will rid me of the poison?"

Ghurran looked at him levelly. "In the time it would take you to reach the docks and return, you will either be able to walk from this room, or you will be dead." The listening smugglers stirred.

"If he dies—" Hordo began threateningly, but Conan cut him off.

"If I die, it will not be Ghurran's fault, will it, Ghurran?"

"Drink," the old man said, "or it will be your own fault."

Conan drank. With the first mouthful a grimace twisted his face, becoming worse with every swallow. As the goblet was taken from his mouth, he gasped, "Crom! It tastes as if a camel bathed in it!" A few of the listeners, those sober enough, laughed.

Ghurran grunted. "Do you want sweetness on the tongue, or the poison counteracted?" His eye fell on the opened chest. Face made even more hollow by a frown, he took some of the leaves, stirring them on his palm with a bony finger.

"Do you know the leaf?" Conan asked. He was not sure if his breathing was easier, or if he just imagined it so. "The man who did this told us they were spices."

"Spices?" Ghurran said absently. "No, I do not think they are spices. But then," he added, letting the leaves fall back into the chest, "I do not know all plants. I would like to look in the other chests. If there are herbs unknown to me in those also, perhaps I will take some of them in payment."

"Look all you want," Hordo said eagerly. "Prytanis, help him open the chests." The Nemedian and the herbalist moved toward the stacked chests, and Hordo dropped his voice to a whisper ranged for Conan's ears. "If he will take herbs rather than a hundred gold pieces, then well enough, I say."

Conan drew a breath; they *were* coming easier. "Help me to my feet, Hordo," he urged. "He said I would walk or die, and by Mitra's bones, I intend to walk."

The two of them exchanged a long look; then the one-eyed man reached down. Conan pulled himself up, putting a hand against the wall to steady himself. Leaning against a wall would not do, though. He took a tottering step. His bones felt ready to bend, but he forced himself to move the other foot forward.

"It is too late for that one," Prytanis' voice came loudly from where he stood beside the chests, dagger in hand. Three already had their lids pried open. "I found some more of those leaves."

Ghurran let the cloak fall back over the corpse's face. "I was curious as to the sort of man who uses a poisoned blade. But I suppose new herbs are more important than dead men. More of the leaves, you say?"

Conan made another step, and another. The weakness was still on him, but he felt firmer in some fashion, less like a figure made of reeds.

Hordo followed him, looking like an anxious bear. "Are you all right, Cimmerian?"

"Right enough," Conan told him, then laughed. "But moments ago

I would have settled for living long enough to know the way of all this. Now I begin to think I may live a bit longer than that after all."

"This body is too frail," Ghurran said suddenly. "Too old!" He knelt, peering into one of the chests. All twenty had been opened, and some of their contents pulled out. There were more dried leaves, exactly like those in the first chest. There were saffron crystals that seemed, from the powder beneath the pile of them on the dirt floor, to crumble almost of their own weight, and tightly corded leather sacks, several of which had been sliced open to spill out what could have been salt except for its crimson color. Two of the chests contained clear vials filled with a verdant liquid and well-packed in linen bags of goose down.

"What ails you?" Conan asked. "I walk, as you said I would, and I will see that you get the gold Hordo promised you." The one-eyed smuggler made a muffled sound of pained protest.

"Gold," Ghurran snorted contemptuously.

"If not gold, then what?" Conan asked. "If any of the herbs or other substances in those chests can be of use to you, take them, leaving only a little for me. It seems we will be not be delivering them to the Za-poroska, but I still want to know why a man would try to kill to keep them hidden. A small portion of the leaves and the rest may help me find out."

"Yes," the herbalist said slowly, "you will want to find out, won't you?" He hesitated. "I do not know exactly how to tell you this. If what I gave you had not been successful, there would have been no need to say anything. I hoped to find something in these chests, or more likely on the body. A man who carries a poisoned weapon will betimes also carry an antidote in case he himself is accidently wounded."

"What need is there of antidotes?" Hordo demanded. "You have already counteracted the poison."

Ghurran hesitated again, eying both Hordo and Conan in turn. "The treatment I have given you, northlander, has only masked the poison for a time."

"But I feel no more than a slight ache in the head," Conan said. "In an hour I will wrestle any man in Sultanapur."

"And you will continue to feel so for another day or two perhaps, then the poison will take hold again. A permanent cure requires herbs that I know, but that can be found only in Vendhya."

"Vendhya!" Hordo exclaimed. "Black Erlik's bowels and bladder!"

Conan motioned Ghurran to speak on, and the old man did so. "You must go to Vendhya, northlander, and I must go with you, for a daily infusion prepared by me will be necessary to keep you alive. The journey is not one I look forward to, for this old body is not suited to such travels. You, however, may find the answers you seek in Vendhya."

"Mayhap I will," Conan said. "It will not be the first time my life has been measured out a day at a time."

"But Vendhya," Hordo protested. "Conan, they do not much like folk from this side of the Vilayet in Vendhya. If you with your accursed eyes are thought strange here, how will they think you there? We'll lose our heads, like as not, and be lucky if we are not flayed first. Ghurran, are you sure there is nothing you can do here in Turan?"

"If he does not go to Vendhya," Ghurran said, "he dies."

"It is all right, my friend," Conan told the one-eyed man. "I will find the antidote there, and answers. Why are those chests worth killing for? Patil was Vendhyan, and I cannot think they were destined elsewhere. Besides, you know I have to leave Sultanapur for a time anyway, unless I want to hide from the City Guard until they find Tureg Amal's killer."

"The chests," Hasan said abruptly. "They can still be taken to the Zaporoska. Whoever was to meet Patil will not know he is dead. They will be waiting there, and they may have answers to our questions. They may even have an antidote."

" 'Tis better than Vendhya," Hordo said quickly. "For one thing, it is closer. No need to travel to the ends of the world if we do not need to."

"It cannot hurt to try," Conan agreed. "An easier trip for your bones, Ghurran." The old man shrugged his thin shoulders noncommittally.

"And if Patil's friends do not have what you need," Hordo added, "then we can think about Vendhya."

"Hold there!" Prytanis strode into the middle of the room, glaring angrily. The other smugglers were listening drunkenly, but he alone seemed sober enough to truly understand what had been said. "Take the chests to the Zaporoska, you say. How are we to find the men we seek? The mouth of the Zaporoska is wide, with dunes and hills to hide an army on both sides."

"When I agreed to carry Patil's goods," Hordo said, "I made sure he told me the signals that would be given by the men ashore, and the signs we must give in return."

"But what profit is there in it?" Prytanis insisted. "The Vendhyan cannot pay. Do you think his companions will when we arrive without him? I say forget these chests and find a load of 'fish' that will put gold in our purses."

"You spineless dog." Hordo's voice was low and seemed all the more deadly for it. "Conan is one of us and we stand together. How deep is the rot in you? Will you now throw goods over the side at the sight of a naval bireme, or abandon our wounded to the excisemen?"

"Call me not coward," the Nemedian snapped. "Many times I have risked having my head put on a pike above the Strangers' Gate, as you well know. If the Cimmerian wants to go, then let him. But do not ask the rest of us to tease the headsman's axe just for the pleasure of the trip."

The jagged scar down Hordo's left cheek went livid as he prepared a blast, but Conan spoke first.

"I do not ask you to come for the pleasure of the trip, Prytanis, nor even for the pleasure of my company. But answer me this. You say you want gold?"

"As any man does," Prytanis said cautiously.

"These chests are worth gold to the men waiting at the Zaporoska. Vendhyans, if Patil is a guide. You have seen other Vendhyans, men with rings on every finger and gems on their turbans. Did you ever see a Vendhyan without a purse full of gold?"

Prytanis' eyes widened as he suddenly realized that Conan spoke not only to him. "But—"

The big Cimmerian went on over the attempted interruption like an avalanche rolling over a hapless peasant. "The Vendhyans waiting on the Zaporoska will have plenty of gold, gold due us when we deliver the chests. And if they will not pay . . ." He grinned wolfishly and touched the hilt of his broadsword. "They'll not be the first to try refusing to pay for their 'fish.' But we did not let the others get away with it, and we'll not let the Vendhyans either."

Prytanis looked as though he wanted to protest further but one of the smugglers cried out drunkenly, "Aye! Cut 'em down and take it all!"

"Vendhyan gold for all of us!" another shouted. Others grunted agreement or laughingly repeated the words. The slit-nosed Nemedian sank into a scowling silence and withdrew sullenly to a corner by himself.

"You still have the gift of making men follow you," Hordo told Conan quietly, "but this time it would have been better to break Prytanis' head and be done with it. He will give trouble before this is done, and we'll have enough of that as it is. Mitra, the old man will likely heave his stomach up at every wave. He looks no happier at the prospect of this shorter journey than he did about traveling to Vendhya." Indeed, Ghurran sat slumped against the chests, staring glumly at nothing.

"I will deal with Prytanis if I must," Conan replied. "And Ghurran can no doubt concoct something to soothe his stomach. The problem now is to find more men." Hordo's vessel could be sailed by fewer than those in the cellar, but the winds would not always be favorable, and rowing against tides and currents would require twice so many at least. The Cimmerian surveyed the men sprawled about the floor and added, "Not to mention sobering this lot enough to walk without falling over their own feet."

"Salted wine," Hordo said grimly. Conan winced; he had personal experience of the one-eyed man's method of ridding a man of drunkenness. "And you cannot risk the streets in daylight," Hordo went on, "I will leave that part of it to you while I try to scrape some more crew out of the taverns. Prytanis! We've work to be done!"

Conan ran his eye over the drunken smugglers once more and grimaced. "Hasan, tell Kafar we need ten pitchers of wine. And a large sack of salt."

The next hour was not going to be pleasant.

VI

The harbor quays were quiet once night had fallen, inhabited only by shadows that transformed great casks of wine and bales of cloth and coiled hawsers into looming, fearsome shapes. Scudding clouds dappled a dull, distant moon. The seaward wind across the bay was as cold as it had been hot during the day, and the watchmen paid by the Merchants' Guild wrapped themselves in their cloaks and found shelter within the waterside warehouses with warming bottles of wine.

There were no eyes to see the men who worked around a trim vessel some sixteen paces long, with a single forward-raked mast stepped amidship. It was tied alongside a dock that leaned alarmingly and creaked at every step on its rough planks. But then the dock creaked whether there were steps or not. All the boats moored there were draped with nets, but few carried more than the faintest smell of fish. Actual fishermen sold small portions of their catch each day for the maintaining of that smell. King Yildiz's customs collectors would seize a fishing boat that did not smell of fish before they even bothered to search it.

Conan stood on the rickety dock with the dark cloak he had from Ghurran pulled about him so that he blended with the night. He was the only one there besides Hordo who knew that the one-eyed man privately called that boat *Karela*, after a woman he had not seen in two years, but looked for still. Conan had known her, too, and understood the smuggler's obsession.

While others loaded the ship, the Cimmerian kept an eye out for the rare watchman who might actually be trying to earn his coin or, more likely, for a chance patrol of the King's excisemen. A slight ache behind his eyes was the only remaining effect of the poison he could detect.

"The old man's potion works well," he said as Hordo climbed up beside him from the boat. "I could almost think the poison was gone completely."

"It had better work," his friend grunted. "You had to promise him those hundred gold pieces when he was ready to settle for herbs."

"My life is worth a hundred gold pieces to me," Conan said dryly. Muffled cursing and thumping rose from the boat. "Hordo, did you truly take on every blind fool you could find for this voyage?"

"We may wish we had twice as many blades before this is done. And with half my men vanished into wine pitchers, I had to take the best of what I could find. Or would you rather wait another day? I hear the City Guard cut an albino into dog meat just at twilight, mistaking him for a northlander. And they've set out to search every tavern and bordello in the city."

"That will take them a century," Conan laughed. A soft cooing caught his ear, and he stared in amazement as a wicker cage of doves was lowered onto the boat, followed by another cage of chickens and three live goats.

"One of the new men suggested it," Hordo said, "and I think it a good idea. I get tired of choosing between dried meat and salt meat when we are at sea."

"As long as they are not more of the crew, Hordo."

"The goats are no randier than some outlanders I know, and the—" The bearded man cut off as a light flared on the boat below. "What in Zandru's Nine Hells . . ."

Conan did not waste time on oaths. Leaping to the deck, he snatched a clay lamp from the hands of a tall, lanky Turanian and threw it over the side.

The man stared at him angrily. "How am I to see where to put anything in this dark?" He was a stranger to Conan, one of Hordo's new recruits, in the turban and leather vest that was the ubiquitous garb of the harbor district.

"What is your name?" the Cimmerian asked.

"I am called Shamil. Who are you?"

"Shamil," Conan said, "I will just assume you are too stupid to realize that a lamp could also be seen by others." His voice grew harder. "I will not even think you might be a spy for the excisemen, trying to draw their attention. But if you do that again, I will make you eat the lamp."

Hordo appeared beside him, testing his dagger on a horny thumb.

"And after he does, I will slit your throat. You understand?" The lanky man nodded warily.

"Blind fools, Hordo," Conan said and turned away before his friend could speak.

The Cimmerian's earlier mirth had soured. Men such as this Shamil might well get them all killed before they ever saw the Zaporoska. And how many others like him were among the newcomers? Even if they were not done in by foolishness like lighting a lamp where stealth was required, how many of the new could be trusted did matters come to a fight on the other side of the Vilayet?

Muttering to himself, Ghurran stumbled his way down the dark deck and thrust a battered pewter cup into Conan's hands. "Drink this. I cannot be sure what effect the pitching of sea travel will have. It is best to have a double dose and be safe."

Conan took a deep breath and emptied the cup in one gulp. "It no longer tastes of camel," he said with a grimace.

"The ingredients are slightly different," the herbalist told him.

"Now it tastes as though a sheep was dipped in it." Conan tossed the cup back to Ghurran as Hordo joined them.

"The chests are lashed below," the smuggler said quietly, "and we are as ready as we are likely to be. Take the tiller, Cimmerian, while I get the men to the oars."

"See if they can keep from braining one another with them," Conan said, but Hordo had already disappeared in the dark, whispering muted commands.

The Cimmerian moved quickly aft, wincing at the clatter of oars as they were laid in the thole pins. As the craft was pushed out from the dock, he threw his weight against the thick wooden haft of the tiller, steering the boat toward open water. The sounds of Hordo quietly calling the stroke came over the creak of the oars. Phosphorescence swirled around the oar blades and in the wake.

Scores of ships in all sizes were anchored in the harbor, galleys and sailing craft from every port on the Vilayet. Conan directed a zig-zag course that kept well clear of all of them. The navy's biremes were berthed in the northern-most part of the bay, but some of the merchantmen would have a man standing watch. None would raise an alarm, however, unless the smugglers' craft came too close. The watches were to guard against thieves or pirates—some of whom were bold enough to enter the harbor of Sultanapur, or even Aghrapur—not to draw unnecessary attention to ships whose captains often carried goods not listed on the manifest.

The offshore wind carried not only the smells of the city, but picked up the harbor's own stenches as well. The aromas of spice ships and the stink of slavers blended with the smell of the water. Slops and offal were tossed over the side whether a ship was at sea or in port, and the harbor of Sultanapur was a cesspool.

The vessel cleared the last of the anchored ships, but instead of relaxing, Conan stiffened and bit back a curse. "Hordo," he called hoarsely. "Hordo, the mole!"

The long stone barrier of the mole protected the harbor against the sharp, sudden storms of the Vilayet that could otherwise send waves crashing in to smash vessels against the quays. Two wide ship channels, separated by more than a thousand paces, were the only openings in the great breakwater, and on either side of each channel was a tall granite tower. The towers were not yet visible in the night and would usually be manned only in time of war. What was visible, however, was the gleam of torchlight through arrow slits.

Pounding a fist into his palm, Hordo slowly backed the length of the deck, staring all the while toward the slivers of light. They became less distant by the moment. He spoke quietly when close enough for Conan and no other to hear. "It must be this Mitra-forsaken assassination, Cimmerian. But if they've manned the towers . . ."

"The chains?" Conan said, and the bearded man nodded grimly.

The chains were another precaution for time of war, like the manning of the towers. Of massive iron links capable of taking a ramming-stroke blow from the largest trireme without breaking, they could be stretched, almost on the surface of the water, to effectively bar the harbor entrances even to vessels as small as the one the smugglers rode.

Conan spoke slowly, letting his thoughts form on his tongue. "There is no reason for the towers to be manned unless the guard-chains have been raised. In the night they are little better than useless as watch posts. But there is no war, only the assassination." He nodded to himself. "Hordo, the chains are not to keep ships out, but to keep them in."

"Keep them in?"

"To try to keep the High Admiral's assassin from escaping," the Cimmerian said impatiently. "There are no city gates here to close and guard, only the chains."

"And if you are right, how does it aid us?" Hordo grunted sourly. "Chains or gates, we are trapped like hares in a cage."

"In war there would be a hundred men or more in each tower. But now . . . They expect no attack, Hordo. And how many men are needed just to guard against someone trying to loose an end of the chain? As many as to guard a gate?"

The one-eyed man whistled tunelessly between his teeth. "A gamble, Cimmerian," he said finally. "You propose a deadly gamble."

"I have no choice. The dice will be tossed, one way or another, and my life is already wagered."

"As you say. But do not ask me to like it, for I do not. We will have to try one of the towers on the part separated from land. Otherwise we might have a few score guardsmen to contend with before our business is done."

"Not you," Conan said. "If we both go, how long do you wager the ship will wait for us? The new men will not outstay the old, and the old are not overly eager for this voyage."

"They all know I would follow any man who left me, and in my own ship," Hordo rumbled. "Follow him to the end of the world, if need be, and rip out his throat with my bare hands." But he took the tiller from the Cimmerian. "See who will go with you. You cannot do it alone."

Conan moved forward to the mast and stood astride the yard on which the sail was furled, lying fore and aft on the deck. The pace of rowing, already ragged without Hordo to call a stroke, slowed further. Even in the dark he knew every eye was on him.

"The trouble in the city has given us a problem," he said quietly. "The guard-chains are up. I intend to lower one and open a way out of the harbor for us. If it is not done, we have come this far for nothing. We will have a few chests of spices—or so I was told they were—that only the Vendhyans want, and the Vendhyans will keep their gold." He waited. Gold was always a good place to end, for the word then loomed large in the listeners' minds.

To his surprise, Hasan drew in his oar and stood silently. Ghurran shifted and wrapped his cloak tighter about himself. No one else moved.

Conan ran his gaze down the two shadowy lines of men, and some of those who had been with Hordo before his coming stirred uncomfortably on their rowing benches. It would not be easy convincing them. Outright cowards did not last long among the Brotherhood of the Coast, but neither did those too eager to seek battle. As well to start with the hardest to convince.

"You, Prytanis?"

The slit-nosed Nemedian's teeth showed white in what could have been a smile or a snarl. "You want this journey, northlander? You lower the chain then. I'd as soon be back ashore with a mug of ale in my fist and a wench on my knee."

"A much safer place, it is true," Conan said dryly and there was a small laugh from the others. Prytanis hunched angrily over his oar.

Shamil, pulling an oar almost by Conan's side, had made no move to rise, but there was an air of watching and waiting about him that was plain even in the dim-mooned night.

"What of you, lighter of lamps?" the Cimmerian asked.

"I merely waited to be asked," the lanky man answered quietly. His oar rattled against the thole pins as it was pulled inboard.

Abruptly two men stood who had been with Hordo when Conan arrived in Sultanapur. "I would not have you think only the newlings are with you," said one, a Kothian named Baltis. Thick old scars were layered where his ears had been none too expertly removed in the distant past. The other, a hollow-faced Shemite who called himself Enam, did not speak but simply drew his tulwar and examined the blade's edge.

"Fools," Prytanis said, but he said it softly.

Conan waved his arm in signal to Hordo, only a gray blur in the stern, and the vessel curved toward the mole. The great breakwater reared before them, a granite wall rising from the dark waters, more than the height of a man, higher than the vessel's deck. Even the new men knew enough of boats to know what was needed now. They backed water smoothly; then those on the side next to the mole raised their oars to fend the craft off from the stone.

The big Cimmerian wasted no time on further words. Putting a foot on the strake, he leaped. His outstretched hands caught the top of the mole, and he pulled himself smoothly up onto the rough granite surface. Grunts and muttered curses announced the arrival of the others, scrambling up beside him. There was no dearth of room, for the breakwater was nearly twenty paces wide.

"We kill them?" Hasan asked in a low voice.

"Perhaps we'll not need to," Conan replied. "Come."

The square, stone watch-tower occupied all of the end of the mole except for a narrow walkway around it. Its crenelated top was fifty feet above them, and only a single heavy wooden door broke the granite walls at the bottom. Arrow slits at the second level showed the yellow gleam of torchlight, but there were none higher.

Motioning the others into the shadows at the base of the tower, Conan drew his dagger and pressed himself flat against the stone wall beside the door. Carefully gauging distance, he tossed the dagger; it clattered on the granite two long paces from the door. For a moment he did not think the sound had carried to those inside. Then came the scrape of the bar being lifted. The door swung open, spilling out a pool of light, and a helmetless guardsman stuck his head through. Conan did not breathe but it was the dagger at the edge of the light that caught the Turanian's eye. Frowning, he stepped out.

Conan moved like a striking falcon. One hand closed over the guardsman's mouth. The other seized the man's sword-belt and heaved. A splash came from below, and then cries.

"Help! Help!"

"The fool's fallen in," someone shouted inside, and in a clatter of booted feet, four more guardsmen rushed from the tower.

Without helmets, one carrying a wooded mug, it was clear they had no presentiment of danger. They skidded to a halt as they became aware of the young giant before them, and hands darted for sword-hilts, but it was too late. A nose crunched under Conan's fist, and even as that man crumpled, another blow took one of his companions in the jaw. The two fell almost one atop the other.

The rest were down as well, Conan saw, and no weapons had been drawn. "Throw their swords in the harbor," he ordered, retrieving his dagger, "and bind them." The cries for help still rose from the water, louder now, and more frantic. "Then make a rope of their belts and tunics, and haul that fool out before he wakes the entire city."

Sword in hand, he cautiously entered the tower. The lowest level was one large room lit by torches, with stone stairs against one wall, leading up. Almost the entire chamber was taken up by a monstrous windlass linked to a complex arrangement of great bronze gears that shone from the fresh grease on them. A long bar ran from the smallest gear to a bronze wheel mounted on the wall below the stairs. Massive iron chain was layered on the windlass drum, the metal of each round link as thick as a man's arm, and unrusted. It was said the ancient Turanian king who commanded that chain to be made had offered the weight in rubies of any smith who could produce iron that would not rust. It was said he had paid it, too, including the weight of the hands and tongue he took from the smith so the secret would not be gained by others.

From the windlass the chain led into a narrow, round hole in the stone floor. Conan ignored that, examining the gears for the means of loosing the chain. One bronze wedge seemed to be all that kept the gears from turning.

"Look out!"

At the shout Conan spun, broadsword leaping into his hand. Toppling from the stairs, a guardsman thudded to the stones at the Cimmerian's feet. A dagger hilt stood out from his chest and a still-drawn crossbow lay by his outstretched hand.

"He aimed at your back," Hasan said from the door.

"I will repay the debt," Conan said, sheathing his blade.

Quickly the Cimmerian worked the wedge free, tossed it aside, and then threw his weight against the bar. It could as well have been set in stone. By the length of the thick metal rod, five men at least were meant to work the windlass. Thick muscles knotted with effort, and the bar moved, slowly at first, then faster. Much more slowly the windlass turned, and huge links rattled into the hole in the floor. Conan strained to rotate the device faster. Suddenly Hasan was there beside him, adding more strength than his bony height suggested.

Baltis stuck his head in at the door. "The chain is below the water as far out as I can see, Cimmerian. And there is stirring on the far side of the channel. They must have heard the shouting for help."

Reluctantly Conan released the bar. A boat would be sent to investigate, and though it would not likely carry many men, the purpose was escape, not a fight. "Our craft draws little water," he said. "It will have to do."

As the three men hurried from the tower, Shamil and Enam straightened from laying the fifth guardsman, bound and gagged with strips torn from his own sopping-wet tunic, in a row with the four who were still unconscious. Without a word they followed Conan onto the narrow walkway that led around the tower. Hordo's one eye, the Cimmerian knew, was as sharp as Baltis's two. And the bearlike man would not waste precious moments.

Before they even reached the channel side of the tower, the soft creak and splash of oars was approaching. The vessel arrived at the same instant they did, backing water as it swung close to the breakwater.

"Jump," Conan commanded.

Waiting only to hear each man thump safely on deck, he leaped after them. He landed with knees flexed, yet staggered and had to catch hold of the mast to keep from falling. His head spun until it seemed as though the ship were pitching in a storm. Jaw clenched, he fought to remain upright.

Ghurran shuffled out of the darkness and peered at the Cimmerian. "Too much exertion brings out the poison," he said. "You must rest, for there is a limit to how much of the potion I can give you in one day."

"I will find the man responsible," Conan said through gritted teeth. "Even if there is no antidote, I will find him and kill him."

From the stern came Hordo's hoarse command. "Stroke! Erlik take the lot of you, stroke!"

Oars working, the slim craft crawled away from Sultanapur like a waterbug skittering over black water.

With a roar Naipal bolted upright on his huge round bed, staring fixedly into the darkness. Moonlight filtered into the chamber through gossamer hangings at arched windows, creating dim shadows. The two women who shared his bed—one Vendhyan, one Khitan, each sweetly rounded and unclothed—cowered away from him among the silken coverlets in fright at the yell. They were his favorites from his *purdhana*, skilled, passionate and eager to please, yet he did not so much as glance at them.

With the tips of his fingers he massaged his temples, trying to remember what it was that had wakened him. From a narrow golden chain about his neck a black opal dangled against his sweat-damp chest. Never was he without it, for that opal was the sole means by which Masrok could signal obedience or ask to be summoned. Now, however, it lay dark and cool against his skin. A dream, he decided. A dream of great portent to affect him so, but portent of what? Obviously it had come as a warning of some . . . *Warning!*

"Katar's teats!" he snapped, and the women cowered from him even farther.

Summoning servants would take too much time. He scrambled from the bed, still ignoring the now-whimpering women. They had many delightful uses, but none now. Hastily he donned his robes, a task he had not performed unaided for years. The narrow golden coffer stood on a table inlaid with turquoise and lapis lazuli. He reached for it, hesitated—no need now to summon Masrok; no need to threaten—then left the coffer and ran.

Desperate wondering filled his mind. What danger could threaten him now? Masrok shielded the eyes of the Black Seers of Yimsha. Zail Bal, the former court wizard and the one man he had ever truly feared, was dead, carried off by demons. If Bhandarkar divined his intent, he might summon other mages to oppose him, but he, Naipal, had men close to the throne, men the King did not know of. He knew what woman Bhandarkar had chosen for the night even before she reached the royal bedchamber. What could it be? What?

The darkness of the high-domed chamber far below the palace was lessened by an unearthly glow from the silver pattern in the floor. Naipal darted to the table where his sorcerous implements were laid out, crystal flasks and beakers, vials that gave off eerie light and others that seemed to draw darkness. His fingers itched to reach for the ebony chest, for the power of the *khorassani*, but he forced himself to lift the lid of the ornately carved ivory box instead. With shaking hands he thrust back the silken coverings.

A harsh breath rasped in his throat like a death rattle. A shadowed image floated on the polished surface, silvery no more. Reflected there was a small ship on a night-shrouded sea, a vessel with a single forward-raked mast, making its way by the rhythmic sweep of oars.

Strange devices of crystal and bone trembled as his fist pounded on the table. As it was meant to, the mirror showed him the source of his danger, yet he cursed its limits. What was the danger here? Across what sea did it come? There were seas to the south and far to the east was the Endless Ocean, said by some to end only at the brink of the world. To the west lay the Vilayet and even farther the great Western Sea. At least Mount Yimsha had been recognizable.

He ground his teeth, knowing it was to keep them from chattering and hating the fact. Like an inky cloud, terror coiled its tendrils around his soul. He had thought himself long beyond such, but now he knew that the years with the mirror standing watch had softened him. He had plotted and acted without fear, thinking he had conquered fear because the emptiness of the mirror had told him his plans were unthreatened. And now this ship! A tiny speck on the waters, by all the gods!

With tremendous effort he forced his features back to their normal outward calm. Forcefully he reminded himself that panic availed nothing. Less than nothing, for it hindered action. He had agents in many places and the means to communicate orders to them more swiftly than flights of eagles. His eyes marked the craft well and fingers that shook only slightly moved among the arcane implements on the table. From whatever direction that vessel came, on whatever shore it landed, there would be men to recognize it. Long before it ever reached him, the danger would be purged as though with fire.

VII

With his feet planted wide against the rise and fall of the deck and one hand on the stay supporting the mast, Conan peered through the night toward the blackness that was the eastern shore of the Vilayet. The vessel ran as close inshore as its shallow draft would allow. Not far to the west were islands of which the most pleasant thing said was that they were the lair of pirates. Other things were said as well, whispered in dark corners, but whatever lurked there, no one wanted to draw its attention.

The Cimmerian shared his vigil in the bow with only the two remaining goats and the wicker cage of pigeons. The chickens had gone the way of the other goat, into the smugglers' stomachs. Most of the crew were sprawled on the deck, heads pillowed on arms or coils of rope. Clouds covered the moon, and only through brief rents was there even a slight lessening of the darkness. The triangular sail was full-bellied with wind, and the rush of water along the hull competed with the occasional snore. But then, he thought, none of them had his reasons for eagerness to be ashore, to find the men for whom the chests below were bound. Keen as his eye was, however, he could make out no details of the land. Worse, there was no sign of the signals Hordo had told him of.

"They must be here," he muttered to himself.

"But will they have the antidote?" Ghurran asked, handing Conan the goblet that had become a nightly ritual.

Conan avoided looking at the muddy liquid in the battered pewter cup. It did not grow to look more appetizing with repeated viewing.

"They will have it." Holding his breath, he emptied the goblet, trying to pour the mixture down his throat rather than let it touch his tongue.

"But if they do not?" the old man persisted. "There seems not even to be anyone there."

The Cimmerian's grimace from the taste of the potion turned to a smile. "They are there." He pointed to three pinpricks of light that had just sprung into being in the blackness of the shoreline on the southern headland of the river mouth. "And they *will* have the antidote."

The herbalist trailed after him as he made his way down the deck. Hordo was kneeling beside a large, open chest of iron-bound oak that was lashed to the mast.

"I saw," the one-eyed man muttered when the Cimmerian appeared. "Now to see if they are the ones we seek." In short order he had assembled a peculiar-looking apparatus, three hooded brass lamps fastened to a long pole. There were hooks for attaching more of the lamps if need be, and pegs for crosspieces if other configurations were desired. This was a not-unusual method of signaling among the smugglers.

Once the lamps were alight, Hordo raised the pole high. Those few of the crew not asleep stood to watch. Ashore, the center light of the three disappeared as though suddenly extinguished. Thrice the bearded smuggler lowered and raised the pole of lamps.

The remaining lights ashore vanished and, with a grunt, Hordo lowered the pole and put out his own lamps. Almost with the breath that extinguished the last flame, he was roaring. "Up, you mangy curs! On your feet, you misbegotten camel spawn! Erlik blast your tainted souls, move!" The ship became an anthill as men lurched out of sleep, some aided by a boot from the one-eyed man.

Conan strode to the tiller and found Shamil manning it. He motioned the lanky newcomer aside and took his place. The lower edge of the sail was just high enough for him to watch the coastline ahead.

"What has happened?" Ghurran demanded. "Were the signals wrong? Are we to land or not?"

"It is a matter of trust," Conan explained without looking away from his task. "The men ashore see a ship, but is it the smuggler they expect? Signals are exchanged, but not with the place of landing. If a shipload of excisemen or pirates lands at the signal lights, they'd find no more than a single man, and that only if he is slow or stupid." Another tiny point of light appeared on the coast, separated from the location of the others by almost a league. "And if we had not given the proper signals in return," the Cimmerian went on, "that would not now be showing us where to come ashore."

Ghurran peered at the bustle among the smugglers. Some eased tulwars and daggers in their sheaths. Others loosed the strings of oilskin bags to check bowstrings and arrow fletchings. "And you trust them as much as they trust you," he said.

"Less," Conan grinned. "Even if those ashore haven't tortured the signals out of the men we are truly here to meet, they could still want what we have without the bother of paying for it."

"I had no idea this could be so dangerous." The herbalist's voice was faint.

"Who lives without danger does not live at all," Conan quoted an old Cimmerian proverb. "Did you think to journey all the way to Vendhya by magic? I can think of no other way to travel so far without danger."

Ghurran did not reply, and Conan turned his whole attention to the matter at hand. The wind carried them swiftly toward the waiting light, but a landing on a night shore was not made under sail. To the creaking of halyards in the blocks, the long yard was lowered and swung fore and aft on the deck, a few hasty lashings being made to keep the sail from billowing across the deck and hindering movement. Men moved to the rowing benches. The rasp of oarshafts on thole-pins, the slow swirl of blades dipping into the black water, and, incongruously, cooing from the cage of pigeons became the only sounds of the vessel.

Conan swung the tiller, and the smugglers' craft turned toward land and the guiding point of light. The vessel began to pitch with the swells rolling to shore, and the faint thrash of breakers drifted to his ear. That there was a safe beach ahead he did not doubt. Even excisemen wanted a smuggler's cargo undamaged for the portion of its value that was theirs in reward. Of what came after the prow had touched shore, however, there was always doubt.

Sand grated under the keel and without the need of orders, every man backed water. To be too firmly aground could mean death. A splash came from the bow as Hordo tossed a stone anchor over the side. It would help hold the lightly beached craft against the tide, but the rope could be cut in an instant.

Even as the shudder of grounding ran through the craft, Conan joined the one-eyed man in the bow. The point of light that had brought them ashore was gone. Varying shades of darkness suggested high dunes and perhaps stunted trees.

392ROBERT JORDAN

Abruptly a click as of stone striking metal came from the beach. Almost directly before them a fire flared, a large fire, some thirty-odd paces from the water. A lone man stood beside the fire, hands outspread to show they were empty. His features could not be seen, but the turban on his head was large, like those favored by Vendhyans.

"We'll discover no more by looking," Conan said and jumped over the side. He landed to his calves in water and more splashed over him as Hordo landed.

The bearded man caught his arm. "Let me do the talking, Cimmerian. You've never been able to lie well, except to women. The truth may serve us here, but it must be used properly."

Conan nodded, and they moved up the beach together.

The waiting man was indeed a Vendhyan, with swarthy skin and a narrow nose. A large sapphire and a spray of pale plumes adorned his turban and a ring with a polished stone was on every finger. Rich brocades and silks made up his garments, though there were stout riding boots on his feet. His dark, deep-set eyes went past them to the boat. "Where is Patil?" he said in badly accented Hyrkanian. His tone was flat and unreadable.

"Patil left Sultanapur before us," Hordo replied, "and by a different way. He did not tell me his route, as you may understand."

"He was to come with you."

Hordo shrugged. "The High Admiral of Turan was slain, you see, and it was said the deed was done by a Vendhyan. The streets of Sultanapur are likely still not safe for one of your country."

The truth, Conan thought. Every word the truth, but handled, as Hordo would put it, properly.

A frown creased the Vendhyan's brow, though he nodded slowly. "Very well. You may call me Lord Sabah."

"You may call me King Yildiz if you need names," Hordo said.

The Vendhyan's face tightened. "Of course. You have the . . . goods— Yildiz?"

"You have the gold? Patil spoke of a great deal of gold."

"The gold is here," Sabah said impatiently. "What of the chests, O King of Turan?"

Hordo raised his right hand above his head, and from the vessel came the grate of the hatch being pushed back. "Let your men come on foot for them," he cautioned, "and no more than four at a time. And I will see the gold before a chest is taken."

Six of the smugglers appeared on the edge of the firelight, bows in hand and arrows nocked. The Vendhyan looked at them levelly, then bowed to Hordo with a dry smile. "It shall be as you wish, of course." Backing around the fire, he faded into the darkness up the beach.

"I mistrust him," Conan said as soon as he was gone.

"Why?" Hordo asked.

"He accepted the tale of Patil too easily. Would you not have asked at least a few more questions if you were he?"

The one-eyed man shook his shaggy head. "Perhaps. But keep your eyes open, and we will get out of this with whole skins whatever he intends."

A dark band of wet about the bottom of his robes, Ghurran puffed up the sandy shelf. "This mode of travel is uncomfortable, inconvenient and damp," he muttered, holding his bony hands out to the fire. "Have you spoken to that man about the antidote, Cimmerian?"

"Not yet."

"Do not. Hear me out," he went on when Conan opened his mouth. "They will be nervous of a man like you with a sword on his hip. And what reason would you give for asking? I have one, you see." To Conan's surprise, the herbalist produce Patil's push-dagger from his sleeve. "I purchased the weapon from Patil, but he said he had none of the antidote. If you said such a thing, they would assume you took the blade from his body. If I say it . . . well, they would sooner believe I had bedded one of their daughters than that these old arms had slain a man." He hastily made the small dagger disappear as Sabah walked into the circle of light.

Two obvious servants followed the Vendhyan, turbaned men in dull-colored cotton, without rings or gems. One carried a dark woolen blanket that he spread beside the fire at Sabah's gesture. The other bore a leather sack, which he upended over the blanket. A cascade of golden coins tumbled to the blanket, bouncing and ringing against each other till a hundred gleaming roundels lay in a scattered heap.

Conan stared in amazement. It was far from the first time he had seen so much gold in one place, but never before offered so casually. If those chests had been filled with saffron, they would not be worth so much. "What is in the chests?" he asked.

The Vendhyan's smile touched only his lips. "Spices."

The tension was broken by Hordo bending to scoop up five of the coins at random. He examined them closely, finally biting each before tossing it back to the blanket. "I will want the sack as well," he said, then shouted over his shoulder, "Bring up the chests!"

Half a score of smugglers appeared from the direction of the ship, each bearing one of the small chests. Hordo motioned, and they set their burdens down off to one side of the fire, then trotted back toward the water. Without a word, Sabah hurried to the chests, the servants at his heels, and two more men ran down the beach to join them. Conan saw Ghurran there as well, but he could not tell if the old man was speaking to anyone. Dropping to his knees, Hordo stuffed coins into the leather sack as fast as he could.

Abruptly a cry of rage rose from the men around the chests. Smugglers coming up the beach with the second load of chests froze where they stood. Conan's hand went to his sword-hilt as Sabah all but hurled himself back into the firelight.

"The seals!" the Vendhyan howled. "They have been broken and resealed!"

Hordo's hand twitched as though he wanted to drop the last coins he held and reach for a weapon. "Patil did it on the day he left," he said hastily. "I do not know why. Check the chests and you will see that we have taken nothing."

The Vendhyan's fists clenched and unclenched, and his eyes darted in furious uncertainty. "Very well," he rasped at last. "Very well. But I will examine each chest." His hands still worked convulsively as he stalked away.

"You were right, Cimmerian," Hordo said. "He should not have accepted that so easily."

"I am glad you agree," Conan said dryly. "Now have you considered that this fire makes us targets a child could hit?"

"I have." The one-eyed man jerked the drawstrings of the sack closed and knotted them to his belt. "Let us get everyone back aboard as quickly as possible."

Sabah was gone, Conan saw, as well as the first ten chests. Turbaned men waited warily for the rest. Ten, not the agreed-upon four, but the Cimmerian was not about to argue the point now. Ghurran was with them, and talking, by his gestures. Conan hoped the herbalist had found what they sought. There was certainly no more time for looking.

With seeming casualness, Conan drifted to the line of smugglers who still waited well down toward the water. Beyond them some of the archers had half-drawn their bows, but all still held their weapons down.

"What was that shouting?" Prytanis demanded.

"Trouble," Conan replied. "But I do not think they will attack until those chests are safely off the beach. Not unless they decide we are suspicious. So take the chests on up, then get back aboard as fast as you can without running. And bring Ghurran."

"And you go back to the ship now?" Prytanis sneered. A ripple of uneasiness ran through the others.

It was an effort for Conan to keep the anger out of his voice. "I stand right here until you get back, as if we trust them like brothers. They are getting impatient, Prytanis. Or do you not want a chance to leave this beach without fighting?"

The Nemedian still hesitated, but another man pushed by him, then another. With a last glare at the big Cimmerian, Prytanis fell in with the file.

Crossing his arms across his chest, Conan tried to give the image of a man at ease, all the while scanning the beach for the attack he was sure must come. The file of smugglers met the clustered Vendhyans, the chests changed hands, and the two groups parted, walking swiftly in opposite directions. The smugglers had the shorter distance to go. Even as the thought came to Conan, one of the Vendhyans looked back, then said something to his fellows, and they all broke into a run made awkward by the chests they carried.

"Run!" Conan shouted to the smugglers, and for once they obeyed with alacrity, two of them dragging Ghurran between them. A rhythmic pounding came to him as he drew his sword, and he stifled a curse to shout to the archers. "Ware horsemen!"

The archers had only time to raise their bows before half a score of mounted men in turbaned helmets and brigantine hauberks galloped out of the dunes with lowered lances. Bowstrings slapped against leather bracers, and five saddles were emptied. The others, one swaying, jerked at their reins and let the charge carry them back into the dark. There were bowmen among the Vendhyans as well, but their target was not men. Flaming arrows arched into the night to fall around the ship. Some hissed into the sea, but others struck wood.

Then Conan had time to worry neither about the ship nor about anyone else. Two horsemen pounded out of the night, bent low in their saddles, seeming to race shoulder to shoulder to see which would lance him first. Snarling, he leaped to the side, away from the long-bladed lances. The two riders tried to wheel on him together, but he closed with them, thrusting at the closer of them. His blade struck a metal plate in quilted brigantine, then slid off and between the plates. The movements of his attack were continuous. Even as his steel pierced ribs and heart, he was scrambling onto the dying man's horse, throwing both the corpse and himself against the second enemy.

The second Vendhyan's eyes bulged with disbelief behind the nasal of his turbaned helmet; he dropped the lance and struggled to reach his tulwar. Conan grappled the live man with one hand while trying to pull his broadsword from the dead one with the other, and the two horses, joined by three linked bodies, danced wildly on the sand. In the same instant, Conan's blade and the Vendhyan's came free. The dark-eyed man desperately raised his weapon to slash. Conan twisted and all three men fell. As they slammed into the ground, the Cimmerian sliced his sword across a dark neck as though he were wielding a dagger and rose from two corpses.

The horses' pavane had carried him well down the beach, and what he saw as he looked back did not appear good. Bodies dotted the sand, though he could not make out how many were smugglers, and neither a standing man nor a mounted one was to be seen. Worse, the stern of the ship was a bonfire. As he watched, a man with a bucket silhouetted himself against the flames. Almost as soon as he appeared, the man dropped the bucket, tried to claw at his back with both hands and toppled into the fire. Not Hordo, Conan thought. The one-eyed man was too smart to do something like that with bowmen about.

The fire had lessened the darkness on the beach considerably, Conan realized. He was not so well lit as the man on the boat but neither could he consider himself shielded by the night from the Vendhyan archers. It was always better to be the hunter than the hunted, and the Easterners were not to be found by staying where he was.

Bent almost double, he ran for the dunes . . . and threw himself flat against a slope of sand as nearly a score of riders appeared above him. This, he thought sourly, was a few more than he had hoped to find at once. He was considering whether or not he could slip away unnoticed when the Vendhyans began talking.

"Are the chests on the pack animals?" a harsh, rasping voice demanded.

"They are."

"And where is Sabah?"

"Dead. He wanted to take the one-eyed man alive to see what he said about the seals under hot irons. The smuggler drowned him in the surf and escaped."

Conan smiled at that, at both parts of it.

"Good riddance," the harsh voice snapped. "I said from the start that we should come down on them as soon as the chests were in sight. Sabah always had to complicate matters. I think he was beginning to believe he really was a lord, with his secrets and his plottings."

"No matter. Sabah is dead, and we will soon hunt down the rest of the vermin."

"You propose to wait that long?" the harsh voice said. "How long do you think the caravan will wait?"

"But Sabah said we must kill all of them. And there is the gold."

"You think of a dead man's orders and a hundred gold pieces?" the harsh voice sneered. "Think instead of our reception if those chests fail to reach Ayodhya safely. Better we all join Sabah now than that."

The silence was palpable. Conan could almost feel agreement radiating from the listeners. As if no further words were necessary, the Vendhyans reined their mounts around and galloped into the dark. Moments later Conan heard other hooves joining these, and all receded to the south.

There was much in what the Cimmerian had heard for him to consider. For one thing, the accursed chests seemed to take on greater importance every time someone spoke of them. For the moment, though, there were more immediate matters to be concerned with.

Half of the boat was burning by the time he reached it. In the light of the fire, Hordo and three others, waist-deep in the surf with buckets, were picked out clearly as they desperately threw water on the flames and watched the shore with equal desperation.

"The Vendhyans are gone!" Conan shouted. Grabbing the strake, he vaulted to the deck. Rivulets of fire ran forward along the sail. "It is too late for that, Hordo!"

"Erlik blast you!" the one-eyed man howled. "This is my ship!"

One of the goats was dead, an arrow through its throat. Food might be in short supply, Conan thought, and tossed the carcass toward the beach. The live goat followed, almost dropping on Hordo's head.

"My ship!" the one-eyed man growled. "Karela!"

"There will be another." Conan lowered the cage of fluttering pigeons and met Hordo's glare over it. "There will be another, my friend, but this one is done."

With a groan, Hordo took the wicker cage. "Get off, Cimmerian, before you burn, too."

Instead, Conan began seizing everything he found loose and not burning—coils of rope, water bags, bundles of personal possessions—and hurled them shoreward. They were stranded in a strange land, which meant it was best to assume a hostile land, and all they would have by way of supplies was what was saved from the flames. The heat became blistering hot as the fire crept closer. Pitch caulking bubbled and fed the conflagration, giving off foul black smoke. Only when there was nothing left unburning within his grasp, however, did Conan leap from the fiery craft.

Splashing to shore, he sank coughing to his knees. After a time he became aware of Ghurran standing over him. The herbalist's parchment-skinned hands clutched a leather bag with a long strap.

"I regret," Ghurran said quietly, "that none of the Vendhyans had the antidote you seek. Though as they apparently planned to slay us, it may be they lied. I will search their dead in any case. You may be assured, however, that I have what is needed to keep you alive until we reach Vendhya."

Conan ran his eyes over the beach. Dead and wounded dotted the sand. A handful of smugglers were tottering hesitantly out of the dark. Behind him the boat was a pyre.

"Until we reach Vendhya," he said bleakly.

As the last flames flickered out on the ruin of the smugglers' craft, Jelal slipped away into the dunes, a coarse-woven bag under his arm. The others were too tired to take notice, he knew, so long as he was quick.

By touch he found dead twigs on the stunted trees scattered in the low hills of sand, and in a spot well-sheltered from the beach, he built a tiny fire. Flint and steel went back into his pouch, and other things came out. A small brass bottle, tightly capped. A short length of goose quill. Strips of parchment, scraped thin. As rapidly as he could without tearing the parchment, he wrote.

> *My Lord, by chance I have perhaps stumbled on to a path to the*
> *answers you seek. To believe otherwise is to believe in too great a*
> *coincidence. I have no answers as yet, only more questions. As you fear,*
> *the path leads to Vendhya, and I will follow it there.*

Something rustled in the night, and Jelal hastily pushed a handful of sand over the tiny fire, quenching the light. A faint aroma of burned wood lingered in the air but that could easily be mistaken for the smell of the charred remains of the ship. For a long moment he listened, holding his breath. Nothing. But there was no reason to take chances at this point. Signing the message by feel, he stowed his paraphernalia and rolled the strip of parchment into a thin tube.

From the coarse-woven sack he took a pigeon. It had been sheer luck, getting the birds brought along, and greater luck that they were not all eaten. Deftly he tied the parchment tube to the pigeon's leg, then tossed the bird aloft. In a flutter of wings it was gone, carrying all he was really sure of thus far to Lord Khalid in Sultanapur. It was little enough, he knew. But if the indications he had seen so far grew much stronger, he vowed to see that this Conan and this Hordo returned to a Turan ready to put their heads on pikes.

VIII

Dawn south of the Zaporoska was gray and dull, for heavy clouds filtered the light of the rising sun to lifelessness. From where he crouched in the dunes behind a twisted scrub oak, Conan watched the Bhalkhana stallion cropping scattered tufts of tough grass and wondered if the animal had settled enough for another try. The tall black's high-pommeled saddle was worked with silver studs and a fringe of red silk dangled from the reins.

Carefully the Cimmerian straightened. The horse flicked an ear but munched in seeming unconcern at another clump of grass. Sand crunched underfoot as Conan approached with slow steps. His hand touched the reins . . . and the stallion seemed to explode.

Fingers tangled in the bridle, Conan was jerked into the air as the ebon animal reared. Like a cat he twisted, throwing his legs around the horse's neck, clutching its mane with his free hand. The stallion dropped, and the added weight of the man pulled it to its knees. Scrambling back to its feet, the horse shook its head furiously. With wild snorts and whinnies, the animal leaped and plunged but Conan clung tenaciously. And as he knew it must, his presence in such an unaccustomed place began to take a toll. The leaps became shorter, the rearings farther apart. Then the stallion was still, nostrils flared and blowing hard.

The animal was not beaten, Conan knew. He was all but staring it in the eye, and that eye was filled with spirit. The question was whether or not it had decided to accept a strange rider. He knew better than to let go of the beast. With infinite caution he pulled himself onto its back, then lifted himself over the high pommel and into the saddle. The stallion only shifted as he took up the red-fringed reins. Finally letting himself relax, Conan patted the glossy arched neck and gently kneed the animal into a trot toward the beach.

The charred ribs of the smugglers' craft, awash in the frothy surf, yet with tendrils of gray smoke still rising, spoke eloquently of the previous night's attack. Some three hundred paces to the north, gray kites screamed and circled above the dunes as they contended with the larger vultures for the pickings below. No one among among the smugglers had considered digging graves for the Vendhyan dead, not after digging three for their own.

The situation on the beach had changed since Conan's leave-taking that morning. Then the smugglers had been gathered around the fire, where the last of the arrow-slain goat still decorated a spit. Now they were in three well-separated knots. The seven survivors of those who had previously sailed with Hordo formed one group, huddled and muttering among themselves, while the men who had joined on the night they left Sultanapur made a second group. All were bedraggled and sooty-faced, and many sported bandages.

The third group consisted of Hordo and Ghurran, standing by the eight Vendhyan horses the smugglers had spent the morning gathering. Hordo glared indiscriminately at newcomers and oldsters alike, while the herbalist looked as though he wished he knew the location of a soft bed.

As Conan swung down from his saddle beside Hordo, Prytanis limped from the cluster of old crew members.

"Nine horses," the Nemedian announced. His tone was loud and ranting but directed only to his six fellows. "Nine horses for three and twenty men."

The newer men stirred uneasily, for the numbers were plain when considered the way Prytanis obviously intended. If they were left out of the calculation, there were horses to go around.

"What happened to his foot?" Conan said softly.

Hordo snorted. "He tried to catch a horse, and it stepped on him. The horse got away."

"Look at us," Prytanis shouted, spinning to face Conan and Hordo. "We came for gold, at your urging, and here we stand, our boat in ashes, three of our number dead, and the width of the Vilayet between us and Sultanapur."

"We came for gold and we have it," Hordo shouted back. He slapped the bulging sack tied at his wide belt; the clinking weight of it pulled the belt halfway down his hip. "As for the dead, a man who joins the

Brotherhood of the Coast expecting no danger would do better to become a real fisherman. Or have you forgotten other times we have had to bury comrades?"

The Nemedian seemed taken aback at the reminder that the gold was still with them. It would be difficult to work up much opposition to Hordo among the smugglers as long as the one-eyed man had gold to hand out. Mouth working, Prytanis cast his eyes about angrily until they landed on Ghurran. "The old man is to blame," he cried. "I saw him among the Vendhyans, talking to them. What did he say to stir them up against us?"

"Fool!" Ghurran spat, and the coldness of that bony face was startling. "Why should I bring them down on us? A sword can split my head as easily as yours, and my desire to live is easily as great as yours. You are a fool, Nemedian, and you rant your foolishness because seeking to blame others for your troubles is easier than seeking solutions to those troubles."

Every man there stared at the unexpected outburst, Prytanis the hardest of all. Face pale with rage, the Nemedian stretched a clawed hand toward the scrawny old man, who stared at him disdainfully.

Conan drew his sword, not threatening anyone, just letting it hang at his side. Prytanis' hand stopped short of the herbalist's coarse brown robes. "If you have something to say," Conan said calmly, "then say it. Touch him, though, and I will cut your head off." The Nemedian jerked his hand back and muttered something under his breath. "Louder," Conan said. "Let everyone hear."

Prytanis took a deep breath. "How are nine horses going to carry three and twenty men back to Sultanapur?"

"They are not," Conan said. "One horse goes to Vendhya with me, and another for Ghurran."

"A horse each for the two of you, while the rest of us—" The Nemedian took a step back as Conan raised his blade.

"If you want the horses badly enough," Conan said grimly, "then take them. Myself, I want the animals very much indeed."

Prytanis' hand moved slowly in the direction of his sword, but his eyes shifted as though he wished he could gauge the support of those behind him without being so obvious as looking over his shoulder.

"Four horses go to Vendhya," Hordo said quickly. "At least. I will ride one, and we will need one for supplies. Anyone else going with us gets a horse, as well, for we have the longer way to go, and the harder. What are left over go to those returning to Sultanapur. I'll give each man his share of the Vendhyan gold before we part. That should buy all the horses you need before you reach Khawarism—"

"Khawarism!" Prytanis exclaimed.

"—Perhaps sooner," Hordo went on as though there had been no interruption. "There should be caravans in the passes of the Colchians."

The Nemedian seemed ready for further argument, but Baltis pushed by him.

"That is fair enough, Hordo," the earless man said. "I speak for the others as well. At least for those of us who have been with you before. It is only Prytanis here who wants all this crying and pulling of hair. As for Enam and myself, we have it in mind to go with you."

"Aye," the cadaverous Shemite agreed. His voice matched his face. "Prytanis can go his own way and take his wailing with him. Straight to Zandru's Ninth Hell for all I care."

The other group, the newcomers, had been stirring and murmuring among themselves all this time. Now Hasan growled, "Enough!" at his fellows and moved away from them. "I want to go with you, too," he said to Hordo. "I will likely never get another chance to see Vendhya."

Shamil was almost on Hasan's heels. "I, also, should like to see Vendhya. I joined you for gold and adventure, and there seems little of either in trudging back to Sultanapur. In Vendhya, though . . . well, we have all heard that in Vendhya even beggars wear gold. Perhaps," he laughed, "some of it will stick to my fingers."

None of the rest of the newlings seemed tempted by tales of Vendhyan wealth and when it came to them that but a single horse was left for those returning to Sultanapur, they lapsed into glum silence, slumping like half-empty sacks on the sand. The experienced smugglers were already seeing to their boots and sandals for the long walk around the Vilayet.

Prytanis seemed stunned by the turn of events. He glared about him at the men, at the ruins of the ship, at the horses, then sighed heavily. "Very well then. I will go as well, Hordo."

Conan opened his mouth to refuse the Nemedian but Hordo rushed in.

"And welcome, Prytanis. You are a good man in tight places. The rest of you see to dividing the supplies. The sooner we travel, the sooner we all reach our destinations. You come with me, Cimmerian. We have plans to make."

Conan let himself be drawn away from the others, but as soon as they were out of earshot, he spoke. "You were right in Sultanapur. I should have broken his head or slit his throat. All he wants is that last horse to himself instead of having to share it. And mayhap a chance to steal the rest of the gold."

"No doubt you speak the truth," Hordo replied. "At least about the horse. But credit me with the one eye I have. While you and Prytanis stared at each other, I was watching the newlings."

"What do they have to do with the Nemedian? I doubt they trust him as much as I do."

"Less, of a certainty. But they are none too sure of setting out afoot either. It would not take much spark—say you and Prytanis attempting to slay each other—for half of them to try for the horses. Then instead of going to Vendhya, we can all kill each other on this Mitra-forsaken bit of coast."

Conan shook his head ruefully. "You see a great deal with that one eye, my old friend. Karela would be proud of you."

The bearded man scrubbed at his nose and sniffed. "Perhaps she would. Come. They will be wanting their gold and likely thinking they should have twice as much."

The gold—three pieces laid in each man's calloused palm—caused no squabble at all, though there were a few sharp looks at the leather bag Hordo tied to his sword-belt. The way it tugged the broad belt down less was clear the proof that he had shared out most of the contents. The division of the supplies was the source of greater friction.

Conan was surprised at how many arguments could arise over dried fruit ruined by heat and immersion, or coils of rope for which no one could think of any use at present. Eventually, however, water bags, blankets and such were parceled out in proportion to numbers. The live goat and the remains of the cooked one would go with the men afoot. The cage of pigeons was lashed to the spare horse, along with a sack of grain for feed.

"Better to give the grain to the horses," Conan grumbled, "and feed ourselves what we can catch." He tossed a stirrup leather up over the silver-studded saddle on the big black and bent to check the girth strap. The two parties had truly become separate now. Those who would ride to Vendhya checked their horses while a short distance away, the men who were returning to Sultanapur bundled and lashed their share of the supplies into backpacks, murmuring doubtfully among themselves.

"Mitra's Mercies, Cimmerian," Hordo told him, "but there are times I think you do your best just to avoid a few comforts. I look forward to a spitted pigeon or two roasting over the fire tonight."

Conan grunted. "If we put less attention to our bellies and more to riding hard, we could catch that caravan by nightfall. The Vendhyans spoke as if it were not far off."

"That," said Ghurran, leading his horse awkwardly by the reins with both hands, "would be a good way to travel to Vendhya. We could journey in safety and in comfort." As though realizing that he intruded on a private conversation, he gave an apologetic smile and tugged his horse on.

"That old man," Hordo muttered, "begins to fray my patience. The Vendhyans nearly kill us, my boat is burned, and through it all nothing seems to matter to him except reaching Vendhya."

"His single-mindedness does not bother me," Conan said, "though I should be glad to be able to do without his potions."

The one-eyed man scratched at his beard. "You know it would be best to forget this caravan, do you not? If the men we fought last night have gone to join it, there will certainly be trouble there for us. We will be strangers, and they members of the caravan already."

"I know," Conan said quietly. "But you must know the antidote is not enough for me. A man has tried to kill me, and perhaps succeeded, over chests that look to be worth more than their contents. I will know the why of it, and the answer lies with those chests."

"But be a little careful, Conan. It will profit you little to be spitted on a Vendhyan lance."

"We tried to be careful last night. From now on, let them be careful of me." Conan swung up into the saddle and had to catch hold of the high pommel as his head spun. Grimly he forced himself erect.

"Let them be careful of me," he repeated and kicked the Bhalkhana stallion into motion.

IX

S and dunes quickly gave way to plains of tough, sparse grass and low, isolated hills. Scrub growth and thorn bushes dotted the land, though to the east taller trees could be seen along the banks of the Zaporoska. To the south the grayness of mountains, the Colchians, rose on the horizon. The sun climbed swiftly, a blazing yellow ball in a cloudless sky, with a baking heat that sucked moisture from man and ground. A puff of dust marked each hoof-fall.

Throughout the day Conan kept a steady pace, one the horses could maintain until nightfall. And he intended to maintain it that long and longer, if need be, despite the heat. His sharp eyes had easily located the tracks left by the Vendhyans and their pack mules. No effort had been made to conceal them. The harsh-voiced man had been concerned with swiftness, not with the unlikely possibility that someone might follow his trail. Enam and Shamil proved to be good hands with a bow, making forays from the line of travel that soon had half a score of lean brown hares hanging from their saddles.

The Cimmerian ignored suggestions that they should stop at midday to cook the hares. Stops to give the horses a drink from cupped hands he tolerated, but no sooner had he pushed the plug back into his water bag than he was mounted again and moving. Always to the south, though drifting slightly to the east as if not to get too far from the Zaporoska. Always following the tracks of two score of mounted men with pack horses.

The sun dropped toward the west, showing a display of gold and purple on the mountains, and still Conan kept on, though the sky darkened rapidly overhead and the faint glimmerings of stars were appearing. Prytanis was no longer the only one muttering. Hordo, and even Ghurran, joined in.

"We will not reach Vendhya by riding ourselves to death," the old herbalist groaned. He shifted on his saddle, wincing. "And it will do you no good if I am too stiff and sore to mix the potion that keeps you alive."

"Listen to him, Cimmerian," Hordo said. "We cannot make the journey in a single day."

"Has one day's riding done you in?" Conan laughed. "You who were once the scourge of the Zamoran plains?"

"I have become more suited to a deck than a saddle," the one-eyed man admitted ruefully. "But, Erlik blast us all, even you can no longer see the tracks you claim to follow. I'll believe much of those accursed northern eyes of yours, but not that."

"I've no need to see the tracks," Conan replied, "while I can see that." He pointed ahead where tiny lights were barely visible through the thickening twilight. "Have you gotten so old you can no longer tell stars from campfires?"

Hordo stared, tugging at his beard, then finally grunted, "A league, perhaps more. 'Tis all but full dark now. Caravan guards will not look with kindness on strangers approaching in the night."

"I will at least be sure it is the right caravan," Conan said.

"You will get us all killed," Prytanis grumbled loudly. "I said it from the first. This is a fool's errand, and you will get us all killed."

Conan ignored him, but he did slow the stallion to a walk as they drew closer to the fires. Those fires spread out like the lights of a small city, and indeed he had seen many respectable towns that covered a lesser expanse. A caravan so large would have many guards. He began to sing, somewhat off tune, a tavern song of Sultanapur, relating the improbable exploits of a wench of even more improbable endowments.

"What in Mitra's name?" Hordo growled perplexedly.

"Sing," Conan urged, pausing in his effort. "Men of ill intent do not announce themselves half a league off. You would not wish a guard to put an arrow in you just because you came on him suddenly in the night. Sing." He took up the song again, and after a moment the others joined in raggedly, all save Ghurran, who sniffed loudly in disapproval of the lyrics.

The bawdy words were ringing through the night when, with a jingle of mail, a score of horsemen burst out of the darkness to surround them with couched lances and aimed crossbows. They wore Turanian armor for the most part, but mismatched. Conan saw a Corinthian breastplate and helmets from three other lands. He let the song trail off—the others had ceased in mid-word—and folded his hands on the pommel of his saddle.

"An interesting song," one of the lancers growled, "but who in Zandru's Nine Hells are you to be singing it here?" He was a tall man, his features hidden in the dark by a nasaled Zamoran helm. At least his voice was not a harsh rasp.

"Wayfarers," Conan replied, "journeying to Vendhya. If you also travel in that direction, perhaps you could use a few extra swords."

The tall lancer laughed. "We have more swords than we can use, stranger. A few days past Karim Singh himself, the *wazam* of Vendhya, joined this caravan with five hundred Vendhyan cavalry sent to escort him from the shores of the Vilayet."

"A great many Vendhyans," Conan said, "to be this close to Turan. I thought they stayed beyond Secunderam."

"I will tell Yildiz of it the next time I speak with him," the lancer replied dryly. A few of his men laughed, but none of the weapons was lowered.

"Do you have other latecomers in your caravan?" Conan asked.

"A strange question. Do you seek someone?"

Conan shook his head as though he had not noticed the creak of leather and mail as the caravan guards tensed. In the long and often lawless passages between cities, caravans protected all of their members against outsiders, no matter the claims or charges. "I seek to travel to Vendhya," he said. "But if there are other latecomers, perhaps some of them need guards. Possibly some of your merchants feel less safe, not more, for the presence of five hundred Vendhyans. Soldiers have been known to have their own ideas of what taxes are due, and how they should be collected."

The lancer's long drawn-out breath told that the idea was not a new one to him. Caravans had paid one tax to the customs men before, and then another to the soldiers supposedly sent to protect them. "Eight swords," he muttered, shaking his head. "Two score and three parties of merchants make up this caravan, stranger, including seven who have joined us since we rounded the southern end of the Vilayet. There are always those—no offense intended—who think to make the journey alone until they see the wastes of the Zaporoska before them and realize the Himelias are yet ahead. Then they are eager to join the first caravan that appears, if they are lucky enough that one does. I will pass the word of your presence, but you must understand that I can allow you to come no closer in the night. How shall I tell them you are called, stranger?"

"Tell them to call me Patil," Conan replied. Hordo groaned through his teeth.

"I am Torio," the lancer said, "captain of the caravan guard. Remember, Patil, keep your men well clear of the caravan until first light." Raising his lance sharply, he wheeled his mount and led the guards away at a gallop toward the caravan's fires.

"I expect this is as good a spot to camp as any," Conan said, dismounting. "Baltis, if you can find something to burn, we can make a good meal on roast hare before sleeping. I could wish we had saved some wine from the ship."

"He is mad," Prytanis announced to the ebon sky. "He gives a name that will bring men after us with blades in their fists, then wishes he had some wine to go with the hare."

"As much as I hate to agree with Prytanis," Hordo rumbled, "he is right this time. If you had to give a name other than your own—though, by Mitra's bones, I cannot see why—could you not have chosen another than that?"

"The Cimmerian is wily," Baltis laughed. "When you hunt rats, you set out cheese. This is cheese our Vendhyan rats cannot fail to sniff."

Conan nodded. "He has the right of it, Hordo. There must be more than a thousand people in that caravan. Now I do not have to search for the men I seek. They will search me out instead."

"And if they search you out with a dagger in the back? Or a few score swordsmen falling on us in the night?" The one-eyed man threw up his hands in exasperation.

"You still do not see," Conan said. "They will want to know who I am, and what I do here, especially using Patil's name. Think of the pains to which they have gone to keep those chests secret. What do I know, and who have I told? They can learn nothing if I am dead."

"You begin to sound as devious as a Stygian," Hordo muttered into his beard.

"For myself," Ghurran said, lowering himself unsteadily to the ground, "I do not care at this moment if Bhandarkar's Lion Guard descends on us." He knuckled the small of his back and stretched, grunting. "After I find myself on the outside of one of those hares, I may feel different, but not now."

"Well?" Conan said, eying the others. "Even if the first man Torio speaks to is one of those I seek, you still have time to be away before they get here."

One by one they got down, Prytanis last of all, and he still muttering. By the time the horses were relieved of their saddles and hobbled, Baltis had a fire going, and Enam and Shamil were skinning and spitting hares. Water, Conan discovered, went very well with roast hare when nothing else was available.

The fire burned low, clean-picked bones were tossed aside, and silence replaced the talk that had prevailed while they ate. Conan offered to take the first watch, but no one seemed to have any interest in wrapping himself in his blankets. One by one all but Conan and Ghurran took out oil and stone to tend their blades. Each tried to act as though this had nothing to do with any possible attack but every man turned his back to the dying fire as he worked. There would be less adjustment for the eyes to the dark that way.

Ghurran fussed about his leather sack, at last thrusting the too-familiar pewter goblet at the big Cimmerian. A anticipatory grimace formed on Conan's face as he took it. As he steeled himself to drink, a clatter of hooves sounded in the night. He leaped to his feet, slopping some of the foul-tasting potion over the rim of the cup, and his free hand went to his sword.

"I thought you were sure there would be no attack," Hordo said, holding his own blade at the ready. Every man around the fire was on his feet, even Ghurran, who twisted his head about as though looking for a place to hide.

"If I was always right," Conan said, "I should be the wealthiest man in Zamora instead of being here." Someone—he was not sure who—sighed painfully.

Seven horses halted well beyond the firelight, and three of the riders dismounted and came forward. Two of them stopped at the very edge of the darkness while the third approached the fire. Dark eyes, seeming tilted because of an epicanthic fold, surveyed the smugglers from a bony, saffron-skinned face.

"I hope that your swords are not for me," the man said in fluent, if overly melodious, Hyrkanian as he tucked his hands into the broad sleeves of a pale-blue velvet tunic embroidered on the chest with a heron. A round cap of red silk topped with a gold button sat on his shaven head. "I am but a humble merchant of Khitai, intending harm to no man."

"They are not for you," Conan said, motioning the others to put up their weapons. "It is just that a man must be on guard when strangers approach in the night."

"A wise precaution," the Khitan agreed. "I am Kang Hou, and I seek one called Patil."

"I am called Patil," Conan said.

The merchant arched a thin eyebrow. "A strange name for a *cheng-li*. Your pardon. It means simply a person with pale skin, one from the lands of the distant west. Such men are considered mythical by many in my land."

"I am no myth," Conan snorted. "And the name suffices me."

"As you say," Kang Hou said blandly. He gave no signal that Conan could see, but the other two figures came forward. "My nieces," the merchant said, "Chin Kou and Kuie Hsi. They accompany me everywhere, caring for an aging man in his dotage."

Conan found himself gaping at two of the most exquisite women he had ever seen. They had oval faces and delicate features that could have been carved by a master striving to show the beauty of Eastern women. Neither looked at all like their uncle, for which the Cimmerian was grateful. Chin Kou seemed a flower fashioned of aged ivory, with downcast almond eyes and a shy smile. Kuie Hsi's dark eyes were lowered, too, but she watched with a twinkle through her lashes, and her skin was like sandalwood-hued satin.

He was not the only one struck by the women, Conan realized. Baltis and Enam appeared to be mentally stripping them of their silken robes, while Prytanis all but drooled with lust. Hasan and Shamil merely stared as if hit in the head. Even Hordo had a gleam in his eye that spoke of calculation as to how to separate one or both of the women from the company of their uncle. As usual, only Ghurran seemed unaffected.

"You are welcome here," the Cimmerian said loudly. "You and your nieces both. The man who offends *any* of you offends me." That got everyone's attention, he noted with approval, and dimmed a few amatory fires by the sour looks he saw on their faces.

"I am honored by your welcome," the merchant said, making a small bow.

Conan returned the bow and smothered a curse as he spilled more of the potion over his hand. Emptying the goblet in one long gulp, he tossed the cup to Ghurran, not quite hurling it at his head. "Filthy stuff," he spat.

"Men doubt the efficacy of medicine without a vile taste," Ghurran said, and Kang Hou turned his expressionless gaze on the herbalist.

"That is an old Khitan proverb. You have journeyed to my land?"

Ghurran shook his head. "No. I had it from the man who taught me herbs. Perhaps he went there, though he never spoke of it to me. Do you know much of herbs? I am always interested in discovering plants new to me, and the uses of them."

"Regrettably, I do not," the merchant replied. "And now, Patil, if I may rush matters unconscionably, I would speak of business."

"Speak of what you will," Conan said when he realized the other man was going to await permission.

"I thank you. I am a poor merchant, a dealer in whatever I can. On this trip, velvets from Corinthia, carpets from Iranistan, and tapestries from Turan. I joined the caravan but two days ago and would not have done so save for necessity. The captain of the vessel that brought me across the Vilayet Sea, a rogue called Valash, had promised to provide ten men as guards. After putting my goods and my animals ashore, however, he refused to honor his agreement. My nieces and I thus must try to tend half a score of camels with only the aid of three servants who, I fear, are of no use at all as protection against brigands."

"I know of Valash," Hordo said, spitting after the name. " 'Tis Hanuman's own luck he did not slit your throat and sell your goods—and your nieces—in Khawarism."

"He attempted no such," the Khitan said. "I was not aware that you were men of the sea."

"We have all been many things in our time," Conan replied. "At the moment we are men with swords who might be hired as guards if enough coin is offered."

Kang Hou tilted his head as though considering. "I think," he said at last, "that two silver coins for each man would be equitable. And a gold coin each if I and my goods reach Ayodhya in safety."

Conan exchanged a look with Hordo, then said, "Done."

"Very good. Until you are ready to ride to the caravan, I will wait with the guards Captain Torio was good enough to lend me. Come, nieces."

As soon as the Khitans were gone, Baltis let out a low laugh. "A gold and two silvers to make a journey we were making for free. The Khitan must have a king's wealth to pay so. There's luck in you, Cimmerian. Take that sour look off your face, Prytanis."

"That," Hasan announced, "was the most beautiful woman I have ever seen."

"Kuie Hsi?" Shamil said jealously.

"The other. Chin Kou."

"That is all we need," Hordo grumbled as he began rolling his blankets, "for those two to lose their heads over this Khitan's nieces. You realize he was lying, do you not? Unless there are two men called Valash captaining ships on the Vilayet, he never got those wenches off that vessel as easily as he makes out."

"I know," Conan said. "I did not hear you refusing him because of it though." The one-eyed man muttered something. "What, Hordo?"

"I said, at least this time you've not gotten us involved with a wizard. You have a bad habit of making wizards annoyed with you."

Shouldering his saddle, Conan laughed. "This time I will not come within a league of a wizard."

X

The music of cithern, flute and tambour sounded softly in the alabaster-columned chamber, the musicians hidden behind a lacy screen carved of ivory. Golden lamps, hanging on silver chains from the vaulted ceiling, cast a sheen on the olive skins of six veiled, supple women, clothed in naught else but tinkling golden bells at their ankles, who danced with finger-cymbals. The smell of incense and attar of roses suffused the air. Other women, as lovely as the dancers and garbed as they, scurried with dainty steps to proffer silver trays of sweetmeats, figs and candied delicacies to Naipal, reclining at his ease on cushions of brocaded silk. Two of their sisters worked long fans of pale ostrich plumes to cool him. The mage merely picked at the offerings and toyed with his goblet of Shirakman wine. He gave as little heed to the women, for his mind was distant from his surroundings.

Near Naipal's head knelt a soft, round-faced man whose tunic of scarlet silk and turban of gold and blue seemed gaudy beside the wizard's soft grays. He, too, gave no eye to the women as he reported in a soft voice on how the day had seen his master's wishes carried out. "And one thousand *pice* were handed out in your name, lord, to the beggars of Ayodhya. An additional one thousand *pice* were . . ."

Naipal stared into his wine, as heedless of its exquisite bouquet as of the eunuch's voice. Five times as the tortuous days passed he had gone to the hidden chamber; twice he actually put his hand on the ornate ivory case. But each time he convinced himself to wait, each time with a new reason. The canker in his bosom was that he well knew the true cause of his hesitancy. To open the case, to gaze on the mirror within, perhaps to see that danger to all his plans was yet reflected there, this was more than he could bear. The fear he had fought off in that night of frenzy was returned a hundredfold to paralyze him. Something whispered in the back of his mind, *wait*. Wait a little longer, and surely the mirror would again be empty, the danger dealt with by his far-flung minions. He knew the whisper was false, yet even as he castigated himself for listening, he waited.

To take his mind from doubts and self-flagellation, he tried to listen to the eunuch. The fat man now murmured of the day's happenings in Ayodhya, such as he thought might interest his master.

"... And finding his favorite wife in the embrace of her two lovers, each a groom from his own stables, Jharim Kar slew the men and flogged his wife. He slew as well three servants who were witness, but the tale is already laughed at in the bazaars, lord. In the forenoon Shahal Amir was slain on the outskirts of the city, by bandits it is said, but two of his wives ..."

Sighing, Naipal let the man's continued burblings pass his ears unheard. Another time the matter of Jharim Kar would have been pleasing, though not of prime importance. A score of deft manipulations to lead a woman to folly and a husband to discovery of that folly, with the result that a man who once gathered other lords around him was now laughed at. A man could not be at once a leader and the butt of bawdy laughter. It was not that Naipal bore Jharim Kar any animus. The nobleman had simply attracted too many others to his side, creating what could have grown into a island of stability in a sea of shifting loyalties and intrigues. The wizard could not allow that. Greater intrigues and increasing turmoil were necessary to his plans. Bhandarkar guarded himself well against his wizard; kings who trusted too much did not long rule, and this king's toenail parings or hair clippings were burned as soon as cut. But Bhandarkar would die, if not from so esoteric a means as he feared, and without his strong hand, turmoil would become chaos, a chaos on which Naipal would impose a new order. Not in his own name, of course. But he would pull the strings, and the king he put on the throne would not even know he danced at another's will.

Lost in dreams of the future, Naipal was startled by the sudden throbbing warmth on his chest. Not quite believing, he clutched at the black opal beneath his robes. Through layers of silk the stone pulsed against his palm. Masrok signaled!

"Be silent!" he roared, throwing the goblet at the eunuch's head for emphasis. The round-faced man snapped his mouth shut as though fearing for his tongue. "Go to Ashok," Naipal ordered. "Tell him that all I have commanded is to be readied at once. At once!"

"I run to obey, lord." The eunuch began shuffling backward on his knees, bumping his forehead to the floor.

"Then run, Katar take you!" Naipal shouted. "Or you will find there is more than can be taken from a man than you have lost!" Babbling terrified compliance, the eunuch scrambled to his feet, still genuflecting, and fled. Naipal's glare swept from the sleek nudity of the dancers to the ivory screen hiding the musicians. At his command for silence, all had frozen, hardly daring to breathe. "Play!" he barked. "Dance! You will all be beaten for laziness!"

The music burst forth desperately, and the dancers writhed in a frenzy to please, but Naipal dismissed them from his awareness and waved away the serving girls. His heart seemed to beat in time with the throbbing of the opal against his hand. The stone was all his mind had room for, the sign from Masrok that the demon should be summoned, and what that must mean. Ashok, chief among the tongueless ones, would quickly prepare the chamber below. In such terror was the wizard held by those who served the gray chambers that he knew they would literally run themselves to death to obey his slightest wish, let alone a command. It could not be done quickly enough to suit him, however. Impatience bubbled in him like the surface of a geyser before eruption.

Able to wait no longer, Naipal flung himself to his feet and stalked from the chamber. Behind him dancers and musicians continued their vain strivings, fearful now to cease without his express command.

To his bedchamber Naipal went first, to fetch the golden coffer containing the demon-wrought dagger. That must be in Masrok's view, not mentioned this time, but no less a reminder that even a demon could be slain.

When he reached the gray-domed chamber beneath the palace, the wizard nodded in satisfaction without even realizing that he had done so. A large, tightly woven basket, its lid lashed firmly in place, stood near his worktable. A bronze gong with a padded mallet hanging from its teakwood frame had been placed near the iron latticework set in one wall.

Naipal paused by the bars. From the door that was part of the iron mesh a ramp led down into a round pit lit by rush torches set high on the walls. On the sand-covered floor of the pit a score of swords in various patterns made an untidy heap. Directly opposite the ramp a massive iron-bound door let into the pit.

For a single test he had used the fires of the *khorassani* to carve out the pit and the cells and connecting corridors beyond. A single test but most necessary, for he had to test the truth of the ancient writings. He did not believe they lied, but none knew better than he that there were degrees of truth, and he must know the exact degree of this truth. But other things must be done first. Beneath his robes the black opal still pulsed against his chest.

Denying his own need for haste, Naipal took greater care than ever before in setting the nine *khorassani* on their golden tripods. Anticipation burned in him like fanned coals as the tenth stone, blacker than midnight, was placed. He settled on the cushions before it, and once more the ancient incantation rolled against the canescent walls.

"*E'las eloyhim! Maraath savinday! Khora mar! Khora mar!*"

Once more bars of fire leaped up. The stones blazed like imprisoned suns, and a pathway was opened to realms unknowable to mortal man.

"Masrok," Naipal called, "I summon you!"

The winds of infinity blew. Thunder roared and the huge obsidian demon floated within the fiery cage. And with it floated another figure, that of a man in armor of studded leather and a spiked helm of a kind unseen in Vendhya for more than a thousand years. Two swords of unbelievable antiquity—one long and straight, one shorter and curved— hung at the armored figure's sides. Almost did Naipal laugh with joy. Success! He did not realize he had spoken aloud until the demon replied in tones like a storm.

"Success you call it, O man? I call it betrayal! Betrayal heaped upon betrayal!"

"Surely a small betrayal only," Naipal said. "And freedom is your eventual reward." A shudder passed through the demon, and its eight arms shook until the wizard feared it might attempt to hurl one of its weapons at him, or even try to fling itself through the flaming barrier. He laid a nervous hand on the golden coffer.

"You speak of what you do not know, O man! A small betrayal? To do your bidding I was forced to slay one of my other selves! For the first time since time itself began, one of the Sivani is slain, and by my hand!"

"And you fear the vengeance of the other two? But surely they do not know, or you would not be here."

"And how long before they discover the deed, O man?"

"Fear not," the mage said. "I will find a way to protect you." Before the demon could speak again, Naipal shouted. "Go, Masrok! I command it!"

With a deafening roar the demon was gone, and only the ancient warrior floated within the bars of the fire.

Now Naipal did permit himself to laugh. Demons, it seemed, could indeed be enmeshed as easily as men.

Swiftly he set about lowering the sorcerous barrier, a task more difficult in some ways than erecting it had been. At last it was done, and he hurried to examine the figure that now stood precisely centered on the arcane pattern in the floor. No breath stirred the ancient warrior's chest, and no light shone in his dark, staring eyes, yet his dusky skin seemed to glow with life. Curious, Naipal touched the warrior's cheek and grunted. Despite what seemed living suppleness to the eye, it was like touching leather stretched tight over wood.

"Now," Naipal murmured to himself.

From the myriad of crystal beakers and vials on his worktable, he chose out five, pouring small, precisely measured portions of their contents into a mortar wrought from the skull of a virgin murdered by her mother. Four of those ingredients were so rare that he begrudged even the tiny amounts needed. With the thigh bone of the virgin's mother for a pestle, he ground and mixed until he had a black paste.

The mage hesitated before turning to the large wicker basket. Then, steeling himself, he tore open the lashings that held its lid. Pity rose in him as he looked down on the ragged boy within, bound and gagged, frozen with fear. Forcefully he stifled emotion and lifted the child from the basket. The small form trembled as he laid it before the shape of the warrior. He could feel the child's eyes on him, though he tried to ignore them.

Hastily now, as if to be done with the thing, Naipal fetched the foul-made mortar. Dipping the little finger of his left hand into the black paste, he drew a symbol on the forehead of the bound child, then again on that of the warrior. The residue he scrubbed carefully from his finger with a cloth.

The warrior, the child and the largest of the *khorassani* lay in a straight line. Naipal lowered himself to the cushions to invoke powers not summoned before.

"Mon'draal un'tar, maran vi'endar!"

The words were softly spoken, yet the walls of the chamber chimed in resonance with them. Thrice Naipal repeated the chant and at the third speaking, rays of light, cold and pale as mountain snow, lanced from the ebon stone, one to strike the dark symbol on the warrior's forehead, the other that on the child's. On and on Naipal spoke the incantation. A third icy beam sprang into being, linking the two symbols directly. The child arched his back and screamed, unable to move his head from beneath the glittering point of that sorcerous triangle. Naipal cried the words loudly to drown out the scream. A whine shimmered from the light like the string of a zither drawn too tight.

Abruptly all was silence; the rays of light vanished. Naipal expelled a long breath. It was done. Getting to his feet, he approached the lifeless body of the child. He had eyes only for that small form.

"You have been freed from a life of misery, pain and hunger," he said. "Your spirit has gone to dwell in a purer realm. Only life was taken from you. It had to be a young life, not yet fully formed." He paused, then added, "I would use the children of nobles and of the wealthy if I could." Funeral fires fit for a lord, he decided. Such would he give this nameless waif.

Slowly his gaze rose to the leather-armored figure. Still no breath stirred in that body. Was there light in the eyes? "Can you hear me?" he demanded. There was no reply. "Step forward!" Obediently the warrior took one pace forward and stood again as a statue. "Of course," Naipal mused. "You are without volition of your own. You obey me, who gave you life again, and only me, unless I command you to heed another. Good. It is as the writings said. So far. Follow me!"

Maintaining the exact distance between them, the warrior obeyed. Naipal unlocked the door in the iron latticework and motioned. The other stepped through, and the wizard closed and relocked the barred door. It was good, Naipal thought, that spoken commands were not necessary. The writings had been unclear.

A hollow tone boomed as Naipal struck the gong with the padded mallet. In the pit the iron-bound door swung open. Moving cautiously, twenty men appeared, eyes going immediately to Naipal and the motionless figure at the head of the ramp. Behind them the door closed silently. When they saw the swords piled on the sand, there was but a moment's hesitation before they rushed for the weapons. The men were as varied as the blades they seized, wearing garb ranging from filthy rags to some noble's cast-off silken finery. They had not been randomly chosen. The test would not be complete then. In that pit were brigands, bandits, deserters from the army, each one familiar with a sword. Freedom and gold had been promised to those who survived. Naipal thought he might even honor the promise.

"Kill them," he commanded.

Even as the words left his mouth, six of the ruffians charged howling up the ramp, blades swinging. His face an expressionless mask, the leather-clad warrior drew his archaic swords and moved smoothly to meet them. The six attacked with a frenzy driven by the promise of freedom; the warrior fought with lightning precision. When the form in ancient armor moved on, a single head rolling down the ramp before it, six corpses littered the way behind.

In the pit two of the deserters hastily chivvied those remaining into two lines as though they were infantry on a battlefield. The warrior neither slowed his approach nor altered his stride. The two ranks of desperate men tensed to meet him. But a pace short of them, the warrior suddenly leaped to his right, attacking. The rogues Naipal had gathered may have thought their formation made them infantry, but they had no shields to protect them. Two fell, bloodied and twitching, before the ranks could wheel under the deserters' shouted instructions. The resurrected warrior did not wait for them, however. As the lines pivoted, he leaped back the other way and dashed into their midst from the flank. The deserters' small order dissolved in a melee of hacking steel, welling blood and screaming men, each fighting frantically for himself alone, each dying as the ancient warrior's flashing blade reached him.

When the leather-armored figure slit the throat of the last kicking wretch, Naipal breathed deep in wondering satisfaction. Twenty corpses littered the crimson-splashed sand, and the reborn warrior stood unharmed. In truth there were rents in the studded leather of his armor, and his teeth could be seen through a gash that laid open his cheek, but not a drop of blood fell from him. He moved among the bodies, making sure that each was actually dead, as though no blade had ever touched him.

Turning his back on the scene below, the wizard sagged against the bars, laughing until he wheezed for breath. Everything the ancient writings had claimed was true. The wounds would heal quickly. Nothing could slay the warrior he had resurrected.

More than two thousand years earlier, a conqueror called Orissa had carved a score of small nations and city-states into the kingdom of Vendhya, with himself as its first king. And when King Orissa died, an army of twenty thousand warriors was entombed with him, a royal bodyguard for the afterlife, preserved so perfectly by intricate thaumaturgies that though they no longer lived, neither were they dead as ordinary men died. With the proper rituals, life could be restored after a fashion, and an army that could not die would march again. All that was necessary was to find the centuries-lost tomb.

"And that," Naipal laughed, loud and mocking, "is all but done, is it not, Masrok, my faithful servant?"

Success so filled him with ebullience that the stupefying fear of the past few days was swept away. Certainly enough time had passed. On whatever waters that vessel rode, if it was near enough to threaten him when he was so close to his goals, it must have made shore by now. And if it had, surely whatever danger it carried had been dealt with by his myrmidons. He would admit no other thought, not when so many victories were already his on this day.

With a firm hand he raised the carven ivory lid and brushed back the silken coverings. Black was the surface of the mirror, and dotted with tiny points of light. It took a moment for Naipal to realize that he saw a vast array of campfires, viewed from a great height. If one small ship had threatened him before, now it seemed that an army did. For his days of fear he was repaid with more fear, and with uncertainty. Had the danger of the ship been disposed of, or had it been transmogrified to this? Was this a new threat, surpassing the old?

Long into the night Naipal's howls of rage echoed in the vast dome.

XI

When the first paleness of dawn appeared on the horizon, Conan was already up and saddling the stallion. The hollow thunk of axes chopping wood drifted to him from the bank of the Zaporoska, not half a league off and lined with tall trees. He shook his head at the Khitan merchant's camels, sharing the picket line with the smugglers' horses. Camels were filthy beasts, to his mind, both in habits and smell, and untrustworthy besides. He would rather have a horse at any time, or even a mule.

"Stinking beast," Hordo grumbled, slapping a camel's flank to make it move aside. Coughing from the cloud of dust he had raised, the one-eyed man edged into the space created to reach his own mount. "And dirty too."

"Have you looked at the goods they carry?" Conan asked quietly.

"I saw no chests, if that's what you mean. We cross the river this morning, you know."

"Pay attention, Hordo. It is all carpets and velvet and tapestries, as the Khitan said. But the value of it, Hordo." The big Cimmerian had been a thief in his youth, and his eye could still gauge the price of anything worth stealing. " 'Tis mainly of the third quality, with only a little of the second. I should not think it worth carrying to Arenjun, much less all the way to Vendhya."

"Distance and rarity increase value," Kang Hou said, approaching silently on felt-slippered feet. His hands were tucked into the sleeves of a pale-blue velvet tunic, this one embroidered with swallows in flight. "It is clear you are no merchant, Patil. The Iranistani carpet that will

422

barely procure a profit in Turan will bring fifty times as much in Vendhyan. Do you think the finest Vendhyan carpets go to Turan? Those grace the floors of Vendhyan nobles, yet a far greater price may be obtained by taking a carpet of the second quality to Aghrapur than by selling one of the first quality in Ayodhya."

"I am no merchant," Conan agreed, backing the black Bhalkhana away from the picket line, "nor wish to be. Yet I am as eager to reach Vendhya as you. If you will excuse me, Kang Hou, I will see when the caravan is to move on. And what else I can discover," he added for Hordo's ears.

Conan rode through the encampment slowly, for though he was indeed eager to travel onward, also did he wish to give his eyes a chance to roam, to see if they might perchance light on some chests like those used for shipping tea.

The caravan was in fact three encampments, though the three camps butting one against the other, and even larger than Conan had supposed. Three and forty merchants, with their servants, attendants and animal tenders, made up nearly the thousand people he thought the entire caravan contained, numbering among them Vendhyans and Khitans, Zamorans and Turanians, Kothians and Iranistanis. Men scurried to collapse and fold tents, to load bales and bundles and wicker panniers on camels and mules under the watchful eyes of finely-clad merchants, who eyed each other as well with surreptitious suspicion, wondering if some other had cut a sharper bargain or aimed for the same markets. Conan received his own share of speculative glances, and more than one merchant called nervously for his guards as the tall Cimmerian rode past.

Vendhyan nobles who had accompanied the *wazam* to Aghrapur had the second encampment, and it was odd enough for a second glance even if the chests were not there. Conan's first thought was that he had stumbled onto a traveling fair, for well over half a thousand people surrounded those gaily striped and pennoned pavilions, being lowered now by turbaned servants. Here, too, were men from many lands, but these were jugglers keeping a dozen balls in the air at once, and acrobats balancing atop limber poles. A bear danced to a flute, tumblers leaped and twisted, and strolling players plucked lute and zither. Skull-capped men in flowing robes and long beards moved through the seeming carnival as if it did not exist, talking in twos and threes, though in truth two of them, screaming insults, were being held from each other's throats by one who, stripped to the waist and with bulging muscles oiled, appeared to be a strongman.

The third encampment had already been struck and taken to the river, where axemen were building rafts for the crossing, but Conan had no intention of approaching that one in any case. It was not that he could imagine no way the chests might have ended up in the baggage of Karim Singh, *wazam* of Vendhya, but five hundred hard-eyed Vendhyan cavalry provided steep odds. Their brigantine hauberks and turbaned helms with mail neck guards were much like those of the Vendhyans on the beach, but these men were very obviously aware of just how far into disputed territory they were. They rode like cats, ready to jump at a sound, and their long-bladed lances swung down if anyone came within a hundred paces.

Abruptly something whistled past Conan's face, close enough for him to feel the breeze. Crossbow bolt, a part of his mind told him even as he instinctively dropped as low as the high pommel would permit and dug his heels into the big black's flanks. The stallion bounded forward and was at a dead run in three strides. Conan sensed rather than saw other quarrels streak by, and once his saddle was jolted by a hit.

As the river drew closer, he finally pulled up and looked back. Nothing in the breaking camp appeared out of the ordinary. No crossbows were in evidence; no one even looked in his direction. Dismounting, he checked the black over. The animal was uninjured and eager to run farther, but in the high cantle of the saddle there was a quarrel thicker than his finger. Conan felt a grim chill. A hand-breadth higher and it would have been in his back. At least there could no longer be any doubt that the chests were in the caravan.

"You there!" came a shout from the direction of the river. "You, Patil!"

Conan looked up and saw Torio, the caravan guard captain, riding toward him. A quick tug pulled the quarrel free. Letting it fall to the ground, he mounted and rode to meet the other man, who began to speak immediately.

"Twice each year for ten years I have made the journey from Aghrapur to Ayodhya and back, and every time there is something new. Now comes something in its own way stranger than any I have seen before."

"And what is this strange thing?"

"His Most Puissant Excellency, Karim Singh, *wazam* of Vendhya, Adviser to the Elephant, wishes your presence, Patil. I mean no offense, but you are obviously no noble, and Karim Singh rarely admits the existence of anyone lower. Why should he suddenly wish to see you, of whom it is most unlikely he has ever heard before?"

"Adviser to the Elephant?" Conan said, partly because he could think of no possible answer to the question and partly from amusement. He had heard of the great gray beasts and hoped to see one on this journey.

"One of the King of Vendhya's titles is the Elephant," Torio replied. "It is no more foolish than Yildiz being called the Golden Eagle, I suppose, or any of the other things kings call themselves."

"Where is this Adviser to the Elephant?"

"Across the river already, and I would watch my tongue around him if I did not want to lose it. That is his pavilion." Torio pointed to a large sprawling tent of golden silk on the opposite bank, encircled by a hundred Vendhyan lancers facing outward. "He cares not at all if we are held up because he wants to talk to you, but his party must be the first in line of march. Karim Singh will breathe no man's dust." The guard captain paused, frowning at nothing, occasionally seeming to study Conan from the corner of his eye. "Mine is a difficult position, Patil. I am responsible for the safety of all in the caravan but must offend no one. What who has said to whom, who seeks advantage and where, these things become important. All the dangers do not come from outside, from Kuigars or Zuagirs. A man can earn silver, and as the sums are not so large as others might offer, only silence as to who was told is required, not total loyalty. Do you understand?"

"No," Conan replied truthfully, and the other man stiffened as though struck.

"Very well then, Patil. Play the game alone if you wish, but remember that only the very powerful can play alone and survive." Jerking the reins viciously, Torio trotted away.

The man belonged with the Vendhyan nobles and the jugglers, Conan thought. He spouted gibberish and was offended when he was not understood.

The tree-lined riverbank was a scene of sweating and shouting. With a crash another thick bole toppled, and laborers rushed with their axes to hew away limbs so it could be lashed to the large raft half-finished at the water's edge. A complement of Vendhyan lancers was leading the horses onto another raft, some fifty feet in length, while a third was in mid-river, making its way along one or a pair of thick cables bowed by the slow current of the Zaporoska. Another heavy cable was already being fastened in place for the raft under construction. Ropes attached to the rafts led to the motive power for the journey in both directions: two score of ragged slaves on either bank for each raft.

The Vendhyan cavalrymen stared at Conan, black eyes unblinking and expressionless, as he led the stallion among them onto the raft. They were tall men, but he was half a head taller than the biggest. Some tried to stand straighter. The only sound on the raft was the occasional stamp of a hoof. Conan could feel the tension in the soldiers. Any one of them would take a direct look as a challenge and being obviously ignored as an insult. As he was not looking for a fight before he even got across the river, the Cimmerian involved himself with pretending to check his saddle girth.

The raft lurched and swayed, swinging out into the current as a strain was taken on the two ropes. It was then that Conan found something to look at in earnest, something on the shore behind them. Well away from the water, Torio rode slowly, peering at the ground. Looking for what he had thrown down, Conan realized. He watched the guard captain until the raft touched the far bank.

XII

Seen close, the huge tent of golden silk was impressive, supported by more than a score of tent poles. The hundred Vendhyan lancers could have fit inside easily, and their horses as well.

The circle of mounted men opened before Conan, seemingly without command. As he rode through, it closed again. He wished he did not feel that those steel-tipped lances were the bars of a cage.

Turbaned servants rushed to meet the Cimmerian, one to take the stallion's bridle, another to hold his stirrup. At the entrance to the pavilion stood a servant with cool, damp towels on a silver tray, to wipe his hands and face. Still another knelt and tried to lave his sandaled feet.

"Enough," Conan growled, tossing back a crumpled towel. "Where is your master?"

A plump man appeared in the entrance, a spray of egret plumes on his large turban of gold and green. Beneath the edge of his gold-brocade tunic peeked the pointed, curling toes of silken slippers. Conan thought this was the *wazam* until the man bowed deeply and said, "Pray follow me, master."

Within, a large chamber had been created by hangings of cloth of gold and floors of Vendhyan carpets fit for the palace of a king. Incense lay thick and heavy in the air. Hidden musicians began to play on flute and cithern as Conan entered, and five women, so heavily veiled and swathed in silk that he could see nothing but their dark eyes, began to dance.

Reclining on a rainbow of silken cushions was a tall man, his narrow olive face topped by a turban of scarlet silk. The servant's snowy plumes were duplicated here in diamonds and pearls. About his neck hung a thick necklace of gold set with emeralds as large as pigeon's eggs, and every finger wore a ring of rubies and sapphires. His dark eyes were deep-set and harder than any of the gems he wore.

"Are *you* Karim Singh?" Conan asked.

"I am." The seated man's deep voice held a note of shock, but he said, "Your lack of the proper forms is strange, but amusing. You may continue it. You are the one called Patil. It is a name of my country and seems odd on one so obviously from distant lands."

"There are many lands," Conan said, "and many names. The name Patil serves me."

The *wazam* smiled as though the Cimmerian had said something clever. "Sit. One must endure the deprivations of travel, but the wine, at least, is tolerable."

Seating himself cross-legged on the cushions, Conan ignored silver trays of candied dates and pickled quail eggs proffered by servants who seemed to appear and vanish by magic, so obsequiously silent were they. He did accept a goblet of heavy gold, ringed by a wide band of amethysts. The wine had a smell of perfume and tasted of honey.

"Word travels quickly," Karim Singh went on. "I soon heard about you, a pale-skinned giant with eyes like. . . . Most disconcerting, those eyes." He did not sound in the least disconcerted. "I know much of the western world, you see, though it is a veiled land to many of my countrymen. Before journeying to Aghrapur to make treaty with King Yildiz, I studied what has been written. While there, I listened. I know of the pale barbarians of the distant north, fierce warriors, stark slayers, ruthless. Such men can be useful."

For the first time in what seemed a very great while, Conan felt he was on ground he knew, if ground he did not particularly like. "I have taken service as far as Ayodhya," he said. "After that my plans are uncertain."

"Ah, yes. The Khitan. He is a spy, of course."

Conan almost choked on the wine. "The merchant?"

"In Vendhya all foreigners are considered spies. It is safer that way." The intent look in Karim Singh's eyes made the Cimmerian wonder for whom he himself was considered to be spying. "But there are spies, and there are spies. One who spies on a spy, for instance. Not all in my land have Vendhya's best interests in their hearts. It might be of interest to me to know to whom in Vendhya the Khitan speaks, and what he says. It might interest me enough to be worth gold."

"I am not a spy," Conan said tightly. "Not for anyone." He felt a moment's confusion as the *wazam* gave a pleased smile.

"Very good, Patil. It is seldom one finds a man faithful to the first buyer."

There was a patronizing tone to his words that made Conan's eyes grow cold. He thought of explaining, but he did not think this man would recognize the concept of honor if it were thrust in his face. As he cast about for a way to change the subject, the Cimmerian's gaze fell on the dancers and his jaw dropped. Opaque veils still covered the faces of the five women to the eyes, but the other swathings of silk now littered the carpets beneath their feet. All of them. Supple curves of rounded olive flesh spun across the chamber, now leaping like gazelles with stretching legs, now writhing as though their bones had been replaced with serpents.

"You appreciate my trinkets?" Karim Singh asked. "They are trophies, after a fashion. Certain powerful lords long opposed me. Then each discovered he was not so powerful as he thought, discovered, too, that even for a lord, life itself could have a price. A favorite daughter, for instance. Each personally laid that price at my feet. Are they not lovely?"

"Lovely," Conan agreed hoarsely. He strove for a smoother tone, lest the other take his surprise for a lack of sophistication. "And I have no doubt their faces will be equally as lovely when the final veil is dropped."

Karim Singh stiffened momentarily. "I forget that you are an outlander. These women are of my *purdhana*. For them to unveil their faces before anyone other than myself would shame them greatly, and me as well."

Considering the soft nudities before him, Conan nodded. "I see," he said slowly. He did not see at all. Different lands, different customs, but this tended toward madness. Taking a deep breath, he set down the goblet and rose to his feet. "I must go now. Kang Hou will soon be crossing the river."

"Of course. And when you reach Ayodhya and no longer serve him, I will send for you. There is always need for a man of loyalty, for a ruthless slayer untroubled by civilized restraints."

Conan did not trust himself to speak. He jerked his head in what he hoped might pass for a bow and stalked out.

Outside the tent the plump man with the egret plumes on his turban was waiting, a silver tray in his hands. "A token from my master," he said, bowing.

There was a leather purse on the tray. It was soft and buttery in Conan's palm and he could feel the coins within. He did not open it to count them or to see if they were gold or silver.

"Thank your master for his generosity," he said, then tossed the purse back to the startled man. "A token from me. Distribute it among the other servants."

He could feel the plump fellow's eyes on his back as he strode to his horse—the two servants were still there; one to hold the bridle, one to hold the stirrup for him to mount—but he did not care. If Karim Singh was insulted by the gesture, so be it. He had had all of His Puissant Excellency, the Adviser to the Elephant, that he could stomach.

The steel-tipped circle opened once more, and Conan rode toward the water. Cursing camel drivers used long switches to drive their laden charges from a raft held tightly against the bank by the slaves on the tow rope. All three of the rafts were in service now. One, loaded with Vendhyan nobles, was in mid-river, and the last, crammed with camels and merchants, was close behind. Two milling masses, merchants in one, nobles and their odd companions in the other, showed the crossings had begun soon after he had reached this side. The far bank was crowded with those waiting.

The Cimmerian did not see Kang Hou or any of the others. If he crossed back, however, it was just as possible as not that they would pass each other on the river. He drew rein where he could watch all three landing places.

As the black stood flicking its tail at flies, stamping its feet with impatience to run, a Vendhyan cavalryman rode up beside him. The silk and velvet of the Vendhyan's garb marked him as an officer, the gem-studded scabbard of his sword and the gilding of his turbaned helmet as an officer of rank. An arrogant sneer was on his face and his eyes were tinged with cruelty. He did not speak, only stared at the big Cimmerian in fierce silence.

He had sought to avoid a fight once this morning, Conan told himself. He could easily do so again. After all, the man but looked at him. Only that. Just looked. Lowering, Conan kept his own gaze on the approaching rafts. The Vendhyan was alone, therefore it had nothing to do with the incident of the purse. In his experience, men like the *wazam* did not reply to perceived insults in such small ways. But then again, this was beginning not to seem so small. Conan's jaw tightened.

"You are the man Patil," the Vendhyan barked suddenly. "You are not Vendhyan."

"I know who and what I am," Conan growled. "Who and what are you?"

"I am Prince Kandar, commanding the bodyguard of the *wazam* of Vendhya. And you will guard your tongue or lose it!"

"I have heard a warning much like that once already today," Conan replied flatly, "but my tongue is still mine, and I will not let go of it easily."

"Bold words," Kandar sneered, "for an outlander with the eyes of a *pan-kur*."

"The eyes of a what?"

"A *pan-kur*. The spawn of a human woman's mating with a demon. The more ignorant among my men believe such bring misfortune with their presence, and evil with their touch. They would have slain you already had I permitted it."

There was a shifting in the Vendhyan's eyes as he spoke. The more ignorant of his men? Conan smiled and leaned toward him. "As I said, I know who and what I am."

Kandar gave a start, and his horse danced a step sideways, but he mastered his face and his mount quickly. "Vendhya is a dangerous land for a foreigner, whoever, or whatever, he is. A foreigner who wished to have no fear of what lay around the next turning or what might come in the night would do well to seek a shielding hand, to cultivate a patron in high places."

"And what would this seeking and cultivating require?" Conan asked dryly.

The Vendhyan moved his horse closer and dropped his voice conspiratorially. "That certain information, the contents of certain conversations, be passed on to the patron."

"I told Karim Singh," Conan replied, biting off each word, "and now I tell you, I will not spy on Kang Hou."

"The Khitan? What are you saying? The *wazam* has an interest in *him*? Bah! I care nothing for merchants!"

The Cimmerian felt as though the other's confusion were contagious. "If not Kang Hou, then who in Zandru's Nine Hells . . ." He paused at a wild thought. "Karim Singh?"

"Aaah," said Kandar, suddenly all urbanity. "That might be pleasing."

"I begin to believe it all," Conan muttered in tones far from belief. "I begin to believe you Vendhyans actually could sign a treaty with Yildiz on one day and kill the High Admiral of Turan the next."

The smoothness that had come to the Vendhyan was as suddenly swept away. He clutched Conan's arm with a swordsman's iron grip, and his teeth were bared in a snarl. "Who says this? Who speaks this lie?"

"Everyone in Sultanapur," Conan said quietly. "I suspect, everyone in Turan. Now take your hand from my arm before I cut it off."

Behind Kandar the raft loaded with nobles had reached the bank, and men were streaming off. Two Vendhyan women riding sidesaddle walked their horses toward Conan and the prince. One was plainly garbed and veiled so that only her eyes showed. The other, riding in advance, had a scarf of sheer red silk over her raven hair, with pearls worked into her tresses, but she wore no veil. Necklaces and bracelets of gold and emeralds adorned her and there were rubies and sapphires on her fingers.

As Kandar, glaring at Conan, opened his mouth, the unveiled woman spoke in a low musical tone. "How pleasant to see you, Kandar. I had thought you avoided me of late."

The Vendhyan prince went rigid. For an instant his eyes stared through Conan, then he rasped, "We will speak again, you and I." Without ever once looking around or acknowledging the women's presence, Kandar kicked his horse to a gallop, spurring toward the *wazam*'s pavilion, which was already being taken down.

Conan was not sorry to see him go, especially not when he was replaced by so lovely a creature as the jewel-bedecked woman. Her skin was dusky satin, and her sloe eyes were large pools in which a man might willingly lose himself. And those dark, liquid eyes were studying him with as much interest as he studied their owner. He returned her smile.

"It seems Kandar does not like you," he said. "I think I like anyone he does not."

The woman's laugh was as musical as her voice. "On the contrary, Kandar likes me much too much." She saw his confusion and laughed again. "He wants me for his *purdhana*. Once he went so far as to try to have me kidnapped."

"When I want a woman, I do not ride away without so much as looking at her." He kept his eyes on her face so she would know it was not of Kandar he spoke at all.

"He has cause. My tirewoman, Alyna," she waved a negligent hand toward the heavily veiled woman, "is his sister."

"His sister!" Conan exclaimed, and once more she laughed. The veiled woman stirred silently on her saddle.

"Ah, I see you are bewildered that the sister of a prince could be my slave. Alas, Alyna dabbled with spies and was to face the headsman's sword until I purchased her life. I then held a masque to which Kandar came, intending to press his suit yet again. For some reason, when he discovered Alyna among the dancing girls, he all but ran from my palace. Such a simple way to rid myself of the bother of him."

Conan stared at that beautiful, sweetly smiling face, appearing so open and even innocent, and only what he had already seen and heard that morning allowed him to credit her words. "You Vendhyans seem to have a liking for striking at your enemies through others. Do none of you ever confront an opponent?"

Her laughter was tinkling bells. "You Westerners are so direct, Patil. Those Turanians! They think themselves devious. They are childlike."

He blinked at that. Childlike? The Turanians? Then something else she had said struck him. "You know my name."

"I know that you call yourself Patil. One must needs be deaf not to hear of a man such as yourself, calling himself by a name of Vendhyan. You interest me."

Her gaze was like a caress running over his broad shoulders and chest, even down to his lean hips and thick-muscled thighs. Many other women had looked at him in like fashion and betimes he enjoyed it. This time he felt like a stallion in the auction barns. "And do you want me to spy on someone, too?" he asked gruffly.

"As I said," she smiled. "Direct. And childlike."

"I am no child, woman," he growled. "And I want no more of Vendhyan deviousness."

"Do you know why so many of King Bhandarkar's court accompanied the *wazam* to Turan? Not as his retinue, as the Turanians seemed to think. For us it was a new land to be looted, in a manner of speaking. I found jugglers and acrobats who will seem new and fresh when they perform at my palace in Ayodhya. I bring a dancing bear with me and several scholars. Though I must say the philosophers of Turan do not compare with those of Khitai."

"Do none of you speak straight out? What has this to do with me?"

"In Vendhya," she said, "the enjoyment of life is a way of life. Men of the court give hunts and revels, though the last are often no more than drunken debauches. In any case, neither is proper for a woman of breeding. Yet for every decision made by men on horseback while lancing wild boars, two are made in the palace of a noblewoman. You may ask how mere women compete with the lords and princes. We gather about us scholars and men of ideas, the finest musicians, the most talented poets, the best artists, whether in stone or metal or paint. The newest plays are performed in our palaces and there may be found strange visitors from far-off, mysterious lands. Nor does it hurt that our serving wenches are chosen for their beauty, though unlike the men, we require discretion in their use."

Conan's face had become more and more grim as he listened. Now he exploded. "That is your 'interest' in me? I am to be a dancing bear or a montebank?"

"I do not believe the women of the court will find you a dancing bear," she said, "although you are nearly as large as one." Suddenly she was looking at him through long kohled lashes, and the tip of her tongue touched a full lip. "Nor can I see you as a montebank," she added throatily.

"Co—Patil!" came a cry, and Conan saw Hordo leading his horse up from the river.

"I must go," the Cimmerian told her roughly, and she nodded as though in some manner she was satisfied.

"Seek my tent tonight, O giant who calls himself Patil. My 'interest' in you is not done with." A smile swept away the seductress to be replaced by the innocent again. "You have not asked my name. I am the Lady Vyndra." And a flick of her gold-mounted riding whip sent her horse leaping away, the veiled woman at her heels.

Behind Hordo, Kang Hou's servants were driving the merchant's camels ashore, aided by the smugglers. One of the humped beasts knelt on the bank while Hasan and Shamil solicitously helped Chin Kou and Kuie Hsi into tented *kajawahs*, conveyances that hung like panniers on the animal's sides.

"Pretty wench," Hordo commented, staring after the galloping Vyndra. "Rides well, too." He looked around to see if anyone was close by, then dropped his voice. "Did you find the chests?"

Conan shook his head. "But they are here. Someone tried to kill me."

"Always a good way to begin a day," Hordo said dryly. "Did you discover anything at all?"

"Three men tried to hire me as a spy and that 'pretty wench' wants to add me to her menagerie."

"Your humor is beyond me, Cimmerian."

"I also found out that my eyes are demon-spawned, and beyond that I learned that Vendhya is a madhouse."

The one-eyed man grunted as he swung into the saddle. "The first I've told you before myself. And the second is known to all. It looks as if we were finally moving."

The *wazam*'s party—Conan remembered Torio saying it had to be

first in the line of march—was beginning to stretch out in a line somewhat east of due south, with Vendhyan lancers in two columns to either
side. Karim Singh himself was in an ornate litter of ebony and gold,
borne between four horses. An arched canopy of gleaming white silk
stretched above the palanquin and hangings of golden gossamer draped
the sides. Kandar rode beside the litter, bending low out of his saddle
to speak urgently to the man within.

"If they tried to kill you," Hordo went on, "at least you have stirred
them up."

"Perhaps I have," Conan said. He pulled his gaze away from the
wazam's litter. "Let us join Kang Hou and the others, Hordo. There
are hours of light left for traveling yet today."

Night and the depths of the earth were necessary for some things. Some doings could not bear the light of day or exposure to witness of the open sky. As it did so often of late, night found Naipal in the gray-domed chamber far below his palace. The air had the very smell of necromancy, a faint, sickly-sweet taint of decay blended with the indefinable yet unmistakable hellish odor of evil. The smell hung about Naipal, a thing it had not done before his last deeds in that chamber, but he did not notice nor would he have cared had he.

He swung from contemplation of the resurrected warrior, standing as still as stone against the canescent wall in the same spot to which Naipal had at last commanded him on the previous night. The wizard's eyes went to his worktable, skipping quickly over the chest of carved ivory. There, in crystal-stoppered flasks, were the five ingredients necessary for the transfer of life, the total quantity of them that he possessed. In King Orissa's tomb beneath the lost city of Maharashtra stood twenty thousand deathless warriors. An undying, ever-conquering army. And he could give life to perhaps twenty.

With a wordless snarl, he began to pace. The ancient mages who prepared Orissa's tomb had complied with the King's commands to set him an ever-lasting bodyguard. But those thaumaturges feared the uses to which that bodyguard could be put if ever it were wakened, and they planned well. Only one of the five ingredients could be obtained in Vendhya. The others, chosen partly because they were little-used in sorceries, could be found only in lands little more than legend in Vendhya even two thousand years later. He had made arrangements, of course, but of what use were they when disaster loomed over his head?

Forcing his eyes to the ornate ivory chest, he clenched his fists and glared as though he wished to smash it, and he was not sure that he did not. When finally he had dragged himself from the chamber on the night before, it had been as one fleeing. Creeping through the corridors of his own palace like a thief, he told himself that this was not the paralysis returning, not the fear. He had conquered that. Merely he needed to rest, to refresh himself. Musicians were summoned, and food and wine, but all tasted like sawdust, and the flutes and citherns clawed at his nerves. He ordered cooks and musicians both to be flogged. By twos and threes the women of his *purdhana* were brought to him and returned, weeping and welted for their failures to please. Five times in the course of the day he had commanded that ten thousand *pice* be distributed to the poor in his name, but even that produced no uplifting of his spirits. Now he was back in his sorcery-carved chambers in the earth's bowels. Here he would deal at last with the source of his danger, whatever or wherever it was.

His hands reached toward the flat ivory box . . . and stopped at the chime of a bell. Quizzically his head swiveled toward the sound. On one corner of the rosewood table, crowded amidst crystal beakers filled with noxious substances and oddly glowing vials sealed with lead, was another flat chest, this of polished satinwood with a silver bell, scribed about with arcane symbols, mounted atop it. Even as he looked, the bell sounded once more.

"So the fool finally found the courage to use it," Naipal muttered. He hesitated, wanting to see to his own problems, but the bell rang again. Breathing heavily, he moved around the table to the satinwood chest.

Its lid came off, and he set it aside to stare down at a mirror that showed his image and that of the chamber in quite ordinary fashion. The mirror slid within the box on rails and props so that it could be set at any angle. He raised it almost upright. Eight tiny bone trays came next, atop silver pegs that fitted into holes on the edge of the box, one at each corner, one in the precise middle of each side.

Again the bell chimed, and he cursed. Powders prepared long in advance and stored with the mirror were carefully ladled onto the tiny trays with a bone spatula. Last to come from the box was a small silver mallet, graven with miniscule renderings of the symbols on the bell.

"*Sa'ar-el!*" Naipal intoned. A blue spark leaped from mallet to bell, and the bell rang. As it did, the powders at the four cardinal points flared in blue flame. Before those tiny berylline fires died in wisps of smoke, he spoke again. *"Ka'ar-el!"* Once more the bell sounded untouched, and blue flame leaped at the minor points. *"Ma'ar-el! Diendar!"* For the third time the chime came and in the mirror Naipal's reflection swirled and dissolved into a maelstrom of color.

Slowly the polychrome whirling coalesced into the image of a narrow-faced man in turban of cloth-of-gold wrapped about with golden chains set with rubies. "Naipal?" the man said. "Asura be praised that it is you."

"Excellency," Naipal said, suppressing his irritation, "how may I serve the Adviser to the Elephant, soon to *be* the Elephant?"

Karim Singh started and stared about him as though fearing who might be behind him. The man could not be fool enough, Naipal thought, to have someone with him while he used the scrying mirror. Could he?

"You should not say such things," the *wazam* said. "Asura alone knows who might overhear. Another wizard perhaps, listening. And now, of all times."

"Excellency, I have explained that only those in the actual presence of these two mirrors . . ." Naipal stopped and drew a deep breath. Explaining to the fool for the hundredth time was useless. "I am Naipal, court wizard to King Bhandarkar of Vendhya. I plot the death of Bhandarkar and spit on his memory. I plot to place His Excellency Karim Singh on the throne of Vendhya. Your Excellency sees. I would not say these things if anyone could overhear."

Karim Singh nodded, though his face was pasty. "I suppose I must . . . trust you, Naipal. After all, you serve me faithfully. I also trust that you know it would be well to give more faithfulness to me than you have given Bhandarkar."

"I am Your Excellency's servant." Naipal wondered if the man had any inkling of how much of his rise to power was the wizard's doing. "And how may I serve Your Excellency now?"

"I . . . do not know exactly," the *wazam* said. "It could be disaster. The treaty is destroyed, without doubt. Our heads may roll. I warn you, Naipal, I will not go to the block alone."

Naipal sighed irritably. The treaty with Turan followed the simple principles he had led Karim Singh to believe were his own. To seize the throne at Bhandarkar's death required a land in turmoil. Outside enemies tended to unify a country. Therefore all nations that might threaten Vendhya—Turan, Iranistan, the nations and city-states of Khitai and Uttara Koru and Kambuja—must be placated, made to feel neither threatened by nor threatening toward Vendhya. The wizard's preferred method was the manipulation of people in key positions, supplemented by sorcery where needed. It was Karim Singh who thought in terms of treaties. Still, the journey to Turan *had* kept him safely out of Naipal's way for a time.

"Excellency, if Yildiz would not sign, it is of no import. Assuredly, even if Bhandarkar holds the failure against Your Excellency, he has no time to—"

"Listen to me, fool!" Karim Singh's eyes bulged hysterically. "The treaty was signed! And perhaps within hours of that signing the High Admiral of Turan was dead! At the hands of Vendhyan assassins! Who else but Bhandarkar himself would dare such a thing? And if it is indeed him, then what game does he play? Do we move against him unseen, or does he merely toy with us?"

Sweat dampened Naipal's palms as he listened, but he would not wipe them while the other could see. His eyes flickered to the ivory chest. An army? With wizards perhaps? But how could such be mobilized without his knowing? "Bhandarkar cannot know," he said at last. "Is Your Excellency sure of all of the facts? Stories often become distorted."

"Kandar was convinced. And this Patil, who told him, is no man for intrigue. Why, he is as devious as a newborn infant."

"Describe . . . this Patil to me," the wizard said softly. Karim Singh frowned. "A barbarian. A pale-skinned giant with the eyes of a *pan-kur*. Where are you going? Naipal!"

Before the description was finished, the wizard leaped to the ivory chest. He threw back the lid, brushed aside the silken coverings and stared at exactly what he had seen the night before, a vast array of fires in the night. Not an army. A huge caravan. So many pieces suddenly fell into place, yet for every answer there was a new question. He became aware again of Karim Singh's shouting.

"Naipal! Katar take you! Where are you? Return instantly or by Asura . . ." The wizard moved again in front of the mirror that contained Karim Singh's now-apoplectic visage. "Just in time to save your head! How dare you leave like that, without so much as craving permission or a word of explanation? I will not tolerate such—"

"Excellency. Please. Your Excellency must listen. This man calling himself Patil, this barbarian giant with the eyes of a *pan-kur*"—in spite of himself, Naipal shuddered at that; could it be an omen, or worse?— "he must die, and everyone with him. Tonight, Excellency."

"Why?" Karim Singh demanded.

"His description," the mage improvised. "Various divinations have brought it to me that a man of that description can bring ruin to all our plans. And as well there is another threat to us in the same caravan with Your Excellency, a threat of which I learned only a short time ago. There is a party of Vendhyan merchants. Their leader is a man called Sabah, though he may use another name. They have pack mules rather than camels, bearing what will appear to be bales of silk."

"I suppose these men must die as well," Karim Singh said and Naipal nodded.

"Your Excellency understands well." Commands had been given and apparently not obeyed. Naipal did not tolerate failure.

"Again, why?"

"The arts of divination are uncertain as to details, Excellency. All that I can say for certain is that every day, every hour that these men live, is a threat to Your Excellency's ascension to the throne." The wizard paused, choosing his words. "There is one other matter, Excellency. Within what appear to be the bales of silk of the Vendhyan merchants will be chests sealed with lead seals. These chests must be brought to me with the seals unbroken. And I must add that the last is more important to Your Excellency's gaining the throne than all the rest, than all we have done so far. The chests must be brought to me with the seals unbroken."

"My gaining the throne," Karim Singh said flatly, "depends on chests being brought to you? Chests that are with the very caravan in which I travel? Chests of which you knew nothing until a short time ago?"

"Before Asura, it is so," Naipal replied. "May my soul be forfeit." It was an easy oath to make; that forfeit had been made long since.

"Very well then. The men will be dead before the sun rises. And the chests will be brought to you. Peace be with you." The silver bell chimed in sympathy with the silver bell in the *wazam*'s tent so far away, and the image in the mirror leaped and was that of Naipal.

"And peace be with you, most excellent of fools," the wizard muttered.

He looked at his palms. The sweat was still there. So many new questions, but death would provide all the answers he needed. Smiling, he wiped his hands on his robes.

XIV

Absolute darkness was pushed back from the night-swathed encampment by hundreds of campfires scattered among a thousand tents. Many of those tents glowed with the light of lamps within, casting moving, mysterious shadows on walls, whether silk or cotton, made less than opaque. The thrum of citherns floated in the air, and the smell of cinnamon and saffron from meals not long consumed.

Conan approached Vyndra's tent with an uncertainty he was not used to. All during the day's march he had avoided her, and if that consisted mainly in staying with Kang Hou's camels rather than seeking her out, it had not been so easily done as it sounded. It was possible she wanted him only as an oddity for her noble friends in Ayodhya, a strange-eyed barbarian at which to gawk, but on the other hand, a woman did not look at an oddity coquettishly through lowered lashes. In any case, she was beautiful, he was young, and therefore he had come as she asked.

Ducking through the tent's entrance flap, he found himself staring Alyna in the eyes, which was still all he could see of her for thick veils and heavy robes. "Your mistress," he began and cut off as a flash of murderous rage flickered through the woman's eyes.

As quickly as it appeared, though, it was gone, and she bowed him deeper into the tent, which, though smaller than Karim Singh's was divided within in much the same fashion by silken hangings.

In a central chamber floored with exquisite Vendhyan carpets and lit by golden lamps, Vyndra stood awaiting him. "You came, Patil. I am glad."

Conan clamped his teeth firmly to keep from gaping. Gold and rubies and emeralds still bedecked her, but the robes she had worn earlier were now replaced by layers of purest gossamer. She was covered from ankles to neck, yet her position in front of a lamp cast shadows of tantalizing mystery on rounded surfaces, and the scent of jasmine floating from her seemed the very distillation of wickedness.

"If this were Turan," he said when he found his tongue, "or Zamora or Nemedia, and there were two women in a room dressed as the two of you, it would be Alyna who was free, and you who were slave. To a man, without doubt, and the delight of his eye."

Vyndra smiled, touching a finger to her lips. "How foolish of those women to let their slaves outshine them. But if you wish to see Alyna, I will have her dance for you. I have no other dancing girls with me, I fear. Unlike Karim Singh and the other men, I do not find them a necessity."

"I would much rather see you dance," he told her, and she laughed low in her throat.

"That is something no man will ever see." Yet she twined her arms above her head and stretched in a motion so supple it cried dancer, and one that dried Conan's throat. That fabric was more than merely sheer when drawn tight.

"If I could have some wine?" he asked hoarsely.

"Of course. Wine, Alyna, and dates. But sit, Patil. Rest yourself."

She pressed him down onto piled cushions of silk and velvet. He was not sure of exactly how she managed this since she had to reach up to put her small hands on his shoulders, but he suspected the perfume had something to do with it.

He tried to put his arms around her then, while she bent over him so enticingly, but she slipped away like an eel and reclined on the cushions just an arm's length away. He settled for accepting a goblet of perfumed wine from Alyna. The cup was as heavy as the one in which the *wazam* had given him wine, though instead of amethysts, it was studded with coral beads.

"Vendhya seems to be a rich land," he said after he had drunk, "though I've not been there yet to see it."

"It is," Vyndra said. "And what else do you know of Vendhya before you have been there?"

"Vendhyans make carpets," he said, slapping the one beneath the cushions, "and they perfume their wine and their women alike."

"What else?" she giggled.

"Women from the *purdhana* are shamed by baring their faces but not by baring anything else." That brought an outright laugh, though the edges of a blush showed about Alyna's veil. Conan liked Vyndra's laughter, but he was already tired of the sport. "Beyond that, Vendhya seems to be famous for spies and assassins."

Both women gasped as one, and Vyndra's face paled. "I lost my father to the Katari. As did Alyna."

"The Katari?"

"The assassins for which Vendhya is so famous. You mean you did not even know the name?" Vyndra shook her head and shuddered. "They kill, sometimes for gold, sometimes for whim it seems, but always the death is dedicated to the vile goddess Katar."

"That name I have heard," he said, "somewhere."

Vyndra sniffed. "No doubt on the lips of a man. It is a favorite oath of Vendhyan men. No woman would be so foolish as to call on one dedicated to endless death and carnage."

She was clearly shaken, and he could sense her withdrawing into herself. Frantically he sought another topic, one fit for a woman's ears. One of her poets would no doubt compose a verse on the spot, he thought bitterly, but all the verse he knew was set to music, and most of it would made a trull blush.

"A man of your country did say something out of the ordinary to me today," he said slowly, and latched on to the one remark out of several that would bear repeating. "He thought my eyes marked me as demonspawn. A *pan-kur*, he called it. You obviously do not believe it, else you'd have run screaming rather than inviting me to drink your wine."

"I might believe it," she said, "if I had not talked to learned men who told me of far-off lands where the men are all giants with eyes like sapphires. And I rarely run screaming from anything." A small smile had returned to play on her lips. "Of course, if you actually claim to be a *pan-kur*, I would never doubt the man who calls himself Patil."

Conan flushed slightly. Everyone seemed to know the name was not his, but he could not bring himself to say that he had lied about it. "I have fought demons," he said, "but I am none of their breed."

"You have fought demons?" Vyndra exclaimed. "Truly? I saw demons once, a score of them, but I cannot imagine anyone actually fighting one, no matter what the legends say."

"You saw a score of demons?" Despite his own experience seemingly to the contrary, Conan was aware that demons—and wizards, for that matter—were not so thick on the ground as most people imagined. It was just that he had bad luck in the matter, though Hordo insisted it was a curse. "A score in one place?"

Vyndra's dark eyes flashed. "You do not believe me? Many others were there. Five years ago in the palace of King Bhandarkar, he who was then the court wizard, Zail Bal, was carried off in full view of scores of people. The demons were *rajaie*, which drink the life from their victims. You see, I know whereof I speak."

"Did I say I did not believe you?" Conan asked. He would believe in twenty demons in one place—much less anyone escaping alive from that place—when he saw it, but he hoped devoutly that his luck was never quite that bad.

A small crease appeared between Vyndra's brows, as though she doubted his sincerity. "If you have truly fought demons—and you see I do not question *your* claim—then you must certainly stay at my palace in Ayodhya. Why, perhaps even Naipal would come to meet a man who has fought demons. What a triumph that would be!"

It might have sounded promising, he thought ruefully, if not for this other man. "Do you wish me there, or this Naipal?"

"I want both of you, of course. Think of the wonderment. You, a huge warrior, obviously from a land shrouded in distance and mystery, a fighter against demons. He, the court wizard of Vendhya, the—"

"A wizard," Conan breathed heavily. Hordo would believe he had done this apurpose, or else he would mutter about the curse.

"I said that," Vyndra said. "He is the most mysterious man in Vendhya. No more than a handful other than King Bhandarkar, and perhaps Karim Singh, know his face. Women have arranged assignations with him merely in the hope they might be able to say they could recognize him."

"I have never met the man," he said, "nor intend to, yet I do not like him."

Her laugh was low and wicked. "He keeps the assignations, too, with those women pretty enough. They are gone for days and return on the point of exhaustion with stories of passion beyond belief, but when they are asked of his features, they grow vague. The visage they describe could belong to any handsome man. Still, the transports of rapture they speak of are such that I myself have considered—"

With a curse Conan hurled the golden goblet aside. Vyndra squeaked as he pounced, catching her face between his hands. "I do not want you to attract some sorcerer," he told her heatedly. "I do not want you because you are from a country distant from mine or because you would seem strange to the people of my land. I want you because you are a beautiful woman and you make my blood burn." There was invitation on her face and when he kissed her, she tangled her hands in his hair as though it were she who held him, not the reverse.

When at last she snuggled against his chest with a sigh, there was a mischevious twinkle in her big dark eyes, and small white teeth indented her full lower lip. "Do you intend to take me now?" she asked softly and then added as he growled in his throat, "With Alyna watching?"

Conan did not take his eyes from her face. "She is still here?"

"Alyna is faithful to me in her fashion and rarely leaves my side."

"And you do not intend to send her away." It was not a question.

"Would you have me separated from my faithful tirewoman?" Vyndra asked with a wide-eyed smile.

Clearing his throat, Conan got to his feet. Alyna was there, bright eyes glinting with amusement above her veil. "I have half a mind," he said conversationally, "to switch both your rumps till you have to be tied across your saddles like bolts of silk. Instead, I think I will see if there is an honest trull in this caravan, for your games bore me."

He stalked out on that, thinking he had quieted her, but laughing words followed him before he let the tent flap fall. "You are a violent man, O one who calls himself Patil. You will be a wonderment to my friends."

XV

There were panderers on the outskirts of the encampment, as Conan had known there would be in a caravan so large and going so far. Two of them. Karim Singh might have his own women along, as would the Vendhyan noblemen and even many of the merchants; but for the rest—for guards and camel drivers and mule handlers—from Khawarism to Secunderam was a long way without a woman. Except for the panderers.

They had set out tables made of planks laid on barrels before their tents, with casks to sit on and drink while a man waited his turn for the use of the tents. Cheap wine they gave away to those who bought their other merchandise, sour wine served by sweet women, slender jades and voluptuous trulls, tall wenches and short. Soft, willing flesh. If the gilded brass girdles low on their hips and their strips of diaphanous silk were more than a *purdhana* dancer wore, all could be removed for a coin, for women were the goods sold here.

And yet, Conan realized, it was not a woman he wanted. He sat on an upended keg before the second panderer's tents, a leathern jack of thin wine in his fist, a slender wench wiggling on his knee as she bit at his neck with small white teeth. He could not pretend disinterest in her, but she seemed a distraction, if a pleasant one. A buxom jade at the first panderer's tent had been the same. Though he was not yet twenty, he had long since learned to curb his anger when need be, but on that day he had held it in check with Karim Singh and lashed it down with Kandar. And then there had been Vyndra. Now he wanted to loose the rage, to strike out at something. He wanted one of the other men fondling a woman to challenge him for the doxy on his lap, or two, or five. Hammering fists, even bloody steel, would drain the anger coiled in his belly like a serpent dripping venom from its fangs.

The slender trull snuggled against him contentedly as he stood with her in his arms, then stared at him in consternation when he plopped her bottom onto the keg. "I am not a Vendhyan," he told her, dropping coins in her hands. "I do not take out my anger on others than those who have earned it." Her look was one of total uncomprehension, but he spoke for his own benefit as much as hers.

The raucous laughter of the panderers' tents followed him into the encampment. Many of the merchants' tents were darkened now, and silence lay even on the picket lines of animals behind each, though the thin sounds of zither and flute, cithern and tambor, drifted from the nobles' portion of the camp. Sleep, he thought. Sleep, then journey on the morrow, then sleep again and journey again. The antidote would be found in Vendhya, and the answers he sought would come, but he would dissipate the tightness of anger with sleep.

The fire burned low in front of the lone tent shared by Kang Hou and his nieces. A Khitan servant poking the embers was all that moved among the blanket-wrapped shapes of smugglers scattered about the merchant's tent. But Conan stopped short of the dim light of that fire, a jangling in the back of his head that he recognized as a warning that something was wrong.

His ears strained for sounds below normal hearing, and his eyes sought the shadows between the other tents. The sounds were all about him now that he listened. The rasp of leather on leather, the soft clink of metal, the pad of softly placed feet. Shadows shifted where they should be still.

"Hordo!" Conan roared, broadsword coming into his hand. "Up, or die in your blankets!" Before the warning was past his lips, smugglers were rolling to their feet with swords in hand. And Vendhyans as well, afoot and mounted, were upon them.

To attempt to make his way to his companions was madness, the Cimmerian knew. They did not fight to hold a piece of ground but to escape, and every man would be seeking to break through the ring of steel. He had no time for thought on the matter. He had killed one man and was crossing swords with a second by the time he shouted the last word.

Jerking his blade free of the second corpse, he all but decapitated another Vendhyan, searching all the while for his path to freedom, ignoring the screams and clanging steel around him as he fought his way away from the Khitan's tent. A turban-helmed horseman appeared in front of him, lance gone but tulwar lifted to slash. The Vendhyan's fierce, killing grin turned to shock as Conan leaped to grapple with him. Unable to use his sword so close, the horseman beat at Conan with the hilt as the horse danced in circles. The big Cimmerian could not use his broadsword either, merely wrapping that arm about the Vendhyan, but his dagger quickly slid between the metal plates of the brigantine hauberk. The horseman screamed, and again as he was toppled from the saddle. Then Conan was scrambling into the other's place, seizing the reins and slamming his heels into the horse's flanks.

The calvary-trained animal burst into a gallop, and Conan, lying low in the saddle, guided it between the tents. Merchants and their servants, roused by the tumult, jumped shouting from the path of the speeding rider. Suddenly there was a man who did not leap aside, a caravan guard who dropped to one knee and planted the base of his spear. The horse shrieked as the long blade thrust into its chest, and abruptly Conan was flying over the crumpling animal's head. All of the breath was driven from him by the fall, yet the Cimmerian struggled to rise. The guard rushed in for an easy kill of the man on his knees, tulwar raised high. With what seemed his last particle of strength, Conan drove his sword into the other's chest. The force of the man's charge carried him into the big Cimmerian, knocking him over. Still fighting for breath, Conan pushed the man away, extricated his blade, and staggered into the shadows. Half-falling, he pressed his back against a tent.

Wakened merchants shouted on all sides.

"What happens?"

"Are we attacked?"

"Bandits!"

"My goods!"

Vendhyan soldiers shoved the merchants aside, beating at them with the butts of their lances. "Go back to your tents!" was their cry. "We seek spies! Go back to your tents, and you will not be harmed! Anyone outside will be arrested!"

Spies, Conan thought. He had found his fight, but there was yet a trickle of his previous anger remaining, a trickle growing stronger. Moments before, escape from the encampment had been paramount in his mind. Now he thought he would first visit the man who considered all foreigners spies.

Like a hunting leopard, the big Cimmerian flowed from shadow to shadow, blending with the dark. Curious eyes were easily avoided, for there were few abroad now. No one moved between the tents save soldiers, announcing their coming with creak of harness and clink of armor and curses that they must search when they would be sleeping. Silently Conan moved into deeper shadows as the Vendhyans appeared, watching with a feral grin as they marched or rode past him, sometimes within arm's reach, yet always unseeing.

Karim Singh's tent glowed with light within, and two fires blazed high before the canopied entrance. The fires made the dim light filtered through golden silk at the rear seem almost as dark as the surrounding light. A score of Vendhyan cavalry sat their horses like statues in a ring about the tent, facing outward, ten paces at least separating each man from the next.

Like statues they were in truth, or else thought they guarded against attack by an army, for on his belly Conan crawled unseen between two at the rear of the tent. As he prepared to slit an entrance in the back wall of the tent with his dagger, voices from inside stopped him.

"Leave us," commanded Karim Singh.

Conan opened a small slit only, parting it with his fingers. A last Vendhyan soldier was bowing himself from the silk-walled chamber within. Karim Singh stood in the middle of the chamber, a cavalryman's sword in his hand, and before him knelt a Vendhyan bound hand and foot. The kneeling man wore the robes of a merchant, though they hardly seemed consistent with his hard face and the long scar that crossed his nose and cheek.

"You are called Sabah?" the *wazam* asked in an easy tone.

"I am Amaur, Excellency, an honest merchant," the kneeling man said, "and even you have no right to simply seize my goods without cause." The harsh, rasping voice made Conan stiffen in memory. The rider in the dunes. He would listen for a while before killing Karim Singh.

The *wazam* set the point of his sword against the other's throat. "You are called Sabah?"

"My name is Amaur, Excellency. I know no one called—" The kneeling man gasped as the point pressed closer, bringing a trickle of blood.

"An honest merchant?" Karim Singh laughed softly. As he spoke, he increased the pressure of the blade. The kneeling man leaned back but the sword point followed. "Within the bales of silk you carry were found chests sealed with lead. You are a smuggler, at least. Who are the chests destined for?"

With a cry, the prisoner toppled. From his back he stared with bulging eyes. The sword still was at his throat and there was no farther he could go to escape it. The hardness of his face had become a mask of fear. "I . . . I cannot say, Excellency. Before Asura, I swear it!"

"You will say or you will face Asura shortly. Or, more likely, Katar." The *wazam's* voice became conspiratorial. "I know the name, Amaur. I know. But I must hear it from your lips if you would live. Speak, Amaur, and live."

"Excellency, he . . . he will kill me. Or worse!"

"*I* will kill you, Amaur. This sword is at your throat, here, and *he* is far away. Speak!"

"N . . . Naipal!" the man sobbed. "Naipal, Excellency!"

"Good," Karim Singh said soothingly. But he did not move the sword. "You see how easy it was. Now. Why? Tell me why he wants these chests."

"I cannot, Excellency." Tears rolled down Amaur's cheeks now and he shook with weeping. "Before Asura, before Katar, I would tell you if I could, but I know nothing! We were to meet the ship, kill all on board and bring the chests to Ayodhya. Perhaps Sabah knew more, but he is dead. I swear, Excellency! I speak truly, I swear!"

"I believe you," Karim Singh sighed. "It is a pity." And he leaned on the sword.

Amaur's attempt to scream became a bubbling gurgle as steel slid through his throat. Karim Singh stared at him as though fascinated by the blood welling up in his mouth and the convulsions that wracked his bound form. Abruptly the *wazam* released the sword. It remained upright, its point thrust through man and carpets into the ground, shaking with Amaur's final twitching.

"Guards!" Karim Singh called, and Conan lowered the dagger with which he had been about to lengthen the slit. "Guards!"

Half a score of Vendhyans rushed into the chamber with drawn blades. Staring at the sight that greeted them, they hastily sheathed their weapons.

"The other spies," the *wazam* said. "The giant, in particular. He has been taken? He cannot be mistaken, for his size and his eyes set him apart."

"No, Excellency," one of the soldiers replied deferentially. "Four of that party are dead, but not the giant. We seek the others."

"So he is still out there." Karim Singh spoke as though to himself. "He seemed a stark man. A slayer born. He will seek me now." He shook himself and glared at the soldiers as if angered that they had overheard. "He must be found! A thousand pieces of gold to the man who finds him. All of you, and ten others, will remain with me until he is dead or in chains. And he who does not die stopping the barbarian from reaching me will die wishing that he had. Have someone dispose of this," he added with a nod toward Amaur's corpse.

The *wazam* strode from the chamber then, the guards clustering about him, and Conan sagged where he crouched outside. Against a score of guards he might not even reach Karim Singh before he was cut down. He had known men who embraced a brave but useless death; he was not one of them. Death was an old acquaintance to him and had been long before he found himself with Patil's poison in his blood. Death was neither to be feared nor sought, and when he met it, the meeting would not be without purpose. Besides, he now had a name, Naipal, the man who had begun all of this. That was another who must die as well as Karim Singh.

Silently Conan slipped back into the night.

XVI

A horse and a water bag were what he needed now, Conan knew. In this land a man afoot and without water was a man dying or dead. There were far more camels than horses in the caravan, however, and many of the horses were animals suitable for show but not for a man who needed to travel far and fast. Moreover, word of the reward must have been spreading quickly, for the soldiers were now more assiduous in their searching. Twice he located suitable mounts only to be forced to abandon them by turban-helmed patrols.

Finally he found himself in the nobles' portion of the encampment. Most of the tents were dark and the silence was as complete as in the merchants' part. He wondered if the soldiers had been as brusque here in quieting curiosity as they had been with the merchants.

Something moved in the darkness, a shadow heaving, and he froze. A grunt came from the shadow, and the rattle of a chain. Conan peered more closely and then stifled a laugh. It was Vyndra's dancing bear. On sudden impulse, he drew his dagger. The bear, sitting in a sprawl, eyed him as he cautiously approached. It did not move as he sawed at the leather collar about its neck.

"It is a harsh land," he whispered, "with many ways to die." He felt foolish in talking to an animal, but there was a need, too. "You may find hunters or stronger bears. If you do not run far enough, they will chain you again and make you dance for Vyndra. The choice is yours, to die free or to dance for your mistress."

The bear stared at him as the collar fell loose, and he held the dagger ready. Just because it had not attacked him so far did not mean it would not, and the shaggy creature was half again as large as he. Slowly the bear got to its feet and lumbered into the dark.

"Better to die free," Conan grinned after the beast.

"And I say I saw something move."

Conan stiffened at the words, cursing his impulses.

"Take ten men around the other way and we will see."

In an instant the Cimmerian's blade made a long slit in the tent wall behind him, and he went through as footsteps rounded the tent. Within was as deep a darkness as outside, though his keen eyes, already used to the night, could make out shadowy shapes and mounds on the carpet spread for flooring. The footsteps halted on the other side of the thin wall, and voices muttered indistinguishably. One of the mounds moved.

Not again, Conan thought. Hoping it was not another bear, he threw himself on the shifting shape. The grunt that came when he landed was nothing at all like that of a bear. Soft flesh writhed against him beneath a thin linen coverlet, and his hand frantically sought a mouth, finding it just in time to stifle a scream. Bringing his face close, he looked into big dark eyes filled with a mixture of fear and rage.

"Alyna is not here now, Vyndra," he whispered and moved his hand from her lips.

As her mouth opened once more for a scream, he stuffed it with the ball of her hair that he had gathered with his other hand. Quickly he felt around the bed mat until he found a long silk scarf, which he tied across her mouth to keep her from spitting the hair out. Bound and gagged, he thought, she could raise no alarm until he was far away. With luck, she would not be found until morning.

Stripping off the linen coverlet, he was forced to stop and stare. Even when covered in shadows, the lush curves of her were enough to take his breath away. He found it quickly, though, jerking his head back barely in time to save his eyes from clawing nails.

"This time the sport is not of your choosing," he said softly, catching her flailing arm and deftly flipping her onto her stomach. He found another scarf and used it to bind her wrists behind her. "You may not dance for me," he chuckled, "but this is almost as enjoyable." He felt her quiver and did not need the angry, muffled sounds coming from behind the gag to tell him it was with rage.

As he searched for something to tie her ankles with, he became aware of voices in the front of the tent. Hastily he dragged his struggling prisoner closer to where he could listen.

"Why do you wish to see my mistress?" came Alyna's voice. "She sleeps."

A man answered with weary patience. "The *wazam* has learned that your mistress entertained a spy earlier tonight. He would talk with her of it."

"Can it not wait until morning? She will be angry if she is wakened."

Conan did not wait to learn the outcome. If Vyndra was found now, the soldiers would know he was close by before her gag was fully out of her mouth. Half-carrying the wriggling woman, he darted to the rear of the tent and peered cautiously through the slit by which he had entered. The searchers were gone. It was possible they were even the same men now in the front of the tent.

"I am sorry," he told her.

He was glad for the gag as he pulled her through the slit. The violent protesting noises she made were bad enough as it was. Despite her struggles, he lifted her into his arms, running as fast as he could manage while making sure he did not speed into the midst of a patrol or trip over tent ropes.

Well away from her tent, he put her on her feet, careful to keep a grip on one slender arm. If they were discovered, he had to be able to fight without being burdened with her. And there would be no need to prevent her escape then.

Finding a horse was still his first concern, but when he tried to start out again, he found he was dragging a bent-over, crouching woman who seemed to be attempting to make herself as small as possible while simultaneously refusing to move her feet.

"Stand up and walk," he said hoarsely, but she shook her head furiously. "Crom, woman, I've no time to ogle your charms." She shook her head again.

A quick look around revealed no evidence of anyone both near and awake. All of the surrounding tents were dark. His full-armed swing landing on her buttock produced a louder smack than he would have liked, not to mention the sounds she produced, but it brought her onto her toes and half-erect. When she tried to crouch again, he held his open hand in front of her face.

"Walk," he whispered warningly.

Her glare was enough to slay lions, but slowly she straightened. Without so much as a glance at the beauties she had revealed, he hurried her on. He was not young enough to be a complete fool over a woman.

Ghosting among the tents, they more than once barely avoided the searching Vendhyan soldiers. At first Conan was surprised that Vyndra made no effort to escape when the turban-helmed warriors were close, nor even to attract them with noise or struggle. In fact, she had become as silent as he, eyes constantly searching for what might trip or betray. Then it came to him. Escaping him was one thing, being rescued while garbed in naught but two scarves quite another. He smiled gratefully, accepting anything that made his own escape easier.

Once more he was in the merchants' area, so deathly still that he knew all there were huddled breathlessly, not daring to make a sound that would attract the soldiers. A destination had come to his mind, a place where there might be horses and a place the soldiers would not be searching if he had but a particle of luck.

Movement in the shadows ahead again sent him to hiding, dragging a compliant Vyndra behind. This was no patrol, he saw quickly, but a lone man padding furtively. Slowly the shadow resolved into Kang Hou, half-crouched with his hands in his sleeves. As Conan opened his mouth, two more shapes appeared behind the first. Vendhyan cavalrymen, afoot and carrying their lances like spears.

"Searching for something, Khitan?" one called.

Smoothly Kang Hou pivoted, hands flickering out of concealment. Something flew through the air, and the two Vendhyans dropped soundlessly. Hastily the merchant ran to crouch above the bodies.

"You are a dangerous man for a merchant," Conan said softly as he stepped into the open.

Kang Hou spun, a throwing knife in each upraised hand, then slowly slid the knives from sight within his sleeves.

"A merchant must often travel in dangerous company," he said blandly. He ran his eyes over Vyndra and raised an eyebrow. "I have heard it said that some warriors favor women above all other loot, but under these circumstances, I find it strange."

"I do not want her," Conan said. Vyndra growled through her gag. "The problem is, where can I leave her and be sure she'll not be found before I have gotten a horse and left this place?"

"A quandary," the Khitan agreed. "You have considered where to find this horse? The soldiers check the picket lines constantly and a missing animal will not go long undiscovered."

"At the last place they will look for one of us," Conan replied. "The picket line behind your tent."

Kang Hou smiled. "Admirable reasoning. Having led my original pursuers a way from the encampment, I am now returning there. Will you accompany me?"

"In but a moment. Hold her."

Thrusting Vyndra at the startled Khitan, Conan hurried to the dead Vendhyans. Quickly he dragged them into the deeper darkness beside a tent—no sense in leaving them to be easily found—and when he returned to the others, he carried one of the soldiers' cloaks. Kang Hou wore a small smile, and Vyndra's eyes were squeezed tightly shut.

"What happened?" the Cimmerian asked. He draped the cloak around the woman as best he could with her hands bound. Her eyes flew open, giving him a look of mingled surprise and gratitude.

"I'm not entirely certain," the merchant said, "but it seems that her belief is that if she cannot see me, I cannot see her." Even in the dark her blush at his words was evident.

"We have no time for foolishness," Conan said. "Come."

A thousand gold pieces was a powerful spur when added to the command of a man such as Karim Singh, but even that spur lost its sharpness when the searchers began to believe their quarry had already escaped from the encamped caravan. Patrols of Vendhyans began to grow fewer, and those who still hunted did so in desultory fashion. Many no longer even went through the motions, gathering instead in easily avoided knots to talk in low voices.

Short of the Khitan's camp Conan halted, still hidden in the darkness among the other merchants' tents. Vyndra obeyed his grip on her arm with seeming docility, but he maintained his hold. The fire was only coals now, and bales of velvet lay ripped open among carpets unrolled and scattered about. If anyone had died there—the Cimmerian remembered the report to Karim Singh of four dead—their bodies had been taken away. The picket line was only a murky mass but some of those shadows moved in ways he did not like Kang Hou started forward, but Conan caught his arm.

"Horses move even in the night," the Khitan whispered, "and the soldiers would not hide. We must hurry."

Conan shook his head. Pursing his lips, he gave the call of a bird found only on the plains of Zamora. For an instant there was silence, then the call came back, from the picket line.

"Now we hurry," Conan said and ran for the horses, hauling Vyndra behind him.

Hordo stepped out to meet him, motioning for greater quickness. "I hoped you had made it, Cimmerian," he said hoarsely. "Hell has come to sup, it seems." Two other shadows became men, Enam and Prytanis.

"I heard there are four dead," Conan said. "Who?"

"Baltis!" Prytanis spat. "The Vendhyan scum cut him to shreds. I *said* you brought us all to our deaths."

"He followed me," Conan agreed, to the slit-nosed man's evident surprise. "It is another debt I owe."

"Baltis died well," Hordo said, "and took an honor guard with him. A man can ask no more of dying than that. The other three," he added to the Khitan, "were your servants. I have not seen your nieces."

"My servants were not fighting men," Kang Hou sighed, "but I had hoped . . . No matter. As for my nieces, Kuie Hsi will care for her sister as well as I could. Might I suggest that we take horses and continue this talk elsewhere?"

"A good suggestion," Conan said.

The stallion was still there; Conan had feared that such a fine mount would have been taken by the Vendhyans. He heaved the saddle onto the animal's back one-handed but fastening the girth would require two hands. Giving Vyndra a warning look, he released her but kept a sharp eye on her as he hastily strapped the saddle tight. To his surprise, she did not move. No doubt, he thought, she still dreaded being found clothed as she was, even if it did mean rescue.

"The wench," Hordo said curiously. "Do you have a purpose with her, or is she just a token to remember this place by?"

"There is a purpose," Conan said, explaining why he could not leave her yet. "It may be I must take her all the way to Vendhya with me, for I doubt she'd survive long if I left her to make her own way on the plain." He paused, then asked with more casualness than he felt, "What of Ghurran?"

"I've not seen the old man since the attack," Hordo replied regretfully. "I am sorry, Cimmerian."

"What is, is," Conan said grimly. "I must saddle a horse for the woman. I fear you must ride astride, Vyndra, for we have no sidesaddle." She merely stared at him, unblinking.

It was a silent procession that made its stealthy way through the tents of the encampment, leading their horses. The animals could walk more quietly without burdens, and they all would have been more noticeable mounted. The Vendhyan patrols, half-hearted and noisy, might as well not have been there. Conan, first in line, had the reins of his horse and Vyndra's in one hand and her arm firmly in the other. Discovery would end the need for keeping her, as he was sure she must know, and he was not about to trust the odd passivity she had shown so far.

The edge of the caravan encampment appeared before him, and ingrained caution made him signal a halt. Prytanis began to speak, but Conan angrily motioned him to silence. There was a faint noise, almost too low to hear. The soft tread of horses. Perhaps all of the Vendhyans had not given up on the hunt.

A glance told Conan the others had heard as well. Swords were in hand—Kang Hou held one of his throwing knives—and each man had moved alongside his horse to be ready to mount. The Cimmerian tensed, ready to heave Vyndra aside to relative safety and vault into his saddle, as the other horses appeared.

Five animals were in the other pary as well, and Conan almost laughed with relief when he saw those leading the beasts. Shamil and Hasan, each with a protective arm about one of Kang Hou's nieces, and old Ghurran hobbling in the rear.

"It is good to see you," Conan called softly.

The two younger men spun, clawing for their swords. Hasan was somewhat hampered by Chin Kou clutching at him, but Kuie Hsi came up with a knife poised to throw. A dangerous family, the Cimmerian thought. Ghurran merely watched expressionessly as though no fear remained in him.

The two groups joined, everyone attempting whispered conversation, but Conan silenced them with a hiss. "We talk when we are safe," he told them softly, "and that is far from here." Lifting Vyndra into her saddle, he adjusted the soldier's cloak to give her a modicum of decency. "I will find you something to wear," he promised. "Perhaps you will dance for me yet." She stared at him above the gag, the expression in her eyes unreadable.

As Conan swung into his own saddle, a wave of dizziness swept over him, and he had to clutch the high pommel to keep from falling.

Ghurran was at his side in an instant. "I will compound the potion as soon as I can," the old herbalist said. "Hang on."

"I've no intention of anything else," Conan managed through gritted teeth. Leading Vyndra's horse by the reins, he kneed his own mount to motion, into the night toward Vendhya. He would not let go.

There were debts to pay, and two men to kill first.

XVII

Naipal looked at the man facing him, a thin, hard-eyed Vendhyan who could have been a soldier, and wondered at what motivated him. Neither personal gain nor power seemed to impress the other man. He showed no signs of love or hate or pride, nor of any other emotion. It made the wizard uneasy, confronting a man who exposed so little by which he might be manipulated.

"You understand, then?" Naipal said. "When Bhandarkar is dead, the oppression will end. Shrines to Katar will be allowed in every city."

"Have I not said that I understand?" the nameless representative of the Katari asked quietly.

They were alone in the round chamber, its shallow-domed ceiling a bas-relief of ancient heroes. Golden lamps on the walls gave soft illumination. No food or drink had been brought, for the Katari would not eat in the dwelling of one who invoked the services of his cult. They stood because the Katari did, and the wizard did not want the other looming over him. A standing man had the advantages of height and position over a seated man.

"You have not said it will be done." Naipal was hard pressed to keep irritation out of his voice. There was so much to be done this day, but this part was as important as any and must be handled delicately.

Along with the other things that did not impress or affect one of the Katari was the power of a sorcerer. Spells could destroy a Katari as quickly as any other man, but that meant little to one who believed to his core that death, however it came, meant instantly being taken to the side of his goddess. It all gave the wizard an ache in his temples.

"It will be done," the Katari said. "In return for what you have promised, Bhandarkar, even on his throne, will be dedicated to the goddess. But if the promises are not kept . . ."

Naipal ignored the threat. That was an aspect he could deal with later. He certainly had no intention of giving additional power to a cult that could, and assuredly would, undermine him. The *khorassani* could certainly protect him against the assassin's knife. Or a bodyguard of resurrected warriors from King Orissa's tomb.

"You understand also," the wizard said, "that the deed must be done when I signal it? Not before. Not an hour before."

"Have I not said that I understand?" the other repeated.

Naipal sighed. The Katari had the reputation of killing in their own time and their own way, but even if Bhandarkar had not protected himself against spells, there could be nothing of sorcery connected with his death. The appearance of clean hands would be essential to Naipal, for he wanted a land united willingly under the supposed leadership of Karim Singh, not one ravaged by opposition and war. And who would believe a wizard would use the Katari when he could slay so easily by other means?

"Very well," Naipal said. "At my sign, Bhandarkar is to die by Katari knives, on his throne, in full view of his nobles and advisers."

"Bhandarkar will die."

With that Naipal had to be satisfied. He offered the Katari a purse of gold, and the man took it with neither change of expression nor word of gratitude. It would go to the coffers of the Katari, the wizard knew, and so was no cord to bind the fellow, but habit made him try.

When the assassin was gone, Naipal paused only to fetch the golden coffer containing the demon-wrought dagger, then made his way hurriedly to the gray-domed chamber far below the palace. The resurrected warrior stood his ceaseless vigil against a wall, unsleeping, untiring. Naipal did not look at him. The newness was gone, and what was a single warrior to the numbers he would raise from the dead?

Straight to the ivory chest he went, unhesitatingly throwing back the lid and brushing aside the silken coverings. In the mirror there was a single campfire, seen from a great height. For seven days the mirror had shown a fire by night and a small party of riders by day, first on the plains beyond the Himelias, now in the very mountains themselves. Almost out of them, in fact. They moved more slowly than was necessary. It had taken some time for him to realize that they actually followed the caravan bringing the chests to him. Salvation and potential disaster would arrive together.

Seven days of seeing the proof of Karim Singh's failure had taken much of the sting away though. It no longer affected him as it had, watching possible doom approach. In truth, except for the pain behind his eyes that had come while talking to the Katari, Naipal felt almost numb. So much to do, he thought as he closed the box, and so little time remaining. The strain was palpable. But he would win, as he always did.

Moving quickly, he arranged the *khorassani* on their golden tripods. The incantations of power were spoken. Fires brighter than the sun leaped and flared and formed a cage. The summoning was cried and with a thunderous clap, Masrok floated before him in the bound void, weapons glowing in five of its eight obsidian fists.

"It is long, O man," the demon cried angrily, "since you have summoned me. Have you not felt the stone pulse against your flesh?"

"I have been busy. Perhaps I did not notice." Days since, Naipal had removed the black opal from about his neck to escape that furious throbbing. Masrok had to be allowed to ripen. "Besides, you yourself said that time did not matter to one such as you."

Masrok's huge from quivered as though on the point of leaping at the fiery barriers constraining it. "Be not a fool, O man! Within the limits of my prison have I been confined, and only its empty vastness on levels beyond your knowing has saved me. My other selves know that one of the Sivani is no more! How long can I flee them?"

"Perhaps there is no need to flee them. Perhaps your day of freedom is close, leaving those others bound for eternity. Bound away from you as well as from the world."

"How, O man? When?"

Naipal smiled as he did when a man brought to hopeless despair by his maneuverings displayed the first cracks before shattering. "Give me the location of King Orissa's tomb," he said quietly. "Where lies the centuries-lost city of Maharastra?"

"No!" The word echoed ten thousand times as Masrok spun into an ebon blur, and the burning walls of its cage howled with the demon's rage. "I will never betray! Never!"

The wizard sat, silent and waiting, until the fury had quieted. "Tell me, Masrok," he commanded.

"Never, O man! Many times have I told you there are limits to your binding of me. Take the dagger that I gave you and strike at me. Slay me, O man, if that is your wish. But I will never betray that secret."

"Never?" Naipal tilted his head quizzically, and the cruel smile returned to his lips. "Perhaps not." He touched the golden coffer, but only for an instant. "I will not slay you, however. I will only send you back and leave you there for all of time."

"What foolishness is this, O man?"

"I will not send you back to those levels vaster than my mind can know, but to that prison you share with your remaining other selves. Can even a demon know fear if its pursuers are also demons? I can only slay you, Masrok. Will they slay you when at last they overtake you? Or can demons devise tortures for demons? Will they kill you, or will you continue to live, to live until the end of time under tortures that will make you remember your prison as the most sublime of paradises? Well, Masrok?"

The huge demon stared at him malevolently, unblinking, unmoving. Yet Naipal knew. Were Masrok a man, that man would be licking his lips and sweating. He *knew!*

"My freedom, O man?" the demon said at last. "Free of serving you as well?"

"When the tomb is located," Naipal replied, "and the army buried there is within my grasp, you will have your freedom. With, of course, a binding spell to make certain you can neither harm nor hinder me in the future."

"Of course," Masrok said slowly.

The part about the binding spell was perfect, Naipal thought. A concern for his own future safety was certain to convince the demon he meant to go through with the bargain.

"Very well, O man. The ruins of Maharastra lie ten leagues to the west of Gwandiakan, swallowed ages past by the Forests of Ghendai."

Victory! Naipal wanted to jump to his feet and dance. Gwandiakan! It must be an omen, for the first city at which Karim Singh's caravan would rest once across the Himelias was Gwandiakan. He must contact the *wazam* with the scrying glass. He would race to meet the chests there and go immediately to the tomb. But no wonder the ruins had never been found. No road had ever been hewn through the Forests of Ghendai, and few had ever tried to cut its tall trees for their wood. Huge swarms of tiny, stinging flies drove men mad and those who escaped the flies succumbed to a hundred different fevers that wracked the body with pain before they killed. Some men would rather die than enter those forests.

"Maps," he said suddenly. "I will need maps so my men will not go astray. You will draw them for me."

"As you command, O man."

The demon's weary defeat was triumphal music to Naipal's ears.

XVIII

From the hills overlooking Gwandiakan, Conan stared at the city in amazement. Alabaster towers and golden domes and columned temples atop tiered, man-made hills of stone spread in vast profusion, surrounded by a towering stone wall leagues in circumference.

" 'Tis bigger than Sultanapur," Enam said in awe.

" 'Tis bigger than Sultanapur and Aghrapur together," Hordo said.

Kang Hou and his nieces seemed to take the city's size as a matter of course, while Hasan and Shamil had eyes only for the Khitan women.

"You judge by the smallness of your own lands," Vyndra mocked. She sat her horse unbound, for Conan had seen no reason to keep her tied once they were away from the caravan. She wore robes of green silk from bundles of clothing the Khitan women had gathered for themselves. They were smaller women than she, and the tightness of her current garb delineated her curves to perhaps greater perfection than she might have wished. "Many cities in Vendhya are as large or larger," she went on. "Why, Ayodhya is three times so great."

"Are we to sit here all day?" Ghurran demanded grumpily. As the others had grown tired with journeying, the herbalist had seemed to gain energy, but all of it went to irritability.

Prytanis jumped in with still nastier tones. "What of this palace she has been telling us of? After days of living on what we can snare, with naught to drink but water, I look forward to wine and delicacies served by a willing wench. Especially as the Cimmerian wants to keep this one for himself."

Vyndra's face colored, but she merely said, "I will take you there."

Conan let her take the lead, though he kept his horse close behind hers as they wended their way out of the hills. He was far from sure of what to make of the Vendhyan woman or her actions. She had made no attempt to escape and ride to the caravan, even when she knew it was just out of sight ahead of them, with a plain trail showing the way. And he often caught her watching him, a strange, unreadable look in her dark eyes. He had made no advances to her, for it seemed wrong after he had carried her away bodily. She would see a threat behind any words he might say, and she had done nothing to earn that. So he watched her in turn, uneasily, wondering when this strange calm she affected would end.

Their way led toward the city for only a short time, then turned to the west. Before they came out of the hills, Conan could see many palaces in that direction, great blocks of pale, columned marble gleaming in the sun in the midst of open spaces scattered over leagues of forest to the north and south. Still farther to the west, the trees grew taller, and there were no palaces there that he could see.

Suddenly the trees through which they rode were gone, and before them was a huge structure of ivory spires and alabaster domes, with rising terraces of fluted columns and marble stairs at the front a hundred paces wide. On each side was a long pool bordered by broad marble walks and reflecting the palace in its mirror-smooth waters.

As they rode toward the great expanse of deep-run stairs, Vyndra spoke suddenly. "Once Gwandiakan was a favored summer resort of the court, but many came to fear the fevers of the forests to the west. I have not been here since I was a child, but I know there are a few servants still, so perhaps it is habitable." She bounced from her saddle and bounded up the broad stairs, needing two paces to a single stairstep.

Conan climbed down from his horse more slowly, and Hordo with him. "Does she play some Vendhyan game with us?" the one-eyed man asked.

Conan shook his head silently; he was as uncertain as his friend. Abruptly a score of men in white turbans and pale cotton tunics appeared at the head of the stairs. The Cimmerian's hand went to his sword, but the men ignored those at the foot of the stair and bent themselves almost double bowing to Vyndra, murmuring words that did not quite reach Conan's ear.

Vyndra turned back to the others. "They remember me. It is as I feared. There are only a few servants, and the palace is much deteriorated, but we may find some bare comforts."

"I know the comforts I want," Prytanis announced loudly. "The three prettiest wenches I can find. Strip them all and I'll choose."

"My serving women are to be gently treated," Vyndra said angrily.

"You forget you are a prisoner, wench!" the slit-nosed man snarled. "Were the Cimmerian not here, I would—"

"But I am here," Conan said in hard tones. "And if she wants her serving girls treated gently, then you will treat them like your own sisters."

Prytanis met the Cimmerian's iron gaze for only a moment, then his dark eyes slid away. "There are tavern wenches in the city, I'll wager," he muttered. "Or do you wish them treated like sisters as well?"

"Have a care if you go into the city," Conan told him. "Remember, foreigners are all considered spies in this land."

"I can look after myself," the Nemedian growled. Sawing at the reins, he jerked his horse around and galloped off in the direction of Gwandiakan.

"Another must go as well," Conan said as he watched Prytanis disappear. "I'd not trust him to discover what we must know, but information is needed. The caravan entered the city, but how long will it remain? And what does Karim Singh do? Hordo, you see that none of Vyndra's servants run off to tell of strangers here. There has been nothing to indicate Karim Singh knows we follow, so let us see that that does not change. I will go into—"

"Your pardon," Kang Hou broke in. "It will take long for an obvious outlander such as yourself to learn anything of interest, for talk will die in your presence. On the other hand, my niece, Kuie Hsi, has often passed as a Vendhyan woman in aid of my business. If she can obtain the proper clothing here . . ."

"I cannot like sending a woman in my place," Conan said but the Khitan only smiled.

"I assure you I would not send her if I thought the danger were too great for her."

Conan looked at Kuie Hsi, standing straight and serene beside Shamil. In her embroidered robes she looked plainly Khitan, but with her dusky coloring and the near lack of an epicanthic fold on her eyes, it seemed barely possible. "Very well," he said reluctantly. "But she is only to look and listen. Asking questions could draw the wrong eyes to her and I'll not let her take that chance."

"I will tell her of your concern," the merchant said.

Servants came—silent turbaned men bowing as they took away the

horses, even more deeply bowing men and women, smiling as they proffered silver goblets of cool wine and golden trays with damp towels for
dusty hands and faces.

A round-faced, swarthy man appeared before Conan, bobbing quick
bows as he spoke. "I am Punjar, master, steward of the palace. My
mistress has commanded me to see personally to your wishes."

Conan looked for Vyndra and could not see her. The servants made
a milling mass about the Cimmerian's party on the stairs, asking how
they might serve, speaking of baths and beds. Momentary thoughts of
devious traps flitted through his mind. But Kang Hou was following a
serving girl in one direction while his nieces were led in another and
Conan had few remaining doubts of the merchant's ability to avoid a
snare. Ghurran, he saw, had retained his horse.

"Do you mistrust this place, herbalist?" Conan asked.

"Less than you, apparently. Of course she is both a woman and a
Vendhyan, which means that she will either guard you with her life or
kill you in your sleep." Days in the open had darkened and weathered
the old man's skin, making it less parchmentlike, and his teeth gleamed
whitely as he grinned at Conan's discomfort. "I intend to ride into
Gwandiakan. It is possible I might find the ingredients for your antidote
there."

"That old man," Hordo grumbled as the herbalist rode away, "seems
to live on sunlight and water, like a tree. I do not think he even sleeps."

"You merely grow jealous as you catch up to him in age," Conan said
and laughed as the one-eyed man scowled into his beard.

The corridors through which Punjar led him made the Cimmerian
wonder at Vyndra's comment that the palace was barely habitable. The
varicolored carpets scattered on polished marble floors, the great tapestries lining the walls, were finer than any he had seen in palaces in
Nemedia or Zamora, lands noted in the West for their luxury. Golden
lamps set with amethyst and opal hung on silver chains from ceilings
painted with scenes of ancient heroes and leopard hunts and fanciful
winged creatures. Cunningly wrought ornaments of delicate crystal and
gold sat on tables of ebony and ivory inlaid with turquoise and silver.

The baths were pools mosaicked in geometric patterns, but among
the multi-hued marble tiles were others of agate and lapis lazuli. The
waters were warm in one pool, cool in another, and veiled serving girls
in their servant's pristine white scurried to pour perfumed oils into the
water, to bring him soaps and soft toweling. He kept his broadsword
close at hand, moving it from the side of one pool to the side of the
next as he changed temperatures, and this set the women twittering

softly to one another behind their veils. He ignored their shocked looks; to disarm himself was to show more trust than he could muster.

Refusing the elaborate silken robes—including, he saw with some amusement, the long lengths of silk to wind into a turban—that they brought to replace his dusty, travel-stained garb, Conan chose out a plain tunic of dark blue and belted on his sword over that. Punjar appeared again, bowing deeply.

"If you will follow me, master?" The round-faced man seemed nervous and Conan kept a hand on his sword-hilt as he motioned the other to lead.

The chamber to which Conan was taken had a high vaulted ceiling and narrow columns worked in elaborate gilded frescoes. Surely such columns were too thin to be meant for support. At the top of the walls intricate latticework had been cut in the marble; the scrolled openings were tiny, Conan noted, but perhaps still large enough for a crossbow bolt.

The floor, of crimson and white diamond-shaped tile of marble, was largely bare, though a profusion of silken cushions was scattered to one side. Placed beside the cushions were low tables of hammered brass bearing golden trays of dates and figs, a ruby-studded golden goblet and a tall crystal flagon of wine. Conan wondered if it were poisoned and then almost laughed aloud at the thought of poisoning a man already dying of poison.

"Pray be seated, master," Punjar said, gesturing to the cushions.

Conan lowered himself but demanded, "Where is Vyndra?"

"My mistress rests from her travels, master, but she has commanded an entertainment for you. My mistress begs that you excuse her absence, and begs also that you remember her request that her serving women be treated gently." Bowing once more, he was gone.

Abruptly music floated from the latticework near the ceiling—the thrum of citherns, the piping of flutes, the rhythmic thump of tambours. Three women darted into the room with quick, tiny steps to stand in the center of the bare floor. Only their hands and feet were not covered by thick layers of many-colored silk, and opaque veils covered their faces from chin to eyes. To the sound of the music they began to dance, finger-cymbals clinking and tiny golden bells tinkling at their ankles.

Even for a Vendhyan, Conan thought, this was too elaborate a way to kill a man. Filling the goblet with wine, he reclined to watch and enjoy.

At first the dancers' steps were slow but by tiny increments their speed increased. In flowing movements they spun and leaped, and with each spin, with each leap, a bit of colorful silk drifted away from them. Graceful jumps in unison they made, with legs outstretched, or they writhed with feet planted and arms twined above their heads. The length and breadth of the floor they covered, now moving away from him, now gliding almost to the cushions. Then all the silks were gone save their veils, and the three lush-bodied women danced in only their satiny skins, gleaming with a faint sheen of perspiration.

At the sharp clap of Conan's hands, the dancers froze, rounded breasts heaving from their exertions. The musicians, unseeing and unaware of what transpired, played on.

"You two go," the Cimmerian commanded, indicating his choices. "You stay and dance." Dark eyes exchanged uncertain glances above veils. "Your mistress commanded an entertainment for me," he went on. "Must I drag the three of you through the palace in search of her to tell her you will not obey?" The looks that passed between the women were frightened now. The two he had pointed out ran from the chamber. The third woman stared after them as though on the point of running also. "Dance for me," Conan said.

Hesitantly, reluctantly, she found her steps again. Before, the dancers had seemed more aware of the music than of Conan, but now this woman's head turned constantly, independent of her dance, to keep her dark eyes on his face. She flowed across the floor, whirling and leaping as gracefully as before, but there was a nervousness, too, as though she felt his gaze as a palpable caress on her nudity.

As she came close to him, Conan grabbed a slim, belled ankle. With a squeal she toppled to the cushions and lay staring at him over her veil with wide eyes. For long moments there was no sound but the music and her agitated breathing.

"Please, master," she whispered finally. "My mistress asks that her serving women—"

"Am I your master then?" Conan asked. Idly he ran a finger from slender calf to rounded thigh, and she shivered. "What if I send for Punjar, saying you have not pleased me? What if I demand he switch you here and now?"

"Then I . . . I would be switched, master," she whispered and swallowed hard.

Conan shook his head. "Truly, Vendhyans are mad. Would you really go so far to hide the truth from me?" Before she could flinch away, he snatched the veil from her face.

For an instant Vyndra stared up at him, scarlet suffusing her cheeks.

Then her eyes snapped shut, and frantically she tried to cover herself with her arms.

"It did not work with Kang Hou," Conan laughed, "and it does not work with me." Her blush deepened and her eyes squeezed tighter. "This time your playing at games has gone awry," he said, leaning over her. "One chance, and one chance only, will I give you to run and then I will show you what men and women do who do not play games."

The crimson did not leave her cheeks, but her eyes opened just enough for her to look at him through long lashes. "You fool," she murmured. "I could have run from you any day since my hands were unbound."

Throwing her arms about his neck, she pulled him down to her.

XIX

As shadows lengthened with the sinking sun, Conan left Vyndra sleeping on the cushions and went in search of more wine.

"Immediately, master," a servant said in response to his request, adding at his next question, "No, master, the two men have not yet returned from the city. I know nothing of the Khitan woman, master."

Finding a chamber with tall, arched windows looking to the west, Conan sat with his foot on the windowsill and his back against its frame. The sun, violent red in a purpling sky, hung its own diameter above the towering trees in the distance. It was a grim sight, fit for his mood. The day had been useless. Waiting in the palace, even making love to Vyndra, however enjoyable, now seemed time wasted. At least in following the caravan this far there had been the illusion of doing something about the poison in his veins, of hunting down the men whose deaths he must see to before his own. One of those men, at least, was in the city, not a league distant, and here he sat, waiting.

"Patil?"

At the soft female voice, he looked around. An unveiled Vendhyan woman stood in the doorway of the chamber, her plain robes of cotton neither those of a servant nor of a noble.

"You do not recognize me," she said with a smile, and abruptly he did.

"Kuie Hsi," he gasped. "I did not believe you could so completely—" Impatiently he put all that aside. "What did you learn?"

"Much, and little. The caravan remained in the city only hours, for the merchants' markets are in Ayodhya and the nobles are impatient to reach the court. Karim Singh, however," she added as he leaped to his feet, "is yet in Gwandiakan, though I could not learn where."

"He will not escape me," Conan growled. "Nor this Naipal, wizard though he be. But why does the *wazam* remain here rather than going on to the court?"

"Perhaps because, according to rumor, Naipal has been in Gwandiakan for two days. As his face is known to few, however, this cannot be confirmed."

Conan's fist smacked into his palm. "Crom, but this cannot be other than fate. Both of them within my grasp. I will finish it this night."

The Khitan woman caught his arm as he started from the chamber. "If you mean to enter Gwandiakan, take care, for the city is uneasy. Soldiers have been arresting the children of the streets, all of the homeless urchins and beggar children, supposedly on the orders of the *wazam*. Many are angered, and the poorer sections of the city need but a spark to burst into flame. The streets of Gwandiakan could run with blood over this."

"I have seen blood before," he said grimly, and then he was striding down the tapestried corridors. "Punjar! My horse!"

But half-awake, Vyndra stretched on the cushions, noting lazily that the lamps had been lit and night was come. Abruptly she frowned. Someone had laid a silken coverlet over her. With a gasp she clutched the covering to her at the sight of Chin Kou. The Khitan woman's arms were filled with folds of many-colored silk.

"I brought garments," Chin Kou said.

Vyndra pulled the coverlet up about her neck. "And what made you think I would need clothing?" she demanded haughtily.

"I am sorry," Chin Kou said, turning to leave. "No doubt when you wish to cover yourself, you will summon servants. I will leave you the coverlet since you seem to desire that."

"Wait!" Blushing, Vyndra fingered the coverlet. "I did not know. As you have brought the garments, you might as well leave them."

Chin Kou arched an eyebrow. "There is no need to take such a tone with me. I know very well what you were doing with the *cheng-li* who calls himself Patil." Vyndra groaned, the scarlet in her cheeks deepening. After a moment the merchant's daughter took pity. "I was doing the same thing with the *cheng-li* who calls himself Hasan. Now I know your secret and you know mine. You fear only shame before your servants. My uncle's switch produces a much greater smarting than mere shame."

Vyndra stared at the other woman as though seeing her for the first time. It was not that she had been unaware of Chin Kou, but the Khitan was a merchant's niece and surely merchants' nieces did not think and feel in the same way as a woman born of the Kshatriya blood. Or did they? "Do you love him?" she asked. "Hasan, I mean?"

"Yes," Chin Kou said emphatically, "though I do not know if he returns my feelings. Do you love the man called Patil?"

Vyndra shook her head. "As well love a tiger. But," she added with a mischievousness she could not control, "to be made love to by a tiger is a very fine thing."

"Hasan," Chin Kou said gravely, "is also very vigorous."

Suddenly the two women were giggling, and the giggles became deep-throated laughter.

"Thank you for the clothing," Vyndra said when she could talk again. Tossing aside the coverlet, she rose. Chin Kou aided her in dressing, though she did not ask it, and once she was garbed, she said, "Come. We will have wine and talk of men and tigers and other strange beasts."

As the Khitan woman opened her mouth to reply, a shrill scream echoed through the palace, followed by the shouts of men and the clang of steel on steel.

Chin Kou clutched at Vyndra's arm. "We must hide."

"Hide!" Vyndra exclaimed. "This is *my* palace and I will not cower in it like a rabbit."

"Foolish pride speaks," the smaller woman said. "Think what kind of bandits would attack a palace! Do you think your noble blood will protect you?"

"Yes. And you also. Even brigands will know that a ransom will be paid, for you and your sister as well, once they know who I am."

"Know who you are?" came a voice from the doorway, and Vyndra jumped in spite of herself.

"Kandar," she breathed. Pride said to stand her ground defiantly, but she could not stop herself from backing away as the cruel-eyed prince swaggered into the chamber, a bloody sword in his fist. In the corridor behind him were turban-helmed soldiers, also with crimson-stained weapons.

He stooped to take something from the floor—the veil she had worn while dancing—and fingered it thoughtfully as he advanced. "Perhaps you think you are a noble-woman," he said, "perhaps even the famous Lady Vyndra, known for the brilliance of her wit and the dazzling gatherings at her palaces? Alas, the tale has been well told already of how the Lady Vyndra fell prey beyond the Himelias to a savage barbarian who carried her off, to death perhaps, or slavery."

"What can you possibly hope to gain by this farce?" Vyndra demanded, but the words faded as six veiled women, swathed in concealing layers of silk, entered the room. And with them was Prytanis.

Smirking, the Nemedian leaned against the wall with his arms crossed. "The gods are good, wench," he said, "for who should I find in Gwandiakan but Prince Kandar, who was interested to learn of the presence of a certain woman nearby. A purse of gold he offered for the nameless jade, and I could only accept his generosity."

Annoyance flashed across Kandar's face, but he seemed otherwise unaware of the other man. "Prepare her," he commanded. "Prepare both of them. I will not refuse an extra trifle when it is put before me."

"No!" Vyndra screamed.

She whirled to run, but before she had crossed half the chamber, three of the veiled women were on her, pushing her to the floor. With a corner of her mind she was aware of the other three holding Chin Kou, but panting desperation flooded every part of her. Frantically, futilely, she fought, but the women rolled her this way and that, stripping away her so-recently donned robes with humiliating ease. When she was naked, they would not allow her to regain her feet but dragged her writhing across the floor with kicking legs trailing behind her. At Kandar's feet they forced her to her knees and his gaze chilled her to the bone, turning her muscles to water, stilling her struggles. Chin Kou was knelt beside her, as naked as she and sobbing with terror, but Vyndra could not take her eyes from Kandar's.

"You cannot hope to get away with this," she whispered. "I am not some nameless—"

"You *are* nameless," he snapped. "I told you, the Lady Vyndra is gone"—slowly he fastened the veil across her face by its tiny silver chain—"and in her place is a new addition to my *purdhana*. I think I will name you Maryna."

"Your sister," Vyndra panted. She had had no trouble with the veil while dancing; now it seemed to restrict her breathing. "I will free Alyna. I will—" His slap jerked her head sideways.

"I have no sister," he growled.

"What of my gold?" Prytanis demanded suddenly. "The wench is yours, and I want my payment."

"Of course." Kandar took a purse from his belt, tossing it to the slit-nosed man. "It is satisfactory?"

Prytanis eagerly untied the purse strings and spilled some of the golden coins into his palm. "It is satisfactory," he said. "If only Conan could see—" His words ended in a grunt as Kandar's sword thrust into his middle. Gold rang on the floor tiles as he grabbed the blade with both hands.

Kandar met the Nemedian's unbelieving gaze levelly. "You gazed on the unveiled faces of two women of my *purdhana*," he explained. The razor steel slid easily from the dying man's grasp, and Prytanis fell atop his gold.

Face smarting, Vyndra gathered the last shreds of her courage. "To kill your own hirelings and take back the gold is like you, Kandar. You were always a fool and a worm." His dark gaze made her realize it *had* been the last of her courage. She clenched her teeth with the effort of facing him.

"He saw your face unveiled," the prince said, "and that of the Khitan woman, so he had to die, for my honor. But he earned the gold and I am no thief. You will be beaten once for that and again for each of the other insults."

"I am of the Kshatriya blood." Vyndra spoke the words for her own benefit, as though to deny what had happened, and no one else seemed to notice them.

"This was the last of your strange companions," Kandar continued. "The others are already dead. All of them."

A whimper rose in Vyndra's throat. The vanishing of a small hope she had not know was there until it was gone, the hope that the huge barbarian would rescue her, left her now truly with nothing. "You will never break me," she whispered and knew the emptiness of the words even as they left her lips.

"Break you?" Kandar said mockingly. "Of course not. But there must be some small training in obedience. Some small humbling of your pride." Vyndra wanted to shake her head in denial, but his eyes held hers like a serpent mesmerizing a bird. "On the morrow you will be placed on a horse, garbed as now, and paraded through the streets of Gwandiakan so that all may see the beauty of my new possession. Bring them!" he snapped at the women.

With all of her heart Vyndra wanted to muster a shout of defiance, but she knew, as she was dragged to the horses, that it was a wail of despair that echoed in the halls of her palace.

XX

At a crude plank table by himself in the corner of a dirt-floored tavern, Conan was reminded of Sultanapur as he tugged the hood of his dark cloak, borrowed from a groom at Vyndra's palace, deeper over his face. Wondering when he would next be in a city without the need to hide his features, he emptied half the cheap wine in his wooden tank in one long swallow.

The others in the tavern were Vendhyans all, though far from the nobles or wealthy of Gwandiakan. Carters who smelled of their oxen rubbed elbows with masons' apprentices in tunics stained with gray splashes of dried mortar. Nondescript turbaned men hunkered over their wine or talked in hushed tones with black eyes darting to see who might overhear. The smell of sour wine warred with incense, and the muted babble of voices did not quite mask the tinkle of bells at the wrists and ankles of sloe-eyed doxies parading through the tavern. Unlike their sisters in the West, their robes covered them from ankle to neck, but those robes were of the sheerest gossamer, concealing nothing. The jades found few customers, though, and the usual frivolity of taverns was absent. The air was filled with a tension darker than the night outside the walls. The Cimmerian was not the only man to keep his face hidden.

Conan signaled for more wine. A serving wench, her garb but a trifle more opaque than that of the trulls, brought a rough clay pitcher, took his coin and hurried away without a word, obviously eager to return to her cubbyhole and hide.

That tightly wound nervousness had been evident in the entire city from his arrival, and it had grown tighter as the night went on. Soldiers were still arresting homeless waifs and beggar children, such few as had not gone to ground like pursued foxes, carrying them off to the fortress prison that stood in the center of Gwandiakan. But even the soldiers could sense the mood of the sullen throngs. Patrols now often numbered a hundred men, and they moved as though expecting attack at any moment.

The streets had been full of talk earlier, full of rumor, and the Cimmerian had no trouble in hearing of the men he sought. Quickly he learned the location of Prince Kandar's palace, one of the few east of the city, and of that where Karim Singh was said to be staying. Before he had gone a hundred paces, however, he heard of another palace said to house the *wazam*, and fifty paces beyond that a third, both widely separated from each other and from the first. Each corner brought a new rumor. Half the palaces of Gwandiakan were said to contain Karim Singh. Tongues could be found to name *every* palace as housing Naipal, and many spoke of an invisible palace constructed in a night by the mage, while still others claimed the wizard watched the city from above, from the clouds. In the end it was frustration that had sent Conan into the tavern.

A wave of dizziness that had nothing to do with the wine swept over him, not for the first time that night, clouding his vision. Grimly he fought it off, and when his eyes cleared, Hordo was sliding onto a bench across the table from him.

"I have been looking for you for hours," the one-eyed man said. "Kandar attacked Vyndra's palace with a hundred lancers and took Vyndra and the Khitan's niece, Chin Kou. Prytanis was with him."

With a snarl Conan smashed his wooden tankard to the dirt floor. Momentary silence rolled through the room, and every eye swiveled to him. Then, hastily, talk began again. It was not a night to become involved in a stranger's anger.

"The men?" Conan asked.

"Nicks and cuts. No more. We managed to get to the horses and Kuie Hsi found us a place to hide, an abandoned temple on something called the Street of Dreams, though miserable dreams they must be. A day or two of rest and healing and we'll see what can be done about the wenches."

Conan shook his head, as much to clear it as in negation. "I do not have a day or two. Best you return to this temple. They will need you if they are to make it back to Turan."

"What are you about?" Hordo demanded, but the Cimmerian only clapped his friend on the shoulder and hurried from the tavern. As Conan trotted down the darkened street, he heard the one-eyed man calling behind him, but he did not look back.

The Bhalkhana stallion was stabled near the city gate by which he had entered Gwandiakan, and a coin retrieved the big black from a wizened liveryman. The city gates themselves were massive, ten times the height of a man, and made of black iron plates worked in fanciful designs. They would not be easily moved, and from the dirt that had accumulated along their bases, it had been years since they were closed. The city's ill ease hung on the turban-helmed gate guards as well, and they only watched him nervously, fingering their spears, as he galloped through.

The one bit of definite information he had learned in his night of listening, the one story that did not change—and the one he had thought least useful even at that—was the location of Kandar's palace. Rage filled him, but it was an icy rage. To die with sword in hand would be much preferable to succumbing to the poison in his veins, but the women must be freed first. Only when they were safe could he allow himself to think of his own concerns.

Short of the palace he rode into a copse of trees and tied the stallion's reins to a branch. Stealth and cunning, bred in his days as a thief, would better serve him now than steel.

Prince Kandar's palace, larger even than Vyndra's, shone in the night with the light of a thousand lamps, a gleaming alabaster intricacy of terraces, domes and spires. Reflection pools stretched on all sides and between them gardens of flowering shrubs reached the very walls of the palace, their myriad blossoms filling the darkness with a hundred perfumes.

Perfumes and blossoms did not interest Conan, but the shrubs served well to cover his silent approach. He was but one shadow among many. Fingers trained by climbing the cliffs of his native Cimmerian mountains found crevices in the seemingly smooth joining of great marble blocks, and he scaled the palace wall as another man might climb a ladder.

Lying flat atop the broad wall, Conan surveyed what he could of the palace—small courtyards with splashing fountains, intricately friezed towers thrusting toward the sky, colonnaded walks lit by lamps of cunningly wrought gold. Breath caught in his throat, and his hand went unbidden to his sword. Past the fluted columns of one of those colonnades walked a man in robes of gold and crimson with another in what seemed black silk. Karim Singh. And, if the gods were with him, Naipal.

With a regretful sigh he released the sword-hilt and watched the two men walk on beyond his sight. The women, he told himself. The women first. Scrambling to his feet, he ran along the wall.

Height was the key, as experience in the cities of Nemedia and Zamora had taught him. A man glimpsed in the upper reaches of a structure, even one who obviously did not belong there, was often ignored. After all, without a right to be there, how could he have traveled so far? Too, entering on the upper levels meant that every step took a man closer to the ground and his route to escape. Escape was especially important this night, for the two women if not for him.

Cornices, friezes and a hundred elaborate workings of alabaster stone made a swift path for the big Cimmerian. Slipping through a narrow window just below the roof, he found himself in a pitch-dark stuffy room. By touch he quickly ascertained that it was a storeroom for carpets and bedding. The narrow door opened onto a corridor dimly lit by brass lamps. No gold hangings or fine tapestries here, for these upper floors were servants' quarters. Snores drifted from some of the rooms. As silent and grim as a hunting cat, Conan padded into the hall. Stairs led him down.

Sounds floated from other parts of the palace—an indistinguishable murmur of voices, the thrum of a cithern. Once the single deep toll of a gong echoed mournfully. The Cimmerian let them pass all but unnoticed, his eyes and ears straining instead for the flicker of shadow or hint of a soft footfall that might betray any who could give an alarm.

It was a bedchamber he sought, he was sure of that. From what he knew of Kandar, such would have been his first stop with the women, and it would no doubt suit his fancy to have them awaiting his return were he not still with them. Conan hoped that he was. Karim Singh and Naipal would certainly escape him this night but it would be good to deal with Kandar at least.

The first three bedchambers he found were empty, though golden lamps cast soft light in wait for their eventual occupants. As he stepped into the fourth, only a sense below the levels of understanding threw him into a forward roll an instant before razor steel slashed through the place where his head had been.

Conan came to his feet with broadsword in hand, and a vigorous cut made his attacker leap back. The Cimmerian stared at his opponent, for he had not seen the man's like before, not even in this strange land. A nasaled helm with a thick spike topped his dark expressionless face, and his armor was of leather studded with brass. A long straight sword was in his gauntleted right hand, a shorter curved blade in his left, and he moved as though he knew well the use of each.

"I am here for the women," Conan said in a taunting voice. If he could make the man exchange words with him, the other might not think to give an alarm even while they strove to slay each other. "Tell me where they are, and I'll not kill you." The man's silent rush forced him to throw up his blade in defense.

And it was defense, the Cimmerian realized in shock. His broadsword flashed and darted as swiftly as ever it had, but it was all in a desperate effort to keep the other's steel from striking him. For the first time in his life he faced a man faster than himself. Slashes with the speed of a striking viper forced him back. Snarling, he gambled, continuing the motion of a block with a smash of his fisted hilt to his opponent's face.

The strangely armored man was thrown back, an inlaid table crushed to splinters by his fall, but before Conan could take more than a single step to follow up his attack, the other sprang to his feet. Conan met him in the center of the room, and sparks were struck as steel wove a deadly lace between them. The Cimmerian poured all of his rage—at Kandar, at Naipal, at Karim Singh—into his attack, refusing this time to yield a step. Abruptly a slicing blow of his broadsword sheared through flesh and bone, but even as it did, he was forced to jump back to avoid a decapitating stroke.

Landing on guard and ready to continue, Conan felt the hair on the back of his neck stir. His last blow had stopped his opponent—and indeed it should have, as the short curved sword now lay on the carpet along with the hand that gripped it—but it was obviously only a temporary halt. That expressionless face had not changed in the least, and the dark flat eyes did not so much as glance at the severed wrist, a wound that gave not a single drop of blood. Sorcery, the Cimmerian thought. Suddenly the silence in which the other had fought took on eerie quality. And then the murderous assault began anew.

If the sorcerous warrior was accustomed to fighting with two swords, he seemed little less able with only one. Conan met each lightning stroke but his own were met as well. He could match the other now, the Cimmerian knew, one blade against one blade, but could mortal flesh outlast the endurance of sorcery?

Abruptly the severed stump struck the side of Conan's head with a force greater than he would have believed possible, flinging him back as though he were a child. It was his turn to find himself on his back amidst the ruins of a table, but before he could rise, his attacker was on him.

Desperately Conan blocked a downward blow that would have split his skull. Among the wreckage of the table his hand closed on a hilt, and he thrust. The other man twisted like a serpent, and the blade cut through his leather armor, slicing across his ribs. As though his bones had melted, the dark warrior collapsed atop Conan.

Quickly the Cimmerian heaved the body from him and sprang to his feet with sword ready, fearing some trick. The leather-armored figure did not move; the flat black eyes were glazed.

In wonder Conan looked at the weapon he had taken up and almost dropped it as he cursed. It seemed a short-sword but the hilt was long enough for two hands, and blade and hilt alike were wrought of some strange silvery metal that glowed with unearthly light.

A smell made his nose twitch and he cursed again. It was the stink of putrefaction. Within the leather armor the corpse of his opponent was already half-decayed, white bone showing through rotted flesh. An ensorcelled warrior slain by an obviously ensorcelled blade. Part of his mind urged Conan to leave the foul thing but another part whispered that such might be useful against a sorcerer like Naipal. Mages were not always so easily slain as other men.

Sheathing his broadsword, he hastily tore silk from the coverlets on the bed and wrapped the silvery weapon, thrusting it behind his sword-belt. As he did so, he heard pounding boots approaching, many of them. The splintered tables, with scattered chests and broken crystal and shattered mirrors, were mute evidence that the battle had not been silent after all. Muttering imprecations, he ran for the windows, climbing through just as a score of Vendhyan soldiers poured into the room.

Once more alabaster ornamentations were his roadway along the wall, but behind him he heard cries of alarm. Upward he climbed, grasping a balustrade to pull himself onto a balcony . . . and stopping with one foot over at the sight of another dozen men in turbaned helms. A thrown spear streaked by his head and he threw himself desperately back as other arms were cocked.

Even with knees bent, the force of landing shook him to the bone. More voices took up the cry of alarm, and the thud of running boots came from both left and right. A spear lanced from above to quiver in the ground not a pace from him. He leaped away from the wall, and another spear shivered where he had stood. Bent double, he ran into the garden between the reflecting pools, becoming one with the shadows.

"Guards!" the cries rose. "Guards!"

"Beat the gardens!"

"Find him!"

From the edge of the trees Conan watched, teeth bared in a snarl. Soldiers milled about the palace like ants about a kicked anthill. There would be no entering that palace again tonight.

Pain ripped through him, muscles spasming, doubling him over. Gasping for breath, he forced himself erect. His hand closed on the silk-shrouded hilt of the strange weapon. "I am not dead yet," he whispered, "and it will not be over until I am." With no more sound than the wind in the leaves, he faded into the darkness.

Naipal stared at the ruin of his bedchamber in shocked disbelief, willing himself not to breathe the smell of decay that hung in the air. The shouts of searching soldiers did not register on his ear. Only the contents of that chamber were real at that moment, and they in a way that turned his stomach with fear and sent blinding pains through his head.

The leather armor held his eye with sickly fascination. A skull grinned up at him from the ancient helm. Bones and dust were all that was left of his warrior. His warrior who could not die. The first of an army that could not die. In the name of all the gods, how had it happened?

With an effort he pulled his gaze from the leather-clad skeleton, but inexorably it fell on the long golden coffer, now lying on its side amid splinters of ebony that had been a table, lying there open and empty. Empty! Shards of elaborately carved ivory were all that was left of the mirror of warning, and naught but a hundred jagged pieces remained of the mirror itself.

Grunting, he bent to pick up half a dozen of the mirror fragments. Each, whatever its size, was filled by an image, an image that would be on all the other pieces as well, an image that would never change now. Wonderingly, he studied that grim face in the fragments, a square-cut black mane held back by a leather cord, strange eyes the color and hardness of sapphire, a feral snarl baring white teeth.

He knew who it had to be. The man who called himself Patil. Karim Singh's simple barbarian. But the mirror, even now at the last, would show only what threatened his plans. Could a simple barbarian do that? Could a simple barbarian seek him out so quickly? Know to break the mirror and steal the demon-wrought dagger? Slay what could not be slain? The pieces fell from Naipal's fingers as he whispered the word he did not want to believe. "Pan-kur."

"What was that?" Karim Singh asked as he entered the room. The wazam carefully kept his eyes from the thing in leather armor on the floor. "You look exhausted, Naipal. Kandar's servants will clean this mess, and his soldiers will deal with the intruder. You must rest. I will not have you collapse before you can serve me as king."

"We must go immediately," Naipal said. He rubbed his temples with the tips of his fingers. The strain of the past days wore at him, and he would not now take the effort to feign servility. "Tell Kandar to gather his soldiers."

"I have been thinking, Naipal. What will it matter if we wait a few days? Surely it will rain soon, and the stinging flies are said to be better after a rain."

"Fool!" the wizard howled, and Karim Singh's jaw dropped. "You will have me serve you as king? Wait and you will not be king, you will be meat for dogs!" Naipal's eyes went to the scattered fragments of mirror and slid away. "And tell Kandar we must have more soldiers. Tell him to strip the fortress if need be. A simple spell will divert your fearsome flies."

"The governor is uneasy," Karim Singh said shakily. "He obeys but I can tell that he does not believe my reasons for ordering the street children arrested. Given the mood of the city, he might refuse such a command and even if he obeys, he will doubtless send riders to Ayodhya, to Bhandarkar."

"Do not fear Bhandarkar. If you must fear someone . . ." Naipal's voice was soft, but his eyes burned so that Karim Singh took a step back and seemed to have trouble breathing. "Tell the governor that if he defies me, I will wither his flesh and put him in the streets as a tongueless beggar to watch his wives and daughters dragged away to brothels. Tell him!" And the *wazam* of Vendhya fled like a servant. Naipal forced his gaze back to the fragments of mirror, back to the hundred-times repeated image.

"You will not conquer, *pan-kur*," he whispered. "I will yet be victorious over you."

XXI

ordo had been right about the Street of Dreams, Conan thought when he first saw it in the gray light of dawn. The stallion picked its way along the dirt roadway between muddy pools of offal and piles of rubble overgrown with weeds. The buildings were skulls, with empty windows for eye sockets. Roofs sagged where they had not fallen in. Walls leaned and some had collapsed, spewing clay bricks across the dirt of the Street, revealing barren, rat-infested interiors. Occasional ragged, furtive shapes appeared in a doorway or darted across the street behind him. The people of the Street of Dreams were like scurrying rodents, fearful to poke their noses into the light. The stench of decay and mold filled the air. Ill dreams indeed, Conan thought. Ill dreams indeed.

The abandoned temple was not hard to find, a domed structure with pigeons fluttering through gaping holes in the dome. Once eight fluted marble columns had stood across its front, but now three had fallen. Two lay in fragments across the street, weeds growing thickly along their edges. Of the third only a stump remained. Part of the front wall had fallen too, revealing that what must have once seemed to be marble blocks were in truth only a stone facing over clay bricks. The opening widened and heightened the temple door enough for a man to enter on horseback. There was no sign of the smugglers but the gloomy interior could have hidden them easily. Or ten times their number of the area's denizens. Conan drew his sword. He had to duck his head as he rode through the gap in the wall.

Within was a large dim room, its cracked floor tiles covered with dust and broken bricks. The thick pillars here were of wood, all splintered with rot. At the far end of the chamber there was a marble altar, its edges chipped and cracked, but of whatever god it had been raised to, there was no evidence.

Before the stallion had taken three paces into the room, Hordo appeared from behind a pillar. "It is about time you got here, Cimmerian. I was all but ready to give you up for dead this time."

Enam and Shamil stepped out, too, with arrows nocked but not drawn. Both had bandages showing. "We did not know it was you," the young Turanian said. "There are pigeons roasting on a spit in the back, if you are hungry."

"We try to hide the smell of them," Enam said, spitting. "The people here are like vermin. They look ready to swarm over anyone with food like a pack of rats."

Conan nodded as he stepped down from the saddle. Once on the ground, he had to hold onto the stirrup leather for a moment; the pains and dizziness had not returned, but weakness had come in their place. "I have seen nothing like them," he said. "In Turan or Zamora it is a far cry from palace to beggar, but here it seems two different lands."

"Vendhya is a country of great contrasts," Kang Hou said, approaching from the rear of the ruined structure.

"It is like a melon rotting from within," Conan replied. "A fruit overripe for plucking." The weakness was lessening. It came in cycles. "Someday perhaps I will return with an army and pluck it."

"Many have said as much," the Khitan replied, "yet the Kshatriyas still rule here. Forgive my unseemly haste, but Hordo has told us you sought Prince Kandar's palace last night. You could not find my niece? Or Lady Vyndra?"

"I could not reach them," Conan said grimly. "But I will before I am done."

Kang Hou's face did not change expression, and all he said was, "Hasan says the pigeons must be taken from the fire. He suggests they be eaten before they grow cold."

"The man must have a heart like stone," Hordo muttered as the other two smugglers followed the Khitan out.

"He is a tough man for a merchant," Conan agreed. He tugged the silk-wrapped weapon from his belt and handed it to his friend. "What do you make of this?"

Hordo gasped as the cloth fell away, revealing the faintly glowing silvery metal. "Sorcery! As soon as I heard there was a wizard in this, I should have turned my horse around." His eye squinted as he peered at the weapon. "This design makes no sense, Cimmerian. A two-handed hilt on a short-sword?"

"It slew a man, or a thing, that my sword did not slow," Conan said.

The one-eyed man winced and hastily rebundled the silk about the weapon. "I do not want to know about it. Here. Take it." He chewed at nothing as the Cimmerian returned the weapon to its place tucked behind his sword-belt, then said, "There has been no sign of Ghurran. How did you pass the night without his potion?"

"Without missing the foul thing," Conan grunted. "Come. I could eat a dozen of those pigeons. Let us get to them before they are gone."

There were two large windowless rooms at the back of the temple, one without a roof. In that room was the fire; the other was used as a stable. Enam and Shamil squatted by the fire, wolfing down pigeon. The Khitan ate more delicately, while Hasan sat against a wall, clasping his knees and scowling at the world.

"Where is Kuie Hsi?" Conan wanted to know.

"She left before first light," Hordo told him around mouthfuls of roast pigeon, "to see what she could discover."

"I have returned," the Khitan woman said from the door, "again leaning much and little. I was slow in returning because the mood of the city is ugly. Angry crowds roam the streets and ruffians take advantage. A woman alone, I was twice almost assaulted."

"You have a light step," Conan complimented her. He would wager that the men who had "almost" assaulted her rued the incident if they still lived. "What is this much and little you have learned?"

Still in her Vendhyan garb, Kuie Hsi looked hesitantly at Kang Hou, who merely wiped his lips with a cloth and waited. "At dawn," she began slowly, "Karim Singh entered the city. The wizard, Naipal, was with him, and Prince Kandar. They took soldiers from the fortress, increasing the number of their escort to perhaps one thousand lances, and left the city, heading west. I heard a soldier say they rode to the Forests of Ghelai. The chests in which you are so interested went with them on mules."

For an instant Conan teetered on the horns of decision. Karim Singh and Naipal might escape him. There was no way to tell how much time he had left before the poison overtook him completely. Yet he knew there was only one way to decide. "If they took so many soldiers," he said, "few can remain at Kandar's palace to guard Vyndra and Chin Kou."

Kuie Hsi let her eyes drop to the floor, and her voice became a whisper. "There were two women with them, veiled but unclothed, and bound to their saddles. One was Chin Kou, the other the Vendhyan woman. Forgive me, uncle. I could see her but could do nothing."

"There is nothing to forgive," Kang Hou said, "for you have in no way failed. Any failure is mine alone."

"Perhaps it is," Conan said quietly, "but I cannot feel but that neither woman would be where she is except for me. And that means it is on me to see them safe. I will not ask any of you to accompany me. Beyond the matter of a thousand soldiers, you know there is a wizard involved, and he will be where I am going."

"Be not a fool," Hordo growled, and Enam added, "The Brotherhood of the Coast does not desert its own. Prytanis never understood that but I do."

"He has Chin Kou," Hasan burst out. "Do you expect me to sit here while he does Mitra alone knows what to her?" He seemed ready to fight Conan if need be.

"As for me," Kang Hou said with an amused smile for Hasan, "she is only my niece, of course." The young Turanian's face colored. "This is a matter of family honor."

Shamil gave a shaky laugh. "Well, I'll not be the only one to stay here. I wanted adventure, and none can say this is not it."

"Then let us ride," Conan said, "before they escape us."

"Patience," Kang Hou counseled. "The Forests of Ghelai are ten leagues distant, and a thousand men ride more slowly than six may. Let us not fail for a lack of preparation. There are stinging flies in the forests, but I know of an ointment that may abate their attack."

"Flies?" Hordo muttered. "Stinging flies? Wizards are not enough, Cimmerian? When we are out of this, you will owe me for the flies."

"And returning to Gwandiakan may not be wise," Kuie Hsi offered. "Soon there may be riots. A league this side of the forests there is said to be a well, thought to be a stopping place for caravans in ancient times but long abandoned. There I will await you with food and clothing for Chin Kou and Vyndra. And word if the city is safe. I will draw maps."

Conan knew they were right. How many times in his days as a thief had he sneered at others for their lack of preparation and the lack of success that went with it? But now he could only grind his teeth with the frustration of waiting an instant. Time and the knowledge of the poison in his veins pressed heavily on him. But he would see Vyndra and Chin Kou free—and Karim Singh and Naipal dead—before he died.

By Crom, he vowed it.

XXII

Riding beneath the tall trees of the Forest of Ghelai, Conan was unsure whether Kang Hou's ointment was not worse than the flies it was meant to discourage. There was no smell to it, but the feel on the skin was much like that after wading in a cesspool. The horses had liked having it smeared on them no more than had the men. He slapped a tiny fly that would not be discouraged—the bite was like a red-hot needle stabbing his arm—and grimaced at the glittering-winged swarms that surrounded the meager column. Then again, perhaps the ointment was not so bad.

The forest canopy was far above their heads, many of the trees towering more than a hundred and fifty feet. The high branches were thickly woven, letting little light through, and that seeming tinged with green. Streams of long-tailed monkeys flowed from limb to limb, a hundred rivers of brown fur rolling in a hundred different directions. Flocks of multicolored birds, some with strange bills or elaborate tail feathers, screamed from high branches while others in a thousand varied hues made brilliant streaks against the green as they darted back and forth.

"There are no such flies on the plains of Zamora," Hordo grumbled, slapping. "I could be there instead of here had I a brain in my head. There are no such flies on the steppes of Turan. I could be there—"

"If you do not shut your teeth," Conan muttered, "the only place you will be is dead, and likely left to rot where you fall. Or do you think Kandar's soldiers are deaf?"

"They could not hear themselves pass wind for those Mitra-accursed birds," the one-eyed man replied, but he subsided into silence.

In truth Conan did not know how close or how far the Vendhyans might be. A thousand men left a plain trail, but the ground was soft and springy with a thousand years of continuous decay, and the chopping that passed for hoofprints could have been five hours old or the hundredth part of that. The Cimmerian did know the day was almost gone though, for all he could not see the sun. The amount of time they had been riding made that plain, and the dim greenish light was fading. He did not believe the soldiers would continue on in the dark.

Abruptly he reined in, forcing the others behind to do so as well, and peered in consternation at what lay ahead. Huge blocks of stone, overgrown with vines as thick as a man's arm, formed a wide wall fifty feet high that stretched north and south as far as the eye could make out in the dim verdant light. Directly before him was a towered gateway, though the gates that once had blocked it had been gone for centuries by the evidence of a great tree rising in its center. Beyond he could make out other shapes among the forest growth, massive ruins among the trees. And the trail they followed passed through that gateway.

"Would they pass the night in there?" Hordo asked. "Even the gods do not know what might be in a place like that."

"I think," Kang Hou said slowly, "that this might be where they were going." Conan looked at him curiously, but the slight merchant said no more.

"Then we follow," the Cimmerian said, swinging down from his saddle. "But we leave the horses here." He went on as mouths opened in protest. "A man hides better afoot, and we must be like ferrets scurrying through a thicket. There are a thousand Vendhyan lancers in this place, remember." That brought them down.

Leaving someone with the animals, Conan decided, was worse than useless. It would reduce their number by one and the man left behind could do nothing if a Vendhyan patrol came on him. All would enter the city together. Conan, sword in hand, was first through the ancient gateway, with Hordo close behind. Enam and Shamil brought up the rear with arrows nocked to their bowstrings. Alone of the small column, Kang Hou seemed unarmed, but the Cimmerian was ready to wager the merchant's throwing knives resided in his sleeves.

Conan had seen ruined cities before, some abandoned for centuries, or even millennia. Some would stand on mountain peaks until the earth shook and buried them. Others endured the sand-laden desert winds, slowly wearing away stone so that in another thousand years or two, unknowing eyes would see only formations of rock and believe chance alone made them resemble an abode of men. This city was different, however, as though some malevolent god, unwilling to wait for the slow wearing away by rain and wind, had commanded the forest to attack and consume all marks of man.

If they crept over the remains of a street, it was impossible to tell, for dirt and a thousand small plants covered all, and everywhere the trees. Much of the city was no more, with no sign that it had ever been. Only the most massive of structures remained—the palaces and the temples. Yet even they fought a loosing battle against the forest. Temple columns were so wreathed in vines that only the regularity of their spacing betrayed their existence. Here the marble tiles of a palace portico bulged with the roots of a giant tree, and there a wall of alabaster, now green with mold, buckled before the onslaught of another huge trunk. Toppled spires lay shrouded by conquering roots and monkeys gamboled on no-longer gleaming domes that might once have sheltered potentates.

The others seemed to feel the oppressiveness of the ruins, but neither Conan nor Kang Hou allowed themselves to be affected, outwardly at least. The Cimmerian would allow no such distractions from whatever time he had left. He ghosted through the fading light with a deadly intensity, eyes striving to pierce the layers of green and shadow ahead. And then there was something to see. Lights. Hundreds of scattered lights, flickering like giant fireflies.

Conan could see little from the ground, but nearby vines like hawsers trailed down from a balcony of what might have once been a palace. Sheathing his sword and shifting the silk-wrapped sorcerous weapon to a place behind his back, the Cimmerian climbed one of the thick vines hand over hand. The others followed as agilely as the monkeys of the forest.

Crouching behind a green-swathed stone balustrade, Conan studied the lights. They were torches atop poles stuck in the ground, forming a great circle. A knot of Vendhyan cavalrymen clustered around each torch, dismounted and fingering their swords nervously as they peered at the wall of growth surrounding them. Oddly, no insects fluttered in the light of the torches.

"Their ointment is better than yours, Khitan," Enam muttered, crushing one of the stinging flies. No one else spoke for the moment.

It was clear enough what the soldiers guarded. The great circle of torches surrounded a building more massive than any Conan had yet seen in the ruined city. Columned terraces and great domes rose more than twice as high as the tallest tree on the forest floor, yet others of the giant trunks rose in turn from those terraces, turning the huge structure into a small mountain.

"If they are in that," Hordo said softly, "how in Zandru's Nine Hells do we find them? It must have a hundred leagues of corridor and more chambers than a man could count."

"They are in there," Kang Hou said. "And I fear we must find them for more than their lives."

Conan eyed the merchant sharply. "What is it you know that I do not?"

"I *know* nothing," Kang Hou replied, "but I fear much." With that he scurried to the vines and began to climb back down. There was nothing Conan could do but follow.

Once on the ground again, the Cimmerian took the lead. The two women would be with Kandar, and Kandar would certainly be with Karim Singh and Naipal. In the huge building, Kang Hou said, and for all the denials, Conan was sure the man knew something. So be it, he thought.

It was a file of wraiths that flitted through the Vendhyan lines, easily avoiding the few soldiers who rode patrol among the clusters at the torches. Bushes and creepers grew from chinks between the marble blocks of the great structure's broad stairs and lifted tiles on the wide portico at their head. Tall bronze doors stood open, a thick wreathing of vines speaking of the centuries since they had been shifted from their present position. With his sword in advance, Conan entered.

Behind him he heard the gasps of the others as they followed but he knew what caused the sounds of astonishment and so did not look back. His eyes were all for the way ahead. From the huge portal a wide aisle of grit-covered tiles led between thick columns, layered with gold leaf, to a vast central chamber beneath a dome that towered hundreds of feet above. In the middle of that chamber stood a marble statue of a man, more than half the height of the dome and untouched by time. Conan's skin prickled at the armor on the figure, stone-carved to represent studded leather. Instead of a nasaled helm, however, a gleaming crown topped the massive head.

"Can that be gold?" Shamil gasped, staring up at the statue.

"Keep your mind to the matter at hand," Hordo growled, "or you'll not live long enough for worrying about gold." His eyes had a glitter though, as if he had calculated the weight of that crown to within a feather.

"I had thought it was but legend," Kang Hou breathed. "I had hoped it was but legend."

"What are you talking about?" Conan demanded. "This is not the first time you have indicated you knew something about this place. I think it is time to tell the rest of us."

This time the Khitan nodded. "Two millennia ago, Orissa, the first King of Vendhya, was interred in a tomb beneath his capital city, Maharastra. For five centuries he was worshiped as a god in a temple built over his tomb and containing a great figure of Orissa wearing a gold crown said to have been made by melting the crowns and scepters of all the lands he had conquered. Then, in a war of succession, Maharastra was sacked and abandoned by its people. With time the very location of the city was lost. Until now."

"That is very interesting," Conan said dryly, "but it has nothing to do with why we are here."

"On the contrary," Kang Hou told him. "If my niece dies, if we all die, we must slay the wizard Naipal before he looses what lies in the tomb beneath this temple. The legends that I know speak vaguely of horrors, but there is a prophecy associated with all of them. 'The army that cannot die will march again at the end of time.' "

Conan looked again at the carved armor, then shook his head stubbornly. "I am here for the women first. Then I will see to Naipal and the other two."

A boot crunched at one side of the chamber and Conan whirled, his broadsword coming up. A Vendhyan soldier, eyes bulging beneath his turbaned helm, clutched at the throwing knife in his throat and fell to lie still on the floor. Kang Hou hurried to retrieve his blade.

"Khitan merchants seem a tough lot," Hordo said incredulously. "Perhaps we should include him when we divide that crown."

"Matters at hand." Conan grunted. "Remember?"

"I do not say leave the women," the one-eyed man grumbled, "but could we not take the crown as well?"

Conan paid no heed. His interest lay in where the soldier had come from. Only one doorway on that side of the chamber, and that the nearest to the corpse, opened onto stairs leading beneath the temple. At the base of those stairs he could see a glimmer of light, as of a torch farther on.

"Hide the Vendhyan," he commanded. "If anyone comes looking for him, they'll not think that wound in his throat was made by a monkey."

Impatiently hefting his sword, he waited for Hasan and Enam to carry the corpse into a dark corridor and return alone. Without a word, then, he started down.

XXIII

In a huge high-ceilinged chamber far beneath the temple once dedicated to Orissa, Naipal again paused in his work to look with longing expectation at the doorway to his power. Many doorways opened into the chamber, letting on the warren of passages that crossed and criss-crossed beneath the temple. This large marble arch, each stone bearing a cleanly incised symbol of sorcerous power, was blocked by a solid mass of what appeared to be smooth stone. Stone it might appear, but a sword rang on it as against steel and left less mark than it would have on that metal. And the whole of the passage from the chamber to the tomb, a hundred paces in length, was sealed with the adamantine substance, so said the strange maps Masrok had drawn.

The wizard swayed with exhaustion, but the smell of success close at hand drove him on, even numbing the ache behind his eyes. Five of the *khorassani* he placed on their golden tripods at the points of a carefully measured pentagon he had scribed on the marble floor tiles with chalk made from the burned bones of virgins. Setting the largest of the smooth ebon stones on its own tripod, he threw wide his black-robed arms and began the first incantation.

"Ka-my'een dai'el! Da-en'var hoy'aarth! Khora mar! Khora mar!"

Louder the chant rose, and louder still, echoing from the walls, ringing in the ears, piercing the skull. Karim Singh and Kandar pressed their hands to their ears, groaning. The two women, naked save for their veils, bound hand and foot, wailed for the pain. Only Naipal reveled in the sound, gloried in the reverberations deep in his bones. It was a sound of power. His power. Eye-searing bars of light lanced from the largest

492

khorassani to each of the others, then from each of those smaller stones to each of its glowing brothers, forming a pentagram of burning brilliance. The air between the lines of fire shimmered and rippled as though flame sliced to gossamer had been stretched there, and the whole hummed and crackled with fury.

"There," Naipal said. "Now the guardian demons, the Sivani, are sealed away from this world unless summoned by name."

"That is all very well," Kandar muttered. Actually seeing the wizard's power had drained some of his arrogance. "But how are we to get to the tomb? My soldiers cannot dig through that. Will your stones' fire melt that which almost broke my blade?"

Naipal stared at the man who would lead the army that was entombed a hundred paces away—at least the man the world would think led it—and watched his arrogance wilt further. The wizard did not like those who could not keep their minds focused on what they were about. Kandar's insistence that the women should witness every moment of his triumph—*his* triumph!—irritated Naipal. For the moment Kandar was still needed, but, Naipal decided, something painfully fitting would make way for the prince's successor. At least Karim Singh, his narrow face pasty and beaded with sweat, had been cowed to a proper view of matters.

Instead of answering the question, Naipal asked one in tones like the caress of a razor's edge. "Are you sure you made the arrangements I commanded? Carts filled with street urchins should have arrived by now."

"They will come," Kandar answered sullenly. "Soon. I sent my body servant to see if they have come, did I not? But it takes time to gather so many carts. The governor might—"

"Pray he does only what he has been told," Naipal snarled.

The wizard rubbed at his temples fretfully. All of his fine plans, now thrown into a hodgepodge of haste and improvisation by that accursed *pan-kur*.

Quickly he took the last four *khorassani* from their ebony chest and placed them on tripods of gold. So close to the demon's prison, they would do for the summoning. He was careful to put the tripods well away from the other five to avoid any interaction. A resonance could be deadly. But there would be no resonance, no failure of any kind. The accursed blue-eyed barbarian, the devil spawn, would be defeated.

"*E'las eloyhim! Maraath savinday! Khora mar! Khora mar!*"

Conan was grateful for the pools of light from the distantly spaced torches, each only just visible from the last. Seemingly hundreds of dark tunnels formed a maze under the temple but the torches made a path to follow. And at the end of that path must lie what he sought.

Suddenly the Cimmerian stiffened. From behind came the sound of pounding feet. Many pounding feet.

"They must have found the body," Hordo said with a disgusted glare that took in Hasan and Enam.

Conan hesitated only an instant. To remain where they were meant a battle they could not in all probability win. To rush ahead meant running headlong into the gods alone knew what. "Scatter," he ordered the others. "Each must find his way as he can. And Hanuman's own luck go with us all."

The big Cimmerian waited only long enough to see each man disappear down a separate dark passage, then chose his own. The last glimmers of light faded behind him quickly. He slowed, feeling his way along a smooth wall, placing each foot carefully on a floor he could no longer see. With the blade of his sword he probed the blackness ahead.

Yet abruptly that blackness did not seem as complete as it had. For a moment he thought his eyes might be adapting, but then he realized there was a light ahead. A light that was approaching him. Pressing his back against the wall, he waited.

Slowly the light drew closer, obviously bobbing in someone's hand. The shape of a man became clear. It was no torch he carried, though he held it like one, but rather what seemed to be a metal rod topped by a glowing ball.

Conan's jaw tightened at this obvious sorcery. But the man coming nearer looked nothing at all like the one he had seen at Kandar's palace, the man he had thought was Naipal. Recognition came to him in the same instant that the man stopped, peering into the darkness toward Conan was though he sensed a presence. It was Ghurran, but a Ghurran whose apparent age had been halved to perhaps fifty.

"It is I, herbalist," the Cimmerian said, stepping away from the wall. "Conan. And I have questions for you."

The no-longer-so-old man gave a start, then stared at him in amazement. "You actually have one of the daggers! How—? No matter. With that I can slay the demon if need be. Give it to me!"

A part of the silk wrapping had scraped loose against the wall, Conan realized, revealing the faintly glowing hilt of silvery metal. With one hand he pushed the cloth back into place. "I have need of it, herbalist. I will pass over how you have made yourself younger, and how that torch was made, but what do you do in this place, at this time? And why did you abandon me to die from the poison after coming so far?"

"There is no poison," Ghurran muttered impatiently. "You must give me the dagger. You know not what it is capable of."

"No poison!" Conan spat. "I have suffered agonies of it. Not a night gone but the pain was enough to twist my stomach into knots and send fire through my muscles. You said you sought an antidote, but you left me to die!"

"You fool! I gave you the antidote in Sultanapur! All you have felt is your body purging itself of the potions I gave you to make you think you were still poisoned."

"Why?" was all Conan said.

"Because I had need of you. My body was too frail to make this journey alone, but as soon as I saw the contents of those chests, I knew I must. Naipal prepares to loose a great evil on the world, and only I can stop him. But I must have that dagger!"

A widening of Ghurran's eyes warned Conan as much as did the increase in light. The Cimmerian dropped to a crouch and threw himself to one side, twisting and stabbing as he did. A Vendhyan tulwar sliced above his head, but his own blade went through the soldier's middle. The dying man fell, and his two fellows, rushing at his heels, went down in a heap atop Conan. The big Cimmerian grappled with them in the light of their fallen torch. Ghurran and his glowing rod had vanished.

In a struggling pile the three men rolled atop the torch. One of the Vendhyans screamed as the flames were ground out against his back, then screamed again as a dagger found his flesh. Conan's hands closed on the head of the soldier who had slain his companion by mistake. The sound of a neck breaking was a loud snap in the dark.

But it need not be total dark Conan thought as he climbed to his feet. Without hesitation he unwrapped the strange weapon. A dagger, Ghurran had called it, but what monstrous hand could use it so, the Cimmerian wondered. And it could slay the demon. What demon? But for whatever hand or purpose the silvery blade had been wrought, its faint glow was light of a sort in the blackness of the tunnel, if light of an eerie grayish-blue. By it Conan recovered his broadsword and again began a slow progress through the tunnels. Soon he heard voices, hollow echoes in the distant passages. With difficulty he determined a direction. Grimly he moved toward the source.

Thunder smote the chamber, and the obsidian form of Masrok floated in the void of its fiery cage. The silvery weapons held in five of its eight arms looked no different, yet in some fashion they had an aura of having been used recently a pulsation that reached into the back of a human mind and whispered of violence and death. Karim Singh and Prince Kandar edged back from the huge figure, no matter that it was confined. The bound women seemed frozen with shock and fear.

"You slice matters too finely, O man," Masrok boomed. Crimson eyes flickered to the blazing pentagram in what could not possibly have been nervousness. "A delay of but another beat of a human heart and my other selves would have been on me. Who would serve you then, O man?"

"Masrok, I command you—" Naipal began when half a score of Vendhyan soldiers burst into the chamber.

"Prince Kandar!" one of them cried. "Someone has—"

"You dare intrude!" Naipal howled. He spoke a word that made even him shiver, and lightning flared from the largest of the *khorassani*. A single shriek rent the air, and a cinder, only vaguely resembling the soldier who had shouted, fell and shattered into charred chunks on the stone floor. Turban-helmed men ran, screaming with terror.

Karim Singh and Prince Kandar both tried to speak at once.

"My men are not to be slain out of hand," Kandar shouted.

"The message could have been important," the *wazam* cried.

Both men clamped their teeth on further words as Naipal's dark eyes came to rest on them. "He dies whom I wish to die, and what is important is what I say is important. *This* is important!" The wizard turned his attention back to the demon, which had watched what had happened immpassively. "You will open the way to the tomb for me, Masrok. I care not how."

"From within this cage?" Masrok replied with a hint of its former sarcasm.

"Open it!"

For a moment scarlet eyes met those of ebon, then the demon's mouth opened, and the sound that emerged sent shudders through human flesh. Only for an instant, however. The sound rose with blinding speed to send a stabbing pain in the ears, and beyond. Yet still Masrok's straining jaws told of a cry continuing.

Suddenly that call was answered. Suddenly there were—*things* in the chamber. What exactly or how many it was impossible to tell, for it pained the eye to gaze on them directly, and under a sidelong glance, the numbers and forms seemed to shift constantly. Impressions were all that could be made out, and they enough to bring a lifetime of nightmares. Fangs dripping spittle that bubbled and hissed on the stone. Razor claws gleaming like steel and needle spines glittering like crystal. Sparkling scales in a thousand hues and leathery wings that seemed to stretch farther than the eye could see, farther surely than the walls of the chamber.

Kandar stood ashen-faced, trembling almost as much as the women, who writhed against their bonds and wailed with frantic despair. Karim Singh's lips moved rapidly and silently, and Naipal realized with considerable amusement that the *wazam* prayed. The wizard realized as well that those monstrous forms, so terrifying to human eyes, cowered beneath Masrok's gaze. Perhaps, he thought, he had summoned and bound a greater power than he knew. It increased his resolve to see the demon returned to the prison it shared with its other selves.

Human skulls, dangling for ornament, swayed as Masrok raised one silvery, glowing spear and pointed with it to the blocked passage. Horrific forms flowed to the adamantine substance, clawing, gouging, devouring, a seething mass that slowly sank into the stone, leaving an open way behind it.

"Impressive," said a voice from one of the many entrances to the great room.

Naipal spun, ready to utter the word that drew lightning from the *khorassani*, and it seemed his heart had turned to ice in his chest. "Zail Bal," he gasped. "You are dead!"

"You never would believe your eyes, Naipal," the newcomer said, "when you wished to believe other than what you saw. Of course you have reason to believe as you do. You saw me carried off by *rajaie* while far from my implements." Zail Bal's dark eyes narrowed. "And some of my amulets had been most cunningly tampered with. Still, I managed to slay the demons, though not without cost, it is true. I found myself deposited on the shores of the Vilayet in an age-riddled body, too frail to travel a league." His gaze went from the imprisoned Masrok, once again watching the humans in silence, to the passage into which the summoned beings had now disappeared. "You have done well for me in my absence, apprentice. I had not managed to locate this place before my . . . accident."

"I am no longer the apprentice," Naipal snarled. "I am the court wizard! I am the master!"

"Are you?" Zail Bal's chuckle was dry. "Karim Singh may have his throne, and Kandar may call himself general, but the army that lies below will march for me, Naipal, not for you. The demon will serve me."

Naipal's eyes flickered to the *khorassani*. Did he dare? He had never known that Zail Bal sought Orissa's tomb, and that fact raised unpleasant possibilities. Could he risk that the former court wizard did not also know the words of power? Would the other have risked confronting him without that knowledge? So. If either began to speak the words, the other would also. The nature of the stones was to accept only one master at a time. If neither man gained control quickly enough, both would perish, as well as every living thing for leagues. Naipal had no interest in taking the other man with him as he died. He wanted victory, not death.

"You said your body was age-riddled," Karim Singh said suddenly in a voice that quavered, "yet you appear younger than I. No more than forty. I remember you well, and you were older than that when . . ." His voice trailed off at Zail Bal's chuckle. It was dry this time as well, like the dust of the grave.

"Yes, I am younger than I was and I will be younger still. But what of you, Naipal? Do you suffer from exhaustion that sleep will not cure? Are there pains behind your eyes, splitting your skull?"

"What have you done?" Naipal whispered, then screamed it. "*What have you done?*"

The other wizard laughed and as he spoke, his voice never lost its sound of amusement. "Did you think I kept no cords to my apprentice, Naipal? They were useless over the distance from Turan but once I was across the Himelias . . . aaah. Now I drain the vitality from you through those cords, Naipal, though not exactly as the *rajaie* drained it from me. You will not grow old. Merely tired. So tired you cannot stand or even hold your head up. But do not fear that I will let you die, Naipal. I would not do such to my *faithful* apprentice. No, I will give you eternal life. I will put you in a safe, dry place, with only the endless thirst to distract you from the pains in your head and the nibbles of the rats. Of course the rats will stop their nibbling when you wither sufficiently. You will be a desiccated husk, holding life until it crumbles to dust. And I assure you I will see that it takes a very long time."

Naipal had neither moved nor spoken during Zail Bal's recitation. The fool should have lulled him, he thought. Now he would have to take the gamble. There would come a moment when the *former* court wizard let his attention lapse and then Naipal would begin the words, in a whisper. By the time Zail Bal realized what was happening, it would be too late. It *must* be too late.

A gasp from Karim Singh caught a corner of Naipal's mind. The shifting mass of beings that Masrok had summoned had returned, flowing from the mouth of the passage to the tomb.

"They are done, O man," the eight-armed demon announced. "The way is clear."

All eyes went to the passage. Zail Bal stepped by the seething horror without looking at it, not as though the sight pained his eyes but rather as if he simply could not be bothered by it at the moment. Even Kandar and Karim Singh overcame their fear enough to move closer. Naipal began to whisper furiously.

Crouching near the end of one of the passages that let into the great underground chamber, Conan weighed the silvery weapon in his hand. A dagger, Ghurran had called it. Or Zail Bal, as he now named himself. And the Cimmerian could see the weapon's twin clasped by the huge eight-armed shape. Much had been said in that chamber that he would ponder later, but it was another thing that Ghurran/Zail Bal had said that was of interest now. The weapon he held could slay the demon, by which Conan assumed he had meant the towering obsidian form. Masrok, he had heard it called. Perhaps it could slay the others as well.

Once more Conan tried to look at the demons and found his eyes sliding away unbidden. Their sudden appearance from the other passage, just when he was on the point of entering while the men argued, had been a shock. But now that all eyes peered into the passage from which the monstrosities had come, it might just be possible for him to reach the women before he was even seen. As for what came then . . . With a fatalistic grimness he hefted his broadsword in one hand and large silvery dagger in the other. Then he must bar pursuit long enough for the women to flee. Treading with light swiftness, he moved into the subterranean chamber.

His eyes shifted constantly from the women to the others. Vyndra and Chin Kou, naked and bound at wrists and ankles, lay trembling with eyes squeezed shut above their veils. Naipal appeared to be muttering under his breath, watching the other men, and they in turn had eyes only for the passage. It led to an army, had Ghurran, or Zail Bal, claimed? Kang Hou's army that would come at the end of time perhaps? Warriors like the one he had faced? He could not waste time in worry over that now. The demons that had come from the tunnel seemed fixed on the huge ebon form floating in nothingness in the center of the chamber, while it—

Conan's breath caught in his throat. Those crimson eyes now followed him. He quickened his pace toward the women. If the demon called a warning, he might still . . . The massive arms holding glowing spears moved back. Conan snarled silently. He could not dodge two thrown spears at once. Flipping the silvery weapon in his hand, he hurled it at the demon and threw himself toward the women.

A titanic blast rocked the chamber, and Conan landed atop the women as the earth heaved beneath his feet. Stunned, he fumbled desperately for his own dagger as he took in the horrific scene. The humans were staggering to their feet where the blast had flung them. Splintered shards of black stone lay in ten small pools of molten gold. And Masrok stood on the stone floor, the glowing dagger it had already held now mirrored by another.

"Free!" Masrok cried, and with gibbering howls of demonic terror, the beings it had summoned fled, flowing up into the ceiling, melting into the floor. Scarlet eyes that now glittered went to Naipal. "You threatened me with this blade, O man." The booming voice was heavy with mockery. "How I wished for you to strike. From the inside your barriers were impervious but from the outside . . . Any unliving thing could cross from the outside easily, and the crossing of this demon-wrought blade, this metal of powers you never dreamed of, shattered all of your bonds. All!"

The cords on the ankles first, Conan told himself as he found his knife. The women could run with hands tied if need be.

"I always intended your freedom," Naipal said hoarsely. "We made a pact."

"Fool!" the demon snarled. "You bound me, made one of the Sivani your servant. And *you!*" The furious rubiate gaze pinned Zail Bal, who had been attempting to edge toward one of the passages. "You intended the same. Know, then, the price for daring such!"

Both wizards shouted incantations, but the glowing spears sped from Masrok's hands, transfixing each man through the chest. Almost in the same instant the silvery weapons leaped back to the demons' grasp, bearing their still-living burdens. Shrieks split the air, and futile hands clutched at glowing hafts now staining with blood.

"Know for all time!" Masrok thundered. And the demon spun, blurring into an obsidian whirlwind streaked with silver.

Then it was still once more and the wizards were gone. But a new skull dangled below the head of each spear, a skull whose empty sockets retained a glow of life, and the shrieks of the wizards, echoing faintly as though from a great distance, could yet be heard.

Slicing the last cord binding a wrist, Conan heaved the women to their feet. Weeping, they tried to cling to him, but he pushed them toward the one passage that showed the light of a torch. The marked path lay there, one they could follow even without his aid.

"You also," Masrok growled, and Conan realized the demon's eyes were now on him. Keeping his face to the creature, he began to follow the women, but slowly. If the worst happened, there must be distance between him and them. "You thought to slay me, puny mortal," the demon said. "You, also, will know—"

A sound like all the winds of the world crying through the maze of passages filled the great room, but no breath of air stirred. The rushing howl died abruptly, and at its ending a mirror image of Masrok stood at either end of the chamber.

"Betrayer!" they shouted with one voice, and it was as though a thunderhead had spoken. "The way that was to open at the end of time is opened beforehand!"

Masrok shifted slightly, that monstrous ebon head swiveling from one form to the other.

"Slayer!" they cried as one. "One of the Sivani is dead, by the deeds of a Sivani!"

Masrok raised its weapons. No particle of the demon's attention remained on Conan. The Cimmerian spun to hasten after the women, and he found them halted before the passage entrance, Kandar confronting them with the curved blade of his tulwar.

The Prince's face was pale and sweaty, and his eyes rolled to the tensing obsidian giants with barely controlled terror. "You can keep the Khitan wench," he rasped, "but Vyndra is mine. Decide quickly, barbarian. If we are still here when their battle begins, none of us will survive."

"I have decided already," Conan said, and his broadsword struck. Twice steel rang on steel and then the Vendhyan Prince was falling with a crimson gash where his throat had been. "Run!" Conan commanded the women. He did not look back as they darted into the tunnel. The ground rumbled beneath his feet. The battle of demons was beginning.

Sound pursued them in their flight through the subterranean passages. The crash of lightnings confined and the roar of thunder imprisoned. The earth heaved, and dirt and rock showered from above.

Sheathing his sword, Conan scooped up the women, one over each shoulder, and redoubled his speed, fleeing from the pool of light into the debris-filled darkness. The flames on distantly spaced torches wavered as the walls on which they hung danced.

Then the stairs were before him. He took them three at a time. In the vast-domed temple chamber, massive columns shivered and the towering statue swayed. Without slowing, Conan ran past the tall bronze doors and into the night.

Outside, the circle of torches remained, swaying as the ground heaved in swells like the sea, but the soldiers were fled. Trees a hundred and fifty feet high cracked like whips.

Conan ran into the forest until a root caught his foot and sent him sprawling with his burdens. He could not rise again, only cling as the earth shook and rippled in waves, but at last he looked back.

Bolts of lightning burst toward the sky from the temple, hurling great blocks of stone into the air, casting a blue illumination over the frenzied forest. And dome by dome, columned terrace by columned terrace, the huge temple fell, collapsing inward, ever sinking as it leaped like a thing alive. Lightning flashes revealed the ruin no higher then the flailing trees surrounding it, then half their height, then only a mound of rubble.

Abruptly there was no more lightning. The ground gave one final tortured heave and was still.

Conan rose unsteadily to his feet. He could no longer see even the mound. In truth he did not believe it was any longer there. "Swallowed by the earth," he said softly, "and the entrance sealed once more."

His arms filled suddenly with naked, weeping women, but his mind was on other matters. Horses. Whether or not the demons had been buried with the tomb, he did not intend to remain long enough to find out.

Epilogue

Conan rode through the dawn with his jaw set grimly, wondering if perhaps he could not find just a few Vendhyan soldiers who would try to contest his passage or perhaps question the Vendhyan cavalry saddle on his horse. It would be better than the icy daggers of silence being hurled against his back by Vyndra and Chin Kou. Of necessity he gripped the reins of their horses in one hand; the fool women would not have left the forest otherwise.

"You must find us garments," Vyndra said suddenly. "I will not be seen like this."

"It is not seemly," Chin Kou added.

Conan sighed. It was not the first time they had made the demand, though they had no idea as to where he might obtain the clothes. The past hour of silence had come from his retort that they had *already* been seen by half the populace of Gwandiakan. He twisted in the saddle to look back at them. The two women still wore the veils, if nothing else. He had asked why, since they obviously hated the small squares of silk, but they had babbled incomprehensively at him about not being recognized, and both had gone into such a frenzy that someone might be watching, for all it had been pitch dark in the middle of the forest at the time, that he did not mention it again. They stared at him now with dark, furious eyes peeping over the top of their veils, yet each sat straight in her saddle, seemingly unaware of the nudity of which she complained.

"We are almost to the old well," he told them. "Kuie Hsi should be there with garb for you both."

"The well!" Vyndra exclaimed, suddenly trying to hide behind the high pommel of her saddle. "Oh, no!"

"There might be people!" Chin Kou moaned as she, too, contorted.

Before they could slip from the saddles and hide—they had done that once already—Conan kicked his horse to a gallop, pulling theirs along behind, heedless of their wails of protest.

The wall of the old well remained, surrounded by trees much smaller than those of the forest. The well itself had long collapsed. A portion of a stone wall still stood nearby, perhaps once part of a caravansary. There were people there as well. Conan grinned as he ran his eye over them. Hordo and Enam tossing dice. Hasan and Shamil seated with their backs against the wall. Kang Hou sipping from a tiny cup held delicately in his fingers, while Kuie Hsi crouched by a fire where a kettle steamed. The men looked the worse for wear, sprouting bandages and poultices, but they sprang to their feet with glad shouts at his appearance.

Kuie Hsi did not shout but rather came running with bundles in her arms. The other two women, Conan saw, had slid from the saddles and were hiding behind their horses. He dismounted, leaving them to their flurry of silks, and went to meet the men.

"I thought you were dead for certain this time," the one-eyed man muttered gruffly.

"Not I," Conan laughed, "nor any of the rest of us it seems. Our luck has not been so bad after all." The smiles faded from their faces, producing a frown on his. "What has happened?"

"A great deal," Kang Hou replied. "My niece brought much news with her. For one thing, King Bhandarkar is dead at the hands of the Katari. Fortunately Prince Jharim Kar managed to rally nobles to Bhandarkar's young son, Bhunda Chand, who has been crowned as the new king, thus restoring order. On the unfortunate side, you, my *cheng-li* friend, have been condemned to death by Royal Edict, signed by Bhunda Chand, for complicity in the assassination of his father."

Conan could only shake his head in amazement. "How did this madness come about?"

The Khitan merchant explained. "One of Jharim Kar's first moves after the coronation—and that was a hasty affair, it seems—was to ride for Gwandiakan with the young King and all the cavalry he could muster. Supposedly he found evidence that Karim Singh was a leader of the plot, and thus must be arrested and executed before he could become a rallying point for disaffection. It is rumored, however, that the Prince blames the *wazam* for an incident involving one of his wives. Whatever the truth, Bhunda Chand's column met the caravan on which we and the *wazam* traveled. And one Alyna, a servant of the Lady Vyndra, gave testimony that her mistress and a pale-skinned barbarian called Patil had plotted with Karim Singh and spoken in her presence of slaying Bhandarkar."

A shriek of fury announced that Vyndra had just had the same information from Kuie Hsi. The Vendhyan noble-woman stormed from behind the horses, clutching half-donned silken robes that fluttered after her. "I will strip her hide! That sow will speak the truth, or I will wear out switches on her!"

"I fear it is too late for any such action on your part," Kang Hou said. "Alyna—perhaps I should say the Lady Alyna—has already been confirmed in your titles and estates. The Royal Edict concerning you not only strips you of those possessions but gifts her with your life and person."

Vyndra's mouth worked silently for a moment, then she rounded on Conan. "You are the cause of this! It is all your fault! What are you going to do about it?"

"I am to blame?" Conan growled. "*I* enslaved Alyna?" Vyndra's eyes almost started from her head in fury and he sighed. "Very well. I will take you to Turan with me."

"Turan!" she cried, throwing up her hands. "It is a pigsty unfit for a civilized woman! It—" Suddenly it dawned on her that her gesture had bared her to the waist. Shrieking, she snatched the still-sliding silk and dashed for the shelter of the horses.

"A woman whose temper equals her great beauty," Kang Hou said, "and whose deviousness and vindictiveness exceed both."

Conan waved the words aside. "What of Gwandiakan? Will it be safe to hide there for a day or two while we recuperate?"

"That will not be possible," Kuie Hsi said, joining them. "The people of Gwandiakan took the earthquake as a sign from the gods, especially when they discovered that carts had been assembled to take the children from the city to an unknown destination. A wall of the fortress had collapsed. The people stormed the fortress, freeing the imprisoned children. Soldiers who tried to stop them were torn limb from limb. Jharim Kar has promised justice in the matter, but in the meanwhile his soldiers patrol the streets heavily. I cannot believe any Western foreigner would long escape their notice."

"I am glad for the children," Conan said, "for all it had nothing to do with me, but this means we must ride for the mountains from here. And the sooner the better, I think. What of you, Kang Hou? Are you, too, proscribed?"

"I am but a humble merchant," the Khitan replied, "and so, no doubt, beneath Alyna's notice. To my good fortune. As for your journey over the mountains, I fear that not all who came with you will return to Turan. You will pardon me?" Bowing, he left before Conan could ask what he meant, but Hasan took his place.

"I must speak with you," the young Turanian said. "Alone." Still frowning after Kang Hou, Conan let himself be drawn off from the others. Hasan pressed a folded square of parchment into the Cimmerian's hand. "When you return to Sultanapur, Conan, take that to the House of Perfumed Doves and say it is for Lord Khalid."

"So you are the one who will not return to Turan," Conan said, turning over the square of parchment in his hands. "And what message is it you send to Yildiz's spy master?"

"You know of him?"

"More is known on the streets of Sultanapur than the lords of Turan would believe. But you have not answered my question."

The Turanian drew a deep breath. "I was sent to discover if a connection exists between the Vendhyans and the death of the High Admiral. Not one question have I asked concerning that, yet I know already this land is so full of intrigues within intrigues that no clear answer can ever be found. I say as much in the letter. As well I say that I can find no evidence connecting the 'fishermen' of Sultanapur with the matter, and that the rumors of a northland giant in the pay of Vendhyans is just that. A rumor. Lord Khalid will recognize my hand, and so know it for a true report. It is unsealed. You may read it if you wish."

Conan stuffed the parchment into his belt pouch. There would be time for reading—and for deciding whether to visit the House of Perfumed Doves—later. "Why are you remaining?" he asked. "Chin Kou?"

"Yes. Kang Hou has no objections to a foreigner marrying into his family." Hasan snorted a laugh. "After years of avoiding it, it seems I will become a spice merchant after all."

"Be careful," Conan cautioned. "I wish you well, but I do not believe the Khitans are much less devious than the Vendhyans."

Leaving the young Turanian, Conan went in search of Kang Hou. The merchant was seated on the wall of the caved-in well. "Soon you will be fleeing Vendhya," the Khitan said as Conan approached. "What of your plans to sack the land with an army at your back?"

"Someday perhaps. But Vendhya is a strange land, mayhap too devious for a simple northlander like me. It makes my thoughts whirl in peculiar fashions."

Kang Hou arched a thin eyebrow. "How so, man who calls himself Patil?"

"Just fragments, spinning. Odd memories. Valash, sitting in the Golden Crescent on the morning the High Admiral died. A very hard man, Valash. He would never have let two such beauties as your nieces leave his ship except to a slaver's block. Unless someone frightened him into it perhaps. But then, you are a very hard man for a poor merchant, are you not, Kang Hou? And your niece, Kuie Hsi, is an extremely able woman. The way in which she passed for a Vendhyan woman to seek information in Gwandiakan. And knowing Naipal was among those who rode to the Forests of Ghelai, though I have heard his face was known but to a handful. Were you aware that a Vendhyan woman was delivered to the High Admiral as a gift on the morning he died? She vanished soon after his death, I understand. But I have never understood why the Vendhyans would sign a treaty with Turan and kill the High Admiral within a day of it. Kandar seemed truly shocked at the news, and Karim Singh as well. Strange, would you not say, Kang Hou?"

All through the rambling discourse the Khitan had listened with an expression of polite interest. Now he smiled, tucking his hands into his broad sleeves. "You weave a very fanciful tale for one who calls himself a simple northlander."

Returning the smile, Conan put his hand on his dagger. "Will you wager you are faster than I?" he asked softly.

For an instant Kang Hou wavered visibly. Then, slowly, he brought his hands into the open. Empty. "I am but a peaceful merchant," he said as though nothing had happened. "If you would care to listen, perhaps I can weave a tale as fanciful as yours. Having, of course, as little to do with reality."

"I will listen," Conan said cautiously, but he did not move his hand from the dagger hilt.

"I am from Cho-Hien," the Khitan began, "a small city-state on the borders of Vendhya. The lifeblood of Cho-Hien is trade, and its armies are small. It survives by balancing its larger, stronger neighbors one against another. Largest, strongest and most avaricious of Cho-Hien's neighbors is Vendhya. Perhaps the land rots from within, as you say, but the ruling caste, the Kshatriyas, are fierce men with eyes for conquest. If those eyes turn to the north, they will fall first on Cho-Hien. Therefore Cho-Hien must keep the Kshatriyas' gaze to the east, or to the west. A treaty with Turan, for instance, might mean that Kshatriyan ambitions would look not toward the Vilayet but toward Khitai. My tale, I fear, has no more point than yours but perhaps you found it entertaining."

"Entertaining," Conan agreed. "But a question occurs to me. Does Chin Kou share Kuie Hsi's talents? That is," he added with a smile, "if Kuie Hsi had any talents out of the ordinary."

"Chin Kou's sole talent is that she remembers and can repeat every word that she hears or reads. Beyond that she is merely a loving niece who comforts an aging man's bones. Though now it seems she will comfort another."

"That brings another question. Does Hasan know of this?"

"Of my fanciful tale? No." A broad grin split the Khitan's face. "But he knew what I was, as I knew what he was, before ever we reached the Himelias. He will make a fine addition to my family. For a foreigner. Now I will ask a question," he added, the grin fading. "What do you intend concerning my fanciful tale?"

"A tale spun by a northlander and another spun by a Khitan merchant," Conan said musingly. "Who in Turan would believe if I told them? And if they did, they would find ten other reasons for war, or near to war. For there to be true peace between Turan and Vendhya, the Vilayet will have to expand to swallow Secunderam, perhaps enough to separate the two lands for all time. Besides, true peace and true war alike are bad for smugglers."

"You are not so simple as you claim, northlander."

"Vendhya is still a strange land," Conan replied with a laugh. "And one I must be leaving. Fare you well, Kang Hou of Cho-Hien."

The Khitan rose and bowed, though he was careful to keep his hands away from his sleeves. "Fare you well . . . Conan of Cimmeria."

Conan laughed all the way to the horses. "Hordo," he roared, "do we ride, or have you grown so old you have put down roots? Enam, to horse! And you, Shamil. Do you ride with us, or remain here like Hasan?"

"I have had my fill of travel and adventure," Shamil replied earnestly. "I return to Sultanapur to become a fisherman. For fish!"

Vyndra pushed her way past the men scrambling into saddles and confronted Conan. "What of me?" she demanded.

"You do not wish to go to Turan," Conan told her, "and you cannot remain in Vendhya. Except as Alyna's . . . guest. Perhaps Kang Hou will take you to Cho-Hien."

"Cho-Hien! Better Turan than that!"

"Since you have asked so nicely, if you keep me warm on the cold nights in the mountains, I will find a place for you dancing in a tavern in Sultanapur."

Her cheeks colored, but she held out her arms for him to lift her to her saddle. As he did, though, she pressed herself against him briefly and whispered, "I would much rather dance for you alone."

Conan handed her her reins and turned away, hiding a smile as he vaulted to his own saddle. There would be problems with this woman yet, but amusing ones he thought.

"What of the antidote?" Hordo asked. "And Ghurran?"

"I saw him," Conan replied. "You might say he saved all of us with what he told me." Ignoring the one-eyed man's questioning look, he went on. "But are we to sit here until the Vendhyans put all our heads on pikes? Come! There's a wench called Tasha waiting for me in Sultanapur." And with a grin for Vyndra's angry squawl, he booted his horse to a gallop, toward the mountains towering to the north.